THE

DRAGON

REPUBLIC

ALSO BY R. F. KUANG

The Poppy War

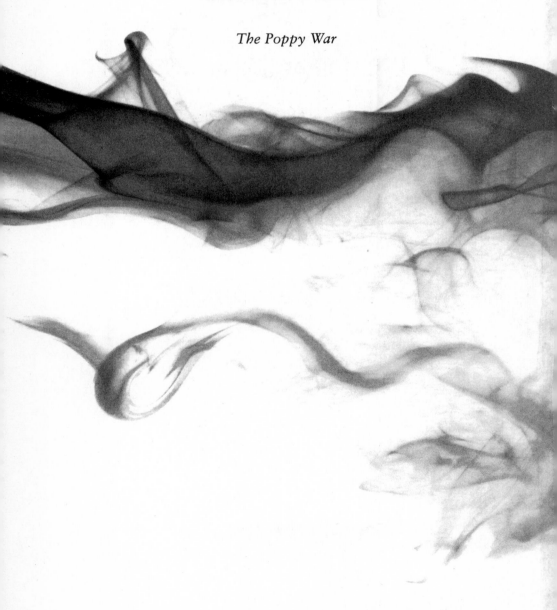

THE
DRAGON
REPUBLIC

THE POPPY WAR, BOOK TWO

R. F. KUANG

HARPER Voyager
An Imprint of HarperCollins*Publishers*

THE DRAGON REPUBLIC. Copyright © 2019 by Rebecca Kuang. All rights reserved. Printed in the United States of America. No part of this book may be used or reproduced in any manner whatsoever without written permission except in the case of brief quotations embodied in critical articles and reviews. For information, address HarperCollins Publishers, 195 Broadway, New York, NY 10007.

HarperCollins books may be purchased for educational, business, or sales promotional use. For information, please email the Special Markets Department at SPsales@harpercollins.com.

Harper Voyager and design are trademarks of HarperCollins Publishers LLC.

FIRST EDITION

Designed by Paula Russell Szafranski

Frontispiece © Jannarong / Shutterstock

Maps by Eric Gunther and copyright © 2017 Springer Cartographics

Library of Congress Cataloging-in-Publication Data has been applied for.

ISBN 978-0-06-266263-7

19 20 21 22 23   LSC   10 9 8 7 6 5 4 3 2 1

To

匡为华

匡萌芽

冯海潮

钟辉英

杜华

冯宝兰

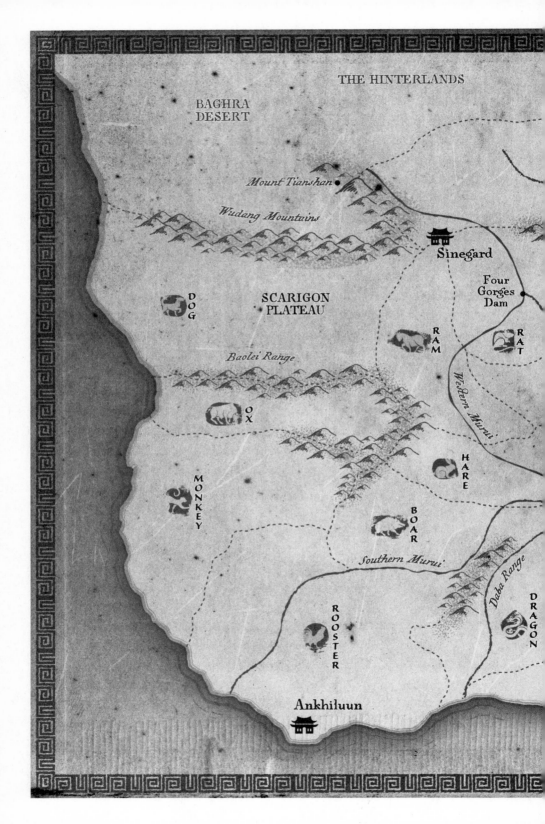

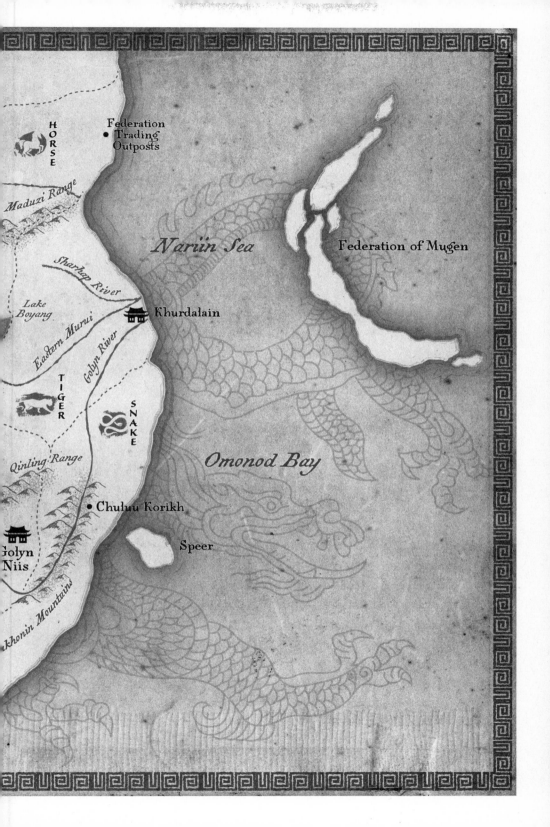

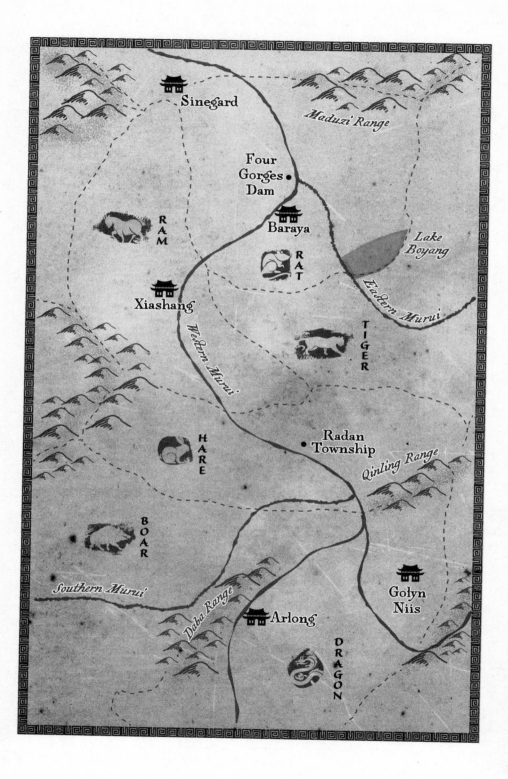

THE

DRAGON

REPUBLIC

ARLONG, EIGHT YEARS PRIOR

"Come on," Mingzha begged. "Please, I want to see."

Nezha seized his brother by his chubby wrist and pulled him back from the shallows. "We're not allowed to go past the lily pads."

"But don't you want to know?" Mingzha whined.

Nezha hesitated. He, too, wanted to see what lay in the caves around the bend. The grottoes of the Nine Curves River had been mysteries to the Yin children since they were born. They'd grown up with warnings of dark, dormant evils concealed behind the cave mouths; of monsters that lurked inside, eager for foolish children to stumble into their jaws.

That alone would have been enough to entice the Yin children, all of whom were adventurous to a fault. But they'd heard rumors of great treasures, too; of underwater piles of pearls, jade, and gold. Nezha's Classics tutor had once told him that every piece of jewelry lost in the water inevitably wound up in those river grottoes. And sometimes, on a clear day, Nezha thought he could see the glimmer of sunlight on sparkling metal in the cave mouths from the window of his room.

He'd desperately wanted to explore those caves for years— and today would be the day to do it, when everyone was too busy to pay attention. But it was his responsibility to protect Mingzha. He'd never been trusted to watch his brother alone before; until today he'd always been too young. But this week Father was in the capital, Jinzha was at the Academy, Muzha was abroad at the Gray Towers in Hesperia, and the rest of the palace was so frazzled over Mother's sudden illness that the servants had hastily passed Mingzha into Nezha's arms and told them both to keep out of trouble. Nezha wanted to prove he was up to the task.

"Mingzha!"

His brother had wandered back into the shallows. Nezha cursed and dashed into the water behind him. How could a six-year-old move so quickly?

"Come *on*," Mingzha pleaded when Nezha grabbed him by the waist.

"We can't," Nezha said. "We'll get in trouble."

"Mother's been in bed all week. She won't find out." Mingzha twisted around in Nezha's grip and shot him an impish smile. "I won't tell. The servants won't tell. Will you?"

"You're a little demon," Nezha said.

"I just want to see the entrance." Mingzha beamed hopefully at him. "We don't have to go in. *Please?*"

Nezha relented. "We'll just go around the bend. We can look at the cave mouths from a distance. And then we're turning back, do you understand?"

Mingzha shouted with delight and splashed into the water. Nezha followed, stooping down to grab his brother's hand.

No one had ever been able to deny Mingzha anything. Who could? He was so fat and happy, a bouncing ball of giggles and delight, the absolute treasure of the palace. Father adored him. Jinzha and Muzha played with him whenever he wanted, and they never told him to get lost the way Jinzha had done so often to Nezha.

Mother doted on him most of all—perhaps because her other sons were destined to be soldiers, but she could keep Mingzha all to herself. She dressed him in finely embroidered silks and adorned him with so many lucky amulets of gold and jade that Mingzha clinked everywhere he walked, weighed down with the burden of good fortune. The palace servants liked to joke that they could always hear Mingzha before they saw him. Nezha wanted to make Mingzha stop to remove his jewelry now, worried it might drag him down under waves that already came up to his chest, but Mingzha charged forward like he was weightless.

"We're stopping here," Nezha said.

They'd gotten closer to the grottoes than they had ever been in their lives. The cave mouths were so dark inside that Nezha couldn't see more than two feet past the entrances, but their walls looked beautifully smooth, glimmering with a million different colors like fish scales.

"Look." Mingzha pointed at something in the water. "It's Father's cloak."

Nezha frowned. "What's Father's cloak doing at the bottom of the river?"

Yet the heavy garment lying half-buried in the sand was undeniably Yin Vaisra's. Nezha could see the crest of the dragon embroidered in silver thread against the rich cerulean-blue dye that only members of the House of Yin were permitted to wear.

Mingzha pointed to the closest grotto. "It came from in there."

An inexplicable, chilly dread crept through Nezha's veins. "Mingzha, get away from there."

"Why?" Mingzha, stubborn and fearless, waded closer to the cave.

The water began to ripple.

Nezha reached out to pull his brother back. "Mingzha, wait—"

Something enormous burst out of the water.

Nezha saw a huge dark shape—something muscled and coiled like a serpent—before a massive wave rose above him and slammed him facedown into the water.

The river shouldn't have been deep. The water had only come up to Nezha's waist and Mingzha's shoulders, had only been getting shallower the closer they moved to the grotto. But when

Nezha opened his eyes underwater, the surface seemed miles away, and the bottom of the grotto seemed as vast as the palace of Arlong itself.

He saw a pale green light shining from the grotto floor. He saw faces, beautiful, but eyeless. Human faces embedded in the sand and coral, and an endless mosaic studded with silver coins, porcelain vases, and golden ingots—a bed of treasures that stretched on and on into the grotto as far as the light went.

He saw a blink of movement, dark against the light, that disappeared as quickly as it came.

Something was wrong with the water here. Something had stretched and altered its dimensions. What should have been shallow and bright was deep; deep, dark, and terribly, hypnotically quiet.

Through the silence Nezha heard the faint sound of his brother screaming.

He kicked frantically for the surface. It seemed miles away.

When at last he emerged from the water, the shallows were mere shallows again.

Nezha wiped the river water from his eyes, gasping. "Mingzha?"

His brother was gone. Crimson streaks stained the river. Some of the streaks were solid, lumpy masses. Nezha knew what they were.

"Mingzha?"

The waters were quiet. Nezha stumbled to his knees and retched. Vomit mixed into bloodstained water.

He heard a clink against the rocks.

He looked down and saw a golden anklet.

Then he saw a dark shape rising before the grottoes, and heard a voice that came from nowhere and vibrated his very bones.

"Hello, little one."

Nezha screamed.

PART I

CHAPTER 1

Dawn saw the *Petrel* sail through swirling mist into the port city of Adlaga. Shattered by a storm of Federation soldiers during the Third Poppy War, port security still hadn't recovered and was almost nonexistent—especially for a supply ship flying Militia colors. The *Petrel* glided past Adlaga's port officers with little trouble and made berth as close to the city walls as it could get.

Rin propped herself up on the prow, trying to conceal the twitching in her limbs and to ignore the throbbing pain in her temples. She wanted opium terribly and couldn't have it. Today she needed her mind alert. Functioning. Sober.

The *Petrel* bumped against the dock. The Cike gathered on the upper deck, watching the gray skies with tense anticipation as the minutes trickled past.

Ramsa drummed his foot against the deck. "It's been an hour."

"Patience," Chaghan said.

"Could be that Unegen's run off," Baji said.

"He hasn't run off," Rin said. "He said he needed until noon."

"He'd also be the first to seize this chance to be rid of us," Baji said.

He had a point. Unegen, already the most skittish by far

among the Cike, had been complaining for days about their impending mission. Rin had sent him ahead overland to scope out their target in Adlaga. But the rendezvous window was quickly closing and Unegen hadn't shown.

"Unegen wouldn't dare," Rin said, and winced when the effort of speaking sent little stabs through the base of her skull. "He knows I'd hunt him down and skin him alive."

"Mm," Ramsa said. "Fox fur. I'd like a new scarf."

Rin turned her eyes back to the city. Adlaga made an odd corpse of a township, half-alive and half-destroyed. One side had emerged from the war intact; the other had been bombed so thoroughly that she could see building foundations poking up from blackened grass. The split appeared so even that half houses existed on the line: one side blackened and exposed, the other somehow teetering and groaning against the ocean winds, yet still standing.

Rin found it hard to imagine that anyone still lived in the township. If the Federation had been as thorough here as they'd been at Golyn Niis, then all that should be left were corpses.

At last a raven emerged from the blackened ruins. It circled the ship twice, then dove straight toward the *Petrel* as if locked on a target. Qara lifted a padded arm into the air. The raven pulled out of its dive and wrapped its talons around her wrist.

Qara ran the back of her index finger over the bird's head and down its spine. The raven ruffled its feathers as she brought its beak to her ear. Several seconds passed. Qara stood still with her eyes shut, listening intently to something the rest of them couldn't hear.

"Unegen's pinned Yuanfu," Qara said. "City hall, two hours."

"Guess you're not getting that scarf," Baji told Ramsa.

Chaghan yanked a sack out from under the deck and emptied its contents onto the planks. "Everyone get dressed."

Ramsa had come up with the idea to disguise themselves in stolen Militia uniforms. Uniforms were the one thing Moag hadn't been able to sell them, but they weren't hard to find. Rotting corpses lay in messy piles by the roadside in every abandoned coastal town, and it took only two trips to scavenge enough clothes that weren't burned or covered in blood.

Rin had to roll up the arms and legs of her uniform. Corpses of her stature were difficult to come by. She suppressed the urge to vomit as she laced on her boots. She'd pulled the shirt off a body wedged inside a half-burned funeral pyre, and three washes still couldn't conceal the smell of charred flesh under salty ocean water.

Ramsa, draped absurdly in a uniform three times his size, gave her a salute. "How do I look?"

She bent down to tie her boot laces. "Why are you wearing that?"

"Rin, please—"

"You're not coming."

"But I want to—"

"*You are not coming*," she repeated. Ramsa was a munitions genius, but he was also short, scrawny, and utterly worthless in a melee. She wasn't losing her only fire powder engineer because he didn't know how to wield a sword. "Don't make me tie you to the mast."

"Come on," Ramsa whined. "We've been on this ship for weeks, and I'm so fucking seasick just walking around makes me want to vomit—"

"Tough." Rin yanked a belt through the loops around her waist.

Ramsa pulled a handful of rockets from his pocket. "Will you set these off, then?"

Rin gave him a stern look. "I don't think you understand that we're not trying to blow Adlaga up."

"Oh, no, you just want to topple the local government, that's so much better."

"With minimal civilian casualties, which means we don't

need you." Rin reached out and tapped at the lone barrel leaning against the mast. "Aratsha, will you watch him? Make sure he doesn't get off the ship."

A blurry face, grotesquely transparent, emerged from the water. Aratsha spent most of his time in the water, spiriting the Cike's ships along to wherever they needed to go, and when he wasn't calling down his god he preferred to rest in his barrel. Rin had never seen his original human form. She wasn't sure he had one anymore.

Bubbles floated from Aratsha's mouth as he spoke. "If I must."

"Good luck," Ramsa muttered. "As if I couldn't outrun a fucking barrel."

Aratsha tilted his head at him. "Please be reminded that I could drown you in seconds."

Ramsa opened his mouth to retort, but Chaghan spoke over him. "Everyone take your pick." Steel clattered as he dumped out a chest of Militia weapons onto the deck. Baji, complaining loudly, traded his conspicuous nine-pointed rake for a standard infantry sword. Suni scooped up an Imperial halberd, but Rin knew the weapon was purely for show. Suni's specialty was bashing heads in with his shield-sized hands. He didn't need anything else.

Rin fastened a curved pirate scimitar to her waist. It wasn't Militia standard, but Militia swords were too heavy for her to wield. Moag's blacksmiths had fashioned her something lighter. She wasn't yet used to the grip, but she also doubted the day would end in a sword fight.

If things got so bad that she needed to get involved, then it would end in fire.

"Let's reiterate." Chaghan's pale eyes roved over the assembled Cike. "This is surgical. We have a single target. This is an assassination, not a battle. You will harm no civilians."

He looked pointedly at Rin.

She crossed her arms. "I know."

"Not even by accident."

"I *know*."

"Come off it," Baji said. "Since when did you get so high and mighty about casualties?"

"We've done enough harm to your people," said Chaghan.

"*You* did enough harm," Baji said. "I didn't break those dams."

Qara flinched at that, but Chaghan acted as if he hadn't heard a word. "We're finished hurting civilians. Am I understood?"

Rin jerked out a shrug. Chaghan liked to play commander, and she was rarely in a state to be bothered. He could boss them around all he liked. All she cared about was that they got this job done.

Three months. Twenty-nine targets, all killed without error. One more head in a sack, and then they'd be sailing north to assassinate their very last mark—the Empress Su Daji.

Rin felt a flush creep up her neck at the thought. Her palms grew dangerously hot.

Not now. Not yet. She took a deep breath. Then another one, more desperate, when the heat only extended through her torso.

Baji clamped a hand on her shoulder. "You all right?"

She exhaled slowly. Made herself count backward from ten, and then up to forty-nine by odd numbers, and then back down by prime numbers. Altan had taught her that trick, and it mostly worked, at least when she took care not to think about Altan when she did it. The fever flush receded. "I'm fine."

"And you're sober?" Baji asked.

"*Yes*," she said stiffly.

Baji didn't take his hand off her shoulder. "You're sure? Because—"

"I've *got this*," she snapped. "Let's go gut this bastard."

Three months ago, after the Cike had first sailed out from the Isle of Speer, they'd faced a bit of a dilemma.

Namely, they had nowhere to go.

They knew they couldn't return to the mainland. Ramsa had pointed out, quite astutely, that if the Empress had been willing to sell the Cike out to Federation scientists, then she wouldn't be happy to see them alive and free. A quick, furtive supply trip to a tiny coastal city in Snake Province confirmed their suspicions. All of their faces were plastered on the village post boards. They'd been named as war criminals. Bounties were out for their arrest—five hundred Imperial silvers dead, six hundred alive.

They'd stolen as many crates of provisions as they could and hurried out of Snake Province before anyone saw them.

Back in Omonod Bay, they'd debated their options. The only thing they could all agree on was that they needed to kill the Empress Su Daji—the Vipress, the last of the Trifecta, and the traitor who had sold her nation to the Federation.

But they were nine people—eight, without Kitay—against the most powerful woman in the Empire and the combined forces of the Imperial Militia. They'd had few supplies, only the weapons they carried on their backs and a stolen skimmer so banged up that they spent half their time bailing water out of the lower decks.

So they'd sailed down south, past Snake Province into Rooster territory, tracing the coastline until they reached the port city Ankhiluun. There they had come into the employ of the Pirate Queen Moag.

Rin had never met anyone she respected as much as she did Moag—the Stone Bitch, the Lying Widow, and the ruthless ruler of Ankhiluun. She was a consort-turned-pirate who went from Lady to Queen when she murdered her husband, and she'd been running Ankhiluun as an illegal enclave of foreign trade for years. She'd skirmished with the Trifecta during the Second Poppy War, and she'd been fending off the Empress's scouts ever since.

She was more than happy to help the Cike rid her of Daji for good.

In return, she demanded thirty heads. The Cike had returned twenty-nine. Most had been low-level smugglers, captains, and mercenaries. Moag's primary income stream came from contraband opium imports, and she liked to keep her eye out for opium dealers who didn't play by her rules—or at least line her pockets.

The thirtieth mark would be harder. Today Rin and the Cike intended to topple Adlaga's local government.

Moag had been trying to break into the Adlaga market for years. The little coastal city didn't offer much, but its civilians, many with lingering addictions to opiates since the days of Federation occupation, would gladly spend their life savings on Ankhiluuni imports. Adlaga had held out against Moag's aggressive opium trade for the past two decades only because of a particularly vigilant city magistrate, Yang Yuanfu, and his administration.

Moag wanted Yang Yuanfu dead. The Cike specialized in assassination. They were a matchmaker's dream.

Three months. Twenty-nine heads. Just one more job and they'd have silver, ships, and enough soldiers to distract the Imperial Guard long enough for Rin to march up to Daji and wrap flaming fingers around her throat.

If port security was lax, wall defense was nonexistent. The Cike passed through Adlaga's walls with no interference—which wasn't hard to do, considering the Federation had blown great holes all across the boundary and none of them were guarded.

Unegen met them behind the gates.

"We picked a good day for murder," he said as he guided them into the alleyway. "Yuanfu's due in the city square at noon for a war commemoration ceremony. He'll be out in broad daylight, and we can pick him off from the alleys without showing our faces."

Unlike Aratsha, Unegen preferred his human form when he wasn't calling down the shape-shifting powers of the fox spirit. But Rin had always sensed something distinctly vulpine in the way he carried himself. Unegen was both crafty and easily startled; his narrow eyes were always darting from side to side, tracking all of his possible escape routes.

"So we've got what, two hours?" Rin asked.

"A little over. There's a warehouse a few blocks down from

here that's fairly empty," he said. "We can hunker down to wait in there. Then, ah, we split pretty easily if things go south."

Rin turned toward the Cike, considering.

"We'll take the corners of the square when Yuanfu shows up," she decided. "Suni in the southwest. Baji northwest, and I'll take the northeast."

"Diversions?" Baji asked.

"No." Normally diversions were a fantastic idea, and Rin loved assigning Suni to wreak as much havoc as possible while she or Baji darted in to slit their target's throat, but during a public ceremony the risk to civilians was too great. "We'll let Qara take the first shot. The rest of us clear a path back to the ship if they put up resistance."

"Are we still trying to pretend we're normal mercenaries?" Suni asked.

"Might as well," Rin said. They'd done a decent job so far of concealing the extent of their abilities, or at least silencing anyone who would spread rumors. Daji didn't know the Cike were coming for her. The longer she believed them dead, the better. "We're dealing with a better opponent than usual, though, so do what you need to. At the end of the day, we want a head in a bag."

She took a breath and ran the plan once more through her mind, considering.

This would work. This was going to be fine.

Strategizing with the Cike was like playing a chess game in which she had several massively overpowered, unpredictable, and bizarre pieces. Aratsha commanded the waters. Suni and Baji were berserkers, capable of leveling entire squadrons without breaking a sweat. Unegen could transform into a fox. Qara not only communed with birds, she could shoot out a peacock's eye from a hundred meters away. And Chaghan . . . she wasn't quite sure what Chaghan did, other than irritate her at every possible turn, but he seemed capable of making people lose their minds.

All of them combined against a single township official and his guards seemed like overkill.

But Yang Yuanfu was used to assassination attempts. You had to be, if you were one of the few uncorrupt officials left in the Empire. He shielded himself with a squadron of the most battle-hardy men in the province wherever he went.

Rin knew, based on Moag's reports, that Yang Yuanfu had survived at least thirteen assassination attempts over the past fifteen years. His guards were well accustomed to treachery. To get past them, you'd need fighters of unnatural ability. You needed overkill.

Once inside the warehouse, the Cike had nothing to do but wait. Unegen kept watch by the slats in the wall, twitching continuously. Chaghan and Qara sat with their backs against the wall, silent. Suni and Baji stood slouched, arms crossed casually as if simply waiting for their dinners.

Rin paced the room, focusing on her breathing and trying to ignore the twinges of pain in her temples.

She counted thirty hours since she'd ingested any opium. That was longer than she'd gone for weeks. She twisted her hands together as she walked, trying to force the twitching to go away.

It didn't help. It didn't stop the headache, either.

Fuck.

At first she'd thought she only needed the opium for the grief. She thought she would smoke it for the relief, until the memories of Speer and Altan dulled to a faint ache, until she could function without the suffocating guilt of what she'd done.

She thought *guilt* must be the word for it. The irrational feeling, not the moral concept. Because she'd told herself she wasn't sorry, that the Mugenese deserved what they got and that she was never looking back. Except the memory loomed like a gaping chasm in her mind where she'd tossed in every human feeling that threatened her.

But the abyss kept calling for her to look in. To fall inside.

And the Phoenix didn't want to let her forget. The Phoenix wanted her to gloat about it. The Phoenix lived on rage, and rage was intricately tied to the past. So the Phoenix needed to claw apart the open wounds in her mind and set fire to them, day after day, because that gave her memories and those memories fueled the rage.

Without opium the visions flashed constantly through Rin's mind's eye, often more vivid than her surrounding reality.

Sometimes they were of Altan. More times they weren't. The Phoenix was a conduit to generations of memories. Thousands upon thousands of Speerlies had prayed to the god in their grief and desperation. And the god had collected their suffering, stored it, and turned it into flames.

The memories could also be deceptively calm. Sometimes Rin saw brown-skinned children running up and down a pristine white beach. She saw flames burning higher on the shore—not funeral pyres, not flames of destruction, but campfires. Bonfires. Hearth fires, warm and sustaining.

And sometimes she saw the Speerlies, enough of them to fill a thriving village. She was always amazed by how *many* of them there were, an entire race of people that sometimes she feared she'd only dreamed up. If the Phoenix lingered, then Rin could even catch fragments of conversations in a language she almost understood, could see glimpses of faces that she almost recognized.

They weren't the ferocious beasts of Nikara lore. They weren't the mindless warriors the Red Emperor had needed them to be and every subsequent regime had forced them to be. They loved and laughed and cried around their fires. They were *people*.

But every time, before Rin could sink into the memory of a heritage she didn't have, she saw on the fading horizon boats sailing in from the Federation naval base on the mainland.

What happened next was a haze of colors, accumulated perspectives that shifted too fast for Rin to follow. Shouts, screams, movement. Rows and rows of Speerlies lined up on the beach, weapons in hand.

But it was never enough. To the Federation, they must have

seemed savages, using sticks to fight gods, and the booms of cannon fire lit up the village as quickly as if someone had held a light to kindling.

Gas pellets launched from the tower ships with terribly innocent popping noises. Where they hit the ground they expelled huge, thick clouds of acrid yellow smoke.

Women fell. Children twitched. The warrior ranks broke. The gas did not kill immediately; its inventors were not so kind.

Then the butchering began. The Federation fired continuously and indiscriminately. Mugenese crossbows could shoot three bolts at a time, unleashing an unceasing barrage of metal that ripped open necks, skulls, limbs, hearts.

Spilled blood traced marble patterns into white sand. Bodies lay still where they fell. At dawn, the Federation generals marched to the shore, boots treading indifferently over crushed bodies, advancing to slam their flag into the bloodstained sand.

"We've got a problem," Baji said.

Rin snapped back to attention. "What?"

"Take a look."

She heard the sudden sound of jangling bells—a happy sound, utterly out of place in this ruined city. She pressed her face to a gap in the warehouse slats. A cloth dragon bobbed up and down through the crowd, held up on tent poles by dancers below. Dancers waving streamers and ribbons followed behind, accompanied by musicians and government officials lifted on bright red sedan chairs. Behind them was the crowd.

"You said it was a small ceremony," Rin said. "Not a fucking parade."

"It was quiet just an hour ago," Unegen insisted.

"And now the whole township's clustering in that square." Baji squinted through the slats. "Are we still going by that 'no civilian casualties' rule?"

"Yes," Chaghan said before Rin could answer.

"You're no fun," Baji said.

"Crowds make targeted assassinations easier," Chaghan said. "It's a better opportunity to get in close. Make your hit without being spotted, then filter out before his guards have time to react."

Rin opened her mouth to say *That's still a lot of witnesses*, but the withdrawal cramps hit her first. A wave of pain tore through her muscles; it started in her gut and flared out, so sudden that for a moment the world turned black, and all she could do was clutch her chest, gasping.

"Are you all right?" Baji asked.

A wave of bile rose up in her throat before she could respond. She heaved. A second swell of nausea racked her gut. Then a third.

Baji put a hand on her shoulder. "Rin?"

"I'm *fine*," she insisted for what seemed like the thousandth time.

She wasn't fine. Her head was throbbing again, and this time the pain was accompanied by a nausea that seized her rib cage and didn't let go until she was doubled over on her knees, whimpering.

Vomit splattered the floor.

"Change of plans," Chaghan said. "Rin, get back to the ship."

She wiped her mouth. "No."

"I'm telling you you're not in any state to be useful."

"And I'm your commander," she said. "So shut up and do as I say."

Chaghan's eyes narrowed. The warehouse fell silent.

Rin had been wrestling Chaghan for control over the Cike for months. He questioned her decisions at every turn; he took every chance he could to make it very clear that he thought Altan had made a stupid decision naming her commander.

And Rin knew, in all fairness, he was right.

She was dreadful at leadership. Most of her attack plans over the past three months had boiled down to "everyone attack at once and see if we come out all right on the other side."

But command ability aside, she had to be here. Had to see Adlaga through. Since they'd left Speer her withdrawals had only been getting worse and worse. She'd been mostly functional during their first few missions for Moag. Then the endless killings, the screams, and the flashbacks to the battlefield kept setting her anger off again and again until she was spending more hours of the day high than she did sober, and even when she *was* sober she felt like she was still teetering on the brink of madness because the fucking Phoenix never shut up.

She needed to pull herself back from the precipice. If she couldn't do this basic, simple task; couldn't kill some township official who wasn't even a shaman, then she would hardly be able to stand up to the Empress.

And she couldn't lose her chance at revenge. Revenge was the only thing she had.

"Don't you jeopardize this," Chaghan said.

"Don't you patronize me," she retorted.

Chaghan sighed and turned to Unegen. "Can you watch her? I'll give you laudanum."

"I thought I was supposed to return to the ship," Unegen said.

"Change of plans."

"Fine." Unegen twitched out a shrug. "If I have to."

"Come on," Rin said. "I don't need a wet nurse."

"You'll wait in the corner of the crowd," Chaghan ordered, ignoring her. "You won't leave Unegen's side. You'll both act as reinforcements, and barring that, you will be the last resort."

She scowled. "Chaghan—"

"The *last resort*," he repeated. "You've killed enough innocents."

The hour came. The Cike dissipated, darting out of the warehouse to join the moving crowd one by one.

Rin and Unegen blended into Adlaga's masses easily enough. The main streets were packed with civilians, all caught up in their own miseries, and so many noises and sights came from all directions that Rin, unsure of where to look, couldn't help but feel a constant state of mild panic.

A wildly discordant mash of gongs and war drums drowned out the lute music from the front of the parade. Merchants hawked their wares every time they turned a corner, screaming prices with the sort of urgency that she associated with evacuation warnings. Celebratory red confetti littered the streets, tossed out in handfuls by children and entertainers, a snowfall of red paper flecks that covered every surface.

"How do they have the funds for this?" Rin muttered. "The Federation left them starving."

"Aid from Sinegard," Unegen guessed. "End-of-war celebration funds. Keeps them happy, keeps them loyal."

Rin saw food everywhere she looked. Huge cubes of watermelon on sticks. Red bean buns. Stalls selling soup dumplings dripping with soy sauce and lotus seed tarts lined the streets. Merchants flipped egg cakes with deft movements, and the crackle of oil under any other circumstances would make her hungry, but now the pungent smells only made her stomach turn.

It seemed both unfair and impossible that there could be such an abundance of food. Just days ago they had sailed past people who were drowning their babies in river mud because that was a quicker and more merciful death than letting them slowly starve.

If all this came from Sinegard, then that meant the Imperial bureaucracy had possessed food stores like this the entire time. Why had they withheld it during the war?

If the people of Adlaga were asking that same question, they didn't show it. Everyone looked so *happy*. Faces relaxed in simple relief because the war was over, the Empire was victorious, and they were safe.

And that made Rin furious.

She'd always had trouble with anger, she knew that. At Sinegard she'd constantly acted in furious, impulsive bursts and dealt with the consequences later. But now the anger was permanent, an unspeakable fury imposed upon her that she could neither contain nor control.

But she also didn't want to make it stop. The anger was a shield. The anger helped her to keep from remembering what she'd done.

Because as long as she was *angry*, then it was okay—she'd acted within reason. She was afraid that if she stopped being angry, she might crack apart.

She tried to distract herself by scanning the crowd for Yang Yuanfu and his guards. Tried to focus on the task at hand.

Her god wouldn't let her.

Kill them, encouraged the Phoenix. *They don't deserve their happiness. They didn't fight.*

She had a sudden vision of the marketplace on fire. She shook her head frantically, trying to tune out the Phoenix's voice. "No, stop . . ."

Make them burn.

Heat flared up in her palms. Her gut twisted. No—not here, not now. She squeezed her eyes shut.

Turn them to ash.

Her heartbeat began to quicken; her vision narrowed to a pinprick and expanded again. She felt feverish. The crowd suddenly seemed full of enemies. In one instant everyone was a blue-uniformed Federation soldier, bearing weapons; and in another they were civilians once again. She took a deep, choking breath, trying to force air into her lungs, eyes squeezed shut while she willed the red haze to go away once more.

This time it wouldn't.

The laughter, the music, the smiling faces standing around her all made her want to scream.

How dare they live when Altan was dead? It seemed horrifically unfair that life could keep on going and these people could be celebrating a war that they hadn't won for themselves, when they hadn't suffered for it . . .

The heat in her hands intensified.

Unegen seized her by the shoulder. "I thought you had your shit under control."

She jumped and spun around. "*I do!*" she hissed. Too loud. The people around her backed away from her.

Unegen pulled her toward the edge of the crowd, into the safety of the shadows under Adlaga's ruins. "You're drawing attention."

"I'm *fine*, Unegen, just let go—"

He didn't. "You need to calm down."

"I know—"

"No. I mean *right now*." He nodded over her shoulder. "She's here."

Rin turned.

And there sat the Empress, borne like a bride on a palanquin of red silk.

CHAPTER 2

The last time Rin had encountered the Empress Su Daji, she had been burning with fever, too delirious to see anything but Daji's face—lovely, hypnotic, with skin like porcelain and eyes like moth's wings.

The Empress was just as arresting as ever. Everyone Rin knew had emerged from the Mugenese invasion looking a decade older, jaded and scarred, but the Empress was as pale, ageless, and unmarked as ever, as if she existed on some transcendent plane untouchable by mortals.

Rin's breath quickened.

Daji wasn't supposed to be here.

It wasn't supposed to happen like this.

Images of Daji's body flashed through her mind. Head cracked against white marble. Pale neck sliced open. Body charred to nothing—but she wouldn't have burned immediately. Rin wanted to do it slowly, wanted to relish it.

A slow cheer went up through the crowd.

The Empress leaned out through the curtains and raised a hand so white it nearly glimmered in the sunlight. She smiled.

"We are victorious," she called out. "We have survived."

Anger flared inside Rin, so thick she almost choked on it. She felt like her body was covered with ant bites that she couldn't scratch at—a kind of frustration bubbling inside her, just begging her to let it explode.

How could the Empress be alive? The sheer contradiction infuriated her, the fact that Altan and Master Irjah and so many others were dead and Daji looked like she'd never even been wounded. She was the head of a nation that had bled millions to a senseless invasion—an invasion *she'd* invited—and she looked like she'd just arrived for a banquet.

Rin barged forward.

Unegen immediately dragged her back. "What are you doing?"

"What do you think?" Rin wrenched her arms out of his grip. "I'm going to get her. Go rally the others, I'll need backup—"

"Are you crazy?"

"She's *right there*! We'll never get a shot this good again!"

"Then let Qara do it."

"Qara doesn't have a clear shot," Rin hissed. Qara's station in the ruined bell towers was too high up. She couldn't get an arrow through—not past the carriage windows, not past this crowd. Inside the palanquin Daji was shielded on all sides; shots from the front would be blocked by the guards standing right before her.

And Rin was more concerned that Qara *wouldn't* shoot. She'd certainly seen the Empress by now, but she might be afraid to fire into a crowd of civilians, or to give away the Cike's location before any of them had a clear shot. Qara might have decided to be prudent.

Rin didn't care for prudence. The universe had delivered her this chance. She could end this all in minutes.

The Phoenix strained at her consciousness, eager and impatient. *Come now, child . . . Let me . . .*

She dug her fingernails into her palms. *Not yet.*

Too much distance separated her from the Empress. If she lit up now, everyone in the square was dead.

She wished desperately that she had better control over the fire. Or any control at all. But the Phoenix was antithetical to control.

The Phoenix wanted a roaring, chaotic blaze, consuming every-thing around her as far as the eye could see.

And when she called the god she couldn't tell her own desire apart from the Phoenix's; its desire, and her desire, was a death drive that demanded more to feed its fire.

She tried to think of something else, anything other than rage and revenge. But when she looked at the Empress, all she saw were flames.

Daji looked up. Her eyes locked on to Rin's. She lifted a hand and waved.

Rin froze. She couldn't look away. Daji's eyes became windows became memories became smoke, fire, corpses, and bones, and Rin felt herself falling, falling into a black ocean where all she could see was Altan as a human beacon igniting himself on a pier.

Daji's lips curved into a cruel smile.

Then the firecrackers set off behind Rin without warning—*pop-pop-pop*—and Rin's heart almost burst out of her chest.

Suddenly she was shrieking, hands pressed to her ears while her entire body shook.

"It's fireworks!" Unegen hissed. He dragged her wrists away from her head. "Just fireworks."

But that didn't mean anything—she *knew* they were fireworks, but that was a rational thought, and rational thoughts didn't matter when she shut her eyes and saw with every blast of sound explosions bursting behind her eyelids, flailing limbs, screaming children—

She saw a man dangling from the floorboards of a building that had been rent apart, trying to hold on with slippery fingers to slanting wooden planks to not fall into the flaming spears of timber below. She saw men and women plastered to the walls, dusted over with faint white powder so she might have thought they were statues if she couldn't see the dark shadow of blood in an outline all around them—

Too many people. She was trapped by too many people. She sank to her knees, face buried in her hands. The last time she'd been inside a crowd of people like this they'd been stampeding away from the horror of the inner city of Khurdalain—her eyes shot up and darted around, searching for escape routes, and found none, just unending walls of bodies packed together.

Too much. Too many sights, the information—her mind collapsed in on itself; bursts and flickers of fire emitted from her shoulders and exploded in the air above her, which just made her tremble harder.

And there were still *so many people*—they were crammed together, a teeming mass of outstretched arms, a nameless and faceless entity that wanted to tear her apart—

Thousands, hundreds of thousands—and you wiped them out of existence, you burned them in their beds—

"Rin, *stop!*" Unegen shouted.

It didn't matter, though. The crowd had formed a wide berth around her. Mothers dragged their children back. Veterans pointed and exclaimed.

She looked down. Smoke furled out from every part of her.

Daji's litter had disappeared. She'd been spirited to safety, no doubt; Rin's presence had been a glaring warning beacon. A line of Imperial guards pushed through the crowded street toward them, shields raised, spears pointed directly at Rin.

"Oh, fuck," Unegen said.

Rin backed away unsteadily, palms held out before her as if they belonged to a stranger. Someone else's fingers sparking with fire. Someone else's will dragging the Phoenix into this world.

Burn them.

Fire pulsed inside her. She could feel the veins straining behind her eyes. The pressure shot little stabs of pain behind her head, made her vision burst and pop.

Kill them.

The guard captain shouted an order. The Militia stormed her. Then her defensive instincts kicked in, and she lost all self-control. She heard a deafening silence in her mind, then a high, keening noise, the victorious cackle of a god that knew it had won.

When she finally looked at Unegen she didn't see a man, she saw a charred corpse, a white skeleton glistening over flesh sloughing away; she saw him decompose to ash within seconds and she was struck by how *clean* that ash was; so infinitely preferable to the complicated mess of bones and flesh that made him up now . . .

"*Stop it!*"

She heard not a scream, but a whimpering beg. For a split second Unegen's face flickered through the ash.

She was killing him. She knew she was killing him, and she couldn't stop.

She couldn't even move her own limbs. She stood immobile, fire roaring out of her extremities, holding her still like she'd been encased in stone.

Burn him, said the Phoenix.

"No, stop—"

This is what you want.

It wasn't what she wanted. But it wouldn't stop. Why would the Phoenix's gift include any inkling of control? It was an appetite that only strengthened; the fire consumed and wanted to consume more, and Mai'rinnen Tearza had warned her about this once but she hadn't listened and now Unegen was going to die. . . .

Something heavy clamped over her mouth. She tasted laudanum. Thick, sweet, and cloying. Panic and relief warred in her head as she choked and struggled, but Chaghan just squeezed the soaked cloth harder over her face as her chest heaved.

The ground swooped under her feet. She loosed a muffled shriek.

"Breathe," Chaghan ordered. "Shut up. Just breathe."

She choked against the sick and familiar smell; Enki had made this for her so many times. She fought not to struggle; pushed down her natural instincts—she had ordered them to do this, this was *supposed* to happen.

That didn't make it any easier to take.

Her legs buckled beneath her. Her shoulders sagged. She swooned into Chaghan's side.

He dragged her upright, slung her arm over his shoulder, and helped her toward the stairs. Smoke billowed in their path; the heat didn't affect Rin, but she could see Chaghan's hair curling, crinkling black at the edges.

"*Fuck*," he muttered under his breath.

"Where's Unegen?" she mumbled.

"He's fine, he'll be fine. . . ."

She wanted to insist on seeing him, but her tongue felt too heavy to form words. Her knees gave way entirely, but she didn't feel herself fall. The sedative worked its way through her bloodstream, and the world was a light and airy place, a fairy's domain. She heard someone yell. She felt someone lift her and place her on the bottom of the sampan.

She managed a last look over her shoulder.

On the horizon, the entire port town was lit up like a beacon—lamps illuminated on every deck, bells and smoke signals going up in the glowing air.

Every Imperial sentry could see that warning.

Rin had learned the standard Militia codes. She knew what those signals meant. They'd announced a manhunt for traitors to the throne.

"Congratulations," Chaghan said. "You've brought the entire Militia down on our backs."

"What are we going to—" Her tongue lolled heavy in her mouth. She'd lost the capacity to form words.

He put a hand on her shoulder and shoved. "Get down."

She tumbled gracelessly into the space under the seats. She opened her eyes wide to see the wooden base of the boat inches from her nose, so close she could count the grains. The lines along the wood swirled into ink images, which she tilted into, and then the ink assumed colors and became a world of red and black and orange.

The chasm opened. That was the only time it could—when she was high out of her mind, too out of control to stay away from the one thing she refused to let herself think about.

She was flying over the longbow island, she was watching the fire mountain erupt, streams of molten lava pouring over the peak, rushing in rivulets toward the cities below.

She saw the lives crushed out, burned and flattened and transformed to smoke in an instant. And it was so easy, like blowing out a candle, like crushing a moth under her finger; she wanted it and it happened; she had willed it like a god.

As long as she remembered it from that detached, bird's-eye view, she felt no guilt. She felt rather remotely curious, as if she had set an anthill on fire, as if she had impaled a beetle on a knife tip.

There was no guilt in killing insects, only the lovely, childish curiosity of seeing them writhe in their dying throes.

This wasn't a memory or a vision; this was an illusion she had conjured for herself, the illusion she returned to every time she lost control and they sedated her.

She wanted to see it—she *needed* to dance at the edge of this memory that she did not have, skirting between the godlike cold indifference of a murderer and the crippling guilt of the deed. She played with her guilt the way a child holds his palm to a candle flame, daring to venture just close enough to feel the stabbing licks of pain.

It was mental self-flagellation, the equivalent of digging a nail into an open sore. She knew the answer, of course, she just couldn't admit it to anyone—that at the moment she sank the island, the moment she became a murderer, she had wanted it.

"Is she all right?" Ramsa's voice. "Why is she laughing?"

Chaghan's voice. "She'll be fine."

Yes, Rin wanted to shout, yes, she was fine; just dreaming, just caught between this world and the next, just enraptured by the illusions of what she had done. She rolled around on the bottom of the sampan and giggled until the laughter turned to loud, harsh sobs, and then she cried until she couldn't see anymore.

CHAPTER 3

"Wake up."

Someone pinched her arm, hard. Rin bolted upright. Her right hand reached to a belt that wasn't there for a knife that was in the other room, and her left hand slammed blindly sideways into—

"Fuck!" Chaghan shouted.

She focused with difficulty on his face. He backed up, hands held out before her to show that he held no weapons, just a washcloth.

Rin's fingers moved frantically over her neck and wrists. She knew she wasn't tied down, she *knew*, but still she had to check.

Chaghan rubbed ruefully at his rapidly bruising cheek.

Rin didn't apologize for hitting him. He knew better than that. All of them knew better than that. They knew not to touch her without asking. Not to approach her from behind. Not to make sudden movements or sounds around her unless they wanted to end up a stick of charcoal floating to the bottom of Omonod Bay.

"How long have I been out?" She gagged. Her mouth tasted like something had died in it; her tongue was as dry as if she had spent hours licking at a wooden board.

"Couple of days," Chaghan said. "Good job getting out of bed."

"Days?"

He shrugged. "Messed up the dosage, I think. At least it didn't kill you."

Rin rubbed at dry eyes. Bits of hardened mucus came off the sides of her eyes in clumps. She caught a glimpse of her face in her bedside mirror. Her pupils weren't red—they took a while to adjust back every time she'd been on any kind of opiates—but the whites of her eyes were bloodshot, full of angry veins thick and sprawling like cobwebs.

Memories seeped slowly into the forefront of her mind, fighting through the fog of laudanum to sort themselves out. She squeezed her eyes shut, trying to separate what had happened from what she'd dreamed. A sick feeling pooled in her gut as slowly, her thoughts formed into questions. "Where's Unegen . . . ?"

"You burned over half his body. Nearly killed him." Chaghan's clipped tone spared her no sympathy. "We couldn't bring him with us, so Enki stayed behind to look after him. And they're, ah, not coming back."

Rin blinked several times, trying to make the world around her less blurry. Her head swam, disorienting her terribly every time she moved. "What? Why?"

"Because they've left the Cike."

That took several seconds to sink in.

"But—but they *can't*." Panic rose in her chest, thick and constricting. Enki was their only physician, and Unegen their best spy. Without them the Cike were reduced to six.

She couldn't kill the Empress with six people.

"You really can't blame them," Chaghan said.

"But they're *sworn*!"

"They swore to Tyr. They were sworn to Altan. They have no obligation to an incompetent like you." Chaghan cocked his head. "I suppose I don't have to tell you that Daji got away."

Rin glared at him. "I thought you were on my side."

"I said I'd help you kill Su Daji," he said. "I didn't say I'd hold your hand while you threatened the lives of everyone on this ship."

"But the others—" A sudden fear seized her. "They're still with me, aren't they? They're loyal?"

"It's nothing to do with loyalty," he said. "They are terrified."

"Of me?"

"You really can't see past yourself, can you?" Chaghan's lip curled. "They're terrified of themselves. It's very lonely to be a shaman in this Empire, especially when you don't know when you're going to lose your mind."

"I know. I understand that."

"You don't understand *anything*. They aren't afraid of going mad. They *know* they will. They know that soon they will become like Feylen. Prisoners inside their own bodies. And when that day comes, they want to be around the only other people who could put an end to it. *That's* why they're still here."

The Cike culls the Cike, Altan had once told her. *The Cike takes care of its own.*

That meant they defended one another. It also meant they protected the world from one another. The Cike were like children playing at acrobatics, perched precariously against one another, relying on the rest to stop them from hurtling into the abyss.

"Your duty as commander is to protect them," Chaghan said. "They are with you because they are scared, and they don't know where else they can go. But you're endangering them with every stupid decision you make and your utter lack of control."

Rin moaned, clutching her head between her hands. Every word was like a knife to her eardrums. She knew she'd fucked up, but Chaghan seemed to take inordinate delight in rubbing it in. "Just leave me alone."

"No. Get out of bed and stop being such a brat."

"Chaghan, please—"

"You're a fucking mess."

"I know that."

"Yes, you've known that since Speer, but you're not getting better, you're getting worse. You're trying to fix everything with opium and it's destroying you."

"I *know*," she whispered. "I just—it's always *there*, it's screaming in my mind—"

"Then control it."

"I *can't*."

"Why not?" He made a noise of disgust. "Altan did."

"But I'm not Altan." She couldn't hold back her tears. "Is that what you wanted to tell me? I'm not as strong as him, I'm not as smart as him, I can't do what he could do—"

He laughed harshly. "Oh, that much is clear."

"*You* take command then. You act like you're in charge already, why don't you just take the post? I don't fucking care."

"Because Altan named you commander," he said simply. "And between us, at least I know how to respect his legacy."

That shut her up.

He leaned forward. "That burden's on you. So you will learn to control yourself, and you will start protecting them."

"But what if that's not possible?" she asked.

His pale eyes didn't blink. "Frankly? Then you should kill yourself."

Rin had no idea how to respond to that.

"If you think you can't beat it, then you should die," Chaghan said. "Because it will corrode you. It will turn your body into a conduit, and it will burn down everything until it's not just civilians, not just Unegen, but everyone around you, everything you've ever loved or cared about.

"And once you've turned your world to ash, you'll *wish* you could die."

She found the others in the mess once she finally recovered the physical coordination to make her way down the passageway without tripping.

"What is this?" Ramsa spat something onto the table. "Bird droppings?"

"Goji berries," Baji said. "You don't like them in porridge?"

"They've got mold on them."

"Everything's got mold on them."

"But I thought we were getting new supplies," Ramsa whined.

"With what money?" Suni asked.

"We are the *Cike*!" Ramsa exclaimed. "We could have stolen something!"

"Well, it's not like—" Baji broke off as he saw Rin standing in the doorway. Ramsa and Suni followed his gaze. They fell silent.

She stared back at them, utterly lost for words. She'd thought she knew what she was going to say to them. Now she only wanted to cry.

"Rise and shine," Ramsa said finally. He kicked a chair out for her. "Hungry? You look horrific."

She blinked at him. Her words came out in a hoarse whisper. "I just wanted to say . . ."

"Don't," said Baji.

"But I just—"

"*Don't*," Baji said. "I know it's hard. You'll get it eventually. Altan did."

Suni nodded in silent agreement.

Rin's urge to cry grew stronger.

"Have a seat," Ramsa said gently. "Eat something."

She shuffled to the counter and tried clumsily to fill a bowl. Porridge slopped out of the ladle onto the deck. She walked toward the table, but the floor kept shifting under her feet. She collapsed into the chair, breathing hard.

No one commented.

She glanced out the porthole. They were moving startlingly fast over choppy waters. The shoreline was nowhere in sight. A wave rolled under the planks, and she stifled the attendant swell of nausea.

"Did we at least get Yang Yuanfu?" she asked after a pause.

Baji nodded. "Suni took him out during the commotion. Bashed his head against the wall and flung his body into the ocean while his guards were too busy with Daji to fend us off. I guess the diversion tactic worked after all. We were going to tell you, but you were, ah, incapacitated."

"High out of your mind," Ramsa supplied. "Giggling at the floor."

"I get it," Rin said. "And we're heading back to Ankhiluun now?"

"As fast as we can. We've got the entire Imperial Guard chasing us, but I doubt they'll follow us into Moag's territory."

"Makes sense," Rin murmured. She worked her spoon through the porridge. Ramsa was right about the mold. The greenish-black blotches were so large that they almost rendered the entire thing inedible. Her stomach roiled. She pushed the bowl away.

The others sat around the table, fidgeting, blinking, and making eye contact with everything except her.

"I heard Enki and Unegen left," she said.

The statement was met with blank stares and shrugs.

She took a deep breath. "So I suppose—what I wanted to say was—"

Baji interrupted before she could continue. "We're not going anywhere."

"But you—"

"I don't like being lied to. And I especially hate being sold. Daji has what's coming for her. I'm seeing this through to the end, little Speerly. You don't have to worry about desertion from me."

Rin glanced around the table. "Then what about the rest of you?"

"Altan deserved better than he got," Suni said simply, as if that much sufficed.

"But you don't have to stay here." Rin turned to Ramsa. Young, innocent, tiny, brilliant, and dangerous. Ramsa. She wanted to make sure he'd remain with her, and knew it'd be selfish to ask. "I mean, you shouldn't."

Ramsa scraped at the bottom of his bowl. He seemed thoroughly disinterested in the conversation. "I think going anywhere else would get a little boring."

"But you're just a kid."

"Fuck off." He dug around his mouth with his little finger,

picking at something stuck behind his back molars. "You've got to understand that we're killers. You spend your life doing one thing, it's very hard to stop."

"That, and our only other option is the prison at Baghra," Baji said.

Ramsa nodded. "I hated Baghra."

Rin remembered that none of the Cike had good track records with Nikara law enforcement. Or with civilized society, for that matter.

Aratsha hailed from a tiny village in Snake Province where the villagers worshipped a local river god that purportedly protected them from floods. Aratsha, a novice initiate to the river god's cult, became the first shaman in generations who succeeded in doing what his predecessors had claimed. He drowned two little girls by accident in the process. He was about to be stoned to death by the same villagers who praised his fraudulent teachers when Tyr, the Cike's former commander, recruited him to the Night Castle.

Ramsa came from a family of alchemists who'd produced fire powder for the Militia until an accidental explosion near the palace had killed his parents, cost him an eye, and landed him in the notorious prison at Baghra for alleged conspiracy to assassinate the Empress, until Tyr pulled him out of his cell to engineer weapons for the Cike instead.

Rin didn't know much about Baji or Suni. She knew they had both been students at Sinegard once, members of Lore classes of years past. She knew they'd been expelled when things went terribly wrong. She knew they'd both spent time at Baghra. Neither of them would volunteer much else.

The twins Chaghan and Qara were equally mysterious. They weren't from the Empire. They spoke Nikara with a lilting Hinterlander accent. But when asked about home, they offered only the vaguest utterances. *Home is very far away. Home is at the Night Castle.*

Rin understood what they were trying to say. They, like the others, simply had no other place to go.

"What's the matter?" Baji asked. "Sounds like you want us gone."

"It's not that," Rin said. "I just—I can't make it go away. I'm scared."

"Of what?"

"I'm scared I'll hurt you. Adlaga won't be the end. I can't make the Phoenix go away and I can't make it stop and—"

"Because you're new to this," Baji interrupted. He sounded so kind. How could he be so kind? "We've all been there. They want to use your body all the time. And you think you're on the brink of madness, you think that this moment is going to be when you finally snap, but it's not."

"How do you know that?"

"Because it gets easier every time. Eventually you learn to exist on the precipice of insanity."

"But I can't promise I won't—"

"You won't. And we'll go after Daji again. And we'll keep doing it, over and over, as many times as it takes, until she's dead. Tyr didn't give up on us. We're not giving up on you. This is why the Cike exists."

She stared at him, stricken. She didn't deserve this, whatever this was. It wasn't friendship. She didn't deserve that. It wasn't loyalty, either. She deserved that even less. But it was camaraderie, a bond formed by a common betrayal. The Empress had sold them to the Federation for a silver and a song, and none of them could rest until the rivers ran red with Daji's blood.

"I don't know what to say."

"Then just shut up and stop being a little bitch about it." Ramsa pushed her bowl back in front of her. "Eat your porridge. Mold is nutritious."

Night fell over Omonod Bay. The *Petrel* spirited down the coast under the cover of darkness, buoyed by a shamanic force so powerful that within hours it had lost its Imperial pursuers. The Cike spread out—Qara and Chaghan to their cabin, where they spent almost all of their time, secluded from the others; Suni and Ramsa onto the front deck for night watch, and Baji to his hammock in the main sleeping quarters.

Rin locked herself inside her cabin to wage a mental battle with a god.

She didn't have much time. The laudanum had nearly worn off. She wedged a chair under the doorknob, sat down on the floor, squeezed her head between her knees, and waited to hear the voice of a god.

She waited to return to the state in which the Phoenix wanted utter command and shouted down her thoughts until she obeyed.

This time she would shout back.

She placed a small hunting knife beside her knee. She pressed her eyes shut. She felt the last of the laudanum pass through her bloodstream, and the numb, foggy cloud left her mind. She felt the curdling clench in her stomach and gut that never disappeared. She felt, along with the terrifying possibility of sobriety, *awareness*.

She always came back to the same moment, months ago, when she'd been on her hands and knees in that temple on the Isle of Speer. The Phoenix relished that moment because to the god it was the height of destructive power. And it kept bringing her back because it wanted her to believe that the only way to reconcile herself with that horror was to finish the job.

It wanted her to burn up this ship. To kill everyone around her. Then to find her way to land, and start burning that down, too; like a small flame igniting the corner of a sheet of paper, she was to make her way inland and burn down everything in her path until nothing was left except a blank slate of ash.

And then she would be clean.

She heard a symphony of screams, voices both collective and individual, Speerly or Mugini voices—it never mattered because wordless agony didn't have a language.

She could not bear how they were numbers and not numbers all at once, and the line kept blurring and it was awful because as long as they were numbers it wasn't so bad but if they were *lives*, then the multiplication was unbearable—

Then the screaming solidified into Altan.

His face splintered apart along cracks of skin turned charcoal, eyes burning orange, black tears opening streaks across his face, fire tearing him open from the inside—and she couldn't do anything about it.

"I'm sorry," she whispered. "I'm sorry, I'm sorry, I *tried* . . ."

"It should have been you," he said. His lips blistered, crackled, fell away to reveal bone. "You should have died. You should have gone up in flames." His face became ash became a skull, pressed against hers; bony fingers around her neck. "It should have been you."

Then she couldn't tell if her thoughts were his or her own, only that they were so loud they drowned out everything in her mind.

I want you to hurt.

I want you to die.

I want you to burn.

"No!" She slammed her blade into her thigh. The pain was only a temporary respite, a blinding whiteness that drove out everything in her mind, and then the fire would be back.

She'd failed.

And she'd failed last time, too, and the time before that. She'd failed every time she tried. At this point she didn't know why she did it, except to torture herself with the knowledge that she could not control the fire raging in her mind.

The cut joined a line of open wounds on her arms and legs that she'd sliced open weeks before—and kept sliced open—because even though it was only temporary, pain was still the only option other than opium that she could think of.

And then she couldn't think anymore.

The motions were automatic now, and it all came so easily—rolling the opium nugget between her palms, the spark of the first flicker of flame, and then the smell of crystallized candy concealing something rotten.

The nice thing about opium was that once she'd inhaled it, everything stopped mattering; and for hours at a time, carved out into her world, she could stop dealing with the responsibility of existence.

She sucked in.

The flames receded. The memories disappeared. The world stopped hurting her, and even the frustration of surrender faded to a dull nothing. And the only thing that remained was the sweet, sweet smoke.

CHAPTER 4

"Did you know that Ankhiluun has a special government office dedicated to figuring out how much weight the city can sustain?" Ramsa asked brightly.

He was the only one of them who could navigate the Floating City with ease. He hopped ahead, effortlessly navigating the narrow footbridges that lined the sludgy canals, while the rest inched warily along the wobbly planks.

"And how much weight is that?" Baji asked, humoring him.

"I think they're approaching maximum capacity," Ramsa said. "Someone's got to do something about the population, or Ankhiluun's going to start sinking."

"You could send them inland," Baji said. "Bet we've lost a couple hundred thousand people in the last few months."

"Or just have them fight another war. Good way to kill people off." Ramsa skipped off toward the next bridge.

Rin followed clumsily behind, blinking blearily under the unforgiving southern sun.

She hadn't left her cabin on the ship for days. She'd taken the smallest possible daily dose of opium that worked to keep her mind quiet while leaving her functional. But even that amount fucked so badly with her sense of balance that she had to cling to Baji's arm as they walked inland.

Rin hated Ankhiluun. She hated the salty, tangy ocean odor that followed her wherever she went; she hated the city's sheer loudness, the pirates and merchants screaming at each other in Ankhiluuni pidgin, an unintelligible mix of Nikara and western languages. She hated that the Floating City teetered over open water, roiling back and forth with each incoming wave, so that even standing still, she felt like she was about to fall.

She wouldn't have come here except out of utter necessity. Ankhiluun was the single place in the Empire where she was close to safe. And it was home to the only people who would sell her weapons.

And opium.

At the end of the First Poppy War, the Republic of Hesperia sat down with delegates from the Federation of Mugen to sign a treaty that established two neutral zones on the Nikara coastline. The first was at the international port of Khurdalain. The second was at the floating city of Ankhiluun.

Back then Ankhiluun had been a humble port—just a smattering of nondescript one-story buildings without basements because the flimsy coastal sands couldn't support any larger architecture.

Then the Trifecta won the Second Poppy War, and the Dragon Emperor bombed half the Hesperian fleet to smithereens in the South Nikan Sea.

In the absence of foreigners, Ankhiluun flourished. The locals occupied the half-destroyed ships like ocean parasites, linking them together to form the Floating City. Now Ankhiluun extended precariously from the coastline like an overreaching spider, a series of wooden planks that formed a web of walkways between the myriad ships anchored to shore.

Ankhiluun was the juncture through which poppy in all its forms entered the Empire. Moag's opium clippers sailed in from the western hemisphere and deposited their cargo in giant, empty husks of ships that served as repositories, from which long, thin smuggling boats picked it up and poured through branches of tributaries spreading out from the Murui River, steadily infusing the Empire's bloodstream like seeping poison.

Ankhiluun meant cheap, abundant opium, and that meant glorious, peaceful oblivion—hours upon hours when she didn't have to think about or remember anything at all.

And that, above all, was why Rin hated Ankhiluun. It made her so terribly afraid. The more time she spent here, locked alone in her cabin while she drifted on Moag's drugs, the less she felt able to leave.

"Odd," said Baji. "You'd think we'd get more of a welcome."

To get to the city center, they'd passed floating markets, garbage piles strewn along the canals, and rows of distinctive Ankhiluuni bars that had no benches or chairs—only ropes strung across walls where patrons could hang drunk by their armpits.

But they had been walking for more than half an hour now. They were well within the heart of the city, in full view of its residents, and no one had intercepted them.

Moag had to know they were back. Moag knew *everything* that happened in the Floating City.

"That's just how Moag likes to play power politics." Rin stopped walking to catch her breath. The shifting planks made her want to vomit. "She doesn't seek us out. We have to go to her."

Getting an audience with Chiang Moag was no easy affair. The Pirate Queen surrounded herself with so many layers of security that no one knew where she was at any given time. Only the Black Lilies, her cohort of spies and assistants, could be counted upon to get word directly to her, and the Lilies could only be found at a gaudy pleasure barge floating in the center of the city's main canal.

Rin looked up, shielding her eyes from the sun. "There."

The *Black Orchid* wasn't so much a ship as it was a floating three-story mansion. Garishly colorful lanterns hung from its sloped pagoda roofs, and bawdy, energetic music drifted constantly from its papered windows. Each day starting at noon, the *Black Orchid* crawled up and down the still canal, picking up patrons who rowed out to its decks in bright red sampans.

Rin dug around in her pockets. "Anyone got a copper?"

"I do." Baji tossed a coin toward the sampan boatman, who guided his vessel toward the shore to ferry the Cike onto the pleasure barge.

A handful of Lilies, perched lightly on the second-story railing, waved insouciantly at them as they approached. Baji whistled back.

"Stop that," Rin muttered.

"Why?" Baji asked. "It makes them happy. Look, they're smiling."

"No, it makes them think you're an easy target."

The Lilies were Moag's private army of terribly attractive women, all with breasts the size of pears and waists so narrow they looked in danger of snapping in half. They were trained martial artists, linguists, and uniformly the most obnoxious group of women Rin had ever met.

A Lily stopped them at the top of the gangplank, her tiny hand stretched out as if she could physically stop them from boarding. "You don't have an appointment."

She was clearly a new girl. She couldn't have been older than fifteen. Her face bore only small dabs of lipstick, her breasts were just little buds poking through her shirt, and she didn't seem to realize she was standing in front of a handful of the most dangerous people in the Empire.

"I'm Fang Runin," said Rin.

The girl blinked. "Who?"

Rin heard Ramsa turn his snicker into a cough.

"*Fang Runin*," she repeated. "I don't need an appointment."

"Oh, love, that's not how it works here." The girl tapped slim fingers against her impossibly narrow waist. "You've got to make an appointment, and we're booked up days in advance." She peered over Rin's shoulder at Baji, Suni, and Ramsa. "Also, it's extra for groups larger than four. The girls don't like it when you share."

Rin reached for her blade. "Look here, you little shit—"

"*Back up.*" Suddenly the girl was holding a fistful of needles she must have concealed in her sleeve. Their tips were purple with poison. "No one touches a Lily."

Rin fought the sudden urge to slap the girl across her face. "If you don't move aside this *second*, I'll shove this blade so far up your—"

"Well, this is a surprise." The silk sheets over the main doors rustled, and a voluptuous figure emerged on deck. Rin stifled a groan.

It was Sarana, a Black Lily of the highest distinction and Moag's personal favorite. She'd been Moag's go-between with the Cike since they landed at Ankhiluun three months ago. She possessed an unbearably sharp tongue, an obsession with sexual innuendo, and—according to Baji—the most perfect breasts south of the Murui.

Rin hated her.

"Fancy seeing you here." Sarana approached, cocking her head to the side. "We thought you weren't interested in women."

She had a way of shimmying when she spoke, accentuating each word with a shake of her hips. Baji made a choking noise. Ramsa was staring unabashedly at Sarana's chest.

"I need to see Moag," Rin said.

"Moag's busy," Sarana replied.

"I think Moag knows better than to keep me waiting."

Sarana raised her finely drawn eyebrows. "She also doesn't like to be disrespected."

"Must I be blunt?" Rin snapped. "Unless you want this boat going up in flames, you go get your mistress and tell her I want an audience."

Sarana feigned a yawn. "Be nice to me, Speerly. Else I'll tattle."

"I could sink your barge in minutes."

"And Moag would have you shot full of arrows before you

could even get off the boat." Sarana gave her a dismissive wave. "Get going, Speerly. We'll send for you when Moag is ready."

Rin saw red.

The fucking *nerve.*

Sarana might have thought it an insult, but Rin *was* a Speerly. She'd single-handedly won the Third Poppy War. She'd sunk a fucking *country.* She hadn't come this far just to banter with some stupid Lily whore.

Her hands shot out and grabbed Sarana by the collar. Sarana moved for her hairpiece, which was no doubt poisoned, but Rin slammed her against the wall, wedged one elbow against her throat, and pinned her right wrist down with the other.

She leaned forward to press her lips against Sarana's ear. "Maybe you think you're safe now. Maybe I'll just turn and walk away. You'll brag to the other bitches how you scared the Speerly off! Lucky you! Then one night, when you've turned off the lanterns and rolled up the gangplank, you'll smell smoke in your quarters. You'll run out onto the deck, but by then the flames will be burning so hot you can't see two feet in front of you. You'll know it's me, but you'll never be able to tell Moag, because a sheet of fire will burn all your pretty skin off, and the last thing you'll see before you leap off the ship into boiling-hot water is my laughing face." Rin dug her elbow deeper into Sarana's pale throat. "Don't *fuck with me,* Sarana."

Sarana patted frantically at Rin's wrists.

Rin tilted her head. "What was that?"

Sarana's voice was a strangled whisper. "Moag . . . might make an exception."

Rin let go. Sarana collapsed back against the wall, frantically fanning her face.

The red haze ebbed from the edges of Rin's vision. She closed a fist and opened it, let loose a long breath, and wiped her palm against her tunic. "That's more like it."

"We're here," Sarana announced.

Rin reached up to remove the blindfold from her face. Sarana had made her come alone—the others were more than happy to stay on the pleasure barge—and her naked vulnerability had kept her twitching and sweating during their entire journey through the canals.

At first she saw nothing but darkness. Then her eyes adjusted to the dim lights, and she saw that the room was lit up with tiny, flickering fire lamps. She saw no windows, no glints of sunshine. She couldn't tell whether they were in a ship or in a building; whether nighttime had fallen or if the room was simply sealed so well that no outside light could get in. The air indoors was much cooler than outside. She thought she could still feel the rocking sea beneath her legs, but only faintly, and she couldn't tell if it was real or imagined.

Wherever she was, the building was massive. A grounded warship? A warehouse?

She saw blocky furniture with curved legs that surely had to be of foreign origin; they didn't carve tables like that in the Empire. Along the walls hung portraits, though they couldn't have been of Nikara men; the subjects were pale-skinned, angry-looking, and all wearing absurdly shaped white wigs. A massive table, large enough to seat twenty, occupied the center of the room.

On the other side, flanked by a squadron of Lily archers, sat the Pirate Queen herself.

"Runin." Moag's voice was a gravelly drawl, deep and oddly compelling. "Always a pleasure."

In the streets of Ankhiluun, they called Moag the Stone Widow. She was a tall, broad-shouldered woman, more handsome than pretty. They said she was a prostitute from the bay who'd married one of Ankhiluun's many pirate captains. Then he died under circumstances that were never properly examined, and Moag rose steadily through the ranks of Ankhiluun's pirate hierarchy and consolidated a fleet of unprecedented strength. She was the first to ever unite the pirate factions of Ankhiluun under one flag. Until her reign, the disparate bandits of Ankhiluun had been at war with one another in the same way the twelve provinces of Nikan had been at war since the death of the Red Emperor. In a way, she had managed to do what Daji never could. She'd convinced disparate factions of soldiers to serve a single cause—herself.

"I don't think you've ever been to my private office." Moag gestured around the room. "Nice place, isn't it? The Hesperians were unbearably annoying, but they knew how to decorate."

"What happened to the original owners?" Rin asked.

"Depends. I assume the Hesperian Navy taught their sailors how to swim." Moag pointed to the chair opposite her. "Sit."

"No, thanks." Rin couldn't bear sitting in chairs anymore. She hated the way that tables blocked her legs—if she jumped or tried to run, her knees would slam against the wood, costing her precious escape time.

"Have it your way, then." Moag cocked her head to the side. "I heard Adlaga didn't go well."

"Got derailed," Rin said. "Had a surprise encounter with Daji."

"Oh, I know," Moag said. "The whole coastline knows about it. You know how Sinegard has spun this, right? You're the rogue Speerly, traitor to the crown. Your Mugenese captors drove you mad, and now you're a threat to everyone you come across. The bounty on your head has been raised to six thousand Imperial silvers. Double if you're alive."

"That's nice," Rin said.

"You don't seem concerned."

"They're not wrong about anything." Rin leaned forward. "Look, Yang Yuanfu is dead. We couldn't bring back his head, but your scouts will confirm everything as soon as they can get to Adlaga. It's time to pay up."

Moag ignored that, resting her chin on her fingertips. "I don't get it. Why go to all this trouble?"

"Moag, come on—"

Moag lifted a hand to cut her off. "Talk me through this. You have power beyond what most people could dream of. You could do anything you want. Become a warlord. Become a pirate. Hell, captain one of my ships if you want to. Why keep picking this fight?"

"Because Daji started this war," Rin said. "Because she killed my friends. Because she remains on the throne and she shouldn't. Because *someone* has to kill her, and I'd rather it be me."

"But *why*?" Moag pressed. "No one hates our Empress as much as I do. But understand this, little girl: you're not going to find allies. Revolution is fine in theory. But nobody wants to die."

"I'm not asking anyone else to risk it. Just give *me* weapons."

"And if you fail? You don't think the Militia will track where your supplies came from?"

"I killed thirty men for you," Rin snapped. "You owe me any supplies I want; those were the terms. You can't just—"

"What can't I do?" Moag leaned forward, ringed fingers circling the hilt of her dagger. She looked deeply amused. "You think I *owe* you? By what contract? Under what laws? What will you do, take me to court?"

Rin blinked. "But you said—"

"'But you said,'" Moag mocked in a high-pitched voice. "People say things they don't mean all the time, little Speerly."

"But we had an agreement!" Rin raised her voice, but her words came out plaintive, not dominant. She sounded childish even to her own ears.

Several Lilies began to titter into their fans.

Rin's hands tightened into fists. The residual opium kept her from erupting into fire, but still a haze of scarlet entered her vision.

She took a deep breath. *Calm.*

Murdering Moag might feel good in the moment, but she doubted even she could get out of Ankhiluun alive.

"You know, for someone of your pedigree, you're incredibly stupid," Moag said. "Speerly abilities, Sinegard education, Militia service, and you still don't understand the way the world works. If you want to get things done, you need brute force. I need you, and I'm the only one who can pay you, which means you need me. Complain all you want. You're not going anywhere."

"But you're *not* paying me." Rin couldn't help it. "So fuck you."

Eleven arrowheads pointed to her forehead before she could move.

"*Stand down,*" Sarana hissed.

"Don't be so dramatic." Moag examined her lacquered nails. "I'm trying to help you, you know. You're young. You've got a whole life ahead of you. Why waste it on revenge?"

"I need to get to the capital," Rin insisted stubbornly. "And if you won't give me supplies, then I'll go elsewhere."

Moag sighed theatrically, pressed her fingers against her temples, and then folded her arms on the table. "I propose a compromise. One more job, and then I'll give you everything you want. Will that work?"

"What, I'm supposed to trust you now?"

"What choice do you have?"

Rin chewed on that. "What kind of job?"

"How do you feel about naval battles?"

"Hate them." Rin didn't like being over open water. She'd only agreed to jobs on land so far, and Moag knew that. Around the ocean, she was too easily incapacitated.

Fire and water didn't mix.

"I'm sure a healthy reward would change your mind." Moag rummaged in her desk, pulled out a charcoal rendering of a ship and slid it across the table. "This is the *Heron*. Standard opium skimmer. Red sails, Ankhiluuni flag, unless the captain's changed it. He's been coming up short in the books for months."

Rin stared at her. "You want me to kill someone based on accounting errors?"

"He's keeping more than his fair share of his profits. He's been very clever about it, too. Got an accountant to fudge the numbers so that it took me weeks to detect. But we keep triple copies of everything. The numbers don't lie. I want you to sink his ship."

Rin considered the rendering. She recognized the ship build.

Moag had at least a dozen skimmers just like it sitting in Ankhiluun's harbor. "Is he still in the city?"

"No. But he's scheduled to return to port in a few days. He thinks I don't know what he's done."

"Then why don't you get rid of him yourself?"

"Under regular circumstances I would," said Moag. "But then I'd have to give him the pirate's justice."

"Since when does Ankhiluun care about *justice*?"

"The fact that we're independent from the Empire doesn't make us an anarchy, dear. We'd hold a trial. It's standard procedure with embezzlement cases. But I don't want to give him a fair trial. He's well-liked, he has too many friends in this city, and punishment by my hand would certainly provoke retaliation. I'm not in the mood for politics. I want him blown out of the water."

"No prisoners?"

Moag grinned. "Not a high priority."

"Then I'll need to borrow a skimmer."

Moag's smile widened. "Do this for me and you can keep the skimmer."

This wasn't optimal. Rin needed a ship with Militia colors, not a smuggling vessel, and Moag might still withhold the weapons and money. No—she had to take it for granted Moag would cheat her, some way or another.

But she had no leverage. Moag had the ships, she had the soldiers, so she could dictate the terms. All Rin had was the ability to kill people, and no one better to sell it to.

She had no better options. She was strategically backed into a corner, and she couldn't think her way out.

But she knew someone who could.

"There's something else I want," she said. "Kitay's address."

"Kitay?" Moag narrowed her eyes. Rin could watch the thoughts spinning in her head, trying to determine if it was a liability, if it was worth the charity.

"We're friends," Rin said as smoothly as she could. "We were classmates. I care about him. That's all it is."

"And you're only asking about him now?"

"We're not going to flee the city, if that's what you're worried about."

"Oh, you'd never manage that." Moag gave her a pitying look. "But he asked me not to tell you where to find him."

Rin supposed she shouldn't have been surprised. It still stung.

"Doesn't matter," she said. "I still want the address."

"I gave him my word I'd keep it a secret."

"Your word means nothing, you old hag." Rin couldn't suppress her impatience. "Right now you're just dithering for the fun of it."

Moag laughed. "Fair enough. He's in the old foreign district. A safe house at the very end of the walkway. You'll see Red Junk Fleet symbols on the doorposts. I've posted a guard there, but I'll tell them to stand down if they see you. Shall I let him know you're coming?"

"Please don't," Rin said. "I'll surprise him."

The old foreign district was still and silent, a rare oasis of calm in the never-ending cacophony that comprised Ankhiluun. Half these houses were abandoned—no one had lived here since the Hesperians left, and the remaining buildings were used only to store inventory. The bright lights that littered the rest of Ankhiluun were absent. This place lay uncomfortably far from the open central square, where Moag's guards had easy access.

Rin didn't like that.

But Kitay had to be safe. Tactically, it would be a terrible idea to let him get hurt. He was a remarkable reserve of knowledge. He read everything and forgot nothing. He was best kept alive as an asset, and Moag had surely realized it since she'd put him under house arrest.

The lone house at the end of the road floated a little ways off from the rest of the bobbing street, tethered only by two long chains and a hazardous floating walkway made of badly spaced planks.

Rin stepped gingerly over the planks, then rapped on the wooden door. No response.

She tried the handle. It didn't even have a lock—she couldn't see a keyhole. They'd made it impossible for Kitay to keep visitors out.

She pushed the door open.

The first thing she noticed was the mess—a sprawl of yellowing books, maps, and ledgers that littered every visible surface. She blinked around in the dim lamplight until she finally saw Kitay sitting in the corner with a thick tome over his lap, nearly buried under stacks of leather-bound books.

"I've already eaten," he said without looking up. "Come back in the morning."

She cleared her throat. "Kitay."

He looked up. His eyes widened.

"Hello," she said.

Slowly he set his books to the side.

"Can I come in?" she asked.

Kitay stared at her for a long moment before waving her inside. "Fine."

She shut the door behind her. He made no move to get up, so she picked her way through the papers toward him, taking care not to step on any pages. Kitay had always hated when anyone disturbed his carefully arranged messes. During exam season at Sinegard, he'd thrown temper tantrums whenever someone moved his inkwells.

The room was so cramped that the only empty space was a patch of floor against the wall right beside him. Taking care not to touch him, she slid down, crossed her legs, and placed her hands on her knees.

For a moment they simply stared at each other.

Rin wanted desperately to reach out and touch his face. He looked weak, and far too thin. He had healed some since Golyn Niis, but even now his collarbone protruded to a frightening degree, and his wrists looked so fragile she might snap them with one hand. He had grown his hair out in a long, curly mess that he'd bunched up at the back of his head, which pulled at the edges of his face and made his cheekbones stick out more than they already did.

He didn't remotely resemble the boy she'd met at Sinegard.

The difference was in his eyes. They used to be so bright, lit up with a feverish curiosity about everything. Now they were just dull and blank.

"Can I stay?" she asked.

"I let you in, didn't I?"

"You told Moag to keep your address from me."

"Oh." He blinked. "Yes. I did do that."

He wouldn't meet her eyes. She knew him well enough to know that this meant he was furious with her, but after all these months, she still didn't know precisely why.

No—she did, she just wouldn't admit that she was wrong about it. The one time they'd fought about it, *really* fought about it, he'd slammed the door shut on her and hadn't spoken to her until they reached dry land.

She hadn't let herself think about it since. It went into the chasm, just like every other memory that made her start craving her pipe.

"How are you doing?" she asked.

"I'm under house arrest. How do you think I'm doing?"

She looked around at the papers splayed out across the table. They littered the floor, pinned down with inkwells.

Her eyes landed on the ledger he'd been scribbling in. "She's kept you busy, at least?"

"'Busy' is a word for it." He slammed the ledger shut. "I'm working for one of the Empire's most wanted criminals, and she's got me doing her *taxes*."

"Ankhiluun doesn't pay taxes."

"Not taxes to the Empire. To Moag." Kitay twirled the ink brush in his fingers. "Moag's running a massive crime ring with a taxation scheme that's just as complicated as any city bureaucracy's. But the record-keeping system they've been using so far, it's . . ." He waved his hands in the air. "Whoever designed this didn't understand how numbers work."

What a brilliant move on Moag's part, Rin thought. Kitay had the mental dexterity of twenty scholars combined. He could add impossibly large sums without blinking, and he had a mind for strategy that had rivaled Master Irjah's. He might be grumpy under house arrest, but he couldn't resist a puzzle when presented with one. The ledgers may as well have been a bucket of toys.

"Are they treating you all right?" she asked.

"Well enough. I get two meals a day. Sometimes more, if I've been good."

"You look thin."

"The food's not very good."

He still wouldn't look at her. She ventured to place a hand on his arm. "I'm sorry Moag's kept you here."

He jerked away. "Wasn't your decision. I'd do the same if I'd taken myself prisoner."

"Moag's really not so bad. She treats her people well."

"And she uses violence and extortion to run a massively illegal city that has been lying to Sinegard for twenty years," said Kitay. "I'm worried you're starting to lose your sense of scale here, Rin."

She rankled at that. "Her people are still better off than the Empress's subjects."

"The Empress's subjects would be fine if her generals weren't running around trying to commit treason."

"Why are you so loyal to Sinegard?" Rin demanded. "It's not like the Empress has done anything for you."

"My family has served the crown at Sinegard for ten generations," said Kitay. "And no, I'm not helping you with your personal vendetta just because you think the Empress got your stupid commander killed. So you can stop pretending to be my friend, Rin, because I know that's all you came for."

"I don't just *think* that," she said. "I *know* it. And I know the Empress invited the Federation onto Nikara land. She wanted this war, she started the invasion, and everything you saw at Golyn Niis was Daji's fault."

"False accusations."

"I heard it from Shiro's mouth!"

"And Shiro didn't have any motivation to lie to you?"

"Daji doesn't have any motivation to lie to *you*?"

"She's the Empress," Kitay said. "The Empress doesn't betray her own. Do you understand how absurd this is? There's literally no political advantage—"

"You should want this!" she yelled. She wanted to shake him, hit him, do anything to make that maddening blankness in his face go away. "Why don't you want this? Why aren't you furious? Didn't you see Golyn Niis?"

He stiffened. "I want you to leave."

"Kitay, please—"

"*Now.*"

"I'm your friend!"

"No, you're not. Fang Runin was my friend. I'm not sure who you are, but I don't want anything to do with you."

"Why do you keep saying that? What did I ever do to you?"

"How about what you did to *them*?" He grabbed for her hand. She was so surprised that she let him. He slammed her palm over the lamp beside him, forced it down directly over the fire. She yelped from the sudden pain—a thousand tiny needles, pressing deeper and deeper into her palm.

"Have you ever been burned before?" he whispered.

For the first time Rin noticed little burn scars dotting his palms and forearms. Some were recent. Some looked inflicted yesterday.

The pain intensified.

"Shit!" She kicked out. She missed Kitay but hit the lamp. Oil spilled over the papers. The fire whooshed up. For a second she saw Kitay's face illuminated in the flame, absolutely terrified, and then he yanked a blanket off the floor and threw it over the fire.

The room went dark.

"What the hell was that?" she screamed.

She didn't raise her fists, but Kitay flinched away as if she had—his shoulder hit the wall, and then he curled toward the ground with his head buried under his arms, raw sobs shaking his thin frame.

"I'm sorry," he whispered. "I don't know what . . ."

The throbbing pain in her hand made her breathless, almost light-headed. Almost as good as it felt when she got high. If she thought about it too hard she would start crying, and if she started crying it might tear her apart, so she tried laughing instead, and that turned into tortured hiccups that shook her entire frame.

"Why?" she finally managed.

"I was trying to see what it was like," he said.

"For who?"

"How *they* felt. In the moment that it happened. In their very last seconds. I wanted to know how they felt when it ended."

"It doesn't feel like anything," she said. A wave of agony shot up her arm again, and she slammed her fist against the floor in an attempt to numb out the pain. She clenched her teeth until it passed.

"Altan told me about it once," she said. "After a bit you're not able to breathe. And then you're gasping so hard you can't feel it hurt anymore. You don't die from the burning, you die from lack of air. You choke, Kitay. That's how it ends."

CHAPTER 5

"Try some ginger rock," Ramsa suggested.

Rin gagged and spat until she was sure her stomach would expel nothing else, and then pulled her head back over the side of the ship. Remnants of her breakfast, a phlegmy, eggy mess, floated in the green waves below.

She took the shards of candy from Ramsa's palm and chewed while fighting the urge to dry-heave. For all their weeks at sea, she'd still never gotten used to the constant sensation that the ground was swirling beneath her feet.

"Expect some choppier waves today," Baji said. "Monsoon season is kicking up in the Omonod. We'll want to avoid going upwind if this keeps up, but as long as we have the shore as a breakwater we should be all right."

He was the only one of them who had any real nautical experience—he'd worked on a transport ship as part of his labor sentence shortly before he'd been sent to Baghra—and he flaunted it obnoxiously.

"Oh, shut up," Ramsa said. "It's not like you do any real steering."

"I'm the navigator!"

"*Aratsha*'s the navigator. You just like the way you look standing at the helm."

Rin was grateful that they didn't have to do much maneuvering themselves. It meant they didn't have to bother with a crew of Moag's hired help. They needed only the six of them to sail up and down South Nikan Sea, doing minimal ship maintenance while blessed Aratsha trailed alongside the hull, guiding the ship wherever they needed to go.

Moag had lent them an opium skimmer named *Caracel*, a sleek and skinny vessel that somehow packed six cannons on each side. They didn't have the numbers to man each cannon, but Ramsa had devised a clever workaround. He'd connected all twelve fuses with the same strip of twine, which meant he could set them all off at once.

But that was only the last resort. Rin didn't intend to win this skirmish with cannons. If Moag didn't want survivors, then Rin only had to get close enough to board.

She folded her arms on the railing and rested her chin on them, staring down at the empty water. Sailing was far less interesting than staking out enemy camps. Battlefields were endlessly entertaining. The ocean was just lonely. She'd spent the morning watching the monotonous gray horizon, trying to keep her eyes open. Moag hadn't been certain when her tax-evading captain would sail back to port. It could be any time from now to past midnight.

Rin didn't understand how the sailors could stand the terrible lack of orientation at sea. To her, every stretch of the ocean looked the same. Without the coast to anchor her, one horizon was indistinguishable from the next. She could read star charts if she tried, but to her naked eye, each patch of greenish blue meant the same thing.

They could be anywhere in Omonod Bay. Somewhere out there lay the Isle of Speer. Somewhere out there was the Federation.

Moag had once offered to take her back to Mugen to survey the damage, but Rin had refused. She knew what she would find there. Millions of bodies encased within hardened rock, charred skeletons frozen in their last living acts.

How would they be positioned? Mothers reaching for their children? Husbands wrapping their arms around their wives? Maybe their hands would be stretched out toward the sea, as if they could escape the deadly thick sulfurous clouds rumbling down the mountainside if they could just get to the water.

She had imagined this too many times, had painted a far more vivid image of it in her mind than reality was likely to be. When she closed her eyes she saw Mugen and she saw Speer; the two islands blurred together in her mind, because in all cases the narrative was the same: children going up in flames, the skin sloughing off their bodies in large black patches, revealing glistening bone underneath.

They burned for someone else's war, someone else's wrongs; someone they had never met had made the decision they should die, so in their last moments they would have had no idea why their skin was scorching off.

Rin blinked and shook her head to clear it. She kept slipping into daydreams. She'd taken a small dose of laudanum last night after her singed palm hurt so much she couldn't sleep, which in retrospect was an awful idea because laudanum exhausted her more than opium did and wasn't half as fun.

She examined her hand. Her skin was puffy and furiously red, even though she'd soaked it in aloe for hours. She couldn't make a fist without wincing. She was grateful she'd only burned her left hand, not her sword hand. She cringed at the thought of grasping a hilt against the tender skin.

She moved her thumbnail over the center of her palm and dug it hard into the open wound. Pain lanced through her arm, bringing tears to her eyes. But it woke her up.

"Shouldn't have taken that laudanum," said Chaghan.

She jerked upright. "I'm awake."

He joined her by the railing. "Sure you are."

Rin shot him an irritated glare, wondering how much effort it would take to toss him overboard. Not very much, she guessed. Chaghan was so terribly frail. She could do it. They wouldn't miss him. Probably.

"You see those rock formations?" Baji, who must have sensed an impending screaming match, edged his way in between them. He pointed toward a series of cliffs on the distant Ankhiluuni shore. "What do they look like to you?"

Rin squinted. "A man?"

Baji nodded. "A drowned man. If you sail to shore during sunset, it looks like he's swallowing the sun. That's how you know you've found Ankhiluun."

"How many times have you been here?" Rin asked.

"Plenty. Came down here with Altan once, two years ago."

"For what?"

"Tyr wanted us to kill Moag."

Rin snorted. "Well, you failed."

"To be fair, it was the *only* time Altan ever failed."

"Oh, I'm sure," she said. "Wonderful Altan. Perfect Altan. Best commander you've ever had. Did everything right."

"Excepting the Chuluu Korikh," Ramsa piped up. "You could call that a disaster of monumental proportions."

"To be fair, Altan used to make some really good tactical decisions." Baji rubbed his chin. "Before, you know, that string of really bad ones."

Ramsa whistled. "Lost his mind near the end, he did."

"Went a little crazy, yeah."

"Shut up about Altan," said Chaghan.

"It's a pity how the best ones snap," Baji continued, ignoring him. "Like Feylen. Huleinin, too. And you remember how Altan started sleepwalking at Khurdalain? I swear, one night I was walking back from taking a piss and he—"

"I said *shut up*!" Chaghan slammed both hands against the railing.

Rin felt a noticeable chill sweep over the deck; goose bumps were forming on her arms. There was a stillness in the air, like the space between lightning and thunder. Chaghan's bone-white hair had begun to curl up at the edges.

His face didn't match his aura. He looked like he might cry.

Baji lifted his palms up. "All right. Tiger's tits. I'm sorry."

"You do not have the right," Chaghan hissed. He pointed a finger at Rin. "*Especially* you."

She bristled. "What's that supposed to mean?"

"You're the reason why—"

"Why *what*?" she asked loudly. "Go on, say it."

"Guys. *Guys.*" Ramsa wedged his way between them. "Great Tortoise, lighten up. Altan's dead. All right? Dead. And fighting about it won't bring him back."

"Look at this." Baji handed Rin his spyglass, directing her attention to a black point just visible on the horizon. "Does that look like a Red Junk ship to you?"

Rin squinted into the eyepiece.

Moag's Red Junk fleet comprised distinctive opium skimmers, built narrow for enough speed to outrun other pirates and the Imperial Navy, possessing deep hulls to transport huge amounts of opium and distinctive battened sails that resembled carp fins. On the open seas they disguised all identifying marks, but when they docked in the South Nikan Sea, they flew the crimson flag of Ankhiluun.

But this ship was a bulky creation, large and squat, much rounder than an opium skimmer. It had white sails instead of red, and no flag in sight. As Rin watched, the ship cut a ridiculously sharp turn in the water toward them that should have been impossible without a shaman's help.

"That's not Moag's," she said.

"That doesn't make it an enemy ship," said Ramsa. He peered out at the ship with a spyglass of his own. "Could be a friendly."

Baji snorted. "We're fugitives working for a pirate lord. Do you think we have a lot of friends right now?"

"Fair enough." Ramsa slammed the spyglass shut and shoved it in his pocket.

"Just open fire," Chaghan suggested.

Baji shot him an incredulous look. "Look, I don't know how much time you've spent at sea, but when you see a foreign warship with no identifying marks and no indication of whether or not it's brought a support fleet, the response is usually not to *just open fire*."

"Why not?" Chaghan asked. "You said it yourself. It can't be a friendly."

"Doesn't mean it's looking for a fight."

Ramsa's head swiveled back and forth between Chaghan and Baji as they spoke. He looked like a very confused baby bird.

"Hold fire," Rin told him hastily. "At least until we know who they are."

The ship was close enough now that she could just make out an etching of characters on the sides of the ship. *Cormorant*. She'd been over the list of Red Junk ships harbored at Ankhiluun. This wasn't one of them.

"Are you seeing this?" Ramsa was peering through his spyglass again. "What the hell is this?"

"What?" Rin couldn't tell what was bothering Ramsa. She couldn't see any armored troops. Or crew of any uniform, for that matter.

Then she realized that was precisely what was wrong.

She couldn't see anyone on board at all.

No one stood at the helm. No one manned the oars. The *Cormorant* was close enough now that they could all see its empty decks.

"That's impossible," said Ramsa. "How are they propelling it?"

Rin leaned over the side of the ship and yelled. "Aratsha! Hard right turn."

Aratsha obeyed, reversing their direction faster than any oared ship would be able to. But the foreign ship veered about immediately to follow their course, cutting an absurdly precise turn. The ship was fast, too—even though the *Caracel* had Aratsha propelling it along, the *Cormorant* had no trouble following their pace.

Seconds later it had almost caught up. It was pulling in parallel. Whoever was on it intended to board.

"That's a ghost ship," Ramsa whimpered.

"Don't be stupid," Baji said.

"They've got a shaman, then. Chaghan's right, we should fire."

They looked helplessly at Rin to confirm the order. She opened her mouth just as a boom split the air, and the *Caracel* shook under their feet.

"You still think it's not hostile?" Chaghan asked.

"Fire," she said.

Ramsa ran belowdecks to light the fuse. Moments later a series of booms rocked the *Caracel* as their starboard-side cannons went off one by one. Blazing metal balls skimmed over the water, scorching bright orange trails behind them—but instead of blowing holes into the sides of the *Cormorant*, they only bounced off metal plating. The warship barely shook from the impact.

Meanwhile the *Caracel* lurched alarmingly to starboard. Rin peeked over the edge—they'd taken damage to their hull, and though she knew nearly nothing about ships, that didn't look survivable.

She cursed under her breath. They'd have to row one of the lifeboats back to shore. If the *Cormorant* didn't dispose of them first.

She could hear Ramsa's footsteps moving frantically around belowdecks, trying to reload. Arrows sailed over her head, courtesy of Qara, but they thudded ineffectively into the sides of the warship. Qara had no target—the warship had no crew on deck, no archers. Whoever it was didn't need archers when they had a row of cannons so powerful they could likely blow the *Caracel* out of the water in minutes.

"Get closer!" Rin shouted. They were outgunned, outmaneuvered. The only chance they had at winning was to board that ship and smoke it out. "Aratsha! Put me on that ship!"

But they weren't moving. The *Caracel* bobbed listlessly in the water.

"Aratsha!"

No response. Rin climbed on the railing and bent to look over-board. She saw an odd stream of black, like a smoke cloud unfurling underwater. Blood? But Aratsha didn't bleed, not when he was in his watery form. And the cloud looked too dark to be blood.

No. It looked like ink.

A projectile shrieked overhead. She ducked. The salvo landed in the water in front of her. Another burst of black emanated from the site of impact.

It *was* ink.

They were firing the pellets into the water. This was intentional. Their attackers knew the Cike had a water shaman, and they had blinded Aratsha on purpose because *they knew what he was.*

Rin's chest tightened. This was no random attack. The warship had targeted them, had prepared for what they could do. This was a calculated ambush planned well in advance.

Moag had sold them out.

Another series of missiles whistled through the air, this time headed for the deck. Rin crouched down, braced for the explosion, but the impact didn't come. She opened her eyes. A delayed explosive?

But no fiery explosion rocked the boat. Instead a cloud of black smoke shot out of the projectiles, unfurling outward with a terri-fying rapidity. Rin didn't bother trying to run. The smoke covered the entire deck within seconds.

It wasn't just a smokescreen, it was an asphyxiate—she tried to suck in air but nothing went through; it was like her throat had closed up, as if someone had pinned her to the wall by the neck. She staggered back, gagging. She could taste something in the air—something sickly sweet and terribly familiar.

Opium.

They know what we are. They know what makes us weak.

Suni and Baji dropped to their knees, utterly subdued. Wherever Qara was, she'd stopped shooting. Rin could just make out Ramsa's and Chaghan's limp forms through the smoke. Only she remained standing, coughing violently, clutching feebly at her throat.

She had smoked opium so many times, the phases of the high were familiar to her by now. It was only a matter of time.

First there was the dizzying sensation of floating, accompanied by an irrational euphoria.

Then the numbness that felt almost as good.

Then nothing.

Rin's arms stung like she'd plunged them inside a beehive. Her mouth tasted like charcoal. She tried to conjure up enough spit to wet her throat and barely managed a repellent lump of phlegm. She forced her eyes open. The sudden attack of light made them water; she had to blink several times before she could look up.

She was tied to a mast, her arms stretched above her. She wiggled her fingers. She couldn't feel them. Her legs were also bound, tied so tightly that she couldn't even bend them.

"She awakens." Baji's voice.

She strained her neck but couldn't see him. When she swiveled her head around she suffered a sudden attack of vertigo. Even tied down, she felt like she was floating. Looking up or down gave her the terrible sensation of falling. She squeezed her eyes shut. "Baji? Where are you?"

"Behind you," he said. "Other side of the . . . the mast."

His words came out in a barely intelligible drawl.

"The others?" she asked.

"All here," Ramsa piped up from her other side. "Aratsha's in that barrel."

Rin sat up straight. "Wait, could he—"

"No go. They sealed the lid. Good thing he doesn't need to breathe." Ramsa must have been wiggling his arms, straining the rope, because she felt her bindings tighten painfully around her own wrists.

"Stop that," she said.

"Sorry."

"Whose ship is this?" she asked.

"They won't tell us," Baji said.

"They? Who are *they*?"

"We don't know. Nikara, I'm assuming, but they won't talk to us." Baji raised his voice to shout at a guard who must have been standing behind her, because Rin couldn't see anyone. "Hey, you! You Nikara?"

No response.

"Told you," said Baji.

"Maybe they're mutes," Ramsa said. "All of them."

"Don't be a fucking idiot," Baji said.

"They could be! You don't know!"

That wasn't remotely funny, but Ramsa devolved into a fit of giggles, leaning forward so that the ropes strained painfully against all of their arms.

"Can you all shut up?" Chaghan's voice. It came from several feet away.

Rin peeked her eyes open for a split second, just long enough to take in the sight of Chaghan, Qara, and Suni bound to the mast opposite her.

Chaghan was slumped against his sister. Suni was still unconscious, head drooped forward. A thick pool of saliva had collected beneath his open mouth.

"Why, hello," said Ramsa. "Good to see you, too."

"Shut your damn mouth," Chaghan grumbled, before he devolved into a string of curses that ended with "Damned Nikara swine."

"Are you high?" Ramsa let out a shrill cackle. "Tiger's tits, Chaghan's high—"

"I'm . . . not . . ."

"Quick, someone ask him if he's always constipated or his face just looks that way."

"At least I've got both eyes," Chaghan snapped.

"Oh, '*I've got both eyes*.' Nice one. At least I'm not so skinny a pigeon could knock me over—"

"Shut up," Rin hissed. She opened her eyes again, trying to take stock of their surroundings. All she could see was the ocean receding behind them. "Ramsa. What do you see?"

"Just the ship's side. Little bit of ocean."

"Baji?"

Silence. Had he fallen asleep again?

"*Baji!*" she shouted.

"Hmm? What?"

"What can you see?"

"Uh. My feet. A bulkhead. The sky."

"No, you idiot—where are we headed?"

"How the fuck should I know—wait. There's a dot. Yeah, that's a dot. An island, I think?"

Rin's heartbeat quickened. Speer? Mugen? But both were a several-weeks journey away; they couldn't be anywhere close. And she didn't remember any islands near Ankhiluun. The old Hesperian naval bases, maybe? But those were long abandoned. If the Hesperians had come back, Nikara foreign relations had changed drastically since she'd last checked.

"Are you sure?" she asked.

"Not really. Hold on." Baji was silent for a moment. "Great Tortoise. That's a nice ship."

"What do you mean, that's a *nice ship?*"

"I mean, if that ship were a person, I would fuck that ship," said Baji.

Rin suspected Baji wouldn't be much help until the opium wore off. But then their vessel took a sharp turn to port, putting Rin in full view of what turned out to be, indeed, a *very* nice ship. They had sailed into the shadow of the largest war vessel she had ever seen: a monstrous, multidecked war junk, with several layers of catapults and portholes, and a massive trebuchet mounted on top of a deck tower.

Rin had studied naval warfare at Sinegard, though never in depth. The Imperial Navy's own fleet had fallen into disrepair, and the only people sent to naval posts were the bottom-feeders of each class. Still, they'd learned enough about naval crafts that Rin knew this was no Imperial ship.

The Nikara couldn't build vessels like this. It had to be a foreign battleship.

Her mind pored sluggishly over possibilities. The Hesperians hadn't taken sides in the Third Poppy War—but if they had, then they would have allied with the Empire, which meant . . .

But then she heard the crew shouting commands to each other, and they were in fluent Nikara. *"Halt. Ready to board."*

What Nikara general had access to a Hesperian ship?

Rin heard shouting, the sound of groaning wood, and heavy footsteps moving about the deck. She strained harder against the ropes, but all that did was chafe at her wrists; her skin stung like it had been scraped raw.

"What's happening?" she screamed. "Who are you?"

She heard someone order a salute formation, which meant they were being boarded by someone of higher rank. A Warlord? A *Hesperian?*

"I think we're about to be handed off," Baji said. "It was nice knowing you all. Except you, Chaghan. You're weird."

"Fuck you," Chaghan said.

"Wait, I've still got a whale bone in my back pocket," said Ramsa. "Rin, you could try igniting just a little bit, burn through the ropes and then I'll get it out—"

Ramsa droned on, but Rin barely heard what he was saying.

A man had just walked into her field of vision. A general, judging from his uniform. He wore a half mask over his face—a Sinegardian opera mask of cerulean-blue ceramic. But it was his tall, lean build that caught her gaze, and his gait: confident, arrogant, like he expected everyone around him to bow before him.

She knew that stride.

"Suni can handle the main guard, and I'll commandeer the cannons, implode the ship or something—"

"Ramsa," Rin said in a strangled voice. *"Shut. Up."*

The general crossed the deck and paused in front of them.

"Why are they bound?" he asked.

Rin stiffened. She knew that voice.

One of the crew hastened over. "Sir, we were warned not to let their hands out of sight."

"These are our people. Not prisoners. Unbind them."

"Sir, but they—"

"I don't enjoy repeating myself."

It had to be him. She'd only ever met one person who could convey so much disdain in so few words.

"You've bound them so tight their limbs will suffer blood loss," the general said. "If you deliver them damaged to my father, he will be very, *very* angry."

"Sir, I don't think you understand the nature of the threat—"

"Oh, I understand. We were classmates. Weren't we, Rin?" The general knelt down before her and pulled off his mask.

Rin flinched.

The boy she remembered was so beautiful. Skin like porcelain, features finer than any sculptor could carve, delicately arched eyebrows that conveyed precisely that mixture of condescension and vulnerability that Nikara poets had been trying to describe for centuries.

Nezha wasn't beautiful anymore.

The left side of his face was still perfect, somehow; still smooth like the glaze on fine ceramic. But the right side . . . the right side was mottled with scars, crisscrossing over his cheek like the plates of a tortoise shell.

Those were not natural scars. They looked nothing like the burn scars Rin had seen on bodies destroyed by gas. Nezha's face should have been twisted and deformed, if not utterly blackened. But his skin remained as pale as ever. His porcelain face had not darkened, but rather looked like glass that had been shattered and glued back together. Those oddly geometric scars could have been drawn over his skin with a fine brush.

His mouth was pulled into a permanent sneer toward the left

side of his face, revealing teeth, a mask of condescension that he couldn't ever take off.

When Rin looked into his eyes, she saw noxious yellow fumes rolling over withering grass. She heard shrieks that dwindled into chokes. And she heard someone screaming her name, over and over and over.

She found it harder and harder to breathe. A buzzing noise filled her ears, and black spots clouded the sides of her vision like ink drops on wet parchment.

"You're dead," she said. "I saw you die."

Nezha looked amused. "And you were always supposed to be the clever one."

CHAPTER 6

"*What the fuck?*" she screamed.

"Hello to you, too," said Nezha. "I thought you'd be happy to see me."

She couldn't do anything but stare at him. It seemed impossible, unthinkable, that he was really alive, standing before her, speaking, *breathing*.

"Captain," Nezha called. "The ropes."

Rin felt the pressure around her wrists tighten briefly, then disappear. Her arms dropped to her sides. Blood rushed back into her extremities, sending a million shocks of lightning through her fingers. She rubbed her wrists and winced when skin came off in her hands.

"Can you stand?" Nezha asked.

She managed a nod. He pulled her to her feet. She took a step forward, and a dizzying spell of vertigo slammed into her like a wave.

"Steady." Nezha caught her arm just as she lurched toward him.

She righted herself. "Don't touch me."

"I know you're confused. But it'll—"

"I said *don't touch me.*"

He backed away, hands out. "It'll all make sense in a minute. You're safe. Just trust me."

"Trust you?" she repeated. "You bombed my ship!"

"Well, it's not technically your ship."

"You could have killed us!" she shrieked. Her brain still felt terribly sluggish, but this fact struck her as very, very important. "You fired opium onto my ship!"

"Would you rather we fired real missiles? We were trying not to hurt you."

"Your men bound us to the mast for hours!"

"Because they didn't want to die!" Nezha lowered his voice. "Look, I'm sorry it came to that. We needed to get you out of Ankhiluun. We weren't trying to hurt you."

His placating tone only made her angrier. She wasn't a fucking child; he couldn't calm her with soothing whispers. "You let me think you were dead."

"What did you want, a letter? It's not like it was terribly easy to track you down, either."

"A letter would have been better than *bombing my ship*!"

"Are you ever going to let that go?"

"It's a rather large thing to let go!"

"I will explain everything if you come with me," he said. "Can you walk? Please? My father's waiting for us."

"Your father?" she repeated dumbly.

"Come on, Rin. You know who my father is."

She blinked at him. Then it hit her.

Oh.

Either she'd been hit by a massive stroke of fortune, or she was about to die.

"Just me?" she asked.

Nezha's eyes flickered toward the Cike, lingering briefly on Chaghan. "I was told you're the commander now?"

She hesitated. She hadn't been acting much like a commander. But the title was hers, even if in name only. "Yes."

"Then just you."

"I'm not going without my men."

"I'm afraid I can't allow that."

She stuck her chin out. "Sucks, then."

"Do you seriously think any of them are in a state for an audience with a Warlord?" Nezha gestured toward the Cike. Suni was still asleep, the puddle of drool widening under his mouth. Chaghan stared open-mouthed at the sky, fascinated, and Ramsa had his eyes squeezed shut, giggling at nothing in particular.

It was the first time Rin had ever been glad she'd developed such a high tolerance for opium.

"I need your word you won't hurt them," she said.

Nezha looked offended. "Please. You're not prisoners."

"Then what are we?"

"Mercenaries," he said delicately. "Think of it that way. You're mercenaries out of a job, and my father has a very generous offer for your consideration."

"What if we don't like it?"

"I really think you will." Nezha motioned for Rin to follow him down the deck, but she remained where she stood.

"Feed my men while we're gone, then. A hot meal, not leftovers."

"Rin, come on—"

"Give them baths, too. And then take them to their own quarters. Not the brig. Those are my terms. Also, Ramsa doesn't like fish."

"He's been operating out of the coast and he doesn't like *fish*?"

"He's picky."

Nezha muttered something to the captain, who adopted a face like he'd been forced to sniff curdled milk.

"Done," Nezha said. "Now will you come?"

She took a step and stumbled. Nezha extended his arm toward her. She let him help her to the edge of the ship.

"Thanks, Commander," Ramsa called behind them. "Try not to die."

The Hesperian warship *Seagrim* loomed huge over their rowboat, swallowing them completely in its shadow. Rin couldn't help but stare in awe at its sheer scale. She could have fit half of Tikany on that warship, temple included.

How did a monstrosity like that stay afloat? And how did it move? She couldn't see any oars. The *Seagrim* appeared to be just like the *Cormorant*, a ghost vessel with no visible crew.

"Don't tell me you've got a shaman powering that thing," she said.

"If only. No, that's a paddle-wheel boat."

"What's that?"

He grinned. "Have you heard the legend of the Old Sage of Arlong?"

She rolled her eyes. "Who's that, your grandfather?"

"Great-grandfather. The legend goes, the old sage was staring at a water wheel watering the fields and thought about reversing the circumstances; if he moved the wheel, then the water must move. Fairly obvious principle, isn't it? Incredible how long it took for someone to apply it to ships.

"See, the old Imperial ships were idiotically designed. Propelled by sculls from the top deck. Problem with that is if your rowers get shot out, you're dead in the water. But the paddle-wheel pushers are on the bottom deck. Entirely enclosed by the hull, totally protected from enemy artillery. A bit of an improvement from old models, eh?"

Nezha seemed to enjoy talking about ships. Rin heard a distinct note of pride in his voice as he pointed out the ridges at the bottom of the warship. "You see those? They're concealing the paddle wheels."

She couldn't help but stare at his face while he talked. Up close his scars weren't so unsettling, but rather oddly compelling. She wondered if it hurt him to talk.

"What is it?" Nezha asked. He touched his cheek. "Ugly, isn't it? I can put the mask back on, if it's bothering you."

"It's not that," she said hastily.

"What, then?"

She blinked again. "I just . . . I'm sorry."

He frowned. "For what?"

She stared at him, searching for evidence of sarcasm, but his expression was open, concerned.

"It's my fault," she said.

He stopped rowing. "It's not your fault."

"Yes, it was." She swallowed. "I could have pulled you out. I heard you calling my name. You *saw* me."

"I don't remember that."

"Yes, you do. Stop lying."

"Rin. Don't do this." Nezha stopped rowing to reach out and grasp her hand. "It wasn't your fault. I don't blame you."

"You should."

"I don't."

"I could have pulled you out," she said again. "I wanted to, I was going to, but Altan wouldn't let me, and—"

"So blame Altan," Nezha said in a hard voice, and resumed rowing. "The Federation was never going to kill me. The Mugenese like to keep prisoners. Someone figured out I was a warlord's son, so they kept me for ransom. They thought they might leverage me into a surrender from Dragon Province."

"How'd you escape?"

"I didn't. I was in the camp when word got out that Emperor Ryohai was dead. The soldiers who had captured me arranged to trade me back to my father in exchange for a safe exit from the country."

"Did they get it?" she asked.

He grimaced. "They got *an* exit."

When they reached the hull of the warship, Nezha hooked four ropes to the ends of the rowboat and whistled at the sky. Seconds later the boat began to rock as sailors hoisted them up.

The main deck hadn't been visible from the rowboat, but now Rin saw that soldiers were posted at every corner of the ship. They were Nikara in their features—they must have been from Dragon Province, but Rin noticed they did not wear Militia uniforms.

The Seventh Division soldiers she had met at Khurdalain wore green Militia gear with the insignia of a dragon stitched into their armbands. But these soldiers were decked out in dark blue, with a silver dragon pattern visible over their chests.

"This way." Nezha led her down the stairs to the second deck and down the passageway until they stopped before a set of wooden doors guarded by a tall, spare man holding a blue-ribboned halberd.

"Captain Eriden." Nezha stopped and saluted, though according to uniform he should have been the higher rank.

"General." Captain Eriden looked like a man who'd never smiled in his life. Deep frown lines seemed permanently etched into his gaunt, spare face. He dipped his head to Nezha, then turned to Rin. "Hold out your arms."

"That's not necessary," said Nezha.

"With all due respect, sir, you are not the one sworn to guard your father's life," Eriden said. "Hold out your arms."

Rin obeyed. "You're not going to find anything."

Normally she kept daggers in her boots and inner shirt, but she could feel their absence; the *Cormorant*'s crew must have removed them already.

"Still have to check." Eriden peered inside her sleeves. "I'm to warn you that if you dare to so much as point a chopstick in the Dragon Warlord's direction, then you'll be shot full of crossbow bolts faster than you can breathe." His hands moved up her shirt. "Do not forget we also have your men as hostages."

Rin shot Nezha an accusing glare. "You said we weren't hostages."

"They aren't," Nezha said. He turned to Eriden, eyes hard. "They *aren't*. They're our guests, Captain."

"Call them whatever you like." Eriden shrugged. "But try anything funny and they're dead."

Rin shifted so that he could feel the small of her back for weapons. "Wasn't planning on it."

Finished, Eriden wiped his hands off on his uniform, turned, and grasped the door handles. "In that case, I'm to extend you a welcome on behalf of the Dragon Warlord."

"Fang Runin, isn't it? Welcome to the *Seagrim*."

For a moment Rin could only gape. She couldn't look at the Dragon Warlord and not see Nezha. Yin Vaisra was a grown version of his son without scars. He possessed all the infuriating beauty of the House of Yin—pale skin, black hair without a single streak of gray, and fine features that looked like they had been carved from marble—cold, arrogant, and imposing.

She'd heard endless gossip about the Dragon Warlord during her years at Sinegard. He ruled the richest province in the Empire by far. He'd single-handedly led the defense of the Red Cliffs in the Second Poppy War, had obliterated a Federation fleet with only a small cluster of Nikara fishing boats. He'd been chafing under Daji's rule for years. When he'd failed to appear at the Empress's summer parade for the third consecutive year, the apprentices had speculated so loudly that he was planning open treason that Nezha had lost his cool and sent one of them to the infirmary.

"Rin is fine." Her words came out sounding frail and tiny, swallowed up by the vast gilded room.

"A vulgar diminutive," Vaisra declared. Even his voice was a deeper version of Nezha's, a hard drawl that seemed permanently coated in condescension. "They're fond of those in the south. But I shall call you Runin. Please, sit down."

She cast a fleeting glance at the oak table between them. It had a low surface, and the high-backed chairs looked terribly heavy. If she sat, her knees would be trapped. "I'll stand."

Vaisra raised an eyebrow. "Have I made you uncomfortable?"

"You bombed my ship," Rin said. "So yes, a little."

"My dear girl, if I wanted you dead, your body would be at the bottom of Omonod Bay."

"Then why isn't it?"

"Because we need you." Vaisra drew out his own chair and sat, gesturing to Nezha to do the same. "It hasn't been easy to find you, you know. We've been sailing down the coast of the Snake Province for weeks now. We even checked Mugen."

He said it like he'd meant to startle her, and it worked. She couldn't help but flinch. He watched her, waiting.

She took the bait. "What did you find?"

"Just a few fringe islands. Of course, they had no clue of your whereabouts, but we stayed a week or so to make sure. People will say anything under torture."

Her fingers tightened into fists. "They're still *alive*?"

She felt like someone had taken a bar to her rib cage. She knew Federation soldiers remained on the mainland, but not that *civilians* were still alive. She'd thought she had put a permanent end to the country.

What if she hadn't? The great strategist Sunzi cautioned to always finish off an enemy in case they came back stronger. What would happen when Federation civilians regrouped? What if she still had a war to fight?

"Their invasion is over," Vaisra reassured her. "You made certain of that. The main islands have been destroyed. Emperor Ryohai and his advisers are dead. A few cities on the edges of the archipelago remain standing, but the Federation has erupted into frothy madness, like ants pouring out of a hill once you've killed the queen. Some of them are sailing off the islands in droves, seeking refuge on Nikara shores, but . . . well. We're getting rid of them as they come."

"How?"

"The usual way." His lips twitched into a smile. "Why don't you sit?"

Reluctantly, she drew the chair out as far from the table as she could and sat at the very edge, knees locked together.

"There," Vaisra said. "Now we're friends."

Rin decided to be blunt. "Are you here to take me back to the capital?"

"Don't be stupid."

"Then what do you want from me?"

"Your services."

"I'm not murdering anyone for you."

"Dream a little bigger, my dear." Vaisra leaned forward. "I want to overthrow the Empire. I'd like you to help."

The room fell silent. Rin studied Vaisra's face, waiting for him to burst into laughter. But he looked so terribly sincere—and so did Nezha—that she couldn't help but cackle.

"Is something funny?" Vaisra asked.

"Are you mad?"

"'Visionary,' I think, is the word you want. The Empire is on the verge of falling apart. A revolution is the only alternative to decades of civil warfare, and someone has to start the ball rolling."

"And you'd bet on your odds against the Militia?" Rin laughed again. "You're one province against eleven. It'll be a massacre."

"Don't be so certain," Vaisra said. "The provinces are angry. They're hurting. And for the first time since any of the Warlords can remember, the specter of the Federation has disappeared. Fear used to be a unifying force. Now the cracks in the foundation grow day by day. Do you know how many local insurrections have erupted in the past month? Daji is doing everything she can to keep the Empire united, but the institution is a sinking ship that's rotted at the core. It may drift for a while, but eventually it will be dashed to pieces against the rocks."

"And you think you can destroy it and build a new one."

"Isn't that precisely what you want?"

"Killing one woman is not the same thing as overthrowing a regime."

"But you can't evaluate those events in a vacuum," said Vaisra. "What do you think happens if you succeed? Who steps into Daji's shoes? And whoever that person is, do you trust them to rule the Twelve Provinces? To be any kinder to people like you than Daji was?"

Rin hadn't thought that far. She had never bothered to think much about life after she'd killed Daji. Once she'd gotten Altan's revenge, she wasn't sure that she even wanted to keep living.

"It doesn't matter to me," she said.

"Then think of it this way," Vaisra said. "I can give you a chance to take your revenge with the full support of an army of thousands."

"Would I have to take orders?" she asked.

"Rin—" Nezha started.

"Would I have to take orders?"

"Yes," Vaisra said. "Of course."

"Then you can fuck off."

Vaisra looked confused. "All soldiers take orders."

"I'm not a soldier anymore," she said. "I put in my time, I gave the Empire my loyalty, and that got me strapped to a table in a Mugenese research lab. I'm done taking orders."

"We are not the Empire."

She shrugged. "You want to be."

"You little fool." Vaisra slammed his hand against the table. Rin flinched. "Look outside yourself for a moment. This isn't just about you, it's about the future of our people."

"*Your* people," she said. "I'm a Speerly."

"You are a scared little girl reacting from anger and loss in the most shortsighted way possible. All you want is to get your revenge. But you could be so much more. *Do* so much more. *Listen to me.* You could change history."

"Haven't I changed history enough?" Rin whispered.

She didn't care about anyone's visions for the future. She'd stopped wanting to be great, to carve out her place in history, a long time ago. She'd since learned the cost.

And she didn't know how to say that she was just so *tired*.

All she wanted was to get Altan's revenge. She wanted to put a blade in Daji's heart.

And then she wanted to disappear.

"Your people died not because of Daji but because of this Empire," Vaisra said. "The provinces have become weak, isolated, technologically inept. Compared to the Federation, compared to Hesperia, we are not just decades but centuries behind. And the problem isn't our people, it's their rulers. The twelve-province system is an antiquated, inefficient yoke dragging the Nikara behind. Imagine a country that was truly united. Imagine an army whose factions weren't constantly at war with one another. Who could possibly defeat us?"

Vaisra's eyes glimmered as he spread his hands across the table. "I am going to transform the Empire into a republic—a great republic, founded on the individual freedom of men. Instead of Warlords, we would have elected officials. Instead of an Empress, we would have a parliament, overseen by an elected president. I would make it impossible for a single person like Su Daji to bring ruin upon this realm. What do you think of that?"

A lovely speech, Rin thought, if Vaisra had been talking to someone more gullible.

Maybe the Empire did need a new government. Maybe a democracy would usher in peace and stability. But Vaisra had failed to realize that she simply did not care.

"I just finished fighting one war," she said. "I'm not terribly interested in fighting another."

"So what is your strategy? To roam up and down the coastline, killing off the only officials who have been brave enough to keep opium outside their borders?" Vaisra made a noise of disgust. "If that's your goal, you're just as bad as the Mugenese."

She bristled. "I'll kill Daji eventually."

"And how, pray tell?"

"I don't have to tell *you*—"

"By renting a pirate ship?" he mocked. "By entering into losing negotiations with a pirate queen?"

"Moag was *going* to give us supplies." Rin felt the blood rushing to her face. "And we would have had the money, too, until you assholes showed up—"

"You're so terribly naive. Don't you get it? Moag was always going to sell you out. Did you think she would pass up that bounty on your heads? You're lucky our offer was better."

"Moag wouldn't," Rin said. "Moag knows my value."

"You're assuming Moag is rational. And she is, until it comes to great sums of money. You can buy her off with any amount of silver, and that I have in abundance." Vaisra shook his head like a disappointed teacher. "Don't you get it? Moag only flourishes while Daji is on the throne, because Daji's isolationist policies create Ankhiluun's competitive advantage. Moag only benefits as long as she operates outside the law, while the rest of the country is in such deep shit that it's more profitable to operate inside her boundaries than without. Once trade becomes legitimized, she's out of an empire. Which means the very last thing she wants is for you to succeed."

Rin opened her mouth, realized she had nothing to say, and closed it. For the first time, she did not have a counterargument.

"Please, Rin," Nezha interjected. "Be honest with yourself. You can't fight a war on your own. You are *six people*. The Vipress is guarded by a corps of elite soldiers that you've never gone up against. And that's not to mention her own martial arts skills, which you know nothing about."

"And you no longer have the advantage of surprise," said Vaisra. "Daji knows you are coming for her, which means you need a way to get closer to her. You need *me*."

He gestured to the walls around them. "Look at this ship. This is the very best that Hesperian naval technology can offer. Twelve cannons lined on every side."

Rin rolled her eyes. "Congratulations?"

"I have ten more ships like it."

That gave her pause.

Vaisra leaned forward. "Now you get it. You're a smart girl; you can run the calculations yourself. The Empire does not have a functioning navy. I do. We will control this Empire's waterways. The war will be over in six months *at worst*."

Rin tapped her fingers against the table, considering. *Could* they win this war? And what if they did?

She couldn't help but balance the possibilities—she'd been trained too well at Sinegard not to.

If what Vaisra said was true, then she had to admit this *was* the perfect time to launch a coup. The Militia at present was fragmented and weak. The provinces had been decimated by Federation battalions. And they might switch sides quickly, once they learned the truth about Daji's deception.

The benefits of joining an army were also obvious. She'd never have to worry about her supplies. She'd have access to intelligence she couldn't get on her own. She'd have free transportation to wherever she wanted to go.

And yet.

"What happens if I say no?" she asked. "Are you going to compel me into service? Make me your own Speerly slave?"

Vaisra didn't take the bait. "The Republic will be founded on freedom of choice. If you refuse to join, then we can't make you."

"Then maybe I'll leave," she said, mostly to see how he would respond. "I'll go into hiding. I'll bide my time. Get stronger."

"You could do that." Vaisra sounded bored, like he knew she was just pulling objections out of her ass. "Or you could fight for me and get the revenge you want. This isn't hard, Runin. And you're not really considering saying no. You're just pretending to think because you like being a little brat."

Rin glared at him.

It was such a rational option. She *hated* that it was a rational option. And she hated more that Vaisra knew that, and knew she'd arrive at the same conclusion, and was now simply mocking her until her mind caught up to his.

"I have more money and resources at my disposal than anyone in this empire," Vaisra said. "Weapons, men, information—anything you need, you can get it from me. Work for me and you will want for nothing."

"I'm not putting my life in your hands," she said. The last time she had pledged her loyalty to someone, she'd been betrayed. Altan had died.

"I will never lie to you," said Vaisra.

"Everybody lies to me."

Vaisra shrugged. "Then don't trust me. Act purely in your own interest. But I think you'll find it clear soon enough that you don't have many other options."

Rin's temples throbbed. She rubbed her eyes, trying desperately to think through all the possibilities. There had to be a catch. She knew better than to take offers like this at face value. She'd learned her lesson from Moag—never trust someone who holds all the cards.

She had to buy herself some time. "I can't make a decision without speaking to my people."

"Do as you like," Vaisra said. "But have an answer for me by dawn."

"Or what?" she asked.

"Or you'll have to find your own way back to shore," he said. "And it's a long swim."

"Just to clarify, the Dragon Warlord does *not* want to kill us?" Ramsa asked.

"No," said Rin. "He wants us in his army."

He wrinkled his nose. "But why? The Federation's gone."

"Exactly that. He thinks it's his opportunity to overthrow the Empire."

"That's actually clever," Baji said. "Think about it. Rob the house while it's on fire, or however the saying goes."

"I don't think that's a real saying," Ramsa said.

"It's a little more noble than that," said Rin. "He wants to build a republic instead. Overthrow the Warlord system. Construct a parliament, appoint elected officials, restructure how governance works across the Empire."

Baji chuckled. "Democracy? Really?"

"It's worked for the Hesperians," said Qara.

"Has it?" Baji asked. "Hasn't the western continent been at war for the past decade?"

"The question isn't whether democracy could work," Rin said. "That doesn't matter. The question is whether we enlist."

"This could be a trap," Ramsa pointed out. "He could be bringing you to Daji."

"He could have just killed us when we were drugged, then. We're dangerous passengers to have on board. It wouldn't be worth the risk unless Vaisra really did think he could convince us to join him."

"So?" Ramsa asked. "Can he convince us?"

"I don't know," Rin admitted. "Maybe."

The more she thought about it, the more it seemed like a good idea. She wanted Vaisra's ships. His weapons, his soldiers, his power.

But if things went south, if Vaisra hurt the Cike, then this fell on her shoulders. And she couldn't let the Cike down again.

"There's still a benefit to going it on our own," said Baji. "Means we don't have to take orders."

Rin shook her head. "We're still six people. You can't assassinate a head of state with six people."

Never mind that she'd been perfectly willing to try just a few hours ago.

"And what if he betrays us?" Aratsha asked.

Baji shrugged. "We could always just cut our losses and defect. Run back to Ankhiluun."

"We can't run back to Ankhiluun," Rin said.

"Why not?"

She told them about Moag's ploy. "She'd have sold us to Daji if Vaisra hadn't offered her something better. He sank our ship because he wanted her to think that we'd died."

"So it's Vaisra or nothing," Ramsa said. "That's just fantastic."

"Is this Yin Vaisra really so bad?" Suni asked. "He's just one man."

"That's true," said Baji. "He can't be any scarier than the other Warlords. The Ox and Ram Warlords weren't anything special. It's nepotism and inbreeding all around."

"Oh, so like how you were produced," said Ramsa.

"Listen, you little bitch—"

"Join them," Chaghan said. His voice was hardly louder than a whisper, but the cabin fell silent. It was the first time he had spoken all evening.

"You're debating this like you get to decide," he said. "You don't. You really think Vaisra's going to let you go if you say no? He's too smart for that. He's just told you his intentions to commit treason. He'll have you killed if there's even the slightest risk you'd go to anyone else." He gave Rin a grim look. "Face it, Speerly. It's join up or die."

"You're gloating," Rin accused.

"I would never," said Nezha. He'd been beaming the entire way down the passageway, showing her around the warship like some ebullient tour guide. "But glad to have you on board."

"Shut up."

"Can't I be happy? I've missed you." Nezha stopped before a room on the first deck. "After you."

"What's this?"

"Your new quarters." He opened the door for her. "Look, it locks from the inside four different ways. Thought you'd like that."

She did like it. The room was twice as large as her quarters on her old ship, and the bed was a proper *bed*, not a cot with lice-ridden sheets. She stepped inside. "I have this all to myself?"

"I told you." Nezha sounded smug. "The Dragon Army has its benefits."

"Ah, that's what you call yourselves?"

"Technically it's the Army of the Republic. Nonprovincial, and all that."

"You'd need allies for that."

"We're working on it."

She turned toward the porthole. Even in the darkness she could see how fast the *Seagrim* was moving, slicing through black waves at speeds faster than Aratsha had ever been capable of. By morning Moag and her fleet would be dozens of miles behind them.

But Rin couldn't leave Ankhiluun like this. Not yet. She had one more thing to retrieve.

"You said Moag thinks we're dead?" she asked.

"I'd be surprised if she didn't. We even tossed some charred corpses in the water."

"Whose bodies?"

Nezha stretched his arms over his head. "Does it matter?"

"I suppose not." The sun had just set over the water. Soon the Ankhiluuni pirate patrol would begin to make its rounds around the coast. "Do you have a smaller boat? One that can sneak past Moag's ships?"

"Of course," he scoffed. "Why, do you need to go back?"

"*I* don't," she said. "But you've forgotten someone."

By all accounts Kitay's audience with Vaisra was an unmitigated disaster. Captain Eriden wouldn't let Rin onto the second deck, so she was unable to eavesdrop, but about an hour after they brought Kitay on board, she saw Nezha and two soldiers dragging him to the lower level. She ran down the passageway to catch up.

"—and I don't care if you're pissed, you can't *throw food* at the *Dragon Warlord*," said Nezha.

Kitay's face was purple with anger. If he was at all relieved to see Nezha alive, he didn't show it. "Your men tried to blow up my house!"

"They tend to do that," Rin said.

"We had to make it look like you'd died," Nezha said.

"I was still in it!" Kitay cried. "And so were my ledgers!"

Nezha looked amazed. "Who gives a shit about your ledgers?"

"I was doing the city's taxes."

"*What?*"

Kitay stuck his lower lip out. "And I was almost done."

"What the fuck?" Nezha blinked. "I don't—Rin, you talk some sense into this idiot."

"I'm the idiot?" Kitay demanded. "*Me? You're* the ones who think it'd be a good idea to start a bloody civil war—"

"Because the Empire needs one," Nezha insisted. "Daji's the reason why the Federation invaded; she's the reason why Golyn Niis—"

"You were not at Golyn Niis," Kitay snarled. "*Don't* talk to me about Golyn Niis."

"Fine—I'm sorry—but shouldn't that justify a regime change? She's hamstrung the Militia, she's fucked our foreign relations, she's not fit to rule—"

"You have no proof of that."

"We do have proof." Nezha stopped walking. "Look at your scars. Look at *me*. The proof's written on our skin."

"I don't care," Kitay said. "I don't give a shit what your politics are, I want to go home."

"And do what?" Nezha asked. "And fight for *whom*? There's a war coming, Kitay, and when it's here, there will be no such thing as neutrality."

"That's not true. I shall seclude myself and live the virtuous life of a scholarly hermit," Kitay said stiffly.

"Stop," Rin said. "Nezha's right. Now you're just being stubborn."

He rolled his eyes at her. "Of course you're in on this madness. What did I expect?"

"Maybe it's madness," she said. "But it's better than fighting for the Militia. Come on, Kitay. You know you can't go back to the status quo."

She could see it in Kitay's eyes, how badly he wanted to resolve the contradiction between loyalty and justice—because Kitay, poor, upright, moral Kitay, always so concerned with doing what was right, couldn't reconcile himself to the fact that a military coup might be justified.

He flung his hands in the air. "Even so, you think I'm in a position to join your republic? My father is the Imperial *defense minister*."

"Then he's serving the wrong ruler," said Nezha.

"You don't understand! My entire family is at the heart of the capital. They could use them against me—my mother, my sister—"

"We could extract them," Nezha said.

"Oh, like you extracted me? Very nice, I'm sure they'll *love* getting abducted in the middle of the night while their house burns down."

"Calm down," Rin said. "They'd still be alive. You wouldn't have to worry."

"Like you'd know how it feels," Kitay snapped. "The closest thing you had to a family was a suicidal maniac who got himself killed on a mission almost as stupid as this one."

She could tell he knew he'd crossed the line, even as he said it. Nezha looked stunned. Kitay blinked rapidly, refusing to meet her eyes. Rin hoped for a moment that he might cave, that he'd apologize, but he simply looked away.

She felt a pang in her chest. The Kitay she knew would have apologized.

A long silence followed. Nezha stared at the wall, Kitay at the floor, and neither of them dared to meet Rin's eyes.

Finally Kitay held out his hands, as if waiting for someone to bind them. "Best get me down to the brig," he said. "Don't want your prisoners running around on deck."

CHAPTER 7

When Rin returned to her private quarters, she locked the door carefully from the inside, sliding all four bolts into place, and propped a chair against the door for good measure. Then she lay back on her bed. She closed her eyes and tried to relax, to make herself internalize a brief sense of security. She was safe. She was with allies. No one was coming for her.

Sleep didn't come. Something was missing.

It took her a moment to realize what it was. She was searching for that rocking feeling of the bed shifting over water, and it wasn't there. The *Seagrim* was such a massive warship that its decks mimicked solid land. For once, she was on stable ground.

This was what she wanted, wasn't it? She had a place to be and a place to go. She wasn't drifting anymore, wasn't desperately scrambling to put together plans she knew would likely fail.

She stared up at the ceiling, trying to will her racing heartbeat to slow down. But she couldn't shake the feeling that something was wrong—a deep-seated discomfort that wasn't just the absence of rolling waves.

It began with a prickling feeling in her fingertips. Then a flush of heat started in her palms and crept up her arms to her chest.

The headache began a minute after that, searing flashes of pain that made her grind her teeth.

And then fire started burning at the back of her eyelids.

She saw Speer and she saw the Federation. She saw ashes and bones blurred and melted into one, one lone figure striding toward her, slender and handsome, trident in hand.

"You stupid cunt," Altan whispered. He reached forward. His hands made a necklace around her throat.

Her eyes flew open. She sat up and breathed in and out, deep and slow and desperate breaths, trying to quell her sudden swell of panic.

Then she realized what was wrong.

She had no access to opium on this ship.

No. Calm. Stay calm.

Once upon a time at Sinegard, back when Master Jiang had been trying to help her shut her mind to the Phoenix, he'd taught her techniques to clear her thoughts and disappear into a void that imitated nonexistence. He'd taught her how to think like she was dead.

She had shunned his lessons then. She tried to recall them now. She forced her mind through the mantras he'd made her repeat for hours. *Nothingness. I am nothing. I do not exist. I feel nothing, I regret nothing . . . I am sand, I am dust, I am ash.*

It didn't work. Surges of panic kept breaking the calm. The prickling in her fingers intensified into twisting knives. She was on fire, every part of her burned excruciatingly, and Altan's voice echoed from everywhere.

It should have been you.

She ran to the door, kicked the chair away, undid the locks, and ran barefoot out into the passageway. Stabs of pain pricked the backs of her eyes, made her vision spark and flash.

She squinted, struggling to see in the dim light. Nezha had said his cabin was at the end of the passage . . . so this one, it had to be . . . She banged frantically against the door until it opened and he appeared in the gap.

"Rin? What are you—"

She grabbed his shirt. "Where's your physician?"

His eyebrows flew up. "Are you hurt?"

"*Where?*"

"First deck, third door to the right, but—"

She didn't wait for him to finish before she started sprinting toward the stairs. She heard him running after her but she didn't care; all that mattered was that she get some opium, or laudanum, or whatever was on board.

But the physician wouldn't let her into his office. He blocked the entrance with his body, one hand against the doorframe, the other clenched on the door handle.

"Dragon Warlord's orders." He sounded like he'd been expecting her. "I'm not to give you anything."

"But I need—the pain, I can't stand it, I need—"

He started to close the door. "You'll have to do without."

She jammed her foot in the door. "Just a little," she begged. She didn't care how pathetic she sounded, she just needed something. Anything. "*Please.*"

"I have my orders," he said. "Nothing I can do."

"Damn it!" she screamed. The physician flinched and slammed the door shut, but she was already running in the opposite direction, feet pounding as she neared the stairs.

She had to get to the top deck, away from everyone. She could feel the pricks of malicious memory pressing like shards of glass into her mind; bits and pieces of suppressed recollections that swam vividly before her eyes—corpses at Golyn Niis, corpses in the research facility, corpses at Speer, and the soldiers, all with Shiro's face, jeering and pointing and *laughing*, and that made her so furious, made the rage build and build—

"Rin!"

Nezha had caught up with her. His hand grasped her shoulder. "What the hell—"

She whirled around. "Where's your father?"

"I think he's meeting with his admirals," he stammered. "But I wouldn't—"

She pushed past him. Nezha reached for her arm, but she ducked away and raced through the passageway and down the stairs to Vaisra's office. She jiggled the handles—locked—then kicked furiously at the doors until they swung open from inside.

Vaisra didn't look remotely surprised to see her.

"Gentlemen," he said, "we'll need some privacy, please."

The men inside vacated their seats without a word. None of them looked at her. Vaisra pulled the doors shut, locked them, and turned around. "What can I do for you?"

"You told the physician not to give me opium," Rin said.

"That is correct."

Her voice trembled. "Look, asshole, *I need my*—"

"Oh, no, Runin." Vaisra lifted a finger and wagged it, as if chiding a small child. "I should have mentioned. A last condition of your enlistment. I do not tolerate opium addicts in my army."

"I'm not an addict, I just . . ." A fresh wave of pain racked her head and she broke off, wincing.

"You're no good to me high. I need you alert. I need someone capable of infiltrating the Autumn Palace and killing the Empress, not some opium-riddled sack of shit."

"You don't get it," she said. "If you don't drug me, I will incinerate everyone on this ship."

He shrugged. "Then we'll throw you overboard."

She could only stare at him. This made no sense to her. How could he remain so infuriatingly calm? Why wasn't he caving in, cowering in terror? This wasn't how it was supposed to work—she was supposed to threaten him and he was supposed to do what she wanted, that was always how it worked—

Why hadn't she scared him?

Desperate, she resorted to begging. "You don't know how much this hurts. It's in my mind—the god is always in my mind, and it *hurts* . . ."

"It's not the god." Vaisra stood up and crossed the room toward her. "It's the anger. And it's your fear. You've seen battle for the first time, and your nerves can't shut down. You're frightened all the time. You think everyone's out to get you, and you *want* them to be out to get you because then that'll give you an excuse to hurt them. That's not a Speerly problem, it's a universal experience of soldiers. And you can't cure it with opium. There's no running from it."

"Then what—"

He put his hands on her shoulders. "You face it. You accept that it's your reality now. You fight it."

Couldn't he understand that she'd tried? Did he think it was easy? "No," she said. "I need—"

He cocked his head to the side. "What do you mean, 'no'?"

Rin's tongue felt terribly heavy in her mouth. Sweat broke out over her body; she could see it beading on her hands.

He raised his voice. "Are you contradicting my orders?"

She took a shuddering breath. "I—I can't. Fight it."

"Ah, Runin. You don't understand. You're my soldier now. You follow orders. I tell you to jump, you ask how high."

"But I *can't*," she repeated, frustrated.

Vaisra lifted his left hand, briefly examined his knuckles, and then slammed the back of his hand across her face.

She stumbled backward, more from the shock than the force. Her face registered no pain, only an intense sting, like she'd walked straight into a bolt of lightning. She touched a finger to her lip. It came away bloody.

"You hit me," she said, dazed.

He grasped her chin tightly in his fingers and forced her to look up at him. She was too stunned to feel any rage. She wasn't angry, she was only afraid. No one dared to touch her like this. No one had for a long time.

No one since Altan.

"I've broken in Speerlies before." Vaisra traced a thumb across her cheek. "You're not the first. Sallow skin. Sunken eyes. You're smoking your life away. Anyone could smell it on you. Do you know why the Speerlies died young? It wasn't their penchant for constant warfare, and it wasn't their god. They were smoking themselves to death. Right now I wouldn't give you six months."

He dug his nails into her skin so hard that she gasped. "That ends now. You're cut off. You can smoke yourself to death after you've done what I need you for. But only after."

Rin stared at him in shock. The pain was starting to seep in, first a little sting and then a great throbbing bruise across her entire face. A sob rose up in her throat. "But it hurts so much . . ."

"Oh, Runin. Poor little Runin." He smoothed her hair out of her eyes and leaned in close. "*Fuck* your pain. What you're dealing with is nothing that a little discipline can't solve. You're capable of blocking out the Phoenix. Your mind can build up its own defenses, and you just haven't done it because you're using the opium as a safe way out."

"Because I need—"

"You need *discipline*." Vaisra forced her head up farther. "You must concentrate. Fortify your mind. I know you hear the screaming. Learn to live with it. Altan did."

Rin could taste blood staining her teeth when she spoke. "I'm not Altan."

"Then learn to be," he said.

So Rin suffered alone in her quarters, with the door bolted shut, guarded from the outside by three soldiers, at her own request.

She couldn't bear lying on her bed. The sheets scratched at her skin and exacerbated the terrible prickling that had spread across her body. She wound up curled on the floor with her head between her knees, rocking back and forth, biting her knuckles to keep from screaming. Her whole body cramped and shivered, racked with wave after wave of what felt like someone stamping slowly on each of her internal organs.

The ship's physician had refused to give her any sedatives on the grounds that she would just trade her opium addiction for a milder substance, so she had nothing to silence her mind, nothing to quell the visions that flashed through her eyes every time she closed them, a combination of the Phoenix's never-ending visual tour of horrors and her own opioid-driven hallucinations.

And, of course, Altan. Her visions always came back to Altan. Sometimes he was burning on the pier; sometimes he was strapped to an operating table, groaning in pain, and sometimes he wasn't injured at all, but those visions hurt the most, because then he would be talking to her—

Her cheek still burned from the force of Vaisra's blow, but in her visions it was Altan who struck her, smiling cruelly as she stared stupidly up at him.

"You hit me," she said.

"I had to," he answered. "*Someone* had to. You deserved it."

Did she deserve it? She didn't know. The only version of the truth that mattered was Altan's, and in her visions, Altan thought she deserved to die.

"You're a failure," he said.

"You can't come close to what I did," he said.

"It should have been you," he said.

And under everything, the unspoken command: *Avenge me, avenge me, avenge me . . .*

Sometimes, fleetingly, the visions became a terribly twisted fantasy where Altan was not hurting her. A version where he loved her instead, and his strikes were caresses. But they were fundamentally irreconcilable because Altan's nature was the same as the fire that had devoured him: if he didn't burn everyone around him, then he wasn't himself.

Sleep came finally through sheer exhaustion, but then only in short, fitful bursts; every time she nodded off she awoke screaming, and it was only by biting her knuckles and pressing herself into the corner that she could remain quiet throughout the night.

"Fuck you, Vaisra," she whispered. "Fuck. Fuck. *Fuck.*"

But she couldn't hate Vaisra, not really. It may have just been the sheer exhaustion; she was so racked with fear, grief, and rage that it was a trial to feel anything more. But she knew she needed this. She'd known for months she was killing herself and that she didn't have the self-control to stop, that the only person who might have stopped her was dead.

She needed someone who was capable of controlling her like no one since Altan could. She hated to admit it, but she knew that in Vaisra she might have found a savior.

Daytime was worse. Sunlight was a constant hammer on Rin's skull. But if she stayed cooped up in her quarters any longer, she would lose her mind, so Nezha accompanied her outside, keeping a tight grip on her arm while they walked along the top deck.

"How are you doing?" he asked.

It was a stupid question, asked more to break the silence than anything, because it should have been *obvious* how she was doing: she hadn't slept, she was trembling uncontrollably from both exhaustion and withdrawal, and eventually, she hoped, she would reach the point where she simply fell unconscious.

"Talk to me," she said.

"About what?"

"Anything. Literally anything else."

So he started telling her court stories in a low murmur that wouldn't give her a headache; trivial tales of gossip about who was fucking this Warlord's wife, who had really fathered that Warlord's son.

Rin watched him while he spoke. If she focused on the most minute details of his face, it distracted her from the pain, just for a little bit. The way his left eye opened just slightly wider than his right now. The way his eyebrows arched. The way his scars curled over his right cheek to resemble a poppy flower.

He was so much taller than she was. She had to crane her head to look up at him. When had he gotten so tall? At Sinegard they had been about the same height, nearly the same build, until their second year, when he'd started bulking up at a ridiculous pace. But then, at Sinegard they had just been *children*, stupid, naive, playing at war games that they had never seriously believed would become their reality.

Rin turned her gaze to the river. The *Seagrim* had moved inland, was traveling upstream on the Murui now. It moved upriver at a snail's pace as the men at the paddle boards wheeled furiously to push the ship through the sludgy mud.

She squinted at the banks. She wasn't sure if she was just hallucinating, but the closer they got, the more clearly she could make out little shapes moving in the distance, like ants crawling up logs.

"Are those people?" she asked.

They were. She could see them clearly now—men and women stooped beneath the sacks they carried over their shoulders, young children staggering barefoot along the riverside, and little babies strapped in bamboo baskets to their parents' backs.

"Where are they going?"

Nezha looked faintly surprised that she had even asked. "They're refugees."

"From where?"

"Everywhere. Golyn Niis wasn't the only city the Federation sacked. They destroyed the whole countryside. The entire time we were holding that pointless siege at Khurdalain they were marching southward, setting villages ablaze after they'd ripped them apart for supplies."

Rin was still hung up on the first thing he'd said. "So Golyn Niis wasn't . . ."

"No. Not even close."

She couldn't even fathom the death count this implied. How many people had lived in Golyn Niis? She multiplied that by the provinces and came up with a number nearing a million.

And now, all across the country, the Nikara refugees were shuffling back to their homes. The tide of bodies that had flowed from the war-ravaged cities to the barren northwest had started to turn.

"'You asked how large my sorrow is,'" Nezha recited. Rin recognized the line—it was from a poem she'd studied a lifetime ago, a lament by an Emperor whose last words became exam material for future generations. "'And I answered, like a river in spring flowing east.'"

As they floated up the Murui, crowds of people lined the banks with their arms outstretched, screaming at the *Seagrim*.

"Please, just up to the edge of the province . . ."

"Take my girls, leave me but take the girls . . ."

"You have space! You have space, damn you . . ."

Nezha tugged gently at Rin's wrist. "Let's go belowdecks."

She shook her head. She wanted to see.

"Why can't someone send boats?" she asked. "Why can't we bring them home?"

"They're not going home, Rin. They're running."

Dread pooled in her stomach. "How many are still out there?"

"The Mugenese?" Nezha sighed. "They're not a single army. They're individual brigades. They're cold, hungry, frustrated, and they have nowhere to go. They're thieves and bandits now."

"How many?" she repeated.

"Enough."

She made a fist. "I thought I brought peace."

"You brought *victory*," he said. "This is what happens after. The Warlords can hardly keep control over their home provinces. Food shortages. Rampant crime—and it's not just the Federation bandits. The Nikara are at each other's throats. Scarcity will do that to you."

"So of course you think it's a good time to fight another war."

"Another war is inevitable. But maybe we can prevent the next big one. The Republic will have growing pains. But if we can fix the foundation—if we can institute structures that make the next invasion less likely and keep future generations safe—then we'll have succeeded."

Foundation. Growing pains. Future generations. Such abstract concepts, she thought; concepts that wouldn't compute for the average peasant. Who cared who sat on the throne at Sinegard when vast stretches of the Empire were underwater?

The children's cries suddenly seemed unbearable.

"Couldn't we give them something?" she asked. "Money? Don't you have stacks of silver?"

"So they could spend it where?" Nezha asked. "You could give them more ingots than you could count, but they've got nowhere to buy goods. There's no supply."

"Food, then?"

"We tried doing that. They just tear each other to pieces trying to get at it. It's not a pretty sight."

She rested her chin on her elbows. Behind them the flock of humans receded; ignored, irrelevant, betrayed.

"You want to hear a joke?" Nezha asked.

She shrugged.

"A Hesperian missionary once said the state of the average Nikara peasant is that of a man standing in a pond with water coming up to his chin," said Nezha. "The slightest ripple is enough to put him underwater."

Staring out over the Murui, Rin didn't find that the least bit funny.

That night she decided to drown herself.

It wasn't a premeditated decision so much as it was an act of sheer desperation. The pain had gotten so bad that she banged on the door to her room, begging for help, and then when the guards opened it she ducked past their arms and ran up the stairs and out the hatch to the main deck.

Guards ran after her, shouting for reinforcements, but she doubled her pace, bare heels slamming against the wood. Splinters lanced little shreds of pain through her skin—but that was *good* pain because it distracted her from her screaming mind, if only for half a second.

The railing of the prow came up to her chest. She gripped the edge and attempted to pull herself up, but her arms were weak— surprisingly weak, she didn't remember getting that weak—and she sagged against the side. She tried again, hoisted herself far enough that her upper body draped over the edge. She hung there facedown for a moment, staring at the dark waves trailing alongside the *Seagrim*.

A pair of arms grasped her around the waist. She kicked and flailed, but they only tightened as they dragged her back down. She twisted her neck around.

"*Suni?*"

He walked backward from the prow, carrying her by the waist like a little child.

"Let go," she panted. "Let me *go!*"

He put her down. She tried to break away but he grabbed her wrists, twisted her arms behind her back, and forced her down into a sitting position.

"Breathe," he ordered. "Just breathe."

She obeyed. The pain didn't subside. The screaming didn't quiet. She began to shake, but Suni didn't let go of her arms. "If you just keep breathing, I'll tell you a story."

"I don't want to hear a fucking story," she said, gasping.

"Don't want. Don't *think*. Just breathe." Suni's voice was quiet, soothing. "Have you heard the story of the Monkey King and the moon?"

"No," she whimpered.

"Then listen carefully." He relaxed his grip ever so slightly, just enough that her arms stopped hurting. "Once upon a time, the Monkey King caught his first glimpse of the Moon Goddess."

Rin shut her eyes and tried to focus on Suni's voice. She'd never heard Suni talk this much. He was always so quiet, drawn into himself, as if he were unused to being in full occupation of his own mind that he wanted to relish the experience as much as possible. She'd forgotten how gentle he could sound.

He continued. "The Moon Goddess had just ascended to the heavens, and she was still drifting so close to Earth that you could see her face on the surface. She was such a lovely thing."

Some old memory stirred in the back of her mind. She did know this story after all. They told it to children in Rooster Province during the Lunar Festival, every autumn when children ate moon cakes and solved riddles written on rice paper and floated lanterns in the sky.

"Then he fell in love," she whispered.

"That's right. The Monkey King was struck with the most terrible passion. He had to possess her, he thought, or he might die. So he sent his best soldiers to retrieve her from the ocean. But they failed, for the moon lived not in the ocean but in the sky, and they drowned."

"Why?" she asked.

"Why did they drown? Why did the moon kill them? Because they weren't climbing to the sky to find her, they were diving into the water toward her reflection. But it was a fucking illusion they were grasping, not the real thing." Suni's voice hardened. It didn't rise above a whisper, but he might as well have been shouting. "You spend your whole life chasing after some illusion you think is real, only to realize you're a damned fool, and that if you reach any further, you'll drown."

He let go of her arms.

Rin turned around to face him. "Suni . . ."

"Altan liked that story," he said. "I first heard it from him. He told it whenever he needed to calm me down. Said it would help if I thought of the Monkey King as just another person, someone gullible and foolish, and not a god."

"The Monkey King is a dick," she said.

"And the Moon Goddess is a bitch," he said. "She sat there in the sky and watched the monkeys drowning over her. What does that say about her?"

That made her laugh. For a moment they both looked up at the moon. It was half-full, hiding behind a wispy dark cloud. Rin could imagine she was a woman, coy and devious, waiting to entice foolish men to their deaths.

She placed her hand over Suni's. His hand was massive, rougher than wood bark, mottled with calluses. Her mind spun with a thousand unanswered questions.

Who made you like this?

And, more importantly, *Do you regret it?*

"You don't have to suffer alone, you know." Suni gave her one of his rare, slow smiles. "You're not the only one."

She would have smiled back, but then a wave of sickness hit her gut and she jerked her head down. Vomit splattered the deck.

Suni rubbed circles on her back while she spat blood-speckled phlegm on the planks. When she was done, he smoothed her vomit-covered hair out of her eyes as she sucked in air in great, racking sobs.

"You're so strong," he said. "Whatever you're seeing, whatever you're feeling, it's not as strong as you are."

But she didn't want to be strong. Because if she were strong then she would be sober, and if she were sober she would have to consider the consequences of her actions. Then she'd have to look into the chasm. Then the Federation of Mugen would stop being an amorphous blur, and her victims would stop being meaningless numbers. Then she would recognize one death, what it meant, and then another, and then another and another and—

And if she wanted to recognize it, then she would have to be something, *feel* something other than anger, but she was afraid that if she stopped being angry then she might shatter.

She started to cry.

Suni smoothed the hair back from her forehead. "Just breathe," he murmured. "Breathe for me. Can you do that? Breathe five times."

One. Two. Three.

He continued to rub her back. "You just have to make it through the next five seconds. Then the next five. Then on and on."

Four. Five.

And then another five. And those five, oddly enough, were just the littlest bit more bearable than the last.

"There you go," Suni said after maybe a dozen counts to five. His voice was so low it was hardly a whisper. "There, look, you've done it."

She breathed, and counted, and wondered how Suni knew exactly what to say.

She wondered if he had done this before with Altan.

"She'll be all right," Suni said.

Rin looked up to see who he was talking to, and saw Vaisra standing in the shadows.

It couldn't have taken him long to respond to the soldiers' calls. Had he been there the entire time, watching without speaking?

"I heard you came out to get some air," he said.

She wiped vomit off her cheek with the back of her hand. Vaisra's gaze flickered to her stained clothing and back to her face. She couldn't read his expression.

"I'll be okay," she whispered.

"Will you?"

"I'll take care of her," Suni said.

A brief pause. Vaisra gave Suni a curt nod.

After another moment Suni helped her up and walked her back to her cabin. He kept one arm around her shoulders, warm, solid, comforting. The ship rocked against a particularly violent wave, and she staggered into his side.

"I'm sorry," she said.

"Don't be sorry," Suni said. "And don't worry. I've got you."

Five days later the *Seagrim* sailed over a submerged town. At first when Rin saw the tops of buildings emerging from the river she thought they were driftwood, or rocks. Then they got close enough that she could see the curving roofs of drowned pagodas, thatched houses lying under the surface. An entire village peeked up at her through river silt.

Then she saw the bodies—half-eaten, bloated and discolored, all with empty sockets because the glutinous eyes had already been nibbled away. They blocked up the river, decomposing at such a rate that the crew had to sweep away the maggots that threatened to climb on board.

Sailors lined up at the prow to shift bodies aside with long poles to make way for the ship. The corpses started piling up on the river's sides. Every few hours sailors had to climb down and drag them into a pile before the *Seagrim* could move—a duty the crew drew lots for with dread.

"What happened here?" Rin asked. "Did the Murui run its banks?"

"No. Dam breach." Nezha looked pale with fury. "Daji had the dam destroyed to flood the Murui river valley."

That wasn't Daji. Rin knew whose handiwork this was.

But did no one else know?

"Did it work?" she asked.

"Sure. It took out the Federation contingents in the north. Holed them up long enough for the northern Divisions to make mincemeat out of them. But then the floodwaters caught several hundred villages, which makes several thousand people who don't have homes now." Nezha made a fist. "How does a ruler do this? To her own *people*?"

"How do you know it was her?" Rin asked cautiously.

"Who else could it be? Something that big had to be an order from above. Right?"

"Of course," she murmured. "Who else would it be?"

Rin found the twins sitting together at the stern of the ship. They were perched on the railing, staring down at the wreckage trailing behind them. When they saw Rin approaching, they both jumped down and turned around, regarding her warily, as if they knew exactly why she had come.

"So how does it feel?" Rin asked.

"I don't know what you're talking about," Chaghan said.

"You did it, too," she said gleefully. "It wasn't just me."

"Go back to sleep," he said.

"Thousands of people!" she crowed. "Drowned like ants! Are you proud?"

Qara turned her head away, but Chaghan lifted his chin indignantly. "I did what Altan ordered."

That made her screech with laughter. "Me too! I was just acting on orders! He said I had to get vengeance for the Speerlies, and so I did, so it's not my fault, because Altan *said*—"

"Shut up," Chaghan snapped. "Listen—Vaisra thinks that Daji ordered the opening of those dikes."

She was still giggling. "So does Nezha."

He looked alarmed. "What did you tell him?"

"Nothing, obviously. I'm not stupid."

"You can't tell anyone the truth," Qara cut in. "Nobody in the Dragon Republic can know."

Of course Rin understood that. She knew how dangerous it would be to give the Dragon Army a reason to turn on the Cike. But in that moment all she could think of was how terribly funny it was that she wasn't the only one with mass murder on her hands.

"Don't worry," she said. "I won't tell. I'll be the only monster. Just me."

The twins looked stricken, but she couldn't stop laughing. She wondered how it had felt, the moment before the wave hit. The civilians might have been making dinner, playing outside, putting their children to bed, telling stories, making love, before a crushing force of water swept over their homes, destroyed their villages, and snuffed out their lives.

This was what the balance of power looked like now. People like her waved a hand and millions were crushed within the confines of some elemental disaster, flung off the chessboard of the world like irrelevant pieces. People like her—shamans, all of them—were like children stomping around over entire cities as if they were mud castles, glass houses, fungible entities that could be targeted and demolished.

On the seventh morning after they'd left Ankhiluun, the pain receded.

She woke up without a fever. No headache. She took a hesitant step toward the door and was pleasantly surprised at how steady her feet felt on the floor, how the world didn't whirl and shift around her. She opened the door, wandered out onto the upper deck, and was stunned by how good the river spray felt on her face.

Her senses felt sharper. Colors seemed brighter. She could smell things she hadn't before. The world seemed to exist with a vibrancy that she hadn't been aware of.

And then she realized that *she had her mind to herself.*

The Phoenix wasn't gone. She felt the god lingering still at the forefront of her mind, whispering tales of destruction, trying to control her desires.

But this time she knew what *she* wanted.

And she wanted control.

She'd been victim to the god's urges because she'd been keeping her own mind weak, dousing away the flame with a temporary and unsustainable solution. But now her head was clear, her mind was present—and when the Phoenix screamed, she could shut it down.

She requested to see Vaisra. He sent for her within minutes.

He was alone in his office when she arrived.

"You're not afraid of me?" she asked.

"I trust you," he said.

"You shouldn't."

"Then I trust you more than you trust yourself." He was acting like an entirely different person. The harsh persona was gone. His voice sounded so gentle, so encouraging that she was suddenly reminded of Tutor Feyrik.

She hadn't thought about Tutor Feyrik in a long time.

She hadn't felt *safe* in a long time.

Vaisra leaned back in his chair. "Go on, then. Try calling the fire for me. Just a little bit."

She opened her hand and focused her eyes on her palm. She recalled the rage, felt the heat of it coil in the pit of her stomach. But this time it didn't come all at once in an uncontrollable torrent, but manifested as a slow, angry burn.

A small burst of flame erupted in her palm. And it was just the burst; no more, no less, though she could increase its size, or if she wanted to, force it even smaller.

She closed her eyes, breathing slowly; cautiously she raised the flame higher and higher, a single ribbon of fire swaying over her hand like a reed, until Vaisra commanded her, "Stop."

She closed her fist. The fire went out.

Only afterward did she realize how fast her heart was beating.

"Are you all right?" Vaisra asked.

She managed a nod.

A smile spread over his face. He looked more than pleased. He looked proud. "Do it again. Make it bigger. Brighter. Shape it for me."

She reeled. "I can't. I don't have that much control."

"You *can*. Don't think about the Phoenix. Look at me."

She met his eyes. His gaze was an anchor.

A fire sparked out of her fist. She shaped it with trembling hands until it took on the image of a dragon, coils undulating in the space between her and Vaisra, making the air shimmer with the heat of the blaze.

More, said the Phoenix. *Bigger. Higher.*

Its screams pushed at the edge of her mind. She tried to shut it down.

The fire didn't recede.

She started to shake. "No, I can't—I can't, you have to get out—"

"Don't think about it," Vaisra whispered. "*Look at me.*"

Slowly, so faintly she was afraid she was imagining it, the red behind her eyelids subsided.

The fire disappeared. She collapsed to her knees.

"Good girl," Vaisra said softly.

She wrapped her arms around herself, rocked back and forth on the floor, and tried to remember how to breathe.

"May I show you something?" Vaisra asked.

She looked up. He crossed the room to a cabinet, opened a drawer, and pulled out a cloth-covered parcel. She flinched when he jerked the cloth off, but all she saw underneath was the dull sheen of metal.

"What is it?" she asked.

But she already knew. She would recognize this weapon anywhere. She had spent hours gazing upon that steel, the metal etched with evidence of countless battles. It was metal all the way through, even at the hilt, which would normally be made of wood, because Speerlies needed weapons that wouldn't burn through when they held them.

Rin felt a sudden light-headedness that had nothing to do with opium withdrawal and everything to do with the sudden and terribly vivid memory of Altan Trengsin walking down the pier to his death.

A harsh sob rose in her throat. "Where did you get that?"

"My men recovered it from the Chuluu Korikh." Vaisra bent down and held the trident out before her. "I thought you might want to have it."

She blinked at him, uncomprehending. "You—why were you there?"

"You've got to stop thinking I know less than I do. We were looking for Altan. He would have been, ah, useful."

She snorted through her tears. "You think Altan would have joined you?"

"I think Altan wanted any opportunity to rebuild this Empire."

"Then you don't know anything about him."

"I knew his people," Vaisra said. "I led the soldiers that liberated him from the research facility, and I helped train him when he was old enough to fight. Altan would have fought for this Republic."

She shook her head. "No, Altan just wanted to make things burn."

She reached out, grasped the trident, and hefted it in her hands. It felt awkward in her fingers, too heavy at the front and oddly light near the back. Altan had been much taller than she, and the weapon seemed too long for her to wield comfortably.

It couldn't function like a sword. It was no good for lateral blows. This trident had to be wielded surgically. Killing strikes only.

She held it away from her. "I shouldn't have this."

"Why not?"

She barely got the words out, she was crying so hard. "Because I'm not him."

Because I should have died, and he should be alive and standing here.

"No, you're not." Vaisra continued to stroke her hair with one hand, though he'd already smoothed it behind her ears. The other hand closed over her fingers, pressing them harder around the cool metal. "You'll be better."

When Rin was sure she could stomach solid food without vomiting, she joined Nezha abovedeck for her first actual meal in more than a week.

"Don't choke." Nezha sounded amused.

She was too busy ripping apart a steamed bun to respond. She didn't know if the food on deck was ridiculously good, or if she was just so famished that it tasted like the best thing she'd ever eaten.

"It's a pretty day," he said while she swallowed.

She made a muffled noise in agreement. The first few days she hadn't been able to bear standing outside in the direct sunlight. Now that her eyes no longer burned, she could look out over the bright water without wincing.

"Kitay's still sulking?" she asked.

"He'll come around," Nezha said. "He's always been stubborn."

"That's putting it lightly."

"Have a little sympathy. Kitay never wanted to be a soldier. He spent half his time wishing he'd gone to Yuelu Mountain, not Sinegard. He's an academic at heart, not a fighter."

Rin remembered. All Kitay had ever wanted to do was be a

scholar, go to the academy at Yuelu Mountain, and study science, or astronomy, or whatever struck his fancy at the moment. But he was the only son of the defense minister to the Empress, so his fate had been carved out before he was even born.

"That's sad," she murmured. "You shouldn't have to be a soldier unless you want to."

Nezha rested his chin on his hand. "Did you want to?"

She hesitated.

Yes. No. She hadn't thought there was anything else for her. She hadn't thought it mattered if she wanted to.

"I used to be scared of war," she finally said. "Then I realized I was very good at it. And I'm not sure I'd be good at anything else."

Nezha nodded silently, gazing out at the river, pulling mindlessly at his steamed bun without eating it.

"How's your . . . uh . . ." Nezha gestured toward his temples.

"Good. I'm good."

For the first time she felt as if she had a handle on her anger. She could think. She could breathe. The Phoenix was still there, looming in the back of her mind, ready to burst into flame if she called it—but *only* if she called it.

She looked down to discover the steamed bun was gone. Her fingers were clutching nothing. Her stomach reacted to this by growling.

"Here," Nezha said. He handed her his somewhat mangled bun. "Have mine."

"You're not hungry?"

"I don't have much of an appetite right now. And you look emaciated."

"I'm not taking your food."

"Eat," he insisted.

She took a bite. It slid thickly down her throat and settled in her stomach with a wonderful heaviness. She hadn't been so full for such a long time.

"How's your face?" Nezha asked.

She touched her cheek. Sharp twinges of pain lanced through her lower face whenever she spoke. The bruise had blossomed while the opium seeped out of her system, as if one had to trade off with the other.

"It feels like it's just getting worse," she said.

"Nah. You'll be fine. Father doesn't hit hard enough to injure."

They sat awhile in silence. Rin watched fish jumping out of the water, leaping and flailing as if begging to be caught.

"And your face?" she asked. "Does it still hurt?"

In certain lights Nezha's scars looked like angry red lines someone had carved all over his face. In other lights they looked like a delicately painted crosshatch of brush ink.

"It hurt for a long time. Now I just can't feel anything."

"What if I touched you?" She was struck by the urge to run her thumb over his scars. To caress them.

"I wouldn't feel that, either." Nezha's fingers drifted to his cheek. "I suppose it scares people, though. Father makes me wear the mask whenever I'm around civilians."

"I thought you were just being vain."

Nezha smiled but didn't laugh. "That too."

Rin ripped large chunks from the steamed bun and barely chewed before swallowing.

Nezha reached out and touched her hair. "That's a good look on you. Nice to see your eyes again."

She'd shorn her hair close to her head. Not until she'd seen her discarded locks on the floor had she realized how disgusting it had become; the scraggly tendrils had grown out greasy and tangled, a nesting site for lice. Her hair was shorter than Nezha's now, close-cropped and clean. It made her feel like a student again.

"Has Kitay eaten anything?" she asked.

Nezha shifted uncomfortably. "No. Still hiding in his room. We don't keep it locked, but he won't come out."

She frowned. "If he's that furious, then why don't you let him go?"

"Because we'd rather have him on our side."

"Then why not just use him as leverage against his father? Trade him as a hostage?"

"Because Kitay's a resource," Nezha said frankly. "You know the way his mind works. It's not a secret. He knows most things and he remembers everything. He has a better grasp on strategy than anyone should. My father likes to keep his best pieces around for as long as he can. Besides, his father was at Sinegard before they abandoned it. There's no guarantee he's alive."

"Oh" was all she could say. She looked down and realized that she had finished Nezha's bun, too.

He laughed. "You think you can handle something more than bread?"

She nodded. He signaled for a servant, who disappeared into the cabin and reemerged a few minutes later with a bowl that smelled so good that a disgusting amount of saliva filled Rin's mouth.

"This is a delicacy near the coast," Nezha said. "We call it the wawa fish."

"Why?" she asked through a full mouth.

Nezha turned it over with his chopsticks, deftly separating the white flesh from the spine. "Because of the way it shrieks. Flails in the water crying like a baby with a rash. Sometimes the cooks boil them to death just for fun. Didn't you hear it in the galley?"

Rin's stomach turned. "I thought there might be a baby on board."

"Aren't they hilarious?" Nezha picked up a slice and put it in her bowl. "Try it. Father loves them."

CHAPTER 8

"If you have an open shot at Daji, take it." Captain Eriden jabbed the blunt end of his spear at Rin's head as he spoke. "Don't give her a chance to seduce you."

She ducked the first blow. The second whacked her on the nose. She shook off the pain, winced, and readjusted her stance. She narrowed her eyes at Eriden's legs, trying to predict his movements by watching only his lower body.

"She'll want to talk," Eriden said. "She always does, she thinks it's funny to watch her prey squirm before she kills it. Don't wait for her to say her piece. You'll be deathly curious because she'll make you, but you must attack before your chance is gone."

"I'm not an idiot," Rin panted.

Eriden directed another flurry of blows at her torso. Rin managed to block about half of them. The rest wrecked her.

He withdrew his spear, signaling a temporary reprieve. "You don't understand. The Vipress is no mere mortal. You've heard the stories. Her face is so dazzling that when she walks outside, the birds fall out of the sky and the fish swim up to the surface."

"It's just a face," she said.

"It is not *just a face*. I've seen Daji beguile and bewitch some of the most powerful and rational men I know. She brings them to their knees with just a few words. More often with just a look."

"Did she ever charm you?" Rin asked.

"She charmed everyone," Eriden said, but didn't elaborate. Rin could never get anything but blunt, literal answers from Eriden, who had the dour visage and personality of a corpse. "Be careful. And keep your gaze down."

Rin knew that. He'd been saying it for days. Daji's preferred weapon was her eyes—those snake's eyes that could ensnare a soul with a simple look, could trap the viewer into a vision of Daji's own choosing.

The solution was to never look her in the face. Eriden was training Rin to fight solely by watching her opponent's lower body.

This turned out to be particularly difficult when it came to hand-to-hand combat. So much depended on where the eyes darted, where the torso was pointed. All motion on oblique planes came from the upper body, but Eriden chided Rin every time her eyes strayed too far upward.

Eriden lunged forward without warning. Rin fared slightly better blocking the next sequence of attacks. She'd learned to watch not just the feet but the hip—often that pivoted first, set into motion the legs and feet. She parried a series of blows before a strong hit got through to her shoulder. It wasn't painful, but the shock nearly made her drop her trident.

Eriden signaled another pause.

While Rin doubled over to catch her breath, he drew a set of long needles out of his pocket. "The Empress is also partial to these."

He flung three of them toward her. Rin hopped hastily to the side and managed to get out of the needles' trajectory but landed badly on her ankle.

She winced. The needles kept coming.

She waved her trident madly in a circle, trying to knock them out of the air. It almost worked. Five clattered against the ground. One struck her on the upper thigh. She yanked it out. Eriden hadn't bothered to blunt the tips. *Asshole.*

"Daji likes her poison," Eriden said. "You're dead now."

"Thanks, I got that," Rin snapped.

She let the trident drop and bent over her knees, sucking in deep draughts of air. Her lungs were on fire. Where had her stamina gone? At Sinegard, she could have sparred for hours.

Right—up in a puff of opium smoke.

Eriden hadn't even broken a sweat. She didn't want to look weak by asking for another break, so she tried distracting him with questions. "How do you know so much about the Empress?"

"We fought by her side. The Dragon Province had some of the best-trained troops during the Second Poppy War. We were almost always with the Trifecta on the front lines."

"What were the Trifecta like?"

"Brutal. Dangerous." Eriden pointed his spear toward her. "Enough talk. You should—"

"But I have to know," she insisted. "Did Daji fight on the battlefield? Did you see her? What was she like?"

"Daji's not a warrior. She's a competent martial artist, they all were, but she's never relied on blunt force. Her powers are more subtle than the Gatekeeper's or the Dragon Emperor's were. She understands desire. She knows what drives men, and she takes their deepest desire and makes them believe that she is the only thing that can give it to them."

"But I'm a woman."

"All the same."

"But that can't make so much of a difference," Rin said, more to convince herself than anything. "That's just—that's *desire*. What is that next to hard power?"

"You think fire and steel can trump desire? Daji was always the strongest of the Trifecta."

"Stronger than the Dragon Emperor?" A memory resurfaced of a white-haired man floating above the ground, beastly shadows circling around him. "Stronger than the Gatekeeper?"

"Of course she was," Eriden said softly. "Why do you think she's the only one left?"

That gave Rin pause.

How *had* Daji become the sole ruler of Nikan? Everyone she'd asked told a different story. All that anyone in the Empire seemed to know for sure was that one day the Dragon Emperor died, the Gatekeeper disappeared, and Daji alone remained on the throne.

"Do you know what she did to them?" she asked.

"I'd give my arms to find out." Eriden tossed his spear to the side and drew his sword. "Let's see how you do with this."

His blade moved blindingly fast. Rin staggered backward, trying desperately to keep up. Several times her trident nearly slipped out of her hands. She gritted her teeth, frustrated.

It wasn't just that Altan's trident was too long, too unbalanced, clearly designed for a taller stature than hers. If that were the problem, she would have just swallowed her pride and swapped it for a sword.

It was her body. She knew the right motions and patterns, but her muscles simply could not keep up. Her limbs seemed to obey her mind only after a two-second lag.

Simply put, *she* didn't work. Months of lying prone in her room, breathing smoke in and out, had whittled her muscles away. Only now had she become aware of how weak, how painfully thin and easily tired she'd become.

"Focus." Eriden closed in. Rin's movements became increasingly desperate. She wasn't even trying to get a blow in herself; it took all her concentration to keep his blade away from her face.

She couldn't win a weapons match at this rate.

But she didn't have to use her trident for the kill. The trident was only useful as a ranged weapon—it kept her opponents at a far enough distance to protect her.

But *she* need only to get close enough to use the fire.

She narrowed her eyes, waiting.

There it was. Eriden struck for her hilt—a low, reaching blow. She let him flip the weapon out of her hands. Then she took advantage of the opening, darted into the space created by their interlocking weapons, and jammed her knee into Eriden's sternum.

He doubled over. She kicked in his knees, dropped down onto his chest, and splayed her palms out before his face.

She emitted the smallest hint of flame—just enough to make him feel the heat on his skin.

"Boom," she said. "You're dead now."

Eriden's mouth pressed into something that almost resembled a smile.

"How's she doing?"

Rin twisted to look over her shoulder.

Vaisra and Nezha emerged on the deck. Eriden pulled himself to a sitting position.

"She'll be ready," he said.

"She'll *be* ready?" Vaisra repeated.

"Give me a few days," Rin said, panting. "Still figuring this out. But I'll get there."

"Good," Vaisra said.

"You're bleeding." Nezha pointed to her thigh.

But she barely heard him. She was still looking at Vaisra, who was smiling more widely than she'd ever seen him. He looked pleased. Proud. And somehow, the jolt of satisfaction that gave her felt better than anything she'd smoked in months.

"You'll accompany the Dragon Warlord into the Autumn Palace for the noon summit," Eriden said. "Remember, you'll be presented as a war criminal. Do not act like he is your ally. Make sure to look afraid."

A dozen of Vaisra's generals and advisers were in the state-room, seated around an array of detailed maps of the palace. Rin sat on Vaisra's right, sweating slightly from the constant attention. The entire plan centered on her, and she had no room to fail.

Eriden held up a pair of iron handcuffs. "You'll be bound and muzzled. I'd get used to the feel of these."

"That's no good," Rin said. "I can't burn through metal."

"They're not completely metal." Eriden slid the handcuffs across the table so that Rin could take a closer look. "The link in the middle is twine. It will burn through with minimal heat."

She fiddled with the handcuffs. "And Daji won't just have me killed? I mean—she'll know what I'm there to do; she saw me try at Adlaga."

"Oh, she'll likely suspect us of treachery the moment we dock in Lusan. We're not trying to ambush her. Daji likes to play with her food before she eats it. And she especially won't want to get rid of *you*. You're too interesting."

"Daji never strikes first," Vaisra said. "She'll want to milk you for as much information as she can, so she'll try to take you somewhere private to talk. Feign surprise at that. Then she'll likely make an offer nearly as tempting as mine."

"Which will be what?" Rin asked.

"Use your imagination. A place in her Imperial Guard. Free rein to scour the Empire of any remaining Federation troops. More glory and riches than you could possibly dream of. It'll all be a lie, of course. Daji has kept her throne for two decades by eliminating people before they become problems. Should you take a position in her court, you will simply be the latest on her long list of political assassinations."

"Or they'll find your body in the sewers minutes after you say yes," said Eriden.

Rin looked around the table. "Does no one else see the gaping flaw in this plan?"

"Pray tell," Vaisra said.

"Why don't I just kill her on sight? Before she opens her mouth? Why even take the risk of letting her talk?"

Vaisra and Eriden exchanged a glance. Eriden hesitated a moment, then spoke. "You, ah, won't be able to."

Rin blanched. "What does *that* mean?"

"We just went over this," Vaisra said. "Once Daji sees you,

she'll know you're there to kill her. And she'll very strongly suspect my own intentions. The only way to get you into the Autumn Palace and close enough to attack without putting the rest of us in danger is if you're sedated first."

"Sedated," Rin repeated.

"We'll have to give you a dose of opium while Daji's guards are watching," Vaisra said. "Enough to pacify you for an hour or two. But Daji doesn't know about your increased tolerance, which helps us. It'll wear off sooner than she expects."

Rin hated this plan. They were asking her to enter the Autumn Palace unarmed, high out of her mind, and completely unable to call the fire. But no matter how she turned it over in her mind, she couldn't find a loophole in the logic. She had to be defanged if she was to get close enough to get a hit.

She tried not to let her fear show as she spoke. "So am I—I mean, will I be alone?"

"We cannot bring a larger guard to the Autumn Palace without arousing Daji's suspicion. You will have hidden but minimal rein-forcements. We can get soldiers in here, here, and here." Vaisra tapped at three points on a map of the palace. "But remember, our objective here is very limited. If we wanted an all-out war, we would have brought the armada up the Murui. We are only here to cut the head off the snake. The battles come after."

"So I'm the only one at risk," Rin said. "Nice."

"We will not abandon you. We will extract you if it goes badly, I promise. Successful or not, you'll use one of these escape routes to get out of the palace. Captain Eriden will have the *Seagrim* ready to depart Lusan in seconds if escape is necessary."

Rin peered down at the map. The Autumn Palace was hope-lessly large, arranged like a maze within a conch shell, a spiraling complex of narrow corridors and dead ends, with twisting hallways and tunnels constructed in every direction.

The escape routes were marked with green lines. She narrowed her eyes, muttering to herself. A few more minutes and she'd have them memorized. She'd always been good at memorizing things, and now that she was off opium she was finding it easier and easier to focus on mental tasks.

She cringed at the thought of giving that up, even for an hour.

"You make this sound so easy," she said. "Why hasn't anyone tried to kill Daji before?"

"She's the Empress," said Vaisra, as if that were explanation enough.

"She's one woman whose sole talent is being very pretty," Rin said. "I don't understand."

"Because you're too young," Eriden said. "You weren't alive when the Trifecta were at the peak of their power. You don't know the fear. You couldn't trust anyone around you, even your own family. If you whispered a word of treason against Emperor Riga, then the Vipress and the Gatekeeper would be sure to have you destroyed. Not just imprisoned—obliterated."

Vaisra nodded. "In those years, entire families were ruined, executed, or exiled, and their lineages wiped from history. Daji oversaw this all without blinking an eye. There is a reason why the Warlords still bow down before her, and it's not just because she is *pretty*."

Something about Vaisra's expression gave Rin pause. Then she realized it was the first time she had ever seen him look scared.

She wondered what Daji had done to him.

Someone knocked on the door just then. She jumped in her seat.

"Come in," Vaisra called.

A junior officer poked his head in. "Nezha sent me to alert you. We've arrived."

Near the end of his reign, the Red Emperor built the Autumn Palace in the northern city of Lusan. It was never meant to be a capital or an administrative center; it was too far removed from the central provinces to properly govern. It served merely as a resort for his favorite concubines and their children, an escape for the days when Sinegard became so scorching hot that their skin threatened to darken within seconds of stepping outside.

Under the Empress Su Daji's regime, Lusan had been a place for court officials to harbor their wives and families safely away from the dangers at court, until it turned into the interim capital after Sinegard and then Golyn Niis were razed to the ground.

As the *Seagrim* sailed toward the city, the Murui narrowed to a thinner and thinner stream, which forced them to move at a slower and slower pace until they weren't sailing so much as crawling toward the Autumn Palace.

Rin could see the city walls from miles off. Lusan seemed to be lit from within by some unearthly afternoon glow. Everything was somehow golden; it was like the rest of the Empire had dulled to shades of black, white, and bloody red during the war, and Lusan had soaked up all the surrounding color, shining brighter than anything she had seen in months.

Close to the city walls Rin saw a woman walking down the riverbank with buckets of dye and heavy rolls of cloth strapped to her back. Rin knew the cloth was silk from the way it glimmered when it was unrolled, so soft that she could almost imagine the butterfly-wing texture on the backs of her fingers.

How could Lusan have silk? The rest of the country was garbed in unwashed, threadbare scraps. All along the Murui, Rin had seen naked children and babies wrapped in lily pads in some effort to preserve their dignity.

Farther downriver, fishing sampans glided up and down the winding waterways. Each boat carried several large birds—white creatures with massive beaks—hooked to the boats on strings.

Nezha had to explain to Rin what the birds were for. "They've got a string around their necks, see? The bird swallows the fish; the farmer pulls the fish out of the bird's neck. The bird goes in again, always hungry, always too dumb to realize that everything it catches goes into the fish basket and that all it'll ever get are slops."

Rin made a face. "That seems inefficient. Why not just use a net?"

"It is inefficient," Nezha agreed. "But they're not fishing for staples, they're hunting for delicacies. Sweetfish."

"Why?"

He shrugged.

Rin already knew the answer. Why *not* hunt for delicacies? Lusan was clearly untouched by the refugee crisis that had swept the rest of the country; it could afford to focus on luxury.

Perhaps it was the heat, or perhaps because Rin's nerves were already always on edge, but she felt angrier and angrier as they made for port. She hated this city, this land of pale and pampered women, men who were not soldiers but bureaucrats, and children who didn't know what fear felt like.

She simmered not with resentment so much as with a nameless fury at the idea that outside the confines of warfare, life could go on and *did* go on, that somehow, still, in pockets scattered throughout the Empire there were cities and cities of people who were dyeing silk and fishing for gourmet dinners, unaffected by the single issue that plagued a soldier's mind: when and where the next attack would come.

"I thought I wasn't a prisoner," said Kitay.

"You're not," said Nezha. "You're a guest."

"A guest who isn't allowed off the ship?"

"A guest whom we'd like to keep with us a little longer," Nezha said delicately. "Can you stop glaring at me like that?"

When the captain announced that they had anchored in Lusan, Kitay had ventured abovedeck for the first time in weeks. Rin had hoped he'd come up for some fresh air, but he was just following Nezha around the deck, intent on antagonizing him in any way possible.

Rin had tried several times to intercede. Kitay, however, seemed determined to pretend she didn't exist by ignoring her every time she spoke, so she turned her attention to the sights on the riverbank instead.

A mild crowd had gathered around the base of the *Seagrim*,

made up mostly of Imperial officials, Lusani merchants, and messengers from other Warlords. Rin surmised from what snatches of conversation she could hear from the top deck that they were all trying to get an audience with Vaisra. But Eriden and his men were stationed at the bottom of the gangplank, turning everyone away.

Vaisra had also issued strict orders that no one was to leave the ship. The soldiers and crewmen were to continue living on board as if they were still out on open water, and only a handful of Eriden's men had been permitted to enter Lusan to purchase fresh supplies. This, Nezha had explained, was to minimize the risk that someone might give away Rin's cover. Meanwhile, she was only allowed on deck if she wore a scarf to cover her face.

"You know you can't keep me here indefinitely," Kitay said loudly. "Someone's going to find out."

"Like who?" Nezha asked.

"My father."

"You think your father's in Lusan?"

"He's in the Empress's guard. He commands her security detail. There's no way she would have left him behind."

"She left everyone else behind," Nezha said.

Kitay crossed his arms. "Not my *father*."

Nezha caught Rin's eye. For the briefest moment he looked guilty, like he wanted to say something that he couldn't, but she couldn't imagine what.

"That's the commerce minister," Kitay said suddenly. "He'll know."

"What?"

Before either Nezha or Rin could register what he meant, Kitay broke into a run at the gangplank.

Nezha shouted for the closest soldiers to restrain him. They were too slow—Kitay dodged their arms, climbed onto the side of the ship, grabbed a rope, and lowered himself to the riverbank so quickly that he must have burned his hands raw.

Rin ran for the gangplank to intercept him, but Nezha held her back with one arm. "Don't."

"But he—"

Nezha just shook his head. "Let him."

They watched from a distance, silent, as Kitay ran up to the commerce minister and seized his arm, then doubled over, panting.

Rin could see them clearly from the deck. The minister recoiled for a moment, hands lifted as if to ward off this unfamiliar soldier, until he recognized Defense Minister Chen's son and his arms dropped.

Rin couldn't tell what they were saying. She could only see their mouths moving, the expressions on their faces.

She saw the minister place his hands on Kitay's shoulders.

She saw Kitay ask a question.

She saw the minister shake his head.

Then she saw Kitay collapse in on himself as if he had been speared in the gut, and she realized that Defense Minister Chen had not survived the Third Poppy War.

Kitay didn't struggle when Vaisra's men marched him back onto the boat. He was white-faced, tight-lipped, and his madly twitching eyes looked red at the rims.

Nezha tried to put a hand on Kitay's shoulder. Kitay shook him off and made straight for the Dragon Warlord. Blue-clad soldiers immediately moved to form a protective wall between them, but Kitay didn't reach for a weapon.

"I've decided something," he said.

Vaisra waved a hand. His guard dispersed. Then it was just the two of them facing each other: the regal Dragon Warlord and the furious, trembling boy.

"Yes?" Vaisra asked.

"I want a position," Kitay said.

"I thought you wanted to go home."

"Don't fuck with me," Kitay snapped. "I want a position. Give me a uniform. I won't wear this one anymore."

"I'll see where we can—"

Kitay cut him off again. "I'm not going to be a foot soldier."

"Kitay—"

"I want a seat at the table. Chief strategist."

"You're rather young for that," Vaisra said drily.

"No, I'm not. You made Nezha a general. And I've always been smarter than Nezha. You know I'm brilliant. I'm a fucking genius. Put me in charge of operations and you won't lose a single battle, I *swear*." Kitay's voice broke at the end. Rin saw his throat bob, saw the veins protruding from his jaw, and knew that he was holding back tears.

"I'll consider it," Vaisra said.

"You knew, didn't you?" Kitay demanded. "You've known for months."

Vaisra's expression softened. "I'm sorry. I didn't want to be the one to have to tell you. I know how much pain you must feel—"

"No. *No*, shut the fuck up, I don't want that." Kitay backed away. "I don't need your fake sympathy."

"Then what would you like from me?"

Kitay lifted his chin. "I want troops."

The Warlords' summit would not commence until after the victory parade, and that stretched over the next two days. For the most part Vaisra's soldiers did not participate. Several troops entered the city in civilian clothes, sketching out final details in their already extensive maps of the city in case anything had changed. But the majority of the crew remained on board, watching the festivities from afar.

Every now and then an armed delegation arrived aboard the *Seagrim*, faces shrouded under hoods to conceal their identities. Vaisra received them in his office, doors sealed, guards posted outside to discourage curious eavesdroppers. Rin assumed the visitors were the southern Warlords—the rulers of Boar, Rooster, and Monkey provinces.

Hours passed without news. Rin grew maddeningly bored. She'd been over the palace maps a thousand times, and she'd already trained so long with Eriden that day that her leg muscles screamed when she walked. She was just about to ask Nezha if they might explore Lusan in disguise when Vaisra summoned her to his office.

"I have a meeting with the Snake Warlord," he said. "On land. You're coming."

"As a guard?"

"No. As proof."

He didn't explain further, but she suspected she knew what he meant, so she simply picked up her trident, pulled her scarf up higher over her face until it concealed all but her eyes, and followed him toward the gangplank.

"Is the Snake Warlord an ally?" she asked.

"Ang Tsolin was my Strategy master at Sinegard. He could be anything from ally to enemy. Today, we'll simply treat him as an old friend."

"What should I say to him?"

"You'll remain silent. All he has to do is look at you."

Rin followed Vaisra across the riverbank until they reached a line of tents propped up at the city borders as if it were an invading army's. When they approached the periphery, a group of green-clad soldiers stopped them and demanded their weapons.

"Go on," Vaisra muttered when Rin hesitated to part with her trident.

"You trust him that much?"

"No. But I trust you won't need it."

The Snake Warlord came to meet them outside, where his aides had set up two chairs and a small table.

At first Rin mistook him for a servant. Ang Tsolin didn't look like a Warlord. He was an old man with a long and sad face, so slender he seemed frail. He wore the same forest-green Militia uniform as his men, but no symbols announced his rank, and no weapon hung at his hip.

"Old master." Vaisra dipped his head. "It's good to see you again."

Tsolin's eyes flickered toward the outline of the *Seagrim*, which was just visible down the river. "So you didn't take the bitch's offer, either?"

"It was rather unsubtle, even for her," Vaisra said. "Is anyone staying in the palace?"

"Chang En. Our old friend Jun Loran. None of the southern Warlords."

Vaisra arched an eyebrow. "They hadn't mentioned that. That's surprising."

"Is it? They're southern."

Vaisra settled back in his chair. "I suppose not. They've been touchy for years."

No one had brought a chair out for Rin, so she remained standing behind Vaisra, hands folded over her chest in imitation of the guards who flanked Tsolin. They looked unamused.

"You've certainly taken your time getting here," Tsolin said. "It's been a long camping trip for the rest of us."

"I was picking up something on the coast." Vaisra pointed toward Rin. "Do you know who she is?"

Rin lowered her scarf.

Tsolin glanced up. At first he seemed only confused as he examined her face, but then he must have taken in the dark hue of her skin, the red glint in her eyes, because his entire body tensed.

"She's wanted for quite a lot of silver," he said finally. "Something about an assassination attempt in Adlaga."

"It's a good thing I've never wanted for silver," said Vaisra.

Tsolin rose from his chair and walked toward Rin until only inches separated them. He was not so much taller than she was, but his gaze made her distinctly uncomfortable. She felt like a specimen under his careful examination.

"Hello," she said. "I'm Rin."

Tsolin ignored her. He made a humming noise under his breath and returned to his seat. "This is a very blunt display of force. You're just going to march her into the Autumn Palace?"

"She'll be properly bound. Drugged, too. Daji insisted on it."

"So Daji knows she's here."

"I thought that'd be prudent. I sent a messenger ahead."

"No wonder she's getting antsy, then," Tsolin said. "She's increased the palace guard threefold. The Warlords are talking. Whatever you're planning, she's ready for it."

"So it will help to have your support," Vaisra said.

Rin noticed that Vaisra dipped his head every time he spoke to Tsolin. In a subtle fashion, he was bowing continuously to his elder, displaying deference and respect.

But Tsolin seemed unresponsive to flattery. He sighed. "You've never been content with peace, have you?"

"And you refuse to acknowledge that war is the only option," said Vaisra. "Which would you prefer, Tsolin? The Empire can die a slow death over the next century, or we can set the country on the right path within the week if we're lucky."

"Within a few bloody years, you mean."

"Months, at the most."

"Don't you remember the last time someone went up against the Trifecta?" Tsolin asked. "Remember how the bodies littered the steps of the Heavenly Pass?"

"It won't be like that," Vaisra said.

"Why not?"

"Because we have her." Vaisra nodded toward Rin.

Tsolin looked wearily in Rin's direction.

"You poor child," he said. "I'm so sorry."

She blinked, unsure what that meant.

"And we have the advantage of time," Vaisra continued quickly. "The Militia is reeling from the Federation attack. They need to recuperate. They couldn't marshal their defenses fast enough."

"Yet under your best-case scenario, Daji still has the northern provinces," Tsolin said. "Horse and Tiger would never defect. She has Chang En and Jun. That's all you need."

"Jun knows not to fight battles he can't win."

"But he can and will win this one. Or did you think you would defeat everyone through a little intimidation?"

"This war could be over in days if I had your support," Vaisra said impatiently. "Together we'd control the coastline. I own the canals. You own the eastern shore. Combined, our fleets—"

Tsolin held up a hand. "My people have undergone three wars in their lifetime, each time with a different ruler. Now they might have their first chance at a lasting peace. And you want to bring a civil war to their doorsteps."

"There's a civil war coming, whether you admit it or not. I only hasten the inevitable."

"We will not survive the inevitable," Tsolin said. True sorrow laced his words. Rin could see it in his eyes; the man looked haunted. "We lost so many men at Golyn Niis, Vaisra. Boys. You know what our commanders made their soldiers do the evening before the siege? They wrote letters home to their families. Told them they loved them. Told them they wouldn't be coming home. And our generals chose the strongest and fastest soldiers to deliver the messages back home, because they knew it wasn't going to make a difference whether we had them at the wall."

He stood up. "My answer is no. We have yet to recover from the scars of the Poppy Wars. You can't ask us to bleed again."

Vaisra reached out and grabbed Tsolin's wrist before he could turn to go. "You're neutral then?"

"Vaisra—"

"Or against me? Shall I expect Daji's assassins at my door?"

Tsolin looked pained. "I know nothing. I help no one. Let's leave it at that, shall we?"

"We're just going to let him go?" Rin asked once they were out of Tsolin's earshot.

Vaisra's harsh laugh surprised her. "You think he's going to report us to the Empress?"

Rin thought this had seemed rather obvious. "It's clear he's not with us."

"He will be. He's revealed his threshold for going to war. Provincial danger. He'll pick a side quick enough if it means the difference between warfare and obliteration, so I will force his hand. I'll bring the fight to his province. He won't have a choice then, and I suspect he knows that."

Vaisra's stride grew faster and faster as they walked. Rin had to run to catch up.

"You're angry," she realized.

No, he was *furious*. She could see it in the icy glare in his eyes, in the stiffness of his gait. She'd spent too much of her childhood learning to tell when someone was in a dangerous mood.

Vaisra didn't respond.

She stopped walking. "The other Warlords. They said no, didn't they?"

Vaisra paused before he answered. "They're undecided. It's too early to tell."

"Will *they* betray you?"

"They don't know enough about my plans to do anything. All they can tell Daji is that I'm displeased with her, which she already knows. But I doubt they'll have the backbone to say even that." Vaisra's voice dripped with condescension. "They are like sheep. They will watch silently, waiting to see how the balance of power falls, and they will align with whoever can protect them. But we won't need them until then."

"But you needed Tsolin," she said.

"This will be significantly harder without Tsolin," he admitted. "He could have tipped the balance. It'll truly be a war now."

She couldn't help but ask, "Then are we going to lose?"

Vaisra regarded her in silence for a moment. Then he knelt down in front of her, put his hands on her shoulders, and looked up at her with an intensity that made Rin want to squirm.

"No," he said softly. "We have you."

"Vaisra—"

"You will be the spear that brings this empire down," he said sternly. "You will defeat Daji. You will set in motion this war, and then the southern Warlords will have no choice."

The intensity in his eyes made her desperately uncomfortable. "But what if I can't?"

"You will."

"But—"

"You will, because I ordered you to." His grip tightened on her shoulders. "You are my greatest weapon. Do not disappoint."

CHAPTER 9

Rin had imagined the Autumn Palace as composed of blocky, abstract shapes, the way it was represented on the maps. But the real Autumn Palace was a perfectly preserved sanctuary of beauty, a sight lifted straight out of an ink brush painting. Flowers bloomed everywhere. White plum blossoms and peach flowers laced the gardens; lily pads and lotus flowers dotted the ponds and waterways. The complex itself was an elegantly designed structure of ornamented ceremonial gates, massive marble pillars, and sprawling pavilions.

But for all that beauty, a stillness hung over the palace that made Rin deeply uncomfortable. The heat was oppressive. The roads looked as if they were swept clean hourly by unseen servants, but still Rin could hear the ubiquitous sound of buzzing flies, as if they detected something rotten in the air that no one could see.

It felt as if the palace hid something foul under its lovely exterior; beneath the smell of blooming lilacs, something was in the last stages of decay.

Perhaps she was imagining it. Perhaps the palace was truly beautiful, and she just hated it because it was a coward's resort.

This was a refuge, and the fact that anyone had hidden alive in the Autumn Palace while corpses rotted in Golyn Niis infuriated her.

Eriden nudged the small of her back with his spear. "Eyes down."

She hastily obeyed. She had come posing as Vaisra's prisoner—hands cuffed behind her back, mouth sealed behind an iron muzzle that clamped her lower jaw tightly upward. She could barely speak except in whispers.

She didn't have to remember to look scared. She was terrified. The thirty grams of opium circulating through her bloodstream did nothing to calm her down. It magnified her paranoia even as it kept her heart rate low and made her feel as if she were floating among clouds. Her mind was anxious and hyperactive but her body was slow and sluggish—the worst possible combination.

At sunrise Rin, Vaisra, and Captain Eriden had passed under the arched gateways of the nine concentric circles of the Autumn Palace. Servants patted them down for weapons at each gate. By the seventh gate, they had been groped so thoroughly that Rin was surprised they hadn't been asked to strip naked.

At the eighth gate an Imperial guard stopped her to check her pupils.

"She took a dose before the guards this morning," Vaisra said.

"Even so," said the guard. He reached for Rin's chin and tilted it up. "Eyes open, please."

Rin obliged and tried not to squirm as he pulled her eyelids apart.

Satisfied, the guard stepped back to let them through.

Rin followed Vaisra into the throne room, shoes echoing against a marble floor so smooth it looked like still water at the surface of a lake.

The inner chamber was a rich and ornate assault of decorations that blurred and swam in Rin's opium-blurred eyesight. She blinked and tried to focus. Intricately painted symbols covered every wall, stretching all the way up to the ceiling, where they coalesced in a circle.

It's the Pantheon, she realized. If she squinted, she could make out the gods she had come to recognize: the Monkey God, mischievous and cruel; the Phoenix, imposing and ravenous. . . .

That was odd. The Red Emperor had hated shamans. After he'd claimed his throne at Sinegard, he'd had the monks killed and their monasteries burned.

But maybe he hadn't hated the gods. Maybe he'd just hated that he couldn't access their power for himself.

The ninth gate led to the council room. The Empress's personal guard, a row of soldiers in gold-lined armor, blocked their path.

"No attendants," said the guard captain. "The Empress has decided that she does not want to crowd the council room with bodyguards."

A flicker of irritation crossed Vaisra's face. "The Empress might have told me this beforehand."

"The Empress sent a notice to everyone residing in the palace," the guard captain said smugly. "You declined her invitation."

Rin thought Vaisra might protest, but he only turned to Eriden and told him to wait outside. Eriden bowed and departed, leaving them without guards or weapons in the heart of the Autumn Palace.

But they were not entirely alone. At that moment the Cike were swimming through the underground waterways toward the city's heart. Aratsha had constructed air bubbles around their heads so they could swim for miles without needing to come up for air.

The Cike had used this as an infiltration method many times before. This time, they would deliver reinforcements if the coup went sour. Baji and Suni would take up posts directly outside the council room, poised to spring in and break Vaisra out if necessary. Qara would station herself at the highest pavilion outside the council room for ranged support. And Ramsa would squirrel himself away wherever he and his waterproof bag of combustible treasures could cause the most havoc.

Rin found a small degree of comfort in that. If they couldn't capture the Autumn Palace, at least they had a good chance of blowing it up.

Silence fell over the council room when Rin and Vaisra walked in.

The Warlords twisted in their seats to stare at her, their expressions ranging from surprise to curiosity to mild distaste. Their eyes roved over her body, lingered on her arms and legs, took stock of her height and build. They looked everywhere except at her eyes.

Rin shifted uncomfortably. They were sizing her up like a cow at market.

The Ox Warlord spoke first. Rin recognized him from Khurdalain; she was surprised that he was still alive. "This little girl held you up for weeks?"

Vaisra chuckled. "The searching ate my time, not the extraction. I found her stranded in Ankhiluun. Moag got to her first."

The Ox Warlord looked surprised. "The Pirate Queen? How did you wrestle her away?"

"I traded Moag for something she likes better," Vaisra said.

"Why would you bring her here alive?" demanded a man at the other end of the table.

Rin swiveled her head around and nearly jumped in surprise. She hadn't recognized Master Jun at first glance. His beard had grown much longer, and his hair was shot through with gray streaks that hadn't been there before the war. But she could find the same arrogance etched into the lines of her old Combat master's face, as well as his clear distaste for her.

He glared at Vaisra. "Treason deserves the death penalty. And she's far too dangerous to keep around."

"Don't be hasty," said the Horse Warlord. "She might be useful."

"*Useful?*" Jun echoed.

"She's the last of her kind. We'd be fools to throw a weapon like that away."

"Weapons are only useful if you can wield them," said the Ox Warlord. "I think you'd have a little trouble taming this beast."

"Where do you think she went wrong?" The Rooster Warlord leaned forward to get a better look at her.

Rin had privately been looking forward to meeting the Rooster Warlord, Gong Takha. They came from the same province. They spoke the same dialect, and his skin was nearly as dark as hers. Word on the *Seagrim* was that Takha was the closest to joining the Republic. But if provincial ties counted for anything, Takha didn't show it. He stared at her with the same sort of fearful curiosity one displayed toward a caged tiger.

"She's got a wild look in her eyes," he continued. "Do you think the Mugenese experiments did that to her?"

I'm in the room, Rin wanted to snap. *Stop talking about me like I'm not here.*

But Vaisra wanted her to be docile. Act stupid, he'd said. Don't come off as too intelligent.

"Nothing so complex," said Vaisra. "She was a Speerly straining against her leash. You remember how the Speerlies were."

"When my dogs go mad, I put them down," Jun said.

The Empress spoke from the doorway. "But little girls aren't dogs, Loran."

Rin froze.

Su Daji had traded her ceremonial robes for a green soldier's uniform. Her shoulder pads were inlaid with jade armor, and a longsword hung at her waist. It seemed like a message. She was not only the Empress, she was also grand marshal of the Nikara Imperial Militia. She'd conquered the Empire once by force. She'd do it again.

Rin fought to keep her breathing steady as Daji reached out and traced her fingertips over her muzzle.

"Careful," Jun said. "She bites."

"Oh, I'm sure." Daji's voice sounded languid, almost disinterested. "Did she put up a fight?"

"She tried," Vaisra said.

"I imagine there were casualties."

"Not as many as you would expect. She's weak. The drug's done her in."

"Of course." Daji's lip curled. "Speerlies have always had their predilections."

Her hand drifted upward to pat Rin gently on the head.

Rin's fingers curled into fists.

Calm, she reminded herself. The opium hadn't worn off yet. When she tried to call the fire, she felt only a numb, blocked sensation in the back of her mind.

Daji's eyes lingered on Rin for a long while. Rin froze, terrified that the Empress might take her aside now like Vaisra had warned. It was too early. If she were alone in a room with Daji, the best she could do was hurl some disoriented fists in her direction.

But Daji only smiled, shook her head, and turned toward the table. "We've much to get through. Shall we proceed?"

"What about the girl?" Jun asked. "She ought to be in a cell."

"I know." Daji shot Rin a poisonous smile. "But I like to watch her sweat."

The next two hours were the slowest of Rin's life.

Once the Warlords had exhausted their curiosity over her, they turned their attention to an enormous roster of problems economic, agricultural, and political. The Third Poppy War had wrecked nearly every province. Federation soldiers had destroyed most of the infrastructure in every major city they'd occupied, set fire to huge swaths of grain fields, and wiped out entire villages. Mass refugee movements had reshaped the human density of the country. This was the kind of disaster that would have taken miraculous effort from a unified central leadership to ameliorate, and the council of the twelve Warlords was anything but.

"Control your damn people," said the Ox Warlord. "I have thousands streaming into my border as we speak and we don't have a place for them."

"What are we supposed to do, create a border guard?" The Hare Warlord had a distinctly plaintive, grating voice that made Rin wince every time he spoke. "Half my province is flooded, we haven't got food stores to last the winter—"

"Neither do we," said the Ox Warlord. "Send them elsewhere or we'll all starve."

"We'd be willing to repatriate citizens from the Hare Province under a set quota," said the Dog Warlord. "But they'd have to display provincial registration papers."

"Registration papers?" the Hare Warlord echoed. "These people had their villages sacked and you're asking for *registration papers*? Right, like the first thing they grabbed when their village started going up in flames was—"

"We can't house everyone. My people are pressed for resources as is—"

"Your province is a steppe wasteland, you've got more than enough space."

"We have space; we don't have food. And who knows what your sort would bring in over the borders . . ."

Rin had a difficult time believing that this council, if one could call it that, was really how the Empire functioned. She knew how often the Warlords went to arms over resources, trade routes, and—occasionally—over the best recruits graduating from Sinegard. And she knew that the fractures had been deepening, had gotten worse in the aftermath of the Third Poppy War.

She just hadn't known it was *this* bad.

For hours the Warlords had bickered and squabbled over details so inane that Rin could not believe anyone could possibly care. And she had stood waiting in the corner, sweating through her chains, waiting for Daji to drop her front.

But the Empress seemed content to wait. Eriden was right—she clearly relished playing with her food before she ate it. She sat at the head of the table with a vaguely amused expression on her face. Every once in a while, she met Rin's eyes and winked.

What was Daji's endgame? Certainly she knew that the opium would wear off in Rin eventually. Why was she running out the clock?

Did Daji *want* this fight?

The sheer anxiety made Rin feel weak-kneed and light-headed. It took everything she had to remain standing.

"What about Tiger Province?" someone asked.

All eyes turned to the plump child sitting with his elbows up on the table. The young Tiger Warlord looked around with an expression equal parts bewildered and terrified, blinked twice, then peered over his shoulder for help.

His father had died at Khurdalain and now his steward and generals ruled the province in his stead, which meant that the power in Tiger Province really lay with Jun.

"We've done more than enough for this war," Jun said. "We bled at Khurdalain for months. We're thousands of men down. We need time to heal."

"Come on, Jun." A tall man sitting at the far end of the room spat a wad of phlegm on the table. "Tiger Province is full of arable land. Spread some of the goodness around."

Rin grimaced. This had to be the new Horse Warlord—the Wolf Meat General Chang En. She'd been briefed extensively on this one. Chang En was a former divisional commander who had escaped from a Federation prison camp near the start of the Third Poppy War, taken up the life of a bandit, and assumed rapid control of the upper region of the Horse Province while the former Horse Warlord and his army were busy defending Khurdalain.

They had eaten anything. Wolf meat. Corpses by the roadside. The rumor was that they had paid good money for live human babies.

Now the former Horse Warlord was dead, skinned alive by Federation troops. His heirs had been too weak or too young to challenge Chang En, so the bandit ruler had assumed de facto control of the province.

Chang En caught Rin's eye, bared his teeth, and slowly licked his upper lip with a thick, mottled black tongue.

She suppressed a shudder and looked away.

"Most of our arable land near the coastline has been destroyed by tsunamis or ash fall." Jun gave Rin a look of utter disgust. "The Speerly made sure of that."

Rin felt a twist of guilt. But it had been either that or extinction at Federation hands. She'd stopped debating that trade. She could function only if she believed that it had been worth it.

"You can't just keep foisting your refugees on me," Chang En said. "They're cramming the cities. We can't get a moment's rest without their whining in the streets, demanding free accommodations."

"Then put them to work," Jun said coldly. "Have them rebuild your roads and buildings. They'll earn their own keep."

"And how are we supposed to feed them? If they starve at the borders, that's your fault."

Rin noticed it was the northern Warlords—the Ox, Ram, Horse, and Dog Warlords—who did most of the talking. Tsolin sat with his fingers steepled under his chin, saying nothing. The southern Warlords, clustered near the back of the room, largely remained silent. They were the ones who had suffered the most damage, lost the most troops, and thus had the least leverage.

Throughout all of this Daji sat at the head of the table, observing, rarely speaking. She watched the others, one eyebrow arched just a bit higher than the other, as if she were supervising a group of children who had managed to continually disappoint her.

Another hour passed and they had resolved nothing, except for a halfhearted gesture by Tiger Province to allocate six thousand catties of food aid to the landlocked Ram Province in exchange for a thousand pounds of salt. In the grander scheme of things, with thousands of refugees dying of starvation daily, this was hardly a drop in the bucket.

"Why don't we take a recess?" The Empress stood up from the table. "We're not getting anywhere."

"We've barely resolved anything," said Tsolin.

"And the Empire won't collapse if we break for a meal. Cool your heads, gentlemen. Dare I suggest you consider the radical option of compromising with each other?" Daji turned toward Rin. "Meanwhile, I shall retire for a moment to my gardens. Runin, it's time for you to head off to your cell, don't you think?"

Rin stiffened. She couldn't help but shoot a panicked glance at Vaisra.

He stared forward without meeting her eyes, betraying nothing.

This was it. Rin squared her shoulders. She dipped her head in submission, and the Empress smiled.

Rin and the Empress exited not through the throne room but by a narrow corridor in the back. The servants' exit. As they walked Rin could hear the gurgling of the irrigation pipes beneath the floors.

Hours had passed since the council began. The Cike should be stationed within the palace by now, but that thought made her no less terrified. For now she was operating alone with the Empress.

But she still didn't have the fire.

"Are you exhausted yet?" Daji asked.

Rin didn't respond.

"I wanted you to watch the Warlords at their best. They're such a troublesome bunch, aren't they?"

Rin continued pretending she hadn't heard.

"You don't talk very much, do you?" Daji glanced over her shoulder at her. Her eyes slid down to the muzzle. "Oh, of course. Let's get this off you."

She placed her slim fingers on either side of the contraption and gently pulled it off. "Better?"

Rin kept her silence. *Don't engage her,* Vaisra had warned her. *Maintain constant vigilance and let her speak her piece.*

She only needed to buy herself a few more minutes. She could feel the opium wearing off. Her vision had gotten sharper, and her limbs responded without delay to her commands. She just needed

Daji to keep talking until the Phoenix responded to her call. Then she could turn the Autumn Palace to ash.

"Altan was the same," Daji mused. "You know, the first three years he was with us, we thought he was a mute."

Rin nearly tripped over a cobblestone. Daji continued walking as if she had noticed nothing. Rin followed behind, fighting to keep her calm.

"I was sorry to hear of his loss," Daji said. "He was a good commander. One of our very best."

And you killed him, you old bitch. Rin rubbed her fingers together, hoping for a spark, but still the channel to the Phoenix remained blocked.

Just a little longer.

Daji led her behind the building toward a patch of empty space near the servants' quarters.

"The Red Emperor built a series of tunnels in the Autumn Palace so that he could escape to and from any room if need be. Ruler of an entire empire, and he didn't feel safe in his own bed." Daji stopped beside a well and pushed hard at the cover, bracing her feet against the stone floor. The cover slid off with a loud screech. She straightened and brushed her hands on her uniform. "Follow me."

Rin crawled after Daji into the well, which had a set of narrow, spiraling steps built into its wall. Daji reached up and slid the stone closed over them, leaving them standing in pitch darkness. Icy fingers wrapped around Rin's hand. She jumped, but Daji only tightened her grip.

"It's easy to get lost if you've never been here before." Daji's voice echoed around the chamber. "Stay close."

Rin tried to keep count of how many turns they had taken— fifteen, sixteen—but soon enough she lost track of where they were, even in her carefully memorized mental map. How far were they from the council room? Would she have to ignite in the tunnels?

After several more minutes of walking, they resurfaced into a garden. The sudden burst of color was disorienting. Rin peered, blinking, at the resplendent array of lilies, chrysanthemums, and plum trees planted in clusters around rows upon rows of sculptures.

This wasn't the Imperial Garden—the layout of the walls didn't match. The Imperial Garden was shaped in a circle; this garden was erected inside a hexagon. This was a private courtyard.

This hadn't been on the map. Rin had no clue where she was.

Her eyes flickered frantically around her surroundings, seeking out possible exit routes, mapping out useful trajectories and planes of motion for the impending fight, making note of objects that could be weaponized if she couldn't get the fire back in time. Those saplings looked fragile—she might break a branch off for a club if she got desperate. Best if she could back Daji up against the far wall. If nothing else, she could use those loose cobblestones to smash the Empress's head in.

"Magnificent, isn't it?"

Rin realized Daji was waiting for her to say something.

If she engaged Daji in conversation, she'd be walking headfirst into a trap. Vaisra and Eriden had warned her many times how easily Daji would manipulate, could plant thoughts in her mind that weren't her own.

But Daji would grow bored of talking if Rin stayed silent. And Daji's interest in playing with her food was the only thing buying Rin time. Rin needed to keep the conversation going until she had the fire back.

"I guess," she said. "I'm not one for aesthetics."

"Of course you're not. You got your education at Sinegard. They're all crude utilitarians." Daji put her hands on Rin's shoulders and slowly turned her about the garden. "Tell me something. Does the palace look new to you?"

Rin glanced around the hexagon. Yes, it had to be new. The lustrous buildings of the Autumn Palace, though designed with the architecture of the Red Emperor, did not bear the stains of

time. The stones were smooth and unscratched, the wooden posts
gleaming with fresh paint.

"I suppose," she said. "Is it not?"

"Follow me." Daji walked toward a small gate built into the far
wall, pushed it open, and motioned for Rin to follow her through.

The other side of the garden looked like it had been smashed
under a giant's heel. The midsection of the opposite wall was in
pieces, as if it had been blown apart by cannon fire. Statues were
strewn across the overgrown grass, limbs shattered, lying at grotesque and awkward angles.

This wasn't natural decay. Wasn't the result of failure to keep
the grounds. This had to be the deliberate action of an invading
force.

"I thought the Federation never reached Lusan," Rin said.

"This wasn't the Federation," Daji said. "This wreckage has
been here for over seventy years."

"Then who . . . ?"

"The Hesperians. History likes to focus on the Federation, but
the masters at Sinegard always gloss over the first colonizers. No
one remembers who started the First Poppy War." Daji nudged a
statue's head with her foot. "One autumn day seventy years ago,
a Hesperian admiral sailed up the Murui and blasted his way into
Lusan. He pillaged the palace, razed it to the ground, poured oil
over the wreckage, and danced in the ashes. By that evening the
Autumn Palace had ceased to exist."

"Then why haven't you rebuilt the garden?" Rin's eyes darted
around the grounds while she spoke. A rake lay in the grass about
half a yard from her feet. After all these years it was certainly
blunt and covered in rust, but Rin might still use it as a staff.

"So we have the reminder," Daji said. "To remember how we
were humiliated. To remember that nothing good can come of
dealing with the Hesperians."

Rin couldn't let her eyes linger on the rake. Daji would notice.
She carefully reconstructed its position from memory. The sharp

end was facing her. If she got close enough, she could kick it up into her grasp. Unless the grass had grown too long . . . but it was just grass; if she kicked hard it shouldn't be a problem . . .

"The Hesperians have always intended to come back," Daji said. "The Mugenese weakened this country using western silver. We remember the Federation as the face of the oppressor, but the Hesperians and Bolonians—the Consortium of western countries—are the ones with real power. They are who you ought to be afraid of."

Rin moved just slightly so her left leg was positioned close enough to kick the rake up. "Why are you telling me this?"

"Don't play dumb with me," Daji said sharply. "I know what Vaisra intends to do. I know he intends to go to war. I'm trying to show you that it's the wrong one."

Rin's pulse began to race. This was it—Daji knew her intentions, she needed to fight, it didn't matter if she didn't have the fire yet, she had to get to the rake—

"*Stop that*," Daji ordered.

Rin's limbs froze suddenly in place, muscles stiffening painfully as if the slightest movement might shatter them. She should be springing to fight. She should have at least crouched down. But somehow her body was arrested where she stood, as if she needed the Empress's permission to even breathe.

"We are not finished talking," said Daji.

"I'm finished listening," Rin hissed through clenched teeth.

"Relax. I haven't brought you here to kill you. You are an asset, one of the few I have left. It would be stupid to let you go." Daji stepped in front of her so that they stood face-to-face. Rin hastily averted her eyes. "You're fighting the wrong enemy, dear. Can't you see it?"

Sweat beaded on Rin's neck as she strained to break out of Daji's hold.

"What did Vaisra promise you? You must know you're being used. Is it worth it? Is it money? An estate? No . . . I don't think you could be swayed by material promises." Daji tapped her lacquered nails against painted lips. "No—don't tell me you *believe* him, do you? Did he say he'd bring you a democracy? And you fell for it?"

"He said he'd depose you," Rin whispered. "That's good enough for me."

"Do you really believe that?" Daji sighed. "What would you replace me with? The Nikara people aren't ready for democracy. They're sheep. They're crude, uneducated fools. They need to be told what to do, even if that means tyranny. If Vaisra takes this nation then he'll run it into the ground. The people don't know what to vote for. They don't even understand what it means to vote. And they certainly don't know what's good for them."

"Neither do you," Rin said. "You let them die in hordes. You invited the Mugenese in yourself and you traded them the Cike."

To her surprise, Daji laughed. "Is that what you believe? You can't trust everything you hear."

"Shiro had no reason to lie. I know what you did."

"You understand *nothing*. I have toiled for decades to keep this Empire intact. Do you think I wanted this war?"

"I think that at least half of this country was disposable to you."

"I made a calculated sacrifice. The last time the Federation invaded, the Warlords rallied under the Dragon Emperor. The Dragon Emperor is dead. And the Federation was readying itself for a third invasion. No matter what I did, they were going to attack, and we were nowhere near strong enough to resist them. So I brokered a peace. They could have slices of the east if they would let the heartland remain free."

"So we'd only be *partially* occupied." Rin scoffed. "That's what you call statecraft?"

"Occupied? Not for long. Sometimes the best offensive is false acquiescence. I had a plan. I would become close to Ryohai. I would gain his trust. I would lure him into a false sense of complacency. And then I would kill him. But in the meantime, while their forces were impenetrable, I would play along. I'd do what it took to keep this nation alive."

"Kept alive only to die at Mugenese hands."

Daji's voice hardened. "Don't be so naive. What do you do when you know that war is inevitable? Who do you save?"

"What did you think *we* were going to do?" Rin demanded. "Did you think we would just lie down and let them raze our lands?"

"Better to rule over a fragmented empire than none at all."

"You sentenced millions of us to death."

"I was trying to *save* you. Without me the violence would have been ten times as devastating—"

"Without you, we would at least have had a choice!"

"That would have been no choice. Do you think the Nikara are so altruistic? What if you asked a village to give up their homes so that thousands of others might live? Do you think they would do it? The Nikara are selfish. This entire country is selfish. *People* are selfish. The provinces have always been so *fucking* parochial, unable to see past their own narrow interests to pursue any kind of joint action. You heard those idiots in there. I let you watch for a reason. I can't work with those Warlords. Those fools don't listen."

At the end Daji's voice trembled—only just barely, and only for a second, but Rin heard it.

And for just that moment she saw through that facade of cool, confident beauty, and she saw Su Daji for what she might truly have been: not an invincible Empress, not a treacherous monster, but rather a woman who had been saddled with a country that she didn't know how to run.

She's weak, Rin realized. *She wishes she could control the Warlords, but she can't.*

Because if Daji could have persuaded the Warlords to follow her wishes, she would have done so. She would have done away with the Warlord system and replaced provincial leadership with branches of the Imperial government. But she had left the Warlords in place because even she was not strong enough to supplant them. She was one woman. She couldn't take on their combined armies. She was just barely clinging to power through the last vestiges of the legacy of the Second Poppy War.

But now that the Federation was gone, now that the Warlords no longer had reason to fear, it was very likely the provinces would realize they had no need for Daji.

Daji didn't sound like she was spinning lies. If anything, Rin thought it more likely that she was telling the truth.

But if so—then what? That didn't change things.

Daji had sold the Cike to the Federation. Daji was the reason why Altan was dead. Those were the only two things that mattered.

"This Empire is falling apart," Daji said urgently. "It's becoming weak, you've seen that. But what if we bent the Warlords to our will? Just imagine what you could do under my command." She cupped Rin's cheek in her hand, drew their faces close together. "There's so much you have to learn, and I can teach you."

Rin would have bitten Daji's fingers off if she could move her head. "There's nothing you can teach me."

"Don't be foolish. You need me. You've been feeling the pull, haven't you? It's consuming you. Your mind is not your own."

Rin flinched. "I don't—you're not—"

"You're scared to close your eyes," Daji murmured. "You crave the opium, because that's the only thing that makes your mind your own again. You're fighting your god at every moment. Every instant you're not incinerating everything around you, you're dying. But I can help you." Daji's voice was so soft, so tender, so gentle and reassuring that Rin wanted terribly to believe her. "I can give you your mind back."

"I have control of my mind," Rin said hoarsely.

"Liar. Who would have taught you? Altan? He was barely sane himself. You think I don't know what that's like? The first time we called the gods, I wanted to die. We all did. We thought we were going mad. We wanted to fling our bodies off Mount Tianshan to end it."

Rin couldn't stop herself from asking, "So what did you do?"

Daji touched an icy finger to Rin's lips. "Loyalty first. Then answers."

She snapped her fingers.

Suddenly Rin could move again; could breathe easily again. She hugged trembling arms around her torso.

"You don't have anyone else," Daji said. "You're the last Speerly. Altan is gone. Vaisra has no clue what you're suffering. Only I know how to help you."

Rin hesitated, considering.

She knew she could never trust Daji.

And yet.

Was it better to serve at the hand of a tyrant, to consolidate the Empire into the true dictatorship that it had always aspired to be? Or should she overthrow the Empire and take her chances on democracy?

No—that was a political question, and Rin had no interest in its answer.

She was interested only in her own survival. Altan had trusted the Empress. Altan was dead. She wouldn't make that same mistake.

She kicked out with her left foot. The rake slammed hard into her hand—the grass offered less resistance than she'd thought—and she sprang forward, spinning the rake in a forward loop.

But attacking Daji was like attacking air. The Empress dodged effortlessly, skirting so fast through the courtyard that Rin could barely track her movements.

"You think this is wise?" Daji didn't sound the least bit breathless. "You're a little girl armed with a stick."

You're a little girl armed with fire, said the Phoenix.

Finally.

Rin held the rake still so she could concentrate on pulling the flame out from inside her, gathering the searing heat in her palms just as something silver flashed past her face and pinged off the brick wall.

Needles. Daji hurled them at her fistfuls at a time, pulling them out from her sleeves in seemingly endless quantities. The fire dissipated. Rin swung the rake in a desperate circle in front of her, knocking the needles out of the air as fast as they came.

"You're slow. You're clumsy." Now Daji was on the attack, forcing Rin backward in a steady retreat. "You fight like you've never seen battle."

Rin struggled to keep her hands on the heavy rake. She couldn't concentrate enough to call the fire; she was too focused on warding off the needles. Panic clouded her senses. At this rate she'd exhaust herself on the defensive.

"Does it ever bother you?" whispered Daji. "That you are only a pale imitation of Altan?"

Rin's back slammed into the brick wall. She had nowhere left to run.

"Look at me." Daji's voice reverberated through the air, echoed over and over again in Rin's mind.

Rin squeezed her eyes shut. She had to call the fire now, she'd never get this chance again—but her mind was leaving her. The world was not quite going dark, but *shifting*. Everything suddenly seemed too bright, everything was the wrong color and the wrong shape and she couldn't tell the grass from the sky, or her hands from her own feet . . .

Daji's voice seemed to come from everywhere. "Look into my eyes."

Rin didn't remember opening her eyes. She didn't remember having the chance to even resist. All she knew was that one instant her eyes were closed and the next she was staring into two yellow orbs. At first they were golden all the way through, and then little black dots appeared that grew larger and larger until they encompassed Rin's field of vision.

The world had turned entirely dark. She was so cold. She heard howls and screams from far away, guttural noises that almost sounded like words but none she could comprehend.

This was the spirit plane. This was where she faced Daji's goddess.

But she was not alone.

Help me, Rin thought. *Help me, please.*

And the god answered. A wave of bright, warm heat flooded the plane. Flames surrounded her like protective wings.

"Nüwa, you old bitch," said the Phoenix.

A woman's voice, much deeper than Daji's, reverberated through the plane. "And you, snippy as always."

What was this creature? Rin strained to see the goddess's form, but the Phoenix's flames illuminated only a small corner of the psychospiritual space.

"You could never challenge me," said Nüwa. "I was there when the universe tore itself out of darkness. I mended the heavens when they split apart. I gave life to man."

Something stirred in the darkness.

The Phoenix shrieked as a snake's head sprang out and sank its fangs into its shoulder. The Phoenix reared its head, flames spinning out at nothing. Rin felt the god's pain just as acutely as if the snake had bitten her, like two red-hot blades had been jammed between her shoulder blades.

"What do you dream of?" Daji's voice now, overwhelming Rin's mind with every word. "Is this it?"

The world shifted again.

Bright colors. Rin was running across an island in a dress she'd never worn before, with a crescent moon necklace she'd seen only in her dreams, toward a village that didn't exist now except as a place of ash and bone. She ran across the sands of Speer as it was fifty years ago—full of life, full of people with dark skin like hers, who stood up and waved and smiled when they saw her.

"You could have that," Daji said. "You could have everything you wanted."

Rin believed, too, that Daji would be that kind, would let her remain in that illusion until she died.

"Or is this what you want?"

Speer disappeared. The world turned dark again. Rin couldn't see anything but a shadowy figure. But she knew that silhouette, that tall, lean build. She could never forget it. The memory of it was scorched in her mind from the last time she had seen him, walking down that pier. But this time he walked toward her. She was watching the moment of Altan's death in reverse. Time was unraveling. She could take it all back, she could have *him* back.

This couldn't possibly be just a dream. He was too solid—she could sense the mortal weight of him filling up the space around her; and when she touched his face it was solid and warm and bloody and *alive* . . .

"Just relax," he whispered. "Stop resisting."

"But it *hurts* . . ."

"It only hurts if you fight."

He kissed her and it felt like a punch. This wasn't what she wanted—this felt wrong, this was all wrong—his grip was too tight around her arms, he was clutching her against his chest like he wanted to crush her. He tasted like blood.

"That's not him."

Chaghan's voice. A split second later Rin felt him in her mind—a cold, harsh presence in blinding white, a shard of ice piercing the spiritual plane. She had never been so relieved to see him.

"It's an illusion." Chaghan's voice cleared her mind like a shower of cold water. "Get a grip on yourself."

The illusions dissipated. Altan faded into nothing. Then there were only the three of them, souls tethered to gods, hanging suspended in primordial darkness.

"What's this?" Nüwa's voice blended together with Daji's. "A Naimad?" Laughter rang across the plane. "Your people should know not to defy me. Did the Sorqan Sira teach you nothing?"

"I don't fear you," Chaghan said.

In the physical world he was a skeletal waif, so frail he seemed only a shadow of a person. But here he emanated raw power. His voice carried a ring of authority, a gravity that pulled Rin toward him. Right then, Chaghan could reach into the center of her mind and extract every thought she'd ever had as casually as if he were flipping through a book, and she would let him.

"You will go back, Nüwa." Chaghan raised his voice. "Return to the darkness. This world no longer belongs to you."

The darkness hissed in response. Rin braced herself for an impending attack. But Chaghan uttered an incantation in words she did not understand, words that pushed Nüwa's presence back so far that Rin could barely see the outlines of the snake anymore.

Bright lights flooded her vision. Wrenched down from the realm of the ethereal, Rin staggered at the sheer solidity, the physicality of the solid world.

Chaghan stood doubled over beside her, gasping.

Across the courtyard, Daji wiped the back of her mouth with her sleeve. She smiled. Her teeth were stained with blood.

"You are adorable," she said. "And here I thought the Ketreyids were only a fond memory."

"Stand back," Chaghan muttered to Rin.

"What are you—"

"Run on my word." Chaghan tossed a dark circular lump onto the ground. It rolled forward several paces and came to a rest at the Empress's feet. Rin heard a faint sizzling noise, followed by an awful, acrid, and terribly familiar smell.

Daji glanced down, puzzled.

"Go," Chaghan said, and they fled just as Ramsa's signature poop bomb detonated inside the Autumn Palace.

A series of explosions followed them as they ran, ongoing blasts that could not have possibly been triggered by the single bomb. Building after building collapsed around them, creating a wall of fire and debris from behind which no one could pursue them.

"Ramsa," Chaghan explained. "Kid doesn't cut corners."

He yanked her behind a low wall. They crouched down, hands clapped over their ears as the last of the buildings erupted mere yards away.

Rin wiped the dust from her eyes. "Daji's dead?"

"Something like that doesn't die so easily." Chaghan coughed and pounded at his chest with his fist. "She'll be after us soon.

We should go. There's a well a block down; Aratsha knows we're coming."

"What about Vaisra?"

Still coughing, Chaghan staggered to his feet. "Are you crazy?"

"He's still in there!"

"And he's likely dead. Daji's guards will have swarmed the council room by now."

"We don't know that."

"So what, you're going to go *check*?" Chaghan grabbed her shoulders and pinned her against the wall. "Listen to me. It's over. Your coup is finished. Daji's going to come for Dragon Province, and when she does, we're going to lose. Vaisra can't protect you. You need to run."

"And go where?" she asked. "And do what?"

What did Vaisra promise you? You must know you're being used.

Rin knew that. She'd always known that. But maybe she *needed* to be used. Maybe she needed someone to tell her when, and who, to fight. She needed someone to give her orders and a purpose.

Vaisra was the first person in a long, long time who had made her feel stable enough to see a point in staying alive. And if he died here, it was on her.

"Are you insane?" Chaghan shouted. "You want to live, you fucking hide."

"Then you hide. I'm fighting." Rin wrenched her wrists from his grasp and pushed him away. She used more force than she'd meant to; she'd forgotten he was so thin. He stumbled backward, tripped on a rock, and toppled to the ground.

"You're crazy," he said.

"We're all crazy," she muttered as she jumped over his sprawled form and set off at a run toward the council room.

Imperial guards had swarmed the council chamber, pressing steadily in against the two-man army that was Suni and Baji. The Warlords had scattered from their seats. The Hare Warlord huddled against the wall, the Rooster Warlord crouched quivering under the table, and the young Tiger Warlord was curled in a corner, head pressed between his knees as blades clashed inches from his head.

Rin faltered at the doors. She couldn't call the fire now. She didn't have enough control to target her flames. If she lit up the room, she'd kill everyone in it.

"Here!" Baji kicked a sword toward her. She scooped it up and jumped into the fray.

Vaisra wasn't dead. He fought at the center of the room, battling both Jun and the Wolf Meat General. For a second it seemed like he might hold them off. He wielded his blade with a ferocious strength and precision that was stunning to watch.

But he was still only one man.

"Watch out!" Rin screamed.

The Wolf Meat General tried to catch Vaisra off guard. Vaisra spun about and disarmed him with a savage kick to the knee. Chang En dropped to the ground, howling. Vaisra reeled back from the kick, trying to regain his balance, and Jun took the opening to push his blade through Vaisra's shoulder.

Baji barreled into Jun's side and tackled him to the ground. Rin ran forward to catch Vaisra just as he crumpled to the floor; blood spilled over her arms, hot and wet and slippery, and she was astounded by how *much* of it there was.

"Are you— Please, are you—"

She prodded frantically around his chest, trying to stanch the blood with her palm. She could barely see the wound, his torso was so slick with blood, but finally her fingers pressed against the entry point in his right shoulder. Not a vital spot.

She dared to hope. If they acted quickly he might still live. But first they had to get out.

"Suni!" she shrieked.

He appeared instantly at her side. She pushed Vaisra into his arms. "Take him."

Suni slung Vaisra over his shoulders the way one might carry a calf and elbowed his way toward the exit. Baji followed closely, guarding their rear.

Rin picked her way past Jun's limp form. She didn't know if he was dead or alive, but that didn't matter now. She ducked under a guard's arm and followed her men out, over the threshold and toward the closest well.

She leaned over the side and screamed Aratsha's name into the dark surface.

Nothing. There was no time to wait for Aratsha's response; he was there or he wasn't, and Daji's guards were feet away. All she could do was plunge into the water, hold her breath, and pray.

Aratsha answered.

Rin fought the urge to flail inside the pitch-black irrigation channels—that would only make it harder for Aratsha to propel her through the water—and instead focused on taking deep and measured breaths in the pocket of air that enveloped her head. Still, she couldn't ward off the clenching fear that the air would run out. Already she could feel the warmth of her own stale breath.

She broke the surface. She clawed her way up the riverbank and collapsed, chest heaving as she sucked in fresh air. Seconds later Suni exploded out of the water, depositing Vaisra on the shore before climbing up himself.

"What happened?" Nezha came running up to them, followed closely by Eriden and his guard. His eyes landed on his father. "Is he—"

"Alive," Rin said. "If we're quick."

Nezha turned to the two closest soldiers. "Get my father on the ship."

They hoisted Vaisra up between them and set off at a dash toward the *Seagrim*. Nezha pulled Rin to her feet. "What just—"

"No time." She spat out a mouthful of river water. "Have your crew weigh anchor. We've got to get out."

Nezha slung her arm over his shoulder and helped her stagger toward the ship. "It failed?"

"It worked." Rin stumbled into his side, trying to keep pace. "You wanted a war. We just started one."

The *Seagrim* had already begun pushing away from its berth. Crewmen at both ends hacked the ropes keeping the ship tethered to the dock, setting it free to drift with the current. Nezha and Rin jumped into one of the rowboats dangling by the hull. Inch by inch the boat began to rise.

Above, deckhands lowered the *Seagrim*'s sails and turned them toward the wind. Below, a loud grinding noise sounded as the paddle wheel began to churn rhythmically against the water, carrying them swiftly away from the capital.

CHAPTER 10

The *Seagrim*'s crew operated under a somber silence. Word had spread that Vaisra was badly injured. But no news emerged from the physician's office and no one dared intrude to ask.

Captain Eriden had issued only one order: to get the *Seagrim* far away from Lusan as quickly as possible. Any soldier not working a paddling shift was sent to the top deck to man the trebuchets and crossbows, ready to fire at first warning.

Rin paced back and forth by the stern. She didn't have a crossbow or a spyglass, and in her state she was more of a hindrance than an asset to deck defense—she was too jumpy to hold a weapon steady, too anxious to comprehend rapid orders. But she refused to go wait belowdecks. She had to know what was happening.

She kept looking down at her body to check that it was still there, was still working. It seemed impossible to her that she had escaped an encounter with the Vipress unscathed. The ship's physician had cursorily examined her for broken bones but found nothing. Aside from some bruising, she felt no serious pain. Yet she was convinced that something was deeply wrong with her; something deep, internal, a poison that had wrapped around her bones.

Chaghan, too, seemed badly shaken. He'd been silent, unresponsive until they pulled out of harbor, and then he had collapsed against Qara and sunk to the floor, knees drawn up against his chest in a miserable huddle while his sister bent over him, whispering words no one else could understand into his ear.

The crew, clearly unsettled, gave them a wide berth. Rin tried to ignore them until she heard gasping noises from the deck. At first she thought he was sobbing, but no—he was just trying to breathe, jagged gasps rocking his frail form.

She knelt down beside the twins. She wasn't sure whether she ought to try to touch Chaghan. "Are you all right?"

"I'm fine."

"Are you sure?"

Chaghan raised his head and took a deep, shuddering breath. His eyes were ringed with red. "She was—I've never . . . I never imagined anyone could be so . . ."

"What?"

He shook his head.

Qara answered for him. "*Stable.*" She whispered the word like it was a horrifying idea. "She shouldn't be so stable."

"What is she?" Rin asked. "What goddess is that?"

"She's old power," Chaghan said. "She's something that's been alive longer than the world itself. I thought she'd be weakened, now that the other two are gone, but she's . . . if that's the Vipress at her weakest . . ." He slammed a palm against the deck. "We were fools to try."

"She's not invincible," Rin said. "You beat her."

"No, I surprised her. And then for only an instant. I don't think things like that can be *beat*. We got lucky."

"Any longer and she would have had your minds," Qara said. "You'd be trapped forever in those illusions."

She'd turned just as pale as her brother. Rin wondered how much Qara had seen. Qara hadn't even been there, but Rin knew the twins were bonded by some odd Hinterlander magic. When

Chaghan bled, Qara hurt. If Chaghan was shaken by Daji, then Qara must have felt it back on the *Seagrim*, a psychic tremble that threatened to poison her soul.

"So we'll find some other way," Rin said. "She's still a mortal body, she's still—"

"She will squeeze your soul in her fist and turn you into a babbling idiot," Chaghan said. "I'm not trying to dissuade you. I know you'll fight her to the end. But I hope you realize you're going to go mad trying."

Then so be it. Rin wrapped her arms around her knees. "Did you see? In there, when she showed me?"

Chaghan gave her a pitying look. "I couldn't help it."

Qara looked away. She must have seen, too.

For some reason, in that moment Rin felt like it was the most important thing in the world for her to explain herself to the twins. She felt guilty, dirty, like she had been caught in a terrible lie. "It wasn't like that. With him. With Altan, I mean—"

"I know," Chaghan said.

She wiped at her eyes. "It was never like that. I mean—I think I wanted—but he never—"

"We know," Qara said. "Trust us, we know."

Rin was stunned when Chaghan reached out and put his arm around her shoulder. She would have cried, but she felt too raw inside, like she had been hollowed out with a carving knife.

Chaghan's arm rested at an odd angle over her back; his bony elbow joint dug painfully into her bone. After a while she shifted her right shoulder, and he withdrew his arm.

Hours passed before Nezha reemerged onto the deck.

Rin searched his face for clues. He looked wan but not grief-stricken, exhausted but not panicked, which meant . . .

She hastened to her feet. "Your father?"

"I think he'll pull through." He rubbed at his temples. "Dr. Sien finally kicked me out. Said to give Father some space."

"He's awake?"

"Sleeping for now. He was delirious for a bit, but Dr. Sien said that was a good sign. Meant he was talking."

She let loose a long breath. "I'm glad."

He sat down and rubbed his hands down his legs with a small sigh of relief. He must have been standing beside his father's bedside for hours.

"Watching something?" he asked her.

"I'm watching nothing." She squinted at the receding outline of Lusan. Only the highest pagoda towers of the palace were still visible. "That's what's bothering me. No one's coming after us."

She couldn't understand why the riverways were so calm, so silent. Why weren't arrows flying through the air? Why weren't they being pursued by Imperial vessels? Perhaps the Militia lay in wait at the gates at the province's edge. Perhaps they were sailing straight toward a trap.

But the gates were open, and no ships came chasing after them in the darkness.

"Who would they send?" Nezha asked. "They don't have a navy at the Autumn Palace."

"And no one in any of the provinces has one?"

"Ah." Nezha smiled. Why was he *smiling*? "You don't understand. We're not going back the same way. We're headed out to sea this time. Tsolin's ships patrol the Nariin coast."

"And Tsolin won't interfere?"

"No. Father's made him choose. He's not going to choose the Empire."

She couldn't understand his logic. "Because . . . ?"

"Because now there's going to be a war, whether Tsolin likes it or not. And he's not putting his money against Vaisra. So he'll let us through unharmed, and I'll bet that he'll be at our council table in under a month."

Rin was frankly amazed by the confidence with which the House of Yin seemed to manipulate people. "That's assuming he gets out of Lusan."

"If he hasn't made contingency plans for this I'll be shocked."

"Did you ask if he had?"

Nezha chuckled. "It's *Tsolin*. Asking would be an insult."

"Or, you know, a decent precaution."

"Oh, we're about to fight a civil war. You'll have plenty of chances to take precautions." His tone sounded ridiculously cavalier.

"You really think we can win this?" she asked.

"We'll be all right."

"How do you know?"

He grinned sideways at her. "Because we've got the best navy in the Empire. Because we have the most brilliant strategist Sinegard has ever seen. And because we've got you."

"Fuck off."

"I'm serious. You know you're a military asset worth your weight in silver, and if Kitay's on strategy, then that gives us excellent chances."

"Is Kitay—"

"He's fine. He's belowdecks. He's been chatting with the admirals; Father gave him full access to our intelligence files, and he's getting caught up."

"I guess he came around pretty quickly, then."

"We thought he might." Nezha's tone confirmed what she already suspected.

"You knew his father was dead."

He didn't bother denying it. "Father told me weeks ago. He said not to tell Kitay. Not until we'd reached Lusan, anyway."

"Why?"

"Because it would mean more if it didn't come from us. Because it would feel less to him like manipulation."

"So you let him think his father was alive for *weeks*?"

"We're not the ones who killed him, were we?" Nezha didn't look sorry in the slightest. "Look, Rin. My father is very good at cultivating talent. He knows people. He knows how to pull their strings. That doesn't mean he doesn't care about them."

"But I don't want to be lied to," she said.

He squeezed her hand. "I would never lie to you."

Rin wanted desperately to believe that.

"Excuse me," said Captain Eriden.

They turned around.

For once, Eriden did not look immaculately groomed, was not standing at perfect attention. The captain was wan and diminished, shoulders slouching, lines of worry etched across his face. He dipped his head toward them. "The Dragon Warlord would like to see you."

"I'll go right now," Nezha said.

"Not you," said Eriden. He nodded to Rin. "Just her."

Rin was surprised to find Vaisra sitting upright behind the table, wearing a fresh military uniform free of blood. When he breathed, he winced, but only slightly; otherwise he looked as if he had never been injured.

"They told me you dragged me out of the palace," he said.

She sat down across from him. "My men helped."

"And why would you do that?"

"I don't know," she said frankly. She was still trying to figure that out herself. She might have left him in the throne room. Alone, the Cike would have a better chance at survival—they didn't need to ally themselves with a province that had declared open war on the Empire.

But then what? Where did they go from here?

"Why are you still with us?" Vaisra asked. "We failed. And I thought you weren't interested in being a foot soldier."

"Why does it matter? Do you want me to leave?"

"I would prefer to know why people serve in my army. Some do it for silver. Some do it for the sheer thrill of battle. I don't think you are here for either."

He was right. But she didn't know how to answer. How could she explain to him why she'd stayed when she couldn't articulate it to herself?

All she knew was that it felt *good* to be part of Vaisra's army, to act on Vaisra's orders, to be Vaisra's weapon and tool.

If she wasn't making the decisions, then nothing could be her fault.

She couldn't put the Cike in danger if she didn't tell them what to do. And she couldn't be blamed for anyone she killed if she was acting on orders.

And she didn't just crave the simple absolution of responsibility. She craved *Vaisra*. She wanted his approval. Needed it. He provided her with structure, control, and direction that she hadn't had since Altan died, and it felt so terribly good.

Since she'd set the Phoenix on the longbow island she'd been lost, spinning in a void of guilt and anger, and for the first time in a long time, she didn't feel like she was drifting anymore.

She had a reason to live past revenge.

"I don't know what I'm supposed to do," she said finally. "Or who I'm supposed to be. Or where I came from, or—or . . ." She broke off, trying to make sense of the feelings swirling through her mind. "All I know is that I'm alone, I'm the only one left, and it's because of her."

Vaisra leaned forward. "Do you want to fight this war?"

"No. I mean—I don't—I *hate* war." She took a deep breath. "At least I think I should. Everyone is supposed to hate war, or there's something wrong with you. Right? But I'm a soldier. That's all I know how to be. So isn't that what I'm supposed to do? I mean, sometimes I think maybe I can stop, maybe I can just run away. But what I've seen—what I've done—I can't come back from that."

She looked at him beseechingly, desperate for him to disagree, but Vaisra only shook his head. "No. You can't."

"Is it true?" she asked in a small, scared voice. "What the Warlords said?"

"What did they say?" he asked gently.

"They said I'm like a dog. They said I'd be better off dead. Does everyone want me dead?"

Vaisra reached out and took her hands in his. His grip was soft. Tender, almost.

"No one else is going to say this to you. So listen closely, Runin. You have been blessed with immense power. Don't guilt yourself for using it. I won't permit it."

She couldn't hold the tears back anymore. Her voice broke. "I just wanted to—"

"Stop crying. You're better than that."

She choked back a sob.

His voice turned steely. "It doesn't matter what you want. Don't you understand that? You are the most powerful creature in this world right now. You have an ability that can begin or end wars. You could launch this Empire into a glorious new and united age, and you could also destroy us. What you don't get to do is remain neutral. When you have the power that you do, your life is not your own."

His fingers tightened around hers. "People will seek to use you or destroy you. If you want to live, you must pick a side. So do not shirk from war, child. Do not flinch from suffering. When you hear screaming, run toward it."

PART II

CHAPTER 11

Nezha pushed her door open. "You awake?"

"What's going on?" Rin yawned. It was still dark outside her porthole, but Nezha was dressed in full uniform. Behind him stood Kitay, looking half-asleep and very crabby.

"Come upstairs," said Nezha.

"He wants to show us the view," Kitay grumbled. "Get a move on so I can go back to sleep."

Rin followed them down the hall, hopping on one foot as she pulled her shoes on.

The *Seagrim* was blanketed in such a dense blue mist that they might have been sailing through clouds. Rin could not see the landmarks surrounding them until they were close enough for shapes to emerge through the fog. On her left, great cliffs guarded the narrow entrance to Arlong: a dark sliver of space inside the yawning stone wall. Against the light of the rising sun, the rock face glimmered a bright crimson.

Those were the famous Red Cliffs of the Dragon Province. The cliff walls were said to shine a brighter red with every failed invasion against the stronghold, painted with the blood of sailors whose ships had been dashed against those stones.

Rin could just make out massive characters etched into the

walls—words that she could see only if she tilted her head the right way and if the faint sunlight hit them just so. "What do those say?"

"Can't you read it?" Kitay asked. "It's just Old Nikara."

She tried not to roll her eyes. "Translate for me, then."

"You actually can't," Nezha said. "All of those characters have layers upon layers of meaning, and they don't obey modern Nikara grammar rules, so any translation must be imperfect and unfaithful."

Rin had to smile. Those were words recited straight from the Linguistics texts they'd both read at Sinegard, back when their biggest concern was the next week's grammar quiz. "So which translation do you think is right?"

"'Nothing lasts,'" said Nezha, at the same time that Kitay said, "'The world doesn't exist.'"

Kitay wrinkled his nose at Nezha. "'Nothing lasts'? What kind of translation is that?"

"The historically accurate one," Nezha said. "The last faithful minister of the Red Emperor carved those words into the cliffs. When the Red Emperor died, his empire fragmented into provinces. His sons and generals snapped up prize pieces of land like wolves. But the minister of the Dragon Province didn't pledge allegiance to any of the newly formed states."

"I assume that didn't end well," Rin said.

"It's as Father says: there's no such thing as neutrality in a civil war," Nezha said. "The Eight Princes came for the Dragon Province and tore Arlong apart. Thus the minister's epigram. Most think it's a nihilistic cry, a warning that nothing lasts. Not friendships, not loyalties, and certainly not empire. Which makes it consistent with your translation, Kitay, if you think about it. This world is ephemeral. Permanence is an illusion."

As they spoke, the *Seagrim* passed into a channel through the cliffs so narrow that Rin marveled that the warship did not breach its hull along the rocks. The ship must have been designed according to the exact specifications of the channel—and even then, it was a remarkable feat of navigation that they slipped through the walls without so much as scraping stone.

As they penetrated the passage, the cliffs themselves appeared to cleave open, revealing Arlong between them like a pearl hidden inside an oystershell. The city within was startlingly lush, all waterfalls and running streams and more green than Rin had ever seen in Tikany. On the other side of the channel, she could just trace the faint outlines of two mountain chains peeking over the mist: the Qinling Mountains to the east and the Daba range to the west.

"I used to climb up those cliffs all the time." Nezha pointed toward a steep set of stairs carved into the red walls that made Rin dizzy just looking at them. "You can see everything from up there—the ocean, the mountains, the entire province."

"So you could see attackers coming from every direction from miles off," Kitay said. "That's very useful."

Now Rin understood. This explained why Vaisra was so confident in his military base. Arlong might be the most impenetrable city in the Empire. The only way to invade was by sailing through a narrow channel or scaling a massive mountain range. Arlong was easy to defend and tremendously difficult to attack—the ideal wartime capital.

"We used to spend days on the beaches, too," said Nezha. "You can't see them from here, but there are coves hidden under the cliff walls if you know where to find them. In Arlong the riverbanks are so large that if you didn't know any better, you'd think you were on the ocean."

Rin shuddered at the thought. Tikany had been landlocked, and she couldn't imagine growing up this close to so much water. She would have felt so vulnerable. Anything could land on those shores. Pirates. Hesperians. The Federation.

Speer had been that vulnerable.

Nezha cast her a sideways look. "You don't like the ocean?"

She thought of Altan pitching backward into black water. She thought of a long, desperate swim and of nearly losing her mind. "I don't like the way it smells," she said.

"But it just smells like salt," he said.

"No. It smells like blood."

The moment the *Seagrim* dropped anchor, a group of soldiers escorted Vaisra off the ship and ensconced him inside a curtained sedan chair to be carted off to the palace. Rin had not seen Vaisra in more than a week, but she'd heard rumors his condition had worsened. She supposed the last thing he wanted was for word to spread.

"Should we be concerned?" she asked, watching as the chair made its way down the pier.

"He just needs some shoreside rest." Nezha's words didn't sound forced, which Rin took as a good sign. "He'll recover."

"In time to lead a campaign north, you think?" Kitay asked.

"Certainly. And if not Father, then my brother. Let's get you to the barracks." Nezha motioned toward the gangplank. "Come on. I'll introduce you to the ranks."

Arlong was an amphibious city composed of a series of inter-connected islands scattered inside a wide swath of the Western Murui. Nezha led Rin, Kitay, and the Cike into one of the slim, ubiquitous sampans that navigated Arlong's interior. As Nezha guided their boat into the inner city, Rin swallowed down a wave of nausea. The city reminded her of Ankhiluun; it was far less shabby but just as disorienting in its reliance on waterways. She hated it. *What was so wrong with dry land?*

"No bridges?" she asked. "No roads?"

"No need. Whole islands linked by canals." Nezha stood at the stern, steering the sampan forward with gentle sweeps of the rudder. "It's arranged in a circular grid, like a conch shell."

"Your city looks like it's halfway to sinking," Rin said.

"That's on purpose. It's nearly impossible to launch a land invasion on Arlong." He guided the sampan around a corner. "This was the first capital of the Red Emperor. Back during his wars with the Speerlies, he surrounded himself with water. He never felt safe without it—he chose to build a city at Arlong for precisely that reason. Or so the myth goes."

"Why was he obsessed with water?"

"How else do you protect yourself from beings who control fire? He was terrified of Tearza and her army."

"I thought he was in love with Tearza," Rin said.

"He loved her *and* feared her," Nezha said. "They're not mutually exclusive."

Rin was glad when they finally pulled up to a solid sidewalk. She felt far more comfortable on land, where the floorboards wouldn't shift under her feet, where she was at no risk of tipping into the water.

But Nezha looked happier over water than she'd ever seen him. He controlled the rudder like it was a natural extension of his body, and he hopped lightly from the edge of the sampan to the walkway as if it were no more difficult than walking through a grassy field.

He led them into the heart of Arlong's military district. As they walked, Rin saw a series of tower ships, vessels that could carry entire villages, mounted with massive catapults and studded with rows and rows of iron cannons shaped like dragons' heads, mouths curled in vicious sneers, waiting to spit fire and iron.

"These ships are stupidly tall," she said.

"That's because they're designed to capture walled cities," Nezha said. "Naval warfare is a matter of collecting cities like gambling chips. Those structures are meant to overtop walls along major waterways. Strategically speaking, most provinces are just empty space. The major cities control economic and political levers, the transportation and communications routes. So control the city and you've controlled the province."

"I know that," she said, slightly irked that he thought she needed a primer on basic invasion strategy. "I'm just concerned about their maneuverability. How much agility do you get in shallow waters?"

"Not much, but that doesn't matter. Most naval warfare is still decided by hand-to-hand combat," Nezha explained. "The tower ships take down the walls. We go in and pick up the pieces."

Ramsa piped up from behind them, "I don't understand why we couldn't have taken this beautiful, giant fleet and blasted the shit out of the Autumn Palace."

"Because we were attempting a bloodless coup," Nezha said. "Father wanted to avoid a war if he could. Sending a massive fleet up to Lusan might have given the wrong message."

"So what I'm hearing is that it's all Rin's fault," said Ramsa. "Classic."

Nezha walked backward so that he could face them as he talked. He looked terribly smug as he gestured to the ships around them. "A few years ago we added crossbeams to increase structural integrity in the hulls. And we redesigned the rudders— they have more mobility now, so they can operate in a broader range of water depths . . ."

"And your rudder?" Kitay inquired. "Still plunging those depths?"

Nezha ignored him. "We've improved our anchors, too."

"How so?" Rin asked, mostly because she could tell he wanted to brag.

"The teeth. They're arranged circularly instead of in one direction. Means they hardly ever break."

Rin found this very funny. "Does that happen often?"

"You'd be surprised," Nezha said. "During the Second Poppy War we lost a crucial naval skirmish because the ship started drifting out to sea without its crew during a maelstrom. We've learned from that mistake."

He continued to elucidate newer innovations as they walked, gesturing with the pride of a newborn parent. "We started building the hulls with the broadest beam aft—makes it easier to steer at slow speeds. The junks have sails divided into horizontal panels by bamboo slats that make them more aerodynamic."

"You know a lot about ships," Rin said.

"I spent my childhood next door to a shipyard. It'd be embarrassing if I didn't."

Rin stopped walking, letting the others pass her until she and Nezha stood alone. She lowered her voice. "Be honest with me. How long have you been preparing for this war?"

He didn't miss a beat. Didn't even blink. "As long as I've been alive."

So Nezha had spent his entire childhood readying himself to betray the Empire. So he had known, when he came to Sinegard, that one day he would lead a fleet against his classmates.

"You've been a traitor since birth," she said.

"Depends on your perspective."

"But I was fighting for the Militia until now. We could have been enemies."

"I know." Nezha beamed. "Aren't you so glad we're not?"

The Dragon Army absorbed the Cike into its ranks with impressive efficiency. A young woman named Officer Sola received them at the barracks. She couldn't have been more than a few years older than Rin, and she wore the green armband that indicated she had graduated from Sinegard with a Strategy degree.

"You trained with Irjah?" Kitay asked.

Sola glanced at Kitay's own faded armband. "What division?"

"Second. I was with him at Golyn Niis."

"Ah." Sola's mouth pressed into a thin line. "How did he die?"

Skinned alive and hung over a city wall, Rin thought.

"With honor," Kitay said.

"He'd be proud of you," Sola said.

"Well, I'm quite sure he would have called us traitors."

"Irjah cared about justice," Sola said in a hard voice. "He would have been with us."

Within the hour Sola had assigned them to bunks in the barracks, given them a walking tour of the sprawling base that occupied three mini islands and the canals in between, and outfitted them with new uniforms. These were made of warmer, sturdier material than any Militia suits Rin had ever seen. The cloth base came with a set of lamellar armor made up of overlapping leather and metal plates so confusing that Sola had to demonstrate in detail what went where.

Sola didn't point them to any changing rooms, so Rin stripped down along with her men, pulled her new uniform on, and stretched her limbs out. She was amazed at the flexibility. The lamellar armor was far more sophisticated than the flimsy uniforms the Militia issued, and likely cost three times as much.

"We have better blacksmiths than they do up north." Sola passed Rin a chest plate. "Our armor's lighter. Deflects more."

"What should we do with these?" Ramsa held up a bundle of his old clothing.

Sola wrinkled her nose. "Burn them."

The barracks and armory were cleaner, larger, and better stocked than any Militia facility Rin had ever visited. Kitay rifled through the gleaming rows of swords and knives until he found a set that suited him; the rest of them turned in their weapons to the blacksmith for refurbishment.

"I was told you had a detonations expert in your squadron." Sola pulled the curtain aside to reveal the full store of the First Platoon's explosives. Stacks upon stacks of missiles, rockets, and fire lances were arranged neatly in pyramidal piles waiting in the cool darkness to be loaded onto warships.

Ramsa made a highly suggestive whimpering noise. He lifted a missile shaped like a dragon head out from the pile and turned it over in his hands. "Is this what I think it is?"

Sola nodded. "It's a two-stage rocket. The main vessel contains the booster. The rest detonates in midair. Gives it a little extra thrust."

"How'd you manage these?" Ramsa demanded. "I've been working on this for at least two years."

"And we've been working on it for five."

Ramsa pointed at another pile of explosives. "What do *those* do?"

"They're fin-mounted winged rockets." Sola sounded amused. "The fins are for guided flight. We see better accuracy with these than the two-stage rockets."

Someone with a bad sense of humor had carved the head to look like a fish with a droopy expression. Ramsa ran his fingers along the fins. "What kind of range do you get on these?"

"That depends," said Sola. "On a clear day, sixty miles. Rainy days, as far as you can get them."

Ramsa weighed the missile in his hands, looking so delighted that Rin suspected he might have gotten an erection. "Oh, we are going to have fun with these."

"Are you hungry?" Nezha knocked on the door frame.

Rin glanced up. She was alone in the barracks. Kitay had left to find the Dragon Province's archives, and the other Cike members' first priority had been finding the mess hall.

"Not very," she said.

"Good. Do you want to see something cool?"

"Is it another ship?" she asked.

"Yes. But you'll really like this one. Nice uniform, by the way."

She smacked his arm. "Eyes up, General."

"I'm just saying the colors look good on you. You make a good Dragon."

Rin heard the shipyard long before they reached it. Over the cacophonous din of screeches and hammering, they had to yell to hear each other. She had assumed what she saw in the harbor was a completed fleet, but apparently several more vessels were still under construction.

Her eyes landed immediately on the ship at the far end. It was still in its initial stages—only a skeleton thus far. But if she imagined the structure to be built around it, it was titanic. It seemed impossible that a thing like that could ever stay afloat, let alone get past the channel through the Red Cliffs.

"We're going to board *that* to the capital?" she asked.

"That one isn't ready. It keeps getting updated with plans from the west. It's Jinzha's pet project; he's a perfectionist about stuff like this."

"A pet project," she repeated. "Your siblings just build massive boats for their *pet projects*."

Nezha shook his head. "It was supposed to be finished in time for the northern campaign, whenever that gets off the ground. Now it'll be much longer. They've changed the design to a defensive warship. It's meant to guard Arlong now, not to lead the fleet."

"Why is it behind schedule?"

"Fire broke out in the shipyard overnight. Some idiot on watch kicked his lamp over. Set construction back by months. They had to import the timber from the Dog Province. Father had to get pretty creative with that—it's hard to ship in massive amounts of lumber and hide the fact that you're building a fleet. Took a few weeks of dealing with Moag's smugglers."

Rin could see blackened edges on some of the skeleton's outer boards. But the rest had been replaced with new timber, smoothed to a shine.

"The whole thing made a big stir in the city," Nezha said. "Some people kept saying it was a sign from the gods that the rebellion would fail."

"And Vaisra?"

"Father took it as a sign that he should go out and get himself a Speerly."

Instead of taking a river sampan back to the military barracks, Nezha led her down the stairs to the base of the pier, where Rin could still hear the noise of the shipyard over the water rushing gently against the posts that kept the pier up. At first she thought they had walked into a dead end, until Nezha stepped from the glassy sand and right onto the river.

"What the hell?"

After a second she realized he was standing not on the water, but rather on a large circular flap that almost matched the river's greenish-blue hue.

"Lily pads," Nezha said before she could ask. Arms spread for balance, he shifted his weight just so as the waves lifted the lily pad under his feet.

"Show-off," Rin said.

"You've never seen these before?"

"Yes, but only in wall scrolls." She grimaced at the pads. Her balance wasn't half as good as Nezha's, and she wasn't keen to fall into the river. "I didn't know they grew so large."

"They don't usually. These will only last a month or two before they sink. They grow naturally in the freshwater ponds up the mountain, but our botanists found a way to militarize them. You'll find them up and down the harbor. The better sailors don't need rowboats to get to their ships; they can just run across the lily pads."

"Calm down," she said. "They're just stepping stones."

"They're militarized lily pads. Isn't that great?"

"I think you just like using the word 'militarized.'"

Nezha opened his mouth to respond, but a voice from atop the pier cut him off.

"Had enough of playing tour guide?"

A man descended the steps toward them. He wore a blue soldier's uniform, and the black stripes on his left arm marked him as a general.

Nezha hastily hopped off the lily pads onto the wet sand and sank to one knee. "Brother. Good to see you again."

Rin realized in retrospect she should have knelt as well, but she was too busy staring at Nezha's brother. Yin Jinzha. She had seen him once, briefly, three years back at her first Summer Festival in Sinegard. Back then she'd thought that Jinzha and Nezha could have been twins, but upon closer inspection, their similarities were not really so pronounced. Jinzha was taller, more thickly built, and he carried himself with the air of a firstborn—a son who knew he was heir to his father's entire estate, while his younger siblings would be left to a fate of squabbling over the refuse.

"I heard you screwed up at the Autumn Palace." Jinzha's voice was deeper than Nezha's. More arrogant, if that was possible. It sounded oddly familiar to Rin, but she couldn't quite place it. "What happened?"

Nezha rose to his feet. "Hasn't Captain Eriden briefed you?"

"Eriden didn't see everything. Until Father recovers I'm the senior ranking general in Arlong, and I'd like to know the details."

It's Altan, Rin realized with a jolt. Jinzha spoke with a clipped, military precision that reminded her of Altan at his best. This was a man used to competence and immediate obedience.

"I don't have anything to add," Nezha said. "I was on the *Seagrim*."

Jinzha's lip curled. "Out of harm's way. Typical."

Rin expected Nezha to lash out at that, but he swallowed the barb with a nod. "How is Father?"

"Better now than last night. He'd been straining himself. Our physician didn't understand how he was still alive at first."

"But Father told me it was just a flesh wound."

"Did you even get a good look at him? That blade went nearly all the way through his shoulder bone. He's been lying to everyone. It's a wonder he's even conscious."

"Has he asked for me?" Nezha asked.

"Why would he?" Jinzha gave his brother a patronizing look. "I'll let you know when you're needed."

"Yes, sir." Nezha dipped his head and nodded. Rin watched this exchange, fascinated. She'd never seen anyone who could bully Nezha the way Nezha tended to bully everyone else.

"You're the Speerly." Jinzha looked suddenly at Rin, as if he had just remembered she was there.

"Yes." For some reason Rin's voice came out strangled, girlish. She cleared her throat. "That's me."

"Go on, then," Jinzha said. "Let's see it."

"What?"

"Show me what you can do," Jinzha said very slowly, as if talking to a small child. "Make it big."

Rin shot Nezha a confused look. "I don't understand."

"They say you can call fire," Jinzha said.

"Well, yes—"

"How much? How hot? To what degree? Does it come from your body, or can you summon it from other places? What does it take for you to trigger a volcano?" Jinzha spoke at such a terribly fast clip that Rin had trouble deciphering his curt Sinegardian accent. She hadn't struggled with that in years.

She blinked, feeling rather stupid, and when she spoke she stumbled over her words. "I mean, it just *happens*—"

"'It just happens,'" he mimicked. "What, like a sneeze? What help is that? Explain to me how to use you."

"I'm not someone for you to use."

"Fancy that. The soldier won't take orders."

"Rin's had a long journey," Nezha cut in hastily. "I'm sure she'd be happy to demonstrate for you in the morning, when she's had some rest . . ."

"Soldiers get tired, that's part of the job," Jinzha said. "Come on, Speerly. Show us what you've got."

Nezha placed a placating hand on Rin's arm. "Jinzha, really . . ."

Jinzha made a noise of disgust. "You should hear the way Father talks about them. Speerlies this, Speerlies that. I told him he'd be better off launching an invasion from Arlong, but no, he thought he could win a bloodless coup if he just had you. Look how that worked out."

"Rin's stronger than you can imagine," Nezha said.

"You know, if the Speerlies were so strong, you'd think they'd be less dead." Jinzha's lip curled. "Spent my whole childhood hearing about what a marvel your precious Altan was. Turns out he was just another dirt-skinned idiot who blew himself up for nothing."

Rin's vision flashed red. When she looked at Jinzha she didn't see flesh but a charred stump, ashes peeling off what used to be a man—she wanted him dying, dead, hurting. She wanted him to scream.

"You want to see what I can do?" she asked. Her voice sounded very distant, as if someone were speaking at her from very far away.

"Rin . . ." Nezha cautioned.

"No, fuck off." She shrugged his hand off her arm. "He wants to see what I can do."

"I don't think that's a good idea."

"Get back."

She turned her palms out toward Jinzha. It took nothing to summon the anger. It was already there, waiting, like water bursting forth from a dam—*I hate, I hate, I hate*—

Nothing happened.

Jinzha raised his eyebrows.

Rin felt a twinge of pain in her temples. She touched her finger to her eyes.

The twinge blossomed into a searing bolt of agony. She saw an explosion of colors branded behind her eyelids: reds and yellows, flames flickering over a burning village, the silhouettes of people writhing inside, a great mushroom cloud over the longbow island in miniature.

For a moment she saw a character she couldn't recognize, swimming into shape like a nest of snakes, lingering just in front of her eyes before it disappeared. She drifted in a moment between the world in her mind and the material world. She couldn't breathe, couldn't see . . .

She sagged to her knees. She felt Nezha's arms hoisting her up, heard him shouting for someone to help. She struggled to open her eyes. Jinzha stood above her, staring down with open contempt.

"Father was right," he said. "We should have tried to save the other one."

Chaghan slammed the door shut behind him. "What happened?"

"I don't know." Rin's fingers clenched and unclenched around the bedsheets while Chaghan unpacked his satchel beside her. Her voice trembled; she had spent the last half hour trying simply to breathe normally, but still her heart raced so furiously that she could barely hear her own thoughts. "I got careless. I was going to call the fire—just a bit, I didn't really want to hurt him, and then—"

Chaghan grabbed her wrists. "Why are you shaking?"

She hadn't realized she was. She couldn't stop her hands from trembling, but thinking about it only made her shake harder.

"He won't want me anymore," she whispered.

"Who?"

"Vaisra."

She was terrified. If she couldn't call the fire, then Vaisra had recruited a Speerly for nothing. Without the fire, she might be tossed away.

She'd been trying since she regained consciousness to call the fire, but the result was always the same—a searing pain in her temples, a burst of color, and flashes of visions she never wanted to see again. She couldn't tell what was wrong, only that the fire remained out of her reach, and without the fire she was nothing but useless.

Another tremor passed through her body.

"Just calm down," Chaghan said. He set the satchel on the floor and knelt beside her. "Focus on me. Look in my eyes."

She obeyed.

Chaghan's eyes, pale and without pupils or irises, were normally unsettling. But up close they were strangely alluring, two shards of a snowy landscape embedded in his thin face that drew her in like some hypnotized prey.

"What is wrong with me?" she whispered.

"I don't know. Why don't we find out?" Chaghan rummaged in his satchel, closed his fist around something, and offered her a handful of bright blue powder.

She recognized the drug. It was the ground-up dust of some dried northern fungus. She'd ingested it once before with Chaghan in Khurdalain, when she'd taken him to the immaterial realm where Mai'rinnen Tearza was haunting her.

Chaghan wanted to accompany her to the inner recesses of her mind, the point where her soul ascended to the plane of the gods.

"Afraid?" he asked when she hesitated.

Not afraid. Ashamed. Rin didn't *want* to bring Chaghan into her mind. She was scared of what he might see.

"Do you have to come?" she asked.

"You can't do it alone. I'm all you've got. You have to trust me."

"Will you promise to stop if I ask you to?"

Chaghan scoffed, reached for her hand, and pressed her finger into the powder. "We'll stop when I say we can stop."

"Chaghan."

He gave her a frank look. "Do you really have another option?"

The drug began to act almost from the moment it hit her tongue. Rin was surprised at how fast and clean the high was. Poppy seeds were so frustratingly slow, a gradual crawl into the realm of spirit that worked only if she concentrated, but this drug was like a kick through the door between this world and the next.

Chaghan grabbed her hand just before the infirmary faded from her vision. They departed the mortal plane in a swirl of colors. Then it was just the two of them in an expanse of black. Drifting. Searching.

Rin knew what she had to do. She homed in on her anger and created the link to the Phoenix that pulled their souls from the chasm of nothing toward the Pantheon. She could almost feel the Phoenix, the scorching heat of its divinity washing over her, could almost hear its malicious cackle—

Then something dimmed its presence, cut her off.

Something massive materialized before them. There was no way to describe it other than a giant word, slashed into empty space. Twelve strokes hung in the air, a great pictogram the shimmering hue of green-blue snakeskin, glinting in the unnatural brightness like freshly spilled blood.

"That's impossible," Chaghan said. "She shouldn't be able to do this."

The pictogram looked both entirely familiar and entirely foreign. Rin couldn't read it, though it had to be written in the Nikara script. It came close to resembling several characters she knew but deviated from all of them in significant ways.

This was something ancient, then. Something old; something that predated the Red Emperor. "What is this?"

"What does it look like?" Chaghan reached out an incorporeal hand as if to touch it, then hastily drew it back. "This is a Seal."

A Seal? The term sounded oddly familiar. Rin remembered fragments of a battle. A white-haired man floating in the air, lightning swirling around the tip of his staff, opening a void to a realm of things not mortal, things that didn't belong in their world.

You're Sealed.

Not anymore.

"Like the Gatekeeper?" she asked.

"The Gatekeeper was *Sealed*?" Chaghan sounded astonished. "Why didn't you tell me?"

"I had no idea!"

"But that would explain so much! That's why he's been lost, why he doesn't remember—"

"What are you talking about?"

"The Seal blocks your access to the world of spirit," Chaghan explained. "The Vipress left her venom inside you. That's what it's made of. It will keep you from accessing the Pantheon. And over time it will grow stronger and stronger, eating away at your mind until you lose even your memories associated with the Phoenix. It'll make you a shell of yourself."

"Please tell me you can get rid of it."

"I can try. You'll have to take me inside."

"Inside?"

"The Seal is also a gateway. Look." Chaghan pointed into the heart of the character, where the glimmering snake blood formed a swirling circle. When Rin focused on it, it did indeed seem to call to her, drawing her into some unknown dimension beyond. "Go inside. I'm betting that's where Daji's left the venom. It exists here in the form of memory. Daji's power dwells in desire; she's conjured the things that you want the most to prevent you from calling the fire."

"Venom. Memory. Desire." Very little of this was making sense to Rin. "Look—just tell me whatever the fuck I'm supposed to do with it."

"You destroy it however you can."

"Destroy *what*?"

"I think you'll know when you see it."

Rin didn't have to ask how to pass the gate. It pulled her in as soon as she approached it. The Seal seemed to fold in over them, growing larger and larger until it enveloped them. Swirls of blood drifted around her, undulating, as if trying to decide what shape to take, what illusion to create.

"She'll show you the future you want," Chaghan said.

But Rin didn't see how that could possibly work for her, because her greatest desires didn't exist in the future. They were all in the past. She wanted the last five years back. She wanted lazy days on the Academy campus. She wanted lackadaisical strolls in Jiang's garden, she wanted summer vacations at Kitay's estate, she wanted, she *wanted* . . .

She was on the sands of the Isle of Speer again—vibrant, beautiful Speer, lush and vivid like she had never seen it before. And there Altan was, healthy and whole, smiling like she had never really seen him smile.

"Hello," he said. "Are you ready to come home?"

"Kill him," Chaghan said urgently.

But hadn't she already? At Khurdalain she'd fought a beast with Altan's face, and she'd killed him then. Then at the research facility she'd let him walk out on the pier, let him sacrifice himself to save her.

She'd already killed Altan, over and over, and he kept coming back.

How could she harm him *now*? He looked so happy. So free

from pain. She knew so much more about him now, she knew what he had suffered, and she couldn't touch him. Not like this.

Altan drew closer. "What are you doing out here? Come with me."

She wanted to go with him more than anything. She didn't even know where he would take her, only that he would be there. Oblivion. Some dark paradise.

Altan extended his hand toward her. "*Come.*"

She steeled herself. "Stop this," she managed. "Chaghan, I can't—stop it—take me back—"

"Surely you're joking," Chaghan said. "You can't even do this?"

Altan took her fingers in his. "Let's go."

"*Stop it!*"

She wasn't sure *what* she did but she felt a burst of energy, saw the Seal contort and writhe around Chaghan, like a predator sniffing out some new and interesting prey, and saw his mouth open in some soundless scream of agony.

Then they weren't on Speer anymore.

This was nowhere she had ever seen.

They were somewhere high up on a mountain, cold and dark. A series of caves were carved into stone, all glowing with candle fire on the inside. And sitting on the ledge, shoulders touching, were two boys: one dark haired and one fair haired.

She was an outsider in this memory, but the moment she stepped closer her perspective shifted and she wasn't the voyeur anymore but the subject. She saw Altan's face up close, and she realized she was looking at him the way Chaghan once had.

Altan's face was entirely too close to hers. She could make out every last terrible and wonderful detail: the scar running up from his right cheek, the clumsy way his hair had been tied up, the dark lids over his crimson eyes.

Altan was awful. Altan was beautiful. And as she looked into his eyes she realized the feeling that overcame her was not love;

this was a total, paralyzing fear. This was the terror of a moth drawn to the flame.

She hadn't thought that anyone else felt that way. It was such a familiar feeling that she almost cried.

"I could kill you," said Altan, muttering the death threat like a love song, and when she-as-Chaghan struggled against him he pressed his body closer.

"So you could," Chaghan said, and that was such a familiar voice, the coy, level voice. She'd always marveled at how Chaghan could speak so casually to Altan. But Chaghan hadn't been joking, she realized, he'd been afraid; he had been constantly terrified every time he was around Altan. "So what?"

Altan's fingers closed over Chaghan's; too hot, too crushing, an attempt at human contact with absolute disregard for the object of his affection.

His lips brushed against Chaghan's ear. She shuddered involuntarily; she thought he might bite her, move his mouth lower against her neck and rip out her arteries.

She realized that Chaghan felt this fear often.

She realized that Chaghan probably enjoyed it.

"Don't," Chaghan said.

She didn't listen; she wanted to stay in this vision, had the sickening desire to watch it play out to its conclusion.

"That's *enough*."

A wave of darkness slammed down onto them, and when she opened her eyes she was back in the infirmary, sprawled on top of her bed. Chaghan sat bolt upright on the floor, eyes wide open, expression blank.

She grabbed him by the collar. "What was that?"

Chaghan stirred awake. His features settled into something like contempt. "Why don't you ask yourself?"

"You *hypocrite*," she said. "You're just as obsessed with him—"

"Are you sure that wasn't you?"

"Don't lie to me!" she shrieked. "I know what I saw, I know

what you were doing, I bet you only wanted to get in my mind because you wanted to see him from another angle—"

He flinched back.

She hadn't expected him to flinch. He looked so small. So *vulnerable.*

Somehow, that made her angrier.

She clenched his collar tighter. "He's dead. All right? Can't you get that in your fucking head?"

"Rin—"

"He's dead, he's gone, and we can't bring him back. And maybe he loved you, maybe he loved me, but that doesn't fucking matter anymore, does it? He's gone."

She thought he might hit her then.

But he just leaned forward, shoulders hunched over his knees, and pressed his face into his hands. When he spoke he sounded like he was on the verge of tears. "I thought I could catch him."

"What?"

"Sometimes before the dead pass on, they linger," he whispered. "Especially your kind. Anger depends on resentment, and your dead exist in resentment. And I think he's still out there, drifting between this world and the next, but each time I try all I get is fragments of memories, and as more time passes I can't even remember the beautiful things, and I thought maybe—with the venom—"

"You don't know how to fix me, do you?" she asked. "You never did."

Chaghan didn't answer.

She released his collar. "Get out."

He packed up his satchel and left without a word. She almost called him back, but she couldn't think of a single thing to say before he slammed the door.

Once Chaghan was gone, Rin shouted down the hallway until she got the attention of a physician, whom she berated until she obtained a sleeping draught in twice the recommended dosage. She swallowed that in two large gulps, crawled back onto her bed, and fell into the deepest sleep she'd had in a long time.

When she woke, the physician refused her another sleeping draught for another six hours. So she waited in fearful apprehension, anticipating a visit from Jinzha or Nezha or even Vaisra himself. She didn't know what to expect, only that it couldn't be anything good. Who had any use for a Speerly who couldn't summon fire?

But her only visitor was Captain Eriden, who instructed her that she was to continue acting as if she were in full command of her abilities. She was still Vaisra's trump card, Vaisra's hidden weapon, and she was still to appear at his side, even if only as a psychological weapon.

He didn't convey Vaisra's disappointment. He didn't have to. Vaisra's absence stung more than anything else.

She chugged down the next sleeping draught they gave her. The sun had set by the time she woke again. She was terribly hungry. She stood up, unlocked the door, and walked down the hallway, barefoot and groggy, with the vague intention of demanding food from the first person she saw.

"Well, fuck you, too!"

Rin stopped walking.

The voice came from a door near the end of the hallway. "What was I supposed to do? Hang myself like the women of Lü? I bet you'd like that."

Rin recognized that voice—shrill, petulant, and furious. She tiptoed down the hall and stood just beyond the door.

"The women of Lü preserved their dignity." A male voice this time, much older and deeper.

"And who put my dignity in my cunt?"

Rin caught her breath. Venka. It had to be.

"Would you prefer I were a lifeless corpse?" Venka screamed. "Would you prefer my spine were broken, my body crushed, just so long as nothing had gone between my legs?"

The male voice again. "I wish you had never been taken. You know that."

"You're not answering the question." A choked noise. Was Venka crying? "Look at me, Father. *Look at me*."

Venka's father said something in response, too softly for Rin to hear. A moment later the door slammed open. Rin ducked around the corner and froze until she heard the footsteps recede down the hall in the opposite direction.

She exhaled in relief. She considered for a moment, then walked toward the door. It was open, hanging slightly ajar. She placed her fingertips on the wooden panel and pushed.

It *was* Venka. She had shorn her hair off completely—and clearly some time ago, because it was starting to grow back in little dark patches. But her face was the same—ridiculously pretty, all sharp angles and piercing eyes.

"What the hell do you want?" Venka demanded. "Can I help you?"

"You were being loud," Rin said.

"Oh, I'm *so* sorry. Next time my father disowns me, I'll keep it down."

"You were disowned?"

"Well. Probably not. It's not like he's got other heirs to spare." Venka's eyes were red around the rims. "I wish he would, it's better than him trying to tell me what to do with my own body. When I was pregnant—"

"You're *pregnant*?"

"*Was*." Venka scowled. "No thanks to that fucking doctor. He kept saying that fucking cunt Saikhara didn't permit abortions."

"Saikhara?"

"Nezha's mother. She's got some funny ideas about religion. Grew up in Hesperia, did you know that? She worships their stupid fucking Maker. She doesn't just pretend for diplomatic reasons, she actually *believes* in that shit. And she runs around obeying everything he wrote in some little book, which apparently includes forcing women to bear the children of their rapists."

"So what did you do?"

Venka's throat pulsed. "Got creative."

"Ah."

They both stared at the floor for a minute. Venka broke the silence. "I mean, it only hurt a little bit. Not as bad as—you know."

"Yeah."

"That's what I thought about when I did it. Kept thinking about their piggy little faces, and then it wasn't difficult. And the Lady Saikhara can go fuck herself."

Rin sat down on the edge of her bed. It felt oddly good to be around Venka—angry, impatient, abrasive Venka. Venka gave voice to the raw anger that everyone else seemed to have patched over, and for that Rin was grateful.

"How are your arms?" she asked. Last time she'd seen Venka her arms were swathed in so many bandages that Rin wasn't sure if she'd lost use of them altogether. But her bandages were gone now, and her arms weren't dangling uselessly by her sides.

Venka flexed her fingers. "Right one's healed. Left one won't, ever. It was bent all funny, and I can't move three fingers on my left hand."

"Can you still shoot?"

"Works just as well as long as I can hold a bow. They had a glove designed for me. Keeps the three fingers bent back so I don't have to. I'd be just fine on the field with a little practice. Not like anyone believes me." Venka shifted in her bed. "But what are *you* doing here? Did Nezha win you over with his pretty words?"

Rin shifted. "Something like that."

Venka was looking at her with something that might have been jealousy. "So you're still a soldier. Lucky you."

"I'm not sure about that," Rin said.

"Why not?"

For a moment Rin considered telling Venka everything—about the Vipress, about the Seal, about what she had seen with Chaghan. But Venka didn't have the patience for details. Venka didn't care that much.

"I just—I can't do what I did anymore. Not like that." She hugged her chest with her arms. "I don't think I'll ever do that again."

Venka pointed to her eyes. "Is that what you've been crying about?"

"No—I just . . ." Rin took a shaky breath. "I don't know if I'm useful anymore."

Venka rolled her eyes. "Well, you can still hold a sword, can't you?"

CHAPTER 12

In the following week, three more provinces announced their independence from the Empire.

As Nezha predicted, the southern Warlords capitulated first. After all, the south had no reason to stay loyal to the Empire or Daji. The Third Poppy War had hit them the hardest. Their refugees were starving, their bandit epidemic had exploded, and the attack at the Autumn Palace had destroyed any chance that they might win concessions or promises of aid at the Lusan summit.

The southern Warlords notified Arlong of their intentions to secede through breathless delegates traveling over land if they were close enough, and by messenger pigeon if they weren't. Days later the Warlords themselves arrived at Arlong's gates.

"Rooster, Monkey, and Boar." Nezha counted the provinces off as they watched Eriden's guards escort the portly Boar Warlord into the palace. "Not bad."

"That puts us at four provinces to eight," Rin said. "Not incredible odds."

"Five to seven. And they're good generals." That was true. None of the southern Warlords had been born into their ranks; they'd all assumed them in the bloodbaths of the Second and Third Poppy Wars. "And Tsolin will come through."

"How are you so sure?"

"Tsolin knows how to pick sides. He'll show up eventually. Cheer up, this is about as good as we expected."

Rin had imagined that once the four-province alliance solidified, they would march on the north immediately. But politics quickly crushed her hopes for rapid action. The southern Warlords had not brought their armies with them to Arlong. Their military forces remained in their respective capitals, hedging their bets, watching before joining the fray. The south was playing a waiting game. By seceding they had insulated themselves from Vaisra's ire, but so long as they didn't commit troops against the Empire, there was still the chance that Daji would welcome them back with open arms, all sins forgiven.

Days passed. The order to ship out didn't come. The four-province alliance spent hours and hours debating strategy in an endless series of war councils. Rin, Nezha, and Kitay were all present at these; Nezha because he was a general, Kitay because he, in a bizarre turn of events, was now considered a competent strategist if not an especially well-liked one, and Rin purely because Vaisra wanted her there.

She suspected her purpose was to intimidate, to give some reassurance that if the island-destroying Speerly was alive and well in Arlong, then this war could not be so difficult to win.

She tried her best to act as if that weren't a lie.

"We need cross-division squadrons, or this alliance is just a suicide pact." General Hu, Vaisra's senior strategist, had long ago given up on masking his frustration. "The Republican Army has to act as a cohesive whole. The men can't think they're still squadrons of their old province."

"I'm not putting my men under the command of soldiers I've never met," said the Boar Warlord. Rin detested Cao Charouk; he seemed to do nothing but complain so fiercely about everything Vaisra's staff suggested that often she wondered why he'd come to Arlong at all. "And those squads won't function. You're asking men who have never met to fight together. They don't know the same command signals, they don't use the same codes, and they don't have time to learn."

"Well, you lot don't seem keen on attacking the north anytime soon, so I imagine they'll have months at the least," Kitay muttered.

Nezha made a choking noise that sounded like a laugh.

Charouk looked as if he would very much like to skewer Kitay on a flagpole if given the chance.

"We can't beat Daji fighting as four separate armies," General Hu said quickly. "Our scouts report she's assembling a coalition in the north as we speak."

"Doesn't matter if they don't have a fleet," said the Monkey Warlord, Liu Gurubai. He was the most cooperative among the southern Warlords; sharp-tongued and clever-eyed, he spent most meetings stroking his thick, dark whiskers while he played both sides at the table.

If they were dealing only with Gurubai, Rin thought, they might have moved north by now. The Monkey Warlord was cautious, but he at least responded to reason. The Boar and Rooster Warlords, however, seemed determined to hunker down in Arlong behind Vaisra's army. Gong Takha had passed the last few days sitting silent and sullen at the table while Charouk continually blustered his suspicion of everyone else in the room.

"But they will. Daji is now commissioning ships from civilian centers for a restored Imperial Navy. They're converting grain transport ships into war galleys, and they've constructed naval yards at multiple sites in Tiger Province." General Hu tapped on the map. "The longer we wait, the more time they have to prepare."

"Who's leading that fleet?" asked Gurubai.

"Chang En."

"That's surprising," Charouk said. "Not Jun?"

"Jun didn't want the job," said General Hu.

Charouk raised an eyebrow. "That'd be a first."

"It's wise on his part," said Vaisra. "No one wants to have to give Chang En orders. When his officers question him, they lose their heads."

"That's certainly a sign the Empire's on the decline," tutted Takha. "That man is wicked and wasteful."

The Wolf Meat General was notorious for his brutality. When Chang En had staged his coup against the previous Horse Warlord, his troops had split skulls in half and hung strings of the severed heads across the capital walls.

"Or it just means, you know, that all the good generals are dead," Jinzha drawled. He had been remarkably restrained in council so far, though Rin had been watching the contempt build on his face for hours.

"You would know," said Charouk. "Did your apprenticeship with him, didn't you?"

Jinzha bristled. "That was five years ago."

"Not so long for such a short career."

Jinzha opened his mouth to retort, but Vaisra cut him off with a raised hand. "If you're going to accuse my eldest son of treachery—"

"No one is accusing Jinzha of anything," said Charouk. "Again, Vaisra, we just don't think Jinzha is the right choice to lead your fleet."

"Your men couldn't be in better hands. Jinzha studied warcraft at Sinegard, he commanded troops in the Third Poppy War—"

"As did we all," said Gurubai. "Why not give one of our generals the job? Or why not one of us?"

"Because you three are too important to spare."

Even Rin couldn't help but cringe at that naked flattery. The southern Warlords exchanged wry looks. Gurubai made a show of rolling his eyes.

"All right, then because the men of the Dragon Province are not prepared to fight under anyone else," Vaisra said. "Believe it or not, I *am* trying to find the solution that best protects you."

"And yet it's *our* troops you want on the front lines," said Charouk.

"Dragon Province is committing more troops than any of you,

asshat," Rin snapped. She couldn't help it. She knew Vaisra had wanted her to simply observe, but she couldn't stand watching this mess of passivity and petty infighting. The Warlords were acting like children, squabbling as if someone else would win their war for them if they only procrastinated long enough.

Everyone stared at her as if she'd suddenly grown wings. When Vaisra didn't cut her off, she kept going. "It's been three fucking days. Why the fuck are we arguing about division makeup? The Empire is weak *now*. We need to send a force up north *now*."

"Then how about we just send you?" asked Takha. "You sank the longbow island, didn't you?"

Rin didn't miss a beat. "You want me to kill off half the country? My powers don't discriminate."

Takha looked to Vaisra. "What is she even doing here?"

"I'm the commander of the Cike," Rin said. "And I'm standing right in front of you."

"You're a little girl with no command experience and hardly a year of combat under your belt," Gurubai said. "Do not presume to tell us how to fight a war."

"I *won* the last war. You wouldn't even be standing here without me."

Vaisra placed a hand on her shoulder. "Runin, hush."

"But he—"

"*Silence*," he said sternly. "This discussion is beyond you. Let the generals talk."

Rin swallowed her protest.

The door creaked open. A palace aide poked his head in through the gap. "The Snake Warlord is here to see you, sir."

"Let him in," Vaisra said.

The aide stepped inside to hold the door open.

Ang Tsolin walked inside, unaccompanied and unarmed. Jinzha moved to his right to let Tsolin stand next to his father. Nezha shot Rin a smug look, as if to say *I told you so.*

Vaisra looked equally vindicated. "I'm glad to see you join us, Master."

Tsolin scowled. "You didn't have to sail through my fleet."

"Going the other way would have taken longer."

"They came for my family first."

"I assume you had the foresight to extricate them in time."

Tsolin folded his arms. "My wife and children will arrive tomorrow morning. I want them set up with your most secure accommodations. If I catch so much as a whiff of a spy in their quarters, I will turn over my entire fleet to the Empire's use."

Vaisra dipped his head. "Whatever you ask."

"Good." Tsolin bent forward to examine the maps. "These are all wrong."

"How so?" Jinzha asked.

"The Horse Province hasn't remained inactive. They're gathering their troops to the Yinshan base." Tsolin pointed to a spot just above Hare Province. "And Tiger Province is bringing their fleet toward the Autumn Palace. They're closing off your attack routes. You don't have much time."

"Then tell me what I ought to do," Vaisra said. Rin was amazed at how his tone could shift—once commanding, but now deferential and meek, a student seeking a teacher's aid.

Tsolin gave him a wary look. "Good men are dead because of you. I hope you know."

"Then they died for a good cause," Vaisra said. "I suspect you know that, too."

Tsolin didn't answer. He simply sat down, pulled the maps toward him, and began to examine the attack lines with the weary, practiced air of a man who had spent his entire life fighting wars.

As the days dragged on, despite the northern offensive's ongoing delay, Arlong itself continued to mobilize for war like a tightening spring. War preparations were integrated into almost every facet of civilian life. Steely-eyed children worked the furnaces at the armory and carried messages back and forth across the city. Their mothers produced immaculately stitched uniforms at an astonishing rate. In the mess hall, grandmothers stirred congee in giant vats while their grandchildren ferried bowls around to the soldiers.

Another week passed. The Warlords continued to shout at each other in the council room. Rin couldn't bear the constant waiting, so she took out her adrenaline with Nezha.

Sparring was a welcome exercise. The skirmish at Lusan had made it abundantly clear to her that she had been relying far too much on calling the fire. Her reflexes had flagged, her muscles had atrophied, and her stamina was pathetic.

So at least once every day, she and Nezha picked up their weapons and hiked up to empty clearings far up on the cliffs. She lost herself in the sheer, mindless physicality of their bouts. When they were sparring, her mind couldn't languish on any one thought for too long. She was too busy calculating angles, maneuvering steel on steel. The immediacy of the fight was its own kind of drug, one that could numb her to anything else she might accidentally feel.

Altan couldn't torture her if she couldn't think.

Blow by blow, bruise by bruise, she relearned the muscle memory that she had lost, and she relished it. Here she could channel the adrenaline and fear that kept her vibrating with anxiety on a daily basis.

The first few days left her wrecked and aching. The next few were better. She filled in her uniform. She lost her hollow, skeletal appearance. This was the only reason she was grateful for the council's slow deliberation—it gave her time to become the soldier she used to be.

Nezha was not a lenient sparring partner, and she didn't want him to be. The first time he held back out of fear of hurting her, she swept out a leg and knocked him to the ground.

He propped himself up on his stomach. "If you wanted to go for a tumble, you could have just asked."

"Don't be disgusting," she said.

Once she stopped losing hand-to-hand bouts in under thirty seconds, they moved on to padded weapons.

"I don't understand why you insist on using that thing," he said after he disarmed her of her trident for the third time. "It's clumsy as hell. Father's been telling me to get you to switch to a sword."

She knew what Vaisra wanted. She was tired of that argument.

"Reach matters more than maneuverability." She wedged her foot under the trident and kicked it up into her hands.

Nezha came at her from the right. "Reach?"

She parried. "When you summon fire, there's no one who's going to get close to you."

He hung back. "Not to state the obvious, but you can't really do that anymore."

She scowled at him. "I'll fix it."

"Suppose you don't?"

"Suppose you stop underestimating me?"

She didn't want to tell him that she'd been trying. That every night she climbed up to this same clearing where no one would see her, took a dose of Chaghan's stupid blue powder, approached the Seal, and tried to burn the ghost of Altan out of her mind.

It never worked. She could never bring herself to hurt him, not that wonderful version of Altan that she'd never known. When she tried to fight him, he grew angry. And then he reminded her why she'd always been terrified of him.

The worst part was that Altan seemed to be getting stronger every time. His eyes burned more vividly in the dark, his laughter rang louder, and several nights he'd nearly choked the breath from her before she got her senses back. It didn't matter that he was only a vision. Her fear made him more present than anything else.

"Look alive." Rin jabbed at Nezha's side, hoping to catch him off guard, but he whipped his blade out and parried just in time.

They sparred for a few more seconds, but she was quickly losing heart. Her trident suddenly seemed twice as heavy in her arms; she felt like she was fighting at a third her normal speed. Her footwork was sloppy, without form or technique, and her swings grew increasingly haphazard and unguarded.

"It's not the worst thing," Nezha said. He batted a wild blow away from his head. "Aren't you glad?"

She stiffened. "Why would I be *glad*?"

"I mean, I just thought . . ." He touched a hand to his temple. "Isn't it at least nice to have your mind back to yourself?"

She slammed the hilt of the trident down into the ground. "You think I'd lost my mind?"

Nezha rapidly backtracked. "No, I mean, I thought—I saw how you were hurting. That looked like torture. I thought you might be a little relieved."

"It's not a relief to be useless," she said.

She twirled the trident over her head, whipped it around to generate momentum. It wasn't a staff—and she should know better than to wield it with staff techniques—but she was angry now, she wasn't thinking, and her muscles settled into familiar but wrong patterns.

It showed. Nezha may as well have been sparring with a toddler. He sent the trident spinning out of her hands in seconds.

"I told you," he said. "No flexibility."

She snatched the trident up off the ground. "Still has longer reach than your sword."

"So what happens if I get in close?" Nezha twisted his blade between the trident's gaps and closed the distance between them. She tried to fend him off, but he was right—he was out of the trident's reach.

He raised a dagger to her chin with his other hand. She kicked savagely at his shin. He buckled to the ground.

"Bitch," he said.

"You deserved it."

"Fuck you." He rocked back and forth on the grass, clutching his leg. "Help me up."

"Let's take a break." She dropped the trident and sat down on the grass beside him. Her lung capacity hadn't returned. She was still tiring too quickly; she couldn't last more than two hours sparring, much less a full day in the field.

Nezha hadn't even broken a sweat. "You're much better with a sword. Please tell me you know that."

"Don't patronize me."

"That thing is useless! It's too heavy for you! But I've seen you with a sword, and—"

"I'll get used to it."

"I just think that you shouldn't make life-or-death choices based on sentimentality."

She glared at him. "What's *that* supposed to mean?"

He ripped a handful of grass from the ground. "Forget it."

"No, say it."

"Fine. You won't trade because it's *his* weapon, isn't it?"

Rin's stomach twisted. "That's idiotic."

"Oh, come on. You're always talking about Altan like he was some great hero. But he wasn't. I saw him at Khurdalain, and I saw the way he spoke to people—"

"And how did he speak to people?" she asked sharply.

"Like they were objects, and he owned them, and they didn't matter to him apart from how they could serve." His tone turned vicious. "Altan was a shitty person and a shittier commander, and he would have let me die, and you *know* that, and here you are, running around with his trident, babbling on about revenge for someone you should hate."

The trident suddenly felt terribly heavy in Rin's hands.

"That's not fair." She heard a faint buzzing in her ears. "He's dead— You can't— That's not fair."

"I know," Nezha said softly. The anger had left him as quickly as it had come. He sounded exhausted. He sat, shoulders slouched, mindlessly shredding blades of grass with his fingers. "I'm sorry. I don't know why I said that. I know how much you cared about him."

"I'm not talking about Altan," she said. "Not with you. Not now. Not ever."

"All right," he said. He gave her a look that she didn't understand, a look that might have been equal parts pity and disappointment, and that made her desperately uncomfortable. "All right."

. . .

Three days later the council finally came to a joint decision. At least, Vaisra and Tsolin came up with a solution short of immediate military action, and then argued the others into submission.

"We're going to starve them out," Vaisra announced. "The south is the agricultural breadbasket of the Empire. If the northern provinces won't secede, then we'll simply stop feeding them."

Takha balked. "You're asking us to reduce our exports by at least a third."

"So you'll bleed income for a year or two," said Vaisra. "And then your prices will jack up in the next year. The north is in no position to become agriculturally self-sufficient now. If you make this one-time sacrifice, that's likely the end of tariffs, too. Beggars have no leverage."

"What about the coastal routes?" Charouk asked.

Rin had to admit that was a fair point. The Western Murui and Golyn River weren't the only rivers that crossed into the northern provinces. Those provinces could easily smuggle food up the coastline by sending merchants down in the guise of southerners to buy up food stores. They had more than enough silver.

"Moag will cover them," said Vaisra.

Charouk looked amazed. "You're trusting the *Pirate Queen*?"

"It's in her best interest," Vaisra said. "For every blockade runner's ship she seizes, her fleet gets seventy percent of the profits. She'd be a fool to double-cross us."

"The north has other grain supplies, though," Gurubai pointed out. "Hare Province has arable land, for instance—"

"No, they don't." Jinzha looked smug. "Last year the Hare Province suffered a blight and ran out of seed grain. We sold them several boxes of high-yielding seed."

"I remember," said Tsolin. "If you were trying to curry favor, it didn't work."

Jinzha grinned nastily. "We weren't. We sold them damaged seeds, which lulled them into consuming their emergency stores.

If we cut off their external supply, a famine should hit in about six months."

For once, the Warlords seemed impressed. Rin saw reluctant nods around the table.

Only Kitay looked unhappy.

"Six months?" he echoed. "I thought we were trying to move out in the next month."

"They won't have felt the blockade by then," said Jinzha.

"It doesn't matter! It's only the threat of the blockade that matters, you don't need them to actually *starve*—"

"Why not?" Jinzha asked.

Kitay looked horrified. "Because then you'd be punishing thousands of innocent people. And because that's not what you told me when you asked me to do the figures—"

"It doesn't matter what you were told," Jinzha said. "Know your place."

Kitay kept talking. "Why starve them slowly? Why wait at all? If we mount an offensive right now, we can end this war before winter sets in. Any later and we'll be trapped up north when the rivers freeze."

General Hu laughed. "The boy presumes to know how to fight a campaign better than we do."

Kitay looked livid. "I actually read Sunzi, so yes."

"You're not the only Sinegard student at the table," said General Hu.

"Sure, but I got in during an era when acceptance actually took brains, so your opinion doesn't count."

"Vaisra!" General Hu shouted. "Discipline this boy!"

"'Discipline this boy,'" Kitay mimicked. "'Shut up the only person who has a halfway viable strategy, because my ego can't take the heat.'"

"Enough," Vaisra said. "You're out of line."

"This plan is out of line," Kitay retorted.

"You're dismissed," Vaisra said. "Stay out of sight until you're sent for."

For a brief, terrifying moment Rin thought Kitay might start mocking Vaisra, too, but he just threw his papers down onto the table, knocking over inkwells, and stalked toward the door.

"Keep throwing fits like that and Father won't have you at his councils anymore," Nezha said.

He and Rin had both followed Kitay out, which Rin thought was a rather dangerous move on Nezha's part, but Kitay was too angry to be grateful for the gesture.

"Keep ignoring me and we won't have a palace to hold councils *in*," Kitay snapped. "A blockade? A fucking *blockade*?"

"It's our best option for now," Nezha said. "We don't have the military capability to sail north alone, but we could just wait them out."

"But that could take years!" Kitay shouted. "And what happens in the meantime? You just let people die?"

"Threats have to be credible to work," Nezha said.

Kitay shot him a disdainful look. "You try dealing with a country with a famine crisis, then. You don't unite a country by starving innocent people to death."

"They're not going to starve—"

"No? They're going to eat wood bark? Leaves? Cow dung? I can think of a million strategies better than murder."

"Try being diplomatic, then," Nezha snapped. "You can't disrespect the old guard."

"Why not? The old guard has no clue what they're doing!" Kitay shouted. "They got their positions because they're good at factional maneuvering! They graduated from Sinegard, sure, but that was when the entire curriculum was just emergency basic training. They don't have a thorough grounding in military science or technology, and they've never bothered to learn, because they know they'll never lose their jobs!"

"I think you're underestimating some rather qualified men," Nezha said drily.

"No, your father is in a double bind," Kitay said. "No, wait, I've got it, here's what it is—the men he can trust aren't competent, but the men who are competent, he must keep on a taut leash, because they might calculate to defect."

"So what, he trusts you instead?"

"I'm the only one who knows what I'm doing."

"And you basically only joined up yesterday, so can you not act so startled that my father trusts you less than men who have served him for decades?"

Kitay stormed off, muttering under his breath. Rin suspected they wouldn't see him emerge from the library for days.

"Asshole," Nezha grumbled once Kitay was out of earshot.

"Don't look at me," Rin said. "I'm on his side."

She didn't care so much about the blockade. If the northern provinces were holding out, then starvation served them right. But she couldn't bear the idea that they were about to kick a hornet's nest—because then their only strategy would be to wait, hide, and hope the hornets didn't sting first.

She couldn't stand the uncertainty. She wanted to be on the attack.

"Innocent people *aren't* going to die," Nezha insisted, though he sounded more like he was trying to convince himself. "They'll surrender before it gets that bad. They'll have to."

"And if they don't?" she asked. "Then we attack?"

"We attack, or they starve," Nezha said. "Win-win."

Arlong's military operations turned inward. The army stopped preparing ships to sail out and focused on building up defense structures to make Arlong completely invulnerable to a Militia invasion.

A defensive war was starting to seem more and more likely. If the Republic didn't launch their northern assault now, then they'd be stuck at home until the next spring. They were more than halfway into autumn, and Rin remembered how vicious the Sinegardian winters were. As the days became colder, it would get harder to boil water and prepare hot food. Disease and frostbite would spread quickly through the camps. The troops would be miserable.

But the south would remain warm, hospitable, and ripe for the picking. The longer they waited, the more likely it was the Militia would sail downriver toward Arlong.

Rin didn't want to fight a defensive battle. Every great treatise on military strategy agreed that defensive battles were a nightmare. And Arlong, impenetrable as it was, would still take a heavy beating from the combined forces of the north. Surely Vaisra knew that, too; he was too competent to believe otherwise. But in meeting after meeting, he chastised Kitay for speaking up, appeased the Warlords, and did nothing close to inciting the alliance to action.

Rin was beginning to think that even independent action by Dragon Province would be better than nothing. But the orders did not come.

"Father's hands are tied," said Nezha, again and again.

Kitay remained holed up in the library, drawing up war plans that would never be used with increasing frustration.

"I knew joining up with you would be treason," he raged at Nezha. "I didn't think it would be *suicide*."

"The Warlords will come around," Nezha said.

"Fat chance. Charouk's a lazy pig who wants to hide behind Republican swords, Takha doesn't have the spine to do anything but hide behind Charouk, and Gurubai might be the smartest of the lot, but he's not sticking his neck out if the other two won't."

There has to be something else, Rin thought. *Something we don't know about.* There was no way Vaisra would just sit back and let winter come without taking the initiative. What was he waiting for?

For lack of better options, she put her blind faith in Vaisra. She sucked it up when her men asked her about the delay. She closed her ears to the rumors that Vaisra was considering a peace agreement with the Empress. She realized she couldn't influence policy, so she poured her focus into the only things she could control.

She sparred more bouts with Nezha. She stopped wielding her trident like a staff. She became familiar with the generals and lieutenants of the Republican Army. She did her best to integrate the Cike into the Dragon Province's military ecosystem, though both Baji and Ramsa rankled at the strict ban on alcohol. She learned the Republican Army's command codes, communications channels, and amphibious attack formations. She prepared herself for war, whenever it came.

Until the day came when gongs sounded frantically across the harbor, and messengers ran up the docks, and all of Arlong was alight with the news that ships were sailing into the Dragon Province. Great white ships from the west.

Then Rin understood what the stalling had been about.

Vaisra hadn't been pulling back from the northern expedition after all.

He'd been waiting for backup.

CHAPTER 13

Rin squeezed through the crowd behind Nezha, who made liberal use of elbows to get them to the front of the harbor. The dock was already thronged with curious civilians and soldiers alike, all angling to get a good look at the Hesperian ship. But no one was looking out at the harbor. All heads were tilted to the sky.

Three whale-sized crafts sailed through the clouds above. Each had a long, rectangular basket strapped to its underbelly, with cerulean flags sewn along the sides. Rin blinked several times as she stared.

How could structures so massive possibly stay aloft?

They looked absurd and utterly unnatural, as if some god were moving them through the sky at will. But it couldn't be the work of the gods. The Hesperians didn't believe in the Pantheon.

Was this the work of their Maker? The possibility made Rin shiver. She'd always been taught that the Hesperians' Holy Maker was a construct, a fiction to control an anxious population. The singular, anthropomorphized, all-powerful deity that the Hesperians believed in could not possibly explain the complexity of the universe. But if the Maker was real, then everything she knew about the sixty-four deities, about the Pantheon, was wrong.

What *if* her gods weren't the only ones in the universe? What if a higher power did exist—one that only the Hesperians had access to? Was that why they were so infinitely more advanced?

The sky filled with a sound like the drone of a million bees, amplified a hundred times over as the flying crafts drew closer.

Rin saw people standing at the edges of the hanging baskets. They looked like little toys from the ground. The flying whales began approaching the harbor to land, looming larger and larger in the sky until their shadows enveloped everyone who stood below. The people inside the baskets waved their arms over their heads. Their mouths opened wide—they were shouting something, but no one could hear them over the noise.

Nezha dragged Rin backward by the wrist.

"Back away," he shouted into her ear.

There followed a brief period of chaos while the city guard wrangled the crowd back from the landing area. One by one the flying crafts thudded to the ground. The entire harbor shook from the impact.

At last, the droning noise died away. The metal whales shriveled and slumped to the side as they deflated over the baskets. The air was silent.

Rin watched, waiting.

"Don't let your eyes pop out of your head," said Nezha. "They're just foreigners."

"Just foreigners to you. Exotic creatures to me."

"They didn't have missionaries down in Rooster Province?"

"Only on the coastlines." Hesperian missionaries had been banned from the Empire after the Second Poppy War. Several dared to continue visiting cities peripheral to Sinegard's control, but most kept their distance from rural places like Tikany. "All I've ever heard are stories."

"Like what?"

"The Hesperians are giants. They're covered in red fur. They boil infants and eat them in soup."

"You know that never happened, right?"

"They're pretty convinced of it where I come from."

Nezha chuckled. "Let's let bygones be bygones. They're coming now as friends."

The Empire had a troubled history with the Republic of Hesperia. During the First Poppy War, the Hesperians had offered military and economic aid to the Federation of Mugen. Once the Mugenese had obliterated any notion of Nikara sovereignty, the Hesperians had populated the coastal regions with missionaries and religious schools, intent on wiping out the local superstitious religions.

For a short time, the Hesperian missionaries had even outlawed temple visits. If any shamanic cults still existed after the Red Emperor's war on religion, the Hesperians drove them even further underground.

During the Second Poppy War, the Hesperians became the liberators. The Federation had committed too many atrocities for the Hesperians, who had always claimed that their occupation benefited the natives, to pretend neutrality was morally defensible. After Speer burned, the Hesperians sent their fleets to the Nariin Sea, joined forces with the Trifecta's troops, pushed the Federation all the way back to their longbow island, and orchestrated a peace agreement with the newly reformed Nikara Empire in Sinegard.

Then the Trifecta seized dictatorial control of the country and threw the foreigners out by the ship. Whatever Hesperians remained were smugglers and missionaries, hiding in international ports like Ankhiluun and Khurdalain, preaching their word to anyone who bothered to entertain them.

When the Third Poppy War began, those last Hesperians had sailed away on rescue ships so fast that by the time Rin's contingent had reached Khurdalain they might never have been there. As the war progressed, the Hesperians had been willful bystanders, watching aloof from across the great sea while Nikara citizens burned in their homes.

"They might have come a little earlier," Rin quipped.

"There's been a war ravishing the entire western continent for the past two decades," said Nezha. "They've been a bit distracted."

This was news to her. Until now, news of the western continent had been so utterly irrelevant to her it might not have existed. "Did they win?"

"You could say that. Millions are dead. Millions more are without home or country. But the Consortium states came out in power, so they consider that a victory. Although I don't—"

Rin grabbed his arm. "They're coming out."

Doors had opened at the sides of each basket. One by one the Hesperians filed out onto the dock.

Rin recoiled at the sight of them.

Their skin was terribly pale—not the flawless porcelain-white shade that Sinegardians prized, but more like the tint of a freshly gutted fish. And their hair looked all the wrong colors—garish shades of copper, gold, and bronze, nothing like the rich black of Nikara hair. Everything about them—their coloring, their features, their proportions—simply seemed *off*.

They didn't look like people; they looked like things out of horror stories. They might have been demon-possessed monsters conjured up for Nikara folk heroes to fight. And though Rin was too old for folktales, everything about these light-eyed creatures made her want to run.

"How's your Hesperian?" Nezha asked.

"Rusty," she admitted. "I hate that language."

They had all been forced to study several years of diplomatic Hesperian at Sinegard. Rules of pronunciation were haphazard at best and its grammar system was so riddled with exceptions it might not exist at all.

None of Rin's classmates had paid much attention to their Hesperian grammar lessons. They had all assumed that as the Federation was the primary threat, Mugini was more important to learn.

Rin supposed things would be very different now.

A column of Hesperian sailors, identical in their close-cropped hair and dark gray uniforms, walked out of the baskets and formed two neat lines in front of the crowd. Rin counted twenty of them.

She examined their faces but couldn't tell one apart from

the next. They all seemed to have the same lightly colored eyes, broad noses, and strong jaws. They were all men, and each held a strange-looking weapon across his chest. Rin couldn't determine the weapon's purpose. It looked like a series of tubes of different lengths, joined together near the back with something like a handle.

A final soldier emerged from the basket door. Rin assumed he was their general by his uniform, which bore multicolored ribbons on the left chest where the others' were bare. He struck Rin immediately as dangerous. He stood at least half a head taller than Vaisra, he sported a chest as wide as Baji's, and his weathered face was lined and intelligent.

Behind the general walked a row of hooded Hesperians clothed in gray cassocks.

"Who are they?" Rin asked Nezha. They couldn't be soldiers; they wore no armor and held no weapons.

"The Gray Company," he said. "Representatives of the Church of the Divine Architect."

"They're missionaries?"

"Missionaries who can speak for the central church. They're highly trained and educated. Think of them like graduates from the Sinegard Academy of religion."

"What, they went to priest school?"

"Sort of. They're scientists, too. In their religion, the scientists and priests are one and the same."

Rin was about to ask what that meant when a last figure emerged from the center basket. She was a woman, slender and petite, wearing a buttoned black coat with a high collar that covered her neck. She looked severe, alien, and elegant all at once. Her attire was certainly not Nikara, but her face was not Hesperian. She seemed oddly familiar.

"*Hello.*" Baji whistled behind Rin. "Who is that?"

"It's Lady Yin Saikhara," said Nezha.

"Is she married?" Baji asked.

Nezha shot him a disgusted look. "That's my *mother.*"

That was why Rin recognized the woman's face. She had met the Lady of Dragon Province once, years ago, on her first day at Sinegard. Lady Saikhara had taken Rin's guardian Tutor Feyrik for a porter, and she had dismissed Rin entirely as southerner trash.

Perhaps the past four years had done wonders for Lady Saikhara's attitude, but Rin was strongly inclined to dislike her.

Lady Saikhara paused before the crowd, eyes roving the harbor as if surveying her kingdom. Her gaze landed on Rin. Her eyes narrowed—in recognition, Rin thought; perhaps Saikhara remembered Rin as well—but then she grasped the Hesperian general's arm and pointed, her face contorted into what looked like fear.

The general nodded and spoke an order. At once, all twenty Hesperian soldiers pointed their barrel tube weapons at Rin.

A hush fell over the crowd as the civilians hastily backed away.

Several cracks split the air. Rin dove to the ground by instinct. Eight holes dotted the dirt in front of her. She looked up.

The air smelled like smoke. Gray flumes unfurled from the tips of the barrel tubes.

"Oh, fuck," Nezha muttered under his breath.

The general shouted something that Rin couldn't understand, but she didn't have to translate what he'd said. There was no way to interpret this as anything but a threat.

She had two default responses to threats. And she couldn't run away, not in this crowd, so her only choice was to fight.

Two of the Hesperian soldiers came running toward her. She slammed her trident against the closest one's shins. He doubled over, just briefly. She jammed an elbow into the side of his head, grabbed him by the shoulders, and barreled forward, using him as a human shield to deter further fire.

It worked until something landed over Rin's shoulders. A fishing net. She flailed, trying to wriggle out, but it only tightened around her arms. Whoever held it yanked hard, knocking her off balance.

The Hesperian general loomed above her, his weapon pointed straight down at her face. Rin looked up the barrel. The smell of fire powder was so thick she nearly choked on it.

"Vaisra!" she shouted. "Help—"

Soldiers swarmed around her. Strong arms pinned her arms over her head; others grabbed her ankles, rendering her immobile. She heard the clank of steel next to her head. She twisted around and saw a wooden tray on the ground beside her, upon which lay a vast assortment of thin devices that looked like torture instruments.

She'd seen devices like that before.

Someone pulled her head back and jerked her mouth open. One of the Gray Company, a woman with skin like alabaster, knelt over her. She pressed something hard and metallic against Rin's tongue.

Rin bit at her fingers.

The woman snatched her hand away.

Rin struggled harder. Miraculously, the grips on her shoulders loosened. She flailed out and upturned the tray, scattering the instruments across the ground. For a single, desperate moment, she thought she might break free.

Then the general slammed the butt of his weapon into her head and Rin's vision exploded into stars that winked out into nothing.

"Oh, good," said Nezha. "You're awake."

Rin found herself lying on a stone floor. She scrambled to her feet. She was unbound. Good. Her hand jumped for a weapon that wasn't there, and when she couldn't find her trident she curled her hands into fists. "What—"

"That was a misunderstanding." Nezha grabbed her by the shoulders. "You're safe, we're alone. What happened out there was a mistake."

"A *mistake*?"

"They thought you were a threat. My mother told them to attack as soon as they reached land."

Rin's forehead throbbed. She touched her fingers to where she knew a massive bruise was forming. "Your mother is a real bitch, then."

"She often is, yes. But you're in no danger. Father is talking them down."

"And if he can't?"

"He will. They're not idiots." Nezha grabbed her hand. "Will you stop that?"

Rin had begun pacing back and forth in the small chamber like a caged animal, teeth chattering, rubbing her hands agitatedly up and down her arms. But she couldn't stand still; her mind was racing in panic, if she stopped moving she would start to shake uncontrollably.

"Why would they think I was a threat?" she demanded.

"It's, ah, a little complicated." Nezha paused. "I guess the simplest way to put it is that they want to study you."

"*Study?*"

"They know what you did to the longbow island. They know what you *can* do, and as the most powerful country on earth of course they're going to investigate it. Their proposed treaty terms, I think, were that they'd get to examine you in exchange for military aid. Mother put it in their heads that you weren't going to come quietly."

"So what, Vaisra's selling me for their aid?"

"It's not like that. My mother . . ." Nezha continued talking, but Rin wasn't listening. She scrutinized him, considering.

She had to get out of here. She had to rally the Cike and get them out of Arlong. Nezha was taller, heavier, and stronger than she was, but she could still take him—she'd go after his eyes and scars, gouge her fingernails into his skin and knee his balls repeatedly until he dropped his guard.

But she might still be trapped. The doors could be locked from the outside. And if she broke the door down, there could be—no, there certainly were guards outside. What about the window? She could tell from a glance they were on the second, maybe third story, but maybe she could scale down somehow, if she could manage to knock Nezha unconscious. She just needed a weapon—the chair legs might do, or a shard of porcelain.

She lunged for the flower vase.

"Don't." Nezha's hand shot out and gripped her wrist. She struggled to break free. He twisted her arm painfully behind her back, forced her to her knees, and pressed a knee against the small of her back. "Come on, Rin. Don't be stupid."

"Don't do this," she gasped. "Nezha, please, I can't stay here—"

"You're not allowed to leave the room."

"So now I'm a prisoner?"

"Rin, please—"

"Let me go!"

She tried to break free. His grip tightened. "You're not in any danger."

"So *let me go*!"

"You'll derail negotiations that have been years in the making—"

"Negotiations?" she screeched. "You think I give a fuck about negotiations? They want to dissect me!"

"And Father won't let that happen! You think he's about to give you up? You think *I'd* let that happen? I'd die before I let anyone hurt you, Rin, calm down—"

That did nothing to calm her down. Every second she was still felt like a vise tightening around her neck.

"My family has been planning this war for over a decade," Nezha said. "My mother has been pursuing this diplomatic mission for years. She was educated in Hesperia; she has strong ties to the west. As soon as the third war was over, Father sent her overseas to solidify Hesperian military support."

Rin barked out a laugh. "Well, then she cut a shitty deal."

"We won't take it. The Hesperians are greedy and malleable. They want resources only the Empire can offer. Father can talk them down. But we must not anger them. We *need* their weapons." Nezha let go of her arms when it was clear she'd stopped struggling. "You've been in the councils. We won't win this war without them."

Rin twisted around to face him. "You want whatever those barrel things are."

"They're called arquebuses. They're like hand cannons, except they're lighter than crossbows, they can penetrate wooden panels, and they shoot for longer distance."

"Oh, I'm sure Vaisra just wants crates and crates of them."

He gave her a frank look. "We need anything we can get our hands on."

"But suppose you win this war, and the Hesperians don't want to leave," she said. "Suppose it's the First Poppy War all over again."

"They have no interest in staying," he said dismissively. "They're done with that now. They've found their colonies too difficult to defend, and the war's weakened them too much to commit the kind of ground resources they could before. All they want is trade rights and permission to dump missionaries wherever they want. At the end of this war we'll make them leave our shores quickly enough."

"And if they don't want to go?"

"I expect we'll find a way," Nezha said. "Just as we have before. But at present, Father's going to choose the lesser of two evils. And so should you."

The doors opened. Captain Eriden walked inside.

"They're ready for you," he said.

"'They'?" Rin echoed.

"The Dragon Warlord is entertaining the Hesperian delegates in the great hall. They'd like to speak to you."

"No," Rin said.

"You'll be fine," Nezha said. "Just don't do anything stupid."

"We have very different ideas of what defines 'stupid,'" she said.

"The Dragon Warlord would prefer not to be kept waiting." Eriden motioned with a hand. Two of his guards strode forward and seized Rin by the arms. She managed a last, panicked glance over her shoulder at Nezha before they escorted her out the door.

The guards deposited Rin in the short walkway that led to the palace's great hall and shut the doors behind her.

She stepped hesitantly forward. She saw the Hesperians sitting in gilded chairs around the center table. Jinzha sat at his father's right hand. The southern Warlords had been relegated to the far end of the table, looking flustered and uncomfortable.

Rin could tell she'd walked into the middle of a heated argument. A thick tension crackled in the air, and all parties looked flustered, red-faced, and furious, as if they were about to come to blows.

She hung back in the hallway for a moment, concealed by the corner wall, and listened.

"The Consortium is still recovering from its own war," the Hesperian general was saying. Rin struggled to make sense of his speech at first, but gradually the language returned to her. She felt like a student again, sitting in the back of Jima's classroom, memorizing verb tenses. "We're in no mood to speculate."

"This isn't speculation," Vaisra said urgently. He spoke Hesperian like it was his native tongue. "We could take back this country in days, if you just—"

"Then do it yourselves," the general said. "We're here to do business, not alchemy. We are not interested in transforming frauds into kings."

Vaisra sat back. "So you're going to run my country like an experiment before you choose to intervene."

"A necessary experiment. We didn't come here to lend ships at your will, Vaisra. This is an investigation."

"Into what?"

"Whether the Nikara are ready for civilization. We do not distribute Hesperian aid lightly. We made that mistake before. The Mugenese seemed even more ready for advancement than you are. They had no factional infighting, and their governance was more sophisticated by far. Look how that turned out."

"If we're underdeveloped, it's because of years of foreign occupation," Vaisra said. "That's your fault, not ours."

The general shrugged, indifferent. "Even so."

Vaisra sounded exasperated. "Then what are you looking for?"

"Well, it would be cheating if we told you, wouldn't it?" The Hesperian general gave a thin smile. "But all of this is a moot point. Our primary objective here is the Speerly. She has purportedly leveled an entire country. We'd like to know how she did it."

"You can't have the Speerly," Vaisra said.

"Oh, I don't think you get to decide."

Rin strode into the room. "I'm right here."

"Runin." If Vaisra looked surprised, he quickly recovered. He stood up and gestured to the Hesperian general. "Please meet General Josephus Tarcquet."

Stupid name, Rin thought. A garbled collection of syllables that she could hardly pronounce.

Tarcquet rose to his feet. "I believe we owe you an apology. Lady Saikhara had us rather convinced that we were dealing with something like a wild animal. We didn't realize that you would be so . . . human."

Rin blinked at him. Was that really supposed to be an apology?

"Does she understand what I'm saying?" Tarcquet asked Vaisra in choppy, ugly Nikara.

"I understand Hesperian," Rin snapped. She deeply wished that she'd learned Hesperian curse words at Sinegard. She didn't have the full vocabulary range to express what she wanted to say, but she had enough. "I'm just not keen on dialoguing with fools who want me dead."

"Why are we even speaking to her?" Lady Saikhara burst out.

Her voice was high and brittle, as if she had just been crying. The pure venom in her glare startled Rin. This was more than contempt. This was a vicious, murderous hatred.

"She is an unholy abomination," Saikhara snarled. "She is a mark against the Maker, and she ought to be dragged off to the Gray Towers as soon as possible."

"We're not dragging anyone off." Vaisra sounded exasperated. "Runin, please, sit—"

"But you *promised*," Saikhara hissed at him. "You said they'd find a way to fix him—"

Vaisra grabbed at his wife's wrist. "Now is not the time."

Saikhara jerked her hand free and slammed a fist down on the table. Her cup toppled over, spilling hot tea across the embroidered cloth. "You swore to me. You said you'd make this right, that if I brought them back they'd find a way to fix him, you *promised*—"

"Silence, woman." Vaisra pointed to the door. "If you cannot calm yourself, then you will leave."

Saikhara shot Rin a tight-lipped look of fury, muttered something under her breath, and stormed out of the room.

A long silence hung over her absence. Tarcquet looked somewhat amused. Vaisra leaned back in his chair, took a draught of tea, then sighed. "You'll have to excuse my wife. She tends to be ill-tempered after travel."

"She's desperate for answers." A woman in a gray cassock, the one who had stood over Rin at the dock, laid her hand on Vaisra's. "We understand. We'd like to find a cure, too."

Rin shot her a curious look. The woman's Nikara sounded remarkably good—she could have been a native speaker if her tones weren't so oddly flat. Her hair was the color of wheat, straight and slick, braided into a serpent-like coil that rested just over her shoulder. Gray eyes like castle walls. Pale skin like paper, so thin that blue veins were visible beneath. Rin had the oddest urge to touch it, just to see if it felt human.

"She's a fascinating creature," said the woman. "It is rare you meet someone possessed by Chaos who yet remains so lucid. None of our Hesperian madmen have been so good at fooling their observers."

"I'm standing right in front of you," Rin said.

"I'd like to get her in an isolation chamber," the woman continued, as if Rin hadn't spoken. "We're close to developing instruments that can detect raw Chaos in sterile environments. If we could bring her back to the Gray Towers—"

"I'm not going anywhere with you," Rin said.

General Tarcquet stroked the arquebus that lay in front of him. "You wouldn't really have a choice, dear."

The woman lifted a hand. "Wait, Josephus. The Divine Architect values free thought. Voluntary cooperation is a sign that reason and order yet prevail in the mind. Will the girl come willingly?"

Rin stared at the two of them in disbelief. Did Vaisra possibly believe that she would say yes?

"You could even keep her on campaign for the time being," the woman said to Vaisra, as if they were discussing something no more pressing than dinner arrangements. "I would only require regular meetings, perhaps once a week. They would be minimally invasive."

"Define 'minimally,'" Vaisra said.

"I would only observe her, for the most part. I'd perhaps conduct a few experiments. Nothing that will affect her permanently, and certainly nothing that would affect her fighting ability. I'd just like to see how she reacts to various stimuli—"

A ringing noise grew louder and louder in Rin's ears. Everyone's voices became both slurred and magnified. The conversation proceeded, but she could decipher only fragments.

"—fascinating creature—"

"—prized soldier—"

"—tip the balance—"

She found herself swaying on her feet.

She saw in her mind's eye a face she hadn't let herself imagine for a long time. Dark, clever eyes. Narrow nose. Thin lips and a cruel, excited smile.

She saw Dr. Shiro.

She felt his hands moving over her, checking her restraints, making sure she couldn't move an inch from the bed he'd strapped her down on. She felt his fingers feeling around in her mouth, counting her teeth, moving down past her jaw to her neck to locate her artery.

She felt his hands holding her down as he pushed a needle into her vein.

She felt panic, fear, and rage all at once and she wanted to burn but she *couldn't*, and the heat and fire just bubbled up in her chest and built up inside her because the fucking Seal had gotten in the way, but the heat just kept building and Rin thought she might implode—

"Runin." Vaisra's voice cut through the fog.

She focused with difficulty on his face. "No," she whispered. "No, I can't—"

He got up from his seat. "This isn't the same as the Mugenese lab."

She backed away from him. "I don't care, I can't do this—"

"What are you debating?" demanded the Boar Warlord. "Hand her to them and be done with it."

"Quiet, Charouk." Vaisra drew Rin hastily into the corner of the room, far from where the Hesperians could hear. He lowered his voice. "They will force you either way. If you cooperate you will garner us sympathy."

"You're trading me for ships," she said.

"No one is trading you," he said. "I am asking you for a favor. Please, will you do this for me? You're in no danger. You're no monster, and they'll discover that soon enough."

And then she understood. The Hesperians wouldn't find anything. They *couldn't*, because Rin couldn't call the fire anymore. They could run all the experiments they liked, but they wouldn't find anything. Daji had ensured that there was nothing left to find.

"Runin, please," Vaisra murmured. "We don't have a choice."

He was right about that. The Hesperians had made it clear that they would study her by force if necessary. She could try to fight, but she wouldn't get very far.

Part of her wanted desperately to say no. To say fuck it, to take her chances and try her best to escape and run. Of course, they'd hunt her down, but she had the smallest chance of making it out alive.

But hers wasn't the only life at stake.

The fate of the Empire hung in the balance. If she truly wanted the Empress dead, then Hesperian airships and arquebuses were the best way to get it done. The only way she could generate their goodwill was if she went willingly into their arms.

When you hear screaming, Vaisra had told her, *run toward it.*

She'd failed at Lusan. She couldn't call the fire anymore. This might be the only way to atone for the colossal wrongs she'd committed. Her only chance to put things right.

Altan had died for liberation. She knew what he would say to her now.

Stop being so fucking selfish.

Rin steeled herself, took a breath, and nodded. "I'll do it."

"Thank you." Relief washed over Vaisra's face. He turned to the table. "She agrees."

"One hour," Rin said in her best Hesperian. "Once a week. No more. I'm free to go if I feel uncomfortable, and you don't touch me without my express permission."

General Tarcquet removed his hand from his arquebus. "Fair enough."

The Hesperians looked far too pleased. Rin's stomach twisted.

Oh, gods. What had she agreed to?

"Excellent." The gray-eyed woman rose from her chair. "Come with me. We'll begin now."

The Hesperians had already occupied the entire block of buildings just west of the palace, furnished residences that Rin suspected Vaisra must have prepared long ago. Blue flags bearing an insignia that looked like the gears of a clock hung from the windows. The gray-eyed woman motioned for Rin to follow her into a small, windowless square room on the first floor of the center building.

"What do you call yourself?" asked the woman. "Fang Runin, they said?"

"Just Rin," Rin muttered, glancing around the room. It was bare except for two long, narrow stone tables that had recently been dragged there, judging from the skid marks on the stone floor. One table was empty. The other was covered with an array of instruments, some made of steel and some of wood, few of which Rin recognized or could guess the function of.

The Hesperians had been preparing this room since they got here.

A Hesperian soldier stood in the corner, arquebus slung over his shoulder. His eyes tracked Rin every time she moved. She made a face at him. He didn't react.

"You may call me Sister Petra," said the woman. "Why don't you come over here?"

She spoke truly excellent Nikara. Rin would have been impressed, but something felt off. Petra's sentences were perfectly smooth and fluent, perhaps more grammatically perfect than those of most native speakers, but her words came out sounding all wrong. The tones were just the slightest bit off, and she inflected everything with the same flat clip that made her sound utterly inhuman.

Petra picked a cup off the edge of the table and offered it to her. "Laudanum?"

Rin recoiled, surprised. "For what?"

"It might calm you down. I've been told you react badly to lab environments." Petra pursed her lips. "I know opiates dampen the phenomena you manifest, but for a first observation that won't matter. Today I'm interested only in baseline measurements."

Rin eyed the cup, considering. The last thing she wanted was to be off her guard for a full hour with the Hesperians. But she knew she had no choice but to comply with whatever Petra asked of her. She could reasonably expect that they wouldn't kill her. She had no control over the rest. The only thing she could control was her own discomfort.

She took the cup and emptied it.

"Excellent." Petra gestured to the bed. "Up there, please.

Rin took a deep breath and sat down at the edge.

One hour. That was it. All she had to do was survive the next sixty minutes.

Petra began by taking an endless series of measurements. With a notched string she recorded Rin's height, wingspan, and the length of her feet. She measured the circumference around Rin's waist, wrists, ankles, and thighs. Then with a smaller string she took a series of smaller measurements that seemed utterly pointless. The width of Rin's eyes. Their distance from her nose. The length of each one of her fingernails.

This went on forever. Rin managed not to flinch too hard from Petra's touch. The laudanum was working well; a lead weight had settled comfortably in her bloodstream and kept her numb, torpid, and docile.

Petra wrapped the string around the base of Rin's thumb. "Tell me about the first time you communed with, ah, this entity you claim to be your god. How would you describe the experience?"

Rin said nothing. She had to present her body for examination. That didn't mean she had to entertain small talk.

Petra repeated her question. Again Rin kept silent.

"You should know," Petra said as she put the tape measure away, "that verbal cooperation is a condition of our agreement."

Rin gave her a wary look. "What do you want from me?"

"Only your honest responses. I am not solely interested in the stock of your body. I'm curious about the possibilities for the redemption of your soul."

If Rin's mind had been working any faster she would have managed some clever retort. Instead she rolled her eyes.

"You seem confident our religion is false," Petra said.

"I know it's false." The laudanum had loosened Rin's tongue, and she found herself spilling the first thoughts that came to her mind. "I've seen evidence of my gods."

"Have you?"

"Yes, and I know that the universe is not the doing of a single man."

"A single man? Is that what you think we believe?" Petra tilted her head. "What do you know about our theology?"

"That it's stupid," Rin said, which was the extent of what she'd ever been taught.

They'd studied Hesperian religion—Makerism, they called it—briefly at Sinegard, back when none of them thought the Hesperians would return to the Empire's shores during their lifetime. None of them had taken their studies of Hesperian culture seriously, not even the instructors. Makerism was only ever a footnote. A joke. Those foolish westerners.

Rin remembered idyllic walks down the mountainside with Jiang during the first year of her apprenticeship, when he'd made her research differences between eastern and western religions and hypothesize the reasons they existed. She remembered sinking hours into this question at the library. She'd discovered that the vast and varied religions of the Empire tended to be polytheistic, disordered, and irregular, lacking consistency even across villages. But the Hesperians liked to invest their worship in a single entity, typically represented as a man.

"Why do you think that is?" Rin had asked Jiang.

"Hubris," he'd said. "They already like to think they are lords of the world. They'd like to think something in their own image created the universe."

The question that Rin had never entertained, of course, was how the Hesperians had become so vastly technologically advanced if their approach to religion was so laughably wrong. Until now, it had never been relevant.

Petra plucked a round metal device about the size of her palm off the table and held it in front of Rin. She clicked a button at the side, and its lid popped off. "Do you know what this is?"

It was a clock of some sort. She recognized Hesperian numbers, twelve in a circle, with two needles moving slowly in rotation. But Nikara clocks, powered by dripping water, were installations that took up entire corners of rooms. This thing was so small it could have fit in her pocket.

"Is it a timepiece?"

"Very good," Petra said. "Appreciate this design. See the intricate gears, perfectly shaped to form, that keep it ticking on its own. Now imagine that you found this on the ground. You don't know what it is. You don't know who put it there. What is your conclusion? Does it have a designer, or is it an accident of nature, like a rock?"

Rin's mind moved sluggishly around Petra's questions, but she knew the conclusion Petra wanted her to reach.

"There exists a creator," she said after a pause.

"Very good," Petra said again. "Now imagine the world as a clock. Consider the sea, the clouds, the skies, the stars, all working in perfect harmony to keep our world turning and breathing as it does. Think of the life cycles of forests and the animals that live in them. This is no accident. This could not have been forged through primordial chaos, as your theology tends to argue. This was deliberate creation by a greater entity, perfectly benevolent and rational.

"We call him our Divine Architect, or the Maker, as you know him. He seeks to create order and beauty. This isn't mad reasoning. It is the simplest possible explanation for the beauty and intricacy of the natural world."

Rin sat quietly, running those thoughts through her tired mind.

It did sound terribly attractive. She liked the thought that the natural world was fundamentally knowable and reducible to a set of objective principles imposed by a benevolent and rational deity. That was much neater and cleaner than what she knew of the sixty-four gods—chaotic creatures dreaming up an endless whirlpool of forces that created the subjective universe, where everything was constantly in flux and nothing was ever written. Easier to think that the natural world was a neat, objective, and static gift wrapped and delivered by an all-powerful architect.

There was only one gaping oversight.

"So why do things go badly?" Rin asked. "If this Maker set everything in motion, then—"

"Then why couldn't the Maker prevent death?" Petra supplied. "Why do things go wrong if they were designed according to plan?"

"Yes. How did you know?"

Petra gave her a small smile. "Don't look so surprised. That is the most common question of every new convert. Your answer is Chaos."

"Chaos," Rin repeated slowly. She'd heard Petra use this word at the council earlier. It was a Hesperian term; it had no Nikara equivalent. Despite herself, she asked, "What is Chaos?"

"It is the root of evil," Petra said. "Our Divine Architect is not omnipotent. He is powerful, yes, but he leads a constant struggle to fashion order out of a universe tending inevitably toward a state of dissolution and disorder. We call that force Chaos. Chaos is the antithesis of order, the cruel force trying constantly to undo the Architect's creations. Chaos is old age, disease, death, and war. Chaos manifests in the worst of mankind—evil, jealousy, greed, and treachery. It is our task to keep it at bay."

Petra closed the timepiece and placed it back on the table. Her fingers hovered over the instruments, deliberating, and then selected a device with what looked like two earpieces and a flat circle attached to a metal cord.

"We don't know how or when Chaos manifests," she said. "But it tends to pop up more often in places like yours—undeveloped, uncivilized, and barbaric. And cases like yours are the worst outbreaks of individual Chaos that the Company has ever seen."

"You mean shamanism," Rin said.

Petra turned back to face her. "You understand why the Gray Company must investigate. Creatures like you pose a terrible threat to earthly order."

She raised the flat circle up under Rin's shirt to her chest. It was icy cold. Rin couldn't help but flinch.

"Don't be scared," Petra said. "Don't you realize I'm trying to help you?"

"I don't understand," Rin murmured, "why you would even keep me alive."

"Fair question. Some think it would be easier simply to kill you. But then we would come no closer to understanding Chaos's evil. And it would only find another avatar to wreak its destruction. So against the Gray Company's better judgment, I am keeping you alive so that at last we may learn to fix it."

"Fix it," Rin repeated. "You think you can fix me."

"I *know* I can fix you."

There was a fanatic intensity to Petra's expression that made Rin deeply uncomfortable. Her gray eyes gleamed a metallic silver when she spoke. "I'm the smartest scholar of the Gray Company in generations. I've been lobbying to come study the Nikara for decades. I'm going to figure out what is plaguing your country."

She pressed the metal disc hard between Rin's breasts. "And then I'm going to drive it out of you."

At last the hour was over. Petra put her instruments back on the table and dismissed Rin from the examination room.

The last of the laudanum wore off just as Rin returned to the barracks. Every feeling that the drug had kept at bay—discomfort, anxiety, disgust, and utter terror—came flooding back to her all at once, a sickening rush so abrupt that it wrenched her to her knees.

She tried to get to the lavatory. She didn't make it two steps before she lurched over and vomited.

She couldn't help it. She hunched over the puddle of her sick and sobbed.

Petra's touch, which had seemed so light, so noninvasive under the effect of laudanum, now felt like a dark stain, like insects burrowing their way under Rin's skin no matter how hard she tried to claw them out. Her memories mixed together; confusing, indistinguishable. Petra's hands became Shiro's hands. Petra's room became Shiro's laboratory.

Worst of all was the violation, the *fucking* violation, and the sheer helplessness of knowing that her body was not hers and she had to sit still and take it, this time not because of any restraints, but due to the simple fact that she'd chosen to be there.

That was the only thing that kept her from packing her belongings and immediately leaving Arlong.

She needed to do this because she deserved this. This was, in some horrible way that made complete sense, atonement. She knew she was monstrous. She couldn't keep denying that. This was self-flagellation for what she'd become.

It should have been you, Altan had said.

She should have been the one who died.

This came close.

After she had cried so hard that the pain in her chest had faded to a dull ebb, she pulled herself to her feet and wiped the tears and mucus off her face. She stood in front of a mirror in the lavatory and waited to come out until the redness had faded from her eyes.

When the others asked her what had happened, she said nothing at all.

CHAPTER 14

War came in the water.

Rin awoke to shouting outside the barracks. She threw her uniform on in a panicked frenzy; blindly attempted to force her right foot into her left shoe before she gave up and ran out the door barefoot, trident in hand.

Outside, half-dressed soldiers ran around and into one another in a confused swarm of activity while commanders shouted contradicting orders. But nobody had weapons drawn, projectiles weren't flying through the air, and Rin couldn't hear the sound of cannon fire.

Finally she noticed that most of the troops were running toward the beachfront. She followed them.

At first she didn't understand what she was looking at. The water was dusted over with spots of white, as if a giant had blown dandelion puffs over the surface. Then she reached the edge of the pier and saw in closer detail the silver crescents hanging just beneath the surface. Those spots of white were the bloated underbellies of fish.

Not just fish. When she knelt by the water she saw puffy, discolored corpses of frogs, salamanders, and turtles. Something had killed every living thing in the water.

It had to be poison. Nothing else could kill so many animals so quickly. And that meant the poison had to be in the water—and all the canals in Arlong were interconnected—which meant that perhaps every drinking source in Arlong was now tainted . . .

But why would anyone from Dragon Province poison the water? For a minute Rin stood there stupidly, thinking, *assuming* that it must have been someone from within the province itself. She didn't want to consider the alternative, which was that the poison came from upriver, because that would mean . . .

"Rin! Fuck—*Rin!*"

Ramsa tugged at her arm. "You need to see this."

She ran with him to the end of the pier, where the Cike were huddled around a dark mass on the planks. A massive fish? A bundle of clothes? No—a man, she saw that now, but the figure was hardly human.

It stretched a pale, skeletal hand toward her. "Altan . . ."

Her breath caught in her throat. *"Aratsha?"*

She had never before seen him in his human form. He was an emaciated man, covered from head to toe in barnacles embedded in blue-white skin. The lower half of his face was concealed by a scraggly beard so littered with sea worms and small fish that it was difficult to parse out the human bits of him.

She tried to slide her arms beneath him to help him up, but pieces of him kept coming away in her hands. A clump of shells, a stick of bone, and then something crackly and powdery that crumbled to nothing in her fingers. She tried not to push him away in disgust. "Can you speak?"

Aratsha made a strangled noise. At first she thought he was choking on his own spit, but then frothy liquid the color of curdled milk bubbled out the sides of his mouth.

"Altan," he repeated.

"I'm not Altan." She reached for Aratsha's hand. Was that something she should do? It felt like something she should do. Something comforting and kind. Something a commander would do.

But Aratsha didn't seem to even notice. His skin had gone from bluish white to a horrible violet color in seconds. She could see his veins pulsing beneath, a sludgy, inky black.

"Ahh, Altan," said Aratsha. "I should have told you."

He smelled of seawater and rot. Rin wanted to vomit.

"What?" she whispered.

He peered up at her through milky eyes. They were filmy like the eyes of a fish at market, oddly unfocused, staring out at two sides like he'd spent so long in the water that he didn't know what to make of the things on land.

He murmured something under his breath, something too quiet and garbled for her to decipher. She thought she heard a whisper that sounded like "misery." Then Aratsha disintegrated in her hands, flesh bubbling into water, until all that was left was sand, shells, and a pearl necklace.

"Fuck," Ramsa said. "That's gross."

"Shut up," Baji said.

Suni wailed loudly and buried his head in his hands. No one comforted him.

Rin stared numbly at the necklace.

We should bury him, she thought. That was proper, wasn't it?

Should she be grieving? She couldn't feel grief. She kept waiting to feel something, but it never hit, and it never would. This was not an acute loss, not the kind that had left her catatonic after Altan's death. She had barely known Aratsha; she'd just given him orders and he had obeyed, without question, loyal to the Cike until the day he died.

No, what sickened her was that she felt *disappointed*, irritated that now that Aratsha was gone they didn't have a shaman who could control the river. All he'd ever been to her was an immensely useful chess piece, and now she couldn't use him anymore.

"What's going on?" Nezha asked, panting. He'd just arrived.

Rin stood up and brushed the sand off her hands. "We lost a man."

He looked down at the mess on the pier, visibly confused. "Who?"

"One of the Cike. Aratsha. He's always in the water. Whatever hit the fish must have hit him, too."

"Fuck," Nezha said. "Were they targeting him?"

"I don't think so," she said slowly. "That's a lot of trouble for one shaman."

This couldn't be about just one man. Fish were floating dead across the entire harbor. Whoever had poisoned Aratsha had meant to poison the entire river.

The Cike were not the target. The Dragon Province was.

Because yes, Su Daji was that crazy. Daji was a woman who had welcomed the Federation into her territory to keep her throne. She would easily poison the southern provinces, would readily sentence millions to starvation, to keep the rest of her empire intact.

"How many troops?" Vaisra demanded.

All of them were crammed into the office—Captain Eriden, the Warlords, the Hesperians, and a smattering of whatever ranked officers were available. Decorum did not matter. The room had turned into a din of frantic shouting. Everyone spoke at once.

"We haven't counted the men who haven't made it to the infirmary—"

"Is it in the aquifers?"

"We have to shut down the fish markets—"

Vaisra shouted over the noise. "How many?"

"Almost the entire First Brigade has been hospitalized," said one of the physicians. "The poison was meant to affect the wildlife. It's weaker on men."

"It's not fatal?"

"We don't think so. We're hoping to see full recovery in a few days."

"Is Daji insane?" General Hu asked. "This is suicide. This doesn't just affect us, it kills everything that the Murui touches."

"The north doesn't care," Vaisra said. "They're upstream."

"But that means they'd need a constant source of poison," said

Eriden. "They'd have to introduce the agent to the stream daily. And it can't be as far as the Autumn Palace, or they screw over their own allies."

"Hare Province?" Nezha suggested.

"That's impossible," Jinzha said. "Their army is pathetic; they barely have defense capabilities. They'd never strike first."

"If they're pathetic, then they'd do whatever Daji told them."

"Are we sure it's Daji?" Takha asked.

"Who else would it be?" Tsolin demanded. He turned to Vaisra. "This is the answer to your blockade. Daji's weakening you before she strikes. I wouldn't wait around to see what she does next."

Jinzha banged a fist on the table. "I *told you*, we should have sailed up a week ago."

"With whose troops?" Vaisra asked coolly.

Jinzha's cheeks turned a bright red. But Vaisra wasn't looking at his son. Rin realized his remarks were meant for General Tarcquet.

The Hesperians had been watching silently at the back of the room, expressions impassive, standing with their arms crossed and lips pursed like teachers observing a classroom of unruly students. Every so often Sister Petra would scratch something into the writing pad she carried around everywhere, her lips curled in amusement. Rin wanted to hit her.

"This neutralizes our blockade," Tsolin said. "We can't wait any longer."

"But water moves steadily out to sea," said Lady Saikhara. "You never step in the same stream twice. In a matter of days the poisonous agent should have washed out into Omonod Bay, and we'll be fine." She looked imploringly around the table for someone to agree. "Shouldn't it?"

"But it's not just the fish." Kitay's voice was a strangled whisper. He said it again, and this time the room fell quiet when he spoke. "It's not just the fish. It's the entire country. The Murui supplies tributaries to all of the major southern regions. We're talking about all agricultural irrigation channels. Rice paddies. The water doesn't stop flowing there; it stays, it lingers. We are talking about massive crop failure."

"But the granaries," Lady Saikhara said. "Every province has stockpiled grain for lean years, yes? We could requisition those."

"And leave the south to eat what?" Kitay countered. "You force the south to give up their grain stores, and you're going to start bleeding allies. We don't have food, we don't even have *water*—"

"We have water," Saikhara said. "We've tested the aquifers, they're untouched. The wells are fine."

"Fine," said Kitay. "Then you'll just starve to death."

"What about them?" Charouk jabbed a finger in Tarcquet's direction. "They can't send us food aid?"

Tarcquet raised an eyebrow and looked expectantly at Vaisra.

Vaisra sighed. "The Consortium will not make investments until they feel better assured of our chances at victory."

There was a pause. The entire council looked toward General Tarcquet. The Warlords wore uniform expressions of desperate, pathetic, pleading hope. Sister Petra continued to scratch at her writing pad.

Nezha broke the silence. He spoke in deliberate, unaccented Hesperian. "Millions of people are going to die, sir."

Tarcquet shrugged. "Then you'd better get this campaign started, hadn't you?"

The Empress's ploy had the effect of setting fire to an anthill. Arlong erupted in a frenzy of activity, finally triggering battle plans that had been in place for months.

A war over ideology had suddenly become a war of resources. Now that waiting out the Empire was clearly no longer an option, the southern Warlords had no choice but to donate their troops to Vaisra's northern campaign.

Executive orders went out to generals, then filtered down

through commanders to squadron leaders to soldiers. Within minutes Rin had orders to report to the Fourteenth Brigade on the *Swallow*, departing in two hours from Pier Three.

"Nice, you're in the first fleet," Nezha said. "With me."

"Joyous day." She stuffed a change of uniform into a bag and hoisted it over her shoulder.

He reached over to ruffle her hair. "Look alive, little soldier. You're finally getting what you wanted."

En route to the pier they dodged through a maze of wagons carrying hemp, jute, lime for caulking, tung oil, and sailing cloth. The entire city smelled and sounded like a shipyard; it echoed everywhere with the same faint, low groan, the noise of dozens of massive ships detaching their anchors, paddle wheels beginning to turn.

"Move!" A wagon driven by Hesperian soldiers narrowly missed running them over. Nezha pulled Rin to the side.

"Assholes," he muttered.

Rin's eyes followed the Hesperians to the warships. "I guess we'll finally get to see Tarcquet's golden troops in action."

"Actually, no. Tarcquet's only bringing a skeleton platoon. The rest are staying in Arlong."

"Then why are they even going?"

"Because they're here to observe. They want to know if we're capable of coming close to winning this war, and if we are, if we're capable of running this country effectively. Tarcquet told Father some babble about stages of human evolution last night, but I think they really just want to see if we're worth the trouble. Everything Jinzha does gets reported to Tarcquet. Everything Tarcquet sees goes back to the Consortium. And the Consortium decides when they want to lend their ships."

"We can't take this Empire without them, and they won't help us until we take the Empire." Rin made a face. "Those are the terms?"

"Not quite. They'll intervene before this war is over, once they're sure it isn't a lost cause. They're willing to tip the scales, but we have to prove first that we can pull our own weight."

"So just another fucking test," Rin said.

Nezha sighed. "More or less, yes."

The sheer arrogance, Rin thought. It must be nice, possessing all the power, so that you could approach geopolitics like a chess game, popping in curiously to observe which countries deserved your aid and which didn't.

"Is Petra coming with us?" she asked.

"No. She'll stay on Jinzha's ship." Nezha hesitated. "But, ah, Father told me to make it clear that your meetings resume as usual when we rejoin my brother's fleet."

"Even on campaign?"

"They're most interested in you on campaign. Petra promised it wouldn't be much. An hour every week, as agreed."

"It doesn't sound like much to you," Rin muttered. "You've never been someone's lab rat."

Three fleets were preparing to sail out from the Red Cliffs. The first, commanded by Jinzha, would go up the Murui through the center of Hare Province, the agricultural heartland of the north. The second fleet, led by Tsolin and General Hu, would race up the rugged coastline around Snake Province to destroy Tiger Province ships before they could be deployed inland to fend off the main vanguard.

Combined, they were to squeeze the northeastern provinces between the inland attack and the coast. Daji would be forced to fight an enemy on two fronts, and both over water—a terrain the Militia had never been comfortable with.

In terms of sheer manpower, the Republic was still outnumbered. The Militia had tens of thousands of men on the Republican Army. But if Vaisra's fleet did its job, and if the Hesperians kept their word, there was a good chance they might win this war.

"Guys! Wait!"

"Oh, shit," Nezha muttered.

Rin turned around to see Venka running barefoot down the pier toward them. She clutched a crossbow to her chest.

Nezha cleared his throat as Venka came to a halt in front of him. "Uh, Venka, this isn't a good time."

"Just take this," Venka panted. She passed the crossbow into Rin's hands. "I took it from my father's workshop. Latest model. Reloads automatically."

Nezha shot Rin an uncomfortable glance. "This isn't really—"

"Beautiful, isn't it?" Venka asked. She ran her fingers over the body. "See this? Intricate trigger latch mechanism. We finally figured out how to get it to work; this is just the prototype but I think it's ready—"

"We're boarding in minutes," Nezha interrupted. "What do you want?"

"Take me with you," Venka said bluntly.

Rin noticed Venka had a pack strapped to her back, but she didn't have a uniform.

"Absolutely not," Nezha said.

Venka's cheeks reddened. "Why not? I'm all better now."

"You can't even bend your left arm."

"She doesn't need to," Rin said. "Not if she's firing a crossbow."

"Are you insane?" Nezha demanded. "She can't run around with a crossbow that big; she'll be exhausted—"

"Then we'll mount it on the ship," Rin said. "And she'll be removed from the heat of the battle. She'll need protection between rounds to reload, so she'll be surrounded by a unit of archers. It'll be safe."

Venka looked triumphantly at Nezha. "What she said."

"*Safe?*" Nezha echoed, incredulous.

"Safer than the rest of us," Rin amended.

"But she's not done . . ." Nezha looked Venka up and down, hesitating, clearly at a loss for the right words. "You're not done, uh . . ."

"Healing?" Venka asked. "That's what you mean, isn't it?"

"Venka, please."

"How long did you think I'd need? I've been sitting on my ass for months. Come on, *please*, I'm ready."

Nezha looked helplessly at Rin, as if hoping she'd make the entire situation dissipate. But what did he expect her to say? Rin didn't even understand the problem.

"There has to be room on the ships," she said. "Let her go."

"That's not your call. She could die out there."

"Occupational hazard," Venka shot back. "We're soldiers."

"*You* are not a soldier."

"Why not? Because of Golyn Niis?" Venka barked out a laugh. "You think once you're raped you can't be a soldier?"

Nezha shifted uncomfortably. "That's not what I said."

"Yes, it is. Even if you won't say it, that's what you're thinking!" Venka's voice rose steadily in pitch. "You think that because they raped me, I'm never going to go back to normal."

Nezha reached for her shoulder. "Meimei. Come on."

Meimei. Little sister. Not by blood, but by virtue of the closeness of their families. He was trying to invoke his ritual concern for her to dissuade her from going. "What happened to you was horrible. Nobody blames you. Nobody here agrees with your father, or my mother—"

"I know that!" Venka shouted. "I don't give a shit about that!"

Nezha looked pained. "I can't protect you out there."

"And when have you *ever* protected me?" Venka slapped his hand away from her shoulder. "Do you know what I thought when I was in that house? I kept hoping someone might come for me, *I really thought someone was coming for me.* And where the fuck were you? *Nowhere.* So fuck you, Nezha. You can't keep me safe, so you might as well let me fight."

"Yes, I can," Nezha said. "I'm a general. Go back. Or I'll have someone drag you back."

Venka grabbed the crossbow back from Rin and pointed it at Nezha. A bolt whizzed out, narrowly missed Nezha's cheek, and embedded itself into a post several feet behind his head, where it quivered in the wood, humming loudly.

"You missed," Nezha said calmly.

Venka tossed the crossbow on the pier and spat at Nezha's feet. "I never miss."

Captain Salkhi of the *Swallow* stood waiting for the Cike at the base of the gangplank. She was a lean, petite woman with closely cropped hair, narrow eyes, and pinkish-brown skin—not the dusky tint of a southerner, but the tanned hue of a pale northerner who had spent too much time in the sun.

"I'm assuming I'm to treat you lot as I would any other soldiers," she said. "Can you handle ground operations?"

"We'll be fine," said Rin. "I'll walk you through their specialties."

"I'd appreciate that." Salkhi paused. "And what about you? Eriden told me about your, ah, problem."

"I've still got two arms and two legs."

"And she has a trident," Kitay said, walking up behind her. "Very helpful for catching fish."

Rin turned around, pleasantly surprised. "You're coming with us?"

"It's either your ship or Nezha's. And frankly, he and I have been getting on each other's nerves."

"That's mostly your fault," she said.

"Oh, it absolutely is," he said. "Don't care. Besides, I like you better. Aren't you flattered?"

That was about as close to a peace offering from Kitay as she was going to get. Rin grinned. Together they boarded the *Swallow*.

The vessel was no multidecked warship. This was a sleek, tiny model, similar in build to an opium skimmer. A single row of cannons armed it on each side, but no trebuchets mounted its decks. Rin, who had gotten used to the amenities of the *Seagrim*, found the *Swallow* uncomfortably cramped.

The *Swallow* belonged to the first fleet, one of seven light, fast skimmers capable of tight tactical maneuvers. They would sail ahead two weeks in advance while the heavier fleet commanded by Jinzha prepared to ship out.

During that time they would be cut off from the chain of command at Arlong.

That didn't matter. Their instructions were short and simple: find the source of the poison, destroy it, and punish every last man involved. Vaisra hadn't specified how. He'd left that up to the captains, which was why everyone wanted to get to them first.

CHAPTER 15

The *Swallow*'s crew planned to keep sailing upstream until they weren't surrounded by dead fish, or until the poison's source became apparent. The facility would have to be near a main river juncture, and close enough to the Murui that there would be no chance the poison would wash out to the ocean or get blocked up in a dead end. They traveled north up the Murui until they reached the border of Hare Province, where the river branched off into several tributaries.

Here the skimmers split up. The *Swallow* took the westernmost route, a lazy bending creek that trailed slowly through the province's interior heartland. They went cautiously with their flag stowed away, disguising themselves as a merchant ship to avoid Imperial suspicion.

Captain Salkhi kept a clean, tightly disciplined ship. The Fourteenth Brigade rotated shifts on deck, either watching the shoreline or paddling down below. The soldiers and crew accepted the Cike into their fold with wary indifference. If they had questions about what the shamans could or couldn't do, they kept them to themselves.

"Seen anything?" Rin joined Kitay at the starboard railing, legs aching after a long paddling shift. She should have gone to sleep, according to the schedule, but midmorning was the only time that their breaks overlapped.

She was relieved that she and Kitay were on friendly terms again. They hadn't returned to normal—she didn't know if they would ever return to normal—but at least Kitay didn't emanate cold judgment every time he looked at her.

"Not yet." He stood utterly still, eyes fixed on the water, as if he could trace a path to the chemical source through sheer force of will. He was angry. Rin could tell when he was angry—his cheeks went a pale white, he held himself too rigidly, and he went long periods without blinking. She was just glad that he wasn't angry with her.

"Look." She pointed. "I don't think this is the right tributary."

Dark shapes moved under the muggy green water. Which meant the river life was still alive and healthy, unaffected by poison.

Kitay leaned forward. "What's that?"

Rin followed his gaze but couldn't tell what he was looking at.

He pulled a netted pole from the bulkhead, scooped it into the water, and plucked out a small object. At first Rin thought he'd caught a fish, but when Kitay deposited it onto the deck she saw it was some kind of dark and leathery pouch, about the size of a pomelo, knotted tightly at the end so that it looked oddly like a breast.

Kitay pinched it up with two fingers.

"That's clever," he said. "Gross, but clever."

"What is it?"

"It's incredible. This has to be a Sinegard graduate's work. Or a Yuelu graduate. No one else is this smart." He held the object toward her. She recoiled. It smelled awful—a combination of rank animal odor and the sharp, acrid smell of poison that brought back memories of embalmed pig fetuses from her medical classes with Master Enro.

She wrinkled her nose. "Are you going to tell me what it is?"

"Pig's bladder." Kitay turned it over in his palm and gave it a shake. "Resistant to acid, at least to some degree. It's why the poison hasn't been diluted before it reached Arlong."

He rubbed the edge of the bladder between his fingers. "This stays intact so the agent doesn't dissolve into the water until it reaches downstream. It was meant to last several days, a week at most."

The bladder popped open under the pressure. Liquid spilled out onto Kitay's hand, making his skin hiss and pucker. A yellow cloud seeped into the air. The acrid odor intensified. Kitay cursed and flung the bladder back out over the side of the ship, then hastily wiped his skin against his uniform.

"Fuck." He examined his hand, which had developed a pale, angry rash.

Rin yanked him away from the gas cloud. To her relief, it dissipated in seconds. "Tiger's tits, are you—"

"I'm fine. It's not deep, I don't think." Kitay cradled his hand inside his elbow and winced. "Go get Salkhi. I think we're getting close."

Salkhi split the Fourteenth Brigade into squads of six that dispersed through the surrounding region for a ground expedition. The Cike found the poison source first. It was visible the moment they emerged from the tree line—a blocky, three-story building with bell towers at both ends, erected in the architectural style of the old Hesperian missions.

At the southern wall, a single pipe extended over the river—a channel meant to move waste and sewage into the water. Instead, it dispensed poisonous pods into the river with a mechanical regularity.

Someone, or something, was dropping them off from inside.

"This is it." Kitay motioned for the rest of the Cike to crouch low behind the bushes. "We've got to get someone in there."

"What about the guard?" Rin whispered.

"What guard? There's no one there."

He was right. The mission looked barely garrisoned. Rin could count the soldiers on one hand, and after half an hour of scoping the perimeter, they didn't find any others on patrol.

"That makes no sense," she said.

"Maybe they just don't have the men," Kitay said.

"Then why poke the dragon?" Baji asked. "If they don't have backup, that strike was idiotic. This whole town is dead."

"Maybe it's an ambush," Rin said.

Kitay looked unconvinced. "But they're not expecting us."

"It could be protocol. They might all just be hiding inside."

"That's not how you lay out defenses. You only do that if you're under siege."

"So you want us to attack a building with minimal intelligence? What if there's a platoon in there?"

Kitay pulled a flare rocket from his pocket. "I know a way to find out."

"Hold on," Ramsa said. "Captain Salkhi said not to engage."

"Fuck Salkhi," Kitay said with a violence that was utterly unlike him. Before Rin could stop him he lit the fuse, aimed, and loosed the flare toward the patch of woods behind the mission.

A bang rocked the forest. Several seconds later Rin heard shouts from inside the mission. Then a group of men armed with farming implements emerged from the doors and ran toward the explosion.

"There's your guard," Kitay said.

Rin hoisted her trident. "Oh, *fuck* you."

Kitay counted under his breath as he watched the men. "About fifteen. There are twenty-four of us." He glanced back at Baji and Suni. "Think you can keep them out of the mission until the others get here?"

"Don't insult us," Baji said. "Go."

Only two guards remained at the mission's doors. Kitay dispatched one with his crossbow. Rin grappled with the other for a few minutes until at last she disarmed him and slammed her trident into his throat. She wrenched it back out and he dropped.

The doors stood wide open before them. Rin peered into the dark interior. The smell of rotting corpses hit her like a wall, so thick and sharp that her eyes watered. She covered her mouth with her sleeve. "You coming?"

Thud.

She turned. Kitay stood over the second guard, crossbow pointed down, wiping flecks of blood off his chin with the back of his hand. He caught her staring at him.

"Just making sure," he said.

Inside they found a slaughterhouse.

Rin's eyes took a moment to adjust to the darkness. Then she saw pig carcasses everywhere she looked—tossed on the floor, piled up in the corners, splayed over tables, all sliced open with surgical precision.

"Tiger's tits," she muttered.

Someone had killed them all solely for their bladders. The sheer waste amazed her. So much rotting meat was piled on these floors, and refugees in the next province over were so thin their ribs pushed through their ragged garments.

"Found them," Kitay said.

She followed his line of sight across the room. A dozen open barrels stood lined up against the wall. They contained the poison in liquid form—a noxious yellow concoction that sent toxic fumes spiraling lazily into the air above them. Above the barrels were shelves and shelves of metal canisters. More than Rin could count.

Rin had seen those canisters before, stacked neatly on shelves just like these. She'd stared up at them for hours while Mugenese scientists strapped her to a bed and forced opiates into her veins.

Kitay's face had turned a greenish color. He knew that gas from Golyn Niis.

"I wouldn't touch that." A figure emerged from the stairwell opposite them. Kitay jerked his crossbow up. Rin crouched back, trident poised to throw as she squinted to make out the figure's face in the darkness.

The figure stepped into the light. "Took you long enough."

Kitay let his arms drop. *"Niang?"*

Rin wouldn't have recognized her. War had transformed

Niang. Even into their third year at Sinegard, Niang had always looked like a child—innocent, round-faced, and adorable. She'd never looked like she belonged at a military academy. Now she just looked like a soldier, scarred and hardened like the rest of them.

"Please tell me you're not behind this," said Kitay.

"What? The pods?" Niang traced her fingers over the edge of a barrel. Her hands were covered in angry red welts. "Clever design, wasn't it? I was hoping someone might notice."

As Niang moved farther into light, Rin saw that the welts hadn't just formed on her hands. Her neck and face were mottled red, as if her skin had been scraped raw with the flat side of a blade.

"Those canisters," Rin said. "They're from the Federation."

"Yes, they really saved us some labor, didn't they?" Niang chuckled. "They produced thousands of barrels of that stuff. The Hare Warlord wanted to use it to invade Arlong, but I was smarter about it. Put it into the water, I said. Starve them out. The really hard part was converting it from a gas into a liquid. That took me weeks."

Niang pulled a canister off the wall and weighed it in her hand, as if preparing to throw. "Think you could do better?"

Rin and Kitay flinched simultaneously.

Niang lowered her arm, snickering. "Kidding."

"Put that down," Kitay said quietly. His voice was taut, carefully controlled. "Let's talk. Let's just talk, Niang. I know someone put you up to this. You don't have to do this."

"I know that," Niang said. "I volunteered. Or did you think I'd sit back and let traitors divide the Empire?"

"You don't know what you're talking about," Rin said.

"I know enough." Niang lifted the canister higher. "I know you threatened to starve out the north so they'd bow to the Dragon Warlord. I know you're going to invade our provinces if you don't get your way."

"So your solution is to poison the entire south?" Kitay asked.

"You're one to talk," Niang snarled. "You made us starve. You sold us that blighted grain. How does it feel getting a taste of your own medicine?"

"The embargo was just a threat," Kitay said. "No one has to die."

"People *have* died!" Niang pointed a finger at Rin. "How many did she kill on that island?"

Rin blinked. "Who gives a fuck about the Federation?"

"There were Militia troops there, too. Thousands of them." Niang's voice trembled. "The Federation took prisoners of war, shipped them over to labor camps. They took my brothers. Did you give them a chance to get off the island?"

"I . . ." Rin cast Kitay a desperate look. "That's not true."

Was it true?

Surely someone would have told her if it were true.

Kitay wouldn't meet her eyes.

She swallowed. "Niang, I didn't know—"

"*You didn't know!*" Niang screamed. The canister swung perilously in her hand. "That makes it all better, doesn't it?"

Kitay held a palm out, crossbow lowered. "Niang, *please*, put that down."

Niang shook her head. "This is your fault. We just fought a war. Why couldn't you just leave us alone?"

"We don't want to kill you," Rin said. "Please—"

"How generous!" Niang lifted the canister over her head. "She doesn't want to kill me! The Republic will take pity on—"

"Fuck this," Kitay muttered. In one fluid movement he lifted his crossbow, aimed, and shot an arrow straight into Niang's left breast.

The thud echoed like a final heartbeat.

Niang's eyes bulged open. She tilted her head down, examined her chest as if idly curious. Her knees gave out beneath her. The canister slipped from her hand and rolled to a halt by the wall.

The canister's lid burst off with a pop. Yellow smoke streamed out from it, rapidly filling the far end of the room.

Kitay lowered his crossbow. "Let's go."

They ran. Rin glanced over her shoulder just as they passed the door. The gas was almost too thick to see clearly, but she couldn't mistake the sight of Niang, twitching and jerking in a shroud of acid eating ravenously into her skin. Red spots blooming mercilessly across her body, as if she were a paper doll dropped in a pool of ink.

Light rain misted the air over the *Swallow* as it drifted down the tributary to rejoin the main fleet.

The crew had argued briefly over what to do with the canisters. They couldn't just leave them in the mission, but none of them wanted to have the gas on board. Finally Ramsa had suggested that they destroy the mission with a controlled burn. This was purportedly to deter anyone from approaching it until Jinzha could send a squadron to retrieve any remaining canisters, but Rin suspected that Ramsa just wanted an excuse to blow something up.

So they'd drenched the place in oil, piled kindling on the roof and in the makeshift slaughterhouse, and then fired flaming crossbow bolts from the ship once they were a safe sailing distance away.

The building had caught fire immediately, a lovely conflagration that remained visible from miles away. The rain hadn't yet managed to smother all of the flame. Little bursts of red still burned at the base of the building and smoke stretched out to embrace the sky from the towers.

A crack of thunder split the sky. Seconds later the light drizzle turned into fat, hard drops that slammed loudly and relentlessly against the deck. Captain Salkhi ordered the crew to set out barrels to capture fresh water. Most of the crew descended to their cabins, but Rin sat down on the deck, pulled her knees up to her chest, and tilted her head back. Raindrops hit the back of her throat, wonderfully fresh and cool. She gargled the rainwater, let it splash over her face and clothes. She knew the poison hadn't tainted her or she would have seen its effects, but somehow she couldn't feel clean.

"I thought you hated water," Kitay said.

She looked up. He stood over her, a miserable, drenched mess. He still had his crossbow clenched in his hands.

"You all right?" she asked.

His eyes were dead things. "No."

"Sit with me."

He obeyed without a word. Only when he was next to her did she see how violently he was trembling.

"I'm sorry about Niang," she said.

He jerked out a shrug. "I'm not."

"I thought you liked her."

"I barely knew her."

"You *did* like her. I remember. You thought she was cute. You told me that at school."

"Yes, and then that bitch went and poisoned half the country."

He tilted his head upward. His eyes were red, and she couldn't tell his tears apart from the rain. He took a long, shuddering breath.

Then he broke.

"I can't keep doing this." The words spilled out of him between choked, sudden sobs. "I can't sleep. I can't go a second without seeing Golyn Niis. I close my eyes and I'm hiding behind that wall again and the screams don't stop because the killing goes on all night—"

Rin reached for his hand. "Kitay . . ."

"It's like I'm frozen in one moment. And no one knows it because everyone else has moved on except me, but to me everything that's happened since Golyn Niis is a dream, and I know it's not real because I'm still behind the wall. And the worst part—the worst part is that I don't know who's causing the screams. It was easier when only the Federation was evil. Now I can't figure out who's right or wrong, and I'm the *smart* one, I'm always supposed to have the right answer, but I don't."

She didn't know what she could possibly say to comfort him, so she curled her fingers around his and held them tight. "Me neither."

"What happened on that island?" he asked abruptly.

"You know what happened."

"No. You never told me." He straightened up. "Was it conscious? Did you think about what you were doing?"

"I don't remember," she said. "I try not to remember."

"Did you know you were killing them?" he pressed. "Or did you just . . ." His fingers clenched into a fist and then unclenched beneath hers.

"I just wanted it to be over," she said. "I wasn't thinking. I didn't want to hurt them, not really, I just wanted it to end."

"I didn't want to kill her. I just—I don't know why I—"

"I know."

"That wasn't me," he insisted, but she wasn't the one he needed to convince.

All she could do was squeeze his hand again. "I know."

Signals were sent, courses were reversed. Within a day the dispersed skimmers had fled hastily down the Murui to rejoin the main armada.

When Rin saw the Republican Fleet from the front it seemed deceptively small, ships arranged in a narrow formation. Then they approached from the side and the full menace of the flotilla was splayed out in front of her, a marvelous and breathtaking display of force. Compared to the warships, the *Swallow* was just a tiny thing, a baby bird returning to the flock.

Captain Salkhi lit several lanterns to signal their return, and the patrol ships at the fore signaled back their permission to break through the line. The *Swallow* slipped into the ranks. An hour later Jinzha boarded their ship. The crew assembled on deck to report.

"We've stopped the poison at the source, but there may be canisters left in the ruins," Salkhi told Jinzha. "You'll want to send a squadron up there to see if you can retrieve it."

"Were they producing it themselves?" Jinzha asked.

"That's unlikely," Salkhi said. "That wasn't a research facility, it was a makeshift slaughterhouse. It seems like that was just the distribution point."

"We think they got it from the Federation facility on the coast," said Rin. "The one where I was— The one they took me to."

Jinzha frowned. "That's all the way out in Snake Province. Why bring it here?"

"They couldn't have set it off in Snake Province," Kitay said. "The current takes the poison out to sea instead of to Arlong. So someone must have gone there recently, retrieved the canisters, and carted them over to Hare Province."

"I hope that's right," said Jinzha. "I don't want to entertain the alternative."

Because the alternative, of course, was terrifying—that they were fighting a war not only against the Empire, but also against the Federation. That the Federation had survived, and had retained its weapons, and was sending them to Vaisra's enemies.

"Did you take prisoners?" Jinzha asked.

Salkhi nodded. "Two guardsmen. They're in the brig. We'll turn them over for interrogation."

"There's no need for that." Jinzha waved a hand. "We know what we need to know. Bring them out to the beach."

"Your brother has a flair for public spectacle," Kitay told Nezha.

The screaming had been going on for more than an hour now. Rin had almost gotten used to it, though it made it difficult to stomach her dinner.

The Hare Province guardsmen were strung up against posts in the ground, beaten for good measure. Jinzha had stripped them, flayed them, then poured diluted poison from one of the pods into a flask and boiled it. Now it ran in rivulets down the guardsmen's skin, tracing a steaming, angrily red path over their cheeks, their collarbones, down toward their exposed genitals, while the Republican soldiers sat back on the beach and watched.

"This wasn't necessary," Nezha said. His dinner rations sat untouched beside him. "This is grotesque."

Kitay laughed, a flat, hollow noise. "Don't be naive."

"What's that supposed to mean?"

"This *is* necessary. The Republic's just taken a massive blow. Vaisra can't undo the poisoning of the river, or the fact that thousands of people are going to starve. But give a few men a little pain, do it in public, and it'll all be all right."

"Does it make it all right to you?" Rin asked.

Kitay shrugged. "They poisoned a fucking river."

Nezha wrapped his arms around his knees. "Salkhi says you were in there for a while."

Rin nodded. "We saw Niang. Meant to tell you that."

Nezha blinked, surprised. "And how is she?"

"Dead," said Kitay. He was still staring at the men on the posts.

Nezha watched him for a moment, then raised an eyebrow at Rin. She understood his question. She shook her head.

"I hadn't thought about fighting our own classmates," Nezha murmured after a pause. "Who else do we know in the north? Kureel, Arda . . ."

"My cousins," Kitay said without turning around. "Han. Tobi. Most of the rest of our class, if they're still alive."

"I suppose it's not easy going to war against friends," Nezha said.

"Yes, it is," Kitay said. "They have a choice. Niang made her choice. She just happened to be dead fucking wrong."

CHAPTER 16

The guardsmen had stopped twitching by sunset.

Jinzha ordered their bodies burned as a final display. But there was far less retributive pleasure in watching corpses burn compared to hearing men scream, and eventually the smell of cooked meat grew so pungent on the beach that the soldiers started migrating back toward their ships.

"Well, that was fun." Rin stood up and brushed the crumbs off her uniform. "Let's go back."

"You're going to sleep already?" Kitay asked.

"I'm not staying here," she said. "It reeks."

"Not so fast," Nezha said. "You're off the *Swallow*. You've been reassigned to the *Kingfisher*."

"Just her?" Kitay asked.

"No, all of you. Cike, too. Jinzha wants you for strategic consultation, and he thinks the Cike can do more damage from a warship. The *Swallow*'s not an attack boat."

Rin glanced toward the *Kingfisher*, where Hesperian soldiers and Gray Company were clearly visible on deck.

"Yes, that's intentional." Nezha inferred the question from the exasperated look on her face. "They wanted to keep a closer eye on you."

"I already let Petra prod me like an animal once a week," Rin said. "I don't want to see them when I'm trying to eat."

Nezha held his hands up. "Jinzha's orders. Nothing we can do."

Rin suspected Captain Salkhi had also requested a transfer on grounds of disobedience. Salkhi had been deeply frustrated that the Cike had stormed the mission without her command, and Baji hadn't helped things by pointing out that they wouldn't have needed the rest of her troops regardless. Rin's suspicion was confirmed when Jinzha took twenty minutes informing her and the Cike that they would follow his orders to the letter or find themselves tossed into the Murui.

"I don't care that my father thinks the sun shines out of your ass," he said. "You'll act like soldiers or you'll be punished as deserters."

"Asshole," Rin muttered as they left his office.

"He's absolutely awful," Kitay agreed. "It's a rare person who makes Nezha look like the pleasant sibling."

"I'm not saying I want him to drown in the Murui," Ramsa said, "but I want him to drown in the Murui."

With the fleet united, the Republic's northern expedition began in earnest. Jinzha set a direct course that cut straight through Hare Province, which was agriculturally rich and comparatively weak. They would pick off the low-hanging fruit and solidify their supply base before taking on the full force of the Militia.

Hesperians aside, Rin found that traveling on the *Kingfisher* was a marked improvement from the *Swallow*. At least a hundred yards long from bow to stern, the *Kingfisher* was the only turtle boat in the fleet, with a closed top deck wrapped over by wood paneling and steel plates that made it nearly immune to cannon fire. The *Kingfisher* functioned as more or less a floating piece of armor, and for good reason—it carried Jinzha, Admiral Molkoi, almost all of the fleet's senior strategists, and most of the Hesperian delegation.

Flanking the *Kingfisher* were a trio of sister galleys known as the Seahawks—warships with floating boards attached to the port and starboard sides shaped like a bird's wings. Two were affectionately named the *Lapwing* and the *Waxwing*. The *Griffon*, commanded by Nezha, sailed directly behind the *Kingfisher*.

The other two galleys guarded the pride and battering ram of the fleet—two massive tower ships that someone with a bad sense of humor had named the *Shrike* and the *Crake*. They were monstrously large and top-heavy, outfitted with two mounted trebuchets and four rows of crossbows each.

The fleet proceeded up the Murui in a phalanx formation, lined up to adjust to the narrowing breadth of the river. The smaller skimmers alternately ducked in between the warships or followed them in a straightforward line, like a trail of ducklings following their mother.

It was such a beauty of riverine warfare, Rin thought, that the troops never had to weary themselves with marching. They just had to wait to be ferried to the Empire's most important cities, which were all close to the water. Cities needed water to survive, just like bodies needed blood. So if they wanted to seize the Empire, they needed only to sail through its arteries.

At dawn the fleet reached the border of Radan township. Radan was one of Hare Province's larger economic centers, targeted by Jinzha because of its strategic location at the junction of two waterways, its possession of several well-stocked granaries, and the simple fact that it barely had a military.

Jinzha ordered an immediate invasion without negotiation.

"Is he afraid they'll refuse?" Rin asked Kitay.

"More likely he's afraid they'll surrender," Kitay said. "Jinzha needs this expedition to be based on fear."

"What, the tower ships aren't scary enough?"

"That's a bluff. This isn't about Radan, it's about the next battle. Radan needs to be used as an example."

"Of what?"

"What happens when you resist," Kitay said grimly. "I'd go get your trident. We're about to start."

The *Kingfisher* was fast approaching Radan's river gates. Rin lifted her spyglass to get a closer look at the township's hastily assembled fleet. It was a laughably pathetic amalgamation of outdated vessels, mostly single-mast creations with sails made of oiled silk. Radan's ships were merchant vessels and fishing boats with no firing capacity. They had clearly never been used for warfare.

The Cike alone could have taken the city, Rin thought. They were certainly eager for it. Suni and Baji had been pacing the deck for hours, impatient to finally see action. The two of them could have likely broken the outer defenses by themselves. But Jinzha had wanted to commit his full resources to breaking Radan. That wasn't strategy, it was showmanship.

Jinzha strode onto the deck, took one look at the Radan defense fleet, and yawned into his hand. "Admiral Molkoi."

The admiral dipped his head. "Yes, sir?"

"Blow those things out of the water."

The ensuing battle was so one-sided that it seemed impossible. It wasn't a fight, it was a comic tragedy.

Radan's men had rubbed their sails down with oil. It was standard practice for merchants, who wanted to keep their sails waterproof and immune to rot. It was not so clever against pyrotechnics.

The Seahawks fired a series of double-headed dragon missiles that exploded midair into a swarm of smaller explosives, which spread a penumbral shower of fire across the Radan fleet. The sails caught fire immediately. Entire sheets of blistering flame engulfed the pathetic armada, roaring so loudly that for an instant it was all anyone could hear.

Rin found it oddly pleasing to watch, the same way it was fun to kick down sandcastles just because she could.

"Tiger's tits," Ramsa said, perched on the prow while flickering flames reflected in his eyes. "It's like they weren't even trying."

Hundreds of men leaped overboard to escape the searing heat.

"Have the archers pick off anyone who gets out of the river," said Jinzha. "Let the rest burn."

The skirmish took less than an hour from start to finish. The *Kingfisher* sailed triumphantly through the blackened remains of Radan's fleet to anchor right at the town border. Ramsa marveled at how thoroughly the cannons had demolished the river gates, Baji complained that he hadn't gotten to do anything, and Rin tried not to look into the water.

Radan's fleet was destroyed and its gates in shambles. The remaining population of the township laid down their weapons and surrendered with little trouble. Jinzha's men poured into the city and evacuated all civilians from their residences to clear the way for plundering.

Women and children lined up in the streets, heads down, quivering with fear as the soldiers marched them out the gates and along the beach. There they huddled in terrified bundles, glassy eyes staring at the remains of Radan's fleet.

The Republican soldiers were careful not to harm the civilians. Jinzha had been very adamant that the civilians were not to be mistreated. "They are not prisoners, and they are not victims," he'd said. "Let's call them potential members of the Republic."

For potential citizens of the Republic, they looked well and truly terrified of their new government.

They had good reason to fear. Their sons and husbands had been lined up in rows along the shore, held at sword point. They were told their fates hadn't yet been decided, that the Republican leadership was debating overnight on whether or not to kill them.

Jinzha intended to let the civilians pass the night unsure of whether they would live until the sun rose.

In the morning, he would announce to the crowd that he had received orders from Arlong. The Dragon Warlord had meditated on their fates. He recognized that it was no fault of their own that they were misled into resistance by their corrupt leaders, seduced by an Empress who no longer served them. He realized this decision was not made by these honest, common people. He would be merciful.

He would put the decision in the hands of the people.

He would have them vote.

"What do you think they're doing?" Kitay asked.

"They're proselytizing," Rin said. "Spreading the good word of the Maker."

"Doesn't seem like fantastic timing."

"I suppose they have to take a captive audience when they can get it."

They sat cross-legged on the shore in the *Kingfisher*'s shadow, watching as the Gray Company's missionaries made their way through the clumps of huddled civilians. They were too far away for Rin to hear what they were saying, but every now and then she saw a missionary kneel down next to several miserable civilians, put his hands on their shoulders even as they flinched away, and speak what was unmistakably a prayer.

"I hope they're talking in Nikara," said Kitay. "Otherwise they'll sound ominous as hell."

"I don't think it matters if they are." Rin found it hard not to feel a sense of guilty pleasure watching the crowds shrinking from the missionaries, despite the Hesperians' best efforts.

Kitay passed her a stick of dried fish. "Hungry?"

"Thanks." She took the fish, worked her teeth around the tail, and jerked off a bite.

There was an art to eating the salted mayau fish that made up the majority of their rations. She had to chew it up just so to make it soft enough that she could extract the meat from around the bones and spit out the spindly things. Too little chewing and the bones lacerated her throat; too much and the fish lost all flavor.

Salted mayau was a clever army food. It took so long to eat that by the time Rin was finished, no matter how little she'd actually consumed, she felt full on salt and saliva.

"Have you seen their penises?" Kitay asked.

Rin nearly spat out her fish. "What?"

He gestured with his hands. "Hesperian men are supposed to be much, ah, bigger than Nikara men. Salkhi said so."

"How would Salkhi know?"

"How do you think?" Kitay waggled his eyebrows. "Admit it, you've thought about it."

She shuddered. "Not if you paid me."

"Have you seen General Tarcquet? He's massive. I bet he—"

"Don't be disgusting," she snapped. "They're horrible. And they smell awful. They're . . . I don't know, it's like something curdled."

"It's because they drink cow's milk, I think. All that dairy is screwing with their systems."

"I just thought they weren't showering."

"You're one to talk. Have you gotten a whiff of yourself recently?"

"Hold on." Rin pointed across the river. "Look over there."

Some of the civilian women had started screaming at a missionary. The missionary stepped hastily away, hands out in a non-threatening position, but the women didn't stop shrieking until he'd retreated all the way down the beach.

Kitay gave a low whistle. "That's going well."

"I wonder what they're saying to them," Rin said.

"'Our Maker is great and powerful,'" he said pompously. "'Pray with us and you shall never go hungry again.'"

"'All wars will be stopped.'"

"'All enemies will fall down dead, smitten by the Maker's great hand.'"

"'Peace will cover the realm and the demon gods will be banished to hell.'" Rin hugged her knees to her chest as she watched the missionary stand on the beach, seeking out another cluster of civilians to terrify. "You'd think they'd just leave us well enough alone."

Hesperian religion wasn't new to the Empire. At the height of his reign, the Red Emperor had frequently received emissaries from the churches of the west. Scholars of the church took up residence in his court at Sinegard and entertained the Emperor with their astronomical predictions, star charts, and nifty inventions. Then the Red Emperor died, the coddled scholars were persecuted by jealous court officials, and the missionaries were expelled from the continent for centuries.

The Hesperians had made intermittent efforts to come back, of course. They'd almost succeeded during the first invasion. But now the common Nikara people remembered only the lies the Trifecta had spread about them after the Second Poppy War. They killed and ate infants. They lured young women to their convents to serve as sex slaves. They'd more or less become monsters in folklore. If the Gray Company hoped to win converts, they had their work cut out for them.

"They've got to try regardless," Kitay said. "I read it in their holy texts once. Their scholars argue that as the Divine Architect's blessed and chosen people, their obligation is to preach to every infidel they encounter."

"'Chosen'? What does that mean?"

"I don't know." Kitay nodded past Rin's shoulder. "Why don't you ask her?"

Rin twisted around.

Sister Petra was striding briskly down the shore toward them.

Rin swallowed her last bite of fish too quickly. It crawled painfully down her throat, each swallow a painful scratch of unsoftened bone.

Sister Petra met Rin's eyes and beckoned with a finger. *Come.* That was an order.

Kitay patted her shoulder as he stood up. "Have fun."

Rin reached for his sleeve. "Don't you dare leave me—"

"I'm not getting in the middle of this," he said. "I've seen what those arquebuses can do."

"Congratulations," Petra said as they returned to the *Kingfisher.* "I'm told this was a great victory."

"'Great' is a word for it," Rin said.

"And the fire did not come to you in battle? Chaos did not rear its head?"

Rin stopped walking. "Would you rather I had burned those people alive?"

"Sister Petra?" A missionary ran up from behind them. He looked startlingly young. He couldn't have been a day over sixteen. His face was open and babyish, and his wide blue eyes were lashed like a girl's.

"How do you say 'I'm from across the great sea'?" he asked. "I forgot."

"Like so." Petra pronounced the Nikara phrase with flawless accuracy.

"I'm from across the great sea." The boy looked delighted as he repeated the words. "Did I get it right? The tones?"

Rin realized with a start that he was looking at her.

"Sure," she said. "That was fine."

The boy beamed at her. "I love your language. It's so beautiful."

Rin blinked at him. What was wrong with him? Why did he look so happy?

"Brother Augus." Petra's voice was suddenly sharp. "What's in your pocket?"

Rin looked and saw a handful of wotou, the steamed cornmeal buns that along with mayau fish comprised most of the soldiers' meals, peeking out the side of Augus's pocket.

"Just my rations," he said quickly.

"And were you going to eat them?" Petra asked.

"Sure, I'm just taking a walk—"

"*Augus.*"

His face fell. "They said they were hungry."

"You're not allowed to feed them," Rin said flatly. Jinzha had made that order adamantly clear. The civilians were to go hungry for the night. When the Republic fed them in the morning, their terror would be transformed into goodwill.

"That's cruel," Augus said.

"That's war," Rin said. "And if you can't follow basic orders, then—"

Petra swiftly intervened. "Remember your training, Augus. We do not contradict our hosts. We are here to spread the good word. Not to undermine the Nikara."

"But they're starving," Augus said. "I wanted to comfort them—"

"Then comfort them with the Maker's teachings." Petra placed a hand on Augus's cheek. "Go."

Rin watched Augus dart back down the beach. "He shouldn't be on this campaign. He's too young."

Petra turned and gestured for Rin to follow her onto the *Kingfisher*. "Not so much younger than your soldiers."

"Our soldiers are trained."

"And so are our missionaries." Petra led Rin down to her quarters on the second deck. "The brothers and sisters of the Gray Company have dedicated their lives to spreading the word of the Divine Architect across Chaos-ridden lands. All of us have been trained at the company academies since we were very young."

"I'm sure it's easy to find barbarians to civilize."

"There are indeed many on this hemisphere that have not found their way to the Maker." Petra seemed to have missed Rin's sarcasm entirely. She motioned for Rin to sit down on the bed. "Would you like laudanum again?"

"Are you going to touch me again?"

"Yes."

At this rate Rin was going to run the risk of backsliding into her opium addiction. But this choice was between the demon she knew and the foreigner she didn't. She took the proffered cup.

"Your continent has been closed off to us for a long time," Petra said as Rin drank. "Some of our superiors argued that we should stop learning your languages. But I've always known we would come back. The Maker demands it."

Rin closed her eyes as the familiar numbing sensation of laudanum seeped through her bloodstream. "So, what, your missionaries are walking up and down that beach giving everyone long spiels about clocks?"

"One need not comprehend the true form of the Divine Architect to act according to his will. We know that barbarians must crawl before they walk. Heuristics will do for the unenlightened."

"You mean easy moral rules for people who are too dumb to understand why they matter."

"If you must be vulgar about it. I am confident that in time, at least some of the Nikara will gain true enlightenment. In a few generations, some of you may even be fit to join the Gray Company. But heuristics must first be developed for the lesser peoples—"

"Lesser peoples," Rin echoed. "What are *lesser peoples*?"

"You, of course," Petra said, utterly straight-faced, as if this were a simple matter of fact. "It's no fault of your own. The Nikara haven't evolved to our level yet. This is simple science; the proof is in your physiognomy. Look."

She pulled a stack of books onto the table and flipped them open for Rin to see.

Drawings of Nikara people covered every page. They were heavily annotated. Rin couldn't decipher the scrawling, flat Hesperian script, but several phrases popped out.

See eye fold—indicates lazy character.

Sallow skin. Malnutrition?

On the last page, Rin saw a heavily annotated drawing of herself that must have been done by Petra. Rin was glad that Petra's handwriting was far too small for her to decipher. She didn't want to read any conclusions about herself.

"Since your eyes are smaller, you see within a smaller periphery than we do." Petra pointed to the diagrams as she explained. "Your skin has a yellowish tint that indicates malnutrition or an unbalanced diet. Now see your skull shapes. Your brains, which we know to be an indicator of your rational capacity, are by nature smaller."

Rin looked at her in disbelief. "You think you're just naturally smarter than me?"

"I don't think that," Petra said. "I know it. The proof is all well-documented. The Nikara are a particularly herdlike nation. You listen well, but independent thought is difficult for you. You reach scientific conclusions centuries after we discover them." Petra shut the book. "But worry not. In time, all civilizations will become perfect in the eyes of the Maker. That is the Gray Company's task."

"You think we're stupid," Rin said, almost to herself. She had the ridiculous urge to laugh. Did the Hesperians really take themselves this seriously? They thought this was *science*? "You think we're all inferior to you."

"Look at those people on the beach," Petra said. "Look at your country, squabbling over the refuse of wars you've been fighting for centuries. Do they look evolved to you?"

"And what, your own wars just happen to be civilized? Millions of you died, didn't they?"

"They died because we were fighting the forces of Chaos. Our wars are not internal. They are crusaders' battles. But look back to your own history, and tell me that any of your internal wars were fought for anything other than naked greed, ambition, or sheer cruelty."

Rin didn't know whether it was the laudanum, or whether Petra was truly correct, but she hated that she didn't have an answer.

In the morning, the remaining men of Radan were walked at sword point to the town square and instructed to cast their votes by throwing tiles into burlap bags. They could pick from two tile colors: white for yes and black for no.

"What happens if they vote against?" Rin asked Nezha.

"They'll die," he said. "Well, most of them. If they fight."

"Don't you think that kind of misses the point?"

Nezha shrugged. "Everyone joins the Republic by their own free choice. We're just, well, tipping the scales a little bit."

The voting took place one man at a time and lasted just over an hour. Rather than counting the tiles, Jinzha dumped the bags out onto the ground so that everyone could see the colors. By an overwhelming majority, the village of Radan had elected to join the Republic.

"Good decision," he said. "Welcome to the future."

He ordered a single skimmer to remain behind with its crew to enforce martial law and collect a monthly grain tax until the war's end. The fleet would confiscate a seventh of the township's food stores, leaving just enough to tide Radan over through the winter.

Nezha looked both pleased and relieved as they departed on the Murui. "That's what you get when the people decide."

Kitay shook his head. "No, that's what you get when you've killed all the brave men and let the cowards vote."

The Republican Fleet's subsequent skirmishes were similarly easy to the point of overkill. More often than not they took over townships and villages without a fight. A few cities put up resistance, but never to any effect. Against the combined strength of Jinzha's Seahawks, resisters usually capitulated within half a day.

As they went north, Jinzha detached brigades, and then entire platoons, to rule over recently liberated territory. Other crews bled soldiers to man those empty ships, until several skimmers had to be grounded and left on shore because the fleet had been spread too thin.

Some of the villages they conquered didn't put up a resistance at all, but readily joined the Republic. They sent out volunteers in boats laden with food and supplies. Hastily stitched flags bearing the colors of Dragon Province flew over city walls in a welcoming gesture.

"Look at that." Kitay pointed. "Vaisra's flag. Not the flag of the Republic."

"Does the Republic even *have* a flag?" Rin asked.

"I'm not sure. It's curious that they think they're being conquered by Dragon Province, though."

On Kitay's advice, Jinzha placed the volunteer ships and sailors in the front of the fleet. He didn't trust Hare Province sailors to fight on their home territory, and he didn't want them in strategically crucial positions in case they defected. But the extra ships were, in the worst-case scenario, excellent bait. Several times Jinzha sent allied ships out first to lure townships into opening their gates before he stormed them with his warships.

For a while it seemed like they might take the entire north in one clean, unobstructed sweep. But their fortunes finally took a turn for the worse at the northern border of Hare Province when a massive thunderstorm forced them to make anchor in a river cove.

The storm wasn't so much dangerous as it was boring. River storms, unlike ocean storms, could just be waited out if they grounded ships. So for three days the troops holed up belowdecks, playing cards and telling stories while rain battered at the hull.

"In the north they still offer divine sacrifices to the wind." The *Kingfisher*'s first mate, a gaunt man who had been at sea longer than Jinzha had been alive, had become the favorite storyteller of the mess. "In the days before the Red Emperor, the Khan of the Hinterlands sent down a fleet to invade the Empire. But a magician summoned a wind god to create a typhoon to destroy the Khan's fleet, and the Khan's ships turned to splinters in the ocean."

"Why not sacrifice to the ocean?" asked a sailor.

"Because oceans don't create storms. This was a god of the wind. But wind is fickle and unpredictable, and the gods have never taken lightly to being summoned by the Nikara. The moment the Khan's fleet was destroyed, the wind god turned on the Nikara magician who had summoned him. He pulled the magician's village into the sky and dropped it down in a bloody rain of ripped houses, crushed livestock, and dismembered children."

Rin stood up and quietly left the mess.

The passageways belowdecks were eerily quiet. Absent was the constant grinding sound of men working the paddle wheels. The crew and soldiers were concentrated in the mess, if they weren't sleeping, and so the passage was empty except for her.

When she pressed her face to the porthole she saw the storm raging outside, the vicious waves swirling about the cove like eager hands reaching to rip the fleet apart. In the clouds she thought she saw two eyes—bright, cerulean, maliciously intelligent.

She shivered. She thought she heard laughter in the thunder. She thought she saw a hand reach from the skies.

Then she blinked, and the storm was just a storm.

She didn't want to be alone, so she ventured downstairs to the soldiers' cabins, where she knew she could find the Cike.

"Hello there." Baji waved her inside. "Nice of you to join."

She sat down cross-legged beside him. "What are you playing?"

Baji tossed a handful of dice into a cup. "Divisions. Ever played?"

Rin thought briefly back to Tutor Feyrik, the man who had gotten her to Sinegard, and his unfortunate addiction to the game. She smiled wistfully. "Just a bit."

Nominally, no gambling of any kind was permitted on the ships. Lady Yin Saikhara, since her pilgrimage to the west, had instituted strict rules about vices such as drinking, smoking, gambling, and consorting with prostitutes. Almost everyone ignored them. Vaisra never enforced them.

It turned out to be a rather vicious game. Ramsa kept accusing Baji of cheating. Baji was not cheating, but they discovered that Ramsa *was* when a handful of dice spilled out of his sleeve, at which point the game turned into a wrestling match that ended only when Ramsa bit Baji on the arm hard enough to draw blood.

"You mangy little brat," Baji cursed as he wrapped a linen around his elbow.

Ramsa grinned, displaying teeth stained red.

All of them were clearly bored, going stir-crazy while waiting out the storm. But Rin suspected that they were also itching for action. She'd cautioned them not to put their full abilities on display where Hesperian soldiers might be watching. Petra knew about one shaman; she didn't need to discover the rest.

Concealment had turned out to be fairly easy on campaign. Suni and Baji's abilities were freakish, yes, but not necessarily in the realm of the supernatural. In the chaos of a melee, they could pass themselves off as hypercompetent soldiers. It had worked so far. As far as Rin knew, the Hesperians suspected nothing. Suni and Baji might be getting frustrated holding themselves back, but at least they were free.

For once, Rin thought, she'd made some decent decisions as commander. She hadn't gotten them killed. The Republican troops treated them better than the Militia ever had. They were getting paid, they were as safe as they'd ever be, and that was as good as she could do for them.

"What are the Gray Company like?" Baji asked as he scooped the dice off the floor for a new game. "I heard that woman talks your ear off every time you're together."

"It's stupid," Rin muttered. "Religious lecturing."

"Load of hogwash?" Ramsa asked.

"I don't know," she admitted. "They might be right about some things."

She wished she could discard the Hesperian faith more easily, but so many parts of it made sense. She wanted to believe it. She wanted to see her catastrophic actions as a product of Chaos, an entropic mistake, and to believe that she could repent for them by reinforcing order in the Empire, reversing devastation the way one pieced together a broken teacup.

It made her feel better. It made every battle she'd fought since Adlaga feel like another step toward putting things right. It made her feel less like a killer.

"You know their Divine Architect doesn't exist," Baji said. "I mean, you understand why that's obvious, right?"

"I'm not sure," she said slowly. Certainly the Maker didn't exist on the same psychospiritual plane as the sixty-four gods of the Pantheon, but was that enough to discount the Hesperians' theory? What if the Pantheon was, in fact, a manifestation of Chaos? What if the Divine Architect truly existed on a higher plane, out of reach of anyone but his chosen and blessed people?

"I mean, look at their airships," she said. "Their arquebuses. If they're claiming religion made them advanced, they might be right about some things."

Baji opened his mouth to respond and promptly closed it. Rin looked up and saw a shock of white hair in the doorway.

No one spoke. The dice clattered loudly to the floor and stayed there.

Ramsa broke the silence. "Hi, Chaghan."

Rin hadn't spoken to Chaghan since Arlong. When the fleet had sailed, she'd partly hoped that Chaghan might just elect to stay on land. He was never one for the thick of battle, and after their falling-out she couldn't imagine why he'd stay with her. But the twins had remained with the Cike, and Rin had found herself crossing the room whenever she saw a hint of white hair.

Chaghan paused by the door, Qara close behind him.

"Having fun?" he asked.

"Sure," Baji said. "You want in?"

"No, thank you," Chaghan said. "But it's nice to see you're all having such a good time."

No one responded to that. Rin knew she was being mocked, she just didn't have the energy to get into it with Chaghan right now.

"Does it hurt?" Qara asked.

Rin blinked. "What?"

"When the gray-eyed one takes you to her cabin," Qara said. "Does it hurt?"

"Oh. It's—it's not so bad. It's just a lot of measurements."

Qara cast her what looked like a glance of sympathy, but Chaghan grabbed his sister by the arm and stormed out of the cabin before she could speak.

Ramsa gave a low whistle and began to pick the dice up off the floor.

Baji gave Rin a curious look. "What happened between you two?"

"Stupid shit," Rin muttered.

"Stupid shit about Altan?" Ramsa pressed.

"Why would you think it was about Altan?"

"Because with Chaghan, it's always about Altan." Ramsa tossed his dice into a cup and shook. "Honestly? I think Altan was Chaghan's only friend. He's still grieving. And there's nothing you can do to make that hurt less."

CHAPTER 17

The storm passed with minimal damage. One skimmer capsized—the force of the winds had ripped it from its anchor. Three men drowned. But the crew managed to salvage most of its supplies, and the drowned men had been only foot soldiers, so Jinzha wrote it off as a minor setback.

The moment the skies cleared, he gave the order to continue upriver toward Ram Province. It was one step closer to the military center of the Empire and, as Kitay anticipated, the first territory that would present a fighting challenge.

The Ram Warlord had holed up inside Xiashang, his capital, instead of mounting a border defense. This was why the Republic encountered little other than local volunteer militias throughout their destructive trek north. The Ram Warlord had chosen to bide his time and wait for Jinzha's troops to tire before fighting a defensive battle.

That should have been a losing strategy. The Republican Fleet was simply *bigger* than whatever force the Ram Warlord could have rounded up. They knew they could take Ram Province; it was only a matter of time.

The only wrinkle was that Xiashang had unexpectedly robust defenses. Thanks to Qara's birds, the Republican forces had a good layout map of the capital's defensive structures. Even the tower ships with their trebuchets would have a difficult time breaching those walls.

As such, Rin spent her next few evenings in the *Kingfisher*'s office, crammed around a table with Jinzha's leadership coterie.

"The walls are the problem. You can't blow through them." Kitay pointed to a ring he'd drawn around the walls of the city. "They're made of packed earth, three feet thick. You could try ramming them with cannonballs, but it'd just be a waste of good fire powder."

"What about a siege?" Jinzha asked. "We could force a surrender if they think we're willing to wait."

"You'd be a fool," said General Tarcquet.

Jinzha bristled visibly. The leadership exchanged awkward looks.

Tarcquet was always present at strategy councils, though he rarely spoke and never offered the assistance of his own troops. He'd made his role clear. He was there to judge their competence and quietly deride their mistakes, which made his input both irreproachable and grating.

"If this were my fleet I'd throw everything I have at those walls," Tarcquet said. "If you can't take a minor capital, you won't take the Empire."

"But this is not your fleet," Jinzha said. "It's mine."

Tarcquet's lip curled in contempt. "You are in command because your father thought you'd at least be smart enough to do whatever I told you."

Jinzha looked furious, but Tarcquet held up a hand before he could respond. "You can't pull off this bluff. They know you don't have the supplies or the time. You'll have to fold in weeks."

Despite herself, Rin agreed with Tarcquet's assessment. She'd studied this precise problem at Sinegard. Of all the successful defensive campaigns on military record, most were when cities had warded off invaders through protracted siege warfare. A siege turned a battle into a waiting game of who starved first. The Republican Fleet had the supplies to last for perhaps a month. It was unclear how long Xiashang could last. It would be foolish to wait and find out.

"They certainly don't have enough food for the entire city," Nezha said. "We made sure of that."

"Doesn't matter," Kitay said. "The Ram Warlord and his people will be fine. They'll just let the peasants starve; Tsung Ho has done that before."

"Do we try negotiating?" Nezha asked.

"Won't work—Tsung Ho hates Father," Jinzha said. "And he has no incentive to cooperate, because he'll just assume that under the Republican regime he'd be deposed sooner or later."

"A siege *might* work," said Admiral Molkoi. "Those walls are not so impenetrable. We'd just have to break them down at a choke point."

"I wouldn't," Kitay said. "That's what they'll be preparing for. If you're going to storm the city, you want the element of surprise. Some gimmick. Like a false peace proposal. But I don't think they'd fall for that; Tsung Ho is too smart."

A thought occurred to Rin. "What about Fuchai and Goujian?" The men stared blankly at her.

"Fuchai and who?" Jinzha asked.

Only Kitay and Nezha looked like they understood. The tale of Fuchai and Goujian was a favorite story of Master Irjah's. They'd all been assigned to write term papers about it during their second year.

"Fuchai and Goujian were two generals during the Era of Warring States," Nezha explained. "Fuchai destroyed Goujian's home state, and then made Goujian his personal servant to humiliate him. Goujian performed the most degrading tasks to make Fuchai believe he bore him no ill will. One time when Fuchai fell sick, Goujian volunteered to taste his stool to tell how bad his illness was. It worked—ten years later, Fuchai set Goujian free. The first thing Goujian did was hire a beautiful concubine and send her to Fuchai's court in the guise of a gift."

"The concubine, of course, killed Fuchai," Kitay said.

Jinzha looked baffled. "You're saying I send the Ram Warlord a beautiful concubine."

"No," Rin said. "I'm saying you should eat shit."

Tarcquet barked out a laugh.

Jinzha reddened. "Excuse me?"

"The Ram Warlord thinks he holds all the cards," Rin said. "So initiate a negotiation. Humiliate yourself, present yourself as weaker than you are, and make him underestimate your forces."

"That won't tear down his walls," said Jinzha.

"But it *will* make him cocky. How does his behavior change if he's not anticipating an attack? If he instead thinks you're running away? Then we have an opening to exploit." Rin cast about wildly in her head for ideas. "You could get someone behind those walls. Open the gates from the inside."

"There's no way you manage that," Nezha said. "You'd need to get an entire platoon to fight through from the inside, and you can't hide that many men in one ship."

"I don't need an entire platoon," Rin said.

"No squadron is capable of that."

She crossed her arms. "I can think of one."

For once, Jinzha wasn't looking at her with disdain.

"Who do we send to negotiate with the Ram Warlord, then?" he asked.

Rin and Nezha both answered at once. "Kitay."

Kitay frowned. "Because I'm a good negotiator?"

"No." Nezha clapped him on the shoulder. "Because you'll be a really, really bad one."

"I was under the impression that I was receiving your grand marshal." The Ram Warlord lounged casually on his chair, tapping his fingers together as he appraised the Republican delegation with sharp, intelligent eyes.

"You'll be meeting with me," Kitay said. He spoke in a perfectly tremulous voice, obviously nervous and pretending not to be. "The Dragon Warlord is indisposed."

The Republican delegation was deliberately shabby. Kitay was guarded only by two infantry soldiers from the *Kingfisher*. His life had to seem cheap. Jinzha hadn't wanted to let Rin come, but she refused to stay behind while Kitay went to face the enemy.

Their delegations had met at a neutral stretch along the shore. The backdrop made the meeting seem more like a competitive fishing match than the site of a war negotiation. This move, Rin assumed, was designed to humiliate Kitay.

The Ram Warlord looked Kitay up and down and pursed his lips. "Vaisra can't be bothered, so he sends a little puppy to negotiate for him."

Kitay puffed himself up. "I'm not a puppy. I'm the son of Defense Minister Chen."

"Yes, I wondered why you looked familiar. You're a far cry from your old man, aren't you?"

Kitay cleared his throat. "Jinzha sent me here with proposed terms for a truce."

"A truce should be settled between leaders. Jinzha does not even afford me the respect that he ought a Warlord."

"Jinzha has entrusted negotiations to me," Kitay said stiffly.

The Ram Warlord's eyes narrowed. "Ah, I understand. Injured then? Or dead?"

"Jinzha is fine." Kitay let his voice tremble just a bit at the end. "He sends his regards."

The Ram Warlord leaned forward in his chair, like a wolf examining his prey. "Really."

Kitay cleared his throat again. "Jinzha instructed me to convey that the truce can only benefit you. We *will* take the north. It's up to you to decide whether or not you want to join our forces. If you agree to our terms then we'll leave Xiashang alone, so long as your men serve in our—"

The Ram Warlord cut him off. "I have no interest in joining Vaisra's so-called republic. It's just a ploy to put himself on the throne."

"That's paranoid," Kitay said.

"Does Yin Vaisra seem like a man inclined to share power to you?"

"The Dragon Warlord intends to implement the representative democracy style of government practiced in the west. He knows the provincial system isn't working—"

"Oh, but it's working very well for us," said the Ram Warlord. "The only dissenters are those poor suckers in the south, led by Vaisra himself. The rest of us see a system that's granted us stability for two decades. There's no need to disrupt that."

"But it *will* be disrupted," Kitay insisted. "You've seen the fault lines yourself. You're weeks away from going to war with your neighbors over riverways, you have more refugees than you can deal with, and you've received no Imperial aid."

"That, you're wrong about," said the Ram Warlord. "The Empress has been exceedingly generous to my province. Meanwhile, your embargo failed, your fields are poisoned, and you're quickly running out of time."

Rin shot Kitay a glance. His face betrayed nothing, but she knew, on the inside, he must be gloating.

As they spoke, a single merchant ship drifted toward Xiashang, marked with smugglers' colors provided to them by Moag. It would claim to have run up from Monkey Province with illegal shipments of grain. Jinzha had packed soldiers into the hold and dressed the few sailors who would remain visible on deck as river traders.

If the Ram Warlord was expecting smuggler ships, then he might very well let it within the city gates.

"There's a way out here that doesn't end in your death," Kitay said.

"Negotiations are a matter of leverage, little boy," said the Ram Warlord. "And I don't see your fleet."

"Maybe your spies should look harder," Kitay said. "Maybe we've hidden it."

They *had* hidden it, deep inside a canyon crevice two miles downstream from Xiashang's gates. Jinzha had sent a smaller fleet of skimmers manned by skeleton crews out toward a different tributary to make it appear that the Dragon Fleet was avoiding Xiashang entirely by sailing east toward Tiger Province instead. They'd done this very conspicuously in broad daylight. The Ram Warlord's spies had to have seen.

The Ram Warlord shrugged. "Perhaps. Or perhaps you've taken the easy route down the Udomsap tributary instead."

Rin fought to keep her expression neutral.

"The Udomsap isn't so far from you," said Kitay. "By river or by ground, you're lying in Jinzha's warpath."

"Bold words from a little boy." The Ram Warlord snorted.

"A little boy speaking for a great army," Kitay said. "Sooner or later, we'll come for you. And then you'll regret it."

The blustering was an act, but Rin suspected the frustration in his voice was real. Kitay was playing his part so well that Rin couldn't help but feel a sudden urge to step in front of him, to protect him. Standing one-on-one before a Warlord, Kitay just looked like a boy: thin, scared, and far too young for his position.

"No. I don't think we will." The Ram Warlord reached over and ruffled Kitay's hair. "I think you're trapped. That storm hit you harder than you'll admit. And you don't have the troops to press on into the winter, and you're running out of supplies, so you want me to throw open my gates and save your skins. Tell Jinzha he can take his truce and shove it up his butt." He smiled, displaying teeth. "Run along down the river, now."

"I admit this might have been a terrible idea," said Kitay.

Rin's spyglass was trained on Xiashang's gates. She had a sick feeling in her stomach. The fleet had been waiting around the bend since dark. The sun had been up for hours. The gates were still closed.

"You don't think he bought it," Rin said.

"I was so sure he'd buy it," said Kitay. "Men like that are so incredibly arrogant that they always need to think that they've outsmarted everyone else. But maybe he *did*."

Rin didn't want to entertain that thought.

Another hour passed. No movement. Kitay started walking in circles, chewing at his thumbnail so hard that it bled. "Someone should suggest a retreat."

Rin lowered her spyglass. "You'd be sentencing my men to death."

"It's been half a day," he said curtly. "Chances are they're dead already."

Jinzha, who had been pacing the length of the deck in agitation, motioned toward them. "It's time to pursue other options. Those men are gone."

Rin's fists tightened. "Don't you dare—"

"They could have captured them." Kitay tried to calm her down. "He could be planning to use them as hostages."

"We don't have anyone important on that ship," Jinzha said, which Rin thought was a rather cruel way of describing some of his best soldiers. "And knowing Tsung Ho, he'd just set it on fire."

The sun crawled to high noon.

Rin fought the creep of despair. The later it got in the day, the worse their chances of storming the walls. They had already lost the element of surprise. The Ram Warlord surely knew they were coming by now, and he'd had half the day to prepare defenses.

But what other choice did the Republic have? The Cike were trapped behind those gates. Any later and their chances of survival dwindled to nothing. Waiting was useless. Escape would be humiliating.

Jinzha seemed to have been thinking the same. "They're out of time. We attack."

"That's what they want, though!" Kitay protested. "This is the battle they want to have."

"Then we'll give them that fight." Jinzha signaled Admiral Molkoi to give the order. For once, Rin was glad that he'd ignored Kitay.

The Republican Fleet surged forward, a symphony of war drums and churning paddle wheels.

Xiashang *had* prepared well to meet the charge. The Militia went on the offensive immediately. A wave of arrows greeted the Republican Fleet as soon as it crossed into range. For an instant it was impossible to hear anything over the sound of arrows thudding into wood, steel, and flesh. And it didn't stop. The artillery assault kept coming in wave after wave from archers who seemed to have an endless supply of arrows.

The Republican archers returned fire, but they might have been shooting aimlessly at the sky. The defenders simply ducked down and let the bolts whiz overhead while Republican rockets exploded harmlessly against the massive city walls.

The *Kingfisher* was safe ensconced within its turtleshell armor, but the other Republican ships had been effectively reduced to sitting ducks. The tower ships floated uselessly in the water. Their trebuchet crews couldn't launch any missiles—they couldn't move without fear of being turned into pincushions.

The *Lapwing*, the Seahawk closest to the walls, sent a double-headed dragon missile screeching through the air only for a Ram archer to shoot it out of the sky. Upon impact it fell sizzling back toward the boat. The *Lapwing*'s crew scattered before the shower of missiles fell upon their own munitions supply. Rin heard one round of explosions, and then another—a chain reaction that engulfed the Seahawk ship in smoke and fire.

The *Shrike*, however, had managed to steer its towers to just beside the city gate. Rin squinted at the ship, trying to gauge its distance from the wall. The towers were just tall enough to clear the parapets, but as long as the wall was manned with archers, the tower was useless. Anyone who scaled the siege engine would just be picked off at the top.

Someone had to take those archers out.

Rin glared at the wall, frustrated, cursing the Seal. If she could call the Phoenix she could have just sent a torrent of flame over the barriers, could have cleared it out in under a minute.

But she didn't have the fire. Which meant she had to get up there herself, and she needed explosives.

She cupped her hands around her mouth. "Ramsa!"

He was crouched ten meters away behind the mast. She screamed his name thrice to no avail. At last she threw a scrap of wood at his shoulder to get his attention.

He yelped. "What the hell?"

"I need a bomb!"

He opened his mouth to respond just as another set of missiles exploded against the turtle boat's side. He shook his head and gestured frantically at his empty knapsack.

"Anything?" she mouthed.

He dug deep in his pocket, pulled out something round, and rolled it across the floor toward her. She picked it up. A pungent smell hit her nose.

"Is this a *shit bomb*?" she yelled.

Ramsa waved his hands helplessly. "It's all I've got left!"

It would have to do. She shoved the bomb into her shirt. She'd worry about ignition when she got to the wall. Now she needed some way to climb up to the top. And a shield, something huge, heavy and large enough to cover her entire body . . .

Her eyes landed on the rowboats.

She turned to Kitay. "Pull a boat up."

"What?"

She pointed to the siege tower. "Get me up in a boat!"

His eyes widened in understanding. He barked a series of orders to the soldiers behind him. They ran out to the mainmast, ducking beneath shields raised over their heads.

Rin jumped into a rowboat with two other soldiers. Kitay directed the men to fasten the ropes at the ends, typically meant to lower the rowboat into the water, onto the mast pulley. The rowboat teetered wildly when they started hoisting it up the mast. It hadn't been secured well. Halfway up it threatened to flip over until they scrambled to redistribute their weight.

An arrow whistled past Rin's head. The Ram archers had seen them.

"Hold on!" She twisted the ropes. The rowboat tilted nearly

horizontal, a functional full-body shield. Rin crouched down, clinging fast to a seat so she wouldn't tumble out. A crossbow bolt slid through the bottom of the boat and cut through the arm of the soldier to her left. He screamed and let go. A second later Rin heard him crunch on the deck.

She held her breath. The boat was almost to the top of the wall.

"Get ready." She bent her knees and rocked the boat so that it would swing forward. Their first swing toward the wall fell short by a yard. Rin caught a brief, dizzying glimpse of the drop beneath her feet.

Another series of arrows studded the rowboat as they swung backward.

Their second swing got them close enough.

"Go!"

They jumped to the wall. Rin slipped on impact. Her knees skidded on solid rock but her feet kicked off into terrifying, empty space. She flung her arms forward and seized a groove cut in the wall. She strained to pull herself up just far enough that she could slam her elbow into the ridge and drag her torso over.

She tumbled gracelessly onto the walkway and staggered to her feet just as a Ram soldier swung a blade at her head. She blocked it with her trident, wrestled it in a circle, sent it spinning uselessly away, and then butted him in the side with the other end. He tumbled down the stairs and smashed into his comrades.

That gave her a temporary reprieve. She scanned the wall of archers. Ramsa's shit bomb wouldn't kill them, but it would distract them. She just needed a way to ignite it.

Again she cursed the Seal. She could have just lit it with a snap of her fingers; it would have been so *easy*.

She cast her eyes about for a lamp, a brazier, something . . . *there*. Five feet away sat a lump of burning coals in a brass pot. The Ram defenders must have been using it to light their own missiles.

She hefted the bomb in her hands, tossed it toward the pot, and prayed.

She heard a faint, dull pop.

She took a deep breath. Acrid, shit-flavored smoke spilled over the parapets, thick and blinding.

"We're in trouble," said the Republican soldier at her left.

She squinted through the smoke at a column of Ram reinforcements approaching fast from the lefthand walkway.

She looked frantically about the wall for a way to get down. She saw a stairwell to her left, but too many soldiers stood crowded at the base. The only other way down was across the other side of the wall, but the walkway didn't go all the way around—a ridge of wall no thicker than her heel stood between her and the other stairwell.

No time to think. She jumped onto the outer edge of the wall, dug her heels in, and began running before she could teeter to either side. Every few steps she felt her balance jerk horrifically to one side. Somehow she righted herself and kept going.

She heard the twangs of several bows. Rather than duck, she took a flying leap toward the stairwell. She landed painfully on her side and skidded to a halt. Her shoulder and hip screamed in protest, but her arms and legs still worked. She crawled frantically down the stairs, arrows whizzing over her head.

Behind the gates was a war zone.

She'd stumbled into a crush of bodies, a clamor of steel. Blue uniforms dotted the crowd. Republican soldiers. Relief washed over her. They weren't dead after all, just late.

"About time!"

Two wonderfully familiar tornadoes of destruction appeared before her. Suni picked up a Ram soldier as if he were a doll, hoisted him over his head, and flung him into the crowd. Baji slammed his rake down into someone's neck, yanked it up, and twirled it in a circle to knock an incoming arrow out of the air.

"Nice," Rin said.

He helped her to her feet. "What took you so long?"

Rin opened her mouth to respond just as someone tried to grapple her from behind. She jammed her elbow back by instinct and felt the rewarding crunch of a shattering nose. Her assailant's grip loosened. She struggled free. "We were waiting for your signal!"

"We gave a signal! Sent a flare up ten minutes ago! Where's the fucking army?"

Rin pointed to the wall. "There."

A thud shook Xiashang's gates. The *Shrike* had landed its siege tower.

Republican soldiers funneled over the wall like a swarm of ants. Bodies hurtled to the ground like tumbling bricks, while grappling hooks flew into the sky and embedded themselves at regular intervals along the wall.

She saw almost as many blue uniforms as green ones now. Slowly the press of Republican soldiers expanded through the center square.

"Get to the gates," Rin told Baji.

"Way ahead of you." Baji scattered the throng of soldiers guarding one suspension wheel with a well-aimed swing of his rake. Suni took the other wheel. Together they dug their heels into the ground and pushed. Republican soldiers formed a protective circle around them, fending off the press of defenders.

"*Push!*" someone screamed.

Rin didn't have the chance to look behind her to see what was happening. The wave of steel was too blinding. Something sliced open her left cheek. Blood splattered across her face. It was in her eyes—she wiped at them with her sleeve, but that only made them sting worse.

She lashed blindly out with her trident. Steel crunched into bone, and her attacker dropped to the ground. Lucky blow. Rin fell back behind the Republican line and blinked furiously until her vision cleared.

She heard a screeching grind from the suspension wheels. She hazarded a glance over her shoulder. With a massive groan, the gates of Xiashang swung open.

Behind them was the fleet.

The tide had turned. Republican soldiers flooded the square, a deluge of so many blue uniforms that for a moment Rin lost sight of the Ram defenders entirely. Somewhere a horn blew, followed by a series of gong strikes that rang so loudly they drowned out any other sound.

Distress signals. But signals to *whom*? Rin clambered up onto a crate, trying to see above the melee.

She spotted movement in the southwest corridor. She squinted. A new platoon of soldiers, armed and battle-fresh, ran toward the square. The local backup militia? No—they were wearing blue uniforms, not green.

But that wasn't the ocean blue of the Republican uniforms.

Rin almost dropped her trident. Those weren't Nikara soldiers.

Those were Federation troops.

For a moment she thought, panicking, that the Federation was still at large, that they had taken this chance to launch a simultaneous invasion on Xiashang. But that made no sense. The Federation had already been behind the city gates. And they weren't attacking the Xiashang city guard, they were only attacking troops clearly marked in Republican uniforms.

Realization hit like a punch to the gut.

The Ram Warlord had allied with the Federation.

The ground tilted beneath her feet. She saw smoke and fire. She saw bodies eaten by gas. She saw Altan, walking backward away from her on a pier—

"Get down!" Baji shouted.

Rin flung herself to the ground just as a spear hit the wall where her head had been.

She struggled to her feet. She couldn't see an end to the column of Federation soldiers. How many were there? Did they equal Republican numbers?

What had seemed like an easy victory was about to turn into a bloodbath.

She raced up the stairway to get a better look at the city's layout. Just past the town square she saw a three-story residence embedded in a massive, sculpture-dotted garden. That had to be the Ram Warlord's private quarters. It was the largest building in Xiashang.

She knew the best way to end this.

"Baji!" She waved her trident to get his attention. When he looked up, she pointed toward the Ram Warlord's mansion. "Cover me."

He understood immediately. Together they forced their bloody way through the throng until they broke out on the other side of the square. Then they ran for the gardens.

The mansion was guarded by two stone lions, mouths open in wide, greedy caverns. The doors were bolted shut.

Good. That meant someone was hiding inside.

Rin aimed a savage kick at the handle, but the doors didn't budge.

"Please," said Baji. She got out of his way. He took three steps back and slammed his shoulder into the doors. Wood splintered. The doors crashed open.

Baji picked himself up off the ground and pointed behind her. "We've got trouble."

Rin turned around to see a fresh wave of Federation soldiers running toward the mansion. Baji planted himself in the doorway, rake raised.

"You good?" Rin asked.

"You go. I've got this."

She ran indoors. The halls were brightly lit but appeared entirely empty—which would have been the worst of outcomes, because that would mean the Ram Warlord's family had already evacuated to somewhere safe. Rin stood still in the center of the hall, heart pounding, straining to listen for any sound of inhabitants.

Seconds later she heard a baby's shrill wail.

Yes. She concentrated, trying to track the noise. She heard it again. This time the baby's cry was stifled, like someone had clamped a sleeve over its mouth, but in the empty house it rang clear as a bell.

The sound came from the chambers to her left. Rin crept forward, shoes moving silently across the marble floor. At the end of the hall she saw a single silkscreen door. The baby's cries were getting louder. She placed a hand on the door and pulled. Locked. She took a step back and kicked it down. The flimsy bamboo frame gave way with no trouble.

A crowd of at least fifteen women stared up at her, tears of terror streaming down their fat and puffy cheeks, clumped together like flightless birds fattened for the slaughter.

They were the Warlord's wives, Rin guessed. His daughters. Their servant girls and nursemaids.

"Where is Tsung Ho?" she demanded.

They huddled closer together, mute and trembling.

Rin's eyes fell on the baby. An old woman at the back of the room had it clutched in her hands. It was swaddled in red cloth. That meant it was a baby boy. A potential heir.

The Ram Warlord would not let that child die.

"Give him to me," Rin said.

The woman frantically shook her head and pressed the child closer to her chest.

Rin leveled her trident at her. "This is not worth dying for."

One of the girls dashed forward, flailing at her with a curtain pole. Rin ducked down and kicked out. Her foot connected with the girl's midriff with a satisfying *whumph*. The girl collapsed on the ground, wailing in pain.

Rin put a foot on the girl's sternum and pressed down, hard. The girl's agonized whimpers gave her a savage, amused satisfaction. She felt a distinct lack of sympathy toward the women. They chose to be here. They were Federation allies, they knew what was happening, this was their fault, they should all be dead . . .

No. Stop. She took a deep breath. The red cleared from her eyes.

"Any of you try that again and I'll gut you," she said. "The baby. *Now.*"

Whimpering, the old woman relinquished the baby into her hands.

He immediately started to scream. Rin's hands moved automatically to cup around his rear and the back of his head. Leftover instincts from days she'd spent carrying around her infant foster brother.

She had a sudden urge to coo to the baby and rock him until his sobbing ceased. She shut it down. She needed the baby to scream, and to scream loudly.

She backed out of the women's quarters, waving her trident in front of her.

"You lot stay here," she warned the women. "If any of you move, I will kill this child."

The women nodded silently, tears streaking their powdered faces.

Rin backed out of the chamber and returned to the center of the main hall.

"Tsung Ho!" she shouted. "Where are you?"

Silence.

The baby quivered in her arms. His cries had diminished to distressed whimpers. Rin briefly considered pinching his arms to make him scream.

There was no need. The sight of her bloody trident was enough. He caught one glimpse of it, opened his mouth, and shrieked.

Rin shouted over the baby, "Tsung Ho! I'll murder your son if you don't come out."

She heard him approaching long before he attacked.

Too slow. Too fucking slow. She spun around, dodged his blade, and slammed the butt of her trident into his stomach. He doubled over. She caught his blade inside the trident's prongs and twisted it out of his hand. He dropped to all fours, scrambling for his weapon. She kicked it out of the way and jammed the hilt of her trident into the back of his head. He dropped to the floor.

"You traitor." She aimed a savage strike at his kneecaps. He howled in pain. She hit them again. Then again.

The baby wailed louder. She walked to a corner, placed him delicately on the floor, then resumed her assault on his father. The Ram Warlord's kneecaps were visibly broken. She moved on to his ribs.

"Please, mercy, *please* . . ." He curled into a pathetic bundle, arms wrapped over his head.

"When did you let the Mugenese into your gates?" she asked. "Before they burned Golyn Niis, or after?"

"We didn't have a choice," he whispered. He made a high keening noise as he drew his shattered knees to his chest. "They were lined up at our gates, we didn't have any options—"

"You could have fought."

"We would have died," he gasped.

"Then you should have died."

Rin slammed her trident butt against his head. He fell silent.

The baby continued to scream.

Jinzha was so pleased by their victory that he temporarily relaxed the army prohibition on alcohol. Jugs of fine sorghum wine, all plundered from the Ram Warlord's mansion, were passed through the ranks. The soldiers camped out on the beach that night in an unusually good mood.

Jinzha and his council met by the shore to decide what to do with their prisoners. In addition to the captured Federation soldiers there were also the men of the Eighth Division—a larger Militia force than any conquered town they had dealt with so far. They were too big of a threat to let loose. Short of a mass execution, their options were to take an unwieldy number of prisoners—far too many to feed—or to let them go.

"Execute them," Rin said immediately.

"More than a thousand men?" Jinzha shook his head. "We're not monsters."

"But they deserve it," she said. "The Mugenese, at least. You know if the tables were turned, if the Federation had taken our men prisoners, they'd be dead already."

She was so sure that it was a moot debate. But nobody nodded in agreement. She glanced around the circle, confused. Was the conclusion not clear? Why did they all look so uncomfortable?

"They'd be good at the wheels," Admiral Molkoi said. "It'd give our men a break."

"You're joking," Rin said. "You'd have to feed them, for starters—"

"So we'll give them a subsistence diet," said Molkoi.

"Our troops need that food!"

"Our troops have survived on less," Molkoi said. "And it is best they don't get used to the excess."

Rin gawked at him. "You'll put *our* troops on stricter rations so men who have committed treason can live?"

He shrugged. "They're Nikara men. We won't execute our own kind."

"They stopped being Nikara the moment they let the Federation stroll into their homes," she snapped. "They should be rounded up. And beheaded."

None of the others would meet her eye.

"Nezha?" she asked.

He wouldn't look at her. All he did was shake his head.

She flushed with anger. "These soldiers were collaborating with the Federation. Feeding them. Housing them. That's *treason*. That should be punishable by death. Forget the soldiers—you should have the whole city punished!"

"Perhaps under Daji's reign," said Jinzha. "Not under the Republic. We can't garner a reputation for brutality—"

"Because they *helped* them!" She was shouting now, and they were all staring at her, but she didn't care. "The Federation! You don't know what they did—just because you spent the war hiding in Arlong, you didn't see what—"

Jinzha turned to Nezha. "Brother, put a muzzle on your Speerly, or—"

"*I am not a dog!*" Rin shrieked.

Sheer rage took over. She launched herself at Jinzha—and didn't manage two steps before Admiral Molkoi tackled her to the ground so hard that for a moment the night stars blinked out of the sky, and it was all she could do to simply breathe.

"That's enough," Nezha said quietly. "She's calmed down. Let her go."

The pressure on her chest disappeared. Rin curled into a ball, choking miserably.

"Someone take her outside of camp," Jinzha said. "Bind her, gag her, I don't care. We'll deal with this in the morning."

"Yes, sir," said Molkoi.

"She hasn't eaten," Nezha said.

"Then have someone bring her food or water if she asks," Jinzha said. "Just get her out of my sight."

Rin screamed.

No one could hear her—they'd banished her to a stretch of forest outside the camp perimeter—so she screamed louder, again and again, bashing her fists against a tree until blood ran down her knuckles while rage built up hotter and hotter in her chest. And for a moment she thought—hoped—that the crimson fury sparking in her vision might explode into flames, real flames, *finally*—

But nothing. No sparks lit her fingers; no divine laughter rippled through her thoughts. She could feel the Seal at the back of her mind, a pulsing, sickly thing, blurring and softening her anger every time it reached a peak. And that only doubled her rage, made her shriek louder in frustration, but it was a pointless tantrum because the fire remained out of her grasp; dancing, taunting her behind the barrier in her head.

Please, she thought. *I need you, I need the fire, I need to burn . . .*

The Phoenix remained silent.

She sank to her knees.

She could hear Altan laughing. That wasn't the Seal, that was her own imagination, but she heard it as clearly as if he were standing right beside her.

"Look at you," he said.

"Pathetic," he said.

"It's not coming back," he said. "You're lost, you're done, you're not a Speerly, you're just a stupid little girl throwing a temper tantrum in the forest."

Finally her voice and strength gave out and the anger ebbed

pathetically, ineffectually, away. Then she was alone with the indifferent silence of the trees, with no company except for her own mind.

And Rin couldn't stand that, so she decided to get as drunk as she possibly could.

She'd picked up a small jug of sorghum wine back at camp. She chugged it down in under a minute.

She wasn't used to drinking. The masters at Sinegard had been strict—the smallest whiff of alcohol was grounds for expulsion. She still preferred the sickly sweetness of opium smoke to the burn of sorghum wine, but she liked how it seared her delightfully from the inside. It didn't make the anger go away, but it reduced it to a dull throb, an aching pain rather than a sharp, fresh wound.

By the time Nezha came out for her she was utterly soused, and she wouldn't have heard him approach if he hadn't shouted for her every step he took.

"Rin? Are you there?"

She heard his voice around the other side of a tree. She blinked for a few seconds before she remembered how to push words out of her mouth. "Yes. Don't come around."

"What are you doing?"

He circled the tree. She hastily yanked her trousers back up with one hand. A dripping jug dangled from the other.

"Are you pissing in a jug?"

"I'm preparing a gift for your brother," she said. "Think he'll like it?"

"You can't give the grand marshal of the Republican Army a jug of urine."

"But it's warm," she mumbled. She shook it at him. Piss sloshed out the side.

Nezha hastily stepped away. "Please put that down."

"You sure Jinzha doesn't want it?"

"*Rin.*"

She sighed dramatically and complied.

He took her clean hand and led her to a patch of grass by the river, far away from the soiled jug. "You know you can't lash out like that."

She squared her shoulders. "And I have been appropriately disciplined."

"It's not about *discipline*. They'll think you're mad."

"They already think I'm mad," she retorted. "Savage, dumb little Speerly. Right? It's in my nature."

"That's not what I . . . Come on, Rin." Nezha shook his head. "Anyhow. I've, uh, got bad news."

She yawned. "Did we lose the war? That was quick."

"No. Jinzha's demoted you."

She blinked several times, uncomprehending. "What?"

"You're unranked. You're to serve as a foot soldier now. And you're not in command of the Cike anymore."

"So who is?"

"No one. There is no Cike. They've all been reassigned to other ships."

He watched her carefully to gauge her reaction, but Rin just hiccupped.

"That's all right. They hardly listened to me anyway." She derived a kind of bitter satisfaction from saying this out loud. Her position as commander had always been a sham. To be fair, the Cike *did* listen to her when she had a plan, but she usually didn't. Really, they'd effectively been running themselves.

"You know what your problem is?" Nezha asked. "You have no impulse control. Absolutely zero. None."

"It's terrible," she agreed, and started to giggle. "Good thing I can't call the fire, huh?"

He responded to that with such a long silence that eventually it began to embarrass her. She wished now that she hadn't drunk so much. She couldn't think properly through her helplessly muddled mind. She felt terribly foolish, crude, and ashamed.

She had to practice whispering her words before she could voice them out loud. "So what's happening now?"

"Same thing as usual. They're gathering up the civilians. The men will cast their votes tonight."

She sat up. "They should not get a vote."

"They're Nikara. All Nikara get the option to join the Republic."

"They helped the Federation!"

"Because they didn't have a choice," Nezha said. "Think about it. Put yourself in their position. You really think you would have done any better?"

"Yes," she snapped. "I *did*. I *was* in their position. I was in worse—they had me strapped down to a bed, they were torturing me and torturing Altan in front of me and I was terrified, I wanted to die—"

"They were scared, too," he said softly.

"Then they should have fought back."

"Maybe they didn't have the choice. They weren't trained soldiers. They weren't shamans. How else were they going to survive?"

"It's not enough just to survive," she hissed. "You have to fight for something, you can't just—just live your life like a fucking coward."

"Some people are just cowards. Some people just aren't that strong."

"Then they shouldn't have *votes*," she snarled.

The more she thought about it, the more ludicrous Vaisra's proposed democracy seemed. How were the Nikara supposed to rule themselves? They hadn't run their own country since before the days of the Red Emperor, and even drunk, she could figure out why—the Nikara were simply far too stupid, too selfish, and too cowardly.

"Democracy's not going to work. Look at them." She was gesturing at trees, not people, but it hardly made a difference to her. "They're cows. Fools. They're voting for the Republic because they're scared—I'm sure they'd vote just as quickly to join the Federation."

"Don't be unfair," Nezha said. "They're just *people*: they've never studied warcraft."

"So then they shouldn't rule!" she shouted. "They need someone to tell them what to do, what to think—"

"And who's that going to be? Daji?"

"Not Daji. But someone educated. Someone who's passed the Keju, who's graduated from Sinegard. Someone who's been in the military. Someone who knows the value of a human life."

"You're describing yourself," said Nezha.

"I'm not saying it would be me," Rin said. "I'm just saying it shouldn't be the people. Vaisra shouldn't let them elect anyone. He should just rule."

Nezha tilted his head to the side. "You want my father to make himself Emperor?"

A wave of nausea rocked her stomach before she could respond. There was no time to get up; she lurched forward onto her knees and heaved the contents of her stomach against the tree. Her face was too close to the ground. A good deal of vomit splashed back onto her cheek. She rubbed clumsily at it with her sleeve.

"You all right?" Nezha asked when she'd stopped dry-heaving.

"Yes."

He rubbed his hand in circles on her back. "Good."

She spat a gob of regurgitated wine onto the dirt. "Fuck off."

Nezha lifted a clump of mud up from the riverbank. "Have you ever heard the story of how the goddess Nüwa created humanity?"

"No."

"I'll tell it to you." Nezha molded the mud into a ball with his palms. "Once upon a time, after the birth of the world, Nüwa was lonely."

"What about her husband, Fuxi?" Rin only knew the myths about Nüwa and Fuxi both.

"Absent spouse, I guess. Myth doesn't mention him."

"Of course."

"Of course. Anyway, Nüwa gets lonely, decides to create some humans to populate the world to keep her company." Nezha pressed his fingernails into the ball of mud. "The first few people she makes are incredibly detailed. Fine features, lovely clothes."

Rin could see where this was going. "Those are the aristocrats."

"Yes. The nobles, the emperors, the warriors, everyone who matters. Then she gets bored. It's taking too long. So she takes a rope and starts flinging mud in all directions. Those become the hundred clans of Nikan."

Rin swallowed. Her throat tasted like acid. "They don't tell that story in the south."

"And why do you think that is?" Nezha asked.

She turned that over in her mind for a moment. Then she laughed.

"My people are mud," she said. "And you're still going to let them run a country."

"I don't think they're mud," Nezha said. "I think they're still unformed. Uneducated and uncultured. They don't know better because they haven't been given the chance. But the Republic will shape and refine them. Develop them into what they were meant to be."

"That's not how it works." Rin took the clump of mud from Nezha's hand. "They're never going to become more than what they are. The north won't let them."

"That's not true."

"You think that. But I've seen how power works." Rin crushed the clump in her fingers. "It's not about who you are, it's about how they see you. And once you're mud in this country, you're always mud."

CHAPTER 18

"You're joking," Ramsa said.

Rin shook her head, and her temples throbbed at the sudden movement. Under the harsh light of dawn, she'd come to deeply regret ever touching alcohol, which made the task of informing the Cike they'd been disbanded very distasteful. "I'm unranked. Jinzha's orders."

"Then what about us?" Ramsa demanded.

She gave him a blank look. "What *about* you?"

"Where are we supposed to go?"

"Oh." She squeezed her eyes shut, trying to remember. "You're being reassigned. You're on the *Griffon*, I think, and Suni and Baji are on the tower ships—"

"We're not together?" Ramsa asked. "Fuck that. Can't we just refuse?"

"No." She pressed a palm into her aching forehead. "You're still Republic soldiers. You have to follow orders."

He stared at her in disbelief. "That's all you've got?"

"What else am I supposed to say?"

"Something!" he shouted. "Anything! We're not the Cike anymore, and you're just going to take that lying down?"

She wanted to cover her ears with her hands. She was so

exhausted. She wished Ramsa would just go away and break the news to the others for her so that she could lie down and go to sleep and stop thinking about anything.

"Who cares? The Cike's not that important. The Cike is dead."

Ramsa grabbed at her collar. But he was so scrawny, shorter even than she, that it only made him look ridiculous.

"What is wrong with you?" he demanded.

"Ramsa, stop."

"We joined this war for you," he said. "Out of loyalty to *you*."

"Don't be dramatic. You entered this war because you wanted Dragon silver, you like blowing shit up, and you're a wanted criminal everywhere else in the Empire."

"I stuck with you because we thought we'd stay *together*." Ramsa sounded like he was about to cry, which was so absurd that Rin almost laughed. "We're always supposed to be together."

"You're not even a shaman. You've got nothing to be afraid of. Why do you care?"

"Why *don't* you care? Altan named you commander. Protecting the Cike is your duty."

"I didn't ask to be commander," she snapped. Altan's invocation brought up feelings of obligation, duty, that she didn't want to think about. "All right? I don't want to be your Altan. I can't."

What had she done since she'd been put in charge? She'd hurt Unegen, driven Enki away, seen Aratsha killed, and gotten her ass kicked so badly by Daji that she couldn't even properly be called a shaman anymore. She hadn't led the Cike so much as encouraged them to make a series of awful decisions. They were better off without her. It infuriated her that they couldn't see that.

"Aren't you angry?" Ramsa asked. "Doesn't this piss you off?"

"No," she said. "I take orders."

She could have been angry. Could have resisted Jinzha, could have lashed out like she'd always done. But anger had only ever helped her when it manifested in flames, and she couldn't call on that anymore. Without the fire she wasn't a shaman, wasn't a proper Speerly, and certainly wasn't a military asset. Jinzha had no reason to listen to or respect her.

And she knew by now that the fire was never coming back.

"You could at least try," Ramsa said. "Please."

There was no fight left in his voice, either.

"Just grab your things," she said. "And tell the others. They want you to report in ten."

In a matter of weeks the last strongholds of Hare and Ram Provinces capitulated to the Republic. Their Warlords were sent back to Arlong in chains to grovel before Vaisra for their lives. Their cities, townships, and villages were all subjected to plebiscites.

When the civilians elected to join the Republic—and they invariably voted to join, for the alternative was that all men over the age of fifteen would be put to death—they became a part of Vaisra's sprawling war machine. The women were put to work sewing Republican uniforms and spinning linens for the infirmaries. The men were either recruited as infantry or sent south to work in Arlong's shipyards. A seventh of their food stores were confiscated to contribute to the northern campaign's swelling supply lines, and Republican patrols stayed behind to ensure regular shipments of grain upriver.

Nezha bragged constantly that this was perhaps the most successful military campaign in Nikara history. Kitay told him to stop getting high on his own hubris, but Rin could not deny their astonishing string of victories.

The daily demands of the campaign were so grueling, however, that she rarely got the chance to revel in their wins. The cities, townships, and villages began to blur together in her mind. Rin stopped thinking in terms of night and day, and started thinking in battle timetables. The days bled into one another, a string of extraordinarily demanding predawn combat assignments and snatched hours of deep and dreamless sleep.

The only benefit was that she managed to temporarily lose

herself in the sheer physical activity. Her demotion didn't affect her as much as she'd thought it would. Most days she was too tired to even remember it had happened.

But she was also secretly relieved that she did not have to think anymore about what to do with her men. That the burden of leadership, which she'd never adequately met, had been lifted entirely from her shoulders. All she had to do was worry about carrying out her own orders, and that she did splendidly.

Her orders were doubling, too. Jinzha might have begun to appreciate her ability, or he might have simply disliked her so much he wanted her dead without having to take the blame, but he began to put her on the front lines of every ground operation. This was typically not a coveted position, but she relished it.

After all, she was terribly good at war. She had trained for this. Maybe she couldn't call the fire anymore, but she could still *fight*, and landing her trident into the right joint of flesh felt just as good as incinerating everything around her.

She gained a reputation on the *Kingfisher* as an eminently capable soldier, and despite herself she started to bask in it. It awakened an old streak of competitiveness that she had not felt since Sinegard, when the only thing getting her through months of grueling and miserable study had been the sheer delight of having her talents recognized by someone.

Was this how Altan had felt? The Nikara had honed him as a weapon, had put him to military uses since he was a small child, but still they'd lauded him. Had that kept him happy?

Of course she wasn't happy, not quite. But she had found some sort of contentment, the satisfaction that came from being a tool that served its purpose quite well.

The campaigns were like drugs in their own right. Rin felt wonderful when she fought. In the heat of battle, human life could be reduced to the barest mechanics of existence—arms and legs, mobility and vulnerability, vital points to be identified, isolated, and destroyed. She found an odd pleasure in that. Her body knew what to do, which meant she could turn her mind off.

If the Cike were unhappy, she didn't know. She didn't speak to them anymore. She barely saw them after they were reassigned. But she found it harder and harder to care because she was losing the capacity to think about much at all.

In time, sooner than she'd expected, she even stopped longing for the fire that she'd lost. Sometimes the urge crept up on her on the eve of battle and she rubbed her fingers together, wishing that she could make them spark, fantasizing about how quickly her troops could win battles if she could call down a column of fire to scorch out the defensive line.

She still felt the Phoenix's absence like a hole carved out of her chest. The ache never quite went away. But the desperation and frustration ebbed. She stopped waking up in the morning and wanting to scream when she remembered what had been taken from her.

She'd long since stopped trying to break down the Seal. Its dark, pulsing presence no longer pained her daily like a festering wound. In the small moments when she did permit herself to linger on it, she wondered if it had begun to take her memories.

Master Jiang had seemed to know absolutely nothing about who he had been twenty years ago. Would the same happen to her?

Already some of her earlier memories were starting to feel fuzzy. She used to remember intricately the faces of every member of her foster family in Tikany. Now they seemed like blurs. But she couldn't tell if the Seal had eaten those memories away, or if they had simply corroded over time.

That didn't worry her as much as it should have. She couldn't pretend that if the Seal stole her past from her little by little—if she forgot Altan, forgot what she'd done on Speer, and let her guilt wash away into a white nothingness until, like Jiang, she was just an affable, absentminded fool—some part of her wouldn't be relieved.

When Rin wasn't sleeping or fighting, she was sitting with Kitay in his cramped office. She was no longer invited to Jinzha's councils, but she learned everything from Kitay secondhand. He, in turn, enjoyed bouncing his ideas off of her. Talking through the multitudes of possibilities out loud gave relief to the frantic activity inside his mind.

He alone didn't share the Republic's delight over their incredible series of victories.

"I'm concerned," he admitted. "And confused. Hasn't this whole campaign felt too easy to you? It's like they're not even trying."

"They *are* trying. They're just not very good at it." Rin was still buzzing from the high of battle. It felt very good to excel, even if excellence meant cutting down poorly trained local soldiers, and Kitay's moodiness irritated her.

"You know the battles you're fighting are too easy."

She made a face. "You could give us a little bit of credit."

"Do you want praise for beating up untrained, unarmed villagers? Good job, then. Very well done. The superiorly armed navy crushes a pathetic peasant resistance. What a shocking turn of events. That doesn't mean you're taking this Empire on a silver platter."

"It could just mean that our navy is superior," she said. "What, you think Daji's giving up the north on purpose? That doesn't get her anything."

"She's not giving it up. They're building a shipyard, we've known that since the beginning—"

"And if their navy were any use, we would have seen it. Maybe we're actually just *winning* this war. It wouldn't kill you to admit it."

But Kitay shook his head. "You're talking about Su Daji. This is the woman who managed to unite all twelve provinces for the first time since the death of the Red Emperor."

"She had help."

"But she's had no help since. If the Empire were going to fracture, you'd think it would have already. Don't get cocky, Rin. We're playing a game of wikki against a woman who's had decades of practice against far more fearsome opponents. I've said this to Jinzha, too. There's a counteroffensive coming soon, and the longer we wait for it, the worse it's going to be."

Kitay was obsessed with the problem of whether the fleet ought to curtail its campaign for the winter or to sail directly to Tiger Province, rendezvous with Tsolin's fleet, and take on Jun and his army. On the one hand, if they could solidify their hold on the coastline through Tiger Province, then they would have a back channel to run supplies and reinforce land columns to eventually encircle the Autumn Palace.

On the other, taking the coastline would involve a massive military commitment from troops that the Republic didn't yet have. Until the Hesperians decided to lend aid, they would have to settle for conquering the inland regions first. But that could take another couple of months—which required time that they also didn't have.

They were racing against time. Nobody wanted to be stuck in an invasion when winter hit the north. Their task was to solidify a revolutionary base and corner the Empire inside its three northernmost provinces before the Murui's tributaries froze over and the fleet was stuck in place.

"We're cutting it close, but we should be up to the Edu pass within a month," Kitay told her. "Jinzha has to make his decision by then."

Rin did the calculations in her head. "Upriver sailing should take us a month and a half."

"You're forgetting about the Four Gorges Dam," Kitay said. "Up through Rat Province the Murui's blocked up, so the current won't be as strong as it should be."

"A month, then. What do you think happens when we get there?"

"We pray to the heavens that the rivers and lakes haven't frozen yet," Kitay said. "Then we see what our options are. At this point, though, Jinzha's wagered this war on the weather."

Rin's weekly meetings with Sister Petra remained the thorn in her side that progressively stung worse. Petra's examinations had become increasingly invasive, but she had also started withholding the laudanum. She was finished with taking baseline measurements. Now she wanted to see evidence of Chaos.

When week after week Rin failed to call the fire, Petra grew impatient.

"You are hiding it from me," she accused. "You refuse to cooperate."

"Or maybe I'm cured," Rin said. "Maybe Chaos went away. Maybe your holy presence scared it off."

"You lie." Petra wrenched Rin's mouth open with more force than she needed and began tapping around her teeth with what felt like a two-pronged instrument. The cold metal tips dug painfully into Rin's enamel. "I know how Chaos works. It never disappears. It disguises itself in the face of the Maker but always it returns."

Rin wished that were the case. If she had the fire back she'd incinerate Petra where she stood, and fuck the consequences. If she had the fire, then she wouldn't be so terribly helpless, bowing down to Jinzha's commands and cooperating with the Hesperians because she was only a lowly foot soldier.

But if she gave in to her anger now, the worst she could do was make a mess in Petra's lab, wind up dead at the bottom of the Murui, and destroy any hope of a Hesperian-Nikara military alliance. Resistance meant doom for her and everyone she cared about.

So even though it tasted like the bitterest bile, she swallowed her rage.

"It's really gone," she said when Petra released her jaw. "I told you it's been Sealed off. I can't call it anymore."

"So you say." Petra looked deeply skeptical, but she dropped the subject. She placed the instrument back on her table. "Raise your right hand and hold your breath."

"Why?"

"Because I asked."

The Sister never lost her temper with Rin, no matter what Rin said. Petra had a freakishly calm composure. She never betrayed any emotion other than an icy professional curiosity. Rin almost wished that Petra would strike her, just so she knew she was human, but frustration seemed to slide off of her like rainwater from a tin roof.

However, as time passed with no results, she did start subjecting Rin to baser and baser experiments. She made Rin solve puzzles meant for children while she kept time with her little watch. She made Rin perform simple tasks of memorization that seemed designed to make her fail, watching without blinking as Rin became so frustrated that she started throwing things at the wall.

Eventually Petra asked her to stand for examinations naked.

"If you wanted to ogle me you could have asked earlier," Rin said.

Petra didn't react. "Quickly, please."

Rin yanked her uniform off and tossed it in a bundle on the floor.

"Good." Petra passed her an empty cup. "Now urinate in this for me."

Rin stared at her in disbelief. "Right now?"

"I'm doing fluids analysis tonight," Petra said. "Go on."

Rin set her jaw. "I'm not doing that."

"Would you like a sheet for privacy?"

"I don't care," Rin said. "This isn't about science. You don't have a clue what you're doing, you're just being spiteful."

Petra sat down and crossed one leg over the other. "Urinate, please."

"Fuck that." Rin tossed the cup onto the floor. "Admit it. You've no idea what you're doing. All your treatises and all your instruments, and you don't have a single clue about how shamanism works or how to measure Chaos, if that really even exists. You're shooting in the dark."

Petra stood up from her chair. Her nostrils flared white.

Rin had finally struck a nerve. She hoped that Petra might hit her then, if only to break that inhuman mask of control. But Petra only cocked her head to the side.

"Remember your situation." Her voice retained its icy calm. "I am asking you to cooperate only out of etiquette. Refuse, and I will have you strapped to that bed. Now. Will you behave?"

Rin wanted to kill her.

If she hadn't been so exhausted, if she had been an ounce more impulsive, then she would have. It would have been so easy to knock Petra to the floor and jam every sharp instrument on the table into her neck, her chest, her eyes. It would have felt so good.

But Rin couldn't act on impulse anymore.

She felt the sheer, overwhelming weight of Hesperia's military might restricting her options like an invisible cage. They held her life hostage. They held her friends and her entire nation hostage.

Against all of that, Sealed off from the fire and the Phoenix, she was helpless.

So she held her tongue and forced down her fury as Petra's requests became more and more humiliating. She complied when Petra made her lean naked against the wall while she drew intricate diagrams of her genitals. She sat still when Petra inserted a long, thick needle into her right arm and drew so much blood that she fainted when she stood up to return to her quarters and couldn't stand back up for half a day. And she bit her tongue and didn't react when Petra waved a packet of opium under her nose, trying to entice her to draw the fire out by offering her favorite vice.

"Go on," Petra said. "I've read about your kind. You can't resist the smoke. You crave it in your bones. Isn't that how the Red Emperor subdued your ancestors? Call the fire for me, and I'll let you have a little."

That last meeting left Rin so furious that the moment she left Petra's quarters, she shrieked in fury and punched the wall so hard that her knuckle split open. For a moment she stood still, stunned, while blood ran down the back of her hand and dripped off her wrist. Then she sank to her knees and started to cry.

"Are you all right?"

It was Augus, the baby-faced, blue-eyed missionary. Rin gave him a wary look. "Go away."

He reached for her bleeding hand. "You're upset."

She jerked it out of his grasp. "I don't want your pity."

He sat down next to her, fished a linen out of his pocket, and passed it to her. "Here. Why don't you wrap that up?"

Rin's knuckle was bleeding faster than she had realized. After getting her blood drawn the week before, the very sight of it made her want to faint. Reluctantly she took the cloth.

Augus watched as she looped it tightly around her hand. She realized she couldn't tie off the knot by herself.

"I can do that," he offered.

She let him.

"Are you all right?" he asked again when he was finished.

"Does it fucking look like—"

"I meant with Sister Petra," he clarified. "I know she can be difficult."

Rin shot him a sideways look. "You don't like her?"

"We all admire her," he said slowly. "But . . . ah, do you understand Hesperian? This language is hard for me."

"Yes."

He switched, speaking deliberately slowly so that she could keep up. "She's the most brilliant Gray Sister of our generation and the foremost expert of Chaos manifestations on the eastern continent. But we don't all agree with her methods."

"What does that mean?"

"Sister Petra is old-fashioned about conversion. Her school believes that the only pathway to salvation is patterning civilizations on the development of Hesperia. To obey the Maker you must become like us. You must stop being Nikara."

"Attractive," Rin muttered.

"But I think that when we wish to win barbarians over and convert them to the greater good, we should use the same strategies that Chaos uses to draw souls to evil," Augus continued.

"Chaos enters through the other's door and comes out his own. So should we."

Rin pressed her bound knuckles against the wall to stem the pain. Her dizziness subsided. "From what I know, you lot are more fond of blowing our doors up."

"Like I said. Conservative." Augus shot her an embarrassed smile. "But the Company has been changing its ways. Take the bow, for instance. I've read about the Nikara tradition of performing deep bows to superiors—"

"That's only for special occasions," she said.

"Even so. Decades ago, the Company would have argued that bowing to a Nikara would be an utter affront to the dignity of the white race. We are chosen by the Maker, after all. We are the highest evolved persons, and we shouldn't show respect to you. But I don't agree with that."

Rin fought the urge to roll her eyes. "That's nice of you."

"We are not equals," Augus said. "But that doesn't mean we can't be friends. And I don't think the path to salvation involves treating you like you're not people."

Augus, Rin realized, really thought that he was being kind.

"I think I'm good now," she said.

He helped her to her feet. "Would you like me to walk you back to your quarters?"

"No. Thank you. I can manage."

When she returned to her room, she drew the packet of opium out from her pocket. She hadn't quite stolen it. Petra had left it in her lap and hadn't commented on it when Rin stood up to leave. She meant for Rin to have it.

Rin yanked up a loose floorboard and hid the drug where no one could see. She wasn't going to use it. She didn't know what sick game Petra was playing, but she couldn't tempt her that far.

Still, it relieved her to know that if it became too much, that if she wanted it all to end and she wanted to float higher, higher, away from her body and shame and humiliation and pain until she left it permanently, then the opium was there.

If any other Hesperians shared Augus's opinions, they didn't show it. Tarcquet's men on the *Kingfisher* kept a chilly distance from the Nikara. They ate and slept by themselves, and every time Rin drifted within earshot of their conversations, they fell quiet until she'd passed. They continued to observe the Nikara without intervening—coldly amused by their incompetence, and mildly surprised by their victories.

Only once did they put their arquebuses to any use. One evening a commotion broke out on the lower deck. A group of prisoners from Ram Province broke out of their holding cell and attacked a handful of missionaries who had been proselytizing in the brig.

They might have been trying to escape. They might have thought to use the Hesperians as hostages. Or they might have simply wanted to lash out at foreigners for getting too close— Ram Province had suffered greatly under occupation and had no great love of the west. When Rin and the other soldiers on patrol reached the source of the shouting, the prisoners had the missionaries pinned to the floor, alive but incapacitated.

Rin recognized Augus, gasping desperately for breath while a prisoner wedged an arm under his throat.

His eyes locked on to hers. "Help—"

"Get back!" the prisoner shouted. "Everyone get back, or they're dead!"

More Republican soldiers crowded the hallway in seconds. The skirmish should have been resolved instantly. The prisoners were unarmed and outnumbered. But they had also been marked for their strength as pedalers. Jinzha had specifically ordered that they be treated well, and no one wanted to attack for fear of causing irreparable injury.

"Please," Augus whispered.

Rin faltered. She wanted to dart forward and pull his attacker off. But the Republican soldiers were holding back, waiting for orders. She couldn't jump alone into the fray; they'd tear her apart.

She stood, trident raised, watching as Augus's face turned a grotesque blue.

"Out of the way!" Tarcquet and his guard pushed through the commotion, arquebuses raised.

Tarcquet took one look at the prisoners and shouted an order. A round of shots rang through the air. Eight men dropped to the ground. The air curdled with the familiar smell of fire powder. The missionaries broke free, gasping for breath.

"What is this?" Jinzha forced his way through the crowd. "What's happened?"

"General Jinzha." Tarcquet signaled to his men, who lowered their weapons. "Good of you to show up."

Jinzha surveyed the bodies on the floor. "You've cost me good labor."

Tarcquet cocked his arquebus. "I would improve your brig security."

"Our brig security is fine." Jinzha looked white-faced with fury. "Your missionaries weren't supposed to be down there."

Augus rose to his feet, coughing. He reached for Jinzha's arm. "Prisoners deserve mercy, too. You can't just—"

"Fuck your mercy." Jinzha pushed Augus away. "You're on my ship. You'll obey orders, or you can take a swim in the river."

"Don't speak to my people like that." Tarcquet stepped in between them. The difference between him and Jinzha was almost laughable—Jinzha was tall by Nikara standards, but Tarcquet towered over him. "Perhaps your father didn't make it clear. We are diplomats on your ship. If you want the Consortium to even consider funding your pathetic war, you will treat every Hesperian here like royalty."

Jinzha's throat bobbed. Rin watched the anger pass through his expression; saw Jinzha shove down the impulse to react. Tarcquet held all the leverage. Tarcquet could not be reproached.

Rin derived some small satisfaction from that. It felt good to see Jinzha humiliated, treated with the same condescension with which he'd always treated her.

"Am I understood?" Tarcquet asked.

Jinzha glared up at him.

Tarcquet cocked his head. "Say 'yes, sir' or 'no, sir.'"

Jinzha had murder written across his face. "Yes, sir."

Tensions ran high for several days afterward. A pair of Hesperian soldiers began following the missionaries around wherever they went, and the Nikara kept their wary distance. But unless one of theirs was in danger, Tarcquet's soldiers did not fire their weapons.

Tarcquet continued his constant assessment of Jinzha's campaign. Rin saw him every now and then on deck, obnoxiously marking notes into a small book while he surveyed the fleet moving up the river. And Rin wondered what he thought of them—their unresponsive gods, their weapons that seemed so primitive, and their bloody, desperate war.

Two months into the campaign, they sailed at last into Rat Province. Here their string of victories came to an end.

Rat Province's Second Division was the intelligence branch of the Militia, and its espionage officers were the best in the Twelve Provinces. By now, it had also had several months of warning time to put together a better defensive strategy than Hare or Ram Provinces had been able to mount.

The Republic arrived to find villages already abandoned, granaries emptied, and fields scorched. The Rat Warlord had either recalled his civilians to metropolitan centers farther upriver or sent them fleeing to other provinces. Jinzha's soldiers found clothing, furniture, and children's toys scattered across the grassy roads. Whatever couldn't be taken was ruined. In village after village they found burned, useless seed grain and rotting piles of livestock carcasses.

The Rat Warlord wasn't trying to mount a defense of his borders. He had simply retreated to Baraya, his heavily barricaded capital city. He planned to starve the fleet out. And Baraya had a better chance of success than Xiashang had—its gates were thicker, its residents better prepared, and it was more than a mile inland, which neutralized the attack capabilities of the *Shrike* and the *Crake*.

"We should just stop here and turn back." Kitay paced his office floor, frustrated. "Ride out the winter. We'll starve otherwise."

But Jinzha had become increasingly irascible, less and less willing to listen to his advisers and more adamant that they had to storm forward.

"He wants to move on Baraya?" Rin asked.

"He wants to press north as fast as we can." Kitay tugged anxiously at his hair. "It's a terrible idea. But he won't listen to me."

"Then who's he listening to?"

"Any of the leadership who agree with him. Molkoi especially. He's in the old guard—I *told* Vaisra that was a bad idea, but who listens to me? Nezha's on my side, but of course Jinzha won't listen to his little brother, it'd mean losing face. This could throw away all of our gains so far. You know, there's a good chance we'll all just starve to death up north. That'd be hilarious, wouldn't it?"

But, as Jinzha announced to the *Kingfisher*, they absolutely would not starve. They would take Rat Province. They would blow open the gates to the capital city of Baraya, and win themselves enough supplies to last out the winter.

Easy orders to give. Harder to implement, especially when they reached a stretch of the Murui so steep that Jinzha had no choice but to order his troops to move the ships over land. The flooded riverbanks earlier had made it possible for them to sail directly over lowland roads. But now they were forced to disembark and roll the ships over logs to reach the next waterway wide enough to accommodate the warships.

It took an entire day of straining against ropes to simply pull the massive tower ships onto dry land, and much longer to cut down enough trees to roll them across the bumpy terrain. One week bled into two weeks of backbreaking, mindless, numbing labor. The only advantage of this was that Rin was so exhausted that she didn't have the time to be bored.

Patrol shifts were slightly more exciting. These were a chance to get away from the din of ships rolling over logs and explore the surrounding land. Thick forests obscured all visibility past a mile, and Jinzha sent out daily parties to root through the trees for any sightings of the Militia.

Rin found these relaxing, until word got back to the base that the noon patrol had caught sight of a Militia scouting party.

"And you just let them *go*?" Jinzha demanded. "Are you stupid?"

The men on patrol were from the *Griffon*, and Nezha hastily interceded on their behalf. "They weren't worth the fight, brother. Our men were outnumbered."

"But they had the advantage of surprise," Jinzha snapped. "Instead, the entire Militia now knows our precise location. Send your men back out. No one sleeps until I have proof every last scout is dead."

Nezha bowed his head. "Yes, brother."

"And take Salkhi's men with you. Yours clearly can't be trusted to get the job done."

The next day, Salkhi and Nezha's joint expedition returned to the *Kingfisher* with a string of severed heads and empty Militia uniforms.

That appeased Jinzha, but ultimately it made no difference. First the Militia scouts returned in larger and larger numbers. Then the attacks began en masse. The Militia soldiers hid in the mountains. They never launched a frontal assault, but maintained a constant stream of arrow fire, picking off soldiers unawares.

The Republican troops fared badly against these scattered, unpredictable attacks. Panic swept through the camp, destroying morale, and Rin understood why. The Republican Army felt out of place on land. They were used to fighting from their ships. They were most comfortable in water, where they had a quick escape route.

They had no escape routes now.

CHAPTER 19

Snow started falling the day that they finally returned to the river. At first it drifted down in fat, lazy flakes. But within hours it had transformed into a blinding blizzard, with winds so fierce that the troops could hardly see five feet in front of them. Jinzha was forced to keep his fleet grounded by the edge of the river while his soldiers holed up in their ships to wait out the storm.

"I've always been amazed by snow." Rin traced shapes into the porthole condensation as she stared out at the endless, hypnotizing flurry outside. "Every winter, it's a surprise. I can never believe it's real."

"They don't have snow down south?" Kitay asked.

"No. Tikany gets so dry that your lips bleed when you try to smile, but never cold enough for the snow to fall. Before I came north, I'd only heard about it in stories. I thought it was a beautiful idea. Little flecks of the cold."

"And how did you find the snow at Sinegard?"

A howl of wind drowned out Rin's response. She pulled down the porthole cover. "Fucking miserable."

The blizzard let up by the next morning. Outside, the forest had been transformed, like some giant had drenched the trees in white paint.

Jinzha announced that the fleet would remain grounded for one more day to pass the New Year's holiday. Everywhere else in the Empire, New Year's would be a weeklong affair involving twelve-course banquets, firecrackers, and endless parades. On campaign, a single day would have to be enough.

The troops disembarked to camp out in the winter landscape, glad for the chance to escape the close quarters of the cabins.

"See if you can get that fire going," Nezha told Kitay.

The three of them sat huddled together on the riverbank, rubbing their hands together while Kitay fumbled with a piece of flint to start a fire.

Somewhere Nezha had scrounged up a small packet of glutinous rice flour. He poured the flour out into a tin bowl, added some water from his canteen, and stirred it together with his fingers until it formed a small ball of dough.

Rin prodded at the measly fire. It fizzled and sputtered; the next gust of wind put it out entirely. She groaned and reached for the flint. They wouldn't have boiling water for at least half an hour. "You know, you could just take that to the kitchen and have them cook it."

"The kitchen isn't supposed to know I have it," said Nezha.

"I see," Kitay said. "The general is stealing rations."

"The general is rewarding his best soldiers with a New Year's treat," Nezha said.

Kitay rubbed his hands up and down his arms. "Oh, so it's nepotism."

"Shut up," Nezha mumbled. He rubbed harder at the ball of dough, but it crumbled to bits in his fingers.

"You haven't added enough water." Rin grabbed the bowl from him and kneaded the dough with one hand, adding droplets of water with the other until she had a wet, round ball the size of her fist.

"I didn't know you could cook," Nezha said curiously.

"I used to all the time. No one else was going to feed Kesegi."

"Kesegi?"

"My little brother." The memory of his face rose up in Rin's mind. She forced it back down. She hadn't seen him in four years. She didn't know if he was still alive, and she didn't want to wonder.

"I didn't know you had a little brother," Nezha said.

"Not a real brother. I was adopted."

No one asked her to elaborate, so she didn't. She rolled the dough into a snakelike strip between both palms, then broke it up piece by piece into thumb-sized lumps.

Nezha watched her hands with the wide-eyed fascination of a boy who'd clearly never been in the kitchen. "Those balls are smaller than the tangyuan I remember."

"That's because we don't have red bean paste or sesame to fill them with," she said. "Any chance you scrounged up some sugar?"

"You have to add sugar?" Nezha asked.

Kitay laughed.

"We'll eat them bland, then," she said. "It'll taste better in little pieces. More to chew."

When the water finally came to a boil, Rin dropped the rice flour balls into the tin cauldron and stirred them with a stick, creating a clockwise current so that they wouldn't stick to each other.

"Did you know that cauldrons are a military invention?" Kitay asked. "One of the Red Emperor's generals came up with the idea of tin cookware. Can you imagine? Before that, they were stuck trying to build fires large enough for giant bamboo steamers."

"A lot of innovations came from the military," Nezha mused. "Messenger pigeons, for one. And there's a good argument that most of the advances in blacksmithing and medicine were a product of the Era of Warring States."

"That's cute." Rin peered into the cauldron. "Proves that war's good for something, then."

"It's a good theory," Nezha insisted. "The country was in chaos during the Era of Warring States, sure. But look at what it brought us—Sunzi's *Principles of War*; Mengzi's theories on governance.

Everything we know now about philosophy, about warfare and statecraft, was developed during that era."

"So what's the tradeoff?" Rin asked. "Thousands of people have to die so that we can get better at killing each other in the future?"

"You know that's not my argument."

"It's what it sounds like. It sounds like you're saying that people have to die for progress."

"It's not progress they're dying for," Nezha said. "Progress is the side effect. And military innovation doesn't just mean we get better at killing each other, it means we get better equipped to kill whoever decides to invade us next."

"And who do you think is going to invade us next?" Rin asked. "The Hinterlanders?"

"Don't rule them out."

"They'd have to stop killing each other off, first."

The tribes of the northern Hinterlands had been at constant war since any of them could remember. In the days of the Red Emperor, the students of Sinegard had been trained primarily to fend off northern invaders. Now they were just an afterthought.

"Better question," Kitay said. "What do you think is the next great military innovation?"

"Arquebuses," Nezha said, at the same moment that Rin said, "Shamanic armies."

Both of them turned to stare at her.

"Shamans over *arquebuses*?" Nezha asked.

"Of course," she said. The thought had just occurred to her, but the more she considered it, the more attractive it sounded. "Tarcquet's weapon is just a glorified rocket. But imagine a whole army of people who could summon gods."

"That sounds like a disaster," Nezha said.

"Or an unstoppable military," Rin said.

"I feel like if that could be done, it would have been," said Nezha. "But there's no written history on shamanic warfare. The only shamans the Red Emperor employed were the Speerlies, and we know how that went."

"But the predynastic texts—"

"—are irrelevant." Nezha cut her off. "Fortification technology and bronze weapons didn't become military standard until well into the Red Emperor's rule, which is about the same time that shamans started disappearing from the record. We have no idea how shamans would change the nature of warfare, whether they could be worked into a military bureaucracy."

"The Cike's done pretty well," Rin challenged.

"When there are fewer than ten of you, sure. Don't you think hundreds of shamans would be a disaster?"

"You should become one," she said. "See what it's like."

Nezha flinched. "You're not serious."

"It's not the worst idea. Any of us could teach you."

"I have never met a shaman in complete control of their own mind." Nezha looked strangely bothered by her suggestion. "And I'm sorry, but knowing the Cike does not make me terribly optimistic."

Rin pulled the cauldron off of the fire. She knew she was supposed to let the tangyuan cool for a few minutes before serving, but she was too cold, and the vapors misting up from the surface were too enticing. They didn't have bowls, so they wrapped the cauldron in leaves to keep their hands from burning and passed it around in a circle.

"Happy New Year," Kitay said. "May the gods send you blessings and good fortune."

"Health, wealth, and happiness. May your enemies rot and surrender quickly before we have to kill more of them." Rin stood up.

"Where are you going?" Nezha asked.

"Gotta go take a piss."

She wandered toward the woods, looking for a large enough tree to hide behind. By now she'd spent so much time with Kitay that she wouldn't have minded squatting down right in front of him. But for some reason, she felt far less comfortable stripping in front of Nezha.

Her ankle twisted beneath her. She spun around, failed to catch her balance, and fell flat on her rear. She spread her hands to catch her fall. Her fingers landed on something soft and rubbery. Confused, she glanced down and brushed the snow away from the surface.

She saw a child's face buried in snow.

His—she thought it was a boy, though she couldn't quite tell—eyes were wide open, large and blank, with long lashes fringed with snow, embedded in dark shadows on a thin, pale face.

Rin rose unsteadily to her feet. She picked up a branch and brushed the rest of the snow off the child's body. She uncovered another face. And then another.

It finally sank in that this was not natural, that she ought to be afraid, and then she opened her mouth and screamed.

Nezha ordered a squadron to walk through the surrounding square mile with torches held low to the ground until the ice and snow had melted enough that they could see what had happened.

The snow peeled away to reveal an entire village of people, frozen perfectly where they lay. Most still had their eyes open. Rin saw no blood. The villagers didn't appear to have died from anything except for the cold, and perhaps starvation. Everywhere she found evidence of fires, hastily constructed, long fizzled out.

No one had given her a torch. She was still shaken from the experience, and every sudden movement made her jump, so it was best that she didn't hold on to anything potentially dangerous. But she refused to go back to camp alone, either, so she stood by the edge of the forest, watching blankly as the soldiers brushed snow off yet another family of corpses. Their bodies were curled in a heap together, the mother's and father's bodies wrapped protectively around their two children.

"Are you all right?" Nezha asked her. His hand wandered hesitantly toward her shoulder, as if he wasn't sure whether to touch her or not.

She brushed it away. "I'm fine. I've seen bodies before."

Yet she couldn't take her eyes off of them. They looked like a set of dolls lying in the snow, perfectly fine except for the fact that they weren't moving.

Most of the adults still had large bundles fastened to their backs. Rin saw porcelain dishes, silk dresses, and kitchen utensils spilling out of those bags. The villagers seemed to have packed their entire homes up with them.

"Where were they going?" she wondered.

"Isn't it obvious?" Kitay said. "They were running."

"From *what*?"

Kitay said it, because no one else seemed able to. "Us."

"But they didn't have anything to fear." Nezha looked deeply uncomfortable. "We would have treated them the way we've treated every other village. They would have gotten a vote."

"That's not what their leaders would have told them," said Kitay. "They would have imagined we were coming to kill them."

"That's ridiculous," Nezha said.

"Is it?" Kitay asked. "Imagine it. You hear the rebel army is coming. Your magistrates are your most reliable sources of information, and they tell you that the rebels will kill your men, rape your women, and enslave your children, because that's what you're always supposed to say about the enemy. You don't know any better, so you pack up everything you can and flee."

Rin could imagine the rest. These villagers would have run from the Republic just as they had once run from the Federation. But winter had come earlier that year than they'd predicted, and they didn't get to the lowland valleys in time. They couldn't find anything to eat. At some point it was too much work to stay alive. So they decided with the rest of the families that this was as good a place as any to end it, and together they lay down and embraced each other, and perhaps it didn't feel so terrible near the end.

Perhaps it felt just like going to sleep.

Through the entire campaign, she had never once paused to consider just how many people they had killed or displaced. The numbers added up so quickly. Several thousand from famine—

maybe several hundred thousand—and then all the soldiers they'd cut down every time, multiplied across villages.

They were fighting a very different war now, she realized. They were not the liberators but the aggressors. They were the ones to fear.

"War's different when you're not struggling for survival." Kitay must have been thinking the same thing she was. He stood still, hands clutching his torch, eyes fixed on the bodies at his feet. "Victories don't feel the same."

"Do you think it's worth it?" Rin asked him quietly so that Nezha couldn't hear.

"Frankly, I don't care."

"I'm being serious."

He considered for a moment. "I'm glad that someone's fighting Daji."

"But the stakes—"

"I wouldn't think too long about the stakes." Kitay glanced at Nezha, who was still staring at the bodies, eyes wide and disturbed. "You won't like the answers you come up with."

That evening the snowstorms started up again and did not relent for another week. It confirmed what everyone had been afraid of. Winter had arrived early that year, and with a vengeance. Soon enough the tributaries would freeze and the Republican Fleet would be stuck in the north unless they turned back. Their options were dwindling.

Rin paced the *Kingfisher* for days, growing more agitated with every passing minute. She needed to move, fight, attack. She didn't like sitting still. Too easy to fall prey to her own thoughts. Too easy to see the faces in the snow.

Once during a late-night stroll she stumbled across the leadership leaving Jinzha's office. None of them looked happy. Jinzha stormed past her without saying a word; he might not have even noticed her. Nezha lingered behind with Kitay, who wore the peeved, tight-lipped expression that Rin had learned meant that he hadn't gotten his way.

"Don't tell me," Rin said. "We're moving forward."

"We're not just moving forward. He wants us to bypass Baraya entirely and take Boyang." Kitay slammed a fist against the wall. *Boyang!* Is he mad?"

"Military outpost on the border of Rat Province and Tiger Province," Nezha explained to Rin. "It's not a terrible idea. The Militia used Boyang as a fortress during the first and second invasions. It'll have built-in defenses, make it easier to last out the winter. We can break the siege at Baraya from there."

"But won't someone already be there?" Rin asked. If the Militia was garrisoned anywhere, it had to be in Tiger or Rat Province. Any farther north and they'd be fighting in Sinegard for the heart of Imperial territory.

"If someone's already there, then we'll fight them off," said Nezha.

"In icy waters?" Kitay challenged. "With a cold and miserable army? If we keep going north, we're going to lose every advantage we've gained by coming so far."

"Or we could cement our victory," Nezha argued. "If we win at Boyang, then we control the delta at the Elehemsa tributary, which means—"

"Yes, yes, you cut around the coast to Tiger Province, you can send reinforcements to either through riverways," Kitay said irritably. "Except you're not going to win Boyang. The Imperial Fleet is almost certainly there, but for some reason Jinzha would prefer to pretend it doesn't exist. I don't know what's wrong with your brother, but he's getting reckless and he's making decisions like a madman."

"My brother is not a madman."

"Oh, no, he might be the best wartime general I've ever seen. No one's denying he's done well so far. But he's only good because he's the first Nikara general who's been trained to think from a naval perspective first. Once the rivers freeze, it's going to turn into a ground war, and then he won't have a clue what to do."

Nezha sighed. "Look, I understand your point. I'm just trying to see the best in our situation. If it were up to me I wouldn't go to Boyang, either."

Kitay threw his hands up. "Well, then—"

"This isn't about strategy. It's about pride. It's about showing the Hesperians that we won't back down from a challenge. And for Jinzha, it's about proving himself to Father."

"These things always come back to your father," Kitay muttered. "Both of you need help."

"So say that to Jinzha," Rin said. "Tell him that he's being stupid."

"There's no possible version of that argument that goes well," Nezha said. "Jinzha decides what he wants. You think I can contradict him and get away with it?"

"Well, if *you* can't," Kitay said, "then we're fucked."

An hour later the paddle wheels creaked into motion, carrying the Republican Fleet through a minor mountain range.

"Look up." Kitay nudged Rin's arm. "Does that look normal to you?"

At first it seemed to her like the sun was gradually coming up over the mountains, the lights were so bright. Then the glowing objects rose higher, and she saw that they were lanterns, lighting up the night sky one by one like a field of blooming flowers. Long ribbons dangled from the balloons, displaying a message easily read from the ground.

Surrender means immunity.

"Did they really think that would work?" Rin asked, amused. "That's like screaming, 'Go away, please.'"

But Kitay wasn't smiling. "I don't think it's about propaganda. We should turn back."

"What, just because of some lanterns?"

"It's what the lanterns mean. Whoever set them up is waiting for us in there. And I doubt they have the firepower to match the fleet, but they're still fighting on their own territory, and they

know that river. They've staked it out for who knows how long."
Kitay motioned to the closest soldier. "Can you shoot?"

"As well as anyone else," said the soldier.

"Good. You see that?" Kitay pointed to a lantern drifting a
little farther out from the others. "Can you hit it? I just want to
see what happens."

The soldier looked confused, but obeyed. His first shot missed.
His second arrow flew true. The lantern exploded into flames,
sending a shower of sparks and coal tumbling toward the river.

Rin hit the ground. The explosion seemed impossibly loud for
such a small, harmless-looking lantern. It just kept going, too—
the lantern must have been loaded with multiple smaller bombs
that went off in succession at various points in the air like intricate
fireworks. She watched, holding her breath, hoping that none of
the sparks would set off the other lanterns. That might spark a
chain reaction that turned the entire cliffside into a column of fire.

But the other lanterns didn't go off—the first had exploded too
far from the rest of the pack—and at last, the explosions started
to fizzle out.

"Told you," Kitay said once they'd ceased completely. He
picked himself off the ground. "We'd better go tell Jinzha we need
a change in route."

The fleet crept down a secondary channel of the tributary, a narrow pass between jagged cliffs. This would add a week to their
travel time, but it was better than certain incineration.

Rin scanned the gray rocks with her spyglass and found crev-
ices, cliff ledges that could easily conceal enemies, but saw no
movement. No lanterns. The pass looked abandoned.

"We're not in the clear yet," Kitay said.

"You think they booby-trapped both rivers?"

"They could have," Kitay said. "*I* would."

"But there's nothing here."

A boom shook the air. They exchanged a look and ran out to
the prow.

The skimmer at the head of the fleet was in full blaze.

Another boom echoed through the pass. A second ship exploded, sending blast fragments up so high that they crashed across the *Kingfisher*'s deck. Jinzha threw himself to the ground just before a piece of the *Lapwing* could skewer his head to the mast.

"Get down!" he roared. "Everybody down!"

But he didn't have to tell them—even from a hundred yards away the burst impacts shook the *Kingfisher* like an earthquake, knocking everyone on deck off their feet.

Rin crawled as close as she could to the edge of the deck, spyglass in hand. She popped up from the railing and glanced frantically about the mountains, but all she saw were rocks. "There's no one up there."

"Those aren't missiles," Kitay said. "You'd see the heat glow in the air."

He was right—the source of the explosions wasn't from the air; they weren't detonating on the decks. The very water itself was erupting around the fleet.

Chaos took over the *Kingfisher*. Archers scrambled to the top deck to open fire on enemies who weren't there. Jinzha screamed himself hoarse ordering the ships to reverse direction. The *Kingfisher*'s paddle wheels spun frantically backward, pushing the turtle boat out of the tributary, only to bump into the *Crake*. Only after a frantic exchange of signal flags did the fleet begin backtracking sluggishly downriver.

They weren't moving fast enough. Whatever was in the water must have been laced together by some chain reaction mechanism, because a minute later another skimmer went up in flames, and then another. Rin could *see* the explosions starting below the water, each one detonating the next like a vicious streak, getting closer and closer to the *Kingfisher*.

A massive gust of water shot out of the river. At first Rin thought it was just the force of the explosions, but the water spiraled, higher and higher, like a whirlpool in reverse, expanding to surround the warships, forming a protective ring that centered around the *Griffon*.

"What the fuck," Kitay said.

Rin dashed to the prow.

Nezha stood beneath the *Griffon*'s mast, arms stretched out to the tower of water as if reaching for something.

He met Rin's gaze, and her heart skipped a beat.

His eyes were shot through with streaks of ocean blue—not the eerie cerulean gleam of Feylen's glare, but a darker cobalt, the color of old gems.

"You too?" she whispered.

Through the protective wave of water she saw explosions, splashes of orange and red and yellow. Warped by the water, they almost seemed pretty, a painting of angry bursts. Shrapnel seemed frozen in place, arrested by the wall. The water hung in the air for an impossibly long time, steady while the explosives went off one by one in a series of deafening booms that echoed around the fleet. Nezha collapsed on the deck.

The wave dropped, slammed inward, and drenched the wretched remains of the Republican Fleet.

Rin needed to get to the *Griffon*.

The great wave had knocked Nezha's ship and the *Kingfisher* together into a dismal wreck. Their decks were separated by only a narrow gap. Rin took a running start, jumped, skidded onto the *Griffon*'s deck, and ran toward Nezha's limp form.

All the color had drained from his face. He was already porcelain pale, but now his skin looked transparent, his scars cracks in shattered glass over bright blue veins.

She pulled him up into a sitting position. He was breathing, his chest heaving, but his eyes were squeezed shut, and he only shook his head when she tried to ask him questions.

"It hurts." Finally, intelligible words—he twisted in her arms, scrabbling at something on his back. "It *hurts* . . ."

"Here?" She put her hand on the small of his back.

He managed a nod. Then a sudden, wordless scream.

She tried to help him pull his shirt off, but he kept thrashing in her arms, so she had to slice it apart with a knife and yank the pieces away. Her fingers splayed over his exposed back. Her breath caught in her throat.

A massive dragon tattoo, silver and cerulean in the colors of the House of Yin, covered his skin from shoulder to shoulder. Rin couldn't remember seeing it before—but then, she couldn't remember seeing Nezha shirtless before. This tattoo had to be old. She could see a rippled scar arcing down the left side where Nezha had once been pierced by a Mugenese general's halberd. But now the scar glistened an angry red, as if freshly branded into his skin. She couldn't tell if she was imagining things in her panic, but the dragon seemed to undulate under her fingers, coiling and thrashing against his skin.

"It's in my mind." Nezha let out another strangled cry of pain. "It's telling me—*fuck*, Rin . . ."

Pity washed over her, a dark wave that sent bile rising up in her throat.

Nezha gave a low moan. "It's in my head . . ."

She had an idea of what that was like.

He grabbed her wrists with a strength that startled her. "Kill me."

"I can't do that," she whispered.

She *wanted* to kill him. All she wanted was to put him out of his pain. She couldn't bear to look at him like this, screaming like it was never going to end.

But she'd never forgive herself for that.

"What's wrong with him?" Jinzha had arrived. He was looking down at Nezha with a genuine concern that Rin had never seen on his face.

"It's a god," she told him. She was certain. She knew exactly what was going through Nezha's head, because she'd suffered it before. "He called a god and it won't go away."

She had a good idea of what had happened. Nezha, watching

the fleet exploding around him, had tried to protect the *Griffon*. He might not have been aware of what he was doing. He might only remember wishing that the waters would rise, would protect them from the fires. But some god had answered and done exactly what he'd wished, and now he couldn't get it to give him his mind back.

"What are you talking about?" Jinzha knelt down and tried to pull Nezha out of her grasp, but she wouldn't let go.

"Get back."

"Don't you touch him," he snarled.

She smacked his hand away. "I know what this is, I'm the only one who can help him, so if you want him to live, then *get back*."

She was astounded when Jinzha complied.

Nezha thrashed in her arms, moaning.

"So help him," Jinzha begged.

I'm fucking trying, Rin thought. She forced herself to calm. She could think of only one thing that might work. If this was a god—and she was almost certain that this was a god—then the only way to silence its voice was to shut off Nezha's mind, close off his connection to the world of spirit.

"Send a man to my bunk," she told Jinzha. "Cabin three. Have him pull up the second floorboard in the right corner and bring me what's hidden under there. Do you understand?"

He nodded.

"Then hurry."

He stood up and started to bark out orders.

"Get out." Nezha was curling in on himself, muttering. He scrabbled at his shoulder blades, digging his nails deep into his skin, drawing blood. "Get out—*get out!*"

Rin grabbed his wrists and forced them away from his back. He wrenched them, flailing, out of her grip. A stray hand hit her across the chin. Her head whipped to the side. For a moment she saw black.

Nezha looked horrified. "I'm sorry." He clutched at his shoulders like he was trying to shrink. "I'm so sorry."

Rin heard a groaning noise. It came from the deck—the ship was moving, ever so slowly. Something was pushing at it from below. She looked up, and her stomach twisted with dread. The waves were swelling, rising around the *Griffon* like a hand preparing to clench its fingers in a fist. They had grown higher than the mast.

Nezha might lose control entirely. He might drown them all.

"Nezha." She grasped his face between her palms. "Look at me. Please, look at me. *Nezha*."

But he wouldn't, or couldn't, listen to her—his seconds of lucidity had passed, and it was all she could do to hold him tight so that he wouldn't shred his own skin while he moaned and screamed.

An eternity later she heard footsteps.

"Here," Jinzha said, pressing the packet into her hand. Rin crawled onto Nezha's chest, pinning down his arms with her knees, and tore the packet open with her teeth. Nuggets of opium tumbled out onto the deck.

"What are you doing?" Jinzha demanded.

"Shut up." Rin scraped up two nuggets and held them tightly in her fist.

What now? She didn't have a pipe on hand. She couldn't call the fire to just light up the opium nuggets and make him inhale, and making a fire would take an eternity—everything on deck was drenched.

She had to get the opium into him *somehow*.

She couldn't think of any other way. She balled the nuggets up in her hand and forced them into his mouth. Nezha thrashed harder, choking. She pinched his jaw shut, then wrenched it open and pushed the nuggets farther into his mouth until he swallowed.

She held his arms down and leaned over him, waiting. A minute passed. Then two. Nezha stopped moving. His eyes rolled up into the back of his head. Then he stopped breathing.

"You could have killed him," said the ship's physician.

Rin recognized Dr. Sien from the *Cormorant*. He was the

physician who had tended to Vaisra after Lusan, and appeared to be the only man permitted to treat the members of the House of Yin.

"I just assumed you'd have something for that," she said.

She stood slouched against the wall, exhausted. She was amazed she'd been allowed into Nezha's cabin, but Jinzha had only given her a tight nod on his way out.

Nezha lay still on the bed between them. He looked awful, paler than death, but he was breathing steadily. Every rise and fall of his chest gave Rin a small jolt of relief.

"Lucky we had the drug on hand," said Dr. Sien. "How did you know?"

"Know what?" Rin asked cautiously. Did Dr. Sien know that Nezha was a shaman? Did *anyone*? Jinzha had seemed utterly confused. Was Nezha's secret his alone?

"To give him opium," Dr. Sien said.

That told her nothing. She hazarded a half truth in response. "I've seen this illness before."

"Where?" he asked curiously.

"Um." Rin shrugged. "You know. Down in the south. Opium's a common remedy for it there."

Doctor Sien looked somewhat disappointed. "I have treated the sons of the Dragon Warlord since they were babies. They have never told me anything about Nezha's particular ailment, only that he often feels pain, and that opium is the only way to calm him. I don't know if Vaisra and Saikhara know the cause themselves."

Rin looked down at Nezha's sleeping face. He looked so peaceful. She had the oddest urge to brush the hair back from his forehead. "How long has he been sick?"

"He began having seizures when he was twelve. They've become less frequent as he's gotten older, but this one was the worst I've seen in years."

Has Nezha been a shaman since he was a child? Rin wondered. How had he never told her? Did he not trust her?

"He's in the clear now," said Dr. Sien. "The only thing he'll need is sleep. You don't have to stay."

"It's all right. I'll wait."

He looked uncomfortable. "I don't think General Jinzha—"

"Jinzha knows I just saved his brother's life. He'll permit it, and he's an ass if he doesn't."

Dr. Sien didn't argue. After he closed the door behind him, Rin curled up on the floor next to Nezha's bed and closed her eyes.

Hours later she heard him stirring. She sat up, rubbed the grime from her eyes, and knelt next to him. "Nezha?"

"Hmm." He blinked at the ceiling, trying to make sense of his surroundings.

She touched the back of her finger to his left cheek. His skin was much softer than she had thought it would be. His scars were not raised bumps like she'd expected, but rather smooth lines running across his skin like tattoos.

His eyes had returned to their normal, lovely brown. Rin couldn't help noticing how long his lashes were; they were so dark and heavy, thicker even than Venka's. *It's not fair*, she thought. He'd always been much prettier than anyone had the right to be.

"How are you doing?" she asked.

Nezha blinked several times and slurred something that didn't sound like words.

She tried again. "Do you know what's going on?"

His eyes darted around the room for a while, and then focused on her face with some difficulty. "Yes."

She couldn't hold back her questions any longer. "Do you understand what just happened? Why didn't you tell me?"

All Nezha did was blink.

She leaned forward, heart pounding. "I could have helped you. Or—or you could have helped me. You should have told me."

His breathing started to quicken.

"Why didn't you tell me?" she asked again.

He mumbled something unintelligible. His eyelids fluttered shut.

She nearly shook him by the collar, she was so desperate for answers.

She took a deep breath. *Stop it.* Nezha was in no state to be interrogated now.

She could force him to talk. If she pressed harder, if she yelled at him to give her the truth, then he might tell her everything.

That would be a secret revealed under opium, however, and she would have coerced him when he was in no state to refuse.

Would he hate her for it?

He was only half-conscious. He might not even remember.

She swallowed down a sudden wave of revulsion. No—no, she wouldn't do that to him. She couldn't. She'd have to get her answers another way. Now was not the time. She stood up.

His eyes opened again. "Where are you going?"

"I should let you rest," she said.

He shifted in his bed. "No . . . don't go . . ."

She paused at the door.

"Please," he said. "Stay."

"All right," she said, and returned to his side. She took his hand in hers. "I'm right here."

"What's happening to me?" he murmured.

She squeezed his fingers. "Just close your eyes, Nezha. Go back to sleep."

The remains of the fleet sat stuck in a cove for the next three days. Half the troops had to be treated for burn wounds, and the repulsive smell of rotting flesh became so pervasive that the men took to wrapping cloth around their faces, covering everything except their eyes. Eventually Jinzha had made the decision to administer morphine and medicine only to the men who had a decent chance of survival. The rest were rolled into the mud, facedown, until they stopped moving.

They didn't have time to bury their dead so they dragged them into piles interlaced with parts of irreparable ships to form funeral pyres and set them on fire.

"How strategic," Kitay said. "Don't need the Empire getting hold of good ship wood."

"Do you have to be like this?" Rin asked.

"Just complimenting Jinzha."

Sister Petra stood before the burning corpses and gave an entire funeral benediction in her fluent, toneless Nikara while soldiers stood around her in a curious circle.

"In life you suffered in a world wreaked by Chaos, but you have offered your souls to a beautiful cause," she said. "You died creating order in a land bereft of it. Now you rest. I pray your Maker will take mercy on your souls. I pray that you will come to know the depths of his love, all-encompassing and unconditional."

She then began chanting in a language that Rin didn't recognize. It seemed similar to Hesperian—she could almost recognize the roots of words before they took on an entirely different shape—but this seemed something more ancient, something weighted down with centuries of history and religious purpose.

"Where do your people think souls go when they die?" Rin murmured quietly to Augus.

He looked surprised she had even asked. "To the realm of the Maker, of course. Where do your people think they go?"

"Nowhere," she said. "We disappear back to nothing."

The Nikara spoke of the underworld sometimes, but that was more a folk story than a true belief. No one really imagined they might end up anywhere but in darkness.

"That's impossible," Augus said. "The Maker creates our souls to be permanent. Even barbarians' souls have value. When we die, he refines them and brings them to his realm."

Rin couldn't help her curiosity. "What is that realm like?"

"It's beautiful," he said. "A land utterly without Chaos; without pain, disease, or suffering. It is the kingdom of perfect order that we spend our lives trying to re-create on this earth."

Rin saw the joyful hope beaming out of Augus's face as he spoke, and she knew that he believed every word he was saying.

She was starting to see why the Hesperians clung so fervently to their religion. No wonder they had won converts over so easily during occupation. What a relief it would be to know that at the end of this life there was a better one, that perhaps upon death you might enjoy the comforts you had always been denied instead of fading away from an indifferent universe. What a relief to know that the world was supposed to make sense, and that if it didn't, you would one day be justly compensated.

A line of captains and generals stood before the burning pyre. Nezha was at the end, leaning heavily on a walking stick. It was the first time Rin had seen him in two days.

But when she approached him, he turned to walk away. She called out his name. He ignored her. She dashed forward—he couldn't outrun her, not with his walking stick—and grabbed his wrist.

"Stop running away," she said.

"I'm not running," he said stiffly.

"Then talk to me. Tell me what I saw on the river."

Nezha's eyes darted around at the soldiers standing within earshot. He lowered his voice. "I don't know what you're talking about."

"Don't lie to me. I saw what you did. You're a shaman!"

"Rin, shut up."

She didn't let go of his wrist. "You moved the water at will. I *know* it was you."

He narrowed his eyes. "You didn't see anything, and you won't tell anyone anything—"

"Your secret is safe from Petra, if that's what you're asking," she said. "But I don't understand why you're lying to *me*."

Without responding, Nezha turned and limped briskly away from the pyres. She followed him to a spot behind the charred hull of a transport skimmer. The questions poured out of her in an unstoppable torrent. "Did they teach you at Sinegard? Does Jun know? Is anyone else in your family a shaman?"

"Rin, stop—"

"Jinzha doesn't know, I figured that out. What about your mother? Vaisra? Did he teach you?"

"*I am not a shaman!*" he shouted.

She didn't flinch. "I'm not stupid. I know what I saw."

"Then draw your own conclusions and stop asking questions."

"Why are you hiding this?"

He looked pained. "Because I don't want it."

"You can control the water! You could single-handedly win us this war!"

"It's not that easy, I can't just—" He shook his head. "You saw what happened. It wants to take over."

"Of course it does. What do you think we all go through? So you control it. You get practice at reining it in, you shape it to your own will—"

"Like *you* can?" he sneered. "You're the equivalent of a spiritual eunuch."

He was trying to throw her off, but she didn't let that distract her. "And I would kill to have the fire back. It's difficult, I know, the gods aren't kind—but you *can* control them! I can help you."

"You don't know what you're talking about, shut up—"

"Unless you're just scared, which is no excuse, because men are dying while you're sitting here indulging in your own self-pity—"

"I said *shut up*!"

His hand went into the skimmer's hull, an inch from her head. She didn't flinch. She turned her head slowly, trying to pretend her heart wasn't slamming against her chest.

"You missed," she said calmly.

Nezha pulled his hand away from the hull. Blood trickled down his knuckles from four crimson dots.

She should have been afraid, but when she searched his face, she couldn't find a shred of anger. Just fear.

She had no respect for fear.

"I don't want to hurt you," he said.

"Oh, trust me." Her lip curled. "You couldn't."

CHAPTER 20

"A puzzle for you," said Kitay. "The water erupts around the ships, blows holes in the sides like cannonballs, and yet we never see a hint of an explosion above the water. How does the Militia do this?"

"I assume you're about to tell me," Rin said.

"Come on, Rin, just play along."

She fiddled with the shrapnel fragments strewn across his worktable. "Could have been archers aiming at the base. They could have fixed rockets on the front ends of their arrows?"

"But why would they do that? The deck's more vulnerable than the hull. And we would have seen them in the air if they were alight, which they'd have to be to explode on impact."

"Maybe they found out a way to hide the heat glow," she said.

"Maybe," he said. "But then why the chain reaction? Why start with the skimmers, instead of aiming directly at the *King-fisher* or the tower ships?"

"I don't know. Scare tactics?"

"That's stupid," he said dismissively. "Here's a hint: The explosives were in the water to begin with. That's why we never saw them. They really were underwater."

She sighed. "And how would they have managed that, Kitay? Why don't you just tell me the answer?"

"Animal intestines," he said happily. He pulled out a rather disgusting translucent tube from under the table, inside of which he'd threaded a thin fuse. "They're completely waterproof. I'm guessing they used cow intestines, since they're longer, but any animal would do, really, because it just has to keep the fuse dry enough to let it burn down. Then they rig up the interior so that slow-burning coils light the fuse on impact. Cool, eh?"

"Sort of like the pig stomachs."

"Sort of. But those were designed to erode over time. Depending on how slow the coils burn, these could keep a fuse dry for days if they were sealed well enough."

"That's incredible." Rin stared at the intestines, considering the implications. The mines were ingenious. The Militia could win riverine battles without even being present, as long as they could guarantee that the Republican Fleet would travel over a given stretch of water.

When had the Militia developed this technology?

And if they had this capability, were any of the river routes safe?

The door slammed open. Jinzha strode in unannounced, holding a rolled-up scroll in one hand. Nezha followed in his wake, still limping on his walking stick. He refused to meet Rin's eye.

"Hello, sir." Kitay cheerfully waved a cow intestine at him. "I've solved your problem."

Jinzha looked repulsed. "What is that?"

"Water mines. It's how they blew up the fleet." Kitay offered the intestine up to Jinzha for inspection.

Jinzha wrinkled his nose. "I'll trust your word for it. Did you figure out how to deactivate them?"

"Yes, it's easy enough if we just puncture the waterproofing. The hard part is finding the mines." Kitay rubbed his chin. "Don't suppose you've got any expert divers on deck."

"I can figure that part out." Jinzha spread his scroll over Kitay's table. It was a closely detailed map of Rat Province, on which he'd circled in red ink a spot just inland of a nearby lake. "I need you to draw up detailed plans for an attack on Boyang. Here's all the intelligence we have."

Kitay leaned forward to examine the map. "This is for a spring-time operation?"

"No. We attack as soon as we can get there."

Kitay blinked twice. "You can't be considering taking Boyang with a damaged fleet."

"A full three-fourths of the fleet is serviceable. We've mostly lost skimmers—"

"And the warships?"

"Can be repaired in time."

Kitay tapped his fingers on the table. "Do you have men to man those ships?"

Irritation flickered over Jinzha's face. "We've redistributed the troops. There will be enough."

"If you say so." Kitay chewed at his thumbnail, staring intensely down at Jinzha's scribbles. "There's still a slight problem."

"And what's that?"

"Well, Lake Boyang's an interesting natural phenomenon—"

"Get to the point," Jinzha said.

Kitay traced his finger down the map. "Usually lake water levels go down during the summer and go up during colder seasons. That should advantage deep-hulled ships like ours. But Boyang gets its water source directly from Mount Tianshan, and during the winter—"

"Tianshan freezes," Rin realized out loud.

"So what?" Jinzha asked. "That doesn't mean the lake drains immediately."

"No, but it means the water level goes down every day," Kitay said. "And the shallower the lake, the less mobility your warships have, especially the Seahawks. I'm guessing the mines were put there to stall us."

"Then how long do we have?" Jinzha pressed.

Kitay shrugged. "I'm not a prophet. I'd have to see the lake."

"I told you it's not worth it." Nezha spoke up for the first time. "We should head back south while we still can."

"And do what?" Jinzha demanded. "Hide? Grovel? Explain to Father why we've come home with our tails tucked between our legs?"

"No. Explain about the territory we've taken. The men we've added to our ranks. We regroup, and fight from a position of strength."

"We have plenty of strength."

"The entire Imperial Fleet will be waiting for us in that lake!"

"So we will take it from them," Jinzha snarled. "We're not running home to Father because we were scared of a fight."

This isn't really an argument, Rin thought. Jinzha had made up his mind, and he would shout down anyone who opposed him. Nezha—the younger brother, the inferior brother—was never going to change Jinzha's mind.

Jinzha was hungry for this fight. Rin could read it so clearly on his face. And she could understand why he wanted it so badly. A victory at Boyang might effectively end this war. It might achieve the final and devastating proof of victory that the Hesperians were demanding. It might compensate for Jinzha's latest string of failures.

She'd known a commander who made decisions like that before. His bones, if any had survived incineration, were lying at the bottom of Omonod Bay.

"Aren't your troops worth more than your ego?" she asked. "Don't sentence us to death just because you've been humiliated."

Jinzha didn't even deign to look at her. "Did I authorize you to talk?"

"She has a point," Nezha said.

"I am warning you, brother."

"She's telling the truth," Nezha said. "You're just not listening because you're terrified that someone else is right."

Jinzha strode over to Nezha and casually slapped him across the face.

The crack echoed around the little room. Rin and Kitay sat frozen in their seats. Nezha's head whipped to the side, where it stayed. Slowly he touched his fingers to his cheek, where a red mark was blooming outward over his scars. His chest rose and fell; he was breathing so heavily that Rin thought for sure he would strike back. But he did nothing.

"We could probably get to Boyang in time if we leave immediately," Kitay said neutrally, as if nothing had happened.

"Then we'll set sail within an hour." Jinzha pointed to Kitay. "You get to my office. Admiral Molkoi will give you full access to scout reports. I want attack plans by the end of the day."

"Oh, joy," Kitay said.

"What's that?"

Kitay sat up straight. "Yes, sir."

Jinzha stormed out of the room. Nezha lingered by the doorway, eyes darting between Rin and Kitay as if unsure of whether he wanted to stay.

"Your brother's losing it," Rin informed him.

"Shut up," he said.

"I've seen this before," she said. "Commanders break under pressure all the time. Then they make shitty decisions that get people killed."

Nezha sneered at her, and for an instant he looked identical to Jinzha. "My brother is not Altan."

"You sure about that?"

"Say whatever you want," he said. "At least we're not Speerly trash."

She was so shocked that she couldn't think of a good response. Nezha stalked out and slammed the door shut behind him.

Kitay whistled under his breath. "Lovers' spat, you two?"

Rin's face suddenly felt terribly hot. She sat down beside Kitay and busied herself by pretending to fiddle with the cow intestine. "Something like that."

"If it helps, I don't think you're Speerly trash," he said.

"I don't want to talk about it."

"Let me know if you do." Kitay shrugged. "Incidentally, you could try being more careful about how you talk to Jinzha."

She made a face. "Oh, I'm aware."

"Are you? Or do you *like* not having a seat at the table?"

"Kitay . . ."

"You're a Sinegard-trained shaman. You shouldn't be a foot soldier; it's below you."

She was tired of having that argument. She changed the subject. "Do we really have a chance at taking Boyang?"

"If we work the paddle wheels to death. If the Imperial Fleet is as weak as our most optimistic estimates say." Kitay sighed. "If the heaven and the stars and the sun line up for us and we're blessed by every god in that Pantheon of yours."

"So, no."

"I honestly don't know. There are too many moving pieces. We don't know how strong the fleet is. We don't know their naval tactics. We've probably got superior naval talent, but they'll have been there longer. They'll know the lake terrain. They had time to booby-trap the rivers. They'll have a plan for us."

Rin searched the map, looking for any possible way out. "Then do we retreat?"

"It's too late for that now," Kitay said. "Jinzha's right about one thing: we don't have any other options. We don't have supplies to last out the winter, and chances are if we escape back to Arlong, then we'll lose all the progress we've made—"

"What, we can't just hunker down in Ram Province for a few months? Have Arlong ship up some supplies?"

"And give Daji the entire winter to build a fleet? We've gotten this far because the Empire has never had a great navy. Daji has the men, but we have the ships. That's the only reason we're at parity. If Daji gets three months' leeway, then this is all over."

"Some Hesperian warships would be great right around now," Rin muttered.

"And that's the root of it all." Kitay gave her a wry look. "Jinzha's being an ass, but I think I understand him. He can't afford to look weak, not with Tarcquet sitting there judging his every move. He's got to be bold. Be the brilliant leader his father promised. And we'll blaze forward right with him, because we simply have no other option."

"How many of you can swim?" Jinzha asked.

Prisoners stood miserably in line on the slippery deck, heads bent as rain poured down on them in relentless sheets. Jinzha paced up and down the deck, and the prisoners flinched every time he stopped in front of them. "Show of hands. Who can swim?"

The prisoners glanced nervously at one another, no doubt wondering which response would keep them alive. No hands went up.

"Let me put it this way." Jinzha crossed his arms. "We don't have the rations to feed everyone. No matter what, some of you are going to end up at the bottom of the Murui. It's only a question of whether you want to starve to death. So raise your hand if you'll be useful."

Every hand shot up.

Jinzha turned to Admiral Molkoi. "Throw them all overboard."

The men started screaming in protest. Rin thought for a second that Molkoi might actually comply, and that they would have to watch the prisoners clawing over each other in the water in a desperate bid to survive, but then she realized that Jinzha didn't really intend to execute them.

He was watching to see who wouldn't resist.

After a few moments Jinzha pulled fifteen men out of the line and dismissed the rest to the brig. Then he held up a water mine wrapped in cow intestine and passed it through the line so the men could take a better look at the fuse.

"The Militia's been planting these in the water. You will swim through the water and disable them. You will be tethered to the ship with ropes, and you will be given sharp rocks to do the job. If you find an explosive, cut the intestine and ensure that water floods the tube. Try to escape, and my archers will shoot you in the water. Leave any mines intact, and you will die with us. It's in your interest to be thorough."

He tossed several lines of rope at the men. "Go on, then."

Nobody moved.

"Admiral Molkoi!" Jinzha shouted.

Molkoi signaled to his men. A line of guards strode forward, blades out.

"Do not test my patience," Jinzha said.

The men scrambled hastily for the ropes.

The storms only intensified in the following week, but Jinzha forced the fleet forward to Boyang at an impossible pace. The soldiers were exhausted at the paddle wheels trying to meet his demands. Several prisoners dropped dead after being forced to paddle consecutive shifts without a night's sleep, and Jinzha had their bodies tossed unceremoniously overboard.

"He's going to tire his army out before we even get there," Kitay grumbled to Rin. "Bet you wish we'd brought those Federation troops along now, don't you?"

The army was both weary and hungry. Their rations had been dwindling. They now received dried fish twice a day instead of three times, and rice only once in the evenings. Most of the extra provisions they'd obtained in Xiashang had been lost in the explosions. Morale drooped by the day.

The soldiers became even more disheartened when scouts returned with details of the lake defense. The Imperial Navy was indeed stationed at Boyang, as all of them had feared, and it was far better equipped than Jinzha had anticipated.

The navy rivaled the size of the fleet that had sailed out from Arlong. The one consolation was that it was nowhere near the technological level of Jinzha's armada. The Empress had hastily constructed it in the months since Lusan, and the lack of preparation time showed—the Imperial Fleet was a messy amalgamation of badly constructed new ships, some with unfinished decks, and conscripted old merchant boats with no uniformity of build. At least three were leisure barges without firing capacity.

But they had more ships, and they had more men.

"Ship quality would have mattered if they were out over the ocean," Kitay told Rin. "But the lake will turn this battle into a crucible. We'll all be crammed in together. They just need to get their men to board our ships, and it'll be over. Boyang's going to turn red with blood."

Rin knew one way the Republic could easily win. They wouldn't even have to fire a shot. But Nezha refused to speak to her. She only ever saw him when he came aboard the *Kingfisher* for meetings in his brother's office. Each time they crossed paths he hastily looked away; if she called his name, he only shook his head. Otherwise, they might have been complete strangers.

"Do we expect anything to come of this?" Rin asked.

"Not really," Kitay said. He held his crossbow ready against his chest. "It's just a formality. You know how aristocrats are."

Rin's teeth chattered as the Imperial flagship drifted closer to the *Kingfisher*. "We shouldn't have even come."

"It's Jinzha. Always worried about his honor."

"Yes, well, he might try worrying more about his *life*."

Against the counsel of his admirals, Jinzha had demanded a last-minute negotiation with the flagship of the Imperial Navy. Gentlemen's etiquette, he called it. He had to at least give the Wolf Meat General a chance to surrender. But the negotiation would not even be a charade; it was only a risk, and a stupid one.

Chang En had refused a private meeting. The most he would acquiesce to was a temporary cease-fire and a confrontation held over the open water, and that meant their ships were forced to draw dangerously close together in the final moments before the firing began.

"Hello, little dragon!" Chang En's voice rang over the still, cold air. For once, the waters were calm and quiet. Mist drifted from the surface of Boyang Lake, shrouding the assembled fleets in a cloudy fog.

"You've done well for yourself, Master," Jinzha called. "Admiral of the Imperial Navy, now?"

Chang En spread his arms. "I take what I want when I see it."

Jinzha lifted his chin. "You'll want to take this surrender, then. You can retain your position in my father's employ."

"Oh, fuck off." Chang En's jackal laughter rang high and cruel across the lake.

Jinzha raised his voice. "There's nothing Su Daji can do for you. Whatever she's promised you, we'll double it. My father can make you a general—"

"Your father will give me a cell in Baghra and relieve me of my limbs."

"You'll have immunity if you lay down your arms now. I give you my word."

"A Dragon's word means nothing." Chang En laughed again. "Do you think me stupid? When has Vaisra ever kept a vow he's made?"

"My father is an honorable man who only wants to see this country unified under a just regime," Jinzha said. "You'd serve well by his side."

He wasn't just posturing. Jinzha spoke like he meant it. He seemed to truly hope that he could convince his former master to switch loyalties.

Chang En spat into the water. "Your father's a Hesperian puppet dancing for donations."

"And you think Daji is any better?" Jinzha asked. "Stand by her, and you're guaranteeing years of bloody warfare."

"Ah, but I'm a soldier. Without war, I'm out of a job."

Chang En lifted a gauntleted hand. His archers lifted their bows.

"Negotiator's honor," Jinzha cautioned.

Chang En smiled widely. "Talks are over, little dragon."

His hand fell.

A single arrow whistled through the air, grazed Jinzha's cheek, and embedded itself in the bulkhead behind him.

Jinzha touched his fingers to his cheek, pulled them away, and watched his blood trickle down his pale white hand as if shocked that he could bleed.

"Let you off easy that time," Chang En said. "Wouldn't want the fun to be over too quick."

Lake Boyang lit up like a torch. Flaming arrows, fire rockets, and cannon fire turned the sky red, while below, smokescreens went off everywhere to shroud the Imperial Navy behind a murky gray veil.

The *Kingfisher* sailed straight into the mist.

"Bring me his head," Jinzha ordered, ignoring his men's frantic shouts for him to duck down.

The rest of the fleet spread out across the lake to decrease their vulnerability to incendiary attacks. The closer they clumped, the faster they would all go up in flames. The Seahawks and trebuchets started to return the fire, launching missile after missile over the *Kingfisher* and into the opaque wall of gray.

But their spread-out formation only made the Republicans weak against Imperial swarming tactics. Tiny, patched-up skimmers shot into the gaps between the Republican warships and pushed them farther apart, isolating them to fight on their own.

The Imperial Navy targeted the tower ships first. Imperial skimmers attacked the *Crake* with relentless cannon fire from all sides. Without its own skimmer support, the *Crake* began shaking in the water like a man in his death throes.

Jinzha ordered the *Kingfisher* to come to the *Crake*'s aid, but it, too, was trapped, cut off from the fleet by a phalanx of old Imperial junks. Jinzha ordered round after round of cannon fire to clear them a path. But even the bombed-out junks took up space in the water, which meant all they could do was stand and watch as the Wolf Meat General's men swarmed aboard the *Crake*.

The *Crake*'s men were exhausted and spread too thin to begin with. The Wolf Meat General's men were out for blood. The *Crake* never stood a chance.

Chang En cut a ferocious path through the upper deck. Rin saw him raise a broadsword over his head and cleave a soldier's skull in half so neatly he might have been slicing a winter melon. When another soldier took the opportunity to charge him from behind, Chang En twisted around and shoved his blade so hard into his chest that it came out clean on the other side.

The man was a monster. If Rin hadn't been so terrified for her life, she might have stood there on the deck and simply *watched*.

"Speerly!" Admiral Molkoi pointed to the empty mounted crossbow in front of her, then waved at the *Crake*. "Cover them!"

He said something else, but just then a wave of cannons exploded against the *Kingfisher*'s sides. Rin's ears rang as she made her way to the crossbow. She could hear nothing else. Hands shaking, she fitted a bolt into the slot.

Her fingers kept slipping. Fuck, *fuck*—she hadn't fired a crossbow since the Academy, she'd never served in the artillery, and in her panic she'd almost forgotten completely what to do . . .

She took a deep breath. *Wind it up. Aim.* She squinted at the end of the *Crake*.

The Wolf Meat General had cornered a captain near the edge of the prow. Rin recognized her as Captain Salkhi—she must have been reassigned to the *Crake* after the *Swallow* was lost in the burning channel. Rin's stomach twisted in dread. Salkhi still had her weapon, was still trading blows, but it wasn't even close. Rin could tell that Salkhi was struggling to hold on to her blade while Chang En hacked at her with lackadaisical ease.

Rin's first shot didn't even make it to the deck. She had the direction right but the height wrong; the bolt pinged uselessly off the *Crake*'s hull.

Salkhi brought her sword up to block a blow from above, but Chang En slammed his blade so strongly against hers that she dropped it. Salkhi was weaponless, trapped against the prow. Chang En advanced slowly, grinning.

Rin fitted a new bolt into the crossbow and, squinting, lined up the shot with Chang En's head. She pulled the trigger. The bolt sailed over the burning seas and slammed into the wood just next to Salkhi's arm. Salkhi jumped at the noise, twisted around by instinct . . .

She had barely turned when the Wolf Meat General slammed his blade into the side of her neck, nearly decapitating her. She dropped to her knees. Chang En reached down and dragged her upright by her collar until she was dangling a good foot above the ground. He pulled her close, kissed her on her mouth, and tossed her over the side of the ship.

Rin stood frozen, watching Salkhi's body disappear under the waves.

Slowly the tide of red took over the *Crake*. Despite a steady stream of arrow fire from the *Shrike* and the *Kingfisher*, Chang En's men dispatched its crew like a pack of wolves falling on sheep. Someone shot a fiery arrow at the masthead, and the *Crake*'s blue and silver flag went up in flames.

The tower ship now turned on its sister ships. Its catapults and incendiaries were no longer aimed at the Imperial Navy, but at the *Kingfisher* and the *Griffon*.

Meanwhile the Imperial skimmers, small as they were, ran circles around Jinzha's fleet. In shallow waters the Republic's massive warships simply didn't have maneuverability. They drifted helplessly like sick whales while a frenzy of smaller fish tore them apart.

"Put us by the *Shrike*," Jinzha ordered. "We have to keep at least one of our tower ships."

"We can't," Molkoi said.

"Why not?"

"The water level's too low on that side of the lake. The *Shrike*'s been grounded. Any farther and we'll get stuck in the mud ourselves."

"Then at least get us away from the *Crake*," Jinzha snapped. "We're about to be stuck as is."

He was right. While Chang En wrestled for control of the *Crake*, the tower ship had drifted so far into shallow waters that it could not extricate itself.

But the *Kingfisher* and the *Griffon* still had more firepower than the Imperial junks. If they just kept shooting, they might cement their hold on the deeper end of the lake. They had to. They had no other way out.

The Imperial Navy, however, had ground to a halt around the *Crake*.

"What on earth are they doing?" Kitay asked.

They didn't seem to be stuck. Rather, Chang En seemed to have ordered his fleet to sit completely still. Rin scoured the decks for any sign of activity—a lantern signal, a flag—and saw nothing.

What were they waiting for?

Something dark flitted across the upper field of her spyglass. She moved her focus up to the mast.

A man stood at the very top.

He wore neither a Militia nor a Republican uniform. He was garbed entirely in black. Rin could hardly make out his face. His hair was a straggly, matted mess that hung into his eyes and his skin was both pale and dark, mottled like ruined marble. He looked as if he'd been dragged up from the bottom of the ocean.

Rin found him oddly familiar, but she couldn't place where she'd seen him before.

"What are you looking at?" Kitay asked.

She blinked into the spyglass, and the man was gone.

"There's a man." She pointed. "I saw him, he was right there—"

Kitay frowned, squinting at the mast. "What man?"

Rin couldn't speak. Dread pooled at the bottom of her stomach. She'd remembered. She knew exactly who that was.

A sudden chill had fallen over the lake. New ice crackled over the water's surface. The *Kingfisher*'s sails suddenly dropped without warning. Its crew looked around the deck, bewildered. No one had given that order. No one had lowered the sails.

"There's no wind," Kitay murmured. "Why isn't there a wind?"

Rin heard a whooshing noise. A blur shot past her eyes, followed by a scream that grew fainter and fainter until it abruptly cut off.

She heard a crack in the air far above her head.

Admiral Molkoi appeared suddenly on the cliff wall, his body bent at grotesque angles like a broken doll on display. He hung there for a moment before skidding down the rock face and into the lake, leaving behind a crimson streak on gray.

"Oh, fuck," Rin muttered.

What seemed like a lifetime ago, she and Altan had freed someone very powerful and very mad from the Chuluu Korikh.

The Wind God Feylen had returned.

The *Kingfisher*'s deck erupted into shouts. Some soldiers ran to the mounted crossbows, aiming their bolts at nothing. Others dropped to the deck and wrapped their arms around their necks as if hiding from wild animals.

Rin finally regained her senses. She cupped her hands around her mouth. "Everybody get belowdecks!"

She grabbed Kitay's arm and pulled him toward the closest hatch, just as a piercing gust of wind slammed into them from the side. They crumpled together against the bulkhead. His bent elbow went straight into her rib cage.

"Ow!" she cried.

Kitay picked himself off the deck. "Sorry."

Somehow they managed to drag themselves toward the hatch and tumbled more than walked down the stairs to the hold, where the rest of the crew huddled in the pitch darkness. There passed a long silence, pregnant with terror. No one spoke a word.

Light filled the chamber. Gust after gust of wind ripped the wooden panels cleanly away from the ship as if peeling off layers of skin, exposing the cowering and vulnerable crew underneath.

The strange man perched before them on the jagged wood like a bird alighting on a branch. Rin could see his eyes clearly now— bright, gleaming, malicious dots of blue.

"What's this?" asked Feylen. "Little rats, hiding with nowhere to go?"

Someone shot an arrow at his head. He waved a hand, annoyed. The arrow jerked to the side and came whistling back into the soldiers' ranks. Rin heard a dull thud. Someone collapsed to the floor.

"Don't be so rude." Feylen's voice was quiet, reedy and thin, but in the eerily still air they could hear every word he said. He hovered above them, effortlessly drifting above the ground, until his bright eyes landed on Rin. "There you are."

She didn't think. If she stopped to think, then fear would catch up. Instead she launched herself at him, screaming, trident in hand.

He sent her spinning to the planks with a flick of his fingers. She got up to rush him again but didn't even get close. He hurled her away every time she approached him, but she kept trying, again and again. If she was going to die, then she'd do it on her feet.

But Feylen was just toying with her.

Finally he yanked her out of the ship and started tossing her around in the air like a rag doll. He could have flung her into the opposite cliff if he'd wanted to; he could have lifted her high into the air and sent her plummeting into the lake, and the only reason he hadn't was that he wanted to play.

"Behold the great Phoenix, trapped inside a little girl," sneered Feylen. "Where is your fire now?"

"You're Cike," Rin gasped. Altan had appealed to Feylen's humanity once. It had almost worked. She had to try the same. "You're one of us."

"A traitor like you?" Feylen chuckled as the winds hurtled her up and down. "Hardly."

"Why would you fight for her?" Rin demanded. "She had you imprisoned!"

"Imprisoned?" Feylen sent Rin tumbling so close to the cliff wall that her fingers brushed the surface before he jerked her back in front of him. "No, that was Trengsin. That was Trengsin and Tyr, the pair of them. They crept up on us in the middle of the night, and still it took them until midday to pin us down."

He let her drop. She hurtled down to the lake, crashed into the water, and was certain she was about to drown just before Feylen yanked her back up by her ankle. He emitted a high-pitched cackle. "Look at you. You're like a little cat. Drenched to the bone."

A pair of rockets shot toward Feylen's head. He swept them carelessly out of the air. They fell to the water and fizzled out.

"Is Ramsa still at it?" he asked. "How adorable. Is he well? We never liked him, we'll rip out his fingernails one by one after this."

He tossed Rin up and down by her ankle as he spoke. She clenched her teeth to keep from crying out.

"Did you really think you were going to fight us?" He sounded amused. "We can't be killed, child."

"Altan stopped you once," she snarled.

"He did," Feylen acknowledged, "but you're a far cry from Altan Trengsin."

He stopped tossing her and held her still in the air, buffeted on all sides by winds so strong she could barely keep her eyes open. He hung before her, arms outstretched, tattered clothes rippling in the wind, daring her to attack and knowing that she couldn't.

"Isn't it fun to fly?" he asked. The winds whipped harder and harder around her until it felt like a thousand steel blades jamming into every tender point of her body.

"Just kill me," she gasped. "Get it over with."

"Oh, we're not going to kill you," said Feylen. "She told us not to do that. We're just supposed to hurt you."

He waved a hand. The winds yanked her away.

She flew up, weightless and utterly out of control, and crumpled against the masthead. She hung there, splayed out like a dissected corpse, for just the briefest moment before the drop. She landed in a crumpled heap on the *Kingfisher*'s deck. She couldn't draw enough breath to scream. Every part of her body was on fire. She tried making her limbs move but they wouldn't obey her.

Her senses came back in blurs. She saw a shape above her, heard a garbled voice shouting her name.

"Kitay?" she whispered.

His arms shifted under her midriff. He was trying to lift her up, but the pain of the slightest movement was enormous. She whimpered, shaking.

"You're okay," Kitay said. "I've got you."

She clutched at his arm, unable to speak. They huddled against each other, watching the planks continue to peel off the *King-fisher*. Feylen was stripping the fleet apart, bit by bit.

Rin could do nothing but convulse with fear. She squeezed her eyes shut. She didn't want to see. The panic had taken over, and the same thoughts echoed over and over in her mind. *We're going to drown. He's going to rip the ships apart and we will fall into the water and we will drown.*

Kitay shook her shoulder. "Rin. *Look.*"

She opened her eyes and saw a shock of white hair. Chaghan had climbed out on the broken planks, was teetering wildly on the edge. He looked like a little child dancing on a roof. Somehow, despite the howling winds, he did not fall.

He lifted his arms above his head.

Instantly the air felt colder. Thicker, somehow. Just as abruptly, the wind stopped.

Feylen hung still in the air, as if some invisible force was holding him in place.

Rin couldn't tell what Chaghan was doing, but she could feel the power in the air. It seemed as if Chaghan had established some invisible connection to Feylen, some thread that only the two of them could perceive, some psychospiritual plane upon which to wage a battle of wills.

For a moment it seemed as if Chaghan was winning.

Feylen's head jerked back and forth; his legs twitched, as if he were seizing.

Rin's grip tightened on Kitay's arm. A bubble of hope rose in her chest.

Please. Please let Chaghan win.

Then she saw Qara hunched over on the deck, rocking back and forth, muttering something over and over under her breath.

"No," Qara whispered. "No, no, *no!*"

Chaghan's head jerked to the side. His limbs moved spastically, flailing without purpose or direction, as if someone who had very little knowledge of the human body was controlling him from somewhere far away.

Qara started to scream.

Chaghan went limp. Then he flew backward, like a little white flag of surrender, so frail that Rin was afraid the winds themselves might rip him apart.

"You think you can contain us, little shaman?" The winds resumed, twice as ferocious. Another gust swept both Chaghan and Qara off the ship into the churning waves below.

Rin saw Nezha watching, horrified, from the *Griffon*, just close enough to be in earshot.

"Do something!" she screamed. "You coward! *Do something!*"

Nezha stood still, his mouth open, eyes wide as if he were trapped. His expression went slack. He did nothing.

A gust of wind tore the *Kingfisher*'s deck in half, ripping the very floorboards from beneath Rin's feet. She fell through the fragments of wood, bumped and dragged along the rough surface, until she hit the water.

Kitay landed beside her. His eyes were closed. He sank instantly. She wrapped her arms around his chest, kicking furiously to keep them both afloat, and struggled to swim toward the *Kingfisher*, but the water kept sweeping them backward.

Her gut clenched.

The current.

Lake Boyang emptied into a waterfall on its southern border. It was a short, narrow drop—small enough that its current had little effect on heavy warships. It was harmless to sailors. Deadly to swimmers.

The *Kingfisher* rapidly receded from Rin's sight as the current dragged them faster and faster to the edge. She saw a rope drifting beside them and grabbed wildly for it, desperate for anything to hang on to.

Miraculously it was still tethered to the fleet. The line went taut; they stopped drifting. She forced her freezing fingers around the cord against the rushing waters, struggled to wrap it in loops around Kitay's torso, her wrists.

Her limbs had gone numb with the cold. She couldn't move her fingers; they were locked tight around the rope.

"Help us!" she screamed. "Someone *help*!"

Someone stood up from the *Kingfisher*'s prow.

Jinzha. Their eyes met across the water. His face was wild, frantic—she wanted to think he had seen her, but maybe his attention was fixed only on his own disappearing chance of survival.

Then he disappeared. She couldn't tell if Jinzha had cut the rope or if he'd simply gone down under another burst of Feylen's attack, but she felt a jerk in the line just before it went slack.

They spun away from the fleet, hurtling toward the waterfall. There was one second of weightlessness, a confusing and delicious moment of utter disorientation, and then the water claimed them.

CHAPTER 21

Rin ran across a dark field, chasing after a fiery silhouette that she was never going to catch. Her legs moved as if treading water— she was too slow, too clumsy, and the farther back she fell from the silhouette, the more her despair weighed her down, until her legs were so heavy that she couldn't run any longer.

"Please," she cried. "Wait."

The silhouette stopped.

When Altan turned around, she saw he was already burning, his handsome features charred and twisted, blackened skin peeled away to reveal pristine, gleaming bone.

And then he was looming above her. Somehow he was still magnificent, still beautiful, even when arrested in the moment of his death. He knelt in front of her, took her face in his scorching hands, and brought their foreheads close together.

"They're right, you know," he said.

"About what?" She saw oceans of fire in his eyes. His grip was hurting her; it always had. She wasn't sure if she wanted him to let her go or to kiss her.

His fingers dug into her cheeks. "It should have been you."

His face morphed into Qara's.

Rin screamed and jerked away.

"Tiger's tits. I'm not that ugly." Qara wiped her mouth with the back of her hand. "Welcome to the world of the living."

Rin sat up and spat out a mouthful of lake water. She was shivering uncontrollably; it took her a while before she could push words out from between numb, clumsy lips. "Where are we?"

"Right by the riverbank," Qara said. "Maybe a mile out of Boyang."

"What about the rest?" Rin fought a swell of panic. "Ramsa? Suni? *Nezha?*"

Qara didn't answer, which meant she didn't know, which meant that the Cike had either gotten away or drowned.

Rin took several deep breaths to keep from hyperventilating. *You don't know they're dead*, she told herself. And Nezha, if any-one, had to be alive. The water protected him like he was its child. The waves would have shielded him, whether he consciously called them or not.

And if the others are dead, there's nothing you can do.

She forced her mind to compartmentalize, to lock up her concern and shove it away. She could grieve later. First she needed to survive.

"Kitay's all right," Chaghan told her. He looked like a living corpse; his lips were the same dark shade as his fingers, which were blue up to the middle joint. "Just went out to get some fire-wood."

Rin pulled her knees up to her chest, still shaking. "Feylen. That was Feylen."

The twins nodded.

"But why—what was he—" She couldn't understand why they looked so calm. "What's he doing with them? What does he *want?*"

"Well, Feylen the man probably wants to die," Chaghan said.

"Then what does—"

"The Wind God? Who knows?" He rubbed his hands up and down his arms. "The gods are agents of pure chaos. Behind the veil they're balanced, each one against the other sixty-three, but if you set them loose in the material world, they're like water bursting from a broken dam. With no opposing force to check them, they'll do whatever they want. And we never know what the gods want. He'll create a light breeze one day, and then a typhoon the next. The one thing you can expect is inconsistency."

"But then why's he fighting for them?" Rin asked. Wars took consistency. Unpredictable and uncontrollable soldiers were worse than none.

"I think he's scared of someone," Chaghan said. "Someone who can frighten him into obeying orders."

"Daji?"

"Who else?"

"Good, you're awake." Kitay emerged into the clearing, carrying a bundle of sticks. He was drenched, curly hair plastered to his temples. Rin saw bloody scratches all over his face and arms where he'd hit the rocks, but otherwise he looked unharmed.

"You're all right?" she asked.

"Eh. My bad arm's feeling a bit off, but I think it's just the cold." He tossed the bundle onto the damp dirt. "Are you hurt?"

She was so cold it was hard to tell. Everything just felt numb. She flexed her arms, wiggled her fingers, and found no trouble. Then she tried to stand up. Her left leg buckled beneath her.

"*Fuck*." She ran her fingers over her ankle. It was painfully tender to the touch, throbbing wherever she pressed it.

Kitay knelt down beside her. "Can you wiggle your toes?"

She tried, and they obeyed. That was a minor relief. This wasn't a break, then, just a sprain. She was used to sprains. They'd been common for students at Sinegard; she'd learned how to deal with them years ago. She just needed something like cloth for compression.

"Does anyone have a knife?" she asked.

"I've got one." Qara fished around in her pockets and tossed a small hunting knife in her direction.

Rin unsheathed it, held her trouser leg taut, and cut off a strip at the ankle. She ripped that longways into two pieces and wrapped them tightly around her ankle.

"At least you don't have to worry about keeping it cool," said Kitay.

She didn't have the energy to laugh. She flexed her ankle, and another tremor of pain shot up her leg. She winced. "Are we the only ones who made it out?"

"If only. We've got a bit of company." He nodded to his left.

She followed his line of sight and saw a cluster of bodies—maybe seven, eight—huddled together a little ways up the riverbank. Gray cassocks, light hair. No army uniforms. They were all from the Gray Company.

She could recognize Augus. She wouldn't have been able to pick the rest out of a line—Hesperian faces looked so similar to her, all pale and sparse. She noticed with relief that Sister Petra was not among them.

They looked miserable. They were breathing and blinking—moving just enough that Rin could tell they were alive, but otherwise they seemed frozen stiff. Their skin was pale as snow; their lips were turning blue.

Rin waved at them and pointed to the bundle of sticks. "Come over here. We'll build a fire."

She may as well try to be kind. If she could save some of the Gray Company from freezing to death, they might win her some political capital with the Hesperians when—if—they made it back to Arlong.

The missionaries made no move to get up.

She tried again in slow, deliberate Hesperian. "Come on, Augus. You're going to freeze."

Augus registered no recognition when she called his name. She might not have been speaking Hesperian at all. The others had either blank stares or vaguely frightened expressions on their faces. She shuffled toward them, and several scuttled backward as if scared she might bite them.

"Forget it," Kitay said. "I've been trying to talk to them for the last hour, and my Hesperian is better than yours. I think they're in shock."

"They'll die if they don't warm up." Rin raised her voice. "Hey! Get over here!"

More scared looks. Three of them leveled their weapons at her.

Shit. Rin stumbled back.

They had arquebuses.

"Just leave them," Chaghan muttered. "I'm in no mood to be shot."

"We can't," she said. "The Hesperians will blame us if they die."

He rolled his eyes. "They don't have to know."

"They'll find out if even one of those idiots ever finds their way back."

"They won't."

"But we don't know that. And I'm not killing them to make sure."

If it weren't for Augus, she wouldn't have cared. But blue-eyed devil or not, she couldn't let him freeze to death. He'd been kind to her on the *Kingfisher* when he hadn't needed to be. She felt obligated to return the favor.

Chaghan sighed. "Then leave them a fire. And then we'll move far enough that they'll feel safe to approach it."

That wasn't a bad idea. Kitay had a small flame going within minutes, and Rin waved toward the Hesperians. "We're going to sit over there," she called. "You can use this one."

Again, no response.

But once she'd moved farther down the bank, she saw the Hesperians inching slowly toward the fire. Augus stretched his hands out over the flame. That was a small relief. At least they wouldn't die of sheer idiocy.

Once Kitay had built a second fire, all four of them stripped their uniforms off without self-consciousness. The air was icy around them, but they were colder in their drenched clothes than without. Naked, they huddled together over the flames, holding their hands as close to the fire as they could get without burning their skin. They squatted in silence for what seemed like hours. Nobody wanted to expend the energy to talk.

"We'll get back to the Murui." Rin finally spoke as she pulled her dry uniform back on. It felt good to say the words out loud. It was something pragmatic, a step toward solid action, and it quelled the panic building in her stomach. "There's plenty of loose driftwood around here. We could make a raft and just float downstream through the minor tributaries until we hit the main river, and if we're careful and only move at night, then—"

Chaghan didn't let her finish. "That's a terrible idea."

"And why's that?"

"Because there's nothing to go back to. The Republic's finished. Your friends are dead. Their bodies are probably lining the bottom of Lake Boyang."

"You don't know that," she said.

He shrugged.

"They're *not* dead," she insisted.

"So run back to Arlong, then." He shrugged again. "Crawl into Vaisra's arms and hide as long as you can before the Empress comes for you."

"That's not what I—"

"That's exactly what you want. You can't wait to go groveling to his feet, waiting for your next command like some trained dog."

"I'm not a fucking dog."

"Aren't you?" Chaghan raised his voice. "Did you even put up a fight when they stripped you of command? Or were you glad? Can't give orders for shit, but you love taking them. Speerlies ought to know what it's like to be slaves, but I never imagined you'd enjoy it."

"I was never a slave," Rin snarled.

"Oh, you were, you just didn't know it. You bow down to anyone who will give you orders. Altan pulled on your fucking heartstrings, played you like a lute—he just had to say the right words, make you think he loved you, and you'd run after him to the Chuluu Korikh like an idiot."

"Shut up," she said in a low voice.

But then she saw what this was all about now. This wasn't about Vaisra. This wasn't about the Republic at all. This was about Altan. All these months later, after everything they'd been through, everything was *still* about Altan.

She could give Chaghan that fight. He'd fucking had it coming.

"Like you didn't worship him," she hissed. "I'm not the one who was obsessed with him. You dropped everything to do whatever he asked you to—"

"But I didn't go with him to the Chuluu Korikh," he said. "You did."

"You're blaming *me* for that?"

She knew where this was going. She understood now what Chaghan had been too cowardly to say to her face all these months—that he blamed Altan's death on her.

No wonder he hated her.

Qara put a hand on her brother's arm. "Chaghan, don't."

Chaghan shook her off. "Someone let Feylen loose. Someone got Altan captured. It wasn't me."

"And *someone* told him where the Chuluu Korikh was in the first place," Rin shouted. "Why? Why would you do that? You knew what was in there!"

"Because Altan thought he could raise an army." Chaghan spoke in a loud, flat voice. "Because Altan thought he could reset the course of history to before the Red Emperor and bring the world back to a time when Speer was free and the shamans were at the height of their power. Because for a time that vision was so beautiful that even I believed it. But *I* stopped. I realized that he'd gone crazy and that something had broken and that that path was just going to lead to his death.

"But you? You followed him right to the very end. You let them capture him on that mountain, and you let him die on that pier."

Guilt coiled tightly in Rin's gut, wrenching and horrible. She had nothing to say. Chaghan was right; she'd known he was right, she just hadn't wanted to admit it.

He cocked his head to the side. "Did you think he'd fall in love with you if you just did what he asked?"

"Shut up."

His expression turned vicious. "Is that why you're in love with Vaisra? Do you think he's Altan's replacement?"

She rammed her fist into his mouth.

Her knuckles met his jaw with a crack so satisfying she didn't even feel where his teeth punctured her skin. She'd broken something, and that felt marvelous. Chaghan toppled over like a straw target. She lunged forward, reaching for his neck, but Kitay grabbed her from behind.

She flailed in his grasp. "Let me go!"

His grip tightened. *"Calm down."*

Chaghan pulled himself to a sitting position and spat a tooth onto the ground. "And she says she's not a dog."

Rin lunged to hit him again, but Kitay yanked her back.

"Let me go!"

"Rin, stop—"

"I'll kill him!"

"No, you won't," Kitay snapped. He forced Rin into a kneeling position and twisted her arms painfully behind her back. He pointed at Chaghan. "You—stop talking. Both of you stop this right now. We're alone in enemy territory. We split up from each other and we're dead."

Rin struggled to break free. "Just let me at him—"

"Oh, go on, let her try," Chaghan said. "A Speerly that can't call fire, I'm *terrified.*"

"I can still break your skinny chicken neck," she said.

"Stop talking," Kitay hissed.

"Why?" Chaghan sneered. "Is she going to cry?"

"No." Kitay nodded toward the forest. "Because we're not alone."

Hooded riders emerged from the trees, sitting astride monstrous warhorses much larger than any steed Rin had ever seen. Rin couldn't identify their uniforms. They were garbed in furs and leathers, not Militia greens, but they didn't seem like friends, either. The riders aimed their bows toward them, bowstrings stretched so taut that at this distance the arrows wouldn't just pierce their bodies, they would fly straight through them.

Rin rose slowly, hand creeping toward her trident. But Chaghan grabbed her wrist.

"Surrender now," he hissed.

"Why?"

"Just trust me."

She jerked her hand out of his grip. "*That's* likely."

But even as her fingers closed around her weapon, she knew they were trapped. Those longbows were massive—at this distance, there would be no dodging those arrows.

She heard a rustling noise from upriver. The Hesperians had seen the riders. They were trying to run.

The riders twisted around and loosed their bowstrings into the forest. Arrows thudded into the snow. Rin saw Augus drop to the ground, his face twisted in pain as he clutched at a feathered shaft sticking out of his left shoulder.

But the riders hadn't shot to kill. Most of the arrows were aimed at the dirt around the missionaries' feet. Only a few of the Hesperians were injured. The rest had collapsed from sheer fright. They huddled together in a clump, arms raised high, arquebuses unfired.

Two riders dismounted and wrenched the weapons out of the missionaries' trembling hands. The missionaries put up no resistance.

Rin's mind raced as she watched, trying to find a way out. If she and Kitay could just get to the stream, then the current would carry them downriver, hopefully faster than the horses could run, and if she held her breath and ducked deep enough then she'd have some cover from the arrows. But how to get to the water before the riders loosed their bowstrings? Her eyes darted around the clearing—

Put your hands up.

No one spoke the order but she heard it—a deep, hoarse command that resonated loudly in her mind.

A warning shot whistled past her, inches from her temple. She ducked down, grabbed a clump of mud to fling at the riders. If she could distract them, just for a few seconds . . .

The riders turned their bows back toward her.

"Stop!" Chaghan ran out in front of the riders, waving his arms over his head.

A sound like a gong echoed through the clearing, so loud that Rin felt her temples vibrating.

A flurry of images from someone else's imagination forced their way into her mind's eye. She saw herself on her knees, arms up. She saw herself stuck through with arrows, bleeding from a dozen different wounds. She saw a vast and dizzying landscape—a sparse steppe, desert dunes, a thunderous stampede as riders set out on horseback to seek something, destroy something . . .

Then she saw Chaghan, facing the riders with his fists clenched, felt the sheer *intent* radiating out from his form—*we're here in peace we're here in peace I am one of you we're here in peace*—and she realized that this wasn't just some psychospiritual battle of wills.

This was a conversation.

Somehow, the riders could communicate without moving their lips. They conveyed images and fragments of intent without spoken language directly into their receivers' minds. Rin glanced at Kitay, checking to make sure that she hadn't gone mad. He was staring at the riders, eyes wide, hands trembling.

Stop resisting, boomed the first voice.

Frantic babbles erupted from the bound Hesperians. Augus doubled forward and yelled, clutching his head. He was hearing it, too.

Whatever Chaghan said in response, it was enough to persuade the riders that they weren't a threat. Their leader lifted a hand and barked out a command in a language Rin didn't understand. The riders lowered their bows.

The leader swung himself off his horse in one fluid motion and strode toward Chaghan.

"Hello, Bekter," Chaghan said.

"Hello, cousin," Bekter responded. He'd spoken in Nikara; his words came out harsh and twisted. He wrenched sounds out of the air like he was ripping meat from bone, as if he were unused to spoken language.

"*Cousin?*" Kitay echoed out loud.

"We're not proud of it," Qara muttered.

Bekter shot her a quick smile. Whatever passed mentally between them happened too fast for Rin to understand, but she caught the gist of it—something lewd, something violent, horrid, and dripping in contempt.

"Go fuck yourself," Qara said.

Bekter called something to his riders. Two of them jumped to the ground, wrenched Chaghan's and Qara's arms behind their backs, and forced them to their knees.

Rin snatched up her trident, but arrows dotted the ground around her before she could move.

"You won't get a third warning," Bekter said.

She dropped the trident and placed her hands behind her head. Kitay did the same. The riders tied Rin's hands together, pulled her to her feet, and dragged her, stumbling miserably, toward Bekter so that the four of them knelt before him in a single line.

"Where is he?" Bekter asked.

"You're going to have to be more specific," Kitay said.

"The Wind God. I believe the mortal's name is Feylen. We are hunting him. Where has he gone?"

"Downriver, probably," said Kitay. "If you know how to fly, you might catch up!"

Bekter ignored him. His eyes roved over Rin's body, lingering in places that made her flinch. Hazy images came unbidden to her mind, too blurry for her to see more than shattered limbs and flesh on flesh.

"Is this the Speerly?" he asked.

"You can't hurt her," Chaghan said. "You're sworn."

"Sworn not to hurt you. Not them."

"They're under my charge. This is my territory."

Bekter laughed. "You've been gone a long time, little cousin. The Naimads are weak. The treaty is shattering. The Sorqan Sira's decided to come down and clean up your mess."

"'Charge'?" Rin repeated. "'Treaty'? Who are you people?"

"They're watchers," Qara murmured.

"Of what?"

"People like you, little Speerly." Bekter pulled off his hood.

Rin flinched back, repulsed.

His face was covered in mottled burns, ropey and raised, a mountainous terrain of pain running from cheek to cheek. He smiled at her, and the way the scars crinkled around the sides of his mouth was a terrible sight.

She spat at his feet. "Had a bad encounter with a Speerly, didn't you?"

Bekter smiled again. More images invaded her mind. She saw men on fire. She saw blood staining the dirt.

Bekter leaned in so close that she could feel his breath, hot and rank on her neck. "I survived it. He did not."

Before Rin could speak, a hunting horn pierced the air.

The thunder of hooves followed. Rin craned her neck to look over her shoulder. Another group of riders approached the clearing, this one far larger than Bekter's contingent. They formed a circle with their horses, surrounding them.

Their ranks parted. A slight little woman, reaching no higher than Rin's elbow, moved through the lines.

She walked the way Chaghan and Qara did. She was delicate, birdlike, as if she were some ethereal creature for whom being anchored to the earth was a mere inconvenience. Her cloud-white hair fell just past her waist, looped in two intricate braids interwoven with what looked like shells and bone.

Her eyes were the opposite of Chaghan's—darker than the bottom of a well, and black all the way through.

"Bow," Qara muttered. "She is the Sorqan Sira."

Rin ducked her head. "Their leader?"

"Our aunt."

The Sorqan Sira clicked her tongue as she strode past Chaghan and Qara, who knelt with their eyes cast down as if in shame. Kitay she ignored completely.

She stopped in front of Rin. Her bony fingers moved over Rin's face, gripping at her chin and cheekbones.

"How curious," she said. Her Nikara was fluent but oddly syncopated in a way that made her words sound laced with poetry. "She looks like Hanelai."

The name meant nothing to Rin, but the riders tensed.

"Where did they find you?" the Sorqan Sira asked. When Rin didn't answer, she smacked her cheek lightly. "I am talking to you, girl. Speak."

"I don't know," Rin said. Her knees throbbed. She wished desperately that they would let her stop kneeling.

The Sorqan Sira dug her fingernails into Rin's cheek. "Where did they hide you? Who found you? Who protected you?"

"I don't know," Rin repeated. "Nowhere. No one."

"You are lying."

"She's not," Chaghan said. "She didn't know what she was until a year ago."

The Sorqan Sira gave Rin a long, suspicious look, but released her.

"Impossible. The Mugenese were supposed to have killed you off, but you Speerlies keep turning up like rats."

"Chaghan has always drawn Speerlies like moths to a candle," Bekter said. "You remember."

"Shut up," Chaghan said hoarsely.

Bekter smiled widely. "Remember what you wrote in your letters? *The Speerly has suffered. The Mugenese were not kind. But he survived, and he is powerful.*"

Was he talking about Altan? Rin fought the urge to vomit.

"*He has his mind for now but he is hurting.*" Bekter's voice took on a high, mocking pitch. "*But I can fix him. Give him time. Don't make me kill him. Please.*"

Chaghan jammed his elbow backward into Bekter's stomach. In an instant Bekter seized Chaghan's bound wrists and twisted them so far behind his back that Rin thought surely he'd broken them.

Chaghan's mouth opened in a silent scream.

A sound like a thunderclap ricocheted through Rin's mind. She saw the riders wince; they'd heard it, too.

"Enough of this," said the Sorqan Sira.

Bekter released Chaghan, whose head lurched forward as if he'd been shot.

The Sorqan Sira bent down before him and brushed his hair back behind his ears, petting it softly like a mother grooming a misbehaved child.

"You've failed," she said softly. "Your duty was to observe and cull when necessary. Not to join their petty wars."

"We tried to stay neutral," Chaghan said. "We didn't intervene, we never—"

"Don't lie to me. I know what you've done." The Sorqan Sira stood up. "There will be no more of the Cike. We are putting an end to your mother's little experiment."

"Experiment?" Rin echoed. "What experiment?"

The Sorqan Sira turned toward her, eyebrows raised. "Precisely what I said. The twins' mother, Kalagan, thought it would be unjust to deny the Nikara access to the gods. The Cike was Kalagan's last chance. She has failed. I have decided there will be no more shamans in the Empire."

"Oh, *you've* decided?" Rin struggled to stand up straight. She still didn't fully understand what was happening, but she didn't need to. The dynamic of this encounter had become abundantly clear. The riders thought her an animal to be put down. They thought they could determine who had access to the Pantheon.

The sheer arrogance of that made her want to spit.

The Sorqan Sira looked amused. "Did I upset you?"

"We don't need your permission to exist," she snapped.

"Yes, you do." The Sorqan Sira cast her a disdainful smile. "You're little children, grasping in a void that you don't understand for toys that don't belong to you."

Rin wanted to slap the contempt off of her face. "The gods don't belong to you, either."

"But we *know* that. And that is the simple difference. You Nikara are the only people foolish enough to call the gods into this world. We Ketreyids would never dream of the folly your shamans commit."

"Then that makes you cowards," Rin said. "And just because you won't call them down doesn't mean that we can't."

The Sorqan Sira threw her head back and began to laugh—a harsh, cackling crow's laugh. "My word. You sound just like them."

"Who?"

"Has no one ever told you?" The Sorqan Sira grasped Rin's face in her hands once more. Rin flinched away, but the Sorqan Sira's fingers tightened around her cheeks. She pressed her face against Rin's, so close that all Rin could see was those dark, obsidian eyes. "No? Then I'll show you."

Visions pierced Rin's mind like knives forced into her temples.

She stood on a desert steppe, in the shadow of dunes stretching out as far as she could see. Sand whipped around her ankles. The wind struck a low and melancholy note.

She looked down at herself and saw white braids woven with shells and bone. She realized she was in the memory of a much younger Sorqan Sira. To her left she saw a young woman who had to be the twins' mother, Kalagan—she had the same high cheekbones as Qara, the same shock of white hair as Chaghan.

Before them stood the Trifecta.

Rin stared at them in wonder.

They were so *young*. They couldn't have been much older than she was. They could have been fourth-years at Sinegard.

Su Daji as a girl was already impossibly, bewitchingly beautiful. She emanated sex even when she was standing still. Rin saw it in the way she shifted her hips back and forth, the way she swept her curtain of hair over her shoulders.

To Daji's left stood the Dragon Emperor. His face was stunningly, shockingly familiar. Sharp angles, a long straight nose, thick and somber eyebrows. Strikingly handsome, pale and perfectly sculpted in a way that didn't seem human.

He had to be from the House of Yin.

He was a younger, gentler Vaisra. He was Nezha without his scars and Jinzha without his arrogance. His face could not be called kind; it was too severe and aristocratic. But it was an open, honest, and earnest face. A face she immediately trusted, because she couldn't see a way that this man was capable of any evil.

She understood now what they meant in the old stories when they said that soldiers defected to him in droves and knelt at his feet. She would have followed him anywhere.

Then there was Jiang.

If she had ever doubted that her old master could possibly be the Gatekeeper, there was no mistaking his identity now. His hair, shorn close to his ears, was still the same unnatural white, his face as ageless as it had been when she'd met him.

But when he spoke, and his face twisted, he became a complete stranger.

"You don't want to fight us on this," he said. "You're running out of time. I'd clear out while you still can."

The Jiang that Rin had known was placid and cheerful, drifting through the world with a kind of detached curiosity. He spoke softly and whimsically, as if he were a curious bystander to his own conversations. But this younger Jiang had a harshness to his face that startled Rin, and every word he spoke dripped with a casual cruelty.

It's the fury, she realized. The Jiang she knew was utterly peaceful, immune to insult. This Jiang was consumed with some kind of poisonous wrath that radiated from within.

Kalagan's voice trembled with anger. "Our people have claimed the area north of the Baghra Desert for centuries. Your Horse Warlord has forgotten himself. This is not diplomacy, it is sheer arrogance."

"Perhaps," Jiang said. "You still didn't have to dismember his son and send the fingers back to the father."

"He dared to threaten us," said Kalagan. "He deserved what he got."

Jiang shrugged. "Maybe he did. I never liked that kid. But do you know what our dilemma is, dearest Kalagan? We need the Horse Warlord. We need his troops and his warhorses, and we can't get those if they're too busy running around the Baghra Desert fending off your arrows."

"Then he should retreat," said the Sorqan Sira.

Jiang inspected his fingernails. "Or perhaps we'll make *you* retreat. Would it be so hard for you to just go settle somewhere else? Ketreyids are all nomads, aren't you?"

Kalagan lifted her spear. "You *dare*—"

Jiang wagged a finger. "I wouldn't."

"Do you think this is wise, Ziya?"

A girl emerged from the ranks of the riders. She bore a remarkable resemblance to Chaghan, but she stood taller, stronger, and her face was flushed with more color.

"Get back, Tseveri," said the Sorqan Sira, but Tseveri walked toward Jiang until they were separated by only inches.

"Why are you doing this?" she asked softly.

"Politics, really," Jiang said. "It's nothing personal."

"We taught you everything you know. Three years ago we took

pity on you and took you in. We've sheltered you, hidden you, healed you, given you secrets no Nikara has ever obtained. Aren't we family to you?"

She spoke to Jiang intimately, like a sister. But if Jiang was bothered, he hid it well behind a mask of amused indifference.

"Would a simple thank-you suffice?" he asked. "Or did you also want a hug?"

"Be careful who you turn your back on," warned Tseveri. "You don't need the Horse Warlord, not truly. You still need us. You need our wisdom. There's so much you still don't know—"

"I doubt it." Jiang sneered. "I've had enough of playing philosopher with a people so timid they shrink from the Pantheon. I need hard power. Military might. The Horse Warlord can give us that. What can you give me? Endless conversations about the cosmos?"

"You've no idea how ignorant you still are." Tseveri gave him a pitying look. "I see you've anchored yourselves. Did it hurt?"

Rin had no idea what that meant, but she saw Daji flinch.

"Don't be surprised," Tseveri said. "You're so obviously bound. I can see it shining out of you. You think it makes you strong, but it's going to destroy you."

"You don't know what you're talking about," Jiang said.

"No?" Tseveri tilted her head. "Then here's a prophecy for you. Your bond will shatter. You will destroy one another. One will die, one will rule, and one will sleep for eternity."

"That's impossible," Daji scoffed. "None of us can die. Not while the others live."

"That's what you think," said Tseveri.

"Enough of this," Riga said. Rin was stricken by how much he even *sounded* like Nezha. "This isn't what we came for."

"You came to start a war you don't need to fight. And you ignore me at your peril." Tseveri reached for Jiang's hand. "Ziya. Please. Don't do this to me."

Jiang refused to meet her eye.

Daji yawned, making a desultory attempt to cover her mouth

with the back of a dainty pale hand. "We can do this the easy way. Nobody needs to get hurt. Or we could just start fighting."

Kalagan leveled her spear at her. "Don't *presume*, little girl."

A crackling energy charged the air. Even through the distance of memory Rin could sense how the fabric of the desert had changed. The boundaries of the material world were thinning, threatening to warp and give way to the world of spirit.

Something was happening to Jiang.

His shadow writhed madly against the bright sand. The shape was not Jiang's own, but something terrible—a myriad of beasts, so many in size and form, shifting faster and faster, with a growing desperation, as if frantic to break free.

The beasts were in Jiang, too. Rin could see them, shadows rippling under his skin, horrible patches of black straining to get out.

Tseveri cried something in her own language—a plea or an incantation, Rin didn't know, but it sounded like despair.

Daji laughed.

"*No!*" Rin shouted, but Jiang didn't hear her—*couldn't* hear her, because all of this had already come to pass. All she could do was watch helplessly as Jiang forced his hand into Tseveri's rib cage and ripped out her still-beating heart.

Kalagan screamed.

"That's enough," said the present Sorqan Sira, and the last things Rin saw were Daji whipping her needles toward the Ketreyids, Jiang and his beasts pinning down the Sorqan Sira, and Riga, standing impassively, watching the carnage with that wise and caring face, arms raised beatifically as if he blessed the slaughter with his presence.

"We gave the Nikara the keys to the heavens, and they stole our land and murdered my daughter." The Sorqan Sira's voice was flat, emotionless, as if she were merely recounting an interesting anecdote, as if her pain had already been processed so many times she could not feel it anymore.

Rin bent over on her hands and knees, gasping. She couldn't

scrub the image of Jiang from her mind. Jiang, her *master*, cackling with his hands covered with blood.

"Surprised?" asked the Sorqan Sira.

"But I *knew* him," Rin whispered. "I know what he's like, he's not like *that* . . ."

"How would you know what the Gatekeeper is like?" The Sorqan Sira sneered. "Have you ever asked him about his past? Did you have *any* idea?"

The worst part was that it all made *sense*—the truth had dawned on Rin, awful and bitter, and the mystery of Jiang was clear to her now; she knew why he'd fled, why he'd hidden in the Chuluu Korikh.

He must have been starting to remember.

The man she had met at Sinegard had been no more than a shade of a person; a pathetic, affable shade of a personality suppressed. He had not been pretending. She was certain of that. No one could pretend that well.

He had simply not *known*. The Seal had stolen his memories, just like it would one day steal hers, and hidden them behind a wall in his mind.

Was it better now that he remained in his stone prison, suspended halfway between amnesia and sanity?

"You see now. You'll understand if we'd rather put an end to you." The Sorqan Sira nodded to Bekter.

Her unspoken command rang clear in Rin's mind. *Kill them.*

"Wait!" Rin struggled to her feet. "Please—you don't have to—"

"I don't entertain begging, girl."

"I'm not begging, I'm bartering," Rin said quickly. "We have the same enemy. You want Daji dead. You want revenge. Yes? So do I. Kill us, and you've lost an ally."

The Sorqan Sira scoffed. "We can kill the Vipress easily enough ourselves."

"No, you can't. If you could, she'd be dead already. You're scared of her." Rin thought frantically as she spoke, spinning an argument together from thin air. "In twenty years you haven't even *ventured* south, haven't attempted to take back your lands. Why? Because you know the Vipress will destroy you. You've lost to her before. You don't dare to face her again."

The Sorqan Sira's eyes narrowed, but she said nothing. Rin felt a desperate stab of hope. If her words angered the Ketreyids, that meant she had touched on a fragment of the truth. It meant she still had a chance of convincing them.

"But you've seen what I can do," she continued. "You know that I could fight her, because you know what Speerlies are capable of. I've faced the Empress before. Set me free, and I'll fight your battles for you."

The Sorqan Sira shot Chaghan a question in her own language. They conversed for a moment. Chaghan's words sounded hesitant and deferential; the Sorqan Sira's harsh and angry. Their eyes darted once in a while to Kitay, who shifted uncomfortably, confused.

"She *will* do it," Chaghan said finally in Nikara. "She won't have a choice."

"I'll do what?" Rin asked.

They ignored her to keep arguing.

"This is not worth the risk," Bekter interrupted. "Mother, you know this. Speerlies go mad faster than the rest."

Chaghan shook his head. "Not this one. She's stable."

"No Speerlies are stable," said Bekter.

"She fought it," Chaghan insisted. "She's off opium. She hasn't touched it in months."

"An adult Speerly who doesn't smoke?" The Sorqan Sira cocked her head. "That'd be a first."

"It makes no difference," Bekter said. "The Phoenix will take her. It always does. Better to kill her now—"

Chaghan spoke over him, appealing directly to his aunt. "I have seen her at her worst. If the Phoenix could, then it would have already."

"He's lying," Bekter snarled. "Look at him, he's pathetic, he's protecting them even now—"

"Enough," said the Sorqan Sira. "I'll have the truth for myself."

Again, she grasped the sides of Rin's face. "Look at me."

Her eyes seemed different this time. They had become dark and hollow expanses, windows into an abyss that Rin did not want to see. Rin let out an involuntary whine, but the Sorqan Sira's fingers tightened under her jaws. "*Look.*"

Rin felt herself pitching forward into that darkness. The Sorqan Sira wasn't forcing a vision into her mind, she was forcing Rin to dredge one up herself. Memories loomed before her, haphazard and jagged fragments of visions that she'd done her best to bury. She was wrought in a sea of fire, she was pitching backward into black water, she was kneeling at Altan's feet, blood pooling in her mouth.

The Seal loomed over her.

It had grown. It was thrice as large as she had last seen it, an expanded and hypnotic array of colors, swirling and pulsing like a heartbeat, arranged like a character she still could not recognize.

Rin could *feel* Daji's presence inside it—sickening, addictive, seductive. Whispers sounded all about her, as if Daji were murmuring into her ear, promising her wonderful things.

I'll take you away from this. I'll give you everything you've ever wanted. I'll give him back to you.

You only have to give in.

"What is this?" the Sorqan Sira murmured.

Rin couldn't answer.

The Sorqan Sira let go of her face.

Rin dropped to her knees, hands splayed against solid ground. The sun spun in circles above her.

It took her a moment to realize the Sorqan Sira was laughing.

"She's afraid of you," the Sorqan Sira whispered. "Su Daji is afraid of *you.*"

"I don't understand," Rin said.

"This changes everything." The Sorqan Sira barked a command. The riders standing nearest Rin seized her by the arms and hoisted her to her feet.

"What are you doing?" Rin struggled against their grip. "You can't kill me, you still need me—"

"Oh, child. We are not going to kill you." The Sorqan Sira reached out and stroked the backs of her fingers down Rin's cheek. "We are going to fix you."

CHAPTER 22

The Ketreyids tied Rin against a tree, though this time they were considerably gentler. They placed her bound wrists in her lap instead of twisting them painfully behind her back, and they left her legs untied once the extent of her ankle injury became obvious.

She couldn't have run far even without a sprained ankle. Her limbs tingled from fatigue, her head was swimming, and her vision had started going fuzzy. She slouched back against the tree, eyes closed. She couldn't remember the last time she'd eaten anything.

"What are they doing?" Kitay asked.

Rin focused with difficulty on the clearing. The Ketreyids were arranging wooden poles to create a latticed dome-like structure, just large enough to accommodate two people. When the dome was finished, they draped thick blankets over its top until it was completely covered.

The Ketreyids had also added logs to their measly campfire. It was a roaring bonfire now, flames leaping higher than the Sorqan Sira's head. Two riders carried a pile of rocks in from the shore, all at least the size of Rin's head, and placed them over the flames one by one.

"They're preparing for a sweat," Chaghan explained. "That's what the rocks are for. You'll go inside that yurt with the Sorqan Sira. They'll put the rocks inside one by one and pour water over them while they're hot. That fills the yurt with steam and drives the temperatures up to just under what will kill you."

"They're going to steam me like a fish," Rin said.

"It's risky. But that's the only way to draw something like the Seal out. What Daji's left inside you is like a venom. Over time it will keep festering in your subconscious and corrupt your mind."

She blinked in alarm. "You could have told me that!"

"I didn't think it was worth scaring you when I couldn't do anything about it."

"You weren't going to tell me I was going mad?"

"You would have noticed eventually."

"I hate you," she said.

"Calm down. The sweat will extract the venom from your mind." Chaghan paused. "Well. It'll give you a better chance than anything else. It doesn't always work."

"That's optimistic," Kitay said.

Chaghan shrugged. "If it doesn't work, the Sorqan Sira will put you out of your misery."

"That's nice of her," Rin mumbled.

"She'd do it swiftly," Qara assured her. "Quick slice to the arteries, so clean you'll barely even feel it. She's done it before."

"Can you walk?" asked the Sorqan Sira.

Rin jerked awake. She didn't remember dozing off. She was still exhausted; her body felt like it was weighted down with rocks.

She blinked the sleep from her eyes and glanced around. She was lying curled on the ground. Thankfully, someone had untied her arms. She pulled herself to a sitting position and stretched the cricks out of her back.

"Can you walk?" the Sorqan Sira repeated.

Rin flexed her ankle. Pain shot up her leg. "I don't think so."

The Sorqan Sira raised her voice. "Bekter. Lift her."

Bekter glanced down at Rin with a look of distaste.

"I hate you, too," she told him.

She was sure that he would lash out. But the Sorqan Sira's command must truly have been law, because he simply knelt down, pulled her into his arms, and carried her to the yurt. He made no effort to be gentle. She jostled uncomfortably in his arms, and her sprained ankle smashed against the yurt's entrance when he deposited her inside.

She bit back a cry of pain to deny him the pleasure of hearing it. He shut the tent flap on her without another word.

The yurt's interior was pitch-black. The Ketreyids had padded its lattice sides with so many layers of blankets that not a single ray of light could penetrate the exterior.

The air inside was cold, silent, and peaceful, like the belly of a cave. If Rin didn't know where she was, she would have thought the walls were made of stone. She exhaled slowly, listening as her breath filled the empty space.

Light flooded the yurt as the Sorqan Sira entered through the flap. She carried a bucket of water in one hand and a ladle in the other.

"Lie down," she told Rin. "Get as close as you can to the walls."

"Why?"

"So you don't fall onto the rocks when you faint."

Rin curled into the corner, back braced against the taut cloth, and pressed her cheek to the cool dirt. The tent flap closed. Rin heard the Sorqan Sira crawling across the yurt to sit right beside her.

"Are you ready?" the Sorqan Sira asked.

"Do I have a choice?"

"No. But you should prepare your mind. This will go badly if you are frightened." The Sorqan Sira called to the riders outside, "First stone."

A shovel appeared through the flap, bearing a single rock glowing a bright, angry red. The rider outside tipped the rock over into a muddy bed at the center of the yurt, withdrew the shovel, and shut the flap.

In the darkness, Rin heard the Sorqan Sira dip the ladle into the water.

"May the gods hear our prayers." Water splashed over the rock. A loud hiss filled the yurt. "May they grant our wishes to commune."

A wave of steam hit Rin's nose. She fought the urge to sneeze.

"May they clear our eyes to see," said the Sorqan Sira. "Second rock."

The rider deposited another rock into the mud bed. Another splash, another hiss. The steam grew thicker and hotter.

"May they give us the ears to hear their voices."

Rin was starting to feel light-headed. Panic clawed at her chest. She could barely breathe. Even though her lungs filled with air, she felt as if she were drowning. She couldn't lie still any longer. She pawed at the edges of the tent, desperate for a whiff of cold air, anything . . . the steam was in her face now, every part of her was burning, she was being boiled alive.

The rocks kept coming—a third, a fourth, a fifth. The steam became unbearable. She tried covering her nose with her sleeve, but that, too, was damp, and trying to breathe through it was the worst form of torture.

"Empty your mind," the Sorqan Sira ordered.

Rin's heart pumped furiously, so hard that she could feel it in her temples.

I'm going to die in here.

"Stop resisting," the Sorqan Sira said urgently. "Relax."

Relax? The only thing Rin wanted to do then was scramble out of the yurt. She didn't care if she burned her feet on the rocks, didn't care if she had to slip through the mud, she just wanted to get out into the open air where she could breathe.

Only years of meditation practice under Jiang stopped her from getting up and running out.

Breathe.

Just breathe.

She could feel her heartbeat slowing, crawling nearly to a stop.

Her vision swirled and sparked. She saw little lights in the darkness, candles that flickered in the edges of her sight, stars that winked away when she looked upon them . . .

The Sorqan Sira's breath tickled her ear. "Soon you will see many things. The Seal will tempt you. Remember that none of what you see is real. This will be a test of your resolve. Pass, and you will emerge intact, in full possession of your natural abilities. Fail, and I will cut your throat."

"I'm ready," Rin gasped. "I know pain."

"This isn't pain," said the Sorqan Sira. "The Vipress never makes you suffer. She fulfills your wishes. She promises you peace when you know you ought to be fighting a war. That's worse."

She pressed her thumb against Rin's forehead. The ground tipped away.

Rin saw a stream of bright colors, bold and gaudy, which resolved themselves into definable shapes only when she squinted. Reds and golds became streamers and firecrackers; blues and purples became fruits, berries, and cups of pouring wine.

She looked around, dazed. She was standing in a massive banquet hall. It was twice the size of the Autumn Palace's throne room, packed with long tables at which sat gorgeously dressed guests. She saw platters of dragon fruit carved like flowers, soup steaming from turtle shells, and entire roasted pigs sitting on tables of their very own, with attendants designated to carve away pieces of meat for the guests. Sorghum wine ran down gilded trenches carved into the table sides so that the diners could fill their cups themselves whenever they wished.

Faces she knew drifted in and out of her sight, faces she hadn't seen for so long that they felt like they were from a different lifetime. She saw Tutor Feyrik sitting two tables away, meticulously picking the bones from a cut of fish. She saw Masters Irjah and Jima, laughing at the high table with the rest of the Academy masters.

Kesegi waved at her from his seat. He was unchanged since

she'd last seen him—still ten years old, tawny-skinned, all knees and elbows. She stared at him. She'd forgotten what a wonderful smile he had, cheeky and irreverent.

She saw Kitay, dressed in a general's uniform. His wiry hair was grown long, pulled into a bun at the back of his head. He was deep in conversation with Master Irjah. When he caught her eye, he winked.

"Hello, you," said a familiar voice.

She turned, and her heart caught in her throat.

Of course it was Altan. It was *always* Altan, lurking behind every corner of her mind, haunting every decision she made.

But this was an Altan who was alive and whole—not the way she'd known him at Khurdalain, when he'd been burdened by a war that he would kill himself winning. This was the best possible version of him, the way she'd tried to remember him, the way he'd rarely ever been. The scars were still on his face, his hair was still messy and overgrown, tied back in a careless knot, and he still wielded that trident with the casual grace of someone who spent more time on the battlefield than off.

This was an Altan who fought because he adored it and was good at it, and not because it was the only thing he had ever been trained to do.

His eyes were brown. His pupils were not constricted. He did not smell of smoke. When he smiled, he almost looked happy.

"You're here." She couldn't manage anything but a whisper. "It's you."

"Of course I am," he said. "Not even a border skirmish could keep me from you today. Tyr wanted to have my head on a stake, but I don't think even he could stand up to Mother and Father's wrath."

A border skirmish?

Tyr?

Mother and Father?

The confusion lasted for only a moment, and then she understood. Dreams came with their own logic, and this was nothing but a beautiful dream. In this world, Speer had never been destroyed. Tearza had not died and abandoned her people to slavery, and her kin had not been slaughtered overnight on the Dead Island.

She almost laughed out loud. In this illusion, their biggest concern was a fucking *border skirmish*.

"Are you nervous?" Altan asked.

"Nervous?" she echoed.

"I'd be surprised if you weren't," he said. His voice dropped to a conspiring whisper. "Unless you're having second thoughts. And—I mean, if you are, it's fine by me. If we're being honest, I've never been too fond of him, either."

"'Him'?" Rin echoed.

"He's just jealous that you're getting married first while nobody wants him." Ramsa shouldered his way between them, chewing on a red bean bun. He dipped his head toward Altan. "Hello, Commander."

Altan rolled his eyes. "Don't you have fireworks to light?"

"That's not until later," said Ramsa. "Your parents said they'll castrate me if I go near them now. Something about safety hazards."

"That sounds about right." Altan ruffled Ramsa's hair. "Why don't you scurry along and enjoy the feast?"

"Because this conversation is much more interesting." Ramsa took a large bite of the bun and spoke with his mouth full. "So what's it going to be, Rin? Will we have a runaway bride? Because I'd like to finish eating first."

Rin's mouth hung open. Her eyes darted between Ramsa and Altan, trying to detect proof that they were illusions—some imperfection, some lack of substance.

But they were so *solid*, detailed and full of life. And they were so, *so* happy. How could they be this happy?

"Rin?" Altan nudged her shoulder. "Are you all right?"

She shook her head. "I don't— This isn't . . ."

Concern crossed his face. "Do you need to lie down for a moment?"

"No, I just . . ."

He took her arm. "I'm sorry I was making fun of you. Come on, we'll go find you a bench."

"No, that's not what I . . ." She shrugged him off and backed away. She was walking backward, she *knew* she was, but somehow every time she took a step she ended up no farther from Altan than she had been to begin with.

"Come with me," Altan repeated, and his voice resonated around the room. The colors of the banquet hall dimmed. The guests' faces blurred. He was the only defined figure in sight.

He extended his hand toward her. "Quickly now."

She knew what would happen to her if she obeyed.

Everything would be over. The illusion might last another few minutes, or an hour, or a week. Time worked differently in illusions. She might enjoy this one for a lifetime. But in reality, she would have succumbed to Daji's poison. Her life would be over. She would never wake up from this spell.

But would that be so wrong?

She wanted to go with him. She wanted to go so badly.

"No one has to die," Altan said, voicing her own thoughts out loud. "The wars never happened in the first place. You can have everything back. Everyone. No one has to go."

"But they *are* gone," she whispered, and the instant she said it, its truth became apparent. The faces in the banquet hall were lies. Her friends were dead. Tutor Feyrik was gone. Master Irjah was gone. Golyn Niis was gone. Speer was gone. Nothing could bring them back. "You can't tempt me with this."

"Then you can join them," Altan said. "Would that be so bad?"

The lights and streamers dimmed. The tables faded to nothing; the guests disappeared. She and Altan were alone, two spots of flame in a dark passage.

"Is this what you want?" His mouth closed over hers before

she could speak. Scorching hands moved on her body and trailed downward.

Everything was so terribly hot. She was burning. She'd forgotten how it felt to truly *burn*—she was immune to her own flame, and she'd never been caught in Altan's fire, but *this* . . . this was an old, familiar pain, terrible and delicious all at once.

"No." She fought to find her voice. "No, I don't want this—"

Altan's hands tightened on her waist.

"You did," he said, pressing closer. "It was written all over your face. Every time."

"Don't touch me." She pressed her hands against his chest and tried to push him away, to no avail.

"Don't pretend you don't want this," said Altan. "You need me."

She couldn't breathe. "No, I don't . . ."

"Don't you?"

He brought his hand to her cheek. She cringed back, but his burning fingers rested firm on her skin. His hands moved down to her neck. His thumbs stopped where her collarbones met, a familiar resting place. He squeezed. Fire lanced through her throat.

"Come back." The Sorqan Sira's voice cut through her mind like a knife, granting her several delicious, cool seconds of lucidity. "Remember yourself. Submit to him and you lose."

Rin convulsed on the ground.

"I don't want this," she moaned. "I don't want to see this—I want to get out—"

"It's the poison," said the Sorqan Sira. "The sweat amplifies it, brings it to a boil. You must purge yourself, or the Seal will kill you."

Rin whimpered. "Just make it stop."

"I can't. It must get worse before it gets better." The Sorqan Sira seized her hand and squeezed it. "Remember, he exists only in your mind. He only has as much power as you give him. Can you do this?"

Rin nodded and gripped the Sorqan Sira's arm. She couldn't find the breath to say the words *send me back*, but the Sorqan Sira nodded. She threw another ladleful of water onto the rocks.

The heat in the yurt redoubled. Rin choked; her back arched, the material world faded away, and the pain returned. Altan's fingers were around her neck again, squeezing, choking her.

He leaned down. His lips brushed against hers. "Do you know what I want you to do?"

She shook her head, gasping.

"Kill yourself," he ordered.

"*What?*"

"I want you to kill yourself," he repeated. "Make things right. You should have died on that pier. And I should have lived."

Was that true?

It must have been true, if it had lingered so long in her subconscious. And she couldn't lie to herself; she *knew*, had always known that if Altan had lived and if she had died then things would have gone much differently. Aratsha would still be alive, the Cike would not have disbanded, they would not have lost to Feylen, and the Republican Fleet might not be in fragments at the bottom of Lake Boyang.

Jinzha had said it first. *We should have tried to save the other one.*

"You are the reason why I died," Altan continued, relentless. "Make this right. Kill yourself."

She swallowed. "No."

"Why not?" His fingers tightened around her neck. "You're not particularly useful to anyone alive."

She reached up for his hands. "Because I'm done taking orders from you."

He was a product of her own mind. He had only as much power as she gave him.

She pried his fingers off her neck. One by one, they came away. She was nearly free. He squeezed harder but she kicked out, nailed him in the shin, and the moment he let go she scrambled backward away from him and sank into a low crouch, poised to strike.

"Really?" he scoffed. "You're going to fight me?"

"I won't surrender to you anymore."

"'Surrender'?" he repeated, like it was such a ludicrous word. "Is that how you've thought of it? Oh, Rin, it was never about that. I didn't want surrender from you. I had to *manage* you. Control you. You're so fucking *stupid*, you had to be told what to do."

"I'm not stupid," she said.

"Yes, you are." He smiled, patronizing and handsome and hateful all at once. "You're nothing. You're useless. Compared to me you're—"

"I'm nothing at all," she interrupted. "I was a terrible commander. I couldn't function without opium. I still can't call the fire. You can tell me everything I hate about myself, but I already know. You can't say anything to hurt me more."

"Oh, I doubt that." Suddenly his trident was in his hand, spinning as he advanced. "How's this, then? You *wanted* me dead."

She flinched. "No. I never."

"You *hated* me. You were afraid of me, you couldn't wait to be rid of me. Admit it, when I died you laughed."

"No, I wept," she said. "I wept for days, until I couldn't breathe anymore, and then I tried to stop breathing, but every time, Enki brought me back to life, and then I hated myself because you said that I had to keep living, and I hated living because *you're* the one who said I had to—"

"Why would you mourn me?" he asked quietly. "You barely even knew me."

"You're right," she said. "I loved an idea of you. I was infatuated with you. I wanted to *be* you. But I didn't know you then, and I'll never really know what you were. I'm finished wondering now, Altan. I'm ready to kill you."

The trident materialized in her hands.

She had a weapon now. She wasn't defenseless against him. She'd never been defenseless. She had just never thought to look.

Altan's eyes flickered to the prongs. "You wouldn't dare."

"You are not real," she said calmly. "He's dead, and I can't hurt him anymore."

"Look at me," he said. "Look at my eyes. Tell me I'm not real."

She lunged. He parried. She disentangled their prongs and advanced again.

He raised his voice. "*Look at me.*"

"I *am*," she said softly. "I see everything."

He faltered.

She stabbed him through the chest.

His eyes bulged open, but otherwise he didn't move. A slow trickle of blood spilled out the side of his mouth. A red circle blossomed on his chest.

It wasn't a fatal blow. She'd stabbed him just under the sternum. She had missed his heart. Eventually he might bleed to death, but she didn't want him gone just yet. She needed him alive and conscious.

She still needed absolution.

Altan peered down at the prongs emerging from his chest. "Would you like to kill me?"

She withdrew her trident. Blood spilled out faster onto his uniform. "I've done it before."

"But could you do it *now*?" he inquired. "Could you end me? If you kill me here, Rin, I'll go."

"I don't want that."

"Then you still need me."

"Not the way I did."

She'd realized, *finally* realized, that chasing the legacy of Altan Trengsin would give her no truth. She couldn't replicate him in her mind, no matter how many times she tortured herself going over the memories. She could only inherit his pain.

And what was there to replicate? Who *was* Altan, really?

A scared boy from Speer who just wanted to go home, a broken boy who had learned that there was no home to return to, and a soldier who stayed alive just to spite everyone who thought he should be dead. A commander with no purpose, nothing to fight for, and nothing to care about except burning down the world.

Altan was no hero. That was so clear to her now, so stunningly clear that she felt as if she'd been doused in ice water, submerged and reborn.

She didn't owe him her guilt.

She didn't owe him anything.

"I still love you," she said, because she had to be honest.

"I know. You're a fool for it," he said. He stepped forward, reached for her hand, and entwined his fingers in hers. "Kiss me. I know you've wanted to."

She touched his blood-soaked fingers against her cheek. She closed her eyes, just for a moment, and thought about what might have been.

"I loved you, too," he said. "Do you believe that?"

"No, I don't," she said, and pressed her trident into his chest once more.

It slid smoothly in with no resistance. Rin didn't know if that was because the vision of Altan was already fading, immaterial, or if Altan within this dream space was deliberately aiding her, sinking the three prongs neatly into that space in his rib cage that stood just over his heart.

When Rin breathed again it was a new and frightening sensation, at once mechanical and also terribly confusing. Was this *her* body, this mortal and clumsy vessel? One finger at a time she learned the inner workings of her body again. Learned the way air moved through her lungs. Learned to hear the sound of her heart pumping inside her.

She saw light all around her and above her, a perfect circle of blue. It took her a moment to realize that it was the roof of the yurt, pulled open to let the steam escape.

"Don't move," said the Sorqan Sira.

The Sorqan Sira placed a hand over Rin's chest, clenched her fingers, and started to chant. Sharp nails dug into Rin's skin.

Rin screamed.

It wasn't over. She felt a terrible pulling sensation, as if the

Sorqan Sira had wrapped her fingers around Rin's heart and wrenched it out of her rib cage.

She looked down. The Sorqan Sira's fingers hadn't broken skin. The tugging came from something within; something sharp and jagged inside her, something that didn't want to let go.

The Sorqan Sira's chanting grew louder. Rin felt an immense pressure, so great she was sure that her lungs were bursting. It grew and grew—and then something gave. The pressure disappeared.

For a moment all she could do was lie flat and breathe, eyes fixed on the blue circle above.

"Look." The Sorqan Sira opened her palm toward Rin. Inside was a clot of blood the size of her fist, mottled black and rotten. It smelled putrid.

Rin shrank instinctively away. "Is that . . . ?"

"Daji's venom." The Sorqan Sira made a fist over the clot and squeezed. Black blood oozed through the cracks between her fingers and dripped onto the glowing rocks. The Sorqan Sira peered curiously at her stained fingers, then shook the last few drops onto the rocks, where they hissed loudly and disappeared. "It's gone now. You're free."

Rin stared at the stained rocks, at a loss for words. "I don't . . ." She choked before she could finish. Then it happened all at once. Her entire body shook, racked with a grief she hadn't even known was there. She buried her head in her hands, whimpering incoherently, fingers thick with tears and snot.

"It's all right to cry," the Sorqan Sira said quietly. "I know what you saw."

"Then fuck you," Rin choked. "*Fuck you.*"

Her chest heaved. She lurched forward and vomited over the stones. Her knees shook, her ankle throbbed, and she collapsed onto herself, face inches from her vomit, eyes squeezed shut to stem the tide of tears.

Her heart slammed against her rib cage. She tried to focus on her pulse, counting her heartbeats with every passing second to calm down.

He's gone.

He's dead.

He can't hurt me anymore.

She reached for her anger, the anger that had always served as her shield, and couldn't find it. Her emotions had burned her out from the inside; the raging flames had died out because they had nothing left to consume. She felt drained, hollowed out and empty. The only things that remained were exhaustion and the dry ache of loss in her throat.

"You are allowed to feel," the Sorqan Sira murmured.

Rin sniffled and wiped her nose with her sleeve.

"But don't feel bad for him," said the Sorqan Sira. "That was never him. The man you know has gone somewhere he'll be at peace. Life and death, they're equal to this cosmos. We enter the material world and we go away again, reincarnated into something better. That boy was miserable. You let him go."

Yes, Rin knew; in the abstract she knew this truth, that to the cosmos they were fundamentally irrelevant, that they came from dust and returned to dust and ash.

And she should have taken comfort in that, but in that moment she didn't want to be temporary and immaterial; she wanted to be forever preserved in the material world in a moment with Altan, their foreheads pressed together, eyes meeting, arms touching and interlacing, trying to meld into the pure physicality of the other.

She wanted to be alive and mortal and eternally temporary with him, and that was why she cried.

"I don't want him to be gone," she whispered.

"Our dead don't leave us," said the Sorqan Sira. "They'll haunt you as long as you let them. That boy is a disease on your mind. Forget him."

"I *can't*." She pressed her face into her hands. "He was brilliant. He was different. You'd have never met anyone like him."

"You would be stunned." The Sorqan Sira looked very sad. "You have no idea how many men are like Altan Trengsin."

"Rin! Oh, *gods*." Kitay was at her side the instant she emerged from the yurt. She knew, could tell from the expression on his face, that he'd been waiting outside, teeth clenched in anxiety, for hours.

"Hold her up," the Sorqan Sira told him.

He slipped an arm around her waist to take the weight off her ankle. "You're all right?"

She nodded. Together they limped forward.

"Are you sure?" he pressed.

"I'm better," she murmured. "I think I'm better than I've been in a long time."

She stood for a minute, leaning against his shoulder, simply basking in the cold air. She had never known that the air itself could taste or feel so sweet. The sensation of the wind against her face was crisp and delicious, more refreshing than cool rainwater.

"Rin," Kitay said.

She opened her eyes. "What?"

He was staring pointedly at her chest.

Rin fumbled at her front, wondering if her clothes had somehow burned away in the heat. She wouldn't have noticed if they had. The sensation of having a physical body still felt so entirely new to her that she might as well have been walking around naked.

"What is it?" she asked, dazed.

The Sorqan Sira said nothing.

"Look down," Kitay said. His voice sounded oddly strangled.

She glanced down.

"Oh," she said faintly.

A black handprint was scorched into her skin like a brand just below her sternum.

Kitay whirled on the Sorqan Sira. "What did you—"

"It wasn't her," Rin said.

This mark was Altan's work and legacy.

That bastard.

Kitay was watching her carefully. "Are you all right with this?"

"No," she said.

She put her hand over her chest, placed her fingers inside the outlines of Altan's.

His hand was so much bigger than hers.

She let her hand drop. "But it doesn't matter."

"Rin . . ."

"He's dead," she said, voice trembling. "He's dead, he's gone, do you understand? He's *gone*, and he's never going to touch me again."

"I know," said Kitay. "He won't."

"Call the flame," the Sorqan Sira said abruptly. She had been standing quietly, observing their exchange, but now her voice carried an odd urgency. "Do it now."

"Hold on," Kitay said. "She's weak, she's exhausted—"

"She must do it now," the Sorqan Sira insisted. She looked strangely frightened, and that terrified Rin. "I have to know."

"Be reasonable—" Kitay began, but Rin shook her head.

"No. She's right. Stand back."

He let go of her arm and stepped several paces backward.

She closed her eyes, exhaled, and let her mind sink into the state of ecstasy. The place where rage met power. And for the first time in months she let herself hope that she might feel the flame again, a hope that had become as unattainable as flying.

It was infinitely easier now to generate the anger. She could plunder her own memories with abandon. There were no more parts of her mind that she didn't dare prod, that still bled like open wounds.

She traversed a familiar path through the void until she saw the Phoenix as if through a mist; heard it like an echo, felt it like the remembrance of a touch.

She felt for its rage, and she pulled.

The fire didn't come.

Something pulsed.

Flashes of light seared behind her eyelids.

The Seal remained, burned into her mind, still present. The ghost of Altan's laughter echoed in her ears.

Rin held the flame in the palm of her hand for only an instant, just enough to tantalize her and leave her gasping for more, and then it disappeared.

There was no pain this time, no immediate threat that she might be sucked into a vision and lose her mind to the fantasy, but still Rin sank to her knees and screamed.

CHAPTER 23

"There's another way," said the Sorqan Sira.

"Shut up," Rin said.

She'd come so close. She'd almost had the fire back, she'd tasted it, only to have it wrenched out of her grasp. She wanted to lash out at *something*, she just didn't know who or what, and the sheer pressure made her feel like she might explode. "You said you'd fixed it."

"The Seal is neutralized," said the Sorqan Sira. "It cannot corrupt you any longer. But the venom ran deep, and it still blocks your access to the world of spirit—"

"Fuck all you know."

"Rin, don't," Kitay warned.

She ignored him. She knew this wasn't the Sorqan Sira's fault, but still she wanted to hurt, to cut. "Your people don't know shit. No wonder the Trifecta killed you off, no wonder you lost to three fucking teenagers—"

A shrieking noise slammed into her mind. She fell to her knees, but the noise kept reverberating, growing louder and louder until it solidified into words that vibrated in her bones.

You dare reproach me? The Sorqan Sira loomed over Rin like a giant, standing tall as a mountain while everything else in the clearing shrank. *I am the Mother of the Ketreyids. I rule the north of the Baghra, where the scorpions are fat with poison and the great-mawed sandworms lie in the red sands, ready to swallow camels whole. I have tamed a land created to wither humans away until they are polished bone. Do not think to defy me.*

Rin couldn't speak for the pain. The shriek intensified for several torturous seconds before finally ebbing away. She rolled onto her back and sucked in air in great, heaving gulps.

Kitay helped her sit up. "This is why we are polite to our allies."

"I will await your apology," said the Sorqan Sira.

"I'm sorry," Rin muttered. "I just—I thought I had it back."

She'd numbed herself to her loss during the campaign. She hadn't realized how desperately she still wanted the fire back until she touched it again, just for a moment, and everything had come rushing back; the thrill, the blaze, the sheer roaring *power*.

"Do not presume that all is lost," said the Sorqan Sira. "You will never access the Phoenix on your own unless Daji removes the Seal. That she will never do."

"Then it's all over," Rin said.

"No. Not if another soul calls the Phoenix for you. A soul that is bound to your own." The Sorqan Sira looked pointedly at Kitay.

He blinked, confused.

"No," Rin said immediately. "I don't—I don't care what you can do, *no*—"

"Let her speak," Kitay said.

"No, you don't understand the risk—"

"Yes, he does," said the Sorqan Sira.

"But he doesn't know anything about the gods!" Rin cried.

"He doesn't *now*. Once you've been twinned, he will know everything."

"Twinned?" Kitay repeated.

"Do you understand the nature of Chaghan and Qara's bond?" the Sorqan Sira asked.

Kitay shook his head.

"They're spiritually linked," Rin said flatly. "Cut him, and she feels the pain. Kill him and she dies."

Horror flitted across Kitay's face. He tried to mask it, but she saw.

"The anchor bond connects your souls across the psychospiritual plane," said the Sorqan Sira. "You can still call the Phoenix if you do it through the boy. He will be your conduit. The divine power will flow straight through him and into you."

"I'm going to become a shaman?" Kitay asked.

"No. You will only lend your mind to one. She will call the god through you." The Sorqan Sira tilted her head, considering the both of them. "You are good friends, yes?"

"Yes," Kitay said.

"Good. The anchor takes best on two souls that are already familiar. It's stronger. More stable. Can you bear a little pain?"

"Yes," Kitay said again.

"Then we should perform the bonding ritual as soon as we can."

"Absolutely not," Rin said.

"I'll do it," Kitay said firmly. "Just tell me how."

"No, I'm not letting you—"

"I'm not asking your permission, Rin. We don't have another choice."

"But you could die!"

He barked out a laugh. "We're soldiers. We're always about to die."

Rin stared at him in disbelief. How could he sound so cavalier? Did he not understand the risk?

Kitay had survived Sinegard. Golyn Niis. Boyang. He'd suffered enough pain for a lifetime. She wasn't putting him through this, too. She'd never be able to forgive herself.

"You have no idea what it's like," she said. "You've never spoken to the gods, you—"

He shook his head. "No, you don't get to talk like that. You don't get to keep this world from me, like I'm too stupid or too weak for it—"

"I don't think you're weak."

"Then why—"

"Because you don't know anything about this world, and you never should." She didn't care if the Phoenix tormented her, but Kitay . . . Kitay was pure. He was the best person she had ever known. Kitay shouldn't know how it felt to call a god of vengeance. Kitay was the last thing in the world that was still fundamentally kind and good, and she'd die before she corrupted that. "You have no idea how it feels. The gods will break you."

"Do you want the fire back?" Kitay asked.

"What?"

"*Do you want the fire back?* If you can call the Phoenix again, will you use it to win us this war?"

"Yes," she said. "I want it more than anything. But I can't ask you to do this for me."

"Then you don't have to ask." He turned to the Sorqan Sira. "Anchor us. Just tell me what I have to do."

The Sorqan Sira was looking at Kitay with an expression that almost amounted to respect. A thin smile spread across her face. "As you wish."

"It's not so bad," Chaghan said. "You take the agaric. You kill the sacrifice. Then the Sorqan Sira binds you, and your souls are linked together forever after. You don't need to do much but exist, really."

"Why a living sacrifice?" Kitay asked.

"Because there's power in a soul released from the material world," Qara said. "The Sorqan Sira will use that power to forge your bond."

Chaghan and Qara had been enlisted to prepare Rin and Kitay for the ritual, which involved a tedious process of painting a line of characters down their bare arms, running from their shoulders to the tips of their middle fingers. The characters had to be written at precisely the same time, each stroke synchronous with its pair.

The twins worked with remarkable coordination, which Rin would have appreciated more if she weren't so upset.

"Stop moving," Chaghan said. "You're making the ink bleed."

"Then write faster," she snapped.

"That would be nice," Kitay said amiably. "I need to pee."

Chaghan dipped his brush into an inkwell and shook away the excess drops. "Ruin one more character and we'll have to start over."

"You'd like that, wouldn't you?" Rin grumbled. "Why don't you just take another hour? With luck the war will be over before you're done!"

Chaghan lowered his brush. "We didn't have a choice in this. You know that."

"I know you're a little bitch," she said.

"You have no other choice."

"Fuck you."

It was a petty exchange, and it didn't make Rin feel nearly as good as she thought it would. It only exhausted her. Because Chaghan was right—the twins had to comply with the Sorqan Sira or they would certainly have been killed, and if they hadn't, Rin would still have no way out.

"It'll be all right," Qara said gently. "An anchor makes you stronger. More stable."

Rin scoffed. "How? It just seems like a good way to lose two soldiers for every one."

"Because it makes you resilient to the gods. Every time you call them down, you are like a lantern, drifting away from your body. Drift too far, and the gods root themselves in your physical form instead. That's when you lose your mind."

"Is that what happened to this Feylen?" Kitay asked.

"Yes," said Qara. "He went out too far, got lost, and the god planted itself inside."

"Interesting," Kitay said. "And the anchor absolutely prevents that?"

He sounded far too excited about the procedure. He drank the twins' words in with a hungry expression, cataloging every new sliver of information into his prodigious memory. Rin could almost see the gears turning in his mind.

That scared her. She didn't want him entranced with this world. She wanted him to run far, far away.

"It's not perfect, but it makes it much harder to lose your mind," Chaghan said. "The gods can't uproot you with an anchor. You can drift as far as you want into the world of spirit, and you'll always have a way to come back."

"You're saying I'll stop Rin from going crazy," Kitay said.

"She's already crazy," Chaghan said.

"Fair enough," Kitay said.

The twins worked in silence for a long while. Rin sat up straight, eyes closed, breathing steadily as she felt the wet brush tip move against her bare skin.

What if the anchor *did* make her stronger? She couldn't help feeling a thrill of hope at the thought. What would it be like to call the Phoenix without fear of losing her mind to the rage? She might summon fire whenever she wanted, for as long as she wanted. She might control it the way Altan had.

But was it worth it? The sacrifice seemed so immense—not just for Kitay, but for *her*. To link her life to his would be such an unpredictable, terrifying liability. She would never be safe unless Kitay was, too.

Unless she could protect him. Unless she could guarantee that Kitay was *never* in danger.

At last Chaghan put his brush down. "You're finished."

Rin stretched and examined her arms. Swirling black script covered her skin, made of words that almost resembled a language that she could understand. "That's it?"

"Not yet." Chaghan passed them a fistful of red-capped toadstools. "Eat these."

Kitay prodded a toadstool with his finger. "What are these?"

"Fly agaric. You can find it near birch and fir trees."

"What's it for?"

"To open up the crack between the worlds," Qara said.

Kitay looked confused.

"Tell him what it's really for," Rin said.

Qara smiled. "To get you incredibly high. Much more elegant than poppy seeds. Faster, too."

Kitay turned the mushroom over in his hand. "Looks poisonous."

"They're psychedelics," Chaghan said. "They're all poisonous. The whole *point* is to deliver you right to the doorstep of the afterworld."

Rin popped the mushrooms in her mouth and chewed. They were tough and tasteless, and she had to work her teeth for several minutes before they were tender enough to go down. She had the unpleasant sensation that she was chewing through a lump of flesh every time her teeth cut into the fibrous chunks.

Chaghan passed Kitay a wooden cup. "If you don't want to eat the mushroom you can drink the agaric instead."

Kitay sniffed it, took a sip, and gagged. "What's in this?"

"Horse urine," Chaghan said cheerfully. "We feed the mushrooms to the horses, and you get the drug after it passes. Goes down easier."

"Your people are *disgusting*," Kitay muttered. He pinched his nose, tossed the contents of the cup back into his throat, and gagged.

Rin swallowed. Dry lumps of mushroom pushed painfully down her throat.

"What happens to you when your anchor dies?" she asked.

"You die," Chaghan said. "Your souls are bound, which means they depart this earth together. One pulls the other along."

"That's not strictly true," Qara said. "It's a choice. You can choose to depart this earth together. Or you may break the bond."

"You can?" Rin asked. "How?"

Qara exchanged a look with Chaghan. "With your last word. If both partners are willing."

Kitay frowned. "I don't understand. Why is this a liability, then?"

"Because once you have an anchor, they become a part of your soul. Your very existence. They know your thoughts. They feel what you feel. They are the *only ones* who completely and fully understand you. Most would die rather than give that up."

"And you'd both have to be in the same place when one of you died," said Chaghan. "Most people aren't."

"But you *can* break it," Rin said.

"You could," Chaghan said. "Though I doubt the Sorqan Sira will teach you how."

Of course not. Rin knew the Sorqan Sira would want Kitay as insurance—not only to ensure that her weapon against Daji kept working, but as a failsafe in case she ever decided to put Rin down.

"Did Altan have an anchor?" she asked. Altan had possessed an eerie amount of control for a Speerly.

"No. The Speerlies didn't know how to do it. Altan was . . . whatever Altan was doing, that was inhuman. Near the end, he was staying sane off of sheer willpower alone." Chaghan swallowed. "I offered many times. He always said no."

"But you already have an anchor," said Rin. "You can have more than one?"

"Not at the same time. A pairwise bond is optimal. A triangular bond is deeply unstable, because unpredictability in reciprocation means that any defection on one end affects the other two in ways that you cannot protect against."

"But?" Kitay pressed.

"But it can also amplify your abilities. Make you stronger than any shaman has the right to be."

"Like the Trifecta," Rin realized. "They're bonded to each other. That's why they're so powerful."

It made so much sense now—why Daji had not killed Jiang if they were enemies. She wouldn't. She *couldn't*, without killing herself.

She sat up with a start. "So that means . . ."

"Yes," said Chaghan. "As long as Daji is alive, the Dragon Emperor and the Gatekeeper are both still alive. It's possible their bond was dissolved, but I doubt it. Daji's power is far too stable. The other two are out there, somewhere. But my guess is that they can't be doing too well, because the rest of the country thinks they're dead."

You will destroy one another. One will die, one will rule, and one will sleep for eternity.

Kitay voiced the question on Rin's mind. "Then what happened to them? Why did they go missing?"

Chaghan shrugged. "You'd have to ask the other two. Have you finished drinking?"

Kitay drained the cup and winced. "Ugh. Yes."

"Good. Now eat the mushrooms."

Kitay blinked. "What?"

"There's no agaric in that cup," Chaghan said.

"Oh, you asshole," Rin said.

"I don't understand," Kitay said.

Chaghan gave him a thin smile. "I just wanted to see if you'd drink horse piss."

The Sorqan Sira waited outside before a roaring fire. The flames seemed alive to Rin; the tendrils jumped too high, reached too far, like little hands trying to pull her into the blaze. If she let her gaze linger, the smoke, turned purple by the Sorqan Sira's powders, started taking on the faces of the dead. Master Irjah. Aratsha. Captain Salkhi. Altan.

"Are you ready?" asked the Sorqan Sira.

Rin blinked the faces away.

She knelt across from Kitay on the frigid dirt. Despite the cold, they were permitted to wear only trousers and undershirts that exposed their bare arms. The inky characters trailing down their skin shone in the firelight.

She was terrified. He didn't look afraid at all.

"I'm ready," he said. His voice was steady.

"Ready," she echoed.

Between them lay two long, serrated knives and a sacrifice.

Rin didn't know how the Ketreyids had managed to trap an adult deer, massive and healthy, without any visible wounds, in just a matter of hours. Its legs were bound tightly together. Rin suspected that the animal had been sedated, because it lay quite still on the dirt, eyes half-open as if it were resigned to its fate.

The effect of the agaric had begun to set in. Everything seemed terribly bright. When objects moved in her field of vision, they left behind trails like streaks of paint that sparked and swirled before they faded away.

She focused with difficulty on the deer's neck.

She and Kitay were to make two cuts, one on either side of the animal, so that neither could bear full responsibility for its death. Alone, each wound would be insufficient to kill. The deer might drag itself away, cover the cut in mud and somehow survive. But wounds on both sides meant certain death.

Rin picked her knife off the ground and gripped it tightly in her hands.

"Repeat after me," said the Sorqan Sira, and uttered a slow stream of Ketreyid words. The foreign syllables sounded clunky and awkward in Rin's mouth. She knew their meaning only because the twins had explained them to her.

We will live as one. We will fight as one.

And we will kill as one.

"The sacrifice," said the Sorqan Sira.

They brought their knives down.

Rin found it harder than she'd expected. Not because she was unused to killing—cutting through flesh was as easy to her now as breathing. It was the fur that offered resistance. She clenched her teeth and pushed harder. The knife sank into the deer's side.

The deer arched its neck and screamed.

Rin's knife hadn't gone in deep enough. She had to widen the cut. Her hands shook madly; the handle was loose between her fingers.

But Kitay dragged his knife across the deer's side with one clean, steady stroke.

Blood pooled, fast and dark, around their knees. The deer stopped writhing. Its head drooped to the ground.

Through the haze of the agaric, Rin *saw* the moment the deer's life left its body—a golden, shimmering aura that lingered over the corpse like an ethereal copy of its physical form before drifting upward like smoke. She tilted her head up, watched it floating higher and higher toward the heavens.

"Follow it," said the Sorqan Sira.

She did. It seemed such a simple matter. Under the agaric's influence her soul was lighter than air itself. Her mind ascended, her material body became a distant memory, and she flew up into the vast and dark void that was the cosmos.

She found herself standing on the periphery of a great circle, its circumference etched with glowing Hexagrams—characters that together spelled the nature of the universe, the sixty-four deities that constituted all that was and would ever be.

The circle tilted and became a pool, inside which swam two massive carp, one white, one black, each with a large dot of the opposite color on its flank. They drifted lazily, chasing each other in a slow-moving, eternal circle.

She saw Kitay on the other side of the circle. He was naked. It was not a physical nakedness; he was made more of light than he was of body—but every thought, every memory, and every feeling he'd ever had shone out toward her. Nothing was hidden.

She was similarly naked before him. All of her secrets, her insecurities, her guilt, and her rage had been laid bare. He saw her cruelest, most brutal desires. He saw parts of her that she didn't even understand herself. The part that was terrified of being alone and terrified of being the last. The part that realized it loved pain, adored it, could find release only in pain.

And she could see him. She saw the way that concepts were stored in his mind, great repositories of knowledge linked together to be called up at a moment's notice. She saw the anxiety that came with being the only person he knew who was *this* smart. She saw how scared he was, trapped and isolated in his own mind, watching his world break down around him because of irrationalities that he could not fix.

And she understood his sadness. The grief; the loss of a father, but more than just that—the loss of an empire, the loss of loyalty, of *duty*, his sole meaning for existence—

She saw his fury.

How had it taken her this long to understand? She wasn't the only one fueled by anger. But where her rage was explosive, immediate and devastating, Kitay's burned with a silent determination; it festered and rotted and lingered, and the strength of his hate stunned her.

We're the same.

Kitay wanted vengeance and blood. Under that frail veneer of control was an ongoing scream of rage that originated in confusion and culminated in an overwhelming urge for destruction, if only so he could tear the world down and rebuild it in a way that made *sense*.

The circle glowed between them. The black carp and white carp began to circle faster and faster until the darkness and brightness were indistinct; not gray, not melded into each other but yet the same entity—two sides of the same coin, necessary complements balancing each other like the Pantheon was balanced.

The circle spun and they spun with it—faster and faster, until the Hexagrams blurred and melded into a glowing hoop. For a moment Rin was lost in the convergence—up became down, right became left, all distinctions were broken . . .

Then she felt the power, and it was magnificent.

She felt like she had when Shiro injected her veins with heroin. It was the same rush, the same dizzying flood of energy. But this time her spirit did not drift farther and farther from the material world. This time she knew where her body was, could return to it in seconds if she wanted. She was halfway between the spirit world and the material world. She could perceive both, affect both.

She had not gone up to meet her god; her god had been drawn down into her. She felt the Phoenix all about her, the rage and fire, so deliciously warm that it tickled as it coursed over her.

She was so delighted that she wanted to laugh.

But Kitay was moaning. He had been for some time now, but she was so entranced with the power that she'd hardly noticed.

"It's not taking." The Sorqan Sira intruded sharply on Rin's reverie. "Stop it, you're overpowering him."

Rin opened her eyes and saw Kitay curled into a ball, whimpering on the ground. He jerked his head back and uttered a long, keening scream.

Her sight blurred and shifted. One moment she was looking at Kitay and the next she couldn't see him at all. All she could see was fire, vast expanses of fire over which only she had control . . .

"You're erasing him," hissed the Sorqan Sira. "Pull yourself back."

But why? She'd never felt so good before. She never wanted this sensation to stop.

"You are going to kill him." The Sorqan Sira's fingers dug into her shoulder. "And then nothing will save you."

Dimly, Rin understood. She was hurting Kitay, she had to stop, but *how*? The fire was so alluring, it reduced her rational mind to just a whisper. She heard the Phoenix's laughter echoing around her mind, growing louder and stronger with every passing moment.

"Rin," Kitay gasped. *"Please."*

That brought her back.

Her grasp of the material world was fading. Before it disappeared entirely she snatched up her knife and stabbed down into her leg.

Spots of white exploded in her vision. The pain chased the fire away, induced a stark clarity back to her mind. The Phoenix fell silent. The void was still.

She saw Kitay across the spirit plane—kneeling, but alive, present, and whole.

She opened her eyes to dirt. Slowly she pulled herself into a sitting position, wiped the soil off the side of her face. She saw Kitay looking around in a daze, blinking as if he were seeing the world for the first time.

She reached for his hand. "Are you all right?"

He took a deep, shuddering breath. "I—I'm fine, I think, I just . . . Give me a moment."

She couldn't help but laugh. "Welcome to my world."

"I feel like I'm living in a dream." He examined the back of his hand, turned it over in the fading sunlight as if he didn't trust the evidence of his own body. "I suppose—I saw the physical proof of your gods. I knew this power existed. But everything I know about the world—"

"The world you knew doesn't exist," she said softly.

"No shit." Kitay's hands clenched the dirt and grass like he was afraid the ground might disappear under his fingertips.

"Try it," said the Sorqan Sira.

Rin didn't have to ask what she meant.

She stood upon shaky legs and turned to face away from Kitay. She opened her palms. She felt the fire inside her chest, a warm presence waiting to pour out the moment she called it.

She summoned it forward. A warm flame appeared in her hands—a tame, quiet little thing.

She tensed, waiting for the pull, the urge to draw out more, *more*. But she felt nothing. The Phoenix was still there. She knew it was screaming for her. But it couldn't get through. A wall had been built in her mind, a psychic structure that repelled and muted the god to just a faint whisper.

Fuck you, said the Phoenix, but even now it sounded amused. *Fuck you, little Speerly.*

She shouted with delight. She hadn't just recovered, she had *tamed a god.* The anchor bond had set her free.

She watched, trembling, as fire accumulated on her palms. She called it higher. Made it leap through the air in arcs like fish jumping from the ocean. She could command it as completely as Altan had been able to. No. She was better than Altan had ever been, because she was sober, she was stable, and she was free.

The fear of madness was gone, but not the impossible power. The power remained, a deep well from which she could draw when she chose.

And now she *could* choose.

She saw Kitay watching her. His eyes were wide, his expression equal parts fear and awe.

"Are you all right?" she asked him. "Can you feel it?"

He didn't answer. He touched a hand to his temple, his gaze fixed so hard on the flames that she could see them reflected bright in his eyes, and he laughed.

That night the Ketreyids fed them a bone broth—scorching hot, musky, tangy, and salty all at once. Rin guzzled it as fast as she could. It scalded the back of her throat, but she didn't care. She'd been subsisting on dried fish and rice gruel for so long that she'd forgotten how good proper food could taste.

Qara passed her a mug. "Drink more water. You're getting dehydrated."

"Thanks." Rin was still sweating despite the cold onset of night. Little droplets beaded all over her skin, soaking straight through her clothing.

Across the fire, Kitay and Chaghan were engaged in an animated discussion which, as far as Rin could tell, involved the metaphysical nature of the cosmos. Chaghan drew diagrams in the dirt with a stick while Kitay watched, nodding enthusiastically.

Rin turned to Qara. "Can I ask you something?"

"Of course," Qara said.

Rin shot Kitay a glance. He wasn't paying her any attention. He'd seized the stick from Chaghan and was scrawling a very complicated mathematical equation below the diagrams.

Rin lowered her voice. "How long have you and your brother been anchored?"

"For our entire lives," Qara said. "We were ten days old when we performed the ritual. I can't remember life without him."

"And the bond has always . . . it's always been equal? One of you doesn't diminish the other?"

Qara raised an eyebrow. "Do you think I've been diminished?"

"I don't know. You always seem so . . ." Rin trailed off. She didn't know how to phrase it. Qara had always been a mystery to her. She was the moon to her brother's sun. Chaghan was such an overbearing personality. He loved the spotlight, loved to lecture everyone around him in the most condescending way possible. But Qara had always preferred the shadows and the silent company of her birds. Rin had never heard her express an opinion that wasn't her brother's.

"You think Chaghan dominates me," Qara said.

Rin blushed. "No, I just—"

"You're worried you'll overpower Kitay," Qara said. "You think your rage will become too much for him and that he'll become only a shade of you. You think that's what has happened to us."

"I'm scared," Rin said. "I almost killed him. And if that—that imbalance, or whatever, is a risk, I want to know. I don't want to strip him of his ability to challenge me."

Qara nodded slowly. She sat silently for a long while, frowning.

"My brother doesn't dominate me," she said at last. "At least, not in a way I could ever possibly know. But I've never challenged him."

"Then how—"

"Our wills have been united since we were children. We desire the same things. When he speaks, he voices both our thoughts. We are two halves of the same person. If I seem withdrawn to you, it is because Chaghan's presence in the mortal world frees me to dwell among the spirit world. I prefer animal souls to mortals, to whom I've never had much to say. That doesn't mean I'm diminished."

"But Kitay's not like you," Rin said. "Our wills *aren't* aligned. If anything, we disagree more often than not. And I don't want to . . . erase him."

Qara's expression softened. "Do you love him?"

"Yes," Rin said immediately. "More than anyone else in the world."

"Then you don't need to worry," Qara said. "If you love him, then you can trust yourself to protect him."

Rin hoped that was true.

"Hey," Kitay said. "What's so interesting over there?"

"Nothing," Rin said. "Just gossip. Have you cracked the nature of the cosmos?"

"Not yet." Kitay tossed his stick onto the dirt. "But give me a year or two. I'm getting close."

Qara stood up. "Come. We should get some sleep."

Sometime during the day the Ketreyids had built several more yurts, clustered together in a circle. The yurt designated for Rin and her companions was at the very center. The message was clear. They were still under Ketreyid watch until the Sorqan Sira chose to release them.

The yurt felt far too cramped for four people. Rin curled up on her side, knees drawn up to her chest, although all she wanted to do was sprawl out, let all of her limbs loose. She felt suffocated. She wanted open air—open sands, wide water. She took a deep breath, trying to stave off the same panic that had crept up on her during the sweat.

"What's the matter?" Qara asked.

"I think I'd rather sleep outside."

"You'll freeze outside. Don't be stupid."

Rin propped herself up on her side. "You look comfortable."

Qara smiled. "Yurts remind me of home."

"How long has it been since you've been back?" Rin asked.

Qara thought for a moment. "They sent us down south when we turned eleven. So it has been a decade, now."

"Do you ever wish you could go home?"

"Sometimes," Qara said. "But there's not much at home. Not for us, anyway. It's better to be a foreigner in the Empire than a Naimad on the steppe."

Rin supposed that was to be expected when one's tribe was responsible for training a handful of traitorous murderers.

"So—what, no one talks to you back home?" she asked.

"Back home we are slaves," Chaghan said flatly. "The Ketreyids still blame our mother for the Trifecta. They will never accept us back into the fold. We'll pay penance for that forever."

An uncomfortable silence filled the space between them. Rin had more questions, she just didn't know how to ask them.

If she were in a different mood, she would have yelled at the twins for their deception. They'd been spies for all of these years, watching the Cike to determine whether or not they would hold stable. Whether they did a good enough job culling their own, immuring the maddest among them in the Chuluu Korikh.

What if the twins had decided that the Cike had grown too dangerous? Would they have simply killed them off? Certainly the Ketreyids felt as if they had the right. They looked down on Nikara shamans with the same supercilious arrogance as the Hesperians, and Rin hated that.

But she held her tongue. Chaghan and Qara had suffered enough.

And she, if anyone, knew what it was like to be an outcast in her own country.

"These yurts." Kitay put his palms on the walls; his outspread arms reached across a third of the diameter of the hut. "They're all this small?"

"We build them even smaller on the steppe," Qara said. "You're from the south; you've never seen real winds."

"I'm from Sinegard," Kitay said.

"That's not the true north. Everything below the sand dunes counts as the south to us. On the steppe, the night gusts can rip the flesh off your face if they don't freeze you to death first. We stay in yurts because the steppe will kill you otherwise."

No one had a response to that. A peaceful quiet fell over the yurt. Kitay and the twins were asleep in moments; Rin could tell by the sound of their steady, even breathing.

She lay awake with her trident clutched close to her chest, staring at the open roof above her, that perfect circle that revealed the night sky. She felt like a little rodent burrowing down in its hole, trying to pretend that if it lay low enough, then the world outside wouldn't bother it.

Maybe the Ketreyids stayed in their yurts to hide from the winds. Or maybe, she thought, with stars this bright, if you believed that above you lay the cosmos, then you had to construct a yurt to provide some temporary feeling of materiality. Otherwise, under the weight of swirling divinity, you might feel you had no significance at all.

CHAPTER 24

A fresh blanket of snow had fallen while they slept. It made the sun shine brighter, the air bite colder. Rin limped outside and stretched her aching muscles, squinting against the harsh light.

The Ketreyids were eating in shifts. Six riders at a time sat by the fire, wolfing down their food while the others stood guard by the periphery.

"Eat your fill." The Sorqan Sira ladled out two steaming bowls of stew and handed them to Rin and Kitay. "You have a hard ride before you. We'll pack you a bag of dried meat and some yak's milk, but eat as much as you can now."

Rin took the proffered bowl. The stew smelled terribly good. She huddled on the ground and pressed next to Kitay for warmth, bony elbows touching bony hips. Little details about him seemed to stand out in stark relief. She had never noticed before just how long and thin his fingers were, or how he always smelled faintly of ink and dust, or how his wiry hair curled just so at the tips.

She'd known him for more than four years by now, but every time she looked at him, she discovered something new.

"So that's it?" Kitay asked the Sorqan Sira. "You're letting us go? No strings attached?"

"The terms are met," she replied. "We have no reason to harm you now."

"So what am I to you?" Rin asked. "A pet on a long leash?"

"You are my gamble. A trained wolf set loose."

"To kill an enemy that you can't face," Rin said.

The Sorqan Sira smiled, displaying teeth. "Be glad that we still have some use for you."

Rin didn't like her phrasing. "What happens if I succeed, and you no longer have use for me?"

"Then we'll let you keep your lives as a token of our gratitude."

"And what happens if you decide I'm a threat again?"

"Then we'll find you again." The Sorqan Sira nodded to Kitay. "And this time, *his* life will be on the line."

Rin had no doubt the Sorqan Sira would put an arrow through Kitay's heart without hesitation.

"You still don't trust me," she said. "You're playing a long game with us, and the anchor bond was your insurance."

The Sorqan Sira sighed. "I am afraid, child. And I have the right to be. The last time we taught Nikara shamans how to anchor themselves, they turned on us."

"But I'm nothing like them."

"You are far too much like them. You have the same eyes. Angry. Desperate. You've seen too much. You hate too much. Those three were younger than you when they came to us, more timid and afraid, and still they slaughtered thousands of innocents. You are older than they were, and you've done far worse."

"That's not the same," Rin said. "The Federation—"

"Deserved it?" asked the Sorqan Sira. "Every single one? Even the women? The children?"

Rin flushed. "But I'm not—I didn't do it because I liked it. I'm not like *them*."

Not like that vision of a younger Jiang, who laughed when he killed, who seemed to delight in being drenched in blood. Not like Daji.

"That's what they thought about themselves, too," said the

Sorqan Sira. "But the gods corrupted them, just as they will corrupt you. The gods manifest your worst and cruelest instincts. You think you are in control, but your mind erodes by the second. To call the gods is to gamble with madness."

"It's better than doing nothing." Rin knew that she was already walking a fine line, that she ought to keep her mouth shut, but the Ketreyids' constant high-minded pacifistic lecturing infuriated her. "I'd rather go mad than hide behind the Baghra Desert and pretend that atrocities aren't happening when I could have done something about them."

The Sorqan Sira chuckled. "You think that we did nothing? Is that what they taught you?"

"I know that millions died during the first two Poppy Wars. And I know that your people never crossed down south to stop it."

"How many people do you think Vaisra's war has killed?" the Sorqan Sira asked.

"Fewer than would have died otherwise," Rin said.

The Sorqan Sira didn't answer. She just let the silence stretch on and on until Rin's answer began to seem ridiculous.

Rin picked at her food, no longer hungry.

"What will you do with the foreigners?" Kitay asked.

Rin had forgotten about the Hesperians until Kitay asked. She peered around the camp but couldn't spot them. Then she saw a larger yurt a little off to the edge of the clearing, guarded heavily by Bekter and his riders.

"Perhaps we will kill them." The Sorqan Sira shrugged. "They are holy men, and nothing good ever comes of the Hesperian religion."

"Why do you say that?" Kitay asked.

"They believe in a singular and all-powerful deity, which means they cannot accept the truth of other gods. And when nations start to believe that other beliefs lead to damnation, violence becomes inevitable." The Sorqan Sira cocked her head. "What do you think? Shall we shoot them? It's kinder than leaving them to die of exposure."

"Don't kill them," Rin said quickly. Tarcquet made her uncomfortable and Sister Petra made her want to put her hand through a wall, but Augus had never struck her as anything other than naive and well-intentioned. "Those kids are missionaries, not soldiers. They're harmless."

"Those weapons are not harmless," said the Sorqan Sira.

"No," Kitay said. "They are faster and deadlier than crossbows, and they are most deadly in inexperienced hands. I would not return their weapons."

"Safe passage back will be difficult, then. We can spare only one steed for the two of you. They will have to walk through enemy territory."

"Would you give them supplies to make rafts?" Rin asked.

The Sorqan Sira frowned, considering. "Can they find their own way back over the rivers?"

Rin hesitated. Her altruism extended only so far. She didn't want to see Augus dead, but she wasn't about to waste time shepherding children who never should have come along in the first place.

She turned to Kitay. "If they can make it to the Western Murui, they're fine, right?"

He shrugged. "More or less. Tributaries get tricky. They could get lost. Could end up at Khurdalain."

She could accept that risk. It did enough to alleviate her conscience. If Augus and his companions weren't clever enough to make it back to Arlong, then that was their own fault. Augus had been kind to her once. She'd made sure the Ketreyids didn't put an arrow in his head. She owed him nothing more than that.

Chaghan was alone when Rin found him, sitting at the edge of the river with his knees pulled up to his chest.

"Don't they think you might run?" she asked.

He gave her a wry smile. "You know I don't run very fast."

She sat down beside him. "So what happens to you now?"

His face was unreadable. "The Sorqan Sira doesn't trust us to watch over the Cike any longer. She's taking us back north."

"And what will happen to you there?"

His throat bobbed. "That depends."

She knew he didn't want her pity, so she didn't burden him with it. She took a deep breath. "I wanted to say thank you."

"For what?"

"You vouched for me."

"I was just saving my own skin."

"Of course."

"I was also rather hoping that you wouldn't die," he admitted.

"Thanks for that."

An awkward silence passed between them. She saw Chaghan's eyes dart toward her several times, as if he was debating whether to broach the next subject.

"Say it," she finally said.

"Do you really want me to?"

"Yes, if you're going to be this awkward otherwise."

"Fine," he said. "Inside the Seal, what you saw—"

"It was Altan," she said promptly. "Altan, alive. That's what I saw. He was alive."

Chaghan exhaled. "So you killed him?"

"I gave him what he wanted," she said.

"I see."

"I also saw him happy," she said. "He was different. He wasn't suffering. He'd never suffered. He was *happy*. That's how I'll remember him."

Chaghan didn't say anything for a long time. She knew he was trying not to cry in front of her; she could see the tears welling up in his eyes.

"Is that real?" she asked. "In another world, is that real? Or was the Seal just showing me what I wanted to see?"

"I don't know," Chaghan said. "Our world is a dream of the gods. Maybe they have other dreams. But all we have is *this* story unfolding, and in the script of this world, nothing's going to bring Altan back to life."

Rin leaned back. "I thought I knew how this world worked. How the cosmos worked. But I don't know anything."

"Most Nikara don't," Chaghan said, and he didn't even try to mask his arrogance.

Rin snorted. "And you do?"

"We know what constitutes the nature of reality," said Chaghan. "We've understood it for years. But your people are fragile and desperate fools. They don't know what's real and what's false, so they'll cling to their little truths, because it's better than imagining that their world might not matter so much after all."

It was starting to become clear to her now, why the Hinterlanders might view themselves as caretakers of the universe. Who else understood the nature of the cosmos like they did? Who even came close?

Perhaps Jiang had known, a long time ago when his mind was still his. But the man she'd known had been shattered, and the secrets he'd taught her were only fragments of the truth.

"I thought it was hubris, what you did," she murmured. "But it's *kindness*. The Hinterlanders maintain the illusion so you can let everyone else live in the lie."

"Don't call us that," Chaghan said sharply. "*Hinterlander* is not a name. Only the Empire uses this word, because you assume everyone who lives on the steppe is the same. Naimads are not Ketreyids. Call us by our names."

"I'm sorry." She crossed her arms against her chest, shivering against the biting wind. "Can I ask you something else?"

"You're going to ask me regardless."

"Why do you hate me so much?"

"I don't hate you," he said automatically.

"Sure seemed like it. Seemed like it for a long time, even before Altan died."

Finally he twisted around to face her. "I can't look at you and not see him."

She knew he would say that. She knew, and still it hurt. "You thought I couldn't live up to him. And that's—that's fair, I never could. And—and if you were jealous, for some reason, I understand that, too, but you should just know that—"

"I wasn't just jealous," he said. "I was angry. At both of us. I was watching you make all the same mistakes Altan did, and I didn't know how to stop it. I saw Altan confused and angry all those years, and I saw him walk down the path he chose like a blind child, and I thought precisely the same was happening to you."

"But I know what I'm doing. I'm not blind like he was—"

"Yes, you are, you don't even realize it. Your kind has been treated as slaves for so long that you've forgotten what it is like to be free. You're easily angered, and you latch quickly onto things—opium, people, ideas—that soothe your pain, even temporarily. And that makes you terribly easy to manipulate." Chaghan paused. "I'm sorry. Do I offend?"

"Vaisra isn't manipulating me," Rin insisted. "He's . . . we're fighting for something good. Something worth fighting for."

He gave her a long look. "And you really believe in his Republic?"

"I believe the Republic is a better alternative to anything we've got," she said. "Daji has to die. Vaisra's our best shot at killing her. And whatever happens next can't possibly be worse than the Empire."

"You really think that?"

Rin didn't want to talk about this anymore. Didn't want her mind to drift in that direction. Not once since the disaster at Lake Boyang had she seriously considered not returning to Arlong, or the idea that there might not be anything to return to.

She had too much power now, too much rage, and she needed a cause for which to burn. Vaisra's Republic was her anchor. Without that, she'd be lost, drifting. That thought terrified her.

"I have to do this," she said. "Otherwise I have nothing."

"If you say so." Chaghan turned to gaze at the river. He seemed to have given up on arguing the point. She couldn't tell if he was disappointed or not. "Maybe you're right. But eventually, you'll have to ask yourself precisely what you're fighting for. And you'll have to find a reason to live past vengeance. Altan never managed that."

"You're sure you know how to ride this?" Qara handed the war-horse's reins to Rin.

"No, but Kitay does." Rin peered up at the black warhorse with trepidation. She'd never been entirely comfortable around horses—they were so much bigger up close, their hooves so poised to split her head open—but Kitay had spent enough of his child-hood riding around on his family's estate that he could handle most animals with ease.

"Keep off the main roads," Chaghan said. "My birds tell me the Empire's taking back much of its territory. You'll run into Mi-litia patrols if you're seen traveling in broad daylight. Stick to the tree line when you can."

Rin was about to ask about the horse's feed when Chaghan and Qara both looked sharply to the left, like two hunting animals alerted to their prey.

She heard the noises a second later. Shouts from the Ketreyid camp. Arrows thudding into bodies. And a moment later, the un-mistakable sound of a firing arquebus.

"*Shit,*" Kitay breathed.

The twins were already racing back. Rin snatched her trident off the ground and followed.

The camp was in chaos. Ketreyids ran about, grabbing at the reins of spooked horses trying to break free. The air was sharp with the acrid smoke of fire powder. Bullet holes riddled the yurts. Ketreyid bodies were strewn across the ground. And the Gray Company missionaries, half of them wielding arquebuses, fired indiscriminately around the camp.

How had they gotten their arquebuses back?

Rin heard a shot and threw herself to the ground as a bullet burrowed into the tree behind her.

Arrows whistled overhead. Each one found its mark with a thickening thud. A handful of Hesperians dropped to the ground, arrows pierced cleanly into their skulls. A few others ran, panicked, from the clearing. No one chased them.

The only one left was Augus. He wielded two arquebuses, one in each hand, their barrels drooping clumsily against the ground.

He'd never fired one. Rin could tell—he was shaking; he had absolutely no idea what to do.

The Sorqan Sira uttered a command under her breath. The riders moved at once. Instantly twelve arrowheads were pointed at Augus, bowstrings stretching taut.

"Don't shoot!" Rin cried. She ran forward, blocking their arrows' paths with her body. "Don't shoot—please, he's confused—"

Augus didn't seem to notice. His eyes locked on Rin's. He raised the arquebus in his right hand. The barrel formed a direct line to her chest.

It didn't matter if he'd never fired an arquebus before. He couldn't miss. Not from this distance.

"Demon," he said.

"Rin, get back," Kitay said tightly.

Rin stood frozen, unable to move. Augus waved his weapons erratically about, pointed them alternately between the Sorqan Sira, Rin, and Kitay. "Maker give me the courage, protect me from these heathens . . ."

"What is he saying?" the Sorqan Sira demanded.

Augus squeezed his eyes shut. "Show them the strength of heaven and smite them with your divine justice . . ."

"Augus, stop!" Rin walked forward, hands raised in what she hoped was a nonthreatening gesture, and spoke in clearly enunciated Hesperian. "You have nothing to be afraid of. These people aren't your enemies, they're not going to hurt you—"

"Savages!" Augus screamed. He waved one arquebus in an arc before him. The Ketreyids hissed and scattered backward; several sank into a low crouch. *"Get out of my head!"*

"Augus, please," Rin begged. "You're scared, you're not yourself. Look at me, you know who I am, you've met me—"

Augus leveled the arquebus again at her.

The Sorqan Sira's silent command rippled through the clearing. *Fire.*

Not a single Ketreyid rider loosed their bow.

Rin glanced around in confusion.

"Bekter!" the Sorqan Sira shouted. "What is this?"

Bekter smiled, and Rin realized with a twist of dread what was happening.

This wasn't an accident. The Hesperians had been set free on purpose.

This was a coup.

A furious flurry of flashing images ricocheted back and forth in the clearing, a silent war of minds between Bekter and the Sorqan Sira blasted to everyone present, like they were wrestlers performing for an audience.

Rin saw Bekter cutting the Hesperians' bonds and placing the arquebuses in their hands. They stared at him, brain-addled in terror. He told them they were about to play a game. He challenged them to outrun his arrows. The Hesperians scattered.

She saw the girl Jiang had murdered—Tseveri, the Sorqan Sira's daughter—riding across the steppe with a little boy seated before her. They were laughing.

She saw a band of warriors—Speerlies, she realized with a start—at least a dozen of them, flames rolling off of their shoulders as they marched through burned yurts and charred bodies.

She felt a scorching fury radiating out of Bekter, a fury that the Sorqan Sira's weakening protests only amplified, and she understood: This wasn't just some ambition-fueled power struggle. This was vengeance.

Bekter wanted to do for his sister Tseveri what the Sorqan Sira never could. He wanted retribution. The Sorqan Sira wanted Nikara shamans controlled, but Bekter wanted them dead.

Too long you've let the Cike run unchecked in the Empire, Mother. Bekter's voice rang loud and clear. *Too long you've shown mercy to the Naimad scum. No more.*

The riders agreed.

They'd long since shifted their loyalties. Now they only had to dispose of their leader.

The exchange was over in an instant.

The Sorqan Sira reeled back. She seemed to have shrunk in on herself. For the first time, Rin saw fear on her face.

"Bekter," she said. "Please."

Bekter spoke an order.

Arrows dotted the earth around Augus's feet. Augus gave a strangled yelp. Rin lunged forward, but it was too late. She heard a click, then a small explosion.

The Sorqan Sira dropped to the ground. Smoke curled from the spot where the bullet had burrowed into her chest. She looked down, then back up at Augus, face contorted in disbelief, before slumping to the side.

Chaghan rushed forward. *"Ama!"*

Augus dropped the arquebus he'd fired and raised the second one to his shoulder.

Several things happened at once.

Augus pulled the trigger. Qara threw herself in front of her brother. A bang split the night and together the twins collapsed, Qara falling back into Chaghan's arms.

The riders turned to flee.

Rin screamed. A rivulet of fire shot from her mouth and slammed into Augus's chest, knocking him over. He shouted, writhing madly to put out the flames, but the fire didn't stop; it consumed his air, poured into his lungs, seized him from inside like a hand until his torso was charcoal and he couldn't scream anymore.

Augus's death throes slowed to an insectlike twitching as Rin sank to her knees. She closed her mouth. The flames died away, and Augus lay still.

Behind her Chaghan was cradling his sister. A dark splotch of blood appeared over Qara's right breast as if painted by an invisible artist, blossoming larger and larger like a blooming poppy flower.

"Qara—Qara, *no* . . ." Chaghan's hands moved frantically over her breast, but there was no arrowhead to pull out; the metal shard had buried itself too deep for him to save her.

"Stop," Qara gasped. She lifted a shaking hand and touched it to Chaghan's chest. Blood bubbled out between her teeth. "Let go. You have to let go."

"I'm going with you," Chaghan said.

Qara's breath came in short, pained gasps. "No. Too important."

"Qara . . ."

"Do this for me," Qara whispered. *"Please."*

Chaghan pressed his forehead against Qara's. Something passed between them, an exchange of thoughts that Rin could not hear. Qara reached a shaking hand to her chest, drew a pattern in her own blood on the pale skin of Chaghan's cheek, and then placed her palm against it.

Chaghan exhaled. Rin thought she saw something pass in the space between them—a gust of air, a shimmer of light.

Qara's head fell to the side. Chaghan pulled her limp form into his arms and dropped his head.

"Rin," Kitay said urgently.

She spun around. Ten feet away, Bekter sat astride his horse, bow raised.

She lifted her trident, but she had no chance. From this close Bekter had an easy shot. They'd be dead in seconds.

But Bekter wasn't shooting. His arrow was nocked to his bow, but the string wasn't pulled taut. He had a dazed look in his eye; his gaze flickered between the bodies of the Sorqan Sira and Qara.

He's in shock, Rin realized. Bekter couldn't believe what he'd done.

She hefted her trident over her head, poised to throw. "Murder's not so easy, is it?"

Bekter blinked, as if just coming to his senses, and then aimed his bow at her.

"Go on," she told him. "We'll see who's faster."

Bekter looked at the gleaming tips of her trident, then down at Chaghan, who was rocking back and forth over Qara's form. He lowered his bow just a fraction.

"You did this," Bekter said. "You killed Mother. That's what I'll tell them. This is your fault." His voice wavered; he seemed to be trying to convince himself. His bow shook in his hands. "All of this is your fault."

Rin hurled her trident. Bekter's horse bolted. The trident flew a foot over his head and shot through empty air. Rin aimed a burst of flame in his direction, but she was too slow—within seconds Bekter was gone from her sight, disappeared into the forest to follow his band of traitors.

For a long time, the only sound in the clearing came from Chaghan. He wasn't crying, not quite. His eyes were dry. But his chest heaved erratically, his breath came out in short, strangled bursts, and his eyes stared wide, down at his sister's corpse as if he couldn't believe what he was looking at.

Our wills have been united since we were children, Qara had said. *We are two halves of the same person.*

Rin couldn't possibly imagine how it felt to have that stripped away.

At last Kitay bent down over the Sorqan Sira's body and rolled her flat on her back. He pulled her eyelids closed.

Then he touched Chaghan gently on the shoulder. "Is there something we should—"

"There's going to be war," Chaghan said abruptly. He laid Qara out on the dirt before him, then arranged her hands on her chest, one clasped over the other. His voice was flat, emotionless. "Bekter's the chieftain now."

"*Chieftain?*" Kitay repeated. "He just killed his own mother!"

"Not by his own hand. That's why he gave the Hesperians those guns. He didn't touch her, and his riders will attest to that. They'll be able to swear it before the Pantheon, because it's true."

There was no emotion on Chaghan's face. He looked utterly, terrifyingly calm.

Rin understood. He'd shut down, replaced his feelings with a focus on calm pragmatism, because that was the only way he could block out the pain.

Chaghan took a deep, shuddering breath. For a moment the facade cracked, and Rin could see pain twisting across his face, but it disappeared just as fast as it came. "This is . . . this changes everything. The Sorqan Sira was the only one keeping the Ketreyids in check. Now Bekter will lead them to slaughter the Naimads."

"Then go," Rin said. "Take the warhorse. Ride north. Go back to your clan and warn them."

Chaghan blinked at her. "That horse is for you."

"Don't be an idiot."

"We'll find another way," Kitay said. "It'll take us a little longer, but we'll figure it out. You need to go."

Slowly, Chaghan stood up on shaky legs and followed them to the riverbank.

The horse was waiting tamely where they'd left it. It seemed completely unbothered by the commotion in the clearing. It had been trained well not to panic.

Chaghan lifted his foot into the stirrup and swung himself up into the saddle in one graceful, practiced movement. He grasped the reins in both hands and looked down at them. He swallowed. "Rin . . ."

"Yes?" she answered.

He looked very small atop the horse. For the first time, she saw him for what he was: not a fearsome shaman, not a mysterious Seer, but just a boy, really. She'd always thought Chaghan so ethereally powerful, so detached from the realm of mortals. But he was human after all, smaller and thinner than the rest of them.

And for the first time in his life, he was alone.

"What am I going to do?" he asked quietly.

His voice trembled. He looked so utterly lost.

Rin reached for his hand. Then she looked at him, really looked him in the eyes. They were so similar when she thought about it. Too young to be so powerful, not close to ready for the positions they had been thrust into.

She squeezed his fingers. "You fight."

PART III

CHAPTER 25

The journey back to Arlong took twenty-nine days. Rin knew because she carved one notch each day into the side of their raft, imagining, as the time stretched on, how the war must be going. Each mark represented a question, another possible alternate outcome. Had Daji invaded Arlong yet? Was the Republic still alive? Was *Nezha*?

She took solace during the journey in the fact that she didn't see the Imperial Fleet on the Western Murui, but that meant little. The fleet might have already passed them. Daji might be marching on Arlong instead of sailing—the Militia had always been far more comfortable with ground warfare. Or the fleet could have taken a coastal route, could have destroyed Tsolin's forces before sailing south for the Red Cliffs.

Meanwhile their raft bobbled insignificantly down the Western Murui, drifting on the current because both of them were too exhausted to row.

Kitay had cobbled the raft together over two days using ropes and hunting knives the Ketreyids had left behind. It was a flimsy thing, tied together from the washed-up remains of the Republican Fleet, and just large enough for the two of them to lie down without touching.

Rafting was slow progress. They kept cautiously to the shores to avoid dangerous currents like the one that had swept them over the falls at Boyang. When they could, they drifted under tree cover to stay hidden.

They had to be careful with their food. They'd salvaged two weeks' worth of dried meat from the Ketreyids' rations, and occasionally they managed a catch of fish, but still their bones became ever more visible under their skin as the days went on. They lost both muscle mass and stamina, which made it even more important to avoid patrols. Even with Rin's reacquisition of her abilities, there was little chance they could win in any real skirmish if they couldn't even run a mile.

They spent their days sleeping to conserve energy. One of them would curl up on the raft while the other kept a lonely vigil by the spear attached to a shield which served as an oar and rudder. One afternoon Rin awoke to find Kitay etching diagrams into the raft with a knife.

She rubbed the sleep from her eyes. "What are you doing?"

Kitay rested his chin on his fist, tapping his knife against the raft. "I've been thinking about how best to weaponize you."

She sat up. "Weaponize?"

"Bad word?" He continued to scratch at the wood. "Optimize, then. You're like a lamp. I'm trying to figure out how to make you burn brighter."

Rin pointed to a wobbly carved circle. "Is that supposed to be me?"

"Yes. That represents your heat source. I'm trying to figure out exactly how your abilities work. Can you summon fire from anywhere?" Kitay pointed across the river. "For instance, could you make those reeds light up?"

"No." She knew the answer without trying it. "It has to come from me. *Within* me."

Yes, that was right. When she called the flame it felt like it was being tugged out from something inside her and through her.

"It comes out my hands and mouth," she said. "I can do it from other places too, but it feels easier that way."

"So *you're* the heat source?"

"Not so much the source. More like . . . the bridge. Or the gate, rather."

"The gate," he repeated, rubbing his chin. "Is that what the Gatekeeper's name means? Is he a conduit to every god?"

"I don't think so. Jiang . . . Jiang is an open door for certain creatures. You saw what the Sorqan Sira showed us. I think that he's only able to call those beasts. All the monsters of the Emperor's Menagerie, isn't that how the story goes? But the rest of us . . . it's hard to explain." Rin struggled to find the words. "The gods are in this world, but they're also still in their own, but while the Phoenix is in me it can *affect* the world—"

"But not in the way that it wants to," Kitay interrupted. "Or not always."

"Because I don't let it," she said. "It's a matter of control. If you've got enough presence of mind, you redirect the god's power for your purposes."

"And if not? What happens if you open the gate all the way?"

"Then you're lost. Then you become like Feylen."

"But what does that *mean*?" he pressed. "Do you have any control over your body left at all?"

"I'm not sure. There were a few times—just a few—I thought Feylen was inside, fighting for his body back. But you saw what happened."

Kitay nodded slowly. "Must be hard to win a mental battle with a god."

Rin thought of the shamans encased in stone within the Chuluu Korikh, trapped forever with their thoughts and regrets, comforted only by the knowledge that this was the least horrible alternative. She shuddered. "It's nearly impossible."

"So we'll just have to figure out how to beat the wind with fire." Kitay pushed his fingers through his overgrown bangs. "That's a pretty puzzle."

There wasn't much else to do on the raft, so they started experimenting with the fire. Day after day they pushed Rin's abilities to see how far she could go, how much control she could manage.

Up until then, Rin had been calling the fire on instinct. She'd been too busy fighting the Phoenix for control of her mind to ever bother examining the mechanics of the flame. But under Kitay's pointed questions and guided experiments, she figured out the exact parameters of her abilities.

She couldn't seize control of a fire that already existed. She also couldn't control fire that had left her body. She could give the fire a shape and make it erupt into the air, but the lingering flames would dissipate in seconds unless they found something to consume.

"What does it feel like for you?" she asked Kitay.

He paused for a moment before he answered. "It doesn't hurt. At least, not so much as the first time. It's more like—I'm aware of something. Something's moving in the back of my head, and I'm not sure what. I feel a rush, like the shot of adrenaline you get when you look over the edge of a cliff."

"And you're sure it doesn't hurt?"

"Promise."

"Bullshit," she said. "You make the same face every time I summon a flame any bigger than a campfire. It's like you're dying."

"Do I?" He blinked. "Just a reflex, I think. Don't worry about it."

He was lying to her. She loved that about him, that he'd care enough to lie to her. But she couldn't keep doing this to him. She couldn't hurt Kitay and not worry about it.

If she could, she'd be lost.

"You have to tell me when it's too much," she said.

"It's really not so bad."

"Cut the crap, Kitay—"

"It's the urges I feel more than anything," he said. "Not the pain. It makes me hungry. It makes me want more. Do you understand that feeling?"

"Of course," she said. "It's the Phoenix's most basic impulse. Fire devours."

"Devouring feels good." He pointed at an overhanging branch. "Try that shooty thing again."

Over the next few days she learned a number of different tricks. She could create balls of fire and hurl them at targets up to ten yards away. She could make shapes out of flame so intricate that she could have put on an entire puppet show with them. She could, by shoving her hands into the river, boil the water around them until steam misted the air and fish bubbled belly-up to the surface.

Most importantly, she could carve out protective spaces in the fire, up to ten feet from her own body, so that Kitay never burned even when everything around them did.

"What about mass destruction?" he asked after a few days of exploring minor tricks.

Rin stiffened. "What do you mean?"

His tone was carefully neutral. Purely academic. "What you did to the Federation, for instance—can we replicate that? How much flame can you summon?"

"That was different. I was on the island. In the temple. I'd . . . I'd just seen Altan die." She swallowed. "And I was angry. I was so angry."

In that moment, she'd been capable of an inhuman, vicious, and terrible rage. But she wasn't sure she could replicate that rage, because it had been sparked by Altan's death, and what she felt now when she thought about Altan wasn't fury, but grief.

Rage and grief were so different. Rage gave her the power to burn down countries. Grief only exhausted her.

"And if you went back to the temple?" Kitay pressed. "If you went back and summoned the Phoenix?"

"I'm not going back to that temple," Rin said immediately. She didn't know what it was, but Kitay's enthusiasm was making her uncomfortable—he was looking at her with the sort of intense curiosity that she had only ever seen in Shiro and Petra.

"But if you had to? If we only had one option, if everything would be lost if you didn't do it?"

"We're not putting that on the table."

"I'm not saying you have to. I'm saying we have to know if it's even an option. I'm saying you have to at least try."

"You want me to practice a genocidal event," she said slowly. "Just to be clear."

"Start small," he suggested. "Then get bigger. See how far you can go without the temple."

"That'll destroy everything in sight."

"We haven't seen signs of human life all day. If anyone lived here, they're long gone. This is empty land."

"What about wildlife?"

Kitay rolled his eyes. "You and I both know that wildlife is the least of your concerns. Stop hedging, Rin. Do it."

She nodded, put her palms out, and closed her eyes.

Flame wrapped her like a warm blanket. It felt good. It felt *too* good. She was burning without guilt or consequence. She was unrestrained power. She could feel herself tipping back into that state of ecstasy, could have lost herself in the dreamy oblivion of the wildfire that surged higher, faster, brighter, if she hadn't heard a high-pitched keening that wasn't coming from her.

She looked down. Kitay lay curled in a fetal position on the raft, hands clutching his mouth, trying to suppress his screams.

She reined the fire back in with difficulty.

Kitay made a choking noise and buried his head in his hands.

She dropped to her knees beside him. "Kitay—"

"I'm fine," he gasped. "Fine."

She tried to put her hands on him, but he pushed her away with a violence that shocked her.

"Just let me breathe." He shook his head. "It's all right, Rin. I'm not hurt. It's just—it's all in my head."

She could have slapped him. "You're supposed to tell me when it's too much."

"It wasn't too much." He sat up straight. "Try that again."

"*What?*"

"I couldn't get a good look at your blast radius just then," he said. "Try it again."

"Absolutely not," she snapped. "I don't care that you've got a death wish. I can't keep doing this to you."

"Then go right up to the edge," he insisted. "The point right before it hurts too much. Let's figure out what the limit is."

"That's insane."

"It's better than finding out on a battlefield. Please, Rin, we won't get a better chance to do this."

"What is wrong with you?" she demanded. "Why does this matter so much?"

"Because I need to know the full extent of what you can do," Kitay said. "Because if I'm strategizing for Arlong's defense then I need to know where to put you, and why. Because if I went through all of this for *you*, then the very least you can do is show me what maximum power looks like. If we've turned you back into a weapon, then you're going to be a damn good one. And stop panicking over me, Rin. I'm fine until I say I'm not."

So she called the flame again and again, pushing the limits every time, until the shores burned pitch-black around them. She kept going even while Kitay screamed because he'd ordered her not to stop unless he said so explicitly. She kept going until his eyes rolled back into his head and he went limp on the raft. And even then, when he revived seconds later, the first thing he said to her was: "Fifty yards."

When at last they reached the Red Cliffs, Rin saw with immense relief that the flag of the Republic still flew over Arlong.

So Vaisra was safe, and Daji was still a distant threat.

Their next challenge was to get back into the city without getting shot. Arlong, expecting a Militia assault, had hunkered down behind its defenses. The massive gates to the harbor past the Red Cliffs were locked. Crossbows were lined up against every flat surface overlooking the channel. Rin and Kitay could hardly march up to the city doors—any sudden, unexpected movement would get them stuck full of arrows. They discovered this when they saw a wild monkey wander too close to the walls and startle a line of trigger-happy archers.

They were so exhausted that they found this ridiculously funny. A month's worth of travel and their biggest concern was *friendly fire*.

Finally they decided to get some sentries' attention in the least threatening way possible. They hurled rocks at the sides of the cliff and waited while pinging noises echoed around the channel until at last a line of soldiers emerged on the cliffside, crossbows pointed down.

Rin and Kitay immediately put their hands up.

"Don't shoot, please," Kitay called.

The sentry captain leaned over the cliff wall. "What the hell do you think you're doing?"

"We're Republican soldiers back from Boyang," Kitay called, gesturing to their uniforms.

"Uniforms are cheap on corpses," said the captain.

Kitay pointed to Rin. "Not uniforms that fit her."

The captain looked unconvinced. "Back away or I'll shoot."

"I wouldn't," Rin called. "Or Vaisra will be asking why you've killed his Speerly."

The sentries hooted with laughter.

"Good one," said the captain.

Rin blinked. Did they not recognize her? Did they not know who she was?

"Maybe he's new," Kitay said.

"Can I hurt him?" she muttered.

"Just a little."

She tilted her head back and opened her mouth. Breathing fire was harder than shooting it from her hands because it gave her less directional control, but she liked the dramatic effect. A stream of fire shot into the air and unfurled itself into the shape of a dragon that hung for a moment in front of the awed soldiers, undulating grandly, before rushing the captain.

He was never in any real danger. Rin extinguished the flames as soon as they made contact. But he still screamed and fell backward as if he were being charged by a bear. When at last he resurfaced over the cliff wall, his face had turned bright pink, and smoke drifted up from his singed eyebrows.

"I should shoot you just for that," he said.

"Why don't you just tell Vaisra that the Speerly's back," Rin said. "And bring us something to eat."

Word of their return seemed to have spread instantly to the entire harbor. A massive crowd of soldiers and civilians alike surrounded them the moment they passed through the gates. Everyone had questions, and they shouted them from every direction so loudly that Rin could barely make out a word.

The questions she did understand were about soldiers still missing from Boyang. The people wanted to know if any others were still alive. If they were on their way back. Rin didn't have the heart to answer.

"Who dragged you out of hell?" Venka elbowed her way through the soldiers. She seized Rin by the arms, looked her up and down, and then wrinkled her pert nose. "You smell."

"Nice to see you, too," Rin said.

"No, really, it's *rank*. It's like you've taken a knife blade to my nose."

"Well, we haven't seen properly clean water in over a month, so—"

"So what's the story?" Venka interrupted. "Did you break out of prison? Take out an entire battalion? Swim the whole length back down the Murui?"

"We drank horse piss and got high," said Kitay.

"Come again?" Venka asked.

Rin was about to explain when she caught sight of Nezha pushing his way to the front of the crowd.

"Hello," she said.

He stopped just before her and stared, blinking rapidly as if he didn't know what he was looking at. His arms hung awkwardly at his sides, slightly uplifted, like he wasn't sure what to do with them.

"Can I?" he asked.

She stretched her arms toward him. He pulled her in against him so hard that she stiffened on instinct. Then she relaxed, because Nezha was so warm, so solid, and hugging him was such a wonderful feeling that she just wanted to bury her face into his uniform and stand there for a very long time.

"I can't believe it," Nezha murmured into her ear. "We thought for sure . . ."

She pressed her forehead against his chest. "Me too."

Her tears were falling thick and fast. The embrace had already stretched on much longer than it should have, and finally Nezha let her go, but he didn't take his arms off her shoulders.

Finally he spoke. "Where is Jinzha?"

"What do you mean?" Rin asked. "He didn't return with you?"

Nezha just shook his head, eyes wide, before he was pushed aside by two massive bodies.

"Rin!"

Before she could speak, Suni wrapped her in a tight hug, lifting her a good foot off the ground, and she had to pound frantically at his shoulder before he released her.

"All right." Ramsa reached up and frantically patted Suni's shoulder. "You're going to crush her."

"Sorry," Suni said, abashed. "We just thought . . ."

Rin couldn't help but grin even as she felt her ribs for bruises. "Yeah. Good to see you, too."

Baji grabbed her hand, pulled her in, and pounded her on the shoulder. "We knew you weren't dead. You're too spiteful to go that easy."

"How did you get back?" Rin asked.

"Feylen didn't just wreck our ships, he whipped up a storm that wrecked everything in the lake," Baji said. "He was aiming for the big ships, though; somehow a few of the skimmers held together.

About a quarter of us managed to get out of the maelstrom. I've no idea how we paddled back out to the river alive, but here we are."

Rin had an idea of how that had happened.

Ramsa's eyes flickered between her and Kitay. "Where are the twins?"

"That's a long story," Rin said.

"Not dead?" Baji asked.

"I . . . ah, it's complicated. Chaghan isn't. But Qara—" She paused, searching for the right words to say next, just as she saw a tall figure approaching from just over Baji's shoulder.

"Later," she said quietly.

Baji turned his head, saw who she was looking at, and immediately stepped aside. A hush fell over the soldiers, who parted ranks to let the Dragon Warlord through.

"You've returned," said Vaisra. He looked neither pleased nor displeased but somewhat impatient, as if he'd simply been expecting her.

Rin instinctively ducked her head. "Yes, sir."

"Good." Vaisra gestured toward the palace. "Go clean yourself up. I'll be in my office."

"Tell me everything that happened at Boyang," Vaisra said.

"Haven't they already told you?" Rin sat down opposite him. She smelled better than she had in weeks. She'd cut her oily, lice-ridden hair; scrubbed herself in cold water; and traded in her stained, pungent clothes for a fresh uniform.

A part of her had been hoping for a warmer welcome—a smile, a hand on her shoulder, at least some indication that Vaisra was glad she was back—but all he gave her was solemn expectation.

"I want your account," he said.

Rin considered pinning the blame on Jinzha's tactical decisions, but there was no point in antagonizing Vaisra by rubbing salt into an open wound. Besides, nothing Jinzha had done could have prevented what had happened once the battle began. He might as well have been fighting the ocean itself.

"The Empress has another shaman in her employ. His name is Feylen. He channels the Wind God. He used to be in the Cike, until that went sideways. He wrecked your fleet. Took him minutes."

"What do you mean, he *used* to be in the Cike?" Vaisra asked.

"He was put down," Rin said. "I mean, he went mad. A lot of shamans do. Altan let him back out of the Chuluu Korikh by accident—"

"By accident?"

"On purpose, but he was stupid to do it. And now I suppose Daji's found a way to lure him onto her side."

"How did she do that?" Vaisra demanded. "Money? Power? Can he be bought?"

"I don't think he cares about any of that. He's . . ." Rin paused, trying to figure out how to explain it to Vaisra. "He doesn't want what humans want. The god has . . . like with me, with the Phoenix—"

"He's lost his mind," Vaisra supplied.

She nodded. "I think Feylen needs to fulfill the god's fundamental nature. The Phoenix needs to consume. But the Wind God needs chaos. Daji's found some way to bend that to her will, but you won't be able to tempt him with anything humans might want."

"I see." Vaisra was silent for a moment. "And my son?"

Rin hesitated. Had they not told him about Jinzha? "Sir?"

"They didn't bring back a body," Vaisra said.

His mask cracked then. For the briefest moment, he looked like a father.

So he did know. He just wouldn't admit to himself that if Jinzha hadn't made his way back to Arlong with the rest of the fleet, then he was probably dead.

"I didn't see what happened to him," Rin said. "I'm sorry."

"There's no point speculating, then," Vaisra said coolly. His mask reassembled itself. "Let's move on. I assume you'll want to rejoin the infantry?"

"Not the infantry." Rin took a deep breath. "I want command of the Cike again. I want a seat at the strategy table. I want direct say in anything you want the Cike to do."

"And why's that?" Vaisra asked.

Because Chaghan can't be right about my being your dog. "Because I deserve it. I broke the Seal. I've gotten the fire back."

Vaisra raised an eyebrow. "Show me."

She turned an open palm toward the ceiling and summoned a fist-sized ball of fire. She made it run up and down the length of her arm, made it twist around her in the air before calling it back into her fingers. Even after a month of practice, she was still amazed at how easy it was, how delightfully natural it felt to control the flame the way she controlled her fingers. She let it take shapes—a rat, a rooster, an undulating orange dragon—and then she closed her fingers over her palm.

"Very nice," Vaisra said approvingly. The mask was gone now; he was finally smiling. She felt a warm rush of encouragement.

"So. Command?"

He waved a hand. "You're reinstated. I'll let the generals know. How did you manage this?"

"That's a long story." She paused, wondering where to start. "We, ah, ran into some Ketreyids."

He frowned. "Hinterlanders?"

"Don't call them that. They're Ketreyids." She gave him a quick account of what the Ketreyids had done, told him about the Sorqan Sira and the Trifecta.

She omitted the part about the anchor bond. Vaisra didn't need to know.

"Then what happened?" Vaisra asked. "Where are they?"

"They're gone. And the Sorqan Sira's dead."

"*What?*"

She told him about Augus. She knew Vaisra would be surprised, but she hadn't expected his reaction. The color drained from his face. His entire body tensed.

"Who else knows?" he demanded.

"Just Kitay. And a couple of Ketreyids, but they're not telling anyone."

"Tell no one this happened," he said quietly. "Not even my son. If the Hesperians find out, our lives are forfeit."

"It was their fault to begin with," she muttered.

"Shut up." He slammed a hand on the table. She flinched back, startled.

"How could you be so stupid?" he demanded. "You should have brought them back safe, that would have ingratiated us to General Tarcquet—"

"Tarcquet made it back?" she interrupted.

"Yes, and many of the Gray Company are with him. They escaped south in one of the skimmers. They are deeply unhappy with our naval capabilities and are *this* close to pulling out of the continent, which is a thought I assume never crossed your mind when you decided to murder one of them."

"Are you joking? They were trying to kill us—"

"So you should have incapacitated him or fled. The Gray Company is untouchable. You couldn't have picked a worse Hesperian to kill."

"This isn't my fault," Rin insisted. "He'd gone mad, he was waving an arquebus around—"

"*Listen to me*," Vaisra said. "You are walking a very fine line right now. The Hesperians are not just upset, they are terrified. They thought you a curiosity before. Then they saw what happened at Boyang. Now they are convinced that each and every one of you is a mindless agent of Chaos who could bring about the end of the world. They're going to hunt down every shaman in this empire and put them in cages if they can. The only reason why they haven't touched *you* is because you volunteered, and they know you'll cooperate. Do you understand now?"

Fear struck Rin. "Then Suni and Baji—"

"—are safe," Vaisra said. "The Hesperians don't know about them. And they'd better not find out, because then Tarcquet will know we've lied to him. Your job is to keep your head down, to cooperate, and to draw the least possible attention to yourself. You have a reprieve for now. Sister Petra has agreed to postpone your meetings until, one way or another, this war has concluded. So behave yourself. Do not give them further reason for irritation. Otherwise we are all lost."

Then Rin understood.

Vaisra wasn't angry at her. This wasn't about her at all. No, Vaisra was frustrated. He'd been frustrated for months, playing an impossible game with the Hesperians where they kept changing the rules.

She dared to ask. "They're never bringing their ships, are they?"

He sighed. "We don't know."

"They still won't give you a straight answer? All this because they're still deciding?"

"Tarcquet claims they haven't finished their evaluation," Vaisra said. "I admit I do not understand their standards. When I ask, they utter idiotic vagaries. They want signs of rational sentience. Proof of the ability to self-govern."

"But that's ridiculous. If they'd just tell us what they wanted—"

"Ah, but then that would be cheating." Vaisra's lip curled. "They need proof that we've independently attained civilized society."

"But that's a paradox. We can't achieve that unless they help."

He looked exhausted. "I know."

"Then that's fucked." She threw her hands up in the air. "This is all just a spectacle to them. They're never going to come."

"Maybe." Vaisra looked decades older then, lined and weary. Rin imagined how Petra might sketch him in her book. *Nikara man, middle-aged. Strong build. Reasonable intelligence. Inferior.* "But we are the weaker party. We have no choice but to play their game. That's how power works."

She found Nezha waiting for her outside the palace gates.

"Hi," she said tentatively. She looked him up and down, trying to get a read on his expression, but he was just as inscrutable as his father.

"Hello," he said back.

She tried a smile. He didn't return it. For a minute they just stood there staring at each other. Rin was torn between running into his arms again and simply running away. She still didn't know where she stood with him. The last time they'd spoken—really spoken—she'd been sure that he would hate her forever.

"Can we talk?" he asked finally.

"We *are* talking."

He shook his head. "Alone. In private. Not here."

"Fine," she said, and followed him along the canal to the edge of a pier, where the waves were loud enough to drown their voices out from any curious eavesdroppers.

"I owe you an explanation," he said at last.

She leaned against the railing. "Go on."

"I'm not a shaman."

She threw her hands up. "Oh, don't fuck with me—"

"I'm *not*," he insisted. "I know I can do things. I mean, I know I'm linked to a god, and I can—sort of—call it, sometimes . . ."

"That's what shamanism *is*."

"You're not listening to me. Whatever I am, it's not what *you* are. My mind's not my own—my body belongs to some—some *thing* . . ."

"That's just it, Nezha. That's how it is for all of us. And I know it hurts, and I know it's hard, but—"

"You're still not listening," he snapped. "It's no sacrifice for you. You and your god want the same damn thing. But I didn't *ask* for this—"

She raised her eyebrows. "Well, it doesn't just happen by *accident*. You had to want it first. You had to ask the god."

"But I didn't. I never asked, and I've never wanted it." The way Nezha said it made her fall quiet. He sounded like he was about to cry.

He took a deep breath, and when he spoke again, his voice was so quiet she had to step closer to hear him. "Back at Boyang, you called me a coward."

"Look, all I meant was that—"

"I'm going to tell you a story," he interrupted. He was trembling. Why was he trembling? "I want you to just listen. And I want you to believe me. *Please.*"

She crossed her arms. "Fine."

Nezha blinked hard and stared out over the water. "I told you once that I had another brother. His name was Mingzha."

When he didn't continue, Rin asked, "What was he like?"

"Hilarious," Nezha said. "Chubby, loud, and incredible. He was everyone's favorite. He was so full of energy, he *glowed.* My mother had miscarried twice before she gave birth to him, but Mingzha was perfect. He was never sick. My mother adored him. She was hugging him constantly. She dressed him up in so many golden bracelets and anklets that he jangled when he walked." He shuddered. "She should have known better. Dragons like gold."

"Dragons," Rin repeated.

"You said you'd listen."

"Sorry."

Nezha was sickly pale. His skin was almost translucent; Rin could see blue veins under his jaw, crisscrossing with his scars.

"My siblings and I spent our childhood playing by the river," he said. "There's a grotto about a mile out from the entrance to this channel, this underwater crystal cave that the servants liked telling stories about, but Father had forbidden us to enter it. So of course all we ever wanted to do was explore it.

"My mother took sick one night when Mingzha was six. During that time my father had been called to Sinegard on the Empress's orders, so the servants weren't as concerned with watching us as they might have been. Jinzha was at the Academy. Muzha was abroad. So the responsibility for watching Mingzha fell to me."

Nezha's voice cracked. His eyes looked hollow, tortured. Rin didn't want to hear any more. She had a sickening suspicion of where this story was headed, and she didn't want it spoken out loud, because that would make it true.

She wanted to tell him it was all right, he didn't have to tell her, they never had to speak about this again, but Nezha was talking faster and faster, like he was afraid the words would be buried inside him if he didn't spit them out now.

"Mingzha wanted to—no, *I* wanted to explore that grotto. It was my idea to begin with. I put it in Mingzha's head. It was my fault. He didn't know any better."

Rin reached for his arm. "Nezha, you don't have to—"

He shoved her away. "Can you please shut up and just listen *for once?*"

She fell silent.

"He was the most beautiful thing I'd ever seen," he whispered. "That's what scares me. They say the House of Yin is beautiful. But that's because dragons like beautiful things, because dragons *are* beautiful and they create beauty. When he emerged from the cave, all I could think about was how bright his scales were, how lovely his form, how magnificent."

But they're not real, Rin thought desperately. *Dragons are just stories.*

Weren't they?

Even if she didn't believe in Nezha's story, she believed in his pain. It was written all over his face.

Something had happened all those years ago. She just didn't know what.

"So beautiful," Nezha murmured, even as his knuckles whitened. "I couldn't stop staring.

"Then he ate my brother. Devoured him in seconds. Have you watched a wild animal eat before? It's not clean. It's brutal. Mingzha didn't even have time to scream. One moment he was there, clutching at my leg, and the next moment he was a mess of blood and gore and shining bones, and then there was nothing.

"But the dragon spared me. He said he had something better for me." Nezha swallowed. "He said he was going to give me a gift. And then he claimed me for his own."

"I'm so sorry," Rin said, because she didn't know what else to say.

Nezha didn't seem to have even heard. "My mother wishes I'd died that day. *I* wish I'd died. I wish it had been me. But it's selfish even to wish I were dead—because if I had died, then Mingzha would have lived, and the Dragon Lord would have cursed him like he cursed me, he would have *touched* him like he touched me."

She didn't dare ask what that meant.

"I'm going to show you something," he said.

She was too stunned to say anything. She could only watch, aghast, as he undid the clasps of his tunic with trembling fingers.

He yanked it down and turned around. "Do you see this?"

It was his tattoo—an image of a dragon in blue and silver. She'd seen it before, but he wouldn't remember.

She touched her index finger to the dragon's head, wondering. Was this tattoo the reason Nezha had always healed so quickly? He seemed able to survive anything—blunt trauma, poisonous gas, drowning.

But at what price?

"You said he claimed you for his own," she said softly. "What does that mean?"

"It means it *hurts*," he said. "Every moment that I'm not with him. It feels like anchors digging into my body; hooks trying to drag me back into the water."

The mark didn't look like a scar that was almost ten years old. It looked freshly inflicted; his skin shone an angry crimson. The glint of sunlight made the dragon seem as if it was writhing over Nezha's muscles, pressing itself deeper and deeper into his raw skin.

"And if you went back to him?" she asked. "What would happen to you?"

"I'd become part of his collection," he said. "He'd do what he wanted to me, satisfy himself, and I'd never leave. I'd be trapped, because I don't think I can die. I've tried. I've cut my wrists, but I never bleed out before my wounds stitch themselves back together. I've jumped off the Red Cliffs, and sometimes the pain is enough for me to think I've managed it this time, but I always wake up. I think the Dragon is keeping me alive. At least until I return to him.

"The first time I saw that grotto, there were faces all along the cave floor. It took me a while to realize I was fated to become one of them."

Rin withdrew her finger, suppressing a shudder.

"So now you know," Nezha said. He yanked his shirt back on. His voice hardened. "You're disgusted—don't say you aren't, I can see it on your face. I don't care. But don't you tell anyone what I've just told you, and don't you *ever* fucking dare call me a coward to my face."

Rin knew what she should have done. She should have said she was sorry. She should have acknowledged his pain, should have begged his forgiveness.

But the way he *said* it—his long-suffering martyr's voice, like she had no right to question him, like he was doing her a favor by telling her . . . that infuriated her.

"I'm not disgusted by that," she said.

"No?"

"I'm disgusted by you." She fought to keep her voice level. "You're acting like it's a death sentence, but it's not. It's also a source of power. It's kept you alive."

"It's a fucking abomination," he said.

"Am *I* an abomination?"

"No, but—"

"So what, it's fine for me to call the gods, but you're too good for it? You can't sully yourself?"

"That's not what I meant—"

"Well, that's the implication."

"It's different for you, you *chose* that—"

"You think that makes it hurt any less?" She was shouting now. "I thought I was going mad. For the longest time I didn't know which thoughts were my own and which thoughts were the Phoenix's. And it fucking *hurt*, Nezha, so don't tell me I don't know anything about that. There were days I wanted to die, too, but we're not *allowed* to die, we're too powerful. Your father said it himself. When you have this much power and this much is at stake you don't fucking *run* from it."

He looked furious. "You think I'm running?"

"All I know is that hundreds of soldiers are dead at the bottom of Lake Boyang, and you might have done something to prevent it."

"Don't you dare pin that on me," he hissed. "I shouldn't have this power. Neither of us should. We shouldn't exist, we're abominations, and we'd be better off dead."

"But we *do* exist. By that logic it's a good thing the Speerlies were killed."

"Maybe the Speerlies *should* have been killed. Maybe every shaman in the Empire should die. Maybe my mother's right— maybe we should get rid of you freaks, and get rid of the Hinterlanders, too, while we're at it."

She stared at him in disbelief. This wasn't Nezha. Nezha—*her* Nezha—couldn't possibly be saying this to her. She was so sure that he would realize he'd crossed the line, would back down and apologize, that she was stunned when his expression only hardened.

"Don't tell me Altan wasn't better off dead," he said.

All shreds of pity she'd felt for him fled.

She pulled her shirt up. "Look at me."

Immediately Nezha averted his eyes, but she grabbed at his chin and forced him to look at her sternum, down at the handprint scorched into her skin.

"You're not the only one with scars," she said.

Nezha wrenched himself from her grasp. "We are not the same."

"Yes, we are." She yanked her shirt back down. Her eyes blurred with tears. "The only difference between us is that I can suffer pain, and you're still a fucking coward."

She couldn't remember how they parted, only that one moment they were glaring at each other and the next she was stumbling back to the barracks in a daze, alone.

She wanted to run after Nezha and say she was sorry, and she also wanted never to see him again.

Dimly she understood that something had broken irreparably between them. They'd fought before. They'd spent their first three years together fighting. But this wasn't like those childish school-yard squabbles.

They weren't coming back from this.

But what was she supposed to do? Apologize? She had too much pride to grovel. She was so sure she was right. Yes, Nezha had been hurt, but hadn't they all been hurt? She'd been through Golyn Niis. She'd been tortured on a lab table. She'd watched Altan die.

Nezha's particular tragedy wasn't worse because it had happened when he was a child. It wasn't worse because he was too scared to confront it.

She'd been through hell, and she was stronger for it. It wasn't her fault that he was too pathetic to do the same.

She found the Cike sitting in a circle on the barracks floor. Baji and Ramsa were playing dice while Suni watched from a top bunk to make sure Ramsa didn't cheat, as he always did.

"Oh, dear," Baji said as she approached. "Who made you cry?"

"Nezha," she mumbled. "I don't want to talk about it."

Ramsa clicked his tongue. "Ah, boy trouble."

She sat down in between them. "Shut up."

"Want me to do something about it? Put a missile in his toilet?"

She managed a smile. "Please don't."

"Suit yourself," he said.

Baji tossed the dice on the floor. "So what happened up north? Where's Chaghan?"

"Chaghan won't be with us for a while," she said. She took a deep breath and willed herself to push Nezha to the back of her mind. *Forget him. Focus on something else.* That was easy enough—she had so much to tell the Cike.

Over the next half hour she spoke to them about the Ketreyids, about Augus, and about what had happened in the forest.

They were predictably furious.

"So Chaghan was spying on us the entire time?" Baji demanded. "That lying fuck."

"I always hated him," Ramsa said. "Always prancing around with his mysterious mutters. Figures he'd been up to something."

"Can you really be surprised, though?" Suni, to Rin's shock, seemed the least bothered. "You had to know they had some other agenda. What else would Hinterlanders be doing in the Cike?"

"Don't call them Hinterlanders," Rin said automatically.

Ramsa ignored her. "So what were the Hinterlanders going to do if Chaghan decided we were getting too dangerous?"

"Kill you, probably," Baji said. "Pity they went back north, though. Would have been nice to have someone deal with Feylen. It'll be a struggle."

"A struggle?" Ramsa repeated. He laughed weakly. "You think last time we tried to put him down was a *struggle*?"

"What happened last time?" Rin asked.

"Tyr and Trengsin lured him into a small cave and stabbed so many knives through his body that even if he could have shamanized, it wouldn't have done a lick of good," Baji said. "It was kind of funny, really. When they brought him back out he looked like a pincushion."

"And Tyr was all right with that?" Rin asked.

"What do you think?" Baji asked. "Of course not. But that was his job. You can't command the Cike if you don't have the stomach to cull."

A cascade of footsteps sounded outside the room. Rin peered around the door to see a line of soldiers marching out, fully equipped with shields and halberds. "Where are they all going? I thought the Militia hadn't moved south yet."

"It's refugee patrol," Baji said.

She blinked. "Refugee patrol?"

"You didn't see all them coming in?" Ramsa asked. "They were pretty hard to miss."

"We came in through the Red Cliffs," Rin said. "I haven't seen anything but the palace. What do you mean, refugees?"

Ramsa exchanged an uncomfortable look with Baji. "You missed a lot while you were gone, I think."

Rin didn't like what that implied. She stood up. "Take me there."

"Our patrol shift isn't until tomorrow morning," Ramsa said.

"I don't care."

"But they're fussy about that," Ramsa insisted. "Security is tight on the refugee border, they're not going to let us through."

"I'm the Speerly," Rin said. "Do you think I give a shit?"

"Fine." Baji hauled himself to his feet. "I'll take you. But you're not going to like it."

CHAPTER 26

"Makes the barracks look nice, huh?" Ramsa asked.

Rin didn't know what to say.

The refugee district was an ocean of people crammed into endless rows of tents stretching toward the valley. The crowds had been kept out of the city proper, hemmed in behind hastily constructed barriers of shipping planks and driftwood.

It looked as if a giant had drawn a line in the sand with one finger and pushed everyone to one side. Republican soldiers wielding halberds paced back and forth in front of the barrier, though Rin wasn't sure who they were guarding—the refugees or the citizens.

"The refugees aren't allowed past that barrier," Baji explained. "The, uh, citizens didn't want them crowding the streets."

"What happens if they cross?" Rin asked.

"Nothing too terrible. Guards toss them back to the other side. It happened more often at the beginning, but a few beatings taught everyone their lesson."

They walked a few more paces. A horrible stench hit Rin's nose—the smell of too many unwashed bodies packed together for far too long. "How long have they been there?"

"At least a month," Baji said. "I'm told they started flooding in as soon as we moved on Rat Province, but it only got worse once we came back."

Rin could not believe that anyone had been living in these camps for that long. She saw clouds of flies everywhere she looked. The buzzing was unbearable.

"They're still trickling in," Ramsa said. "They come in waves, usually at night. They keep trying to sneak past the borders."

"And they're all from Hare and Rat Provinces?" she asked.

"What are you talking about? These are *southern* refugees."

She blinked at him. "I thought the Militia hadn't moved south."

Ramsa exchanged a glance with Baji. "They're not fleeing the Militia. They're fleeing the Federation."

"*What?*"

Baji scratched the back of his head. "Well, yes. It's not like the Mugenese soldiers all just laid down their weapons."

"I know, but I thought . . ." Rin trailed off. She felt dizzy. She'd known Federation troops remained on the mainland, but she'd thought they were contained to isolated units. Rogue soldiers, scattered squadrons. Roving mercenaries, forming predatory coalitions with provincial cities if they were large enough, but not enough to displace the entire south.

"How many are there?" she asked.

"Enough," Baji said. "Enough that they constitute an entirely separate army. They're fighting for the Militia, Rin. We don't know how; we don't know what deal she brokered with them. But soon enough we'll be fighting a war on two fronts, not one."

"Which regions?" she demanded.

"They're everywhere." Ramsa listed the provinces off on his fingers. "Monkey. Snake. Rooster."

Rin flinched. *Rooster?*

"Are you all right?" Ramsa asked.

But she was already running.

She knew immediately these were her people. She knew them by their tawny skin that was almost as dark as hers. She knew them by the way they talked—the soft country drawl that made her feel nostalgic and uncomfortable at the same time.

That was the tongue she had grown up speaking—the flat, rustic dialect that she couldn't speak without cringing now, because she'd spent years at school beating it out of herself.

She hadn't heard anyone speak the Rooster dialect in so long.

She thought, stupidly, that they might recognize her. But the Rooster refugees shrank away when they saw her. Their faces grew closed and sullen when she met their eyes. They crawled back into their tents if she approached.

It took her a moment to realize that they weren't afraid of her, they were afraid of her uniform.

They were afraid of Republican soldiers.

"You." Rin pointed to a woman about her height. "Do you have a spare set of clothes?"

The woman blinked at her, uncomprehending.

Rin tried again, slipping clumsily into her old dialect like it was an ill-fitting pair of shoes. "Do you have another, uh, shirt? Pants?"

The woman gave a terrified nod.

"Give them to me."

The woman crawled into her tent. She reappeared with a bundle of clothing—a faded blouse that might have once been dyed with a poppy flower pattern, and wide slacks with deep pockets.

Rin felt a sharp pang in her chest as she held the blouse out in front of her. She hadn't seen clothes like this in a long time. They were made for fieldworkers. Even the poor of Sinegard would have laughed at them.

Stripping off her Republican uniform worked. The Roosters stopped avoiding her when they saw her. Instead, she became effectively invisible as she navigated through the sea of tightly packed bodies. She shouted to get attention as she moved down the rows of tents.

"Tutor Feyrik! I'm looking for a Tutor Feyrik! Has anyone seen him?"

Responses came in reluctant whispers and indifferent mutters. *No. No. Leave us alone. No.* These refugees were so used to hearing desperate cries for lost ones that they'd closed their ears to them. Someone knew a Tutor Fu, but he wasn't from Tikany. Someone else knew a Feyrik, but he was a cobbler, not a teacher. Rin found it pointless trying to describe him; there were hundreds of men who could have fit his description—with every row she passed she saw old men with gray beards who turned out not to be Tutor Feyrik after all.

She pushed down a swell of despair. It had been stupid to hope in the first place. She'd known she'd never see him again; she'd resigned herself to that fact long ago.

But she couldn't help it. She still had to try.

She tried broadening her search. "Is anyone here from Tikany?"

Blank looks. She moved faster and faster through the camp, breaking into a run. "Tikany? Please? Anyone?"

Then at last she heard one voice through the crowd—one that was laced not with casual indifference but with sheer disbelief.

"Rin?"

She stumbled to a halt. When she turned around she saw a spindly boy, no more than fourteen, with a mop of brown hair and large, downward-sloping eyes. He stood with a sodden shirt dangling from one hand and a bandage clutched in the other.

"Kesegi?"

He nodded wordlessly.

Then she was sixteen years old again herself, crying as she held him, rocking him so hard they almost fell to the dirt. He hugged her back, wrapping his long and scrawny limbs all the way around her like he used to.

When had he gotten so tall? Rin marveled at the change. Once, he'd barely come up to her waist. Now he was taller than she by about an inch. But the rest of him was far too skinny, close to starved; he looked like he'd been stretched more than he had grown.

"Where are the others?" she asked.

"Mother's here with me. Father's dead."

"The Federation . . . ?"

"No. It was the opium in the end." He gave a false laugh. "Funny, really. He heard they were coming, and he ate an entire pan of nuggets. Mother found him just as we were packing up to leave. He'd been dead for hours." He gave her an awkward smile. A *smile*. He'd lost his father, and he was trying to make her feel better about it. "We just thought he was sleeping."

"I'm sorry," she said. Her voice came out flat. She couldn't help it. Her relationship with Uncle Fang had been one between master and servant, and she couldn't conjure up anything that remotely resembled grief.

"Tutor Feyrik?" she asked.

Kesegi shook his head. "I don't know. I saw him in the crowd when we left, I think, but I haven't seen him since."

His voice cracked when he spoke. She realized that he was trying to imitate a deeper voice than he possessed. He stood up overly straight, too, to appear taller than he was. He was trying to pass himself off as an adult.

"So you've come back."

Rin's blood froze. She'd been walking blindly without a destination, assuming Kesegi had been doing the same, but of course they'd been walking back to his tent.

Kesegi stopped. "Mother. Look who I found."

Auntie Fang gave Rin a thin smile. "Well, look at that. It's the war hero. You've grown."

Rin wouldn't have recognized her if Kesegi hadn't introduced her. Auntie Fang looked twenty years older, with the complexion of a wrinkled walnut. She had always been so red-faced, perpetually furious, burdened with a foster child she didn't want and a husband addicted to opium. She used to terrify Rin. But now she seemed shriveled dry, as if the fight had been drained from her completely.

"Come to gloat?" Auntie Fang asked. "Go on, look. There's not much to see."

"*Gloat?*" Rin repeated, baffled. "No, I . . ."

"Then what is it?" Auntie Fang asked. "Well, don't just *stand* there."

How was it that even now Auntie Fang could still make her feel so stupid and worthless? Under her withering glare Rin felt like a little girl again, hiding in the shed to avoid a beating.

"I didn't know you were here," she managed. "I just—I wanted to see if—"

"If we were still alive?" Auntie Fang put bony hands on narrow hips. "Well, here we are. No thanks to you soldiers—no, you were too busy drowning up north. It's Vaisra's fault we're here at all."

"Watch your tone," Rin snapped.

It shocked her when Auntie Fang cringed backward like she was expecting to be hit.

"Oh, I didn't mean that." Auntie Fang adopted a wheedling, wide-eyed expression that looked grotesque on her leathery face. "The hunger's just getting to me. Can't you get us some food, Rin? You're a soldier, I bet they've even made you a *commander*, you're so important, surely you could call in some favors."

"They're not feeding you?" Rin asked.

Auntie Fang laughed. "Not unless you're talking about the Lady of Arlong walking around handing out tiny bowls of rice to the skinniest children she can find while the blue-eyed devils follow her around to document how wonderful she is."

"We don't get anything," Kesegi said. "Not clothes, not blankets, not medicine. Most of us forage for our own food—we were eating fish for a while, but they'd all been poisoned with something, and we got sick. They didn't warn us about that."

Rin found that impossible to believe. "They haven't opened any kitchens for you?"

"They have, but those kitchens feed perhaps a hundred mouths before they close." Kesegi shrugged his bony shoulders. "Look around. Someone starves to death every day in this camp. Can't you see?"

"But I thought—surely, Vaisra would—"

"Vaisra?" Auntie Fang snorted. "You're on a first-name basis, are you?"

"No—I mean, yes, but—"

"Then you can talk to him!" Auntie Fang's beady eyes glittered. "Tell him we're starving. If he can't feed all of us, just have them deliver food to me and Kesegi. We won't tell anyone."

"But that's not how it works," Rin stammered. "I mean—I can't just—"

"Do it, you ungrateful cunt," Auntie Fang snarled. "You owe us."

"I *owe* you?" Rin repeated in disbelief.

"I took you into our home. I raised you for sixteen years."

"You would have sold me into marriage!"

"And then you would have had a better life than any of us." Auntie Fang pointed a skinny, accusing finger at Rin's chest. "You would never have lacked for anything. All you had to do was spread your legs every once in a while, and you would have had anything you wanted to eat, anything you wanted to wear. But that wasn't enough for you—*you* wanted to be special, to be important, to run off to Sinegard and join the Militia on its merry adventures."

"You think this war has been *fun* for me?" Rin shouted. "I watched my friends die! *I* almost died!"

"We've all nearly died," Auntie Fang scoffed. "Please. You're not special."

"You can't talk to me like that," Rin said.

"Oh, I know." Auntie Fang swept into a low bow. "You're so *important*. So *respected*. Do you want us to grovel at your feet, is that it? Heard your old bitch of an aunt was in the camps, so you couldn't pass up the chance to rub it in her face?"

"Mother, stop," Kesegi said quietly.

"That's not why I came," Rin said.

Auntie Fang's mouth twisted into a sneer. "Then why *did* you come?"

Rin didn't have an answer for her.

She didn't know what she'd expected to find. Not home, not belonging, not Tutor Feyrik—and not this.

This was a mistake. She shouldn't have come at all. She'd cut her ties to Tikany a long time ago. She should have kept it that way.

She backed away quickly, shaking her head. "I'm sorry," she tried to say, but the words stuck in her throat.

She couldn't look either of them in the eyes. She didn't want to be here anymore, she didn't want to feel like this anymore. She backed out onto the main path and broke into a quick walk. She wanted to run away, but couldn't out of pride.

"Rin!" Kesegi shouted. He dashed out after her. "Wait."

She halted in her tracks. *Please say something to make me stay. Please.*

"Yes?"

"If you can't get us food, can you ask them for some blankets?" he asked. "Just one? It gets so cold at night."

She forced herself to smile. "Of course."

Over the next week a torrent of people poured into Arlong on foot, in rickety carts, or on rafts hastily constructed of anything that could float. The river became a slow-moving eddy of bodies packed against each other so tightly that the famous blue waters of the Dragon Province disappeared under the weight of human desperation.

Republican soldiers checked the new arrivals for weapons and valuables before corralling them in neat lines to whichever quarters of the refugee district still had space.

The refugees met with very little kindness. Republican soldiers, Dragons especially, were terribly condescending, shouting at the southerners when they couldn't understand the rapid Arlong dialect.

Rin spent hours each day walking the docks with Venka. She was glad to have escaped processing duty, which involved standing guard over miserable lines while clerks marked the refugees' arrivals and issued them temporary residence papers. That was probably more important than what she and Venka were doing, which was fishing out the refuse from the segments of the Murui near the refugee chokepoints, but Rin couldn't bear to be around the large crowds of brown skin and accusing eyes.

"We're going to have to cut them off at some point," Venka remarked as she lifted an empty jug from the water. "They can't possibly all fit here."

"Only because the refugee district is tiny," Rin said. "If they opened up the city barriers, or if they funneled them into the mountainside, there would be plenty of space."

"Plenty of *space*, maybe. But we haven't got enough clothes, blankets, medicine, grain, or anything else."

"Up until now the southerners were producing the grain." Rin felt obligated to point that out.

"And now they've run from home, so no one is producing food," Venka said. "Doesn't really help us. Hey, what's this?"

She reached gingerly into the water and drew a barrel out onto the dock. She set it on the ground. Out tumbled what at first looked like a soggy bundle of clothing. "Gross."

"What is it?" Rin stepped closer to get a better look and immediately regretted it.

"It's dead, look." Venka held the baby out to show Rin the infant's sickly yellow skin, the bumpy evidence of relentless mosquito attacks, and the red rashes that covered half its body. Venka slapped its cheeks. No response. She held it over the river as if to throw it back in.

The infant started to whimper.

An ugly expression twisted across Venka's face. She looked so suddenly, murderously hateful that Rin was sure she was about to hurl the infant headfirst into the harbor.

"Give it to me," Rin said quickly. She pulled the infant from Venka's arms. A sour smell hit her nose. She gagged so hard she nearly dropped the infant, but got a grip on herself.

The baby was swaddled in clothes large enough to fit an adult. That meant someone had loved it. They wouldn't have parted with the clothes otherwise—it was now the dead of winter, and even in the warm south, the nights got cold enough that refugees traveling without shelter could easily freeze to death.

Someone had wanted this baby to survive. Rin owed it a fighting chance.

She strode hastily to the end of the dock and handed the bundle off to the first soldier she saw. "Here."

The soldier stumbled under the sudden weight. "What am I supposed to do with this?"

"I don't know, just see to it that it's cared for," Rin said. "Take it to the infirmary, if they'll let you."

The soldier gripped the infant tightly in his arms and set off at a run. Rin returned to the river and resumed dragging her spear halfheartedly through the water.

She wanted very badly to smoke. She couldn't get the taste of corpses out of her mouth.

Venka broke the silence first. "What are you looking at me like that for?"

She looked defensive. Furious. But that was Venka's default reaction to everything; she'd rather die than admit vulnerability. Rin suspected Venka was thinking about the child that she'd lost, and she wasn't sure what to say, only that she felt terribly sorry for her.

"You knew it was alive," Rin said finally.

"Yes," Venka snapped. "So what?"

"And you were going to kill it."

Venka swallowed hard and jabbed her spear back into the water. "That thing doesn't have a future. I was doing it a favor."

Wartime Arlong was an ugly thing. Despair settled over the capital like a shroud as the threat of armies closing in from both the north and the south grew closer every day.

Food was strictly rationed, even for citizens of Dragon Province. Every man, woman, and child who wasn't in the Republican Army was conscripted for labor. Most were sent to work in the forges or the shipyards. Even small children were put to task cutting linen strips for the infirmary.

Sympathy was the greatest scarcity. The southern refugees, crammed behind their barrier, were uniformly despised by soldiers and civilians alike. Food and supplies were offered begrudgingly, if at all. Rin discovered that if soldiers weren't positioned to guard the supply deliveries, they would never reach the camps.

The refugees latched on to any potentially sympathetic advocates they could. Once word of Rin's connection to the Fangs spread, she became an involuntarily appointed, unofficial champion of refugee interests in Arlong. Every time she was near the district she was accosted by refugees, all pleading for a thousand different things that she couldn't obtain—more food, more medicine, more materials for cooking fires and tents.

She hated the position they'd thrown her into because it led only to frustration from both sides. The Republican leadership grew irritated because she kept making impossible requests for basic human necessities, and the refugees started resenting her because she could never deliver.

"It doesn't make sense," Rin complained bitterly to Kitay. "Vaisra's the one who always said we had to treat prisoners well. And this is how we treat our own people?"

"It's because the refugees have no strategic advantage to them whatsoever, unless you count the mild inconvenience that their stacked-up bodies might present Daji's army," Kitay said. "If I may be blunt."

"Fuck off," she said.

"I'm just reporting what they're all thinking. Don't kill the messenger."

Rin should have been angrier, but she understood, too, just how pervasive that mind-set was. To most Dragons, the southerners barely registered as Nikara. She could see through a northerner's eyes the stereotypical Rooster—a cross-eyed, buck-toothed, swarthy idiot speaking a garbled tongue.

It shamed and embarrassed her terribly, because she used to be exactly like that.

She'd tried to erase those parts of herself long ago. At fourteen she'd been lucky enough to study under a tutor who spoke near-standard Sinegardian. And she'd gone to Sinegard young enough that her bad habits were quickly and brutally knocked out of her. She'd adapted to fit in. She'd erased her identity to survive.

And it humiliated her that the southerners were now seeking her out, that they had the audacity to wander close to her, because they made her more like them by sheer proximity.

She'd long since tried to kill her association with Rooster Province, a place that had given her few happy memories. She'd almost succeeded. But the refugees wouldn't let her forget.

Every time she came close to the camps, she saw angry, accusing stares. They all knew who she was now. They made a point of letting her know.

They'd stopped shouting invectives at her. They'd long since passed the point of rage; now they lived in resentful despair. But she could read their silent faces so clearly.

You're one of us, they said. *You were supposed to protect us. You've failed.*

Three weeks after Rin's return to Arlong, the Empress sent a direct message to the Republic.

About a mile from the Red Cliffs, the Dragon Province border patrol had captured a man who claimed to have been sent from the capital. The messenger carried only an ornamented bamboo basket across his back and a small Imperial seal to verify his identity.

The messenger insisted he would not speak unless Vaisra received him in the throne room with the full audience of his generals, the Warlords, and General Tarcquet. Eriden's guards stripped him down and checked his clothes and baskets for explosives or poisonous gas, but found nothing.

"Just dumplings," the messenger said cheerfully.

Reluctantly they let him through.

"I bear a message from the Empress Su Daji," he announced to the room. His lower lip flopped grotesquely when he spoke. It seemed infected with something; the left side was thick with red, pus-filled blisters. His words were barely understandable through his thick Rat accent.

Rin's eyes narrowed as she watched him approach the throne. He wasn't a Sinegardian diplomat or a Militia representative. He didn't carry himself like a court official. He had to be a common soldier, if even that. But why would Daji leave diplomacy up to someone who could barely even speak?

Unless the messenger wasn't here for any real negotiations. Unless Daji didn't need someone who could think quickly or speak smoothly. Unless Daji only wanted someone who would take the most delight in antagonizing Vaisra. Someone who had a grudge against the Republic and wouldn't mind dying for it.

Which meant this was not a truce. This was a one-sided message.

Rin tensed. There was no way the messenger could harm Vaisra, not with the ranks of Eriden's men blocking his way to the throne. But still she gripped her trident tight, eyes tracking the man's every movement.

"Speak your piece," Vaisra ordered.

The messenger grinned broadly. "I come to deliver tidings of Yin Jinzha."

Lady Saikhara stood up. Rin could see her trembling. "What has she done with my son?"

The messenger sank to his knees, placed his basket on the marble floor, and lifted the lid. A pungent smell wafted through the hall.

Rin craned her head, expecting to see Jinzha's dismembered corpse.

But the basket was filled with dumplings, each fried to golden perfection and pressed in the pattern of a lotus flower. They had clearly gone bad after weeks of travel—Rin could see dark mold crawling around their edges—but their shape was still intact. They had been meticulously decorated, brushed with lotus seed paste and inked over with five crimson characters.

The Dragon devours his sons.

"The Empress enjoins you to enjoy a dumpling of the rarest meat," said the messenger. "She expects you might recognize the flavor."

Lady Saikhara shrieked and slumped across the floor.

Vaisra met Rin's eyes and jerked a hand across his neck.

She understood. She hefted her trident and charged toward the messenger.

He reeled backward just slightly, but otherwise made no effort to defend himself. He didn't even lift his arms. He just sat there, smiling with satisfaction.

She buried her trident into his chest.

It wasn't a clean blow. She'd been too shocked, distracted by the dumplings to aim properly. The prongs slid through his rib cage but didn't pierce his heart.

She yanked them back out.

The messenger gurgled a laugh. Blood bubbled through his crooked teeth, staining the pristine marble floor.

"You will die. You will all die," he said. "And the Empress will dance upon your graves."

Rin stabbed again and this time aimed true.

Nezha rushed to his mother and lifted her in his arms. "She's fainted," he said. "Someone, help—"

"There's something else," General Hu said while palace attendants gathered around Saikhara. He pulled a scroll out of the basket with remarkably steady hands and brushed the crumbs off the side. "It's a letter."

Vaisra hadn't moved from his throne. "Read it."

General Hu broke the seal and unrolled the scroll. "*I am coming for you.*"

Lady Saikhara sat up and gave a low moan.

"Get her out of here," Vaisra snapped to Nezha. "Hu. Read."

General Hu continued. "*My generals sail down the Murui River as you dawdle in your castle. You have nowhere to flee. You have nowhere to hide. Our fleet is larger. Our men are more numerous. You will die at the base of the Red Cliffs like your ancestors, and your corpses will feed the fish of the Murui.*"

The hall fell silent.

Vaisra seemed frozen to his chair. His expression betrayed nothing. No grief, no fear. He could have been made of ice.

General Hu rolled the scroll back up and cleared his throat. "That's all it says."

Within a fortnight Vaisra's scouts—exhausted, horses ridden half to death—returned from the border and confirmed the worst. The Imperial Fleet, repaired and augmented since Boyang, had begun its winding journey south carrying what seemed like the entire Militia.

Daji intended to end this war in Arlong.

"They've spotted the ships from the Yerin and Murin beacons," reported a scout.

"How are they already this close?" General Hu asked, alarmed. "Why weren't we told earlier?"

"They haven't reached Murin yet," the scout explained. "The fleet is simply massive. We could see it through the mountains."

"How many ships?"

"A few more than they had at Boyang."

"The good news is that the larger warships will get stuck wherever the Murui narrows," Captain Eriden said. "They'll have to roll them on logs to move over land. We have two, maybe two and a half weeks yet." He reached over to the map and tapped a point on Hare Province's northwestern border. "I'm guessing they'll be here by now. Should we send men up, try to stall them at the narrow bends?"

Vaisra shook his head. "No. This doesn't alter our grand strategy. They want us to split our defenses, but we won't take the bait. We concentrate on fortifying Arlong, or we lose the south altogether."

Rin stared down at the map, at the angry red dots representing both Imperial and Federation troops. The Republic was wedged in on both sides—the Empire from the north, the Federation from the south. It was hard not to panic as she imagined Daji's combined forces closing in around them like an iron fist.

"Deprioritize the northern coastline. Bring Tsolin's fleet back to the capital." Vaisra sounded impossibly calm, and Rin was grateful for it. "I want scouts with messenger pigeons positioned at mile intervals along the Murui. Every time that fleet moves, I want to know. Send messengers to Rooster and Monkey. Recall their local platoons."

"You can't do that," Gurubai said. "They're still dealing with the Federation remnants."

"I don't care about the Federation," Vaisra said. "I care about Arlong. If everything we've heard about this fleet is true, then this war is over unless we can hold our base. We need all of our men in one place."

"You're leaving entire villages to die," Takha said. "Entire provinces."

"Then they will die."

"Are you joking?" demanded Charouk. "You think we're just going to stand here while you renege on your promises? You said that if we defected, you would help us eradicate the Mugenese—"

"And I will," Vaisra said impatiently. "Can't you see? We beat Daji and we win back the south, too. Once their backer is gone, the Mugenese will surrender—"

"Or they will understand that the civil war has weakened us, and they'll pick off the pieces no matter what happens," Charouk countered.

"That won't happen. Once we've won Hesperian support—"

"'Hesperian support,'" Charouk scoffed. "Don't be a child. Tarcquet and his men have been loitering in the city for quite some time now, and that fleet isn't showing up on the horizon."

"They will come if we crush the Militia," Vaisra said. "And we cannot do that if we're wasting time fighting a war on two fronts."

"Forget this," said Gurubai. "We should take our troops and return home now."

"Go right ahead," Vaisra said calmly. "You wouldn't last a week. You need Dragon troops and you know that, or you'd have never come in the first place. None of you can hold your home provinces, not with the numbers you have. Otherwise you would have gone back a long time ago."

There was a short silence. Rin could tell from Gurubai's expression that Vaisra was right. He'd called their bluff.

They had no choice now but to follow his lead.

"But what happens after you win Arlong?" Nezha asked suddenly.

All heads turned in his direction.

Nezha lifted his chin. "We unite the country just to let the Mugenese tear it apart again? That's not a democracy, Father, that's a suicide pact. You're ignoring a massive threat just because it's not Dragon lives at stake—"

"Enough," Vaisra said, but Nezha spoke over him.

"Daji invited the Federation here in the first place. You don't need to finish us off."

Father and son glared at each other over the table.

"Your brother would never have defied me like this," Vaisra said quietly.

"No, Jinzha was rash and reckless and never listened to his best strategists, and now he's dead," said Nezha. "So what are you going to do, Father? Act out of some petty sense of revenge, or do something to help the people in your Republic?"

Vaisra slammed his hands on the table. "*Silence.* You will not contradict me—"

"You're just throwing your allies to the wolves! Does no one realize how horrific this is?" Nezha demanded. "General Hu? *Rin?*"

"I . . ." Rin's tongue was lead in her mouth.

All eyes were suddenly, terrifyingly on her.

Vaisra folded his arms over his chest as he watched her, eyebrows raised as if to say, *Go on.*

"They're invading your home," Nezha said.

Rin flinched. What did he expect her to say to that? Did he think that just because she was from the south, she would contradict Vaisra's orders?

"It doesn't matter," she said. "The Dragon Warlord is right—we split our forces and we're dead."

"Come on," Nezha said impatiently. "Of all people, you should—"

"Should what?" she sneered. "I should hate the Federation the most? I *do*, but I also know that dispatching troops south plays right into Daji's hands. Would you rather we simply deliver Arlong to her?"

"You're unbelievable," Nezha said.

She gave him her best imitation of Vaisra's level stare. "I'm just doing my job, Nezha. You might try doing yours."

CHAPTER 27

"I've outlined a number of tactics in this." Kitay handed Rin a small pamphlet. "Captain Dalain will have her own ideas, but based on historical record, these have worked the best, I think."

Rin flipped through the pages. "Did you rip these out of a book?"

He shrugged. "Didn't have time to copy it all down, so I just annotated."

She squinted to read his scrawling handwriting in the margins. "Logging?"

"It's a lot of time and manpower, I know, but you don't have many other good options." He tugged anxiously at his bangs. "It'll be more of an annoyance to them than anything, but it does save us a few hours."

"You've scratched out the guerrilla tactics," she observed.

"They won't do you much good. Besides, you shouldn't be trying to destroy the fleet, or even parts of it."

Rin frowned. That was exactly what she had been planning to do. "Don't tell me you think it's too dangerous."

"No, I think you simply *can't*. You don't understand just how

492   R. F. KUANG

big the fleet is. You can't burn them all before they catch on to you, not with your range of fire. Don't try anything clever."

"But—"

"When you take risks, you're gambling with my life, too," Kitay said sternly. "No stupid shit, Rin, I mean it. Keep to the directive. Just slow them down. Buy us some time."

Vaisra had ordered two platoons to sail up the Murui and obstruct the Imperial Navy's progress. They were racing against the clock, scrambling for extra time so that they could continue fortifying Arlong and wait for Tsolin's fleet on the northern shore to race back down the coastline. If they could delay the Imperial Navy for at least a few days, if Arlong could muster its defenses in time, and if Tsolin's ships could beat Daji's back to the capital, then they might have a fighting chance against the Empire.

It was a lot of *ifs*.

But it was all they had.

Rin had immediately volunteered the Cike for the task of delaying the fleet. She couldn't stand being around the refugees anymore, and she wanted to get Baji and Suni well away from the Hesperians before their restlessness manifested in disaster.

She wished she could bring Kitay with her. But he was too valuable to send out on what was most likely a suicide mission for anyone who wasn't a shaman, and Vaisra wanted him behind city walls to rig up defense fortifications.

And while Rin was glad that Kitay would be out of harm's way, she hated that they were about to be separated for days without a means of communication.

If danger came, she wouldn't be able to protect him.

Kitay read the look on her face. "I'll be all right. You know that."

"But if anything happens—"

"*You're* the one going into a war zone," he pointed out.

"Everywhere is a war zone." She folded the manual shut and stuffed it into her shirt pocket. "I'm scared for you. For both of us. I can't help that."

"You haven't got time to be scared." He squeezed her arm. "Just keep us alive, won't you?"

Rin made one last stop by the forge before she left Arlong.

"What can I do for you?" The blacksmith shouted at her over the furnace. The flames had been burning nonstop for days, mass-producing swords, crossbow bolts, and armor.

She handed him her trident. "What do you make of this metal?"

He ran his fingers over the hilt and felt around the prongs to test their edges. "It's fine stuff. But I don't do many battle tridents. You don't want me to mess around with this too much, I'd ruin the balance. But I can sharpen the prongs if you need."

"I don't want to sharpen it," she said. "I want you to melt it down."

"Hmm." He tested the trident's balance over his palm. "Speerly-built?"

"Yes."

He raised an eyebrow. "And you're sure you want this reforged? I can't find anything wrong with it."

"It's ruined for me," she said. "Destroy it completely."

"This is a very unique weapon. You won't get a trident like this again."

Rin shrugged. "That's fine."

He still looked unsure. "Speerly craft is impossible to replicate. No one's alive now who knows how they made their weapons. I'll do my best, but you might just end up with a fisherman's tool."

"I don't want a trident," she said. "I want a sword."

Two skimmers departed from the Red Cliffs that morning. The *Harrier*, led by Nezha, raced upriver to hold the city of Shayang, situated on a crucial, narrow bend in the upper river delta. Shayang's inhabitants had long since evacuated down to the capital, but the city itself used to be a military base—Nezha needed only garrison the old cannon forts.

Rin's crew, headed by Captain Dalain, a lean, handsome woman, followed at a slower pace, paddling at a crawl in what was supposed to have been Jinzha's warship.

It wasn't close to finished. They hadn't even named it. Jinzha was supposed to choose a name when construction was done, and now no one could bring themselves to do it in his stead. The bulkheads of the upper deck hadn't been put in, the bottom decks were sparse and unfurnished, and cannons hadn't been fitted to the sides.

But none of that mattered, because the paddle wheels were functional. The ship had basic maneuverability. They didn't need to sail it into enemy territory, they just had to get it twenty miles up the river.

Kitay's pamphlet turned out to be brilliant. He'd sketched a series of little tricks to create maximal delays. Once they anchored Jinzha's warship, the Cike and Captain Dalain's crew spread out over a span of ten miles, and with incredible efficiency, implemented each one of them.

They erected a series of dams using a combination of logs and sandbags. Realistically these would buy them only half a day or so, but they would still tire out the soldiers forced to dive into deep water to clear them away.

Upriver from those, they planted wooden stakes in the river to tear holes in the bottom of enemy ships. Kitay, with Ramsa's enthusiastic support, had wanted to plant the same sort of water mines that the Empire had used on them, but they'd run out of time before he could figure out how to dry the intestines properly.

They stretched multiple iron cables across the river, usually right after bends. If the Wolf Meat General was smart, he would just send soldiers out to disassemble the posts instead of trying to hack through the cables. But the posts were hidden well behind reeds and the cables were invisible underwater, so they might cause a destructive backlog if the fleet rammed into them unawares.

They set up a number of garrisons at three-mile intervals of the Murui. Each would be manned by ten to fifteen soldiers armed with crossbows, cannons, and missiles.

Those soldiers were most likely going to die. But they might manage to pick off a handful of Militia troops, or at best damage a ship or two before the Wolf Meat General blew them apart. And in terms of bodies and time, the tradeoff was worth it.

Near the northern border of the Dragon Province, right before the Murui forked into the Golyn, they sank Jinzha's warship into the water.

"That's a pity," said Ramsa as they evacuated their equipment onto land. "I heard it was supposed to be the greatest warship ever built in the Empire's history."

"It was Jinzha's ship," Rin said. "Jinzha's dead."

The warship had been a conquest vessel built for a massive invasion of northern territory. There would be no such invasion now. The Republic was fighting for its last chance at survival. Jinzha's warship would serve best by sitting heavy in the Murui's deep waters and obstructing the Imperial Fleet for as long as it could.

They smashed in the paddles and hacked apart the masts before they disembarked, just to make sure the warship was destroyed beyond the point of any possibility that the Imperial Fleet might repurpose it to sail on Arlong.

Then they rowed small lifeboats to the shore and prepared for a hasty march inland.

Ramsa had laced the two bottom decks with several hundred pounds of explosives, all rigged to destroy the warship's fundamental structures. The fuses were linked together for a chain reaction. All they needed now was a light.

"Everyone good?" Rin called.

From what she could see, the soldiers had all cleared the beach. Most them had already set off at a run toward the forest as ordered.

Captain Dalain gave her a nod. "Do it."

Rin raised her arms and sent a thin ribbon of fire dancing across the river.

The flame disappeared onto the warship, where the fuse had

been laid just where Rin's range ran out. She didn't wait to check if it caught.

Ten yards past the tree line, she heard a series of muffled booms, followed by a long silence. She stumbled to a halt and looked over her shoulder. The warship wasn't sinking.

"Was that it?" she asked. "I thought it'd be louder."

Ramsa looked similarly confused. "Maybe the fuses weren't linked properly? But I was sure—"

The next round of blasts threw them off their feet. Rin hit the dirt, hands clamped over her ears, eyes squeezed shut as her very bones vibrated. Ramsa collapsed beside her, shaking madly. She couldn't tell if he was laughing or trembling.

When at last the eruptions faded, she hauled herself to her feet and dragged Ramsa up to higher ground. They turned around. Just over the tree line, they could just see the Republican flag flying high, shrouded by billowing black smoke.

"Tiger's tits," whispered Ramsa.

For a long, tense moment it seemed like the warship might stay afloat. The sails remained perfectly upright, as if suspended from the heavens by a string. Rin and Ramsa stood side by side, fingers laced together, watching the smoke expand outward to envelop the sky.

At last the sound of splintering wood echoed through the still air as the support beams collapsed one by one. The middle mast disappeared suddenly, as if the ship had folded in on itself, devouring its own insides. Then with a creaking groan, the warship turned on its side and sank into the black water.

They made camp that night to the sound of more explosions, though these were coming from at least seven miles away. The Imperial Navy had reached the border town at Shayang. The noise was impossible to escape. The bombing went on through the night. Rin heard so many rounds of cannon fire that she could not imagine anything still remained of Shayang except for smoke and rubble.

"Are you all right?" Baji asked.

The crew was supposed to be grabbing a few hours' sleep before their journey downriver, but Rin could barely even close her eyes. She sat upright, hugging her knees, unable to look away from the flashing lights in the night sky.

"Hey. Calm down." Baji put a hand on her shoulder. "You're shaking. What's wrong?"

She nodded in Shayang's direction. "Nezha's over there."

"And you're afraid for him?"

She whispered without thinking. "I'm always afraid for him."

"Ah. I get it." Baji gave her a curious look. "You're in love."

"Don't be disgusting. Just because you think the whole world is tits and—"

"No need to get defensive, kiddo. He's a good-looking fellow."

"We're done talking."

Baji snickered. "Fine. Don't engage. Just answer this. Would you be here without him?"

"What, camping out by the Murui?"

"Fighting this war," he clarified. "Serving under his father."

"I serve the Republic," she said.

"Whatever you say," he said, but she could see from the look in his eyes that he hardly believed her.

"Why are you still here, then?" she asked. "If you're so skeptical. I mean—you've got no allegiance to the Republic, and gods know the Cike barely still exists. Why haven't you just run?"

Baji looked somber for a moment. He never looked this serious; he always had such an outsize personality, an endless series of dirty jokes and lewd comments. Rin had never bothered to consider that that might be a front.

"I did think about that for a minute," he said after a pause. "Suni and I both. Before you got back we thought seriously about splitting."

"But?"

"But then we'd have nothing to do. I'm sure you can understand,

Rin. Our gods want blood. That's all we can think about. And it doesn't matter that when we're not high, we've nominally got our minds back. You know that's not how it works. To anyone else a peaceful life would be heaven right now, but for us it'd just be torture."

"I understand," she said quietly.

She knew it would never end for Baji, either; that constant urge to destroy. If he didn't kill enemy combatants then he would start taking it out on civilians and do whatever he'd done to get himself into Baghra in the first place. That was the contract the Cike had signed with their gods. It ended only in madness or death.

"I have to be on a battlefield," Baji said. He swallowed. "Wherever I can find one. There's nothing else to it."

Another explosion rocked the night so hard that even from seven miles away they could feel the ground shake beneath them. Rin drew her knees closer to her chest and trembled.

"You can't do anything about that," Baji told her after it had passed. "You'll just have to trust that Nezha knows how to do his job."

"Tiger's fucking tits," Ramsa shouted. He was standing farther uphill, squinting through his spyglass. "Are you guys seeing this?"

Rin stood up. "What is it?"

Ramsa motioned frantically for them to join him at the top of the hill. He handed Rin his spyglass and pointed. "Look there. Right between those two trees."

Rin squinted through the lens. Her gut dropped. "That's not possible."

"Well, it's not a fucking illusion," Ramsa said.

"What isn't?" Baji demanded.

Wordlessly, Rin handed him the spyglass. She didn't need it. Now that she knew what to look for, even her naked eye could see the outline of the Imperial Navy winding slowly through the trees.

She felt like she was watching a mountain range move.

"That thing's not a ship," Baji said.

"No," Ramsa said, awed. "That's a fortress."

The centerpiece of the Imperial Navy was a monstrous structure: a square, three-decked fortress that looked as if the entire siege barrier at Xiashang had come detached from the ground to slowly float down the river.

How many troops could that fortress hold? Thousands? *Tens* of thousands?

"How does that thing stay afloat?" Baji demanded. "It can't have any mobility."

"They don't need mobility," Rin said. "The rest of the fleet exists to guard it. They just need to get that fortress close enough to the city. Then they'll swarm it."

Ramsa said what they were all thinking. "We're going to die, aren't we?"

"Cheer up," said Baji. "Maybe they'll take prisoners."

We can't fight them. Rin's chest constricted with sharp and suffocating dread. Their entire mission seemed so pointless now. Logs and dams might stall the Militia for a few hours, but a fleet that powerful could eventually barrel its way through anything.

"Question," Ramsa said. He was peering through his spyglass again. "What do Tsolin's flags look like?"

"*What?*"

"Have they got green snakes on them?"

"Yes—"

A terrible suspicion hit her. She seized the spyglass from him, but she already knew what she would see. The ships trailing at the rearguard bore the unmistakable coiled insignia of the Snake Province.

"What's going on?" Baji asked.

Rin couldn't speak.

It wasn't just a handful of ships that belonged to Tsolin. She'd seen six by her count now. Which meant one of two things— either Tsolin had skirmished and lost early to the Imperial Navy, and his ships had been repurposed for Imperial use, or Tsolin had defected.

"I will take your silence to mean the worst," Baji said.

. . .

Captain Dalain ordered an immediate retreat back to Arlong. The soldiers dismantled their camp in minutes. Paddling downstream, they could be back to warn Arlong within a day, but Rin didn't know if advance warning would even make a difference. The addition of Tsolin's ships meant the Imperial Navy had nearly doubled in size. It didn't matter how good Arlong's defenses were. They couldn't possibly fight off a fleet that big.

Cannon fire from Shayang continued throughout the night, then stopped abruptly just before dawn. At sunrise they saw a series of smoke signals from Nezha's soldiers unfurling in the distant sky.

"Shayang's gone," Dalain interpreted. "The *Harrier*'s grounded, but the survivors are falling back to Arlong."

"Should we go to their aid?" someone asked.

Dalain paused. "No. Row faster."

Rin pulled her oar through the muddy water, trying not to imagine the worst. Nezha might be fine. Shayang hadn't been a suicide mission—Nezha had been instructed to hold the fort for as long as he could before escaping into the forest. And if he were seriously injured, the Murui would come to his aid. His god wouldn't desert him. She had to believe that.

Around noon, they heard a distant round of cannon fire once more.

"That'll be the warship," Ramsa said. "They're trying to blow their way through."

"Good," Rin said.

Sinking the warship had perhaps been Kitay's best idea. The Imperial Fleet couldn't simply blast it to bits—the bulk of the structure lay underwater, where cannon fire couldn't touch it. Exploding the top layers would only make it harder to extract the sunken bottom from the Murui.

Half an hour later, the cannon fire stopped. The Militia must have caught on. Now they would have to send in divers with hooks to trawl and clear the river. That might take them two days, three at the most.

But after that, they would resume their slow but relentless journey to Arlong. And without Tsolin, there was nothing left to stop them.

"We know," Kitay said upon Rin's return. He'd rushed out to greet her at the harbor. He looked utterly disheveled; his hair stood up in every direction as if he'd spent the last few hours pacing and tugging at his bangs. "Found out two hours ago."

"But *why*?" she cried. "And when?"

Kitay shrugged helplessly. "All I know is we're fucked. Come on."

She followed him at a run to the palace. Inside the main stateroom, Eriden and a handful of officers stood clustered around a map that was no longer even close to accurate, because it had simply erased Tsolin's ships from the board.

But the Republic hadn't just lost ships. This wasn't a neutral setback. It would have been better if Tsolin had simply retreated, or if he had been killed. But this defection meant that the entire fleet they had relied on now augmented Daji's forces.

Captain Eriden replaced the pieces meant to represent Tsolin's fleet with red ones and stood back from the table. "That's what we're dealing with."

No one had anything to say. The numbers differential was almost laughable. Rin imagined a glistening snake coiling its body around a small rodent, squeezing until the light dimmed from its eyes.

"That's a lot of red," she muttered.

"No shit," Kitay said.

"Where's Vaisra?" she asked.

Kitay drew her to the side and murmured into her ear so Eriden wouldn't hear. "Alone in his office, probably hurling vases at the wall. He asked not to be disturbed." He pointed to a scroll lying on the edge of the table. "Tsolin sent that letter this morning. That's when we found out."

Rin picked the scroll up and unrolled it. She already knew its contents, but she needed to read Tsolin's words herself out of some morbid curiosity, the same way she couldn't help taking a closer look at decomposing animal carcasses.

This is not the future I wished for either of us.

Tsolin wrote in a thin, lovely script. Each stroke tapered carefully to a fine point, an effortless calligraphic style that took years to master. This wasn't a letter written in haste. This was a letter written laboriously by a man who still cared about decorum.

All across the page Rin saw characters crossed out and rewritten where water had blotted the ink. Tsolin had wept as he wrote.

You must recognize that a ruler's first obligation is to his people. I chose the path that would lead to the least bloodshed. Perhaps this has stifled a democratic transition. I know the vision you dreamed of for this nation and I know I may have destroyed it. But my first obligation is not to the unborn people of this country's future, but the people who are suffering now, who pass their days in fear because of the war that you have brought to their doorstep.

I defect for them. This is how I will protect them. I weep for you, my student. I weep for your Republic. I weep for my wife and children. You will die thinking I have abandoned you all. But I do not hesitate to say that I value the lives of my people far more than I have ever valued you.

CHAPTER 28

The Imperial Navy was due to reach the Red Cliffs in forty-eight hours. Arlong became a swarm of desperate, frantic activity as the Republican Army hastened to finish its defensive preparations in the next two days. The furnaces burned at all hours, day and night, turning out mountains of swords, shields, and javelins. The Red Cliffs became a chimney for the engines of war.

The blacksmith sent for Rin the evening of the first day.

"The ore was a marvel to work with," he said as he handed her a sword. It was a lovely thing—a thin, straight blade with a crimson tassel fixed to the pommel. "You wouldn't happen to have more like it, would you?"

"You'd have to sail back to the island," she murmured, turning the blade over in her hands. "Root around the skeletons, see what you find."

"Fair enough." The blacksmith produced a second blade, identical to the first. "Fortunately, there was enough excess metal for a backup. In case you lose one."

"That's useful. Thank you." She held the first blade out, arm straight, to test its weight. The hilt felt molded perfectly to her grasp. The blade was a tad longer than anything she'd ever used, but it was lighter than it looked. She swung it in a circle over her head.

The blacksmith backed out of her range. "I thought you'd want the extra reach."

She tossed the hilt from hand to hand. She'd been afraid the length would feel awkward, but it only extended her reach, and the light weight more than made up for it. "Are you calling me short?"

He chuckled. "I'm saying your arms aren't very long. How does it feel?"

She traced the tip of her blade through the air and let it pull her through the familiar movements of Seejin's Third Form. She was surprised at how good it felt. Nezha had been right—she really was much better with a sword. She'd fought her first battles with one. She'd made her first kill with one.

Why had she been using a trident for so long? That seemed so stupid in retrospect. She'd practiced with the sword for years at Sinegard; it felt like a natural extension of her arm. Wielding one again felt like trading a ceremonial gown for a comfortable set of training clothes.

She gave a yell and hurled the sword toward the opposite wall. It stuck into the wood right where she'd aimed, perfectly angled, hilt quivering.

"How is it?" asked the blacksmith.

"It's perfect," she said, satisfied.

Fuck Altan, fuck his legacy, and fuck his trident. It was time she started using a weapon that would keep her alive.

The sun had gone down by the time she returned to the barracks. Rin moved hastily through the canals, arms sore from hours of lugging sandbags into empty houses.

"Rin?" A small figure emerged from the corner just before she reached the door.

She jumped, startled. Her new blades clattered to the floor.

"It's just me." The figure stepped into the light.

"Kesegi?" She swiped the swords off the ground. "How'd you get past the barrier?"

"I need you to come with me." He reached out to seize her hand. "Quick."

"Why? What's going on?"

"I can't tell you here." He bit his lip, eyes darting nervously around the barracks. "But I'm in trouble. Will you come?"

"I . . ." Rin glanced distractedly toward the barracks. This could go terribly badly. She'd been ordered not to interact with the refugees unless she was on duty, and given the current tensions in Arlong, she would be the last to receive the benefit of the doubt. What if someone saw?

"*Please*," Kesegi said. "It's bad."

She swallowed. What was she thinking? This was Kesegi. Kesegi was family, the very last family that she had. "Of course. Lead the way."

Kesegi set off at a run. She followed close behind.

She assumed something had happened behind the barrier. Some brawl, some accident or skirmish between guards and refugees. Auntie Fang would be at the bottom of it; she always was. But Kesegi didn't take her back to the camps. He led her behind the barracks, past the clanging shipyards to an empty warehouse at the far end of the harbor.

Behind the warehouse stood three dark silhouettes.

Rin halted. None of those figures could be Auntie Fang; they were all too tall.

"Kesegi, what's going on?"

But Kesegi pulled her straight toward the warehouse.

"I brought her," he called loudly.

Rin's eyes adjusted to the dim light, and the strangers' faces became clear. She groaned. Those weren't refugees.

She turned to Kesegi. "What the hell?"

He looked away. "I had to get you here somehow."

"You lied to me."

He set his jaw. "Well, you wouldn't have come otherwise."

"Just hear us out," said Takha. "Please don't go. We'll only get this one chance to speak."

She crossed her arms. "We're hiding from Vaisra behind warehouses now?"

"Vaisra has done enough to ruin us," said Gurubai. "That much is obvious. The Republic has abandoned the south. This alliance must be aborted."

She fought the impulse to roll her eyes. "And what's your alternative?"

"Our own revolution," he said immediately. "We revoke our support for Vaisra, defect from the Dragon Army, and return to our home provinces."

"That's suicide," Rin said. "Vaisra is the only one protecting you."

"You can't even say that with a straight face," Charouk said. "Protection? We've been duped from the beginning. It is time to stop hoping Vaisra will throw us scraps from the table. We must return home and fight the Mugenese off on our own. We should have done that from the beginning."

"You and what army?" Rin asked coolly.

This entire conversation was moot. Vaisra had called this bluff months ago. The southern Warlords couldn't go home. Alone, their provincial armies would be destroyed by the Federation.

"We'll need to build an army," Gurubai acknowledged. "It won't be easy. But we'll have the numbers. You've seen the camps. You know how many of us there are."

"I also know that they are untrained, unarmed, and starving," she said. "You think they can fight Federation troops? The Republic is your only chance at survival."

"Survival?" Charouk scoffed. "We're all going to die within the week. Vaisra's gambled our lives on the Hesperians, and they will never come."

Rin faltered. She didn't have a good answer to that. She knew, just as they did, that the Hesperians were unlikely to ever find the Nikara worthy of their aid.

But until General Tarcquet declared explicitly that the Consortium had refused, the Republic still had a fighting chance.

Defecting to the south was certain suicide—especially because if Rin abandoned Vaisra, then no one was left to protect her from the Gray Company. She might run from Arlong and hide. She might elude the Hesperians for a long time, if she was clever, but they would track her down eventually. They wouldn't relent. Rin understood now that people like Petra would never let challenges to the Maker slip away so easily. They would hunt down and kill or capture every shaman in the Empire for further study. Rin might still fight them off, might even hold her own for a while— fire against airships, the Phoenix against the Maker—but that confrontation would be terrible. She didn't know if she'd come out alive.

And if the southern Warlords defected from the Republic, then no one was left to protect them from the Militia *or* the Federation. That calculation was so obvious. Why couldn't they see it?

"Give up this fool's hope," Gurubai urged her. "Ignore Vaisra's nonsense. The Hesperians are staying away on purpose, just as they did during the Poppy Wars."

"What are you talking about?" Rin demanded.

"You really think they didn't have a single piece of information about what was happening on this continent?"

"What does that matter?"

"Vaisra sent his wife to them," Gurubai said. "Lady Saikhara spent the second and third Poppy Wars tucked safely away on a Hesperian warship. The Hesperians had full knowledge of what was happening. And they didn't send a single sack of grain or crate of swords. Not when Sinegard burned, not when Khurdalain fell, and not when the Mugenese raped Golyn Niis. These are the allies you're waiting for. And Vaisra knows that."

"Why don't you just say what you're suggesting?" Rin asked.

"Has this really never crossed your mind?" Gurubai asked. "This war has been orchestrated by Vaisra and the Hesperians to put him in a prime position to consolidate control of this country. They didn't come during the third war because they wanted to see the Empire bleed. They won't come now until Vaisra's challengers are dead. Vaisra is no true democrat, nor a champion of the people. He's an opportunist building his throne with Nikara blood."

"You're mad," Rin said. "No one is crazy enough to do that."

"You'd have to be crazy *not* to see it! The evidence is right in front of you. The Federation troops never made it as far inland as Arlong. Vaisra lost nothing in the war."

"He nearly lost his *son*—"

"And he got him back with no trouble at all. Face it, Yin Vaisra was the only victor of the Third Poppy War. You're too smart to believe otherwise."

"Don't patronize me," Rin snapped. "And even if that's all true, that doesn't change anything. I already know the Hesperians are assholes. I'd still fight for the Republic."

"You shouldn't fight for an alliance with people who think we're barely human," said Charouk.

"Well, that still gives me no reason to fight for *you*—"

"You should fight for us because you're one of us," said Gurubai.

"I am not one of you."

"Yes, you are," Takha said. "You're a Rooster. Just like me."

She stared at him in disbelief.

The sheer hypocrisy. He'd disowned her easily enough at Lusan, had treated her like an animal. Now he wanted to claim they were one and the same?

"The south would rise for you," Gurubai insisted. "Do you have any idea how much power you hold? You are the last *Speerly*. The entire continent knows your name. If you raised your sword, tens of thousands would follow. They'd fight for you. You'd be their goddess."

"I'd also be a traitor to my closest friends," she said. They were asking her to abandon Kitay. *Nezha.* "Don't try to flatter me. It won't work."

"Your friends?" Gurubai scoffed. "Who, Yin Nezha? Chen Kitay? Northerners who would spit on your very existence? Are you so desperate to be like them that you'll ignore everything else at stake?"

She bristled. "I don't want to be like them."

"Yes, you do," he sneered. "That's all you want, even if you don't realize it. But you're southern mud in the end. You can butcher the way you talk, you can turn away from the stench of the refugee camps and pretend that you don't smell, too, but they are *never* going to think you're one of them."

That did it. Rin's sympathy evaporated.

Did they really believe they could sway her with provincial ties? Rooster Province had never done anything for her. For the first sixteen years of her life, Tikany had tried to grind her into the dirt. She'd lost her ties to the south the moment she'd left for Sinegard.

She'd escaped the Fangs. She'd carved out a place for herself in Arlong. She was one of Vaisra's best soldiers. She wouldn't go back now. She *couldn't*.

For her, the south had only ever meant abuse and misery. She owed it nothing. Certainly not a suicide mission. If the Warlords wanted to throw their lives away, they could do that by themselves.

She saw the way Kesegi was looking at her—stricken, disappointed—and she willed herself not to care.

"I'm sorry," she said. "But I'm not one of you. I'm a Speerly. And I know where my loyalties lie."

"If you stay here you'll die for nothing," Gurubai said. "We all will."

"Then go back," she sneered. "Take your troops. Go home. I won't stop you."

They didn't move. Their faces—stricken, ashen—confirmed she'd called their bluff. They couldn't run. Alone in their provinces, they didn't have a chance. They might—*might*, though Rin strongly doubted they had the numbers—be able to fight off the Mugenese troops on their own. But if Arlong fell, it was only a matter of time until Daji came for them, too.

Without her support, their hands were tied. The southern War-lords were trapped.

Gurubai's hand moved to the sword at his waist. "Will you tell Vaisra?"

Her lip curled. "Don't tempt me."

"Will you tell Vaisra?" he repeated.

Rin gave him an incredulous smile. Was he really going to fight her? Was he really even going to *try*?

She couldn't help relishing this. For once she held all the power; for once, she held their fates in her hands and not the other way around.

She could have killed them right there and been done with it. Vaisra might have even praised her for the demonstration of loyalty.

But it was the eve of battle. The Militia was creeping to their doorstep. The refugees needed some sort of leadership if they were going to survive—certainly no one else was looking out for them. And if she murdered the Warlords now, the resulting chaos would hurt the Republic. The southern armies' numbers weren't great enough to win the battle, but their defection was more than enough to guarantee defeat, and that wasn't something Rin wanted on her hands.

She loved that this was her decision—that she could disguise this cruel calculation as mercy.

"Go to sleep," she said softly, as if speaking to children. "We've a battle to fight."

She escorted Kesegi back to the refugee quarters over his pro-tests. She took him the long way around the city, trying to keep as much distance from the barracks as possible. For ten minutes they walked in stony silence. Every time Rin looked at Kesegi he stared angrily forward, pretending he hadn't seen her.

"You're angry with me," she said.

He didn't respond.

"I can't give them what they want. You know that."

"No, I don't," he said curtly.

"Kesegi—"

"And I don't know *you* anymore."

She had to admit that was true. Kesegi had said farewell to a sister and found a soldier in her place. But she didn't know him anymore, either. The Kesegi she'd left had been just a tiny child. This Kesegi was a tall, sullen, and angry boy who had seen too much suffering and didn't know who to blame for it.

They resumed walking in silence. Rin was tempted to turn around and head back, but she didn't want Kesegi caught alone on the wrong side of the barrier. The night patrol had lately taken to flogging refugees who wandered out of bounds to set an example.

Finally Kesegi said, "You could have written."

"What?"

"I kept waiting for you to write. Why didn't you?"

Rin didn't have a good response to that.

Why *hadn't* she written? The Masters had permitted it. All of her classmates had regularly written home. She remembered watching Niang send eight separate letters to each of her siblings every week, and being amazed that anyone had so much to say about their grueling coursework.

But the thought of writing the Fangs had never even crossed her mind. Once she reached Sinegard, she'd locked her memories of Tikany tightly away in the back of her mind and willed herself to forget.

"You were so young," she said after a pause. "I guess I didn't think you'd remember me."

"Bullshit," Kesegi said. "You're my sister. How could I not remember you?"

"I don't know. I just . . . I thought it'd be easier if we made a clean break with each other. I mean, it's not like I was ever coming home once I got out—"

His voice hardened. "And you didn't ever think I wanted to get out, too?"

She felt a wave of irritation. How had this suddenly become her fault? "You could have if you wanted to. You could have studied—"

"When? When you left it was just me and the shop; and after Father started getting worse, I had to do everything around the house. And Mother isn't kind, Rin. You knew that—I begged you to not leave me with her—but you left anyway. Off in Sinegard on your adventures—"

"They weren't adventures," she said coldly.

"But you were in *Sinegard*," he said plaintively, with the voice of a child who had only heard stories of the former capital, who still thought it was a land of riches and marvels. "And I was stuck in Tikany, hiding from Mother every chance I got. And then the war started and all we did every single day was huddle terrified in underground shelters and hope that the Federation hadn't come to our town yet, and if they did, then they might not kill us immediately."

She stopped walking. "Kesegi."

"They kept saying you were going to come for us." His voice cracked. "That a fire goddess from the Rooster Province had destroyed the longbow island, and that you were going to come back home to liberate us, too."

"I wanted to. I would have—"

"No, you wouldn't have. Where were you all those months? Launching a coup in the Autumn Palace. Starting another war." Venom crept into his voice. "You don't get to say you don't want any part of this. This is your fault. Without you we wouldn't be here."

She could have replied. She could have argued with him, said it wasn't her fault but the Empress's, told him there were political forces at play that were much larger than any of them.

But she simply couldn't form the sentences. None of them felt genuine.

The simple truth was that she'd abandoned her foster brother and hadn't thought about him for years. He'd barely crossed her mind until they'd met in the camp. And she would have forgotten him again if he weren't standing right here before her.

She didn't know how to fix that. She didn't know if fixing it was even possible.

They turned the corner toward a line of single-story stone buildings. They had made it to the Hesperian quarters. A few more minutes and they'd be back at the refugee district. Rin was glad of it. She wanted to get away from Kesegi. She couldn't bear the full brunt of his resentment.

From the corner of her eye, she saw a blue uniform disappear around the back of the closest building. She would have dismissed it, but then she heard the sounds—a rhythmic shuffle, a muffled moan.

She'd heard those noises before. She'd delivered parcels of opium to Tikany's whorehouses plenty of times. She just couldn't imagine how this could be the time or the place.

Kesegi heard it, too. He stopped walking.

"Run to the barrier," she hissed.

"But—"

"I'm not asking." She pushed him. "*Go.*"

He obeyed.

She broke into a run. She saw two half-naked bodies behind the building. Hesperian soldier, Nikara girl. The girl whimpered, trying to scream, but the soldier covered her mouth with one hand, grasped her hair with the other, and jerked her head back to expose her neck.

For a moment all Rin could do was stand and watch.

She'd never seen a rape before.

She'd heard about them. She'd heard too many stories from the women who had survived Golyn Niis, had imagined it vividly so many times that they invaded her nightmares and made her wake up shaking in rage and fear.

And the only thing she could think about was whether this was how Venka had suffered at Golyn Niis. Whether Venka's face had contorted like this girl's, mouth open in a silent scream. Whether the Mugenese soldiers who had pinned her down had been laughing like the Hesperian soldier was now.

Bile rose up in Rin's throat. "Get off of her."

The soldier couldn't, or refused to, understand her. He just kept going, panting like an animal.

Rin couldn't believe those were noises of *pleasure.*

She threw herself into the soldier's side. He twisted around and flung an awkward fist toward her face, but she ducked easily, grabbed his wrists, kicked in his kneecaps, and wrestled him into submission until he was lying on the ground, pinned down between her knees.

She reached down, feeling for his testicles. When she found them, she squeezed. "Is this what you wanted?"

He writhed frantically beneath her. She squeezed harder. He made a gurgling noise.

She dug her fingernails into soft flesh. "No?"

He screeched in pain.

She called the flame. His screams grew louder, but she grabbed his discarded shirt off the ground, shoved it into his mouth, and didn't let him go until his member had turned to charcoal in her hands.

When he finally stopped moving, she climbed off his chest, sat down next to the trembling girl, and put her arm around her shoulders. Neither of them spoke. They just huddled together, watching the soldier with cold satisfaction as he twitched, mewling feebly, on the dirt.

"Is he going to die?" the girl asked.

The soldier's whimpers were getting softer. Rin had burned half of his lower body. Some of the wounds were cauterized. It might take a long while for the blood loss to kill him. She hoped he was conscious for it. "Yes. If no one takes him to a physician."

The girl didn't sound scared, just idly curious. "Will you take him?"

"He's not in my platoon," Rin said. "Not my problem."

More minutes passed. Blood pooled slowly beneath the soldier's waist. Rin sat with the girl in silence, heart hammering, mind racing through the consequences.

The Hesperians would know the killer was her. The burn marks would give her away—only the Speerly killed with fire.

Tarcquet's retaliation would be terrible. He might not settle for Rin's death—if he found out what had just happened, he might abandon the Republic altogether.

Rin had to get rid of that body.

Eventually the soldier's chest stopped rising and falling. Rin shuffled forward on her knees and felt his neck for a pulse. Nothing. She stood up and extended a hand to the girl. "Let's get you cleaned up. Can you walk?"

"Don't worry about me." The girl sounded remarkably calm. She'd stopped trembling. She bent forward to wipe the blood and fluids off of her legs with the hem of her torn dress. "It's happened before."

CHAPTER 29

"Tiger's fucking tits," Kitay said.

"I know," Rin said.

"And you just dumped him in the harbor?"

"Weighed him down with rocks first. I picked a pretty deep stretch by the docks; no one's going to find him—"

"Holy shit." Kitay ran a hand through his bangs and yanked as he paced around the library. "You're going to die. We're all going to die."

"It might be all right." Rin tried to convince herself as she said it, but she still felt terribly light-headed. She'd come to Kitay because he was the one person she trusted to figure out what to do, but now both of them were panicking. "Look, no one saw me—"

"*How do you know?*" he asked shrilly. "No one caught you dragging a Hesperian corpse halfway across the city? No one was looking out their windows? You'd be willing to stake your life on the fact that *not a single person saw?*"

"I didn't drag it, I dumped it in a sampan and rowed out to shore."

"Oh, *that* solves everything—"

"Kitay. Listen." She took a deep breath, trying to get her mind to slow down enough to work properly. "It's been over an hour. If they'd seen, don't you think I'd be dead by now?"

"Tarcquet could be biding his time," Kitay said. "Waiting until morning to set an army on you."

"He wouldn't wait." Rin was certain of that. The Hesperians didn't fuck around. If Tarcquet found out that a shaman, of all people, had killed one of his men, then her body would already be riddled with bullet holes. He wouldn't have given her the chance to escape.

The more time that passed, the more she hoped—believed—that Tarcquet didn't know. Vaisra didn't know. They might never know. Rin wasn't telling anyone, and the refugee girl would certainly keep her mouth shut.

Kitay rubbed his palms against his temples. "When did this happen?"

"I told you. Just over an hour ago, when I was walking Kesegi back to the barriers from the old warehouses."

"What on earth were you doing by the warehouses?"

"Southern Warlords ambushed me. Wanted to talk. They're thinking of defecting back to their home provinces to deal with the Federation armies and they wanted me to come along, and they had this insane theory about the Hesperians, and—"

"What did you say?"

"Of course I refused. That'd be a death sentence."

"Well, at least you didn't commit treason." Kitay managed a shaky laugh. "And then, what, you just wandered back to the barracks and murdered a Hesperian on the way?"

"You didn't see what he was doing."

He threw his hands up. "Does it fucking matter?"

"He was on a girl," she said angrily. "He had her by her neck and he wouldn't stop—"

"So you decided to scorch any possible chance we have of surviving the Red Cliffs?"

"The Hesperians aren't fucking coming, Kitay."

"They're still here, aren't they? If they really didn't care they'd have packed up and gone. Did that ever cross your mind? When your back is to the wall there's a massive difference between zero and one percent but no, you'd rather *guarantee* it's zero—"

Her cheeks burned. "I didn't think—"

"Of course not," Kitay snapped. His knuckles had gone white. "You never think, do you? You always just pick whatever fights you want, whenever you want, and fuck the consequences—"

Rin raised her voice. "Would you rather I had let him rape her?"

Kitay fell silent.

"No," he said after a long pause. "I'm sorry, I didn't—I didn't mean that."

"I didn't think so."

He pressed his face into his hands. "*Gods*, I'm just scared. And you didn't have to kill him, you could have—"

"I know," she said. She felt drained. All the adrenaline had gone out of her at once, and now she only wanted to collapse. "I know, I wasn't thinking, I saw it happening and I just—"

"It's my life on the line now, too."

"I'm sorry."

"I know." He sighed. "I don't think— You didn't have— Fine. It's fine. I understand."

"I really don't think anyone saw."

"Fine." He took a deep breath. "Are you going to go back to the barracks?"

"No."

"Me neither."

They sat together on the floor for a long while in silence. He rested his head against her shoulder. She clutched at his hands. Neither of them could sleep. They were both watching the library windows, waiting to see Hesperian troops lined up at the door, to hear the fall of heavy boots in the hallway. Rin couldn't help but feel a twinge of relief at every additional moment that passed.

It meant the Hesperians weren't coming. It meant that, for now, she was safe.

But what happened when the Hesperians woke up in the morning and discovered a missing soldier? What happened when they started to search? They wouldn't find him for days at least, she'd made sure of that, but the sheer fact that a soldier was missing might derail Hesperian negotiations regardless.

If the fallout didn't land on Rin, then would they punish the entire Republic?

The southern Warlords' words rose unbidden to her mind. *You shouldn't fight for an alliance with people who think we're barely human.*

"Tell me what the southern Warlords said," Kitay said, startling her.

She sat up. "About what?"

"The Hesperians. What's this theory?"

"Just the usual. They don't trust them, they think they'll bring a second coming of the occupation, and . . . Oh." She frowned. "They also think that the Hesperians let the Mugenese invade on purpose. They think Vaisra knew the Federation was going to launch an invasion, and that the Hesperians knew, too, but neither of them acted because they wanted the empire weakened and ripe for the taking."

Kitay blinked. "Really."

"I know. That's crazy."

"No," he said. "That makes sense."

"You can't be serious. That would be awful."

"But it tracks with everything we know, doesn't it?" Kitay gave a short laugh that bordered on manic. "I'd been thinking it from the start, actually, but I thought, 'Nah, no one could be that insane. Or evil.' But think about the Republic's ships. Think about how long it took to build that entire fleet. Vaisra's been planning his civil war for years—that's obvious. But he never launched an attack until now. Why?"

"Maybe he wasn't ready," she said.

"Or maybe he needed the country weakened if he was ever going to wage a successful war against the Vipress. Needed us shattered so he could pick up the pieces."

"He needed someone else to attack first," she said slowly.

He nodded. "And the Federation was the best pawn for that task. I bet he laughed when they marched on Sinegard. I bet he'd been wanting that war for years."

Rin wanted to say no, say *of course* Vaisra wouldn't let innocent people die, but she knew that wasn't true. She knew Vaisra was more than happy to wipe entire provinces off his map as long as it meant he kept his Republic.

Gods, as long as he kept his *city*.

Which meant Hesperian passivity during the Second Poppy War had not been some political mistake, or a delay in communications, but entirely deliberate. Which meant that Vaisra had known the Federation would kill hundreds, thousands, tens of thousands, and he'd let it happen.

When she thought about it now, it should have been so easy to realize that they'd been manipulated. They had been trapped in a geopolitical chess game that had been years, perhaps decades in the making.

And she hadn't simply been fooled. She'd been deliberately blind to the clues around her, and she'd sat back and let everything happen.

She'd been stupidly, passively asleep for such a long time. She'd spent so much effort fighting in the trenches for Vaisra's Republic that she'd barely considered what might happen after.

If they won, what price would the Hesperians demand for their aid? Would Petra's experiments escalate once Vaisra no longer needed Rin on the battlefield?

It seemed so foolish now to imagine that as long as Vaisra vouched for her, she was safe from those arquebuses. Months ago she'd been lost and afraid, desperate to find an anchor, and that had primed her to trust him. But she'd also seen, over and over again by now, how easily Vaisra manipulated those around him like shadow puppets.

How quickly would he trade her away?

"Oh, Kitay." She exhaled slowly. She suddenly felt very, very afraid. "What are we going to do?"

He shook his head. "I don't know."

She thought through the possibilities out loud. "We have no good options. If we defect to the south, we're dead."

"And if you leave Arlong, then the Hesperians will hunt you down."

"But if we stay loyal to the Republic, we're just building a cage for ourselves."

"And none of that even matters if we don't survive the day after tomorrow."

They stared at each other. Rin heard a heartbeat echoing against the silence; hers or Kitay's, she didn't know.

"Tiger's tits," she said. "We're going to die. None of this even matters because Feylen is going to wreck us under the Red Cliffs and we're all going to die."

"Not necessarily." Kitay stood up abruptly. "Come with me."

She blinked up at him. "What?"

"You'll see. I've been meaning to show you something ever since you got back." He clasped her hands and pulled her to her feet. "I just haven't had the chance. Follow me."

Somehow they ended up in the armory. Rin wasn't entirely sure they were supposed to be there, because Kitay had kicked through the lock to get in, but at this point she didn't care.

He led her to a back storage room, pulled a bundle wrapped in a canvas sheet out from a corner, and dropped it on the table. "This is for you."

She peeled the sheet back. "A pile of leather. Thank you. I love it."

"Just unfold it," he said.

She held up the contraption, a confusing combination of riding straps, iron rods, and long sheets of leather. She peered at it from all angles but couldn't make sense of what she was looking at. "What is this?"

"You know how none of us have been able to defeat Feylen?" Kitay asked.

"Because he keeps flinging us into cliff walls? Yes, Kitay, I remember that."

"Listen." He had a manic glint in his eye. "What if he couldn't? What if you could fight him on his turf? Well, *turf* doesn't really apply, but you know what I mean."

She stared at him, uncomprehending. "I have no idea what you're talking about."

"You've got far more control of that fire now, yes?" he asked. "Could probably call it without thinking?"

"Sure," she said slowly. The fire felt like a natural extension of her now; she could extend it farther, burn hotter. But she was still confused. "You already know that. What does that have to do with anything?"

"How hot can you make it?" he pressed.

She frowned. "Isn't all fire the same temperature?"

"Actually, no. You get different sorts of flames on different surfaces. There's a difference between a candle flame and a blacksmith's fire, for instance. I'm not an expert, but—"

"Why does that matter?" she interrupted. "I couldn't get close enough to burn Feylen anyway, and I don't have that kind of reach."

He shook his head impatiently. "But what if you could?"

"We're not all geniuses like you," she snapped. "Just tell me what you're going on about."

He grinned. "Remember the signal lanterns before Boyang? The ones that would have exploded?"

"Of course, but—"

"Do you want to know how they work?"

She sighed and resigned herself to giving him free rein to talk as much as he wanted. "No, but I think you're about to tell me."

"Hot air rises," he said gleefully. "Cool air sinks. The balloons trap the hot air in a small space and it lifts up the entire apparatus."

She considered this for a moment. She was starting to understand where he was going, but she wasn't sure if she liked the conclusion. "I weigh a lot more than a paper balloon."

"It's about the ratio," Kitay insisted. "For instance, heavier birds need larger wings."

"But even the largest bird is *tiny* compared to—"

"So you'd need even bigger wings. And you'll need a hotter fire. But you have the strongest heat source in existence, so all we had to do was get you an apparatus to turn that into flying power. The wings, if you will."

She blinked at him, and then looked down at the pile of leather and metal. "You've got to be joking."

"Not in the slightest," he said happily. "Do you want to try it on?"

She gingerly unfolded the apparatus. It was surprisingly light, the leather smooth under her hands. She wondered where Kitay had found the material. She held it up, marveling at the neat stitching.

"You did this all in a week?"

"Yeah. I'd been thinking about it for a while, though. Ramsa came up with the idea."

"*Ramsa* did?"

He nodded. "Half of munitions is aerodynamics. He's spent a long time figuring out how to make things fly right."

Rin was somewhat wary of gambling her life on the designs of a boy whose greatest passion in life was watching things explode, but she supposed that at this point she had very few options.

With Kitay's help, she fastened the strap over her chest as tightly as she could manage. The iron rods shifted uncomfortably against her back, but otherwise the wings were surprisingly flexible, greased to rotate smoothly with every movement of her arms.

"You know, Altan used to give himself wings," she said.

"He *did*? Could he fly?"

"I doubt it. They were made of fire. I think he just did it to look pretty."

"Well, I think I can give you some functional ones." He tightened the straps around her shoulders. "Everything fit okay?"

She lifted her arms, feeling somewhat like an overgrown bat. The leather wings looked pretty, but they seemed far too thin to sustain her body weight. The interlacing rods that kept the apparatus together also looked so terribly fragile she was sure she could snap them in half over her knee. "You sure that's going to be enough to keep me up?"

"I didn't want to add too much to your weight. The rods are as slender as they'll go. Any heavier and you'll sink."

"They could also break and send me plummeting to my death," she pointed out.

"Have a little faith in me."

"It's gonna hurt *you* if I crash."

"I know." He sounded far too giddy for her comfort. "Shall we go try this out?"

They found an open clearing up on the cliffs, well out of range of anything that was remotely flammable. Kitay had wanted to test his invention by pushing Rin off a ledge, but reluctantly agreed to let her try levitating over level ground first.

The sun was just beginning to rise over the Red Cliffs, and Rin would have found it exceptionally lovely if she weren't so terrified that she could hear her heartbeat slamming in her eardrums.

She stepped out into the middle of the clearing, arms raised stiffly over her sides. She felt both exceedingly scared and stupid.

"Well, go on." Kitay backed up several paces. "Give it a try."

She gave the wings an awkward flap. "So I just . . . light up?"

"I think so. Try to keep it localized to your arms. You want the heat trapped in the air pockets under the wings, not dispersed in the air."

"All right." She willed the flame to dance up her palms and into her neck and shoulders. Her upper body felt deliciously warm, but almost immediately her wings began to smoke and sizzle.

"Kitay?" she called, alarmed.

"That's just the binding agent," said Kitay. "It'll be fine, it'll just burn off—"

Her voice rose several pitches. "It's fine if the *binding agent burns off*?"

"That's just the excess substance. The rest should hold—I think." He didn't sound convincing in the least. "I mean, we tested the solvent at the forge, so in theory . . ."

"Right," she said slowly. Her knees were shaking. Her head felt terribly light. "Why do I let you do this?"

"Because if you die, I die," he said. "Can you make those flames a little larger?"

She closed her eyes. Her leather wings lifted at her sides, expanding from the hot air.

Then she felt it—a heavy pressure yanking on her upper body, like a giant had reached down and jerked her up by the arms.

"Shit," she breathed. She looked down. Her feet had risen off the ground. "Shit. *Shit!*"

"Go higher!" Kitay called.

Great Tortoise. She *was* rising higher, without even trying—no, she was practically shooting upward. She kicked her legs, wobbling in the air. She had no lateral directional control, and she couldn't figure out how to slow her ascent, but holy gods, *she was flying.*

Kitay shouted something at her, but she couldn't hear him over the rush of the flames surrounding her.

"What?" she yelled back.

Kitay flapped his arms and ran in a zigzag motion.

Did he want her to fly sideways? She puzzled over the mechanics of it. She could decrease the heat on one side. As soon as she tried it she nearly flipped over and ended up hanging awkwardly in midair with her hip level with her head. She hastily righted herself.

She couldn't drift laterally, then. But how did birds change direction? She tried to remember. They didn't move straight to one side, they tilted their wings. They didn't drift, they swooped.

She beat her wings down several times and rose several feet into the air. Then she adjusted the curve of her arms so that the wings beat to the side, not downward, and tried again.

Immediately she careened to the left. The swift change in direction was terribly disorienting. Her stomach heaved; her flames flickered madly. For a moment she lost sight of the ground, and didn't right herself until she was mere feet away from the dirt.

She jerked herself out of the dive, gasping. This was going to take some practice.

She flapped her wings to regain altitude. She shot up faster than she'd anticipated. She flapped them again. Then again.

How far could she go? Kitay was still shouting something from the ground, but she was too far up to understand him. She rose higher and higher with each steady beat of her wings. The ground became dizzyingly far away, but she had eyes only for the great expanse of sky above her.

How far could the fire take her?

She couldn't help but laugh as she soared, a high, desperate, frantic laugh of relief. She rose so high that she could no longer make out Kitay's face, until Arlong turned into little splotches of green and blue, until she had even passed through a layer of clouds.

Then she stopped.

She hung alone in an expanse of blue.

A calm washed over her then, a calm that she couldn't ever remember feeling. There was nothing up here she could kill. Nothing she could hurt. She had her mind to herself. She had the *world* to herself.

She floated in the air, suspended at the point between heaven and earth.

The Red Cliffs looked so beautiful from up here.

Her mind wandered to the last minister of the Red Emperor, who had etched those ancient words into the cliffside. He'd written a scream to the heavens, an open plea to future generations, a message for the Hesperians who would one day sail into that harbor and bomb it.

What had he wanted to tell them?

Nothing lasts.

Nezha and Kitay had both been wrong. There was another way

to interpret those carvings. If nothing lasted and the world did not exist, all that meant was that reality was not fixed. The illusion she lived in was fluid and mutable, and could be easily altered by someone willing to rewrite the script of reality.

Nothing lasts.

This was not a world of men. It was a world of gods, a time of great powers. It was the era of divinity walking in man, of wind and water and fire. And in warfare, she who held the power asymmetry was the inevitable victor.

She, the Last Speerly, called the greatest power of all.

And the Hesperians, no matter how hard they tried, could never take this from her.

Landing was the tricky part.

Her first instinct was to simply extinguish the fire. But then she dropped like a rock, plummeting at a breakneck speed for several heart-stopping moments until she managed to get her wings spread and a fire lit beneath them. That made her come to a lurching halt so rough she was shocked the wings didn't rip right off her arms.

She drifted back up, heart hammering.

She'd have to glide down somehow. She thought through the movements in her head—she'd decrease the heat, little by little, until she was close enough to the ground.

It almost worked. She hadn't counted on how fast her velocity would increase. Suddenly she was thirty feet from the ground and hurtling far too quickly toward Kitay.

"*Move!*" she shouted, but he didn't budge. He just reached his hands out, grabbed her wrists, and swung her about until they collapsed in a tangled, laughing heap of leather and silk and limbs.

"I was right," he said. "I'm always right."

"Well, don't be so smug about it."

He groaned happily and rubbed his arms. "So how was it?"

"Incredible." She flung her arms around him and hugged him tight. "You genius. You wonderful, wonderful genius."

Kitay leaned back, arms raised. "Careful, you'll break the wings."

She twisted her head around to check them and marveled at the thin, careful craftsmanship that held the apparatus together. "I can't believe you did this in a week."

"I had some time on my hands," said Kitay. "Wasn't out there trying to stop a fleet or anything."

"I love you," she said.

Kitay gave her a tired smile. "I know."

"We still don't know what we're going to do after—" she started, but he shook his head.

"I know," he said. "I don't know what to do about the Hesperians. For once, I haven't the faintest idea, and I hate it. But we'll figure our way out of it. We've figured our way out of this, we're going to survive the Red Cliffs, we're going to survive Vaisra, and we'll keep surviving until we're safe and the world can't touch us. One enemy at a time. Agreed?"

"Agreed," she said.

Once her legs had stopped shaking, he helped her strip out of her gear. Then they climbed back down the cliff, still light-headed and giddy with victory, laughing so hard that their sides hurt.

Because yes, the fleet was still coming, and yes, they might very well die the next morning, but in that instant it didn't matter, because fuck it, she could *fly*.

"You'll need some air support," Kitay said after a while.

"Air support?"

"You'll be a very conspicuous, very obvious target. You'll want someone fending off the people shooting at you. They throw rocks, we throw them back. A line of archers would be nice."

Rin snorted. Arlong's defenses were spread thin as things were. "They're not going to give us a line of archers."

"Yeah, probably not." He shot her a sideways look, considering. "Should we try Eriden before the last council starts? See if he'll lend us at least one of his men?"

"No," she said. "I have a better idea."

Rin found Venka the first place she looked—training in the archery yard, furiously decimating straw targets. Rin stood in the corner for a moment, watching her from behind a post.

Venka hadn't fully learned yet to compensate for her stiff arms, which seemed to spasm uncontrollably and to bend only with effort. They must have hurt badly—her face tightened every time she reached for her quiver.

She hadn't taken her left arm brace off. She'd just locked her upper wrist into place instead. She was shooting while overcorrecting for a hyperextended arm, Rin realized. But for the amount of control she had left, Venka had a stunning degree of accuracy. Her speed was also absurd. By Rin's count she could shoot twenty arrows a minute, maybe more.

Venka was no Qara, but she'd do.

"Nice go," Rin called at the end of a fifteen-arrow streak.

Venka doubled over, panting. "Don't you have anything better to do?"

In response, Rin crossed the archery range and handed Venka a silk-wrapped parcel.

Venka glared at it suspiciously, then placed her bow on the ground so she could accept. "What's this?"

"A present."

Venka's lip curled. "Is it someone's head?"

Rin laughed. "Just open it."

Venka unwrapped the silk. After a moment she looked up, eyes hard, flinty and suspicious. "Where did you get this?"

"Picked it up in the north," Rin said. "It's Ketreyid-made. You like it?"

Before they'd returned to Arlong, she and Kitay had bundled all the weapons they could scavenge onto the raft. Most of them had been short knives and hunting bows that neither of them could use.

"This is a silkworm thorn bow," Venka declared. "Do you know how *rare* this is?"

Rin wouldn't have known silkworm thorn from driftwood, but

she took that as a good sign. "I thought you'd like it better than those bamboo creations."

Venka turned the bow over in her hands, then held it up to her eyes to examine the bowstring. Her arms shook. She glanced down at her trembling elbows, openly disgusted. "You don't want to waste a silkworm thorn bow on me."

"It's not a waste. I saw you shoot."

"That?" Venka snorted. "That's nowhere close to before."

"The bow will help. Silkworm thorn's lighter, I think. But we can also get you a crossbow, if it'll help with distance."

Venka squinted at her. "What exactly are you saying?"

"I need air support."

"Air . . . ?"

"Kitay's built a contraption to help me fly," Rin said bluntly.

"Oh, *gods*." Venka laughed. "Of course he has."

"He's Chen Kitay."

"Indeed he is. Does it work?"

"Shockingly, yes. But I need backup. I need someone with very good aim."

She was absolutely sure Venka would say yes. She could read longing all over Venka's face. She was looking at the bow the way some might a lover.

"They won't let me fight," she said finally. "Not even from the parapets."

"So fight for me," Rin said. "The Cike's not in the army and the Republic can't tell me who I can recruit. And we're down a few men."

"I heard." A smile cracked across Venka's face. Rin hadn't seen her look so genuinely happy in a long, long time. Venka held the bow tight to her chest, caressing the carved grip. "Well, then. I'm at your service, Commander."

CHAPTER 30

At dawn, Arlong's civilians began clearing out of the city. The evacuation proceeded with impressive efficiency. The civilians had been packed and prepared for this for weeks. All families were ready to go with two bags each of clothing, medical supplies, and several days' worth of food.

By midafternoon the city center had been hollowed out. Arlong became a shell of a city. The Republican Army quickly transformed the larger residences into defense bases with sandbags and hidden explosives.

Soldiers accompanied the civilians to the base of the cliffs, where they began a long, winding climb up to the caves inside the rock face. The pass was narrow and treacherous, and some heights could not be scaled except by using several stringy rope ladders embedded into the rock with nails.

"That's a rough climb," Rin said, looking doubtfully up the rock wall. The ladders were so narrow the evacuees would have to go up one by one, with no one to aid them. "Can everyone make it?"

"They'll get over it." Venka walked up behind her with two small, sniffling children in tow, a brother and sister who'd been separated from their parents in the crowd. "Our people have been using those hills as hideouts for years. We hid there during the Era of Warring States. We hid there when the Federation came. We'll survive this, too." She hoisted the girl up onto her hip and jerked her brother along. "Come on, hurry up."

Rin glanced backward over her shoulder at the masses of people moving below.

Maybe the caves would keep the Dragons safe. But the southern refugees had been ordered to occupy the valley lowlands, and that was just open space.

The official word was that the caves were too small to accommodate everyone, and so the refugees would have to make do. But the valley provided no shelter at all. Exposed to the elements, with no natural or military barriers to hide behind, the refugees would have no protection from the weather or the Militia—and certainly not from Feylen.

But where else were they going to go? They wouldn't have fled to Arlong if home were safe.

"I'm hungry," complained the boy.

"I don't care." Venka tugged at his skinny wrist. "Stop crying. Walk faster."

"This battle will take place primarily in three stages," said Vaisra. "One, we will fend them off at the outer channel between the Red Cliffs. Two, we win the ground battle in the city. Three, they will try to retreat along the coast, and we will pick them off. We'll get to that stage if we are miraculously lucky."

His officers nodded grimly.

Rin glanced around the council room, amazed by how many faces she'd never seen before. A good half of the officers were newly promoted. They wore the stripes of senior leadership, but they looked five years older than Rin at most.

So many young, scared faces. The military command had been killed off at the top. This was rapidly becoming a war fought by the children.

"Can that warship even get through the cliffs?" asked Captain Dalain.

"Daji's familiar with the channel," said Admiral Kulau, the young navy officer who had replaced Molkoi. He sounded as if he were deepening his voice to seem older. "She'll have designed it so it can."

"It doesn't matter," Eriden said. "If their warship even starts depositing troops outside the channel, then we're in trouble." He leaned over the map. "That's why we have archers stationed here and here—"

"Why aren't there any back-end fortifications?" Kitay interrupted.

"The invasion will come from the channel," Vaisra said. "Not the valley."

"But the channel's the obvious avenue of attack," Kitay said. "They know you're expecting them. If I'm Daji, and I have a numerical advantage *that* large, then I split my troops and send a third column round the back while everyone's distracted."

"No one's ever attacked Arlong from land routes," Kulau said. "They'd be eviscerated on the mountaintops."

"Not if they're unguarded," Kitay insisted.

Kulau cleared his throat. "They're not unguarded. They've got fifty men guarding them."

"Fifty men can't beat a column!"

"Chang En's not going to send a full column of his crack troops round the back. You have a fleet that big, you man it."

No one spoke the more obvious answer, which was that the Republican Army simply didn't have the *troops* for better fortifications. And if any part of Arlong warranted a defense, then it was the palace and military barracks. Not the valley lowlands. Not the southerners.

"Of course, Chang En will want this to turn into a land battle," Vaisra continued smoothly. "There they have the sheer advantage in numbers. But this fight remains winnable as long as we keep it amphibious."

The channel had already been blocked up with so many iron chains and underwater obstacles that it almost functioned as a dam. The Republic was banking on mobility over numbers—their armed skimmers could dart between the Imperial ships, breaking up formations while the munitions crews shot bombs down from their cliffside stations.

"What's the makeup of their fleet?" asked a young officer Rin didn't recognize. He sounded terribly nervous. "Which ships do we target?"

"Aim for the warships, not the skimmers," Kulau said. "Anything that has a trebuchet should be a target. But the bulk of their troops are on that floating fortress. If you can sink any ships, sink that first."

"You want us in a fan formation at the cliffs?" Captain Dalain asked.

"No," said Kulau. "If we spread out then they'll just obliterate us. Stay in a narrow line and plug up the channel."

"We're not worried about their shaman?" Dalain asked. "If we clump our ships together, he's just going to blast our fleet against the cliffs."

"I'll take care of Feylen," Rin said.

The generals blinked at her. She looked around the table, eyes wide open. "What?"

"Last time you ended up stranded for a month," said Captain Eriden. "We'll be fine against Feylen—we have fifteen squadrons of archers positioned across the cliff walls."

"And he'll just fling them off the cliffs," said Rin. "They won't be more than an annoyance."

"And you won't be?"

"No," she said. "This time, I can fly."

The generals looked as if they were unsure whether to laugh. Only General Tarcquet, sitting silently as usual in the back of the room, looked mildly curious.

"I built her a, uh, flying kite sort of contraption," Kitay explained. He made some gestures with his hands that clarified nothing. "It's made up of some leather wings with rods, and she can generate flames hot enough to levitate herself using the same principle that lifts a lantern—"

"Have you tried it?" Vaisra asked. "Does it work?"

Rin and Kitay nodded.

"Wonderful," Gurubai said drily. "So, assuming she's not mad, that's the Wind God taken care of. There's still the rest of the Imperial Navy to deal with, and we're still outnumbered three to one."

The officers shifted uneasily.

It was easier for Rin if she compartmentalized the battle to simply dealing with Feylen. She didn't want to think about the rest of the fleet, because the truth was there *was* no easy way to deal with the fleet. They were outnumbered, they were on the defensive, and they were trapped.

Kitay sounded far calmer than she felt. "There's a number of different tactics we can try. We can try to break them up and storm their warships. The important thing is that we don't let that fortress get to the shore, because then it turns into a land battle for the city."

"And Jun's forces won't be so formidable," Kulau added. "They'll be exhausted. The Militia isn't used to naval battles, they'll be seasick and dizzy. Meanwhile our army was designed for riverine warfare, and our soldiers are fresh. We'll just outfight them."

The room looked unconvinced.

"Here's an option we haven't considered," General Hu said after a short pause. "We could surrender."

Rin found it disheartening that this wasn't immediately met with a general outcry.

Several seconds passed in silence. Rin glanced sideways at Vaisra but couldn't read his expression.

"That wouldn't be a terrible idea," Vaisra said finally.

"It wouldn't." General Hu glanced desperately around the room. "Look, I'm not the only one thinking it. They're going to slaughter us. No one's come back from a numbers disadvantage like this in history. If we cut our losses now, we still come out of this alive."

"As always," Vaisra said slowly, "you are the voice of reason, General Hu."

General Hu looked profoundly relieved, but his smile faded as Vaisra continued to speak. "Why *not* surrender? The consequences couldn't possibly be so terrible. All that would happen is that every single person in this room would be flayed alive, Arlong destroyed, and any hope of democratic reform would be quashed in the Empire for at least the next few centuries. Is that what you want?"

General Hu had turned pale. "No."

"I have no place in my army for cowards," Vaisra said softly. He nodded to the soldier standing beside Hu. "You there. You're his aide?"

The boy nodded, eyes huge. He couldn't have been older than twenty. "Yes, sir."

"Ever been in battle?" Vaisra asked.

The boy's throat bobbed as he swallowed. "Yes, sir. I was at Boyang."

"Excellent. And what is your name?"

"Zhou Anlan, sir."

"Congratulations, General Zhou. You've been promoted." Vaisra turned to General Hu. "You can leave."

General Hu forced his way through the crowded bodies and left without another word. The door swung shut behind him.

"He's going to defect," said Vaisra. "Eriden, see that he's stopped."

"Permanently?" Eriden asked.

Vaisra considered that briefly. "Only if he struggles."

After the council had been dismissed, Vaisra motioned for Rin to stay behind. She exchanged a panicked glance with Kitay as he filtered out with the others. Once the room had emptied, Vaisra closed the door behind him.

"When this is over I want you to go pay a visit to our friend Moag," he said quietly.

She was so relieved that he hadn't mentioned the Hesperians that for a moment all she did was blink at him, uncomprehending. "The Pirate Queen?"

"Make it quick," Vaisra said. "Leave the corpse and bring back the head."

"Wait. You want me to kill her?"

"Was I not sufficiently clear?"

"But she's your biggest naval ally—"

"The *Hesperians* are our biggest naval ally," Vaisra said. "Do you see Moag's ships in the bay?"

"I don't see any Hesperian ships in the bay," Rin pointed out.

"They will come. Give them time. But Moag's going to be nothing but trouble once this war's over. She's operated extralegally for too long, and she couldn't get used to a naval authority that isn't her own. Smuggling's in her blood."

"So let her smuggle," Rin said. "Keep her happy. What's the problem with that?"

"There's no way to keep her happy. Ankhiluun exists because of the tariffs. Once we have free trade with the Hesperians, that makes the entire premise of Ankhiluun irrelevant. All she'll have left is opium smuggling, and I don't intend to be half as lenient toward opium as Daji is. There's a war coming once Moag realizes all her income streams are drying up. I'd rather nip it in the bud."

"And this request has nothing to do with the fact that she hasn't sent ships?" Rin asked.

Vaisra smiled. "An ally's only useful if they do as they're told. Moag's proven herself unreliable."

"So you want me to commit preemptive murder."

"Let's not be as dramatic as that." He waved a hand. "We'll call it insurance."

"I think the wall's ready," Kitay said, rubbing his eyes. He looked exhausted. "I wanted to triple-check the fuses, but there wasn't time."

They stood at the edge of the cliffs, watching the sun set between the two sides of the channel like a ball falling down a ravine. Dark water shimmered below, reflecting crimson rock and a burnt-orange sun. It looked like a flood of blood gushing out from a freshly sliced artery.

When Rin squinted at the opposite cliff, she could just see the lines where fuses had been strung together and tucked with nails into the rock, like a sprawling, ugly patchwork of protruding veins.

"What are they chances they don't go off?" she asked.

Kitay yawned. "They'll probably go off."

"Probably," she repeated.

"You're just going to have to trust Ramsa and I did our jobs. If they don't go off, we're all dead."

"Fair enough." Rin hugged her arms across her chest. She felt tiny standing over the massive precipice. Empires had been won and lost under these cliffs. They were on the brink of losing another one.

"Do you think we can win tomorrow?" she asked quietly. "I mean, is there even the slightest chance?"

"I've done the math seven different ways," Kitay said. "Compiled all the intelligence we have and compared the probabilities and everything."

"And?"

"And I don't know." His fists clenched and unclenched, and Rin could tell he was resisting the urge to start tugging at his hair. "That's the frustrating part. You know the one thing that all the great strategists agree upon? It actually doesn't matter what numbers you have. It doesn't matter how good your models are, or how brilliant your strategies are. The world is chaotic and war is fundamentally unpredictable and at the end of the day you don't know who will be the last man standing. You don't know anything going into a battle. You only know the stakes."

"Well, they're pretty fucking high," Rin said.

If they lost, their rebellion would be vanquished and Nikan would descend into darkness for another several decades at least, rent apart by factional warfare and a lingering Federation presence.

But if they won, the Empire would become a Republic, primed to hurtle into the new and glorious future with Vaisra at the helm and the Hesperians at his side.

And then Rin would have to worry about what happened after.

An idea struck her then—just the smallest tendril of one, but it was there; a fierce, burning spark of hope. Vaisra might have just handed her a way out.

"How do you get to the rookery?" she asked.

"I can take you," Kitay said. "Who do you want to send a letter to?"

"Moag." Rin turned to begin the climb back toward the city.

Kitay followed. "What for?"

"There's something she should know." She was already composing the message in her head. If—no, *when*—she left the Republic, she would need an ally. Someone who could get her out of the city fast. Someone who wasn't linked to the Republic.

Moag was a liar, but Moag had ships. And now, Moag had a death sentence over her head that she didn't know about. That gave Rin leverage, which gave her an ally.

"Call it insurance," she said.

Traveling at its current pace, the Imperial Navy would breach the channel at dawn. That gave Arlong six more hours to prepare. Vaisra ordered his troops to sleep in rotating two-hour shifts so they would meet the Militia with as much stamina as possible.

Rin understood the rationale, but she couldn't see how she was possibly supposed to close her eyes. She vibrated with nervous energy, and even sitting still made her uneasy—she needed to be moving, running, hitting something.

She paced around the field outside the barracks. Little rivulets of fire danced through the air around her, swirling in perfect circles. That made her feel the slightest bit better. It was proof that she still had control over *something*.

Someone cleared his throat. She turned around. Nezha stood at the door, bleary-eyed and disheveled.

"What's happened?" she asked sharply. "Did anything—"

"I had a dream," he mumbled.

She raised an eyebrow. "And?"

"You died."

She made her flames disappear. "What is going on with you?"

"You died," he repeated. He sounded dazed, only half-present, like a little schoolboy disinterestedly reciting his Classics. "You—they shot you down over the water, and I saw your body floating up in the water. You were so still. I saw you drown, and I couldn't save you."

He started to cry.

"What the fuck," she muttered.

Was he drunk? High? She didn't know what she was supposed to do, only that she didn't want to be alone with him. She glanced toward the barracks. What would happen if she just left?

"Please don't leave," Nezha said, as if reading her mind.

She folded her arms against her chest. "I didn't think you ever wanted to see me again."

"Why would you think that?"

"'It would be best if we died,'" she said. "Who said that?"

"I didn't mean that—"

"Then what? Where do you draw the line? Suni, Baji, Altan—we're all monsters in your book, aren't we?"

"I was angry that you called me a coward—"

"Because you are a coward!" she shouted. "How many men died at Boyang? How many are going to die today? But no, Yin Nezha has the power to stop the river and he won't do it, because he's fucking scared of a tattoo on his back—"

"I told you, it *hurts*—"

"It always hurts. You call the gods anyway. We're soldiers—we make the sacrifices we must, no matter what it takes. But I suppose you would put your own *comfort* over a chance to crush the Empire—"

"Comfort?" Nezha repeated. "You think it's about comfort? Do you know how it felt, when I was in his cave? Do you know what he did to me?"

"Yes," she said. "Exactly the same thing the Phoenix did to me."

Rin knew Nezha's pain. She just didn't have the sympathy for it.

"You're acting like a fucking child," she said. "You're a general, Nezha. Do your job."

Anger darkened his face. "Just because you've decided to worship *your* abuser doesn't mean we all—"

Rin stiffened. "No one abused me."

"Rin, you know that's not true."

"Fuck you."

"I'm sorry." He held up his hands in surrender. "Look—I really am. I didn't come here to talk about that. I don't want to fight."

"Then why are you here?"

"Because you could die out there," he said. "We both could." His words poured out in a torrent, as if he were afraid that if he stopped speaking they would run out of time, as if he would only ever get this one chance. "I saw it happen, I saw you bleeding out in the water, and I couldn't do anything about it. That was the worst part."

"Are you high?" she demanded.

"I just want to make things right between us. What's that going to take?" Nezha spread his arms. "Should I let you hit me? Do you want to? Go ahead, take a swing. I won't move."

Rin almost took him up on the offer. But the moment she made a fist, her anger dissipated.

Why was it that whenever she looked at Nezha, she wanted to either kill him or kiss him? He made her either furious or deliriously happy. The one thing he did not make her feel was secure.

With him there was no neutrality, no in between. She loved him or she hated him, but she didn't know how to do both.

She lowered her fist.

"I really am sorry," Nezha said. "Please, Rin. I don't want us to end like this."

He tried to say something else, but the sudden boom of the signal gongs drowned out his voice. They reverberated through the barracks with such loud urgency that Rin could feel the ground trembling beneath her feet.

The familiar taste of blood filled her mouth. Panic, fear, and adrenaline flooded her veins. But this time they didn't make her collapse; she didn't want to curl into a ball and rock back and forth until it was over. She was used to this now, and she could use it as a fuel. Turn it into bloodlust.

"We should be in position," she said. She tried to walk past him into the barracks to get her equipment, but he grabbed at her arm.

"Rin, please—you have more enemies than you think you do—"

She shrugged him off. "Let me go!"

He blocked her path. "I don't want this to be the last conversation we ever have."

"Then don't die out there," she said. "Problem solved."

"But Feylen—"

"We're not going to lose to Feylen this time," she said. "We're going to win, and we're going to live."

He sounded like a terrified child woken up from a bad dream. "But how do you know?"

She didn't know what made her do it, but she put her hand on Nezha's shoulder. It wasn't an apology or forgiveness, but it was a concession. An acknowledgment.

And for just a moment, she felt a hint of that old camaraderie, a flicker she'd felt once, a year ago at Sinegard, when he'd thrown her a sword and they'd fought back to back, enemies turned to comrades, firmly on the same side for the first time in their lives.

She saw the way he was looking at her. She knew he felt it, too.

"Between us, we have the fire and the water," she said quietly. "I'm quite sure that together, we can take on the wind."

CHAPTER 31

"I can feel my heartbeat in my temples." Venka leaned over her mounted crossbow and checked the gears for what seemed like the hundredth time. It was cranked to maximum, fitted in with twelve reloading bolts. "Don't you love this part?"

"I hate this part," Kitay said. "Feels like we're waiting for our executioner."

His hairline sported visible bald patches. He was going mad waiting for the Imperial Navy to show up, and Rin knew why. They both liked it so much better when they were on the offensive, when they could decide when to attack and where.

They'd been taught at Sinegard that fighting a defensive battle by sitting behind fixed fortifications was courting disaster because it just gave the enemy the advantage of initiative. Unless a siege was at play, sitting behind defenses was almost always a doomed strategy, because there were no locks that couldn't be broken, and no fortresses that were impregnable.

And this would not be a siege. Daji had no interest in starving them out. She didn't need to. She intended to smash right through the gates.

"Arlong hasn't been taken for centuries," Venka pointed out.

Kitay's hands twitched. "Well, its luck had to run out sometime."

The Republic was as prepared as it ever would be. The generals had set their defensive traps. They'd divided and positioned their troops—seven artillery stations all along the upper cliffs, the majority stationed on the Republican Fleet in formation inside the channel, and the rest either guarding the shore or barricading the heavily fortified palace.

Rin wished that the Cike could be up on the cliff fighting by her side, but neither Baji nor Suni could offer much air support against Feylen. They were both stationed on warships at the center of the Republican Fleet where, right in the brunt of enemy fire, their abilities might stay hidden from Hesperian observers, and also where they'd be able to cause the most damage.

"Is Nezha in position?" Kitay peered over the channel.

Nezha was assigned to the front of the fleet, leading one of the three remaining warships that could hold its own in a naval skirmish. He was to drive his ship directly into the center of the Imperial Fleet and split it apart.

"Nezha's always in position," said Venka. "He's sprung like a—"

"Don't be vulgar," Kitay said.

Venka grinned.

They could hear a faint series of booms echoing from beyond the mouth of the channel. In truth, the battle had already begun—a flimsy handful of riverside forts that constituted Arlong's first line of defense had already engaged the Militia, but they were manned with only enough soldiers to keep the cannons firing.

Kitay had estimated those would buy them all of ten minutes.

"There," Venka said sharply. "I see them."

They stood up.

The Imperial Navy sailed directly into their line of sight. Rin caught her breath, trying not to panic at the sheer size of Daji's fleet combined with Tsolin's.

"What's Chang En doing?" Kitay demanded.

The Wolf Meat General had lashed his boats together, tied them stern to stern into a single, immobile structure. The fleet had become a single, massive battering ram, with the floating fortress at the very center.

"To fight the seasickness, you think?" Venka asked.

Rin frowned. "Has to be."

That seemed like a clever move. The Imperial troops weren't used to fighting over moving water, so they might do better on a locked platform. But a static formation was also particularly dangerous where battling Rin was concerned. If one ship went up in flames, so did the rest of them.

Had Daji not discovered that Rin had figured a way around the Seal?

"It's not seasickness," Kitay said. "It's so Feylen won't blow them out of the water. And it gives them the advantage if we try to board. They get troop mobility between ships."

"We're not going to board," said Rin. "We're going to torch that thing."

"That's the spirit," Venka said with an optimism that nobody felt.

The locked fleet crawled toward the cliffs at a maddeningly slow pace. War drums echoed around the channel as the fortress moved inexorably forward.

"I wonder how many men it takes to propel that thing," Venka mused.

"They don't need much paddling force," Rin said. "They're sailing downstream."

"Okay, but what about lateral movement—"

"Please stop talking," Kitay snapped.

Rin knew their chattering was idiotic, but she couldn't help it. She and Venka had the same problem. They had to keep running their mouths, because the wait would drive them crazy otherwise.

"The gates aren't going to hold," Rin said despite Kitay's glare. "It'll be like kicking down a sandcastle."

"You're giving it five minutes, then?" Venka asked.

"More like two. Get ready to fire that thing."

Venka patted Kitay's shoulder. "Don't be so hard on yourself."

He rolled his eyes. "The gate wasn't my idea."

In a last-ditch effort, Vaisra had ordered his troops to chain the gates of the channel shut with every spare link of iron in the city. It might have deterred a pirate ship, but against this fleet, it was little more than a symbolic gesture. From the sounds of it, the Militia intended to simply knock the gates over with a battering ram.

Boom. Rin felt stone vibrating beneath her feet.

"How old are those gates?" she wondered out loud.

Boom.

"Older than this province," said Venka. "Maybe as old as the Red Emperor. Lot of architectural value."

"That's a pity."

"Isn't it?"

Boom. Rin heard the sharp crack of fracturing wood, and then a noise like fabric ripping.

Arlong's gates were down.

The Imperial Navy poured through. The channel lit up with pyrotechnics. Massive twenty-foot cannons embedded into Arlong's cliff walls went off one by one, sending scorching, boulder-sized balls shrieking into the sides of Chang En's ships. Each one of Kitay's carefully planted water mines went off in lovely, timed succession to the sound of firecrackers magnified by a thousand.

For a moment the Imperial Fleet was hidden behind a massive cloud of smoke.

"Nice," Venka marveled.

Kitay shook his head. "That's nothing. They can absorb the losses."

He was right. When the smoke cleared, Rin saw that there had been more noise than damage. The fleet pressed on through the explosions. The floating fortress remained untouched.

Rin paced toward the cliff edge, sword in hand.

"Patience," Kitay muttered. "Now's not the time."

"We should be down there," she said. She felt like a coward waiting up on the cliff, hiding out of sight while soldiers burned below.

"We're only three people," Kitay said. "We'd be cannon fodder. You dive in now, you'll just get shot full of iron."

Rin hated that he was right.

The cliffs shook continuously under their feet. The Imperial Navy was returning fire. Loaded missiles shot out of the siege towers, showering tiny rockets onto the cliffside artillery stations. Shielded Militia archers returned two crossbow bolts for every one that reached their decks.

Rin's stomach twisted with horror as she watched. The Militia was using precisely the same siege-breaking strategy that Jinzha had employed on the northern campaign—eviscerate the archers first, then barrel through land resistance.

The Republican warships took the worst damage. One had already been blown so thoroughly out of the water that its fragmented remains were blocking the paths of its sister ships.

The Imperial cannons fired low to aim at the paddle wheels. The Republican ships tried to rotate in the water to keep their back paddles out of the line of fire, but they were rapidly losing mobility. At this rate, Nezha's ships would be reduced to sitting ducks.

Rin still saw no sign of Feylen.

"Where is he?" Kitay muttered. "You'd think they would bring him out right away."

"Maybe he's bad with orders," Rin said. Feylen had seemed so terrified of Daji, she didn't want to think about the kind of torture it took to persuade him to fight.

But at this rate, the Militia didn't even need to bring Feylen out. Two artillery stations had gone down. The other five were running out of ammunition and had slowed their rate of fire. Most of Nezha's warships were dead in the water, while the core of the Imperial Navy had sustained very little fire damage.

Time to rectify that. Rin stood up. "I'm going in."

"Now's the time," Kitay agreed. He handed her a jug of oil from a tidy pile stocked next to the crossbow, and then pointed down at the channel. "I'm thinking center left of that tower ship.

You want to split that formation apart. Get the ropes going and the rest will catch fire."

"And don't look down," Venka said helpfully.

"Shut up." Rin stepped backward, dug her feet against the ground, and broke into a run. The wind whipped against her face. Her wings rippled against the drag. Then the cliff disappeared under her feet, her head pitched downward, and there was no fear, no sound, only the thrilling and sickening lurch of the drop.

She let herself dive for a moment before she opened her wings. When she spread her arms the resistance hit her like a punch. Her arms felt like they were being torn from their sockets. She gasped—not from the pain, but from the sheer exhilaration. The river was a blur, ships and armies dissolving into solid streaks of browns and blues and greens.

Arrows emerged in her line of sight. They looked like needles from a distance; gaining in size at a frightening pace. She veered to the left. They whizzed harmlessly past her.

She'd gotten within range of the tower ship. She leveled off the dive. She opened her mouth and palms; a stream of fire shot out from her extremities, setting ablaze everything she passed.

She dropped the oil just before she pulled up.

She heard the glass shatter as the jar hit the deck, the crackle as the flames caught. She smiled as she soared upward to the opposite cliff wall. When she hazarded a glance backward she saw arrows lose momentum and drop back to the ground as they struggled to reach her.

Her feet found solid earth. She dropped to her knees and doubled over on all fours, panting while she surveyed the damage below.

The ropes had caught a steady, spreading fire. She could see them blackening and fraying where she'd dropped the oil.

She looked up. Across the channel, Venka methodically shoved another round of bolts into her crossbow loading mechanism, while Kitay waved for her to return.

The muscles in her arms burned, but she couldn't afford too much time for recovery. She crawled to the edge of the cliff and hauled herself to her feet.

She squinted, mapping out her next flight pattern. She caught Venka's attention and pointed toward a cluster of ships untouched by the fire. Venka nodded and redirected her crossbow.

Rin took a deep breath, jumped off the cliff, and swooped down, basking again in the rush of adrenaline. Javelins came whistling in her direction, one after another, but all she had to do was swerve and they soared uselessly into empty air.

She felt giddy as she set sails ablaze and felt the warm heat of the fire buoying her up as it spread. Was this how Altan had always felt in the heat of battle? She understood now why he'd summoned himself wings, even though he couldn't fly with them.

It was symbolic. Ecstatic. In this moment she was invincible, divine. She hadn't just summoned the Phoenix, she'd become it.

"Nice job," Kitay said once she'd landed. "The fire's spread to three ships, they haven't managed to put it out—wait, can you breathe?"

"I'm okay," she gasped. "Just—give me a moment . . ."

"Guys," Venka said sharply. "This is bad."

Rin staggered to her feet and joined her near the precipice.

Burning the ropes had worked. The Imperial formation had begun to splinter, its outward ships drifting away from the center. Nezha had seized the opening to wedge his warship straight through the main cluster, where he'd managed to blow smoking holes into the side of the floating fortress.

But now he was stuck. The Imperial Navy had lowered wide planks onto his ship's sides. Nezha was about to get swarmed.

"I'm going down there," Rin said.

"To do what?" Kitay asked. "Burn them and you burn Nezha."

"Then I'll land and fight. I can direct fire more accurately from the ground, I just have to get there."

Kitay looked reluctant. "But Feylen—"

"We don't know where Feylen is. Nezha's in trouble. *I'm going.*"

"Rin. Look at the hills." Venka pointed toward the lowland valleys. "I think they've sent ground troops."

Rin exchanged a glance with Kitay.

Before he could speak she launched herself into the sky.

The ground column was impossible to miss. Rin could see them so clearly through the forest, a thick band of troops marching on Arlong from behind. They were barely half a mile from the refugee evacuation areas. They'd reach them in minutes.

She cursed into the wind. Eriden had claimed his scouts hadn't seen anything in the valley.

But how did one miss an entire *brigade*?

Her mind raced. Venka and Kitay were both screaming at her, but she couldn't hear them.

Should she go? How much good could she do? She couldn't destroy a column of soldiers on her own. And she couldn't abandon the naval battle—if Feylen appeared while she was miles away he could sink the entirety of their fleet before she could return.

But she had to tell *someone*.

She scanned the channel. She knew Vaisra and his generals were ensconced behind fortifications near the shore where they could oversee the battle, but they would refuse to do anything even if she warned them. The naval battle had few enough soldiers to spare.

She had to warn the Warlords.

They were scattered throughout the battleground with their troops, she just didn't know *where*.

No one could hear her shout from this high up. Her only option was to write them a message in the sky. She beat her wings twice to gain altitude and flew forward until she hung right over the channel, in clear sight but high out of range.

She decided on two words.

Valley invaded.

She pointed down. Flames poured from her fingers and lingered for a few seconds where she'd placed them before they dissipated. She wrote the two characters over and over, going over strokes that had faded from the air, praying that someone below would see the message.

For a long moment, nothing happened.

Then, near the shoreline, she saw a line of soldiers peeling away from the front. Someone had noticed.

She redirected her attention to the channel.

Nezha's ship had been almost completely overrun by Imperial troops. The ship's cannons had gone silent. By now its crew had to be mostly dead or incapacitated.

She didn't stop to think. She dove.

She landed badly. Her dive was too steep and she hadn't pulled up in time. She skidded forward on her knees, yelping in pain as her skin scraped along the deck.

Militia soldiers converged on her instantly. She called down a column of flame, a protective circle that incinerated everything within a five-foot radius and pushed the approaching soldiers back.

Her eyes fell on a blue uniform in a sea of green. She barreled through the burning bodies, arms shielding her head, until she reached the single Republican soldier in sight.

"Where's Nezha?" she asked.

He stared past her with unfocused eyes. Blood trickled in a single line from his forehead across his face.

She shook him hard. "Where's Nezha?"

The officer opened his mouth just as an arrow embedded itself in his left eye. Rin flung the body away, ducked, and snatched a shield up from the deck just before three arrows thudded into the space where her head had been.

She advanced slowly along the deck, flames roaring out of her in a semicircle to repel Militia troops. Soldiers crumpled in her path, twitching and burning, while others hurled themselves into the water to escape the fire.

Through the blaze she heard the faint sound of clashing steel.

She dimmed the wall of flame just for a moment to see Nezha and a handful of remaining Republican soldiers dueling with General Jun's platoon on the other end of the deck.

He's still alive. Warm hope filled her chest. She ran toward Nezha, shooting targeted ribbons of flame into the melee. Tendrils of fire wrapped around Militia soldiers' necks like whips while balls of flame consumed their faces, blinding their eyes, scorching their mouths, asphyxiating them. She kept going until all soldiers in her vicinity had dropped to the ground, either dead or dying. It felt bizarrely, exhilaratingly good to know she had so much control over the flame, that she now possessed such potent and novel ways of killing.

When she pulled the fire back in, Nezha had fought Jun to submission.

"You're a good soldier," said Nezha. "My father doesn't want you dead."

"Don't bother." A sneer twisted Jun's face. He raised his sword to his chest.

Nezha moved faster. His blade flashed through the air. Rin heard a thick chop that reminded her of a butcher shop. Jun's severed hand dropped to the ground.

Jun stumbled forward on his knees, staring at his bloody stump like he couldn't believe what he was looking at.

"It won't be that easy for you," said Nezha.

"You ingrate," Jun seethed. "I *created* you."

"You taught me the meaning of fear," Nezha said. "Nothing more."

Jun made a wild grab for the dagger in Nezha's belt, but Nezha kicked out—one short, precise blow against Jun's severed stump. Jun howled in pain and fell over onto his side.

"Do it," Rin said. "Quickly."

Nezha shook his head. "He's a good prisoner—"

"He tried to kill you!" Rin shouted. She summoned a ball of flame to her right hand. "If you won't, then I will—"

Nezha grabbed her shoulder. *"Stop!"*

Jun struggled to his feet and made a mad scramble for the edge of the ship.

"No!" Nezha rushed forward, but it was too late. Rin saw Jun's feet disappear over the railing. She heard a splash several seconds later. She and Nezha hurried to the railing to look over the edge, but Jun didn't resurface.

Nezha whirled on her. "We could have taken him prisoner!"

"Look, I didn't hurl him off the side." She couldn't see how this was her fault. "And I just saved your life. You're welcome, by the way."

Rin saw Nezha open his mouth to retort just before something wet and heavy slammed into her from above and knocked her to the deck. Her wings jammed painfully into her shoulders. She was caught under a water-soaked canvas, she realized. Her fire did nothing but fill the inside of the canvas with scorching steam. She had to call it back in before she choked.

Someone was holding the canvas down, trapping her inside. She kicked frantically, trying to wriggle out to no avail. She twisted harder until her head broke through the side.

"Hello." The Wolf Meat General leered down at her.

She roared flames at his face. He slugged the back of his gauntleted hand against her head. She slammed back against the deck; her vision exploded into sparks. Dimly she saw Chang En lift his sword over her neck.

Nezha hurled himself into Chang En's side. They landed sprawled in a heap. Nezha scrambled to his feet and backed away, sword raised. Chang En picked his sword off the deck, cackling, and then attacked.

Rin lay flat on her back, blinking at the sky. All of her extremities tingled, but they wouldn't obey when she tried to move them. From the corner of her eye she caught glimpses of a fight; she heard a deafening flurry of blows, steel raining down on steel.

She had to help Nezha. But her fists wouldn't open; the fire wouldn't come.

Her vision started fading to black, but she couldn't lose consciousness. Not now. She bit down hard on her tongue, willing the pain to keep her awake.

Finally she managed to lift her head. Chang En had backed Nezha into a corner. Nezha was flagging, clearly struggling simply to stand up straight. Blood soaked the entire left side of his uniform.

"I'll saw your head off," Chang En sneered. "Then I'll feed it to my dogs, just like I did your brother's."

Nezha screamed and redoubled his assault.

Rin groaned and rolled over onto her side. Flames sparked and burst in her palms—just tiny lights, nowhere near the intensity she needed. She squeezed her eyes shut, trying to concentrate. To pray.

Please, I need you . . .

Nezha's strikes came nowhere close to landing. Chang En disarmed him with ease and kicked his sword across the deck. Nezha scrambled for the hilt. Chang En swept a leg behind his knees, kicking him to the ground, and placed a boot on his chest.

Hello, little one, said the Phoenix.

Flames burst out of every part of her. The fire was no longer localized to her control points—her hands and mouth—but blazed around her entire body like a suit of armor, glowing and untouchable.

She pointed a finger at Chang En. A thick stream of fire slammed into his face. He dropped his sword and buried his head in his hands, trying to smother the flames, but the blaze only extended across his entire body, burning brighter and brighter as he screamed.

Rin stopped just short of killing him. She didn't want to make this easy for him.

Chang En had stopped moving. He lay flat on his back, covered in grotesque burns. His face and arms had turned black, shot through with cracks that revealed blistered, bubbling skin.

Rin stood over him and opened her palms downward.

Nezha grabbed her shoulder. "Don't."

She shot him an exasperated look. "Don't tell me you want to take him prisoner, too."

"No," he said. "I want to do it."

She stepped back and gestured to Chang En's limp form. "All yours."

"I'll need a sword," he said.

Wordlessly, she handed hers over.

Nezha traced the tip of the blade over Chang En's face, jabbing it into the blistered skin between his crackled cheekbones. "Hey. Wake up."

Chang En's eyes opened.

Nezha forced the sword point straight down into Chang En's left eye.

Chang En grabbed at empty air, trying to wrench the blade from Nezha's grasp, but Nezha gave him a savage kick to the ribs, then several more to the face.

Nezha wanted to watch Chang En bleed. Rin didn't try to stop him. She wanted to watch, too.

Nezha pressed the sword point to Chang En's neck. "Stop moving."

Whimpering, Chang En lay still. His gouged eye dangled grotesquely on the side of his face, still connected by lumpy strings. The other eye blinked furiously, drenched in blood.

Nezha grasped the hilt with both hands and brought it down hard. Blood splashed across both of their faces.

Nezha let the sword drop and backed away slowly. His chest heaved. Rin put her hand on his back.

He leaned into her, shaking. "It's over."

"No, it's not," she whispered.

It had barely just begun. Because the air had suddenly gone still—so still that every flag in the channel dropped, and the sound of every shout and clash of steel was amplified in the absence of wind.

She reached out and grabbed Nezha's fingers in hers, just as the ship ripped out from beneath them.

CHAPTER 32

The force of the gale tore them apart.

For a moment Rin hung weightless in the air, watching driftwood and bodies floating absurdly beside her, and then she dropped into the water with the rest of what used to be the ship's upper deck.

She couldn't see Nezha. She couldn't see anything. She sank fast, weighted down by the wreckage. She flailed desperately around in the black water, trying to find some path to the surface.

And there it was—a glimmer of light through the mass of bodies. Her lungs burned. She had to get up there. She kicked, but something tugged at her legs. She'd gotten tangled in the flag, and wet cloth underwater was strong as iron steel. Panic fogged her mind. The flag only ensnared her more the harder she kicked, dragging her down to the riverbed.

Calm. She forced herself to empty her mind. *Calm down.* No anger, no panic, just nothingness. She found that silent place of clarity that allowed her to think.

She wasn't drowned yet. She still had the strength to kick her way to the surface. And the cloth wasn't tied in such a hopeless knot, it was simply looped twice around her leg. She reached forward. A few quick movements and she broke free. Relieved, she swam upward, forcing herself not to panic, focusing on the simple act of pushing herself through the water until her head broke the surface.

She didn't see Nezha as she dragged herself to shore. She scanned the wreckage, but she couldn't find him. Had he surfaced at all? Was he dead? Crushed, impaled, drowned—

No. She had to trust that he was fine. He could control the water itself; it couldn't possibly kill him.

Could it?

The howl of unnatural wind pierced the channel and lingered, punctuated only by the sound of splintering wood.

Oh, gods.

Rin looked up.

Feylen hung suspended in the air above her, slamming ships against the cliff wall with mere sweeps of his arm. Driftwood and debris swirled in a hazardous circle around him. With winds as fast as these, any one of those pieces might kill her.

Rin's mouth had gone dry. Her knees buckled. All she wanted was to find a hole and hide. She stood paralyzed by fear and despair. Feylen was going to batter their fleet around the channel until there was nothing left. Why fight? Death would be easier if she didn't resist . . .

She ground her fingernails into her palm until the pain brought her to her senses.

She couldn't run.

Who else was going to fight him? Who else possibly *could*?

She'd lost her sword in the water, but she spied a javelin on the ground. Fat lot of good it would do against Feylen, but it felt better to hold a weapon. She scooped it up, opened her wings, and summoned a flame around her arms and shoulders. Steam fizzled around her, a choking cloud of mist. Rin waved it away, hoping desperately her wings were waterproof.

She focused on generating a steady, concentrated stream of flame around her sides, so searingly hot that the air around her blurred, and the grass at her feet wilted and shriveled into gray ash.

Slowly she rose up toward the Wind God.

Up close, Feylen looked miserable. His skin was pallid, pockmarked, overgrown with sores. They hadn't given him new clothes—his black Cike uniform was ripped and dirty. Face-to-face he was no fearsome deity. Just a man with tattered garb and broken eyes.

Her fear faded away, replaced by pity. Feylen should have died a long time ago. Now he was a prisoner in his own body, sentenced to watch and suffer while the god he detested manipulated him as a gateway to the material world.

Without the Seal, without Kitay, Rin might have turned into something just like him.

The man is gone, she reminded herself. *Defeat the god.*

"Hey, asshole!" she shouted. "Over here!"

Feylen turned. The winds calmed.

She tensed, anticipating a sudden blast. She had only Kitay's guarantee that she could correct course with her wings if Feylen sent her spinning, but that was a better chance than anyone else had.

But Feylen only hung still in the air, head cocked to the side, watching her rise to meet him like a child curiously observing the antics of a little bug.

"Cute trick," he said.

A piece of driftwood shot past her left arm. She wobbled and righted herself.

Feylen's cerulean eyes met hers. She shuddered. She was acutely aware of how *fragile* she was. She was fighting the Wind God in his own domain, and she was a little thing held in the air by nothing more than two sheets of leather and a cage of metal. He could tear her apart and dash her against those cliffs so easily.

But she didn't just have her wings. She had a javelin. And she had the fire.

She opened her mouth and palms and shot every bit of flame she had at him—three lines of fire roaring from her body all at once. Feylen disappeared behind a wall of red and orange. The winds around him stilled. Debris began dropping out of the air, a rain of wreckage that dotted the waters below.

His retaliatory blow caught her off guard. A gust of force hit her so hard and fast that she hadn't braced herself, hadn't even tensed. She hurtled backward, tumbling through the air in circles until the cliff wall appeared perilously close before her eyes. Her nose scraped the rock before she managed to redirect her momentum and pull herself right-side up.

She drifted back toward Feylen, heart hammering.

She hadn't burned him to death, but she'd come close. Feylen's face and hair had turned black. Smoke wafted out from his scorched robes.

He looked shocked.

"Try again," she called.

His next attack was a series of unrelenting winds blasting her from different, unpredictable directions so she couldn't just ride out the current. One moment he forced her toward the ground, and the next he buoyed her upward, just to let her drop again.

She maneuvered the winds as well as she could, but it was like swimming against a waterfall. She was a little bird caught in a storm. Her wings were nothing against his overwhelming force. All she could do was keep from plummeting to the ground.

She suspected the only reason Feylen hadn't yet flung her against the rocks was because he was toying with her.

But he hadn't finished her off at Boyang, either. *We're not going to kill you,* he'd said. *She told us not to do that. We're just supposed to hurt you.*

The Empress had commanded him to bring her in alive. That gave her an advantage.

"Careful," she shouted. "Daji won't be happy with broken goods."

Feylen's entire demeanor changed when she spoke Daji's name. His shoulders hunched; he seemed to shrink into himself. His eyes darted around, as if petrified that Daji could see him even so high in the air.

Rin stared at him, amazed. What had Daji *done* to him?

How was Daji so powerful that she could terrify a god?

Rin took the chance to fly in closer. She didn't know how Daji had subdued Feylen, but she was now sure that Feylen couldn't kill her.

Daji still wanted her alive, and that gave her her only advantage.

How did one kill a god? She and Kitay had puzzled over the dilemma for hours. She'd wished they could bring him into the Chuluu Korikh. Kitay had wished they could just bring the Chuluu Korikh to him.

In the end, they'd compromised.

Rin eyed the web of fuses lining the opposite cliff wall. If she couldn't kill Feylen with fire, then she'd bury him under the mountain.

She only had to get him close enough to the rocks.

"I know you're still in there." She drifted closer to Feylen. She needed to distract him, if only for a few seconds' reprieve. "I know you can hear me."

He took the bait. The winds calmed.

"I don't care how powerful your god is. You still own this body, Feylen, and you can take it back."

Feylen stared wordlessly at her, unmoving, but she saw no dimming of the blue, no twitch of recognition in his eyes. His expression was an inscrutable wall, behind which she had no idea if the real Feylen was still alive.

She still had to try.

"I saw Altan in the afterlife," she said. A lie, but one shrouded in the truth, or at least her version of it. "He wanted me to pass something on to you. Do you want to know what he said?"

Cerulean flickered to black. Rin saw it—she hadn't imagined it, it wasn't a trick of the light, she *knew* she'd seen it. She continued to fly forward. Feylen was afraid now; she could read it all over his face. He drifted backward every time she drew closer.

They were so close to the cliff wall.

She was mere feet away from him. "He wanted me to tell you he's sorry."

The winds ceased entirely. A silence descended over the channel. In the still air Rin could hear everything—every haggard breath Feylen took, every round of cannon fire from the ships, every wretched scream from below.

Then Feylen laughed. He laughed so hard that corresponding pulses of wind shot through the air, alternating blasts so fierce that she had to flap frantically to stay afloat.

"*This* was your plan?" he screeched. "You thought he would care?"

"You *do* care." Rin kept her voice calm, level. Feylen was in there. She'd seen him. "I saw you, you remember us. You're Cike."

"You mean nothing to us." Feylen sneered. "We could destroy your world—"

"Then you would have done it. But you're still bound, aren't you? *She's* bound you. You gods have no power except what we give you. You came through that gate to take your orders. And I'm ordering you to go back."

Feylen roared. "Who are you to presume?"

"I'm your commander," she said. "I cull."

She shot her fire not at him, but the cliff wall. Feylen shrieked with laughter as the flames streamed harmlessly past him.

He hadn't seen the fuses. He didn't know.

Rin flapped frantically backward, trying to put as much distance between herself and the cliff as she could.

For a long, torturous instant, nothing happened.

And then the mountain moved.

Mountains weren't supposed to shift like that. The natural world wasn't supposed to reshape itself so completely in seconds. But this was real; this was an act of men, not gods. This was Kitay and Ramsa's handiwork come to fruition. Rin could only stare as the entire top ledge of the cliff slipped down like roofing tiles cascading to the ground.

A shrieking howl pierced through the cascade of tumbling rock.

Feylen was whipping up a tornado. But even those last, desperate gusts of wind could not stop thousands of tons of exploded rock jerked downward with the inevitable force of gravity.

When their rumbling stopped, nothing moved beneath them.

Rin sagged in the air, chest heaving. The fire still burned through her arms, but she couldn't sustain it for long, she was so exhausted. She was struggling just to breathe.

The blood-soaked channel beneath her could have been a meadow of flowers. She imagined that the crimson waves were fields of poppy blossoms, and the moving bodies were just little ants scurrying pointlessly about.

She thought it looked so beautiful.

Could they be winning? If *winning* meant killing as many people as they could, then yes. She couldn't tell which side had control over the river, only that it was awash with blood, and that broken ships were dashed against the cliff sides. Feylen had been killing indiscriminately, destroying Republican and Imperial ships alike. She wondered how high the casualty rate had climbed.

She turned toward the valley.

The destruction there was enormous. The palace was on fire, which meant the Militia troops had long ago slashed their way through the refugee camps. The troops would have cut the southerners down like reeds.

Drown in the channel, or burn in the city. Rin had the hysterical urge to laugh, but breathing hurt too much.

She realized suddenly she was losing altitude.

Her fire had gone out. She'd been falling without noticing. She forced flames back into the wings and beat frantically even as her arms screamed in protest.

Her descent halted—she was close enough to the cliffs that she could see Kitay and Venka waving at her.

"I did it!" she screamed to them.

She saw Kitay's mouth moving, but couldn't hear him. He pointed.

Too late she turned around. A javelin shot past her midriff, passed harmlessly under her wing. *Fuck.* Her stomach lurched. She wobbled but righted herself.

The next javelin struck her shoulder.

For a moment, she simply felt confused. Where was the pain? Why was she still hanging in the air? Her own blood floated around her face in great fat drops that for some reason hadn't fallen, little bulbous things that she couldn't believe had come from her.

Then her flames receded into her body. Gravity resumed its pull. Her wings creaked and folded against her back. Then she was just deadweight plummeting headfirst into the river.

Her senses shut down upon impact. She couldn't breathe, couldn't hear, and couldn't see. She tried to swim, kick herself to the surface, but her arms and legs wouldn't obey her, and besides, she didn't know which way was up. She choked involuntarily. A torrent of water flooded her mouth.

I'm going to die, she thought. *I'm really going to die.*

But was this so bad? It was wonderfully, peacefully silent under the surface. She couldn't feel any pain in her shoulder—her whole body had gone numb. She relaxed her limbs and drifted helplessly toward the river bottom. Easier to give up control, easier to stop struggling. Even her burning lungs didn't bother her so much. In a moment she would open her mouth, and water would rush in, and that would be the end.

This wasn't such a bad way to go. At least it was quiet.

Someone seized her hard. Her eyes shot open.

Nezha pulled her head toward his and kissed her hard, his lips forming a seal around hers. A bubble of air passed into her mouth. It wasn't much, but her vision cleared, her lungs stopped burning, and her limbs began to respond to her commands. Adrenaline kicked in. She needed more air. She grabbed at Nezha's face.

He pushed her away, shaking his head. She started to panic. He seized her wrists and held her until she stopped flailing madly in the water. Then he wrapped his arms around her torso and pulled them both toward the surface.

He didn't kick his legs. He didn't have to swim at all. He only held her against him while a warm current bore them gently upward.

Something shrieked in the air above them just as they broke the surface. A javelin slammed into the water several feet away. Nezha yanked them back down into the depths, but Rin kicked and struggled. All she wanted to do was get to the surface, she was so desperate to breathe . . .

Nezha grasped her face with his hands.

Too exposed, he mouthed.

She understood. They needed to come up somewhere near a broken ship, something that would give them cover. She stopped thrashing. Nezha guided them several yards farther downriver. Then the current buoyed them up and deposited them safely onto the shore.

Her first breath above the surface was the best thing she'd ever tasted. She doubled over, coughing and vomiting river water, but she didn't care because she was *breathing*.

Once her lungs were empty of water, she lay back and summoned the fire. Little flames lit up her wrists, danced across her entire body, and bathed her in delicious warmth. Steam hissed as her clothes dried.

Groaning, she rolled over onto her side. Her right shoulder was a bloody mess. She didn't want to look at it. She knew her wings were a crumpled disaster. Something sharp shoved deeper into her skin every time she moved. She struggled to rip the contraption off, but the metal harness had twisted and bent. It wouldn't give.

She felt for where it pressed into her lower back. Her fingers came away bloody.

She tried not to panic. Something was stuck, that was all. She knew she wasn't supposed to pull it out until she was with a physician, that the object piercing her back was the only thing stopping her blood spilling out. And she couldn't see well enough from this angle—she'd be stupid to try to remove it herself.

But she could barely move without digging the rod deeper into her back. She might end up severing her own spine.

Nezha was in no state to help her. He had curled into a small, trembling ball, his arms wrapped around his knees. She crawled toward him and tried to hoist him into a sitting position using her good arm. "Hey. *Hey.*"

He didn't respond.

He was twitching all over. His eyes fluttered madly while little whimpering noises escaped his mouth. He raised his hands, trying to claw at the tattoo on his back.

Rin glanced at the river. The water had started moving in eerie, erratic patterns. Odd little waves ran against the current. Blood-soaked columns rose out of the river at random. A handful splashed harmlessly near the shore, but one was growing larger and larger near the center of the river.

She had to knock Nezha out. That, or she had to get him high—but this time she had no opium . . .

"I brought it," he gasped.

"What?"

He placed a trembling hand over his pocket. "Stole it—brought it here, just in case . . ."

She shoved her hand into his pocket and drew out a fist-sized packet wrapped tightly in bamboo leaves. She tore it open with her teeth, choking at the familiar, sickly sweet taste. Her body ached with an old craving.

Nezha sucked in air through clenched teeth. "Please . . ."

She clutched two nuggets in her hand and ignited a small fire beneath them. With her other hand she hoisted Nezha upright and tilted his head over the fumes.

He inhaled for a long time. His eyes fluttered closed. The water began to calm. The little waves sank beneath the surface. The columns lowered slowly and disappeared. Rin exhaled in relief.

Then Nezha shrank away from the smoke, coughing. "No—no, I don't want that much—"

She gripped him tighter. "I'm sorry."

He'd only smoked several whiffs. That would wear off in under an hour. That wasn't enough time. She needed to make sure the god was gone.

She forced the opium under his nose and clamped a hand over his mouth to force him to inhale. He thrashed in protest, but he was already weak and his struggles grew more and more feeble as he inhaled more of the smoke. Finally he lay still.

Rin threw the half-burned nuggets into the dirt. She brushed a hand over Nezha's forehead, pushed strands of wet hair out of his eyes.

"You'll be all right," she whispered. "I'll send someone out after you."

"Stay," he murmured. "Please."

"I'm sorry." She leaned forward and lightly kissed his forehead. "We've got a battle to win."

His voice was so faint she had to lean down to hear it. "But we've won."

She choked with desperate laughter. He hadn't seen the burning city. He didn't know that Arlong barely existed anymore. "We haven't won."

"No . . ." His eyes opened. He struggled to raise his arm. He pointed at something past her shoulder. "Look. There."

She turned her head.

There on the seam of the horizon sailed a fleet, waves and waves of warships. Some glided over water; some floated through the air. There were so many that they almost seemed like a mirage, endless doubles of the same row of white sails and blue flags against a brilliant sun.

CHAPTER 33

"How lovely," spoke a voice, familiar and beautiful, that made Rin's heart sink and her mouth fill with the taste of blood.

She lowered Nezha onto the sand and forced herself to stand up. Metal shifted beneath her flesh, and she bit back a cry of pain. The agony in her back and shoulder was almost unbearable. But she was not going to die lying down.

How could the Empress still terrify her like this? Daji was just a lone woman now, without an army or a fleet. Her general's garb was ripped and drenched. She limped when she walked, and her shoes left behind imprints of blood. Yet she approached with her chin lifted high, her eyebrows arched, and her lips curved in an imperious smile as if she had just won a great victory, emanating a dark, seductive beauty that made irrelevant her sodden robes, her shattered ships.

Rin hated that beauty. She wanted to drag her nails across it until white flesh gave way under her fingers. She wanted to gouge Daji's eyes out of their sockets, crush them in her fists, and drip the gelatinous ruin over her porcelain skin.

And yet.

When she looked at Daji her entire body felt weak. Her pulse raced. Her face felt hot. She couldn't tear her eyes from Daji's face. She had to look and keep looking, otherwise she would never be satisfied.

She forced herself to focus. She needed a weapon—she snatched a sharp piece of driftwood off the ground.

"Get back," she whispered. "Come any closer and I'll burn you."

Daji only laughed. "Oh, my darling. Haven't you learned?"

Her eyes flashed.

Suddenly Rin felt the overwhelming urge to kill herself, to drag the driftwood against her own wrists until red lines opened along her veins, and twist.

Hands shaking, she pressed the sharpest edge of the driftwood to her skin. *What am I doing?* Her mind screamed for her to stop, but her body didn't care. She could only watch as her hands moved on their own, preparing to saw her veins apart.

"That's enough," Daji said lightly.

The urge disappeared. Rin dropped the driftwood, gasping.

"Will you listen now?" Daji asked. "I'd like you to stand still, please. Arms up."

Rin immediately put her arms up over her head, stifling a scream as her wounds tore anew.

Daji limped closer. Her eyes flickered over the remains of Rin's harness, and her right lip curled up in amusement. "So that's how you dealt with poor Feylen. Clever."

"Your best weapon is gone," Rin said.

"Ah, well. He was a pain to begin with. One moment he'd try to sink our own fleet, and the next all he wanted to do was float among the clouds. Do you know how absurdly difficult it was to get him to do *anything*?" Daji sighed. "I suppose I'll have to finish the job myself."

"You've lost," Rin said. "Hurt me, kill me, it's still over for you. Your generals are dead. Your ships are driftwood."

A round of cannon fire punctuated her words, a roar so loud that it drowned out every other sound along the shore. It went on for so long that Rin couldn't imagine that anything remained floating in the channel.

But Daji didn't look faintly bothered. "You think that's winning? You aren't the victors. There are no victors in this fight. Vaisra has ensured that civil war will continue for decades. He's only deepened the fractures. No man can stitch this country back together now."

She continued to limp forward until they were separated by only several feet.

Rin's eyes darted around the shore. They stood on an isolated stretch of sand, hidden behind the wreckage of great warships. The only other soldiers in sight were corpses. No one was coming to her rescue. It was just her and the Empress now, facing off in the shadows of the unforgiving cliffs.

"So how did you manage the Seal?" Daji asked. "I was rather convinced that it was unbreakable. It can't have been one of the twins; they would have done it long ago if they could." She tilted her head. "Oh, no, let me guess. Did you find the Sorqan Sira? Is that old bat still alive?"

"Fuck you, murderer," Rin said.

"I presume that means you've found yourself an anchor, too?" Daji's eyes flitted toward Nezha. He wasn't moving. "I do hope it's not him. That one's almost gone."

"Don't you dare touch him," Rin hissed.

Daji knelt over Nezha, fingers tracing over the scars on his face. "He's very pretty, isn't he? Despite everything. He reminds me of Riga."

I must get her away from him. Rin strained to move, eyes bulging, but her limbs remained fixed in place. The flame wouldn't come, either; when she reached for the Phoenix, all her rage crashed pointlessly against her own mind, like waves crashing against cliffs.

"The Ketreyids showed me what you've done," she said loudly, hoping it would distract Daji.

It worked. Daji stood up. "Really."

"The Sorqan Sira showed us everything. You can try to convince me that you're trying to save the Empire, but I know what kind of person you are—you betray those who help you and you throw lives away like they're nothing. I saw you attack them, I saw you three murder Tseveri—"

"Be quiet," Daji said. "Don't say that name."

Rin's jaw locked shut.

Rin stood frozen, heart slamming against her ribs, as Daji approached her. She had just been spinning words out of the air, hurling everything she could to get Daji away from Nezha.

But something had pissed Daji off. Two high spots of color rose in her cheeks. Her eyes narrowed. She looked furious.

"The Ketreyids should have surrendered," she said quietly. "We wouldn't have hurt them if they weren't so fucking stubborn."

Daji stretched a pale hand out and ran her knuckles over Rin's cheeks. "Always such a hypocrite. I acted from necessity, just like you. We are precisely the same, you and I. We've acquired more power than any mortal should have the right to, which means we have to make the decisions no one else can. The world is our chessboard. It's not our fault if the pieces get broken."

"You hurt everything you touch," Rin whispered.

"And you've killed in numbers exponentially greater than we ever managed. What really separates us, darling? That you committed your war crimes by accident, and mine were intentional? Would you really do things differently, if you had another chance?"

The hold on Rin's jaw loosened.

Daji had given her permission to answer.

She couldn't say yes. She could lie, of course, but it wouldn't matter; not here, where no one but Daji was listening, and Daji already knew the truth.

Because if she had another chance, if she could go back to that moment in time when she stood in the temple of the Phoenix and faced her god, she would make the same decision. She would release the volcano. She would encase Mugen in tons of molten stone and choking ash.

She would destroy the country completely and without mercy, the same way that its armies had treated her. And she'd laugh.

"Do you understand now?" Daji tucked a strand of hair behind Rin's ear. "Come with me. We've much to discuss."

"Fuck off," Rin said.

Daji's mouth pressed in a thin line. The compulsion seized Rin's legs and forced her to move, shuddering, toward Daji. One by one Rin's feet dragged through the sand. Sweat beaded on her temples. She tried to shut her eyes and couldn't.

"Kneel," Daji commanded.

No, spoke the Phoenix.

The god's voice was terribly quiet, a tiny echo across a vast plain. But it was there.

Rin struggled to remain standing. A horrible pain shot through her legs, forcing them down, growing stronger every moment that she refused. She wanted to scream but couldn't open her mouth.

Daji's eyes flashed yellow. *"Kneel."*

You will not kneel, said the Phoenix.

The pain intensified. Rin gasped, fighting the pull, her mind split between two ancient gods.

Just another battle. And, as always, anger was her greatest ally.

Rage drowned out the Vipress's hypnosis. Daji had sold out the Speerlies. Daji had killed Altan, and Daji had started this war. Daji didn't get to lie to her anymore. Didn't get to torture and manipulate her like prey.

The fire came in fits and bursts, little balls of flame that Rin hurled desperately from her palms. Daji only dodged daintily to the side and flicked a wrist out. Rin jerked aside to avoid a needle that wasn't there. The sudden movement pulled the broken contraption deeper into her back.

She yelped and doubled over.

Daji laughed. "Had enough?"

Rin screeched.

A thin stream of fire lanced over her entire body—enveloping her, protecting her, amplifying her every movement.

This was power like she'd never felt.

That's a state of ecstasy, Altan told her once. *You don't get tired. . . . You don't feel pain. All you do is destroy.*

Rin had always felt so unhinged—volleying between power-lessness and utter subjugation to the Phoenix—but now the fire was hers. Was *her*. And that made her feel so giddy that she almost screamed with laughter because for the first time ever, she had the upper hand.

Daji's resistance was nothing. Rin backed her easily up against the hull of the nearest beached ship. Her fist smashed into the wood next to Daji's face, missing it by an inch. Wood cracked, splintered, and smoked under her knuckles. The entire ship groaned. Rin drew her fist back again and slammed it into Daji's jaw.

Daji's head jerked to the side like a broken doll's. Rin had split her lip; blood trickled down her chin. Yet still she smiled.

"You're so weak," she whispered. "You have a god but you have no idea what you're doing with it."

"Right now, I know exactly what I want to do with it."

She placed her glowing-hot fingers around Daji's neck. Pale flesh crackled and burned under her touch. She started to squeeze. She thought she'd feel a thrill of satisfaction.

It didn't come.

She couldn't just kill her. Not like this. This was too quick, too easy.

She had to destroy her.

She moved her hands up. Placed her thumbs under the bases of Daji's eye sockets. Dug her nails into soft flesh.

"Look at me," Daji hissed.

Rin shook her head, eyes squeezed tight.

Something popped under her left thumb. Warm liquid streamed down her wrist.

"I'm already dying," Daji whispered. "Don't you want to know who I am? Don't you want to know the truth about us?"

Rin knew she should end things right then.

She couldn't.

Because she *did* want to know. She'd been tortured by these questions. She had to understand why the Empire's greatest heroes—Daji, Riga, and Jiang, *her* Master Jiang—had become the monsters they had. And because here, at the end of things, she doubted now more than ever that she was fighting for the right side.

Her eyes fluttered open.

Visions swarmed her mind.

She saw a city burning the way Arlong burned now; buildings charred and blackened, corpses lining the streets. She saw troops marching in uniform lines of terrifying numbers, while the city's surviving inhabitants crouched by their doorsteps, heads bent and arms raised.

This was the Nikara Empire under Mugenese occupation.

"We couldn't do anything," Daji said. "We were too weak to do anything when their ships arrived at our shores. And for the next five decades, when they raped us, beat us, spat on us and told us we were worth less than dogs, we couldn't do anything."

Rin squeezed her eyes shut, but the images wouldn't go away. She saw a beautiful little girl standing alone before a heap of bodies, soot across her face, tears streaming down her cheeks. She saw a young boy lying in a starved, broken heap in the corner of the alley, curled around jagged, shattered bottles. She saw a white-haired boy screaming profanities and waving his fists at the retreating backs of soldiers who did not care.

"Then we escaped, and we had power within our hands to change the fate of the Empire," Daji said. "So what do you think we did?"

"That doesn't excuse anything."

"It explains and justifies *everything*."

The visions shifted again. Rin saw a naked girl shrieking and crying beside a cave while snakes writhed over her body. She saw a tall boy crouching on the shore while a dragon encircled him, whipping up higher and higher waves that surrounded his body like a tornado. She saw a white-haired boy on his hands and knees, beating his fists against the ground while shadows writhed and stretched out of his back.

"Tell me you wouldn't have given up everything," Daji said. "Tell me you wouldn't sacrifice everything and everyone you knew for the power to take back your country."

Months flashed before Rin's eyes. Next she saw the Trifecta, fully grown, kneeling by the body of Tseveri, who was *just one girl*, and the choice seemed so clear and obvious. Against the suffering of a teeming mass of millions, what was one life? Twenty lives? The Ketreyids were so few; how hard could the comparison be?

What difference could it possibly make?

"We didn't want to kill Tseveri," Daji whispered. "She saved us. She convinced the Ketreyids to take us in. And Jiang loved her."

"Then why—"

"Because we had to. Because our allies wanted that land, and the Sorqan Sira said no, and we needed to win it through force and fear. We had one chance to unite the Warlords and we weren't going to throw it away."

"But then you gave it away!" Rin cried. "You didn't take it back! You sold it to the Mugenese—"

"If your arm were rotting, wouldn't you cut it off to save your body? The provinces were rebelling. Corrupt. Diseased. I would have sacrificed it all for a united core. I knew we weren't strong enough to defend the whole country, only a part of it. So I culled. You know that; you command the Cike. You know what rulers must sometimes do."

"You sold us."

"I did it for them," Daji said softly. "I did it for the empire Riga left me. And you don't understand the stakes, because you don't know the meaning of true fear. You don't know how much worse it could have been."

Daji's voice broke.

And for the second time, Rin saw the facade break, saw through the carefully crafted mirage that Daji had been presenting to the world for decades. This woman wasn't the Vipress, wasn't the scheming ruler Rin had learned to hate and fear.

This woman was afraid. But not of her.

"I'm sorry I hurt you," Daji whispered. "I'm sorry I hurt Altan. I wish I'd never had to. But I had a plan to protect my people, and you simply got in the way. You didn't know your true enemy. You wouldn't listen."

Rin was so furious with her then, because she couldn't hate her anymore. Who was she supposed to fight for now? What side was she supposed to be on? She didn't believe in Vaisra's Republic, not anymore, and she certainly didn't trust the Hesperians, but she didn't know what Daji wanted her to do.

"You can go ahead and kill me," said Daji. "You probably could. I'd fight back, of course, but you'd probably win. *I* would kill me."

"Shut up," Rin said.

She wanted to tighten her fists and choke the life out of Daji. But the rage had drained away. She didn't have the will to fight anymore. She wanted to be angry—things were so much easier when she was just blindly angry—but the anger wouldn't come.

Daji twisted out from her grip, and Rin didn't try to stop her.

Daji was as good as dead regardless. Her face was a grotesque ruin—black liquid gushed out from her gouged eye. She stumbled to the side, fingers feeling for the ship.

Her good eye locked on to Rin's. "What do you think happens to you after I'm gone? Don't imagine for a moment you can trust Vaisra. Without me, Vaisra has no use for you. Vaisra discards his allies without blinking when they are no longer convenient, and if you don't believe me when I say you're next, then you're a fool."

Rin knew Daji was right.

She just didn't know where that left her.

Daji shook her head and held her hands out, open and unthreatening. "Come with me."

Rin took a small step forward.

Wood groaned above her head. Daji skirted backward. Too late, Rin looked up just in time to see the ship's mast crashing down on her.

Rin couldn't even scream. It took everything she had just to breathe. Air came in hoarse, painful bursts; it felt like her throat had been reduced to the diameter of a pin. Her entire back burned with agony.

Daji knelt down in front of her. Stroked her cheek. "You'll need me. You don't realize it now, but you'll figure it out soon. You need me far more than you need them. I just hope you survive."

She leaned down so close that Rin could feel her hot breath on her skin. Daji grabbed Rin by the chin and forced her to look up, into her good eye. Rin stared into a black pupil inside a ring of yellow, pulsing hypnotically, an abyss daring her to fall inside.

"I'll leave you with this."

Rin saw a beautiful young girl—Daji, it had to be—in a huddled heap on the ground, naked, clothes clutched to her chest. Dark blood dripped down pale thighs. She saw the young Riga sprawled on the ground, unconscious. She saw Jiang lying on his side, screaming, as a man kicked him in the ribs, over and over and over.

She dared to look up. Their tormenter was not Mugenese.

Blue eyes. Yellow hair. The soldier brought his boot down, over and over and over, and each time Rin heard another set of cracks.

She leaped forward in time, just a few minutes. The soldier was gone, and the children were clinging to each other, crying, covered in each other's blood, crouching in the shadow of a different soldier.

"Get out of here," said the soldier, in a tongue she was far too familiar with. A tongue she would have never believed would utter a kind word. "Now."

Then Rin understood.

It had been a Hesperian soldier who raped Daji, and a Mugenese soldier who saved her. That was the frame the Empress had been locked into since childhood; that was the crux that had formed every decision afterward.

"The Mugenese weren't the real enemy," Daji murmured. "They never were. They were just poor puppets serving a mad emperor who started a war that he shouldn't have. But who gave them those ideas? Who told them they could conquer the continent?"

Blue eyes. White sails.

"I warned you about everything. I told you this from the beginning. Those devils are going to destroy our world. The Hesperians have a singular vision for the future, and we're not in it. You already know this. You must have realized it, now that you've seen what they're like. I can see it in your eyes. You know they're dangerous. You know you'll need an ally."

Questions formed on Rin's tongue, too many to count, but she couldn't summon the breath to speak them. Her vision was tunneling, turning black at the edges. All she could see was Daji's pale face, dancing above her like the moon.

"Think about it," Daji whispered, tracing her cool fingers over Rin's cheek. "Figure out who you're fighting for. And when you know, come find me."

"Rin? *Rin!*" Venka's face loomed over her. "Fucking hell. Can you hear me?"

Rin felt a great weight lifting off her back and shoulders. She lay flat, eyes open wide, sucking in great gulps of air.

"Hey." Venka snapped her fingers in front of her. "What's my name?"

Rin moaned. "Just help me up."

"Close enough." Venka wedged her arms under her stomach and helped Rin roll onto her side. Every tiny movement sent fresh spasms of pain rippling through her back. She collapsed into Venka's arms, breathless with agony.

Venka's hands moved over her skin, feeling for injuries. Rin felt her fingers pause on her back.

"Oh, that's not good," Venka murmured.

"What?"

"Uh. Can you breathe all right?"

"Ribs," Rin gasped. "My—*ow*!"

Venka pulled her hands away from Rin. They were slippery with blood. "There's a rod stuck under your skin."

"I know," Rin said through gritted teeth. "Get it out." She reached back to try again to yank it out herself, but Venka grabbed her wrist before she could.

"You'll lose too much blood if it comes out now."

Rin knew that, but the thought of the rod digging deeper inside her was making her panic spiral. "But I'm—"

"Just breathe for a minute. All right? Can you do that for me? Just breathe."

"How bad is it?" Kitay's voice. *Thank the gods.*

"Several ribs broken. Don't move, I'll get a stretcher." Venka set off at a run.

Kitay knelt down beside her. His voice dropped to a whisper. "What happened? Where's the Empress?"

Rin swallowed. "She got away."

"Obviously." Kitay's fingers tightened on her shoulder. "Did you let her go?"

"I . . . *what*?"

Kitay gave her a hard look. "Did you let her go?"

Had she?

She found that she couldn't answer.

She could have killed Daji. She'd had plenty of opportunities to burn, strangle, stab, or choke the Empress before the beam fell. If she'd wanted to, she could have ended everything then and there.

Why hadn't she?

Had the Vipress manipulated her into letting her go? Was Rin's reluctance a product of her own thoughts or Daji's hypnosis? She could not remember if she had chosen to let Daji escape, or if she had simply been outsmarted and defeated.

"I don't know," she whispered.

"You don't know," Kitay asked, "or you don't want to tell me?"

"I thought it'd be so clear," she said. Her head swam; her eyes fluttered closed. "I thought the choice was obvious. But now I really don't know."

"I think I understand," Kitay said after a long pause. "But I'd keep that to yourself."

CHAPTER 34

Rin jolted awake to the sound of gongs. She tried to spring out of bed, but the moment she lifted her head, a searing pain rippled through her back.

"Whoa." Venka's blurry face came into view. She put a hand on Rin's shoulder and forced her back down. "Not so fast."

"But the morning alarm," Rin said. "I'm going to be late."

Venka laughed. "To what? You're off duty. We're all off duty."

Rin blinked. "What?"

"It's over. We *won*. You can relax."

After months of warfare, of sleeping and eating and waking on the same strict schedule, that statement was so incredible to Rin that for a moment the words themselves sounded like they'd been spoken in a different language.

"We're finished?" she asked faintly.

"For now. But don't be too disappointed, you'll have plenty to do once you're up and moving." Venka cracked her knuckles. "Soon we'll be running cleanup."

Rin struggled to prop herself up on her elbows. The pain in her lower back pulsed along with her heartbeat. She clenched her teeth to stave it off. "What else is there? Update me."

"Well, the Empire hasn't exactly surrendered. They're decapitated, but the strongest provinces—Tiger, Horse, and Snake—are still holding out."

"But the Wolf Meat General's dead," Rin said. Venka already knew that—she'd seen it happen—but saying it out loud made her feel better.

"Yeah. We captured Tsolin alive, too. Jun made it out, though." Venka picked up an apple from Rin's bedside. She began paring it with rapid, sure movements, fingers moving so fast that Rin was amazed she didn't peel her own skin off. "Somehow he swam out of the channel and got away—he's well on his way back to Tiger Province now. Horse and Snake are loyal to him, and he's a better strategist than Chang En was. They'll put up a good fight. But the war should be over soon."

"Why?"

Venka pointed out the window with her paring knife. "We have help."

Rin shifted around in her bed to peer outside, clutching the windowsill for support. A seemingly infinite number of warships crowded the harbor. She tried to calculate how many Hesperian troops that entailed. Thousands? Tens of thousands?

She should have been relieved the civil war was as good as over. Instead, when she looked at those white sails, all she could feel was dread.

"Something wrong?" Venka asked.

Rin took a breath. "Just . . . disoriented a bit, I think."

Venka handed the peeled apple to Rin. "Eat something."

Rin wrapped her fingers around it with difficulty. It was amazing how hard the simple act of *chewing* was; how much it hurt her teeth, how it strained her jaw. Swallowing was agony. She couldn't manage more than a few bites. She put the apple down. "What happened to the Militia deserters?"

"A couple tried to flee over the mountains, but their horses got scared when the dirigibles came," Venka said. "Trampled them underfoot. Their bodies are still stuck in the mud. We'll probably send a crew to get those horses back. How's your . . . well, how's everything feeling?"

Rin reached backward to feel at her wounds. Her back and shoulder were covered in a swath of bandages. Her fingers kept brushing against raised skin that hurt to touch. She winced. She didn't want to see what lay beneath the wrappings. "Did they tell you how bad it was?"

"Can you still wiggle your toes?"

Rin froze. "*Venka.*"

"I'm kidding." Venka cracked a smile. "It looks worse than it is. It'll take you a while, but you'll get full mobility back. Your biggest concern is scarring. But you were always ugly, so it's not like that will make a difference."

Rin was too relieved to be angry. "Go fuck yourself."

"There's a mirror inside that cabinet door." Venka pointed to the back corner of the room and stood up. "I'll give you some time alone."

After Venka closed the door, Rin pulled off her shirt, climbed gingerly to her feet, and stood naked in front of the mirror.

She was stunned by how repulsive she looked.

She'd always known that nothing could make her attractive; not with her mud-colored skin, sullen face, and short, jagged hair that had never been styled with anything more sophisticated than a rusty knife.

But now she just looked like a broken and battered thing. She was an amalgamation of scars and stitches. On her arm, dotted white reminders of the hot wax she'd once used to burn herself to stay awake studying. On her back and shoulders, whatever lay behind those bandages. And just under her sternum, Altan's handprint, as dark and vivid as the day she'd first seen it.

Exhaling slowly, she pressed her left hand to the spot over her stomach. She couldn't tell if she was only imagining it, but it felt hot to the touch.

"I should apologize," said Kitay.

She jumped. She hadn't heard the door open. "Fucking hell—"

"Sorry."

She scrambled to pull her shirt back on. "You might have knocked!"

"I didn't realize you'd be up." He crossed the room and perched himself on the side of her bed. "Anyway, I wanted to apologize. That wound is my fault. Didn't put padding around the gears—I didn't have time, so I was just going for something functional. The rod went in about three inches at a slant. The physicians said you're lucky it didn't sever your spine."

"Did you feel it, too?" she asked.

"Just a little," Kitay said. He was lying, she knew that, but in that moment she was just grateful he would even try to spare her the guilt. He lifted his shirt and twisted around to show her a pale white scar running across his lower back. "Look. They're the same shape, I think."

She peered enviously at the smooth white lines. "That's prettier than mine will be."

"Don't get too jealous."

She moved her hands and arms about, gingerly testing the temporary boundaries of her mobility. She tried to raise her right arm above her head, but gave up when her shoulder threatened to tear itself apart. "I don't think I want to fly for a while."

"I gathered." Kitay picked her unfinished apple up off the windowsill and took a bite. "Good thing you won't have to."

She sat back down on the bed. It hurt to stand for too long.

"The Cike?" she asked.

"All alive and accounted for. None with serious injuries."

She nodded, relieved. "And Feylen. Is he . . . you know, properly dead?"

"Who cares?" Kitay said. "He's buried under thousands of tons of rock. If there's anything alive down there, it won't bother us for a millennium."

Rin tried to take comfort in that. She wanted to be sure Feylen was dead. She wanted to see a body. But for now, this would have to do.

"Where's Nezha?" she asked.

"He's been in here. Constantly. Wouldn't leave, but I think someone finally got him to go take a nap. Good thing, too. He was starting to smell."

"So he's all right?" she asked quickly.

"Not entirely." Kitay tilted his head at her. "Rin, what did you do to him?"

She hesitated.

Could she tell Kitay the truth? Nezha's secret was so personal, so intensely painful, that it would feel like an awful betrayal. But it also entailed immense consequences that she didn't know how to grapple with, and she couldn't stand keeping that to herself. At least not from the other half of her soul.

Kitay said out loud what she had been thinking. "We're both better off if you don't hide things from me."

"It's an odd story."

"Try me."

She told him everything, every last painful, disgusting detail.

Kitay didn't flinch. "It makes sense, doesn't it?" he asked.

"What do you mean?"

"Nezha's been a prick his whole life. I imagine it's hard to be pleasant when you're in chronic pain."

Rin managed a laugh. "I don't think that's entirely it."

Kitay was silent for a moment. "So am I to understand that's why he's been moping for days? Did he call the dragon at the Red Cliffs?"

Rin's stomach twisted with guilt. "I didn't *make* him do it."

"Then what happened?"

"We were in the channel. We were—I was drowning. But I didn't force him. That wasn't me."

What she wanted was for Kitay to tell her she hadn't done anything wrong. But as usual, all he did was tell her the truth. "You didn't have to force him. You think that Nezha would let you die? After you'd called him a coward?"

"The pain's not so bad," she insisted. "Not so bad that you want to die. You've felt it. We both survived it."

"You don't know how it feels for him."

"It can't possibly be worse."

"Maybe it is. Maybe it's worse than you could even imagine."

She drew her knees up to her chest. "I never wanted to hurt him."

Kitay's voice held no judgment, only curiosity. "Why'd you say those things to him, then?"

"Because his life is not his own," she said, echoing Vaisra's words from so long ago. "Because when you have *this* much power, it's selfish to sit on it just because you're scared."

But that wasn't entirely it.

She was also jealous. Jealous that Nezha might have access to such enormous power and never consider using it. Jealous that Nezha's entire identity and worth did not hinge on his shamanic abilities. Nezha had never been referred to solely by his race. Nezha had never been someone's weapon. They had both been claimed by gods, but Nezha got to be the princeling of the House of Yin, free from Hesperian experimentation, and she got to be the last heir of a tragic race.

Kitay knew that. Kitay knew everything that crossed her mind. He sat quietly for a long time.

"I'm going to tell you something," he finally said. "And I don't want you to take it as a judgment, I want you to take it as a warning."

She gave him a wary look. "What?"

"You've known Nezha for a few years," he said. "You met him when he'd perfected his masks and pretensions. But I've known him since we were children. You think that he's invincible, but he is more fragile than you think. Yes, I know he's a prick. But I also know that he'd throw himself off a cliff for you. Please stop trying to break him."

The trial of Ang Tsolin took place the next morning on a raised dais before the palace. Republican soldiers crowded the courtyard below, wearing uniform expressions of cold resentment. Civilians had been barred from attendance. Word of Tsolin's betrayal was common knowledge by now, but Vaisra didn't want a riot. He didn't want Tsolin to die in chaos. He wanted to give his old master a precise, cleanly executed death, every silent second drawn out as long as possible.

Captain Eriden and his guards led Tsolin to the top of the platform. They'd let him keep his dignity—he was neither blindfolded nor bound. Under different circumstances he might have been receiving the highest honors.

Vaisra met Tsolin at the center of the dais, handed him a wrapped sword, and leaned forward to murmur something into his ear.

"What's happening?" Rin murmured into Kitay's ear.

"He's giving him the option of suicide," Kitay explained. "A respectable end for a disgraceful traitor. But only if Tsolin confesses to and repents for his wrongs."

"Will he?"

"Doubt it. Even an honorable suicide can't overcome that kind of disgrace."

Tsolin and Vaisra stood still on the dais, silently regarding each other. Then Tsolin shook his head and handed the sword back.

"Your regime is a puppet democracy," he said aloud. "And all you have done is hand your country over to be ruled by the blue-eyed devils."

A murmur of unease swept through the soldiers.

Vaisra's eyes roved the crowd and fell on Rin. He beckoned to her with one finger.

"Come here," he said.

She glanced around her, hoping he was pointing to someone else.

"Go," Kitay muttered.

"What does he want with me?"

"What do you think?"

She blanched. "I'm not doing this."

He gave her a gentle nudge. "It's best if you don't think too much about it."

She shuffled forward, leaning heavily on her cane. She could still only barely walk. The worst was the pain in her lower back, because it wasn't localized. The node seemed connected to every muscle in her body—every time she took a step or moved her arms, she felt like she'd been stabbed.

The soldiers parted to clear her a path to the platform. She ascended with slow, shaking steps. Every step pulled painfully at the stitches in her lower back.

Finally she stopped before the Snake Warlord. He met her gaze with tired eyes. Even now, even when he was completely at her mercy, he still looked like he pitied her.

"A puppet to the end," Tsolin whispered, so softly that only she could hear. "When are you going to learn?"

"I'm not a puppet," she said.

He shook his head. "I thought you might be the smart one. But you let him take everything he needed from you and just rolled over like a whore."

She would have responded, but Vaisra spoke over her.

"Do it," he said coldly.

She didn't have to ask what he meant. She knew what he wanted from her. Right now, unless she wanted to arouse suspicion, she needed to be Vaisra's obedient weapon of the Republic.

She placed her right palm on Tsolin's chest, just over his heart, and pushed. Her curled fingers seared with flames so hot her nails went straight into his flesh as if she were clawing at soft tofu.

Tsolin twitched and jerked but kept his mouth shut. She paused, marveling at how long he managed not to scream.

"You're brave," she said.

"You're going to die," he gasped. "You fool."

Her fingers closed around something that she thought might be his heart. She squeezed. Tsolin's head dropped. Over his slumped shoulder, she saw Vaisra nod and smile.

Rin wanted to get out of Arlong immediately after that. But Kitay argued, and she reluctantly agreed, that they wouldn't make it a mile out of the channel. She still couldn't walk properly, much less run. Her open wounds required daily checkups in the infirmary that neither of them had the medical knowledge to conduct on their own.

They also didn't have an escape plan. They'd heard only silence from Moag. If they left now, they'd have to travel on foot unless they could steal a riverboat, and Arlong's dock security was too good for them to manage that.

They had no choice other than to wait, at least until Rin had healed up enough to hold her own in a fight.

Everything hung in a tense equilibrium. Rin received no word from Vaisra or the Hesperians. Sister Petra hadn't summoned her for an examination in months. Rin and Kitay made no overt moves to escape. Vaisra didn't have any reason to suspect her allegiances had shifted, so she was operating on a fairly loose leash. That gave her time to figure out her next move. She was a mouse inching closer to a trap. It would spring when she moved to escape, but only then.

A week after Tsolin's execution, the palace servants delivered a heavy, silk-wrapped package to her room. When she unwrapped it she found a ceremonial dress with instructions to put it on and appear on the dais in an hour.

Rin still couldn't lift her hands all the way over her head, so she enlisted Venka's assistance.

"What the fuck do I do with this?" Rin held up a loose rectangle of cloth.

"Calm down. It's a shawl, you drape it just under your shoulders." Venka took the cloth from Rin and wrapped it loosely over Rin's upper arms. "Like so. So that it flows like water, see?"

Rin was getting too hot and frustrated to care how well her clothes flowed. She snatched up another loose rectangle that looked identical to her shawl. "Then what about this?"

Venka blinked at her as if she were an idiot. "You tie that around your waist."

The biggest injustice, Rin thought, was that despite her injuries, they were still forcing her to walk in the victory parade. Vaisra had insisted it was crucial for decorum. He wanted to put on a show for the Hesperians. A display of Nikara gratitude and etiquette. Proof they were civilized.

Rin was so tired of having to prove her humanity.

The robe was quickly wearing down her patience. The damned thing was hot, stifling, and so tight it restricted her mobility in ways that made her breathing quicken. Putting it on required so many moving pieces she was tempted to throw the whole pile in the corner and set it on fire.

Venka made a noise of disgust as she watched Rin fasten the sash around her waist with a quick sailor's knot. "That looks horrendous."

"It's going to come undone otherwise."

"There's more than one way to tie a knot. And that's far too loose besides. You look like you've been caught getting frisky with a courtier."

Rin pulled at the sash until it pressed into her ribs. "Like this?"

"Tighter."

"But I can't breathe."

"That's the point. Stop only when it feels like your ribs are going to crack."

"I think my ribs *have* cracked. Twice over now."

"Then a third time can't do much more damage." Venka took the sash out of Rin's hands and began retying the knot herself. "You are incredible."

"What's that supposed to mean?"

"How did you come this far without learning any feminine wiles?"

That was such an absurd phrase that Rin snorted into her sleeve. "We're soldiers. Where did *you* learn feminine wiles?"

"I'm *aristocracy*. My whole life my parents were determined to get me married to some minister." Venka smirked. "They were a little miffed when I joined the military instead."

"They didn't want you at Sinegard?" Rin asked.

"No, they hated the idea. But I insisted on it. I wanted glory and attention. Wanted them to write stories about me. Look how that turned out." Venka yanked the knot tight. "You have a visitor, by the way."

Rin turned around.

Nezha stood in the doorway, hands dangling awkwardly by his sides. He cleared his throat. "Hello."

Venka patted Rin's shoulder. "Have fun."

"That's a pretty knot," Nezha said.

Venka winked as she flounced past him. "Even prettier on the wearer."

The creak as the door swung shut might have been the loudest noise Rin had ever heard.

Nezha crossed the room to stand beside her in front of the mirror. They looked at each other in the glass. She was struck by the imbalance between them—how much taller he was, how pale his skin looked next to hers, how elegant and natural he looked in ceremonial garb.

She looked ridiculous. He looked like he belonged.

"You look good," he said.

She snorted. "Don't lie to my face."

"I would never lie to you."

The following silence felt oppressive.

It seemed obvious what they should be talking about, but she didn't know how to raise the subject. She *never* knew how to bring things up around him. He was so unpredictable, warm one minute and cold to her the next. She never knew where she stood with him; never knew if she could trust him, and that was so damn frustrating because aside from Kitay he was the one person whom she wanted to tell *everything*.

"How do you feel?" she finally asked.

"I'll live," he said lightly.

She waited for him to continue. He didn't.

She was terrified to say anything more. She knew a chasm had opened between them, she just didn't know how to close it.

"Thank you," she tried.

He raised an eyebrow. "For what?"

"You didn't have to save me," she said. "You didn't have to . . . do what you did."

"Yes, I did." She couldn't tell if the lightness in his tone was forced or not. "How would it go over if I let our Speerly die?"

"It hurt you," she said. *And I had you smoke enough opium to kill a calf.* "I'm sorry."

"It's not your fault," he said. "We're fine."

But they weren't fine. Something had shattered between them, and she was sure that it was her own fault. She just didn't know how to make it right.

"Okay." She broke the silence. She couldn't stand this anymore; she needed to flee. "I'm going to go find—"

"Did you see her die?" Nezha asked abruptly, startling her.

"Who?"

"Daji. We never found a body."

"I gave your father my report," she said. She'd told Vaisra and Eriden that Daji was dead, drowned, sunk at the bottom of the Murui.

"I know what you told him. Now I want you to tell me the truth."

"That's the truth."

Nezha's voice hardened. "Don't lie to me."

She crossed her arms. "Why would I lie about that?"

"Because they haven't found a body."

"I was trapped under a fucking mast, Nezha. I was too busy trying not to die to *think*."

"Then why did you tell Father that she's dead?"

"Because I think she is!" Rin quickly pulled an explanation out of thin air. "I saw Feylen crash that ship. I saw her fall into the water. And if you can't find a body that just means she's buried down there with the other ten thousand corpses clogging up your channel. What I *don't* understand is why you're acting like I'm a traitor when I just killed a god for you."

"I'm sorry." Nezha sighed. "No, you're right. I just—I want us to be able to trust each other."

His eyes looked so sincere. He'd really bought it.

Rin exhaled, marveling at how narrowly she'd gotten away.

"I've never lied to you." She placed a hand on his arm. It was so easy to act. She didn't have to fake her affection for him. It felt good to tell Nezha what he wanted to hear. "And I never will. I swear."

Nezha gave her a smile. A real smile. "I like when we're on the same side."

"Me too," she said, and that, finally, wasn't a lie. How desperately she wished they could stay that way.

The parade turnout was pathetic. That didn't surprise Rin. In Tikany, people came out for festivals only because they bore the promise of free food and drink, but battle-wrecked Arlong didn't have the resources to spare either. Vaisra had ordered an extra ration of rice and fish distributed across the city, but to civilians who had just lost their homes and relatives, that was little cause to celebrate.

Rin still could only barely walk. She'd stopped using her cane, but she couldn't move more than fifty yards without getting exhausted, and both her arms and legs were riddled by a tight, sore ache that seemed to only be getting worse.

"We can have you ride on a sedan chair if you need," Kitay said when she faltered on the dais.

Rin clutched his proffered arm. "I'll walk."

"But you're hurting."

"Entire city's hurting," she said. "That's the point."

She hadn't seen the city outside the infirmary until now, and the devastation was painful to look at. The fires in the outer city had burned for nearly a day after the battle, extinguished only by rainfall. The palace remained intact, though blackened at the bottom. The lush greenery of the canal islands had been replaced by withered dead trees and ash. The infirmaries were overcrowded with the wounded. The dead lay in neat lines by the beach, awaiting a proper burial.

Vaisra's parade wasn't a testament to victory, but an acknowledgment of sacrifice. Rin appreciated that. There were no gaudy musicians, no flagrant displays of wealth and power. The army walked the streets to show that they had survived. That the Republic was alive.

Saikhara headed the procession, breathtaking in robes of cerulean and silver. Vaisra strode just behind her. His hair was streaked with far more white than it had been months ago, and he walked with just the barest hint of a limp, but even those signs of weakness seemed only to add to his dignity. He was dressed like an Emperor, and Saikhara looked like his Empress. She was their divine mother and he was their savior, father, and ruler all at once.

Behind that celestial couple stood the entire military might of the west. Hesperian soldiers lined the streets. Hesperian dirigibles drifted slowly through the air above them. Vaisra may have promised to usher in a democratic government, but if he intended to stake his claim to the entire Empire, Rin doubted that anyone could stop him.

"Where are the southern Warlords?" Kitay asked. He kept twisting around to get a look at the line of generals. "Haven't seen them all day."

Rin searched the crowd. He was right; the Warlords were absent. She couldn't see a single southern refugee, either.

"Do you think they've left?" she asked.

"I know they haven't. The valleys are still full of refugee camps. I think they chose not to come."

"What for, a show of protest?"

"I suppose it makes sense," he said. "This wasn't their victory."

Rin could understand that. The victory at the Red Cliffs had solved very few of the south's problems. Southern troops had bled for a regime that only continued to treat them as a necessary sacrifice. But the Warlords were sacrificing prudence for symbolic protest. They needed Hesperian troops to clear out the Federation enclaves in their home provinces. They should have been doing their best to win back Vaisra's favor.

Instead, they'd made clear their loyalties, just as they had to her in that alley days ago.

She wondered what that meant for the Republic. The south hadn't submitted an open declaration of war. But they'd hardly demonstrated obedient cooperation, either. Would Vaisra now send those armed dirigibles to conquer Tikany?

Rin planned to be gone long before it came to that.

The procession culminated in a funeral rite for the dead on the riverbank. The turnout for this was much larger. A mass of civilians lined up under the cliffs. Rin couldn't tell if the water was only reflecting the Red Cliffs, but it seemed as if the channel was still shot through with blood.

Vaisra's generals and admirals stood in a straight line on the beach. Ribbons on posts marked those with rank who were absent. Rin counted more ribbons than people.

"That's a hell of a lot of digging." She looked out over the stacks of drenched, rotting corpses. The soldiers had spent days trawling the water for bodies, which otherwise would have poisoned the water with the foul taste of decay for years.

"They don't bury their dead in Arlong," Kitay said. "They send them out to sea."

They watched as soldiers loaded pyramids of bodies onto rafts, then pushed them out into the water one by one. Each pyre was draped with a funeral shroud dipped in oil. At Vaisra's command, Eriden's men shot a barrage of flaming arrows onto the fleet of bodies. Each one found its target. The pyres caught fire with a sharp, satisfying crackle.

"I could have done that," Rin said.

"It means less when you do it."

"Why?"

"Because the only thing that makes it significant is the possibility that they don't aim true." Kitay nodded over her shoulder. "Look who's here."

She followed his line of sight to find Ramsa, Baji, and Suni standing by the edge of the shore a little ways away from a huddle of civilians. They were looking back at her. Ramsa gave her a little wave.

She couldn't help grinning in relief.

She hadn't gotten a chance to talk to the Cike since the eve of the battle. She'd known they were all right, but they hadn't been permitted in the infirmary, and she didn't want to make a fuss for fear of arousing Hesperian suspicion. This might be their only chance to talk privately.

She leaned close to murmur in Kitay's ear. "Is anyone looking?"

"I think you're fine," he said. "Hurry."

She shuffled, limping, as quickly as she could down the shore.

"I see they finally let you out of the death farm," Baji said in greeting.

"'Death farm'?" she repeated.

"Ramsa's nickname for the infirmary."

"It's because they'd roll out corpses every day in grain wagons," Ramsa said. "Glad you weren't in one of them."

"How bad is it?" Baji asked.

She instinctively brushed her fingers over her lower back. "Manageable. Hurts, but I can walk without assistance now. You all got through unscathed?"

"More or less." Baji showed her his bandaged shins. "Scraped those when I was jumping off a ship. Ramsa threw a fuse too late, got a bad burn on his knee. Suni's completely fine. The man can survive anything."

"Good," she said. She glanced quickly around the beach. No one was paying attention to them; the crowd's eyes were fixed on the funeral pyres. She lowered her voice regardless. "We can't stay here anymore. Get ready to run."

"When?" Baji asked. None of them looked surprised. Rather, they all seemed to have been expecting it.

"Soon. We're not safe here. Vaisra doesn't need us anymore

and we can't count on his protection. The Hesperians don't know you and Suni are shamans, so we have a bit of leeway. Kitay doesn't think they'll move in immediately. But we shouldn't drag our feet."

"Thank the gods," Ramsa said. "I couldn't stand them. They smell horrible."

Baji gave him a look. "Really? That's your biggest complaint? The smell?"

"It's rank," Ramsa insisted. "Like tofu gone sour."

Suni spoke up for the first time. "If you're worried, why don't we get out tonight?"

"That works," Rin said.

"Any particulars?" Ramsa asked.

"I don't have a plan beyond escape. We tried to get Moag on board, but she hasn't responded. We'll have to just make our way out of the city on our own."

"One problem," Baji said. "Suni and I are on night patrol. Think it'll tip them off if we go missing?"

Rin assumed that was precisely the reason why they had been put on night patrol.

"When do you get off?" she asked.

"An hour before dawn."

"So we'll go then," she said. "Make straight for the cliffs. Don't wait at the gates, that'll only attract attention. We'll figure out what to do once we're out of the city. Does that work?"

"Fine," Baji said. Ramsa and Suni nodded.

There was nothing else to discuss. They stood together in a cluster, watching the funeral in silence for a few minutes. The flames on the pyres had grown to a full blaze. Rin didn't know what was propelling the pyres farther out to sea, but the way the flames blurred the air above them was oddly hypnotizing.

"It's pretty," Baji said.

"Yeah," she said. "It is."

"You know what's going to happen to them, right?" Ramsa said. "They'll float for about three days. Then the pyres will start to break apart. Burned wood is weak and bodies are heavy as shit. They sink into the ocean, and they'll bloat and crumble unless the fish nibble everything but the bones first."

His brittle voice carried over the still morning air. Heads were turning.

"Will you stop?" Rin muttered.

"Sorry," said Ramsa. "All I'm saying is that they should have just burned them on land."

"I don't think they got all the bodies," Baji said. "I saw more corpses in the river than that. How many Imperial soldiers do you think are still down there?"

Rin shot him a look. "Baji, please—"

"You know, it's funny. The fish will feed on the corpses. Then you'll eat the fish, and you'll literally be feeding on the bodies of your enemies."

She glared at him through blurry eyes. "Do you have to do that?"

"What, you don't think it's funny?" He put his arm around her. "Hey. Don't cry—I'm sorry."

She swallowed hard. She hadn't meant to cry. She wasn't even sure why she was crying—she didn't know any of the bodies on the pyre, and she didn't have any reason to grieve.

Those bodies weren't her fault. She still felt miserable.

"I don't like feeling this way," she whispered.

"Me neither, kid." Baji rubbed her shoulder. "But that's war. You might as well be on the winning side."

CHAPTER 35

Rin couldn't sleep that night. She sat upright in her infirmary bed, staring out the window at the still harbor, counting down the minutes until dawn. She wanted to pace the hallway, but didn't want the infirmary staff to find her behavior odd. She also wished desperately she could be with Kitay, poring over every possible contingency one last time, but they'd been sleeping in separate rooms every night. She couldn't risk giving away any sign that she intended to leave until she'd made it out of the city gates.

She'd packed nothing. She owned very little that mattered—she'd bring along her backup longsword, the one that wasn't lost at the bottom of the channel, and the clothes on her back. She'd leave everything else behind in the barracks. The more she took with her, the faster Vaisra would realize that she had left for good.

Rin had no idea what she was going to do once she got out. Moag still hadn't returned her missive. She might not have even received it. Perhaps she had and elected to ignore it. Or she might have taken it straight to Vaisra.

Ankhiluun might have been a terrible gamble. But Rin simply had no other options.

All she knew was that she needed to get out of the city. For once, she needed to be a step ahead of Vaisra. No one suspected that she might leave, which meant no one was keeping her from going.

She had no advantages past that, but she'd figure out the rest once the Red Cliffs were well behind her.

"Fancy a drink?" asked a voice.

She jumped, hands scrabbling for her sword.

"Tiger's tits," Nezha said. "It's just me."

"Sorry," she breathed. Could he read the fear on her face? She hastily rearranged her features into some semblance of calm. "I'm still twitchy. Every noise I hear sounds like cannon fire."

"I know that feeling." Nezha held up a jug. "This might help."

"What is that?"

"Sorghum wine. We're off duty for the first time since any of us can remember." He grinned. "Let's go get smashed."

"Who's us?" she asked cautiously.

"Me and Venka. We'll go grab Kitay, too." He extended his hand to her. "Come on. Unless you've got something better to do?"

Rin wavered, mind racing furiously.

It was a horrible idea to get drunk on the eve of her escape. But Nezha might suspect something if both she and Kitay refused. He was right—neither she nor Kitay had a plausible excuse to be anywhere else. All of them had been off duty since the Hesperians docked in the harbor.

If she wasn't planning to turn traitor, why on earth would she say no?

"Come on," Nezha said again. "A few drinks won't hurt."

She managed a smile and took his hand. "You read my mind."

She tried to calm her racing heartbeat as she followed him out of the barracks.

This was all right. She could afford this one liberty. Once she left Arlong, she might never see Nezha again. She knew, despite their bond, that he could never leave his father's side. She didn't want him to remember her as a traitor. She wanted him to remember her as a friend.

She had at least until the hour before dawn. She might as well say a proper goodbye.

Rin didn't know where Nezha and Venka had found so much liquor in a city that prohibited its sale to soldiers. When she'd made it outside the infirmary, Venka was waiting on the street with an entire wagon of sealed jugs. Nezha retrieved Kitay from the barracks. Then they pushed the wagon together up to the highest tower of the palace, where they sat overlooking the Red Cliffs, surveying the wreckage of the fleets floating below.

For the first few minutes they didn't speak. They just drank furiously, trying to get as inebriated as possible. It didn't take very long.

Venka kicked at Nezha's foot. "You sure we're not getting jailed for this?"

"We just won the most important battle in the history of the Empire." Nezha gave her a lazy smile. "I think you're fine to imbibe."

"He's trying to frame us," Rin said.

She hadn't meant to start drinking. But Venka and Nezha had kept urging her, and she hadn't known how to say no without drawing suspicion. Once she started it was harder and harder to stop. Sorghum wine was only horrible for the first few swallows, when it felt like it was burning away at her esophagus, but very quickly a delicious, giddy numbness settled over her body and the wine began tasting like water.

It'll wear off in a few hours, she thought dimly. She'd be fine by dawn.

"Believe me," Nezha said. "I wouldn't need this to frame any of you."

Venka sniffed at her jug. "This stuff is gross."

"What do you like better?" Nezha asked.

"Bamboo rice wine."

"The lady is demanding," Kitay said.

"I'll procure it," Nezha vowed.

"'I'll procure it,'" Kitay mimicked.

"Problem?" Nezha asked.

"No, just a question. Have you ever considered being less of a pretentious fuck?"

Nezha put his jug down. "Have you ever considered how close you're standing to the roof?"

"Boys, boys." Venka twirled a strand of hair between her fingers, while Kitay flicked droplets of wine at Nezha.

"Stop it," Nezha snapped.

"Make me."

Rin drank steadily, watching with lidded eyes as Nezha scooted on his knees across the tower and tackled Kitay to the floor. She supposed she should be afraid that they might fall off the edge, but drunk as she was, it just seemed very funny.

"I learned something," Kitay announced abruptly, shoving Nezha off of him.

"You're always learning things," said Venka. "Kitay the scholar."

"I'm an intellectually curious man," Kitay said.

"Always hunkering down in the library. You know, I made a wager once at Sinegard that you spent all that time jerking off."

Kitay spat out a mouthful of wine. "*What?*"

Venka propped her chin up on her hands. "Well, were you? Because I'd like to get my money back."

Kitay ignored her. "My point being—*listen*, guys, this is actually interesting. You know why the Militia troops were fighting like they'd never held a sword before?"

"They were fighting with a bit more skill than that," Nezha said.

"I don't want to talk about troops," said Venka.

Nezha elbowed her. "Indulge him. Else he'll never shut up."

"It's *malaria*," Kitay said. He sounded at first like he was hiccupping, but then he rolled on his side, giggling so hard his entire frame shook. He was drunk, Rin realized; perhaps more drunk than she was, despite the risk.

Kitay must be feeling the way she did—happy, deliriously so, for once in the company of friends who weren't in danger, and she suspected that he, too, wanted to suspend reality and break the rules, to ignore the fact that they were about to part forever and just share these last jugs of wine.

She didn't want dawn to come. She would draw this moment out forever if she could.

"They're not used to southern diseases," Kitay continued. "The mosquitoes weakened them more than anything we did. Isn't that amazing?"

"Marvelous," Venka said drily.

Rin wasn't paying attention. She scooted closer to the edge of the tower. She wanted to fly again, to feel that precipitous drop in her stomach, the sheer thrill of the dive.

She dangled one foot over the edge and relished the feeling of the wind buffeting her limbs. She leaned forward just the slightest bit. What if she jumped right now? Would she enjoy the fall?

"Get away from there." Kitay's voice cut through the fog in her mind. "Nezha, grab her—"

"On it." Strong arms wrapped around her midriff and dragged her away from the edge. Nezha gripped her tightly, anticipating a struggle, but she just hummed a happy note and slouched back against his chest.

"Do you have any idea how much trouble you are?" he grumbled.

"Hand me another jug," she said.

Nezha hesitated, but Venka readily obliged.

Rin took a long draught, sighed, and lifted her fingertips to her temples. She felt as if a current were running through her limbs, like she had stuck her hand in a bolt of lightning. She rested her head back against the wall and squeezed her eyes shut.

The best part of being drunk was how nothing mattered.

She could dwell on thoughts that used to hurt too much to think about. She could conjure memories—Altan burning on the pier, the corpses in Golyn Niis, Qara's body in Chaghan's arms—all without cringing, without the attendant torment. She could reminisce with a quiet detachment, because nothing mattered and nothing hurt.

"Sixteen months." Kitay had started counting aloud on his fingers. "That's almost a year and a half we've been at war now, if you start from the invasion."

"That's not that long," said Venka. "The First Poppy War took three years. The Second Poppy War took five. The succession battles after the Red Emperor could take as long as seven."

"How do you fight a war for *seven years*?" Rin asked. "Wouldn't you get bored of fighting?"

"Soldiers get bored," Kitay said. "Aristocrats don't. To them, it was all a big game. I guess that's the problem."

"Here's a thought experiment." Venka waved her hands in a small arc like a rainbow. "Imagine some alternate world where this war hadn't happened. The Federation never invaded. No, scratch that, the Federation doesn't even exist. Where are you?"

"Any particular point in time?" Kitay asked.

Venka shook her head. "No, I meant, what are you doing with your life? What do you wish you were doing?"

"I know what Kitay's doing." Nezha tilted his head back, shook the last drops from his jug into his mouth, then looked disappointed when it refused to yield any more. Venka passed him another jug. Nezha attempted to pop the cork, failed, muttered a curse under his breath, and smashed the neck against the wall.

"Careful," said Rin. "That's premium stuff."

Nezha lifted the broken edges to his lips and smiled.

"Go on," Kitay said. "Where am I?"

"You're at Yuelu Academy," Nezha said. "You're conducting groundbreaking research on—on some irrelevant shit like the movement of planetary bodies, or the most effective accounting methods across the Twelve Provinces."

"Don't mock accounting," Kitay said. "It's important."

"Only to you," Venka said.

"Regimes have fallen because rulers didn't balance their accounts."

"Whatever." Venka rolled her eyes. "What about the rest of you?"

"I'm good at war," Rin said. "I'd still be doing wars."

"Against who?" Venka asked.

"Doesn't matter. Anyone."

"There might not be any wars left to fight now," Nezha said.

"There's always war," Kitay said.

"The only thing permanent about this Empire is war," Rin said. The words were so familiar she said them without thinking, and it took her a long moment to realize she was reciting an aphorism from a history textbook she'd studied for the Keju. That was incredible—even now, the vestiges of that exam were still burned into her mind.

The more she thought about it, the more she realized that the only permanent thing about *her* might be war. She couldn't imagine where she'd be if she weren't a soldier anymore. The past four years had been the first time in her life that she'd felt like she was worth something. In Tikany, she'd been an invisible shopgirl, far beneath everyone's notice. Her life and death had been utterly insignificant. If she'd been run over by a rickshaw on the street, no one would have bothered to stop.

But now? Now civilians obeyed her command, Warlords sought her audience, and soldiers feared her. Now she spoke to the greatest military minds in the country as if they were equals—or at least as if she belonged in the room. Now she was drinking sorghum wine on the highest tower of the palace of Arlong with the son of the Dragon Warlord.

No one would have paid so much attention to her if she weren't so very good at killing people.

A twinge of discomfort wormed through her gut. Once she left Vaisra's employ, what on earth was she supposed to do?

"We could all just switch to civilian posts now," Kitay said. "Let's all be ministers and magistrates."

"You have to get elected first," Nezha said. "Government by the people, and all that. People have to like you."

"Rin's out of a job, then," Venka said.

"She can be a custodian," said Nezha.

"Did you want someone to rearrange your face?" Rin asked. "Because I'll do it for free."

"Rin's never going to be out of a job," Kitay said hastily. "We'll always need armies. There'll always be another enemy to fight."

"Like who?" Rin asked.

Kitay counted them off on his fingers. "Rogue Federation units. The fractured provinces. The Hinterlanders. Don't look at me like that, Rin; you heard Bekter, too. The Ketreyids want war."

"The Ketreyids want to go to war with the other clans," Venka said.

"And what happens when that spills over? We'll be fighting another border war within the decade, I promise."

"That's just mop-up duty," Nezha said dismissively. "We'll get rid of them."

"Then we'll create another war," said Kitay. "That's what militaries *do*."

"Not a military controlled by a Republic," Nezha said.

Rin sat up. "Have any of you pictured it? A democratic Nikan? Do you really think it'll work?"

The prospect of a functioning democracy had rarely bothered her during the war itself. There was always the more pressing threat of the Empire at hand. But now they'd actually *won*, and Vaisra had the opportunity to turn his abstract dream into a political reality.

Rin doubted he would. Vaisra had too much power now. Why on earth would he give it away?

She couldn't say she blamed him. She still wasn't convinced democracy was even a good idea. The Nikara had been fighting among themselves for a millennium. Were they going to stop just because they could vote for their rulers? And who was going to vote for those rulers? People like Auntie Fang?

"Of course it'll work," Nezha said. "I mean, imagine all the senseless military disputes the Warlords get into every year. We'll end that. All arguments get settled in council, not on a battlefield. And once we've united the entire Empire, we can do anything."

Venka snorted. "You actually believe that shit?"

Nezha looked miffed. "Of course I believe it. Why do you think I fought this war?"

"Because you want to make Daddy happy?"

Nezha aimed a languid kick at her ribs.

Venka dodged and swiped another jug of wine from the wagon, cackling.

Nezha leaned back against the tower wall. "The future is going to be glorious," he said, and there wasn't a trace of sarcasm in his voice. "We live in the most beautiful country in the world. We have more manpower than the Hesperians. We have more natural resources. The whole world wants what we have, and for the first time in our history we're going to be able to use it."

Rin rolled onto her stomach and propped her chin up on her hands.

She liked listening to Nezha talk. He was so hopeful, so optimistic, and so stupid.

He could spout all the ideology he wanted, but she knew better. The Nikara were never going to rule themselves, not peacefully, because there was no such thing as a Nikara at all. There were Sinegardians, then the people who tried to act like Sinegardians, and then there were the southerners.

They weren't on the same side. They'd never been.

"We're hurtling into a bright new era," Nezha finished. "And it'll be magnificent."

Rin spread her arms. "Come here," she said.

He leaned into her embrace. She held his head against her chest and rested her chin on the top of his head, silently counting his breaths.

She was going to miss him so much.

"You poor thing," she said.

"What are you talking about?" he asked.

She just hugged him tighter. She didn't want this moment to end. She didn't want to have to go. "I just don't want the world to break you."

Eventually Venka started retching off the side of the tower.

"It's okay," Kitay said when Rin moved to stand up. "I've got her."

"You're sure?"

"We'll be fine. I'm not close to as drunk as the rest of you." He draped Venka's arm over his shoulder and guided her carefully toward the stairs.

Venka hiccupped and mumbled something incomprehensible.

"Don't you dare puke on me," Kitay told her. He looked over his shoulder at Rin. "You shouldn't be staying out with wounds like that. Go get some sleep soon."

"I will," Rin promised.

"You're sure?" Kitay pressed.

She read the concern on his face. *We're running out of time.*

"I'll be out here for an hour," she said. "Tops."

"Good." Kitay turned to leave with Venka. Their footsteps faded down the staircase, and then it was just Rin and Nezha left on the rooftop. The night air had suddenly become very cold, which at that point seemed to Rin like a good excuse to sit closer to Nezha.

"Are you all right?" he asked her.

"Splendid," she said, and repeated the word twice when the consonants didn't seem to come out right. "Splendid. *Splendid.*" Her tongue sat heavy in her mouth. She'd stopped drinking hours ago, had nearly sobered up by now, but the evening chill had numbed her extremities.

"Good." Nezha stood up and offered her his hand. "Come with me."

"But I like it here," she whined.

"We're freezing here," he said. "Just come on."

"Why?"

"Because it'll be fun," he said, which at that point sounded like a good reason to do anything.

Somehow they ended up on the harbor. Rin lurched into Nezha's side as she walked. She hadn't sobered up as quickly as she'd hoped. The ground tilted treacherously beneath her feet every time she moved. "If you're trying to drown me, then you're being a little obvious about it."

"Why do you always think someone's trying to kill you?" Nezha asked.

"Why wouldn't I?"

They stopped at the end of the pier, farther out than any of the fishing crafts were docked. Nezha jumped into a little sampan and gestured for her to follow.

"What do you see?" he asked as he rowed.

She blinked at him. "Water."

"And illuminating the water?"

"That's moonlight."

"Look closely," he said. "That's not just the moon."

Rin's breath caught in her throat. Slowly her mind made sense of what she was seeing. The light wasn't coming from the sky. It was coming from the river itself.

She leaned over the side of the sampan to get a closer look. She saw darting little sparks among a milky background. The river was not just reflecting the stars, it was adding its own phosphorescent glow—lightning flashes breaking over minuscule movements of the waves, luminous streams washing over every ripple. The sea was on fire.

Nezha pulled her back by the wrist. "Careful."

She couldn't take her eyes off the water. "What is it?"

"Fish and mollusks and crabs," he said. "When you put them in the shadow they produce light of their own, like underwater flames."

"It's beautiful," she whispered.

She wondered if he was going to kiss her now. She didn't know much about being kissed, but if the old stories were anything to judge by, now seemed like a good time. The hero always took his maiden somewhere beautiful and declared his love under the stars.

She would have liked Nezha to kiss her, too. She would have liked to share this final memory with him before she fled. But he only stared thoughtfully at her, his mind fixed on something she couldn't guess at.

"Can I ask you something?" he asked after a pause.

"Anything," she said.

"Why did you hate me so much at school?"

She laughed, surprised. "Wasn't it obvious?"

She had so many answers, it seemed a ridiculous question. Because he was obnoxious. Because he was rich and special and popular, and she wasn't. Because he was the heir to the Dragon Province, and she was a war orphan and a mud-skinned southerner.

"No," said Nezha. "I mean—I understood I wasn't the nicest to you."

"That's an understatement."

"I know. I'm sorry about that. But, Rin, we managed to hate each other so much for three years. That's not normal. That goes back to first-year jitters. Was it all because I made fun of you?"

"No, it's because you scared me."

"I scared you?"

"I thought you were going to be the reason why I'd have to leave," she said. "And I didn't have anywhere else to go. If I'd been expelled from Sinegard, then I might well have died. So I feared you, I hated you, and that never really went away."

"I didn't realize," he said quietly.

"Bullshit," she said. "Don't act like you didn't know."

"I swear that never crossed my mind."

"Really? Because it had to. We *weren't* on the same level, and you knew it, and that's how you got away with everything you did, because you knew I could never retaliate. You were rich and I was poor and you exploited it." She was surprised by how quickly the words came, how easily she could still feel her lingering resentment toward him. She'd thought she'd put it behind her a long time ago. Perhaps not. "And the fact that it's never fucking *crossed your mind* that the stakes were vastly different between us is frustrating, to be frank."

"That's fair," Nezha said. "Can I ask you another question?"

"No. I get to ask my question first."

Whatever game they were playing suddenly had rules, was suddenly open to debate. And the rules, Rin decided, meant reciprocity. She stared at him expectantly.

"Fine." Nezha shrugged. "What is it?"

She was glad she had the liquid courage of lingering alcohol to say what came next. "Are you ever going to go back to that grotto?"

He stiffened. "What?"

"The gods can't be physical things," she said. "Chaghan taught me that. They need mortal conduits to affect the world. Whatever the dragon is . . ."

"That thing is a monster," he said flatly.

"Maybe. But it's beatable," she said. Perhaps she was still flush with the victory of defeating Feylen, but it seemed so obvious to her, what Nezha had to do if he wanted to be freed. "Maybe it was a person once. I don't know how it became what it is, and maybe it's as powerful as a god should be now, but I've buried gods before. I'll do it again."

"You can't beat that thing," Nezha said. "You have no idea what you're up against."

"I think have some idea."

"Not about this." His voice hardened. "You will never ask me about this again."

"Fine."

She leaned backward and let her fingers trail through the

luminous water. She made flames trickle up her arms, delighting in how their intricate patterns were reflected in the blue-green light. Fire and water looked so lovely together. It was a pity they destroyed each other by nature.

"Can I ask another question now?" he asked.

"Go ahead."

"Did you mean it when you said we should raise an army of shamans?"

She recoiled. "When did I say that?"

"New Year's. Back on the campaign, when we were sitting in the snow."

She laughed, amused that he had even remembered. The northern campaign felt like it had been lifetimes ago. "Why not? It'd be marvelous. We'd never lose."

"You understand that's precisely what the Hesperians are terrified of."

"For good reason," she said. "It'd fuck them up, wouldn't it?"

Nezha leaned forward. "Did you know that Tarcquet is seeking a moratorium on all shamanic activity?"

She frowned. "What does that mean?"

"It means you promise never to call on your powers again, and you'll be punished if you do. We report every living shaman in the Empire. And we destroy all written knowledge of shamanism so it can't be passed down."

"Very funny," she said.

"I'm not joking. You'd have to cooperate. If you never call the fire again, you'll be safe."

"Fat chance," she said. "I've *just* gotten the fire back. I don't intend to give it up."

"And if they tried to force you?"

She let the flames dance across her shoulders. "Then good fucking luck."

Nezha stood up and moved across the sampan to sit down beside her. His hand grazed the small of her back.

She shivered at his touch. "What are you doing?"

"Where's your injury?" he asked. He pressed his fingers into the scar in her side. "Here?"

"That hurts."

"Good," he said. His hand moved behind her. She thought he was going to pull her into him, but then she felt a pressure at the small of her back. She blinked, confused. She didn't realize that she had been stabbed until Nezha drew his hand away, and she saw the blood on his fingers.

She slumped to the side. He pulled her into his arms.

His face ebbed in and out of her vision. She tried to speak, but her lips were heavy, clumsy; all she could do was push air out in incoherent whispers. "You . . . but you . . ."

"Don't try to speak," Nezha murmured, and he brushed his lips against her forehead as he drove the knife deeper into her back.

CHAPTER 36

The morning sun was a dagger to Rin's eyes. She moaned and curled onto her side. For a single, blissful moment, she couldn't remember how she had ended up there. Then awareness came slowly and painfully—her mind lapsed into flashes of images, fragments of conversations. Nezha's face. The sour aftertaste of sorghum wine. A knife. A kiss.

She rolled over into something wet, sticky, and putrid. She had vomited in her sleep. A wave of nausea racked her body, but when her stomach heaved nothing came out. Everything hurt. She reached to feel at her back, terrified. Someone had stitched her up—blood was crusted around the wound, but it wasn't bleeding.

She might be fucked, but she wasn't dying just yet.

Two bolts chained her to the wall—one around her right wrist, and one between her ankles. The chains had some slack, but not very much; she couldn't crawl farther than halfway across the room.

She tried to sit up, but a wave of dizziness forced her back onto the floor. Her thoughts moved in slow, confused strains. She tried without hope to call the fire. Nothing happened.

Of course they'd drugged her.

Slowly, her tired mind worked through what had happened.

She'd been so stupid, she wanted to kick herself. She'd been *this* close to getting out, until she'd caved to sentiment.

She'd known Vaisra was a manipulator. She'd known the Hesperians would come after her. But never had she dreamed that Nezha might hurt her. She should have incapacitated him in the barracks and snuck out of Arlong before anyone saw. Instead, she'd hoped they could have one last night together before they parted forever.

Fool, she thought. *You loved him and you trusted him, and you walked straight into his trap.*

After Altan, she should have known better.

She glanced around the room. She was alone. She didn't want to be alone—if she was a prisoner then she needed to at least know what was coming for her. Minutes passed and no one entered the room, so she screamed. Then she screamed again and kept screaming, on and on until her throat burned.

The door slammed open. Lady Yin Saikhara walked into the room. She carried a whip in her right hand.

Fuck, Rin thought sluggishly, just before the whip lashed across her left shoulder to the right side of her hip. For a moment Rin lay frozen, the crack ringing in her ears. Then the pain sank in, so fierce and white-hot that it brought her to her knees. The whip came down again. Right shoulder this time. Rin couldn't bite back her screams.

Saikhara lowered the whip. Rin could just see the barest tremble in her hands, but otherwise the Lady of Arlong stood stiff, imperious, pale with that raw hate that Rin had never understood.

"You were supposed to tell them," Saikhara said. Her hair was loose and disheveled, her voice a tremulous snarl. "You were supposed to help them fix him."

Rin crawled toward the far corner of the room, trying to get out of Saikhara's striking range. "What the fuck are you talking about?"

"You creature of Chaos," Saikhara hissed. "You snake-tongued deceiver, you pawn of the greatest evil, this is all your fault . . ."

Rin realized for the first time that the Lady of Arlong might not be entirely sane.

She raised her hands over her head and crouched against the back corner in case Saikhara decided to bring the whip down again. "What do you think is my fault?"

Saikhara's eyes looked wide and unfocused; she spoke staring at a point a yard to Rin's left. "They were going to fix him. Vaisra promised. But they came back from the campaign and they said they've come no closer to knowing the truth, and you're still *here*, you dirty little thing—"

"Wait," Rin said. Puzzle pieces fitted slowly together in her mind; she couldn't believe she hadn't seen this connection before. "Fix *who*?"

Saikhara only glared.

"Did they say they'd fix *Nezha*?" Rin demanded. "Did the Hesperians say they could cure his dragon mark?"

Saikhara blinked. A mask froze over her features, the same mask her son and husband were so adept at.

But she didn't have to say anything. Rin understood the truth now; it was lying so obviously before her.

"*You promised,*" Saikhara had hissed at Vaisra. "*You swore to me. You said you'd make this right, that if I brought them back they'd find a way to fix him.*"

Sister Petra had promised Saikhara a cure for her son's affliction—this was the entire reason Saikhara had fought so hard to bring the Gray Company to the Empire. Which meant Vaisra and Saikhara had both known Nezha was a shaman all this time.

But they hadn't traded him to the Hesperians.

No, they'd only jeopardized every other shaman in the empire. They'd handed her to Petra to repeat what Shiro had put her through, just for some hope of saving their boy.

"I don't know what you think they'll learn," Rin said quietly. "But hurting me can't fix your son."

No, Nezha was likely going to suffer the dragon's curse until he died. That curse had to be beyond Hesperian knowledge. That thought gave her some small, vicious satisfaction.

"Chaos deceives masterfully." Saikhara moved her hand rapidly over her chest, forming symbols with her fingers that Rin had never seen. "It conceals its true nature and imitates order to subvert it. I know I cannot elicit the truth from you. I am only a novice initiate. But the Gray Company will have their turn."

Rin watched her warily, paying close attention to the whip. "Then what do you want?"

Saikhara pointed toward the window. "I'm here to watch."

Rin followed her gaze, confused.

"Go ahead," Saikhara said. She looked oddly, viciously triumphant. "Enjoy the show."

Rin stumbled toward the window and peered outside.

She saw that she was being held in a third-story room of the palace, facing the center courtyard. Underneath, a crowd of troops—Republican and Hesperian both—had assembled in a semicircle around a raised dais. Two blindfolded prisoners walked slowly up the stairs, arms tied behind their backs, flanked on both sides by Hesperian soldiers.

The prisoners stopped at the edge of the dais. The soldiers prodded them with their arquebuses until they stepped forward to stand at the center. The one on the left tilted his head up to the sun.

Even with the blindfold, Rin recognized that dark, handsome face.

Baji stood straight, unyielding.

Beside him, Suni hunched down between his shoulders as if he could make himself a smaller target. He looked terrified.

Rin twisted around. "What is this?"

Saikhara's gaze was fixed on the window, eyes narrowed, mouth pressed in the thinnest of lines. "*Watch.*"

Someone struck a gong. The crowd parted. Rin watched, veins icy with dread, as Vaisra ascended the dais and took a position several feet in front of Suni and Baji. He raised his arms. He shouted something that Rin couldn't make out over the crowd. All she heard was the soldiers roaring in approval.

"Once upon a time, the Red Emperor had all the monks in his realm put to death." Saikhara spoke quietly behind her. "Why do you think he did it?"

Four Hesperian soldiers lined up in front of Baji, arquebuses leveled at his torso.

"What are you doing?" Rin screamed. "*Stop!*"

But of course Vaisra couldn't hear her down there, not over the shouting. She strained helplessly against her chains, screeching, but all she could do was watch as he lifted his hand.

Four staggered shots punctuated the air. Baji's body jerked from side to side in a horrible dance with each bullet, until the last one caught him dead center in the chest. For a long, bizarre minute he remained standing, teetering back and forth, like his body couldn't decide which way to fall. Then he collapsed to his knees, head bent, before a last round of gunfire knocked him to the floor.

"So much for your gods," Saikhara said.

Below, the soldiers reloaded their arquebuses and fired a second round of bullets into Suni.

Slowly Rin turned around.

Rage filled her mind, a visceral urge not just to defeat but to *destroy*, to incinerate Saikhara so thoroughly that not even her bones would remain, and to do it *slowly*, to make the agony last as long as possible.

She reached for her god. At first there was no response, only an opium-dulled nothing. Then she heard the Phoenix's reply—a distant shriek, ever so faint.

That was enough. She felt the heat in her palms. She had the fire back.

She almost laughed. After all the opium she had smoked, her tolerance had become much, much higher than the Yins had imagined.

"Your false gods have been discovered," Saikhara said softly. "Chaos will die."

"You know nothing of the gods," Rin whispered.

"I know enough." Saikhara raised the whip again. Rin moved faster. She turned her palms toward Saikhara and fire burst out—just a small stream, not even a tenth of her full range, but it was enough to set Saikhara's robes aflame.

Saikhara skirted backward, screeching for help while the lash fell repeatedly against Rin's shoulder, slicing across open wounds. Rin raised her arms to shield her head, but the whip lacerated her wrists instead.

The doors opened. Eriden burst inside, followed by two soldiers. Rin redirected the flames at them, but they held damp, fireproof tarps in front of them. The fire sizzled and failed to catch. One kicked her to the ground and pinned her down by the arms. The other forced a wet cloth over her mouth.

Rin tried not to inhale, but her vision dimmed and she convulsed, gasping. The thick taste of laudanum invaded her mouth, cloying and potent. The effect was immediate. Her flames died away. She couldn't sense the Phoenix—could barely even hear or see at all.

The soldiers let go of her. She lay limp on the floor, dazed, drool leaking out the side of her mouth as she blinked blankly at the door.

"You shouldn't be here," Eriden said to Nezha's mother.

Saikhara spat in Rin's direction. "She should be sedated."

"She *was* sedated. You were reckless."

"And you were incompetent," Saikhara hissed. "This is on your head."

Eriden said something in response, but Rin could no longer understand him. Eriden and Saikhara were only vague, blurry streaks of colors, and their voices were distorted, meaningless babbles of nonsense.

Vaisra came for her hours later. She watched the door open through bloated eyelids, watched him cross the room to kneel down beside her.

"You," she croaked.

She felt his cool fingertips brush against her forehead and push her tangle of hair past her ears.

He sighed. "Oh, Runin."

"I did everything for you," she said.

His expression was uncharacteristically kind. "I know."

"Then why?"

He pulled his hand back. "Look out at the channel."

She glanced, exhausted, toward the window. She didn't have to look—she knew what he wanted her to see. The battered ships lying in pieces along the channel, a fourth of the fleet crushed beneath an avalanche of rocks, the bodies drowned and bloated drifting as far as the river ran.

"That's what happens when you bury a god," she said.

"No. That's what happens when men are fool enough to toy with heaven."

"But I'm not like Feylen."

"It doesn't matter," he said gently. "You could be."

She pulled herself to a sitting position. "Vaisra, please—"

"Don't beg. There's nothing I can do. They know about the man you killed. You burned him and dumped his body in the harbor." Vaisra sounded so disappointed. "Really, Rin? After everything? I told you to be careful. I wished you'd listened."

"He was raping a girl," she said. "He was *on* her, I couldn't just—"

"I thought," Vaisra said slowly, as if talking to a child, "I taught you how the balance of power fell."

She struggled to stand up. The floor tilted under her feet—she had to push herself against the wall. She saw double every time she moved her head, but at last she managed to look Vaisra in the eye. "Do it yourself, then. No firing squads. Use a sword. Grant me that respect."

Vaisra raised an eyebrow. "Did you think we were going to kill you?"

"You're coming with us, sweetheart." General Tarcquet's voice, a slow, indifferent drawl.

Rin flinched. She hadn't heard the door open.

Sister Petra stepped inside and stood just a little behind Tarcquet. Her eyes were like flint beneath her shawl.

"What do you want?" Rin growled at her. "Here to get more urine samples?"

"I admit I thought you could still be converted," Petra said. "This saddens me, truly. I hate to see you like this."

Rin spat at her feet. "Go fuck yourself."

Petra stepped forward until they were standing face-to-face. "You did have me fooled. But Chaos is clever. It can disguise itself as rational and benevolent. It can make us merciful." She lifted her hand to stroke the side of Rin's face. "But in the end, it must always be hunted down and destroyed."

Rin snapped at her fingers. Petra jerked her hand back. Too late. Rin had drawn blood.

Petra skirted back and Rin laughed, let blood drip from her teeth. She saw sheer terror reflected in Petra's eyes, and that alone was so oddly gratifying—Petra had never shown fear before, had never shown *anything*—that she didn't care about the disgust on Tarcquet's face or the disapproval on Vaisra's.

They all already thought her a mad animal. She'd only fulfilled their expectations.

And why shouldn't she? She was done playing the Hesperians' game of hiding, pretending she wasn't lethal when she was. They wanted to see a beast. She'd give them one.

"This isn't about Chaos." She grinned at them. "You're all so terrified, aren't you? I have power that you don't, and you can't stand it."

She opened her palms out. Nothing happened—the laudanum still weighed thick on her mind—but Petra and Tarcquet jumped back nonetheless.

Rin cackled.

Petra wiped her bloody hand on her dress, leaving behind thick, red streaks on gray cloth. "I will pray for you."

"Pray for yourself." Rin lunged forward again, just to see what Petra would do.

The Sister turned on her heels and fled. The door slammed behind her. Rin slunk back, snorting with mirth.

"Hope you got your kicks in," Tarcquet said drily. "Won't be a lot of laughs where you're going. Our scholars like to keep busy."

"I'll bite my tongue out before they touch me," Rin said.

"Oh, it won't be so bad," Tarcquet said. "We'll toss you some opium every once in a while if you behave. They told me you like that."

Her pride fled her.

"Don't give me to them," she begged Vaisra. She couldn't posture anymore, couldn't conceal her fear; her entire body trembled with it, and although she wanted to be defiant, all she could think of was Shiro's laboratory, of lying helpless on a hard table while hands she couldn't see probed at her body. "Vaisra. Please. You still need me."

Vaisra sighed. "I'm afraid that's no longer true."

"You wouldn't have won this war without me. I'm your best weapon, I'm the steel behind your rule, you *said*—"

"Oh, Runin." Vaisra shook his head. "Look outside the window. That fleet is the steel behind my rule. See those warships? Imagine the size of those cargo holds. Imagine how many arquebuses those ships are carrying. You think I really need you?"

"But I'm the only one who can call a god—"

"And Augus, an idiotic boy without the least bit of military training, went up against one of the Hinterlands' most powerful shamans and killed her. Oh yes, Runin, I told them. Now imagine what scores of trained Hesperian soldiers could do. My dear, I assure you I don't need your services any longer." Vaisra turned to Tarcquet. "We're done here. Cart her off whenever you wish."

"I am not keeping that thing on my ship," Tarcquet said.

"We'll deliver her before you depart, then."

"And you can guarantee she won't sink us into the ocean?"

"She can't do anything as long as you give her regular doses of laudanum," said Vaisra. "Post a guard. Keep her doped up and covered in wet blankets, and she'll be tame as a kitten."

"Too bad," Tarcquet said. "She's entertaining."

Vaisra chuckled. "She is that."

Tarcquet gave Rin a last, lingering glance. "The Consortium's delegates will be here soon."

Vaisra dipped his head. "And I would hate to keep the Consortium waiting."

They turned their backs toward her and moved to the door.

Rin rushed forward, panicked.

"I did everything for you." Her voice came out shrill, desperate. "I killed Feylen for you."

"And history will remember you for it," Vaisra said softly over his shoulder. "Just as history will praise me for the decisions I make now.

"Look at me!" she screamed. "Look at me! *Fuck you!* Look at me!"

He didn't respond.

She still had one card left to play, and she hurled it wildly at him. "Are you going to let them take Nezha, too?"

That made him stop.

"What's this?" Tarcquet asked.

"Nothing," said Vaisra. "She's drugged, she's babbling—"

"I know everything," Rin said. Fuck Nezha, fuck his secrets—if he was going to backstab her then she would do the same. "Your son is one of us, and if you're going to kill us all then you'll have to kill him, too."

"Is this true?" Tarcquet asked sharply.

"Clearly not," said Vaisra. "You've met the boy. Come, we're wasting time—"

"Tarcquet saw," Rin breathed. "Tarcquet was on the campaign. Remember how those waters moved? That wasn't the Wind God, General. That was Nezha."

Vaisra said nothing.

She knew she had him.

"You knew, didn't you?" she demanded. "You've always known. Nezha went to that grotto because you let him."

Because how else did two little boys escape the palace guard to explore a cave they were forbidden from entering? How, without the Dragon Warlord's express permission?

"Were you hoping he'd die? Or—no." Her voice shook. "You *wanted* a shaman, didn't you? You knew what the dragon could do and you wanted a weapon of your own. But you wouldn't take the chance on Jinzha. Not your firstborn. But your second son? Your third? They were expendable. You could experiment."

"What is she talking about?" Tarcquet demanded.

"That's why your wife hates me," Rin said. "That's why she hates all shamans. And that's why your son hates you. And you can't hide it. Petra already knows. Petra said she was going to fix him—"

Tarcquet raised an eyebrow. "Vaisra . . ."

"This is nothing," Vaisra said. "She's raving. Your men will have to put up with that on the ship."

Tarcquet laughed. "They don't speak the language."

"Be glad. Her dialect is an ugly one."

"*Stop lying!*" Rin tried to rush Vaisra. But the chains jerked painfully at her ankles and flung her back onto the floor.

Tarcquet gave a last chuckle as he left. Vaisra lingered for a moment in the doorway, watching her impassively.

Finally he sighed.

"The House of Yin has always done what it has needed to," he said. "You know that."

When she woke again she decided she wanted to die.

She considered dashing her head against the wall. But every time she knelt facing the window, hands braced against stone, she started shaking too badly to finish the job.

She wasn't afraid to die; she was afraid she wouldn't bash her head in hard enough. That she'd only shatter her skull but not lose consciousness, that she'd be subject to hours of crushing pain that didn't kill her but left her to a life of unbearable agony and half of her original capacity to think.

In the end, she was too much a coward. She gave up and curled up miserably on the floor to await whatever came next.

After a few minutes she felt a sharp jabbing sensation in her left arm. She jerked her head up, eyes darting around the room to find what had bitten her. A spider? A rat? She saw nothing. She was alone.

The prickling intensified into a sharp lance of pain. She yelped out loud and scrambled to sit up.

She couldn't find the cause of the pain. She squeezed her arm tight, rubbed frantically up and down, but the pain wouldn't disappear. She felt it as acutely as if someone were carving deep gashes into her flesh, but she couldn't see blood bubbling up on her skin or lines splitting the surface.

At last she realized that this wasn't happening to her.

This was happening to Kitay.

Did they have him? Were they hurting him? Oh, *gods*. The only thing worse than being tortured was knowing that Kitay was being tortured—to *feel* it happening, to know that it was ten times worse on his end, and to be unable to stop it.

Thin, scratchy white lines that looked like scars from a long-healed wound materialized under her skin.

Rin squinted at their shape. They weren't random cuts to inflict pain—the pattern was too deliberate. They looked like words.

Hope flared up in her chest. Was Kitay doing this to himself? Was he trying to *write* to her? She closed her fists, teeth clenched against the pain, while she watched the white lines form a single word.

Where?

She crawled to the window and peered outside, counting the windows that led up to hers. Third floor. First room in the center hallway, just above the courtyard dais.

Now she just had to write back. She cast her eyes around the room for a weapon but knew she'd find nothing. The walls were too smooth, and her cell had been stripped of furniture.

She examined her fingernails. They were untrimmed, sharp

and jagged. That might do the trick. They were terribly dirty—
that might cause infection—but she'd worry about that later.

She took a deep breath.

She could do this. She'd scarred herself before.

She managed just three characters before she couldn't bring
herself to scratch any more. *Palace 1–3*.

She watched her arm with bated breath. There was no response.

That wasn't necessarily bad. Kitay had to have seen. Maybe he
just had nothing else to say.

Quickly she smeared the blood over her arms to hide the cuts,
just in case any guards ventured in to check on her. And if they
saw, then she would simply pretend she had gone mad.

CHAPTER 37

Something clanged against the window.

Rin jerked her head up. She heard a second clang. She half ran, half crawled to the windowsill and saw a grappling hook lodged against the iron bars. She peeked over the edge. Kitay was scaling up the wall on a single rope. He grinned up at her, teeth gleaming in the moonlight. "Hi there."

She stared back, too relieved to speak, hoping desperately that she wasn't hallucinating.

Kitay hoisted himself through the window, dropped soundlessly to the floor, and fished a long needle out of his pocket. "How many locks?"

She jangled her chains at him. "Just two."

"Right." Kitay knelt by her ankles and set to work. A minute later the bolt sprang free. Rin kicked the shackles off her legs, relieved.

"Stop that," he whispered.

"Sorry." She was still drowsy from the laudanum. Moving felt like swimming and thinking took twice as long.

Kitay moved on to the bolt around her right wrist.

She sat quietly, trying her best not to move. Half a minute

later she heard something outside the door. She strained her ears. She heard it again—footsteps. "Kitay—"

"I know." His sweaty fingers slipped and fumbled as he worked the needle around the lock. "Stop moving."

The footsteps grew louder.

Kitay yanked at the bolt, but the chains held firm.

"Fuck!" He dropped the needle. "Fuck, *fuck*—"

Panic squeezed at Rin's chest. "They're coming."

"I know." He glared at the iron cuff for a moment, breathing heavily. Then he yanked his shirt over his head, twisted it into a thick knot, and pressed it at her face. "Open your mouth."

"What?"

"So you don't bite off your tongue."

She blinked. *Oh.*

She didn't argue. There was no time to think about it, no time to come up with a better plan. This was it. She let Kitay wedge the cloth into her mouth as far back as it would go until it was pressed down on her tongue, holding her teeth immobile.

"Should I tell you when?" he asked.

She squeezed her eyes shut and shook her head.

"Fine." Several seconds passed. Then he stomped down on her hand.

Her mind flashed white. Her body jerked. She arched her back, legs kicking uncontrollably at nothing. She heard herself screaming through the cloth, but it seemed to come from very far away. For a few seconds she was detached from herself; it was someone else's scream, someone else's hand in pieces. Then her mind reconciled with her body and she began bashing her other hand against the floor, desperate for some secondary pain to mask the intensity of the first.

"Stop that— Rin, *stop*!" Kitay grabbed her shoulder and held her still.

Tears leaked out the sides of her eyes. She couldn't speak; she could barely breathe.

"Did you hear that?" The voices from the hallway sounded terribly close. "I'm going in."

"Suit yourself, but I'm not coming with you."

"She's sedated—"

"Does she *sound* sedated? Go get the captain."

Footsteps echoed down the hallway.

"We have to do this fast," Kitay hissed. He'd turned a ghastly pale. He was feeling this, too; he had to be in agony, and Rin had no idea how he'd suppressed it.

She nodded and shut her eyes again, gasping while he yanked at her hands. Fresh stabs of pain lanced up her arm.

She made the mistake of looking and saw white bone piercing through her flesh. Her vision pulsed black.

"Try wriggling free," Kitay said.

She gave her arm a tentative pull and nearly screamed in frustration. She was still stuck.

"Put that rag back in," he said.

She obeyed. He stomped down again.

This time the hand broke clean through. She felt it, a clean crack that reverberated through the rest of her body. Kitay clenched her wrist firmly and extricated her hand with one vicious pull.

Somehow all the pieces came through still attached to her arm. He wrapped her mangled fingers in his shirt. "Tuck this into your elbow. Press down when you can, it'll stanch the bleeding."

She was so dizzy from the pain that she couldn't stand. Kitay hoisted her up by the armpits to a standing position. "Come on."

She leaned against him, unresponsive. Kitay lightly slapped the sides of her face until her eyes blinked open.

"Can you climb?" he asked. "Please, Rin, we've got to go."

She groaned. "I have one arm and I'm still high."

He dragged her toward the window. "I know. I feel it, too."

She looked at him and realized his hand was hanging limp by his side. That his face was drawn, pale, and slick with sweat. They were tied together. Her pain was his pain. But he was fighting through it.

Then she could, too. She owed him that.

"I can climb," she said.

"It'll be easy," he said. Relief shone clear on his face. "We learned this at Sinegard. Twist the rope around your foot to make a little platform. You'll be standing on about an inch of it. Slide down a little bit at a time." He ripped a square off of the shirt and pressed it into her good hand. "That's for the rope burn. Wait until I'm all the way down so I can catch you."

He patted her cheeks several times to drag her back to alertness and then hauled himself out the window.

Rin had no idea how she made it down the wall. Her limbs moved with dreamlike slowness, and the stones kept swimming before her eyes. Several times the rope threatened to come free from her leg and she spun terrifyingly in the air until Kitay yanked it taut. When she couldn't hold on any longer, she jumped the last six feet and crashed into Kitay. Pain shot up her ankles.

"*Quiet.*" Kitay clamped a hand over her mouth before she could gasp. He pointed out into the darkness. "There's a boat waiting that way, but you've got to get across the dais unnoticed."

She realized then that they were standing on the execution stage. She glanced behind her. She saw two bodies. They hadn't bothered to remove them.

"Don't look," Kitay whispered.

But she *couldn't* not look, not when they were standing so close. Suni and Baji lay bent and broken in browning piles of their own blood. The last two shamans of the Cike, victims of her stupidity.

She glanced around the courtyard. She couldn't see the night patrol, but surely they would be circling back around the palace any moment. "Won't they see us?"

"We have a distraction," Kitay said.

Before she could ask, he stuck his fingers into his mouth and whistled.

A figure appeared at the other end of the courtyard on cue. He stepped into the moonlight, and his profile came into sharp relief. Ramsa.

Rin started toward him, but Kitay yanked her back by the arm. Ramsa met her eyes, shook his head, and pointed to a line of guards emerging from the far corner.

Rin froze. They were three against twenty guards, half of whom were Hesperians armed with arquebuses, and she couldn't call the fire.

Ramsa calmly pulled two bombs out of his pocket.

"What's he doing?" Rin strained against Kitay's grip. "He's going to get himself killed."

Kitay didn't budge. "I know."

"Let me go, I have to help him—"

"You can't."

A shout rang through the night. One of the guards had seen Ramsa. The patrol group broke into a run, swords drawn.

Ramsa knelt on the ground. His fingers worked desperately at the fuse. Sparks flew all around him, but the bombs didn't light.

Rin tugged at Kitay's hands. "Kitay, *please*—"

He dragged her farther back into the shadow. "He's not the one we're trying to save."

She saw a flash of fire powder. The Hesperian guards had fired.

Ramsa stood up. Somehow the first round of shots had missed him. He'd managed to get the fuse to light. He laughed in delight, holding his bombs over his head.

The second round of fire tore him apart.

Time dilated terribly. Rin saw everything happen in slow, deliberate, and intricate detail. One bullet smashed through Ramsa's jaw and came out the other side in a spray of red. One burrowed through his neck. One embedded itself in his chest. Ramsa stumbled back. The bombs fell out of his hands and hit the ground.

Rin thought she could see the barest hint of a flame at the point of ignition. Then a ball of fire expanded out like a blooming flower, and then the blast radius consumed the courtyard.

"Ramsa . . ." She sagged against Kitay's shoulder, arms stretched toward the blast site. Her mouth worked and she pushed air through her throat, but she didn't hear her own voice until a long moment after she spoke. "Ramsa, no—"

Kitay jerked her upright. "He's bought us an escape window. Let's go."

The sampan that awaited them behind the canal bend was hidden so well in the shadows that Rin thought for a few terrifying seconds that it wasn't there at all. Then the boatman steered the craft out from under the willow leaves, stopped before them, and extended his hand. He wore a Hesperian military uniform, but his face was hidden under a Nikara archer's helmet.

"Sorry we couldn't get to you earlier." The boatman was a her. Venka lifted up her helmet for a brief moment and winked. "Get in."

Rin, too exhausted to feel bewildered, stumbled hastily into the sampan. Kitay jumped in after her and tossed the side rope overboard.

"Where'd you get that uniform?" he asked. "Nice touch."

"Went corpse-hunting." Venka kicked the boat away from shore and steered them swiftly down the canal.

Rin collapsed onto a seat, but Venka nudged her with her foot. "Down on the floor. Cover yourself with that tarp."

She crouched down in the space between seats. Kitay helped drag the tarp over her head.

"How did you know to find us?" Rin asked.

"Father tipped me off," Venka said. "I knew something weird was happening on the tower, I just wasn't able to place *what*. The moment I caught the gist of what was going on I ran and found Kitay before Vaisra's men could, but we couldn't figure out where they were keeping you until Kitay tried that thing with his skin. Neat trick, by the way."

"You realize you've just declared treason on your country," Rin said.

"Seems like the least of our concerns," Venka said.

"You can still go back," Kitay said. "I'm serious, Venka. Your whole family is here, you've got no business running away with us. I can take the sampan from here, you can hop off—"

"No," she said curtly.

"Think hard about this," he insisted. "You've still got plausible deniability. You can leave now; no one knows you're on this boat. But you come with us and you can never go back."

"Pity," Venka said dismissively. She turned to Rin. Her voice took on a hard edge. "I heard what you did to that Hesperian soldier."

"Yeah," Rin said. "So?"

"So well done. I hope it hurt."

"It looked like it did."

Venka nodded in silence. Neither of them had anything else to say about it.

"Any luck with the others?" Venka asked Kitay after a pause.

He shook his head. "Wasn't time. The only one I could reach was Gurubai. He should be with the ship now if he got past the guards—"

"Gurubai?" Rin repeated. "What are you talking about?"

"Vaisra's going after the southern Warlords," Kitay explained. "He's won his Empire. Now he's consolidating his power. He started with you, and now he's just cleaning up the others. I tried to give them some warning, but couldn't reach them in time."

"They're dead?"

"Not all of them. They've got Charouk in the cells. Don't know if they'll execute him or let him languish, but they'll certainly never set him free. The Rooster Warlord put up a fight, so they shot him when the riots started—"

"*Riots?* What the hell is going on?"

"The camps have turned into a war zone," Venka said. "They'd doubled the guard all around the refugee district—said it was for safety, but the moment the troops came in for the Warlords they all knew what was happening. The southern troops started the revolt. We've been hearing fire powder going off all night—I think Vaisra set the Hesperians loose on them."

Rin struggled to take all of this in. The world, it seemed, had turned upside down in the span of several hours. "They're just *killing* them? Civilians too?"

"That's likely."

"Then what about Kesegi?" Rin asked. "Did he get out?"

Venka frowned. "Who?"

"I—no one." Rin swallowed. "Never mind."

"Think about it this way," Venka said brightly. "At least it's bought you a distraction."

Rin retreated back under the tarp and lay still, counting her breaths to distract herself from the mess that was her hand. She wanted to look at it, survey the damage in her mangled fingers, but she couldn't bring herself to unwrap the bloody cloth. She knew there would be no salvaging that hand. She'd seen the cracked bones.

"Venka?" Kitay's voice, urgent.

"What?"

"I thought you covered your bases."

"I did."

Rin sat up. They'd moved faster than she thought—the palace was a distant sight, and they were already sailing past the shipyard. She twisted around to see what Venka and Kitay were staring at.

Nezha stood alone at the end of the pier.

Rin scrambled upright, her good hand flung outward. She was still reeling from the laudanum, but she could just elicit the smallest whispers of flame in her palm, could probably jerk out a larger torrent if she focused—

Kitay tackled her back down under the tarp. "Get down!"

"I'll kill him." Fire burst out from her palm and her lips. "*I'll kill him*—"

"No, you won't." He moved to pin her wrists down.

Without thinking she pummeled at Kitay with both fists, trying to break free. Then her injured hand whacked against the side of the boat, and the pain was so horrendous that for a moment everything went white. Kitay clamped a hand over her mouth before she could scream. She collapsed into his arms. He held her against him and rocked her back and forth while she muffled her shrieks into his shoulder.

Venka fired two arrows in rapid succession across the harbor. They both missed by a yard. Nezha jerked his head to the side when they whistled past him, but otherwise stood his ground. He didn't move the entire time the sampan crossed the shipyard toward the dark cover of cliff shadows on the other side of the channel.

"He's letting us go," said Kitay. "Hasn't even sounded the alarm."

"You think he's on our side?" Venka asked.

"He's not," Rin said flatly. "I know he's not."

She knew with certainty that she'd lost Nezha forever. With Jinzha killed and Mingzha long dead, Nezha was the last male heir to the House of Yin. He stood to inherit the most powerful nation this side of the Great Ocean and become the ruler he'd prepared his entire life to be.

Why would he throw that away for a friend? She wouldn't.

"This is my fault," she said.

"It's not your fault," Kitay said. "We all thought we could trust that bastard."

"But I think he tried to warn me."

"What are you talking about? He *stabbed* you."

"The night before the fleet came." She took a deep breath. "He came to find me. He said I had more enemies than I thought I did. I think he was trying to warn me."

Venka pursed her lips. "Then he didn't try very hard."

Two ships with deep builds and slender sides awaited them outside the channel. Both bore the flag of Dragon Province.

"Those are opium skimmers," Rin said, confused. "Why are they—"

"Those are fake flags. They're Red Junk ships." Kitay helped her to her feet as the sampan bumped up against the closest skimmer's hull. Kitay whistled up at the deck. Several seconds later, four ropes dropped into the water around them.

Venka fastened them to hooks on the four sides of the sampan. Kitay whistled again, and slowly they began to rise.

"Moag sends her regards." Sarana winked at Rin as she helped her aboard. "We got your message. Figured you'd want a ride farther south. Just didn't think things would get this bad."

Rin was both deeply relieved and frankly amazed that the Lilies had come for her at all. She couldn't remember why she'd ever hated Sarana; right now she only wanted to kiss her. "So you decided to pick a fight with a giant?"

"You know how Moag is. Always wants to snatch up trump cards, especially when they've been tossed out."

"Did Gurubai make it?" Kitay asked.

"The Monkey Warlord? Yes, he's belowdecks. Little bit blood-ied up, but he'll be fine." Sarana's gaze landed on Rin's wrapped hand. "Tiger's tits. What's under there?"

"You don't want to see," Rin said.

"Do you have a physician on board?" Kitay asked. "I have tri-age training otherwise, but I'll need equipment—boiling water, bandages—"

"Downstairs. I'll take her." Sarana put her arm around Rin and helped her across the deck.

Rin glanced over her shoulder as they walked, peering at the re-ceding cliffs. It seemed incredible that they had not been followed out of the channel. Vaisra certainly knew she'd escaped by now. Troops should be pouring out of the barracks. She'd be surprised if the entire city weren't put under lockdown. The Hesperians would scour the city, the cliffs, and the waters until they had her back in custody.

But the Red Junk skimmers were so clearly visible under the moonlight. They hadn't bothered to hide. Hadn't even turned their lamps off.

She stumbled over a bump in the floor panels.

"All right there?" Sarana asked.

"They're going to catch us," Rin said. Everything felt so idiotically meaningless—her escape, Ramsa's death, the river rendezvous. The Hesperians were going to board them in an hour. What was the point?

"Don't underestimate an opium skimmer," said Sarana.

"Your fastest skimmer couldn't outrun a Hesperian warship," Rin said.

"Probably not. But we have a little time. Command miscommunications always happen when you have two armies and leaders who aren't familiar with each other. The Hesperians don't know it's not a Republican ship and the Republicans won't know if the Hesperians have given permission to fire, or if they even need it. Everyone assumes that someone else is taking care of it."

Sarana's plan was to escape through command chain inefficiency. Rin didn't know whether to laugh or cry. "That doesn't buy you escape, it buys you maybe half an hour."

"Sure." Sarana pointed to the other skimmer. "Thus the second ship."

"What is that, a decoy?"

"Pretty much. We stole the idea from Vaisra," Sarana said cheerfully. "In a second we're going to cloak all of our abovedeck lights, but that ship's going to posture like it's ready for a fight. It's rigged up with twice the firepower of a usual skimmer. They won't get close enough to board, so they'll be forced to blow it out of the water."

That was clever, Rin thought. If the Hesperians didn't notice the second skimmer escaping into the night, they might conclude that she'd drowned.

"Then what about its crew?" she asked. "That thing is crewed, right? You're just going to sacrifice Lilies?"

Sarana's smile looked carved into her face. "Cheer up. With luck, they'll think it's you."

. . .

The Lilies' physician laid Rin's hand on a table, gingerly unwrapped it, and took a sharp breath when she saw the damage.
"You sure you don't want any sedatives?"

"No." Rin twisted her head around to face the wall. The look
on the physician's face was worse than the sight of her mangled
fingers. "Just fix it."

"If you move, I'll have to sedate you," the physician warned.

"I won't." Rin clenched her teeth. "Just give me a gag. Please."

The physician barely looked older than Sarana, but she acted
with practiced, efficient movements that set Rin slightly more at
ease.

First she doused the wounds with some kind of clear alcohol
that stung so badly that Rin nearly bit through the cloth. Then
she stitched together the places where the flesh had split apart to
reveal the bone. Rin's hand was already stinging so badly from the
alcohol that it almost masked the pain, but the sight of the needle
dipping repeatedly into her flesh made her so nauseated she had to
stop in the middle to dry-heave.

At last, the physician prepared to set the bones. "You'll want to
hold on to something."

Rin grasped the edge of the chair with her good hand. Without
warning, the physician pressed down.

Rin's eyes bulged open. She couldn't stop her legs from kicking
madly at the air. Tears streamed down her cheeks.

"You're doing well," the physician murmured as she tied a
cloth splint over the set hand. "The worst part's over."

She pressed Rin's hand between two wooden planks and tied
them together with several loops of twine to render the hand immobile. Rin's fingers were splayed outward, frozen in position.

"See how that feels," said the physician. "I'm sorry it looks so
clumsy. I can build you something more lightweight, but it'll take
a few days, and I don't have the supplies on the ship."

Rin raised the splint to her eyes. Between the planks she could see only the tips of her fingers. She tried to wiggle her fingers, but she couldn't tell if they were obeying her or not.

"Am I all right to remove the gag?" the physician asked.

Rin nodded.

The physician pulled it out of her mouth.

"Will I be able to use this hand?" she asked the moment she could speak.

"There's no telling how this might heal. Most of your fingers are actually fine, but the center of your hand is cracked straight through the middle. If—"

"Am I losing this hand?" Rin interrupted.

"That's likely. I mean, you can never quite predict how—"

"I understand." Rin sat back, trying not to panic. "All right. That's—that's okay. That . . ."

"You'll want to consider getting it amputated if it heals and you still don't have mobility." The physician attempted to sound soothing, but her quiet words only made Rin want to scream. "That might be better than walking around with . . . ah, dead flesh. It's more prone to infections, and the recurring pain might be so bad that you want it gone entirely."

Rin didn't know what to say. Didn't know how she was supposed to absorb the information that she was now effectively one-handed, that she'd have to relearn everything if she wanted to fight with a sword again.

This couldn't be happening. This couldn't be happening to *her*.

"Breathe slowly," said the physician.

Rin realized she'd been hyperventilating.

The physician put a hand on her wrist. "You'll be all right. It's not as bad as you think it is."

Rin raised her voice. "*Not as bad?*"

"Most amputees learn to adjust. In time, you'll—"

"I'm supposed to be a soldier!" Rin shouted. "What the fuck am I supposed to do now?"

"You can summon fire," said the physician. "What do you need a sword for?"

. . .

"I thought the Hesperians were only here for military support and trade negotiations. This treaty basically turns us into a colony." Venka was talking when Rin, despite the physician's protests, walked into the captain's quarters. She glanced up. "Aren't you supposed to be asleep?"

"Didn't want to," Rin said. "What are we talking about?"

"The physician said the laudanum would have you out for hours," Kitay said.

"I didn't take it." She sat down beside him. "I've had enough of opiates for a while."

"Fair enough." He glanced over at her splint, then flexed his own fingers. Rin noticed the sweat drenching his uniform, the half-moon marks where he'd dug his nails into his palm. He'd felt every second of her pain.

She cleared her throat and changed the subject. "Why are we talking about treaties?"

"Tarcquet has staked his claim to the continent," said the Monkey Warlord. Gurubai looked awful. Flecks of dried blood covered both his hands and the left side of his face, and his expression was hollow and haggard. He'd escaped the crackdown, but just barely. "The treaty terms were atrocious. The Hesperians got their trade rights—we've waived our rights to any tariffs, but they get to keep theirs. They also won the right to build military bases anywhere they want on Nikara soil."

"Bet they got permission for missionaries, too," Kitay said.

"They did. And they wanted the right to market opium in the Empire again."

"Surely Vaisra said no," Rin said.

"Vaisra signed every clause," Gurubai said. "He didn't even put up a fight. You think he had a choice? He doesn't even have full control over domestic affairs anymore. Everything he does has to be approved by a delegate from the Consortium."

"So Nikan's fucked." Kitay threw his hands up in the air. "Everything's fucked."

"Why would Vaisra want this?" Rin asked. None of this made sense to her. "Vaisra hates giving up control."

"Because he knows it's better to be a puppet Emperor than to have nothing at all. Because this arrangement plies him with so much silver he'll choke on it. And because now he has the military resources necessary to take the rest of the Empire." Gurubai leaned back in his chair. "You're all too young to remember the days of joint occupation. But things are going right back to how they were seventy years ago."

"We'll be slaves in our own country," Kitay said.

"'Slave' is a strong way of putting it," Gurubai said. "The Hesperians aren't much into forced labor, at least on this continent. They prefer relying on forces of economic coercion. The Divine Architect appreciates rational and voluntary choice, and all that nonsense."

"That's fucked," Rin said.

"It was inevitable the moment Vaisra invited them to his hall. The southern Warlords saw this coming. We tried to warn you. You wouldn't listen."

Rin shifted uncomfortably in her seat. But Gurubai's tone wasn't accusatory, simply resigned.

"We can't do anything about it now," he said. "We need to go back down to the south first. Clean out the Federation. Make it safe for our people to come home."

"What's the point?" Kitay asked. "You're the agricultural center of the Empire. Fight off the Federation and you'll just be doing Vaisra a favor. He's going to come for you sooner or later."

"Then we'll fight back," Rin said. "They want the south, they'll have to bleed for it."

Gurubai gave her a grim smile. "That sounds about right."

"We're going to take on Vaisra and the entire Consortium."

Kitay let that sink in for a moment, and then let out a mad, high-pitched giggle. "You can't be serious."

"We don't have any other options," said Rin.

"You could all run," Venka said. "Go to Ankhiluun, get the Black Lilies to hide you. Lie low."

Gurubai shook his head. "There's not a single person in the Republic who doesn't know who Rin is. Moag's on our side, but she can't keep every lowlife in Ankhiluun from talking. You'd all last at most a month."

"I'm not running," Rin said.

She wasn't going to let Vaisra hunt her down like a dog.

"You're not fighting another war, either," Kitay said. "Rin. You have one functional hand."

"You don't need both hands to command troops," she said.

"*What* troops?"

She gestured around the ship. "I'm assuming we'll have the Red Junk Fleet."

Kitay scoffed. "A fleet so powerful that Moag's never dared to move on Daji."

"Because Ankhiluun's never been at stake," Rin said. "Now it is."

"Fine," Kitay snapped. "You've got a fleet maybe a tenth of the size of what the Hesperians could bring. What else you got? Farm boys? Peasants?"

"Farm boys and peasants become soldiers all the time."

"Yes, given time to train and weapons, neither of which you have."

"What would you have us do, then?" Rin asked softly. "Die quietly and let Vaisra have his way?"

"That's better than getting more idiots killed for a war that you can't win."

"I don't think you realize how big our power base is," said Gurubai.

"Really?" Kitay asked. "Did I just miss the army you've got hidden away somewhere?"

"The refugees you saw at Arlong don't represent even a thousandth of the southern population," said Gurubai. "There are a hundred thousand men who picked up axes to fend off the Federation when it became clear we weren't getting aid. They'll fight for us."

He pointed at Rin. "They'll fight especially for *her*. She's already become myth in the south. The vermilion bird. The goddess of fire. She's the savior they've been waiting for. She's the symbol they've been waiting this whole war to follow. What do you think happens when they see her in person?"

"Rin's been through enough," Kitay said. "You're not turning her into some kind of figurehead—"

"Not a figurehead." Rin cut him off. "I'll be a general. I'll lead the entire southern army. Isn't that right?"

Gurubai nodded. "If you'll do it."

Kitay gripped her shoulder. "Is that what you want to be? Another Warlord in the south?"

Rin didn't understand that question.

Why did it matter what she *wanted* to be? She knew what she *couldn't* be. She couldn't be Vaisra's weapon anymore. She couldn't be the tool of any military; couldn't close her eyes and lend her destructive abilities to someone else who told her where and when to kill.

She had thought that being a weapon might give her peace. That it might place the blame of blood-soaked decisions on someone else so that she was not responsible for the deaths at her hands. But all that had done was make her blind, stupid, and so easily manipulated.

She was so much more powerful than anyone—Altan, Vaisra— had ever let her be. She was finished taking orders. Whatever she did next would be her sole, autonomous choice.

"The south is going to go to war regardless," she said. "They'll need a leader. Why shouldn't it be me?"

"They're untrained," Kitay said. "They're unarmed, they're probably starving—"

"Then we'll steal food and equipment. Or we'll get it shipped in. Perks of allying with Moag."

He blinked at her. "You're going to lead peasants and refugees against Hesperian dirigibles."

Rin shrugged. She was mad to be so cavalier, she knew that. But they were backed against a wall, and their lack of options was almost a relief, because it meant simply that they fought or they died. "Don't forget the pirates, too."

Kitay looked like he was on the verge of ripping out every strand of hair left on his head.

"Do not assume that because the southerners are untrained they will not make good soldiers," said Gurubai. "Our advantage lies in numbers. The fault lines of this country don't lie at the level that Vaisra was prepared to engage. The real civil war won't be fought at the provincial level."

"But Vaisra's not the Empire," Kitay said. "The split was with the Empire."

"No, the split is with people like us," Rin said suddenly. "It's the north and the south. It always was."

The pieces had been working slowly through her opium-addled mind, but when they finally clicked, the epiphany came like a shock of cold water.

How had it taken her this long to figure this out? There was a reason why she'd always felt uncomfortable championing the Republic. The vision of a democratic government was an artificial construct, teetering on the implausibility of Vaisra's promises.

But the real base of opposition came from the people who had lost the most under Imperial rule. The people who, by now, hated Vaisra the most.

Somewhere out there, hiding within the wreckage of Rooster Province, was a little girl, terrified and alone. She was choking on her hopelessness, disgusted by her weakness, and burning with rage. And she would do anything to get the chance to fight, to *really* fight, even if that meant losing control of her own mind.

And there were millions more like her.

The magnitude of this realization was dizzying.

The maps of war rearranged themselves in Rin's mind. The provincial lines disappeared. Everything was merely black and red—privileged aristocracy against stark poverty. The numbers rebalanced, and the war she'd thought she was fighting suddenly looked very, very different.

She'd seen the resentment on the faces of her people. The glare in their eyes when they dared to look up. They were not a people grasping for power. Their rebellion would not fracture over stupid personal ambitions. They were a people who refused to be killed, and that made them dangerous.

You can't fight a war on your own, Nezha had once told her.

No, but she could with thousands of bodies. And if a thousand fell, then she would throw another thousand at him, and then another thousand. No matter what the power asymmetry, war on this scale was a numbers game, and she had lives to spare. That was the single advantage that the south had against the Hesperians—that there were so, so many of them.

Kitay seemed to have realized this, too. The incredulity slid off his face, replaced by grim resignation.

"Then we're going to war against Nezha," he said.

"The Republic's already declared war on us," she said. "Nezha knows what side he chose."

She didn't have to debate this any longer. She *wanted* this war. She wanted to go up against Nezha again and again until at the end, she was the only one standing. She wanted to watch his scarred face twist in despair as she took away from him everything he cared about. She wanted him tortured, diminished, weakened, powerless, and begging on his knees.

Nezha had everything she used to want. He was aristocracy, beauty, and elegance. Nezha *was* the north. He had been born into a locus of power, and that made him feel entitled to use it, to make decisions for millions of people whom he considered inferior to himself.

She was going to wrench that power away from him. And then she'd pay him back in kind.

Finally, spoke the Phoenix. The god's voice was dimmed by the Seal, but Rin could hear clearly every ring of its laughter. *My darling little Speerly. At last we agree.*

All shreds of affection she'd once felt for Nezha had burned away. When she thought of him she felt only a cruel, delicious hatred.

Let it smolder, said the Phoenix. *Let it grow.*

Anger, pain, and hatred—that was all kindling for a great and terrible power, and it had been festering in the south for a very long time.

"Let Nezha come for us," she said. "I'm going to burn his heart out of his chest."

After a pause, Kitay sighed. "Fine. Then we'll go to war against the strongest military force in the world."

"They're not the strongest force in the world," Rin said. She felt the god's presence in the back of her mind—eager, delighted, and at last perfectly aligned with her intentions.

Together, spoke the Phoenix, *we will burn down this world.*

She slammed her fist against the table. "I am."

DRAMATIS PERSONAE

THE CIKE

Fang Runin: a war orphan from Rooster Province; commander of the Cike; and the last living Speerly

Ramsa: a former prisoner at Baghra; current munitions expert

Baji: a shaman who calls on an unknown god that gives him berserker powers

Suni: a shaman who calls on the Monkey God

Chaghan Suren: a shaman of the Naimad clan; and the twin brother of Qara

Qara Suren: a sharpshooter; speaker to birds; and twin sister of Chaghan

Unegen: a shape-shifter who calls on a minor fox spirit

Aratsha: a shaman who calls the river god

*Altan Trengsin: a Speerly, formerly the commander of the Cike

THE DRAGON REPUBLIC AND ITS ALLIES

The House of Yin

Yin Vaisra: the Dragon Warlord and leader of the Republic

Yin Saikhara: the Lady of Arlong; and the wife of Yin Vaisra

Yin Jinzha: the oldest son of the Dragon Warlord; and the grand marshal of the Republican Army

Yin Muzha: Jinzha's twin sister, studying abroad in Hesperia

Yin Nezha: the second son of the Dragon Warlord

*Yin Mingzha: the third son of the Dragon Warlord; drowned in an accident as a child

Chen Kitay: son of the defense minister; and the last heir to the House of Chen

Sring Venka: daughter of the finance minister

Liu Gurubai: the Monkey Warlord

Cao Charouk: the Boar Warlord

Gong Takha: the Rooster Warlord

Ang Tsolin: the Snake Warlord and Yin Vaisra's old mentor

THE NIKARA EMPIRE AND ITS ALLIES

Su Daji: the Empress of Nikan and the Vipress; calls on the Snail Goddess of Creation Nüwa

Tsung Ho: the Ram Warlord

Chang En: the Horse Warlord, aka the "Wolf Meat General," and later leader of the Imperial Navy

Jun Loran: formerly Combat master at Sinegard; currently the de facto Tiger Warlord

Feylen: formerly a shaman of the Cike who calls the Wind God; imprisoned at the Chuluu Korikh and set free by Altan Trengsin

Jiang Ziya: the Gatekeeper, calls on the beasts of the Emperor's Menagerie; currently self-immured in the Chuluu Korikh

***Yin Riga:** the former Dragon Emperor; presumed dead since the end of the Second Poppy War

THE HESPERIANS

General Josephus Tarcquet: the leader of the Hesperian troops in Nikan

Sister Petra Ignatius: a representative of the Gray Company (the Hesperian religious order) in Nikan; one of the most brilliant religious scholars of her generation

Brother Augus: a young member of the Gray Company

THE KETREYIDS

The Sorqan Sira: the leader of the Ketreyid clan; the older sister of Chaghan and Qara's mother

Bekter: son of the Sorqan Sira

***Tseveri:** daughter of the Sorqan Sira; murdered by Jiang Ziya

THE RED JUNK FLEET

Chiang Moag: Pirate Queen of Ankhiluun; aka the Stone Bitch and the Lying Widow

Sarana: a highly ranked Black Lily and one of Moag's favorites

* Deceased

ACKNOWLEDGMENTS

So many people helped me turn this book into something I'm proud of. Hannah Bowman saw this manuscript in its early stages and helped me in the nicest way possible to realize it was trash. It is still trash, but the fun kind. Thank you for always advocating for me, believing in me, and pushing, sometimes dragging, me forward. We burn on, boats against the current, hurtling into the future! David Pomerico and Natasha Bardon not only whipped this manuscript into a much better story than I could have come up with on my own, they helped me grow as a writer and saw me through an awful case of second-book syndrome. JungShan Ink created the cover illustrations and, as usual, somehow reached straight into my mind to depict Rin the way I've always imagined her. Thank you also to the teams at Liza Dawson Associates and Harper Voyager—Havis Dawson, Joanne Fallert, Pamela Jaffee, Caroline Perny, Jack Renninson, and Emilie Chambeyron. I'm lucky I get to work with you!

I'm blessed to be surrounded by friends, mentors, and teachers who encourage me to do more than I ever could have imagined, and who believe in me when I don't. Bennett, the Scarigon Plateau, was named after Scarigon. A great warrior. There you go. Shkibludibap! Maybe one day we will learn the fate of Gicaldo Marovi and his friend Rover . . . Farah Naz Rishi is my shining desert flower, my warm cup of stew on a cold day, the cheese to my bread, the strongest and most beautiful person I know, and the K to my J.B. May we grow old and petty together. Alyssa Wong, Andrea Tang, and Fonda Lee are incredible role models who set the standard for grace and hard work, and who inspire me to unapologetically write *me*. Professors John Glavin, Ananya Chakravarti, Carol Benedict, Katherine Benton-Cohen, John McNeill, James Millward, and Howard Spendelow turned me into the scholar that I am. I'm grateful to the Marshall Commission for its incredible generosity; the Marshall Class of 2018 are complete badasses and I want to be like all of you when I grow up. Adam Mortara reminds me through his shining example to never pull the ladder up after myself, but to reach down and pull others up. Jeanne Cavelos and Kij Johnson remain the best writing teachers I've ever encountered. Port is a very good beverage.

Huge, huge shout-out to the book bloggers, booktubers, bookstagrammers, and reviewers who talk about my work. (Incorrect Poppy War, I'm looking at you.) The fact that people get so excited about my characters is absolutely unreal. You have no idea how much encouragement and support you've given me, and I'm so glad I get to share my stories with you. #FireDick Forever. Burn on, my trash children.

And finally: if I am anything, it is because my parents gave me everything.

ABOUT THE AUTHOR

R. F. Kuang immigrated to the United States from Guangzhou, China, in 2000. She currently resides in the United Kingdom, where she is pursuing a graduate degree in Modern Chinese Studies at the University of Cambridge on a Marshall Scholarship. Her two great loves are corgis and port.